LORD of the
SILENT KINGDOM

Tor Books by Glen Cook

An Ill Fate Marshalling
Reap the East Wind
The Swordbearer
The Tower of Fear

THE BLACK COMPANY
The Black Company (The First Chronicle)
Shadows Linger (The Second Chronicle)
The White Rose (The Third Chronicle)
Shadow Games (The First Book of the South)
Dreams of Steel (The Second Book of the South)
The Silver Spike
Bleak Seasons (Book One of Glittering Stone)
She Is the Darkness (Book Two of Glittering Stone)
Water Sleeps (Book Three of Glittering Stone)
Soldiers Live (Book Four of Glittering Stone)
Chronicles of the Black Company
(Comprising *The Black Company, Shadows Linger,* and *The White Rose*)
The Books of the South
(Comprising *Shadow Games, Dreams of Steel,* and *The Silver Spike*)
The Return of the Black Company
(Comprising *Bleak Seasons* and *She Is the Darkness*)
The Many Deaths of the Black Company
(Comprising *Water Sleeps* and *Soldiers Live*)

THE INSTRUMENTALITIES OF THE NIGHT
The Tyranny of the Night
Lord of the Silent Kingdom

LORD of the SILENT KINGDOM

BOOK TWO
OF THE INSTRUMENTALITIES OF THE NIGHT

GLEN COOK

TOR®

A Tom Doherty Associates Book
New York

LORD OF THE SILENT KINGDOM

Copyright © 2007 by Glen Cook

Edited by Patrick Nielsen Hayden

A Tor Book
Published by Tom Doherty Associates, LLC
175 Fifth Avenue
New York, NY 10010

www.tor-forge.com

Tor® is a registered trademark of Tom Doherty Associates, LLC.

The Library of Congress has catalogued the hardcover edition as follows:

Cook, Glen.
    Lord of the silent kingdom / Glen Cook.—1st ed.
        p. cm.—(Instrumentalities of the night ; bk. 2)
    "A Tom Doherty Associates book."
    ISBN 978-0-7653-0685-2
    I. Title.

  PS3553.O5536L67   2007
  813'.54—dc22

                                                    2006033984

ISBN 978-0-7653-2605-8 (trade paperback)
ISBN 0-7653-2605-1

First Edition: February 2007
First Trade Paperback Edition: August 2010

Printed in the United States of America

P 1

LORD of the SILENT KINGDOM

The ice advances every winter. The world grows colder. The seas grow shallower. In northernmost Andoray the reindeer herds and mystic Seatts have disappeared. The farms and pastures, hills and fjords that supported the warlike Andorayans, two centuries gone, are entombed under ice so thick the wild, tall mountains are lost. Across the world—though less so amongst the Wells of Ihrian—the wells of power are weakening.

Till recently dramatic change has been confined to the far rims of civilization. Lately, though, they have begun to have a real impact round the Mother Sea. A flood of refugees has made it possible to raise armies at bargain prices. Just when the Episcopal Church is ruled by an obsessed Patriarch confident that he is *the* divine instrument meant to expunge heresy and crush unbelievers so all mankind can enjoy God's grace and salvation. As others have done, overlooking the fact that an omnipotent God can handle those sorts without mortal assistance.

The influx of the displaced causes instability everywhere. No one is concerned about the problem. No one *sees* the problem—except at the local level, where folks grumble about the increase in crime and violence, compared to the good old days. Their response to theft or violence is often ferociously violent itself.

Wars are being fought every day, even where armies are not on the march. And wars within wars. And wars behind wars.

There is the endless struggle on behalf of God, the war for heaven fought on earth. It is the war that never ends because the divine touches no two minds the same and few men credit any revelation but their own.

There is the war for daily survival in a world with neither the means nor any philosophical inclination to make abundant resources commonly available.

And there is the incessant, silent war against the Tyranny of the Night. This most deadly and most vile of wars is the struggle least well known. Not one man in five hundred becomes aware of the conflict, yet to be born is to become a conscript in the struggle with the Instrumentalities of the Night. On one side or the other.

1. Caron ande Lette, in the End of Connec

The enemy came out of the forest on the Ellow Hills, sudden as a spring squall. There had been no rumor of their coming. Brock Rault, the Seuir ande Lette, thought they were bandits when the first handful appeared. Then his conscience threw up the fear that they might represent Tormond of Khaurene. The Duke of the End of Connec had forbidden the construction of new fortifications except under ducal charter. Unfinished, Lette was just the sort of fastness that Tormond had proscribed.

Fortifications were appearing throughout the End of Connec. And caused more despair than comfort. The universal inclination seemed to be, once a man was confident of his own defenses, to hire mercenaries and become a plague upon his neighbors.

The Seuir ande Lette was an exception. Barely twenty-one, nevertheless, he had been with Count Raymone Garete at the Black Mountain Massacre and was a veteran of the Calziran Crusade. He had smelled the cruel beast War's foul breath. He had tasted blood. He loathed his family's enemies but never so much that he felt compelled to gift them with terror, death, or pain.

Peace was the root of his faith, though he was a warrior born and consecrated.

Brock Rault was Maysalean, a Seeker After Light. Peaceable by belief and a heretic by declaration of the Brothen Episcopal Church. He did not hide his beliefs.

The enemy drew closer, too quickly for some peasants to get safely inside Caron ande Lette. The Seuir realized that the invaders were no brigands. But neither were they much more, except in numbers. A banner identified them as followers of the Grolsacher mercenary captain, Haiden Backe. Backe operated under letters of marque from Patriarch Sublime V. He roamed the northeastern marches of the Connec, supposedly punishing heretics. In actuality, he plundered anyone who would not buy an exemption.

For his troubles, Haiden Backe received a third of the plunder, which he had to share with his troops. The rest went to the Church.

The Church was desperate for funds. Sublime had to repay loans taken during the Calziran Crusade. Any default meant there would be no loans in future. Nor had he yet finished paying for votes he had bought during the Patriarchal election. *And* he wanted to raise new armies to launch another crusade against the Pramans occupying much of the Holy Lands.

Past crusades had established Brothen Episcopal footholds amongst the Wells of Ihrian, as Crusader principalities and kingdoms. During the last decade, though, those states had been under severe pressure from the Kaifate of Qasr al-Zed and its great champion, Indala al-Sul Halaladin. Sublime desperately wanted history to acclaim him the Patriarch who wrested the Holy Lands from the Unbeliever forever. His extermination of heresy at home would finance the glorious mission overseas.

Honario Benedocto, who had schemed and bribed his way into the Patriarchy, was loathed with enthusiasm by millions.

THE SEUIR ANDE LETTE TURNED TO HIS NEAREST COMPANION, A GRAY MAN in his early sixties. "What say you, Perfect Master? It seems the hour of despair has arrived sooner than you forethought."

The Perfect Master of the Path, Brother Candle from Khaurene, bowed his head. "I'm tempted to declare my shame. As though my coming conjured this pestilence. As to advice, I can only repeat the admonition of the Synod of St. Jeules. Let no Seeker After Light be first to raise his hand against another man. But let no Seeker strengthen evil through any failure to resist it."

Brother Candle had argued against that stance. He was a pacifist at heart. But once the synod reached its decision he set out to prepare his Seeker brethren to defend themselves. Some would destroy them rather than recognize their special relationship with the Divine.

The young knight told Brother Candle, "He'll talk first. His men won't want a real fight or a long siege. Get away from Lette while you can."

Brother Candle stared out at the raiders. Few of them were driven by their devotion to the Episcopal faith. They were mercenaries because they could do nothing else. Without this marginally religious pretense they would be simple brigands.

More than one darkness stalks the earth.

"No stain of cowardice would attach to you, Master," Brock Rault promised. "We'd all rather that one so rare as you be removed from harm's way. Haiden Backe will offer you no respect." Rault's brothers and cousins nodded as they prepared to fight. "And you can carry our plea for help to Count Raymone."

Brother Candle went to stand alone, to meditate. To seek the best path. To discover how he could best serve. To let the Light move him.

The flesh was loath to go. The flesh dreaded what secret thoughts others might entertain if he chose flight. Yet he would do no one any good, ever, if he let himself be butchered at Caron ande Lette. The Church would crow because one of the Adversary's most favored had fallen—while insisting that it had nothing to do with Haiden Backe's campaign. Slipping the Grolsacher a bonus for having disposed of one of those pesky Maysalean Perfects.

Rault said, "I'll have a fast horse brought to the water postern."

"I arrived on foot," the holy man replied. "So shall I depart."

No one argued. A man afoot, in tattered clothing, would be ignored. The outlanders did not understand Maysalean vows of poverty.

BROCK RAULT ENGAGED THE GROLSACHER WARLORD IN POINTLESS DIS-course. He hinted that, offered the right terms, Caron ande Lette might yield without an exchange of blows. Haiden Backe would not find nego-tiations unusual. Connectens seldom chose to fight in the face of supe-rior numbers. Then Brock's youngest brother, Thurm, reported, "The Perfect Master is out of sight."

Rault grunted, gave the signal. The result would stain his soul in-delibly. But he knew that soul would return for another turn around the wheel. He did not hesitate to greet evil with unexpected evil. He had learned that from Count Raymone Garete.

Archers sprang up and let fly. Backe's standard bearer and herald fell from their horses, as did two priests in dun cassocks. A third priest, of substance because he wore armor, survived the hail but had to extricate himself from his wounded mount.

Haiden Backe flung a hand into the path of an arrow streaking to-ward his face. Which exposed the gap in armor under his arm. An arrow found it, broke as its head hit a rib, and turned. It failed to reach his heart.

A companion snatched the reins of Backe's horse. The remaining raiders galloped away, pursued by missiles. A ballista shaft slammed through one, deep into the neck of his mount.

Only the armored priest escaped unscathed.

Brock's sister Socia, just sixteen, observed, "Sublime will use this against us."

"Of course he will. But these men, who don't work for the Patriarch, were here already, without just cause. They mean to steal our lives, our fortunes, and our good names. What else can their not-employer take away?"

Thurm sneered, "He could always excommunicate us."

Everyone in earshot laughed.

Brock said, "None of those people appear to have perished. Let's help them get to this heaven they're determined to force upon us."

Even the fallen priests were disinclined to meet their God today. One volunteered to renounce Sublime V in favor of the Anti-Patriarch, Immaculate II.

Brock let that one inscribe a letter confessing the Brothen Church's Grolsacher connections. He had the rest bound to stakes and left to the mercy of their deity. Within easy bowshot. Should their fellows be over-whelmed by an impulse to rescue them.

The mercenary force surrounded Caron ande Lette.

"Wow!" Socia said. Fearfully. "There's a lot of them."

"But in disarray," Brock replied. "They don't know what to do now. And Haiden Backe can't tell them."

That situation persisted for three days. Backe's underlings launched several clumsy attacks. Each failed.

Haiden Backe lost his struggle with fever and sepsis. The Bishop of Strang, the Grolsacher priest who could afford armor, declared himself Backe's successor. The mercenaries quickly expressed their confidence in the Bishop and the aims of the Brothen Patriarch. That night more than thirty resigned under cover of darkness.

Morcant Farfog, Bishop of Strang, was one of countless corrupt, incompetent bishops associated with the Brothen Patriarchy. Sublime had found that he could ease his fiscal woes by selling new bishoprics.

A rudimentary bureaucracy meant to raise funds through sales of livings, pardons, bequests, and indulgences was in its formative stage.

Sublime needed the money.

The Anti-Patriarch, Immaculate, at Viscesment, moaned and carried on but never really seized the moral opportunity. He was close to abandoning the struggle against the Usurpers of the Mother City.

The mercenaries besieging Caron ande Lette had little to recommend them. But most were not stupid. Few failed to see through Bishop Farfog's bluster. He was supremely incompetent, completely self-involved, and certain to cause fatalities amongst those dim enough to remain in his vicinity.

Desertions continued apace.

Two hours of brisk hiking took Brother Candle to Artlan ande Brith. Seuir Lanne Tuldse was a skeletal, elderly Maysalean knight. Seuir Lanne had kept faith with Khaurene. He had observed the letter of Duke Tormond's proclamation against erecting fortifications.

"Come," Seuir Lanne told the Perfect Master. "We'll go up to the house. From there you'll be able to see the smoke if they fire Caron ande Lette."

"The house" was a stone manor balanced precariously atop a tall, bristling outcrop of weathered limestone. Not, strictly, a fortress. But difficult to enter if the inhabitants preferred that you stay out.

Fifteen minutes after the Perfect Master's arrival Lanne Tuldse's grandson galloped south toward Antieux. He would raise alarums along the way.

The boy ran into one of Count Raymone's patrols. They led him to an encampment on the Old Brothen military highway, the Inland Road, which followed the western bank of the Dechear River. Here the river marked the traditional boundary between the End of Connec and Ormienden, a hodgepodge of counties and minuscule principalities of mixed and varied allegiance, some to the Grail Empire, some to the Patriarchy, some to kingdoms in nearby Firaldia. A few, by marriage, even owed fealty to the ruling houses of Arnhand and Santerin. The harsh vistas of Grolsach lay only eight leagues away, beyond a tongue of Ormienden occupied by entities called Imp and Manu. Count Raymone meant to confront would-be invaders who chose to use the Inland Road. That being the route selected by previous invaders from Arnhand. He felt compelled to resist vigorously. Occupation of the Connec's eastern marches would isolate the rest of the province from the assistance of the Empire.

The Count's spies in Grolsach had learned the truth about Sublime's secret letters of marque. Raymone meant to smash anyone who took them up before they reached the cities of the eastern Connec.

Antieux was a magnet for invaders. Antieux had delivered embarrassments to several forces trying to perpetrate the Patriarch's villainies.

Count Raymone did not have the blessing of Duke Tormond. The Duke clung tenaciously to the illusion that Sublime would keep promises he had made in exchange for Connecten support in his crusade against Calzir. Tormond could not understand that Sublime did not feel obligated to keep faith with heretics. Lying was no sin when you lied to Unbelievers.

Count Raymone moved as soon as he received word. He reached Artlan ande Brith two days later. While the Count's soldiers made camp Brother Candle responded to a summons from the hotheaded, headstrong lord of Antieux.

Count Raymone greeted him warmly. "Desperate hours bring us together again, eh, Master?"

"Existence consists of cycles and convergences," Brother Candle replied. "Even in the upwelling of wickedness. Not to mention demands upon our respective professions."

"Tell me about these Grolsachers."

"I can't."

"Won't?" Count Raymone was accustomed to the vagaries of the Maysalean conscience. Some were determined to remain pacifist, whatever befell them.

"Cannot. The young seuir hustled me out the back door as soon as he recognized the threat."

"Brock Rault is the perfect knight. He fought well against the Arnhanders. He'd have done well in Shippen if the damned Calzirans had bothered to fight back."

"Just as well they didn't. The inevitable would have devoured them."

"Good for us, too." Because Connectens had served in the Calziran Crusade they had established certain rights. Though they had won no honors from the Patriarch, they had helped deliver vast new territories into the realm of Peter, King of Navaya. King Peter, whose queen was Duke Tormond's sister, was now a protector of the Connec.

"Yes. So?"

"Are you going to preach to me, Master?" Count Raymone was intimidating. He was tall, lean, dark, and seemed older than his twenty-four and a half years. He had a long scar over his left eye that made him look more ferocious than he was. Swollen and discolored, it was still healing.

Brother Candle raised a brushy gray eyebrow. "I'd rather you call me Brother."

"I have Maysalean evangelists in my family, Brother. I recognize the light in your eye that means a bout of holy instruction is due to begin." The Count was known for his sardonic sense of humor.

Brother Candle's other eyebrow jumped up. Then he chuckled.

"That won't work, either, Brother. I feel no need to be your pal. You people are transparent manipulators."

"Then I bow to youth's need to make its own mistakes."

"Transparent."

Brother Candle gave up. Count Raymone would give him no foothold. It was too late, anyway. Hell's tendrils had been creeping into the End of Connec for years. Ill-tempered time had begotten evil pups. He was wasting it trying to stem the cruel tide. His obligation now was to preserve and cherish what little he could.

He snorted. A Seeker After Light, a Perfect, did not entertain such conceits as Hell. Hell existed only in the Episcopal mind. The more primitive Chaldarean cults, on the far reaches of the world, believed in an Adversary but not in a Pit of Eternal Torment. Brother Candle did not know how the Hell concept had crept into the western form of Chaldareanism. In other strains, as was the case in the ancestral Devedian and Dainshau religions, all punishment and reward happened right here, right now, in this world.

The Deves and Dainshaus should have had the wickedness hammered out of them by now. Their God and the Chaldareans had been punishing them forever.

"You are amused, Master?"

"Brother. My thoughts veered to the plight of those who reject the Path. These days they must believe their gods particularly spiteful and callous."

"And no less do they deserve, bending their knees to the Tyranny of the Night."

And there lay the paradox of the world.

God was real, if long unseen. All gods were real. Sometimes they reached into the mortal world. Every demon, devil, and sprite ever imagined was real, somewhere. Spirits of tree and river and stone were real. Things that lay in wait in the dark were painfully real and still found even in lands where the ruling faith officially denied them. Even in the End of Connec, which had been acclaimed as tame since the days of the Old Empire, night things were hidden away. The little ones remained where they'd always been, in the forests, in the mountains, in ancient stone circles ignorant people thought had been erected by giants. They avoided notice because in the End of Connec they were far from any source of power. They would never grow into anything more terrible than what they were. They avoided notice because whenever their presence became obvious Episcopal spirit hunters came to destroy them.

Bigger things of the Night were bound into statues or stones and buried beneath crossroads, or into magical swords or enchanted rings seldom used because they were inherently treacherous, or into the tombstones and gateway arches of old-time pagan cemeteries. Such few as had survived the cleansing unleashed by the sorcerer-captains of the Old Brothen Empire.

Once there had been those powerful enough to be accounted gods or godlings. Those were dead or their power and being had been scattered in a thousand fragments of broken stone by the conquering world-tamers of old. The world preferred them scattered and harmless if they could not be permanently destroyed.

Permanent was difficult when belief could quicken the most lost from any stray wisps of power.

There were individuals who could pull them back together. Sorcerers hungry for power. Though in the west no man had become that powerful for more than a dozen centuries. Here, men of talent were, inevitably, drawn into the Collegium. Where they endured constant monitoring by others like themselves. Or they perished.

Brother Candle said, "My creed won't let me bless what you do, Count Raymone. And yet, what you do, however ruthless, has to be done to stem the tide of darkness."

Where darkness and the Night were real forces, not personifications of evil. They could not be that. They were neither good nor evil. Not till someone decided and painted the label on, like a caste mark on the forehead. Or until someone used them to evil purpose.

Brother Candle was at peace with his conscience. He had done all that he could do. But he was troubled, even so. More was wakening than just the rage, greed, and lust of mortal men.

*   *   *

TWO DOZEN SOLDIERS DEMONSTRATED SOUTH OF CARON ANDE LETTE, drawing the attention of the mercenaries. Bishop Farfog moved to confront them, contemptuous of their numbers. The villains who remained with him were not bright enough to worry about a handful of men who seemed determined to bait them.

The Bishop himself did not see that—though he was *supposed* to think these few wanted to lead him into a trap. Count Raymone Garete's clever strategy nearly foundered because his enemy was too stupid to be suspicious.

Inertia and laziness kept the Grolsachers from charging. Plus a dim fear that the defenders of Caron ande Lette, all twenty-two, might fall on them from behind.

While the few demonstrated and the Raults waited, Count Raymone's troops slipped past, out of sight, to the west, taking care to raise no dust. A few passed to the east, too, filtering through the trees along the river's edge. The demonstrators withdrew. The Grolsachers resumed taunting the besieged and dodging the occasional arrow.

The demonstrators reappeared next morning. With two hundred friends. When some mercenaries considered following the example of friends smart enough to take off earlier, they discovered Connecten companies behind them. They watched their pathetic camp be overrun.

There was not much of a fight. The Grolsachers scattered, suffering their casualties on the run.

The Connectens only pursued those who did not flee in the direction they wanted. Back along the river, toward home. Where they found themselves ambushed, pinned down by archers, then set upon by heavy infantry.

That left the river. The Connectens let them be once they entered the water.

Bishop Farfog was one of the few who swam well enough to reach the far bank. Having abandoned his armor and plunder.

Brother Candle arrived while Count Raymone's men were burying the mercenary dead, some of whom had not yet stopped breathing. They had no need to lay down any of their own. The rabble had scattered before the Connectens suffered any damage.

The Perfect Master saw no one who had died of wounds from the front. Many looked like they had been murdered after their capture. Few prisoners had been retained.

Which fit Count Raymone's character. The Count believed that the best way to discourage attacks on the Connec was to obliterate anyone inclined to attack, leaving the corpses to the scavengers.

Brock Rault and his brothers were behind what courtesy was being shown the fallen.

The Perfect Master walked the killing fields in sadness. The mercenaries, refugees and Grolsachers alike, were the poorest of the poor. The dead often even lacked weapons worth looting. They had counted on arming themselves with weapons taken from their victims.

Nor was that new. Grolsach in particular produced poor, would-be killers the way Ormienden produced wines and the End of Connec generated songs, poetry, paintings, and marvelous tapestries.

Grolsachers led by Adolf Black had joined the ill-fated Arnhander incursion that ended with the Black Mountain Massacre. Two years before that, thousands of Grolsachers, again in service to Arnhand, perished in that kingdom's defeat at Themes, when the King of Arnhand tried to enforce his dubious rights in Tramaine.

Brother Candle joined Brock Rault and his siblings, Booth, Socia, and Thurm. Brock and Booth were thoughtful, Thurm unsettled. Socia was totally bloodthirsty. She wanted to put heads on poles facing the Grolsach border.

Brother Candle observed, "The human species has an attention span like that of a bluebottle." Flies became more numerous by the hour. Had Brother Candle entertained any strain of paganism he might have recalled that pre-Chaldarean Instrumentality known as Lord of Flies, Lord of Maggots, Prince of Ravens, or Rook. Rook was the last god who visited battlefields. He followed Ordnan, god of battles, Death, and Hilt, or the Choosers of the Slain. The latter collected the greatest heroes, whole. Hilt collected only the souls of those deemed unworthy of the Hall of Heroes.

Rook was Corruption incarnate.

Rook's thoughts summoned all flies and carrion eaters when men gathered for war. Before the coming of the Episcopal Chaldarean faith. Those old Instrumentalities were gone, now. Supposedly. More or less. Modern man hoped. And prayed to his newer, gentler gods.

The ghosts of the harsher gods never left the collective consciousness. They would be reborn if enough people needed them and called them forth. If the wells of power produced sufficient surplus for Instrumentalities to grow.

Socia offered a disquieting thought. "Maybe the Connec itself is a corpse, drawing flies."

Brother Candle shuddered. There was a mad edge to the girl-child's voice. Perhaps she was sensitive to the Instrumentalities of the Night. He observed, "The Grolsachers never learn. Their adventures all turn into catastrophes. The people who hire them will not learn, either. Why don't they notice that anyone who hires Grolsachers always stumbles into a disaster?"

Socia laughed. "You'd have to figure they're due for a win. Wouldn't you?"

Brother Candle exchanged looks with the girl's brothers. Brock Rault shook his head. Socia had seen the elephant nose to trunk. She had helped abuse the mercenaries cut down in front of the gate. None of that had disturbed her in the least.

The girl had no grasp of Maysalean principles. Brother Candle reminded himself that all religions came plentifully stocked with people who paid no attention to what they were about. Some became powerful in the hierarchy of their faith. And had to swim rivers when their villainy flashed back in their faces.

The Usurper Patriarch Sublime V was the man Brother Candle had in mind, though the accusation could have been laid at the feet of most of the Brothen Episcopal Collegium.

ON ANOTHER LEVEL, BROTHER CANDLE WAS DEEPLY CONCERNED ABOUT the supernatural impact on the conflict. There had been a sharp increase in encounters with things of the Night since the Black Mountain Massacre, in that region. The violence and emotion here was sure to attract the eyes of the Night, as well.

2. Brothe, with the Captain-General

Piper Hecht swore in the Episcopal fashion. "God's Blood! Can't those people leave me alone for a single night?"

Anna Mozilla's full lips twisted in a sneer. "You missed the night, eh? And the afternoon before it? And this morning? I'm wondering if my feelings ought to be hurt, Mr. Captain-General."

Piper took a second to make certain his mistress was teasing. Anna did demonstrate occasional, unpredictable fits of self-pity.

She said, "It's Pinkus Ghort. His own self." Imitating Ghort's Grolsacher speech habits. "So it must be serious."

Hecht's old campaigning companion commanded the Brothen City Regiment, a task as thorny and thankless as herding cats. Ghort faced constraints and demands as distracting as those plaguing the Captain-General himself. Ghort would have a good reason for appearing in person, in the rain.

"It must be." Hecht went to the door. Anna had admitted no one. Only Piper Hecht and one maid ever entered her home. Ghort and his man Polo waited on the tiny stoop.

The warm rain had wakened the rich aromas of the street. Sadly, it was not heavy enough to wash anything away.

"Some major shit coming down, Pipe. We need to jump on it. Fast."

"What?"

"Clearenza. Fon Dreasser repudiated his oaths to the Patriarchy. They haven't heard at the Castella. Yet. Sublime's gonna shit himself."

There would be more. Clearenza's defection was not unexpected. Duke Germa fon Dreasser was inconstant, to be generous. His allegiance shifted between the Grail Empire and the Patriarchy with every change in the political breeze. But this time the change could have more than indifferent consequences. Sublime V owed Germa and the syndics of Clearenza eighteen thousand gold ducats against past-due loans taken to finance the Calziran Crusade. Which had been expected to be self-financing through plunder. That expectation having been stillborn. The little wealth to be found had gotten into the hands of Sublime's Imperial and Direcian allies. Lately, Sublime had stopped even pretending that he would meet his obligations. He had stopped making interest installments to the Clearenzan consortium.

"And?"

"He's asked for the Emperor's protection."

Although unsurprising, that made no immediate sense. The Grail Emperor, Lothar, was a sickly boy not expected to survive the year. Though he had not been expected to survive any of his previous fifteen.

Hecht said, "I smell Ferris Renfrow. I don't have a horse." Hecht seldom rode inside the city, despite his standing.

"Renfrow. Got it first toss, I'll bet. We brought extra mounts." A dozen horsemen waited up the narrow street, only now aware that the Captain-General had come out.

"Let me get . . ."

Anna handed him his winter cloak. It was heavy for the season but would keep him dry during the ride to the Chiaro Palace. She kissed him. Ghort chuckled. Skinny old Polo averted his gaze and reddened.

The horsemen came up. Hecht recognized none of them. No doubt their loyalties lay with Pinkus and his sponsor, Principaté Bronte Doneto. But Hecht had no reason to mistrust Ghort. No reason to be uncomfortable with the situation.

Ferris Renfrow was a sinister figure close to the Grail Emperor. He had been close to Lothar's father, Johannes, as well. Renfrow's work in the shadows had made Johannes Blackboots powerful and kept his fragile successor free of challengers now, within the Empire and without.

The Patriarch, Sublime V, had anticipated a respite. The Imperial crown would pass to Lothar's sister, Katrin, next. But Lothar refused to die. And his Empire kept after the Patriarchy like a pack of hounds, trying to reduce the Church's temporal power. More so now than had been while Johannes was alive.

The young Emperor blamed Sublime for his father's death. And Renfrow fed his bitterness.

That contest would not end while the New Brothen Empire survived.

Hecht could not imagine the Chaldarean Episcopal Church collapsing into history's dust. Much as he might long for that end, secretly. Too many men had too much invested in the institution.

Hecht swung aboard a gray palfrey. He thought some of Ghort's men looked unusually nervous. "What's the trouble?"

"You don't know? You need to pay more attention, Pipe. The Night's been active lately. Even by day. There's been a string of mystery murders. Really violent. Really messy. Victims all torn up. The rumors blame night monsters. People are praying that that's really the cause."

These men were veterans. They should not be troubled. Should they? "There's a less pleasant alternative?"

"Yes."

"A madman?"

"The kind who kills to conjure ugly spirits. Eaters of souls."

Hecht shivered. He had seen and suffered a lot during his thirty-some years. But there were worse things out there, uglier, more evil things, than ever he had seen. Worse things waiting in the night.

"That sounds like Sheard savages, Pinkus. Not Brothens."

"I don't think that's it. I mention it for the sake of completeness. People mostly *want* to look on the dark side. And there ain't no Grand Marshes anymore, way I hear tell."

"What?"

"I know you don't pay attention to anything but Anna and your job. Word is, the marshes are drying up. Principaté Delari could tell you. He has priests all over sending in reports about the changes going on. Like the ice and snow piling up in the high mountains. Like the water level in the Shallow Sea dropping the height of a man. So that all those marshes up there are draining out and drying up. And freezing over permanent on their northern side."

"That makes sense. I guess. It wasn't obvious when I left."

Ghort shrugged. He did not much care about changes going on a thousand miles away. He did not have that kind of mind.

Piper Hecht was glad the man he was around most was shallow and self-absorbed. When talk grew uncomfortable he could divert it just by mentioning wine or the hippodrome. Ghort and the grape got on much too well. And the hippodrome preoccupied most everyone in season.

"So what's special about this killer? What makes him a celebrity?"

Brothe was the world's second largest city, first honors going to Hypraxium in the Eastern Empire. Hypraxium enjoyed a thoroughly decadent reputation. But Brothe had its dark side. Murder was a fact of life. Law was mostly a private matter.

Some murders always fell outside common understanding.

"I can't tell you anything more than I have. I don't get out to find out what the poor and the squatters are saying these days. I just know people are scared. And the Collegium won't take it seriously."

"Is it like when the soultaken were here?" That part of his past Hecht understood only because his current mentor, Principaté Delari, had taken pains to find out what he could about those divinely possessed butchers. Which had been very little. .

"They just killed people to make money to get by till they could do whatever it was that their managing Instrumentalities wanted done."

Only the soultaken knew they had been elected by their gods to destroy a mortal those Old Ones called the Godslayer, a slave-soldier of far Dreanger. Else Tage, one of the most capable captains among the Sha-lug. Sent to Firaldia by Gordimer the Lion on behalf of the Kaif of al-Minphet, to blunt Sublime V's lust for new crusades.

Else Tage never learned that he was a target of ancient gods. He did suspect that the Instrumentalities of the Night had a marked interest in him, however. With only the vaguest notion why.

Else Tage survived the soultaken. Else Tage now wore the name Piper Hecht. He had risen amongst the Episcopal Chaldareans to become Captain-General of the armies being raised by the one man most determined to loose fire and sword upon the Unbelievers of the Holy Lands.

Few knew the truth.

Piper Hecht would have been more comfortable if those few were fewer still.

Hecht said, "Pinkus, you see Doneto all the time. Does he have any idea what's going on inside Sublime's head? Will he want Clearenza punished?"

"Probably. There's a history between Germa fon Dreasser and Honario Benedocto." The latter having been the Patriarch's name before his elevation.

"These Firaldians have been dishonoring each other's wives and daughters and using that to excuse assassinations since . . ."

"Not to mention their sons and catamites."

"Why are we going this way, Pinkus? Especially on a rainy day?"

They had entered an area of tenements so closely crowded that two horsemen could not pass in opposite directions. The unpaved streets were slick and deep in a mix of manure and human ordure. It made sucking noises when the horses lifted their hooves. Water filled their hoofprints instantly.

The grooms in the regimental stables would have plenty to do once these animals returned. "Just Plain Joe will love you." Hooves and legs would need special attention to prevent disease.

"Ogier! Aubero! What the hell is it with this romp through a shit pile? Who told you to go this way?" Ghort tried to bully his way forward.

Half a minute later Hecht emerged into a small square. Those who had preceded him were looking round warily, weapons drawn.

"Something besides the shit stinks," Ghort declared. "Ogier and Aubero have disappeared. Those assholes."

"I deduced as much when I saw your blade bare to the weather."

"Polo will rub the rust out. That's what he gets paid for. That and for spying on all of us for Paludan Bruglioni."

Polo overheard. He did not protest. Ghort never showed any concern for his feelings.

Ghort gave orders. Men dismounted and moved out along the walls facing the square and its central cistern. The emptiness of the square was not a good omen. Ghort muttered, "I never should've taken those two into the lifeguard."

"Who?" Hecht asked.

"Ogier and Aubero. Twins, would you believe? From back home. They had a letter of introduction from my uncle Ornis. I should've listened to my gut instead of figuring I owed family."

A nasty bumblebee whir silenced Ghort's lament. Like Hecht, he dove aside. He had heard the distinctive *thunk!* of a crossbow. He splashed and rolled and got behind the only available cover, a wooden pillar scarcely seven inches wide. "You see where that came from?"

"No." Piper Hecht had acquired similar shelter. Without getting filthy. His pillar was as thick as it was wide. A good thing, because one iron quarrel had bitten into the hard old wood already. "But your men are on to something."

Those Ghort had ordered forward rushed a doorway. They were professionals, all veterans of the Calziran Crusade and the fighting in the streets of al-Khazen.

Bolts continued to streak around and miss till one of Ghort's men got hit in the foot by a ricochet. His man Polo, who had been Hecht's servant at one time, crouched behind the Captain-General, wringing his hands and whining, not in terror but about the amount of work he was going to have to do after this was over.

"Put a stopper in it, Polo." Hecht had located the snipers, now. There were three of them. He didn't think Ghort's wayward bodyguards were among them. No doubt those two were headed north in a hurry, arguing about how to spend their bounties.

Hecht picked a moment when all three snipers would be rewinding their weapons, surged up to go to the attack. Polo grabbed his right arm, trying to keep him from exposing himself. Hecht lurched left, trying to break the servant's grip.

A bolt of darkness streaked down from the rooftop. Hecht saw the spellcaster in momentary silhouette. The bolt was the size and shape of a hammer handle, in infinite black. It would hit him in the chest. He flung his left hand up. His left wrist exploded in sudden, fiery agony.

The clot of darkness curved aside. It struck Polo's outstretched arm. The man shrieked.

It happened in a blink. Polo's arm withered into a leathery, desiccated black stick, a dead mockery of a human limb.

The mutilation was complete before Polo finished his first scream.

One of Ghort's men appeared behind the sorcerer-assassin. A veteran for sure. He wasted no time. He grabbed the assassin and flung him off the roof.

The would-be killer landed on his head. He died instantly, neck broken and skull crushed.

"Shit!" Ghort swore. "Now we'll never know what this was about. He'll be the only one who knew." His men dragged a prisoner into the square. "Can you make him stop howling?" He meant Polo. "That shrieking could get on my nerves."

Hecht said, "Find the soldiers who led us here. You know who they are and where they're from. Have them brought back. Bo Biogna would be the man to send." He massaged his left wrist. It had not been bad this time. "I want to talk to them." The amulet he wore, invisible since its installation by the Dreangean master sorcerer er-Rashal al-Dhulquarnen, protected him well but at the cost of harsh pain. "Bring that corpse. Somebody in the Collegium may be able to get something out of it."

Ghort did not argue although, strictly speaking, the Captain-General of Patriarchal forces had no standing with the Brothen City Regiment. "What the hell just happened, Pipe? I mean, I'm fucking glad it did, but there ain't no way you shouldn't be all over looking like Polo's arm now." Ghort had Polo down, now, trying to examine his arm. Polo would not lie still. "That black bolt shoulda plugged you in the brisket. But it turned off. And got this poor bastard."

"I don't know. I'm glad it did. Though I'm sorry about Polo's arm."

"No shit. Hold still, goddamnit! Garnier! Arnoul! Get those damned horses under control! Aaron's Hairy Balls! They're worse than kids. You have to tell them everything."

Piper Hecht burst into laughter.

"What?"

"Grade Drocker said the same about you not that long ago."

"When? I was always a self-starter."

"When we were in the Connec. At Bishop Serifs's manor, besieging Antieux."

"That was different. You didn't want to stick your neck out around those Brotherhood of War assholes. They didn't care what you did, it was fucked up. You were always wrong just because you didn't belong to their crazy man club."

Pinkus Ghort always had an answer. It might not ring true or make sense, but he had one.

"The corpse," Hecht reminded gently.

"Izzy. Buchie. Search the dead guy. And don't pocket anything. It could kill you later." Softly, he said, "They wouldn't take nothing, no how. They're all guys from out in the sticks. So superstitious and scared of the Night it'll be a miracle if they keep it together now long enough to find the kind of priest who'll pretend to pull the imaginary supernatural leeches off them."

Ghort was exaggerating. That was a matter of course. But Hecht had run into people who were that afraid of the hidden world. People who could not draw a breath without praying and calculating how much attention that might draw from the Instrumentalities of the Night.

Brothe being the Holy Mother City of the Episcopal strain of Chaldareanism, its streets ever boasted floods of religious pilgrims. Many were the sort who held intimate discourse with their deity every waking moment. They wandered in a perpetual daze, babbling constantly.

God must find them annoying. They suffered more misfortunes than the less devout.

Ghort helped Polo onto his mount. Sensitive to the Night, the animal grew skittish. Men, forced to walk because their mounts were carrying a dead sorcerer, a wounded ambusher, or had run away, kept Polo's horse under control.

Polo was incoherent.

He needed a healing brother. Soon.

PINKUS GHORT DID NOT DISPUTE POSSESSION OF THE PRISONERS. "JUST LET me have one healthy one, Pipe. A trophy. So I don't have to listen to Principaté Doneto bark."

"Take your pick. Take two if you want." Hecht was confident that nothing useful could be gained from any of the prisoners. "That'll ease my budget." Working for Sublime, even indirectly, included an endless, thankless, continuous scramble for money. The Patriarch had no comprehension of economics. He could not be made to understand that he had to have income if he wanted to spend. He resented any effort to explain by those whose wages had to be paid and whose costs had to be underwritten.

Sublime was convinced that the Lord would provide. And that hired hands should be happy with what the Lord provided.

They were crossing the vast limestone sprawl of the Closed Ground, so-called since antiquity because the wings of the Chiaro Palace enfolded it completely. The Palace was three and four stories high, its limestone architecture classically simple. The eastern face, in the direction of the Holy Lands, boasted balconies where the Patriarch and senior Principatés presented themselves on Holy Days. There were always scaffoldings somewhere around the marges of the Closed Ground. The Chiaro Palace was under continuous rehabilitation.

The Palace was built of stone from the same quarry as the pavements but the coloring did not match. The pavements had been in place for only three centuries. Parts of the Palace went back fifteen centuries. They showed the effects of all those years of weather and bad air. The stone was streaked brown, yellow, or pale pink.

The first foundations of the Chiaro Palace had been laid down before the Old Brothen Empire recognized itself as such.

Parts of Brothe were older, still. But Hecht was not impressed. His boyhood had passed in a city where structures still in daily use were three times the age of the oldest in Brothe.

The rain continued, growing heavier. Thunder mouthed off north of the Teragi River. There was a pre-Chaldarean superstition about thunder's location being some sort of omen. Hecht could not recall details. He was too wet and uncomfortable to focus on much but the ambush and getting into dry clothing.

His batman came out to help. "What's all this, sir?" Redfearn Bechter was a pensioner of the Brotherhood of War. And, surely, still its agent.

"They ambushed us, Sergeant."

"Bad decision on their part. I know that one there."

"What?"

"Not personally. I've seen him before. He was with Duke Tormond of the Connec when he visited the Patriarch a few years ago."

Bechter had a scary knack for recalling names and faces. "Rainard. That's his name. I remember thinking he was either too stupid or too smart for the job he was doing."

"And that was what?"

"He was one of the varlets managing their animals. But he didn't do much work. He kept sneaking off to hang out in low places. So he was a shirker. Or a spy. I figure spy. A shirker wouldn't get away with it for long."

"You listening, Pinkus?"

"Plenty. You want to keep him? I'll take the other two."

"We do have better interrogators here."

"Let me know what you find out. Look, I came after you for a reason. The screaming high shits really do want to talk about Clearenza. Now."

Being Captain-General had its perquisites. A dozen varlets and stablemen came for the animals and prisoners and casualties. Ghort lied to them. "The guy with the bad arm is related to Principaté Bruglioni. See he gets treated like it."

Polo did come from the Bruglioni household, originally, and likely continued spying for them. But he was a hireling. Even so, invoking the name of one of the Five Families got results.

Ten minutes later, Hecht entered a room he found depressingly familiar. Each time he visited, it was to face irate members of the Collegium, the Princes of the Church. This looked like no exception. The dozen most powerful Principatés had gathered. A bitter squabble was under way, along the usual political lines. The one friendly face he saw belonged to Principaté Delari.

"About damned time!" Principaté Madisetti bellowed. "Where the hell have you been? We sent for you hours ago."

And the Cologni Principaté wanted to know, "Why do you have to come here filthy, smelling like a dung heap?"

"We were ambushed. Four men. Three equipped with our own standard-issue crossbows. The fourth a sorcerer of some skill but very little luck. The corpse is downstairs. If you want to examine it. Who, other than Colonel Ghort and yourselves, knew that I'd been summoned?" Professionally, he had to admire the quickness with which the ambush had been put together. Though, certainly, the ambush team had been around, waiting for an opportunity, for some time.

It did not occur to Hecht that he might not have been the target. He thought he knew who was behind the attempt. He did not know why.

He watched the churchmen closely, not expecting anyone to betray himself. None were major suspects, anyway. Their crime, if any, would be the sin of talking too much.

Only Principaté Delari reacted strongly. His response was vast anger tightly reined. He had, to all intents, adopted Piper Hecht. This ambush was a direct assault on his family.

Piper Hecht had not plumbed the relationship deeply enough to understand. The man he had worked for from his earliest mercenary days, Grade Drocker, had become his mentor during the Calziran Crusade. Drocker was one of the top dozen men in the Brotherhood of War. And the warrior priest had been the illegitimate son of Principaté Muniero

Delari. Who assumed the mentor role with a passion following Drocker's death.

Hecht did not understand but he did not scruple to exploit the situation.

"I'll return shortly," Muniero Delari said. He was a sallow stick figure of a man in his seventies. He moved as easily as men thirty years younger. He left in a rush. The air seemed to go out with him.

The Madisetti Principaté, Donel Madisetti, presumed to pick up his attack. For reasons as obscure as Delari's favor, the Madisetti family had developed an antipathy toward Hecht. The Bruglioni and Arniena families were firm supporters, though they disagreed with one another about Sublime V. The Cologni family waffled. More often than not, though, they opposed the Captain-General because he had worked for the Bruglioni before his elevation. And the Bruglioni may have been behind the assassination of Principaté-designate Rodrigo Cologni. Which had taken place before Hecht's arrival in Brothe.

The relationships and balances between the Five Families seldom made sense to outsiders.

Strange bedfellows. Always. Piper Hecht now worked for Honario Benedocto, the Patriarch Sublime V. The Benedocto were sworn enemies of the Bruglioni. This decade. The Madisetti had marched shoulder to shoulder with the Benedocto for a generation.

The Captain-General was immune to most of the feuding. He was not supposed to be part of city politics, only Church politics. Though the former became the latter at every Patriarchal election.

He turned his back on Donel Madisetti. He addressed details of the ambush to Principaté Bronte Doneto, the Patriarch's cousin. And one of Sublime's few friends.

Doneto asked, "Why would these men want to kill you?"

Hecht shrugged. "That will become more clear once we know who they are."

Doneto's gaze shifted to Pinkus Ghort. Ghort said, "I don't have any ideas."

"You'll have to answer for the men who led you into the ambush." Meaning that, while Ghort was beholden to Bronte Doneto already, he was about to be pushed in a whole lot deeper.

"We're on that already, Your Grace. They'll be brought back. I'll see that they talk." Ghort had sent for his man Bo Biogna. Biogna should be headed north before nightfall.

Hecht said, "I understand there's a problem in Clearenza."

Doneto replied, "I doubt there's a connection."

"I doubt it myself. There'd be no state interest at this point. Would there?"

"Just so. Donel. For Aaron's sake, stop whining. You're a grown man." He tossed that at the Madisetti Principaté. To Hecht, he said, "That bolt would have been better spent sped at another target."

Donel Madisetti shut up. Appalled. He did not expect to be chastised by an ally.

With Principaté Delari absent and Principaté Hugo Mongoz lapsed into a drooling nap, Principaté Doneto took charge. Though he was not the eldest.

Doneto was the sort who wanted to be in charge.

Most of the time he was not unpleasant about it.

Doneto said, "I sent Colonel Ghort to get you at the same time I alerted the crisis committee. They arrived first because they didn't have to go out into the weather or fight anyone to get here." Doneto disdained most of the Princes of the Church. The world might be terrified of the Collegium and its supposed wizards, but Bronte Doneto knew most of his colleagues were incompetents appointed via nepotism or bribe.

There were powerful sorcerers amongst the brethren of the Collegium, however. Who was, and who was not, was a puzzle that interested outsiders constantly strove to solve. While the Principatés strove to stay masked.

Even Sublime, who had come out of the Collegium but whose qualifications mainly included family connections and being stone deaf and blind to the Instrumentalities of the Night, was kept in the dark.

Doneto said, "My cousin is worried about Clearenza because he worries about everything. Too much. For him it's all personal. And an insult to God and all the Holy Founders. All blasphemy, heresy, or something."

Hecht had worked for Principaté Doneto for a year. Doneto liked to think that Hecht worked for him still. Undercover. The Bruglioni and Arniena families, likewise, thought they had a claim on the Captain-General's loyalty because he had worked for them, too. Hecht felt he owed them nothing. He did not say so. Their silent patronage was useful.

He asked, "Is there some military cause for alarm? Or am I just here because His Holiness is in a snit?" He needed to show little respect here. These men had known Honario Benedocto since childhood.

Doneto nodded. "There is. The Grail Emperor is probably behind fon Dreasser's defection. With an eye to extending his influence into the Aco floodplain."

"Is that more of a problem now than the last time fon Dreasser switched allegiances?"

For a moment the Patriarch's cousin seemed unwilling to share secrets. Then he shrugged. "This puts another Imperial stronghold at our backs."

"So. His Holiness still wants to plunder the Connec."

The Empire had neutralized a parade of Patriarchs by forcing them to concentrate on protecting the Patriarchal States. The spate of cooperation during the Calziran Crusade was an anomaly. That truce lasted only till the last Praman kingdom on the Firaldian peninsula fell.

"I'm afraid so."

"Not good, Principaté." Clearenza was ideally sited for interdicting traffic on both the central north-south military road and the east-west highway skirting the foothills of the Jago Mountains and the Ownvidian Knot. Nor would it be a long ride to interfere with barge traffic on the Aco River, or traffic on the eastern military road, which swung inland to cross the most downriver bridge spanning the Aco. "Especially if Clearenza's neighbors harbor grievances of their own."

Principaté Doneto appeared slightly embarrassed. Principaté Madisetti sneered.

Hecht asked, "His Holiness owes them money, too?"

"*All* of them," Madisetti growled.

"I don't want to seem defeatist. But if His Holiness won't pay his debts, yet keeps on spending, how can he not expect difficulties? Won't he listen to Your Graces?"

"No," Donel Madisetti admitted. "Voting for that man may have been the biggest mistake I ever made."

Interesting. This was the sort of news Gordimer the Lion hoped to glean when he sent his best captain over here. Though he meant to distance a potential threat as well.

Captain Else Tage had been too popular with the Sha-lug.

Principaté Doneto grumbled, "Sometimes I wish Honario wasn't family. But he does have a flair for intrigue. He has something going in the Connec. He says it will take care of his debts." Doneto did not sound convinced. "And Lothar Ege's obstruction . . ." He stopped. Secrets escaped even the deepest heart of the Chiaro Palace.

Hecht wished Principaté Delari had not gone down to question the prisoners.

Principaté Delari had a taste for boys. His current favorite was Armand. Armand was an agent of Ferris Renfrow. And of Dreanger. Gordimer had presented the boy to Renfrow during one of the Imperial spymaster's visits to al-Qarn. Armand's real name was Osa Stile. He had been trained and rendered permanently youthful by er-Rashal al-Dhulquarnen.

The old man shared everything with his lover. Who, most observers assumed, was too self-absorbed and scatterbrained to care the slightest about things political, religious, or military. Armand just wanted to be spoiled with sweet scents, rich foods, and pretty clothes.

Piper Hecht saw the boy seldom and was glad of it. What had been done to Osa Stile was too terrible. The slavery of the Sha-lug should not be that cruel.

Osa gave every indication of enjoying his life.

Er-Rashal had known what he was doing when he chose the boy.

Principaté Delari returned, still angry. "They knew nothing. Of course. They were hirelings. Two belonged to the City Regiment, Colonel Ghort. The deathmage and his brother were outsiders."

Pinkus Ghort showed color in throat and cheeks, anger and embarrassment alike. "Who paid them? Who recruited them? Would the two who got away know anything more?"

"Unlikely," Delari said. "But we do know where they're headed, now. The Knight of Wands. An inn in a town named Alicea. The entire team was supposed to reassemble there."

Hecht and Ghort produced skeptical scowls. Both knew Alicea. They had first met not far from Alicea. Hecht said, "The West Way runs through the town. Crossing the trace running east from Sonsa. Pinkus, if you sent Bo by sea he could be there waiting for them."

"I changed my mind. They know Bo. They'd recognize anybody I trust."

"You have to send somebody who'll recognize them."

"I don't know. I'm thinking some of your Deve pals might be the answer."

Grumbling from Donel Madisetti reminded them that they were not brainstorming in their quarters.

Hecht's too-friendly association with the Devedian community did cause stress with some Collegium members. "Won't work. They're only trying to stay out of the way of a crusade themselves." Which was true, well known, and no doubt would, someday, constitute sufficient excuse itself for a Patriarch with Sublime's twist of mind to go after them.

Devedians, and their less numerous and far stranger religious ancestors the Dainshaukin, were loathed by Episcopal Chaldareans. The more because western society could not function without them. Deves provided an inordinate proportion of the lettered and artisan classes. They kept the records and wrote the letters, made the paper those were written on, and manufactured the pens that did the writing. Not all, of course, but better than anyone else. And so they were hated.

Hecht mused, "Then again, I know one who might. But we're here because of Clearenza. Where do we stand?"

He hoped there would be no punitive expedition. The Patriarchal army was not up to it. As always, it was tied up in garrison wherever Sublime feared rebellion or some encroachment by the Grail Emperor. It was a purely defensive force and the Captain-General was not being given the resources to change that. Not fast.

Principaté Doneto broke Hecht's heart. "I'm sure my cousin will insist on something. As a demonstration."

"It can't happen. Not now. He's too far in arrears to the troops."

"He'll send the City Regiment, then."

Ghort snorted.

Hecht said, "The City Regiment isn't his to send. It was raised for the Calziran Crusade. That's over. The men who financed it didn't get any loot out of that. They won't take the same hook twice."

Doneto replied, "I know. But I have to read my lines."

Interesting. The Patriarch's number one supporter was not inspired by his cousin's behavior.

"Would it help if someone he trusted drove each point home?"

"He pays no attention to what I say if it's something he doesn't want to hear."

"I was thinking more like his father or mother. Or somebody he especially respected when he was a kid."

"That hadn't occurred to me. I'll do what I can. But don't expect much."

Hecht nodded, disgruntled. This gathering, slapped together with such suggested high drama, was typical. Every day he had to deal with crises that existed only in the minds of the Patriarch and his henchmen. And with their implacable blindness to the needs of the men they expected to work their wills.

One irony of the world round the Mother Sea was that only during periods of peace and security was there economic activity sufficient to generate the revenues princes needed to finance their wars. The Church, in particular, needed money because the Patriarchy did not have enough fiefdoms whose feudal obligations could be exploited. The Church used mostly hired soldiers. But those mercenaries were seldom dedicated or reliable. Or even very effective. As all the defeats suffered by Grolsachers so frequently demonstrated.

Principaté Doneto suggested, "Let's break this up. We've done His Holiness's bidding. We agree that punishing Clearenza may be more painful for us than them. Hecht, put together the best show you can. Ghort, catch your traitors. Donel. Wake Mongoz so he can close this officially."

Several Principatés wanted to protest but were not inclined to argue with the Patriarch's cousin.

*   *   *

PRINCIPATÉ DELARI TOLD HECHT, "COME WITH ME, PLEASE."

Hecht did so, though he wanted to stay with Ghort, to manufacture a scheme for catching the fugitives. He was uncomfortable being alone with Muniero Delari. Despite his intellectual confidence that the man was not interested in him. He was far too elderly. He was thirty-five.

Principaté Delari sensed his discomfort. And did nothing to allay it. "It's time to bring you into the inner circle."

"Your Grace?"

"The Collegium is more than a clatch of doddering old farts squabbling over bribes." A popular notion underlying an entire cycle of contemptuous jokes.

"Well, of course."

"We occasionally do things we hope will do some good for humanity. Some of us. Sometimes. Even people here in the Palace don't realize."

"All right."

"You sound skeptical."

"Your Grace, I judge only by what I've seen."

"And that is?"

"What the man in the street thinks. Only more so. Because I've met the beast face-to-face."

Delari chuckled. "And that isn't far off the mark. Particularly my brethren from the Patriarchal States. They exist to indulge their own pleasures. They have their capes and miters because they bought them. Or because they're Brothens whose families always have members in the Collegium. If for no better reason than to make sure the Patriarch is always Brothen."

"Yes. I've never understand how Ornis of Cedelete got elected." Hecht meant Worthy VI, the first Anti-Patriarch. Worthy VI was elected legitimately—then run out of town by the Brothen mob. The people of the Mother City believed the Patriarchal seat was Brothen by right and preeminent over the Chaldarean world. In fact, however, the earlier Brothen Patriarchs had been but one of nine equal Fathers of the Church. The Praman Conquest overwhelmed five. Three others went with the Eastern Rite in the schism after the Second Synod of Hypraxium.

"He was elected because an angry Collegium, including Principatés from the Five Families, were fed up with a string of arrogant Bruglioni Patriarchs."

Hecht did not comment.

"The lesson seems to have gone to waste."

Hecht held his tongue. Delari held Honario Benedocto in high disdain.

The Principaté led him to the baths for which the Chiaro Palace was infamous. In Hecht's eye. He used them himself only to avert suspicion. The way he ate pork and broke countless other religious laws. So he told himself.

Never again would he be the hard, razor-edged warrior who had captained the best company of special fighters ever fielded by the Shalug. Brothe had ruined him.

Delari's boy Armand awaited his master. He smirked as he helped Delari disrobe. "Would you like someone to assist you, Captain-General?" The boy's voice had yet to break. He was an excellent singer.

"Herrin and Vernal will be along." Those being the youngsters who bathed him regularly. He made no personal demands on them—though the rules did not permit a bather to force himself on the orphans who served there.

The baths were a sort of charity, providing employment for Brothe's more comely orphans.

The rules were tested occasionally. Principaté Delari was in mild violation by bringing his own catamite in. There would be no complaints. The whole Chiaro Palace feared Muniero Delari. He was reputed to be a powerful sorcerer.

Principaté Muniero Delari was famous for, and sometimes hated for, his determination to do what best served the Church as a whole.

Hecht was repelled by Delari unclad. The man was a pallid old stick figure veined with ugly blue, like an Arnhander cheese. He resembled an artist's caricature of death, as in some paintings hanging in the Palace's miles of hallways. He *smelled* old, even after his baths.

Hecht could not imagine how Osa Stile had congress with that.

Delari said, "If you're as unlucky as I am and survive as long as I have, you'll be a repulsive old man yourself."

Hecht started. Delari had a disconcerting knack for knowing what he was thinking.

Osa sneered.

Herrin and Vernal arrived. Both were tall and thin. Both were of an age where they would be expected to find other employment soon. Herrin had blossomed dramatically of late. She was an attractive blonde burdened by a dour personality. An eventuation Hecht thought ought to mar all children compelled to serve in order to survive. Then reflected that he had not turned out badly despite having been kidnapped and sold into slavery as a toddler.

Vernal lived up to her name. She was bright and cheerful. Evil fortune could not crush her natural optimism. Hecht had, occasionally, considered sending Vernal to serve Anna Mozilla. Anna could use the help. Being what she was, and having who she had for a lover, though, left her unwilling to have anyone stay in full time.

Vernal shared a birthday with Herrin and was as tall but had not yet bloomed. Hecht suspected that she would not change much once she did.

Osa and the girls led Delari and Hecht to an unoccupied hot pool. Once he settled, Hecht asked, "How do you think Sublime will respond to Clearenza's defection?"

Armand's ears pricked up. Delari seemed puzzled by the question.

Hecht said, "The others think he'll do something stupid. You've known him since he was a pup. Will he?"

"Probably. Thinking he's being clever."

"But he will insist on doing something? Even if Lothar is serious about protecting fon Dreasser?"

Armand paid close attention.

"Even more certainly if the Grail Empire gets involved. He's sure Lothar is a weakling. Despite the evidence so far. He's also sure the boy won't live much longer. Despite the contrary evidence there. If he could hasten Lothar's passage into the hereafter, he'd probably do it. Thinking the sisters will be weaker than the boy."

"I don't know about Katrin. I saw Helspeth on the battlefield. She's young and female but that apple didn't fall far from the tree."

"As may be. Right now I want you to see what we do that could be of more enduring consequence."

"Since it's so secret that I don't know about it already, should we talk about it here?"

Armand donned a sour look.

Delari said, "The Empire couldn't put a spy in here. Children aren't that motivated. But what a coup if they could. *Everything* gets discussed here."

"Uhm."

"Later, then. If that makes you more comfortable."

"I have the evening free."

"Take supper with me, then."

Hecht accepted. Anna and Redfearn Bechter alike would pout.

Bechter wanted him to spend more time with the staff in the Castella dollas Pontellas. Hoping to seduce him into the warrior Brotherhood.

The Brothers there were preparing to welcome a new castellan. He would replace Grade Drocker. Though Drocker had been but acting head of the local chapter. The true castellan, Hawley Quirke, had been summoned to the Brotherhood's home base, the Castella Anjela dolla Picolena on the island of Staklirhod, in the eastern reaches of the Mother Sea. Quirke had been lost in a sea battle with a Praman fleet. The position of castellan had gone unfilled since.

"Send word to Bechter about when and where."

"You're in a hurry to go?"

"No. I want to see how Polo is. And I want to talk to Colonel Ghort."

HECHT ASKED, "YOU EVER HAVE TROUBLE WITH THOSE TWO BEFORE?"

"Not really. They belonged to the Cologni company." The City Regiment was a conglomerate of forces subsidized by wealthy benefactors. "And, no, I don't think the Cologni put them up to it. They don't have the imagination."

Having worked with senior members of all the Five Families, Hecht agreed. "They are a dim lot. They're lucky there aren't any bright outsiders around to take advantage."

"Those idiots just saw a chance to grab some extra money."

That was not hard to understand. The poor generally were very poor and desperate indeed. Thinking past tomorrow was a waste of time.

Hecht shrugged. "I'd like to go after those cousins of yours myself."

"Not cousins." Ghort meant to distance himself. "Just guys from back home. How would you get away? Especially with this Clearenza shit?"

"I can't. I'd just like to. To talk to them before anyone else."

"What do you want to find out before anybody else?"

"Who sent them."

"You know they won't know that."

"Don't underestimate the reservoirs of stupid in this world. The man who's supposed to pay them will turn up there. Maybe to pay them, maybe to cut their throats."

"It was me, I'd send some other guys to do that."

"That's possible, too."

"So. I'd really better have somebody get there first. You gonna lend me your Deves?"

"They aren't mine. They're still part of the City Regiment."

"All but the best ones. You took them with you."

"Yes. I did. And I mean to keep them close."

"But . . ."

"I'll talk to Titus. If he sees any advantage for his people, he'll help. Was I you, I wouldn't count on it."

"Well, shit. I didn't want to use my own guys. The finance board will kick my ass for operating outside the city. 'Course, they'll kick it if I don't do nothing, too."

"I feel your pain, brother. I don't have it any better. It's a full-time job just getting my troops paid." He had a sudden notion. He suggested it.

"I like it, Pipe. How long till you could find out if Consent would cover you?"

"Not long."

"I know a ship. The Donetos own her. She's waiting for a cargo. She's supposed to be greased lightning. She trades in places where the republics think they own a monopoly."

"A smuggler."

"Technically. Her master would argue, though."

"He'd sail up the Sawn to Sonsa?"

"Why not? If he ain't carrying contraband?"

Hecht thought there might be a problem, anyway. If he took up his notion. He had been to Sonsa before.

Ghort said, "Unless the gods intervene, we can afford another day. If we use the *Lumberer*."

"The what?"

"That's the name of the boat. A joke. Like calling a big guy Tiny."

Hecht understood without comprehending. It was a western thing. "Uhm. I wonder. Think we could pull it off?"

"What?"

"Sneaking out. To make the pickup ourselves."

"Sure. But your excuse is gonna raise a stink like a year-old latrine." Ghort smirked.

"But if we say we did it ourselves because we didn't have the money to pay our men to, we shame them before the people."

"If we pull it off."

"Yes. We wouldn't dare fail." Hecht knew what he was proposing was not bright. But sometimes you bull ahead in full knowledge that you are doing something dumb.

"Goo! Hey! Back to the fun days when we didn't have no responsibilities."

"We could get things done right the first time."

"Let's do." Ghort was not obsessive about being responsible. "Just cancel everything and go, Pipe."

"I'm tempted." He was. "I'll think about that, too."

THE VISIT TO THE BATHS, THE CONFERENCE WITH PINKUS GHORT, AND A visit to Polo in the Chiaro Palace hospital left the Captain-General two hours late for his daily staff conference. "I'm sorry. The Clearenza situation has the Collegium in a snit." They would know that he had been called in.

Five senior staffers waited in the master planning center at the Castella dollas Pontellas. They included Hecht's new second in command, Colonel Buhle Smolens. Smolens had not been appointed by the

Captain-General. Hecht did not know the man. He came from the Patri-archal garrison at Maleterra and was related to somebody Sublime owed money. He did, however, have a solid military reputation.

Clej Sedlakova was an observer for the Brotherhood. They insisted. The Captain-General was using their facilities.

Hecht could not operate without their approval and support.

Sedlakova was new, too, but there was no doubt he knew his way around a battlefield. He had lost his shield arm. His face bore two ugly scars, one down the right side and one across his forehead. The latter was permanently purple. He did not say much. Nor did he interfere.

The other three men had been with Hecht since he had taken over the City Regiment in the run-up to the Calziran Crusade. They were Hagan Brokke, a Krogusian who had been a private soldier at the time of the first pirate attacks. He had risen swiftly by demonstrating out-standing abilities. He was Hecht's planning officer.

The others were Titus Consent and Tabill Talab, chief intelligence officer and lead quartermaster. Both were Devedian, which made folks like Clej Sedlakova uncomfortable. Consent was in his early twenties.

Sedlakova might be uncomfortable but he was implacably tolerant. Both Deves were exceptionally competent. And unobtrusive with their religion.

All five men were accompanied by assistants. Managing the Patri-arch's armed forces was not a minor enterprise.

Hagan Brokke said, "We're working on that, sir." He indicated a vast wall map of Firaldia. That was a permanent feature of the room. Every little county, dukedom, principality, city-state, kingdom, and re-public was delineated. Political entities were identified by color, in a dozen shades. Isolated parts of the same entity were connected by black strings. Each entity was tagged with a numbered piece of paper. That referenced a sheet listing significant local personalities, the number and sorts of soldiers available, quality of fortifications, and useful political, marital, and family alliance information.

Brokke said, "If we have to attempt the absurd we have garrisons here, here, and here that can support us. I've sent warning orders."

"Excellent."

Titus Consent said, "The Imperials will expect that. It shouldn't worry them. They won't expect anything to come of it. Our side talks loud but never actually does anything."

"We might break that precedent this time."

Consent continued. "Couriers will alert our intelligence assets in the region, too." He tended to talk that way.

"Good again." Consent meant messages had been sent to the Deve-dian ghettoes.

There were Deves everywhere. Going unnoticed, they saw and heard most of the inner workings. And their elders, for the moment, were willing to feed information to Captain-General Piper Hecht.

Which was useful but embarrassing. Deves were little more popular than demons. They were too educated. Too prosperous. Too smart. You did not want to associate too intimately with that sort. They were the source of all the world's evil—if there were no handy Pramans or Maysaleans, other loathsome Unbelievers or heretics, or the Instrumentalities of the Night, to blame. Being literate, Deves wrote things down. Often things you did not want recalled accurately later.

The literate were as mistrusted as those who had congress with the Night. Either could destroy you with arcane knowledge.

Hecht said, "Bring me up to date. Can fon Dreasser protect himself?"

Titus Consent was a tall youth, slim, dark of mien, usually cheerful. He was talented in the extreme and thoroughly competent. He was not obviously Devedian. He handled rampant prejudice mainly by refusing to acknowledge it. He was a solid family man. Early on he had told Hecht that he had been raised from infancy to become a sort of savior for the Deves of the western diaspora.

He said, "We haven't had time to find out. I can tell you that it would be smart to get some arrears money to the garrisons out that way. Blatantly obvious, but every time we pry back pay out of the Patriarch we win more friends among the men with the sharp iron."

That sort of thinking had gotten Hecht exiled from Dreanger when he was Else Tage. Else Tage had been popular with the soldiers.

"Any chance we can find some money?"

"We talked to the Fiducian, Joceran Cuito." Cuito was director of the Patriarchal treasury. He was a Direcian archbishop who was in line to join the Collegium. On merit, and because he had Peter of Navaya as a sponsor. "He means to employ a battery of limited, secured loans."

Sublime was inclined to avoid securing his loans with anything more substantial than a signature. But ink was no longer enough for Brothe's moneylenders.

"Property?" The Church was the biggest landowner in Firaldia. Since earliest Old Brothen times land had been *the* critical measure of wealth. Only land could provide a stream of income.

"Fiducian Cuito would rather pawn art treasures and rare books from the Krois Palace. He won't say why, but he's sure the Church is going to receive a substantial windfall before long."

"Then something's going on under the table. And Sublime's kept it inside his inner circle."

"Exactly."

"Considering the time of year and general economy, I'd say they're going to steal something. Or sell something. Big. They've already sold all the seats in the Collegium that they can. And all the livings that anybody will pay for." A thought. "Could it be a fat bequest?"

"I don't know of anyone with one foot in the grave and the inclination to bribe the guardians at Heaven's gates."

"Would they hurry somebody off to the Promised Land early?" Sublime had not yet been accused of murder for profit. But his predecessors had.

"We don't have access to their records. We haven't heard of any pending legacies."

"Keep an eye on it." Hecht settled in to listen to other reports, not just about Clearenza. He had some responsibilities regarding the ongoing effort to suppress diehard Praman partisans in Calzir.

Calzir would never reclaim its independence. If Sublime recalled his garrisons the Grail Empire and Navaya would flood the vacuum. Making Sublime's two biggest competitors even stronger.

Fate conspired to thwart Sublime at every turn. But he refused to see the stumbling blocks as an expression of God's will.

Few men took their own reverses as God's will. Instead, they worked hard to adjust God's will to reflect their own.

Sublime probably spent a lot of time asking God why it all had to be so hard.

Moving close, Titus Consent asked, "Can I see you privately after we're done?"

"Absolutely. I need a word with you, too. Colonel Smolens, are you confident enough to take over if I take a few days off?"

Smolens showed surprise, then curiosity. "I know my way around, now."

"Your biggest problem would likely be having to deal with our masters. None of them are the least bit reasonable."

"No problem, Captain-General. I can pretend they're my extended family." Buhle Smolens was perfectly formal. He demonstrated the ideal military courtesy, uphill and down, always. He had brought his family to Brothe. Nobody had met them yet. Smolens mentioned them only in passing. His eldest son supposedly wanted a subaltern's position, if one came open.

Smolens had several interesting ideas for installing a more professional attitude in the Patriarchal armies. His big fault was his conviction concerning the earthly and moral supremacy of the Episcopal vein of the Chaldarean faith. Though he did not buy the doctrine of Patriarchal Infallibility.

Hard to do with Sublime V in front of you every day.

Tabill Talab was troubled. He wasted no time once Hecht recognized him. "I'm having a problem no one else seems to notice. I feel a bleak future closing in. For everyone."

Talab was the eternal pessimist, chosen to balance Titus Consent's overconfidence. "Do explain."

"I talk to our couriers. I talk to merchants. I talk to refugees. I ask for reports from our agents in the republics because their ships visit all the ports of the Mother Sea."

Hecht nodded. No point hurrying the man. Talab could get where he was going only along an engineered path.

"No matter where the reports originate, they always mention upswings in the activities of the Night. Not big stuff. Not yet. Just more sightings, more encounters, more malicious mischief getting more virulent."

"Only the minor spirits remain unbound."

"Unbound and unconstrained. But becoming more numerous. They're running from the ice, too."

"Which we expected. Right?"

"Yes, sir. But what hasn't been considered is the fact that the things of the Night have always been more common along the edges of the ice, where societies are more primitive. Out there some of the big ones are still running loose. When the ice advances, and establishes itself permanently in places like the high mountains, all the wildest surviving free shades are pushed into tamer country."

Hecht nodded. No one talked about it much—yet—but that was a logical and obvious development. "That's generally recognized. It's started already."

"Yes, sir, it has. What I don't hear discussed is what that means for the Night."

"Yes?" Talab might be headed where most people were afraid to go.

"When people get pressed together you get what we already have here in Brothe. Worse poverty. More violence that's deadlier. More organized criminal activity. More racism and prejudice. All because you have more people trying to live off the same limited resources.

"The same thing happens with the things of the Night. Only they start to combine into stronger entities. Not often willingly. They just keep getting bigger and stronger if they can devour their own kind. They get angrier, more hateful, and malicious. When they're strong enough, and big enough, they turn into the Night things from old scary stories."

"The ice will gift us with a new round of monster gods?"

"If it advances far enough. Possibly a crop as ugly as those who cursed the earth before modern religions hammered their deities into a more benign shape."

The God of the Pramans, the Chaldareans, the Devedians, and the Dainshaukin enjoyed the same lineage. The Dainshaukin saw Him fierce and psychotic and disinclined to be a nurturer or giver of rewards. He was a punisher, the Punisher, the source of all misfortune, and would happily do you in because He did not like your haircut.

Devedians had a better deal. Their vision of the Almighty visited miseries only when they were earned. He could be appeased without a human sacrifice.

"It isn't something we can do much about. Except keep our heads down and hope. . . . What?"

Titus Consent said, "You're forgetting the soultaken."

"I haven't forgotten. They . . ." Hecht noted what had to be a warning glance from Talab to Consent, nearly invisible in its subtlety, reminding him that his staff had other loyalties.

The soultaken had been men from another age conscripted by their gods so they could open a pathway out of a northern sort of hell. The dead heroes preserved there could then storm forth and destroy what those gods feared most: the Godslayer. Someone who, by happenstance, had learned that even the greatest of the Instrumentalities of the Night could be rendered subject to the wrath of men.

Else Tage had slain a bogon, a baron of the Night, in Esther's Wood in the Holy Lands, saving his war band from an attack initiated by a source he never identified. Later, he and the Devedians of Brothe destroyed one of the soultaken meant to silence him before knowledge he did not know he possessed became general.

The All-Father god of the pre-Chaldarean north himself perished trying to extinguish that knowledge. Prophecy fulfilled.

Piper Hecht remained largely unaware of the full implications of what he had done. The Devedians were not unaware. Their Elders knew who Piper Hecht used to be. They knew what he had done. They knew he had won a fierce reputation amongst the Instrumentalities of the Night, and that those forces would have exterminated him long since had they been better able to distinguish one mortal from another.

The biggest had to use something like the soultaken to find an individual.

Although a brilliant commander and leader, Piper Hecht, under whatever name, sailed through life in near ignorance of what he really was. He was feared by powers and people of which and whom he was unaware or was insufficiently suspicious.

"What about them?" Hecht did know that he was woefully ignorant about all that. Other than that a string of murders had culminated in the emergence and passing of major Instrumentalities during the Calziran Crusade.

Hagan Brokke observed, "The soultaken were just a foretaste of what's coming, I think. The gods themselves have begun to take a real interest in mundane events."

"Gods?" Clej Sedlakova demanded. "There is only one God!"

"Excuse me. For want of another label. High Demons, if you prefer. To borrow from the Dainshaukin."

Those monotheists recognized a mind-boggling array of lesser supernatural entities arranged in several parallel and inimical hierarchies.

Hecht smiled. "I don't much care." No one took exception. Even Sedlakova was disinclined to insist on strict conformance to dogma. "I'll think about it. Though that's something more suited to the Collegium. Colonel Smolens. To my earlier point. I'll be out of touch. You'll have to deal with whatever comes up. I shouldn't be gone long."

Smolens asked, "Do we know where you are? Do we admit that you're not around?"

"If you're pressed say I'm not available. You really won't know where I am." Though he would not bet against the Deves keeping track.

"How long? At the most?" Titus Consent asked.

"As long as it takes to finish what I need to do." Meaning do not get up to anything he should not. "Good. Enjoy yourselves. Oh. You wanted a private word, Titus?"

Consent betrayed what might have been a glimmer of fear. He whispered, "Outside the Castella. I'll walk with you."

Hecht nodded. Not inside the keep of the Chaldarean religion's most ferocious defenders? What a surprise.

HECHT WAITED TILL AFTER THEY CROSSED TO THE SHORE AND WERE HEADED downriver, toward the Memorium. "More problems with the Elders?" The Seven, the Elders of the Brothen Deves, were a pain as big as the heads of the Five Families, or members of the Collegium. They could not leave Titus Consent alone to get on with his sacred work.

"Not yet. I'm sure there will be. That isn't it. Yet."

"Well?"

"Noë is almost to term."

"Uhm." Hecht knew Consent's wife and sons by name but had yet to meet them. Deves did not mix with Chaldareans socially. "Congratulations."

Consent stopped. He shuddered. Hecht halted, back to the jungle of monuments to Old Brothen emperors, generals, and dictators, and their triumphs. "What is it?"

"Noë and I have discussed this for months. We want you to be the baby's godfather. And Principaté Delari to sponsor us. If he will."

Hecht did not get it right away. He still had to get the hang of being Episcopal Chaldarean. "Godfather? I didn't know Deves did that."

"Not the Chaldarean way. My brother would do it. If I had one. Since I don't, my uncles should get the job."

Hecht finally caught on. "Are you talking about converting?"

"I am. If you'll be the baby's godfather. And if Principaté Delari will sponsor us. We've been studying in secret. We already know most of what we need to."

Hecht was stunned. "But you're the Elect."

"They never asked *me*. I don't want to be the Elect. It's eaten me up for twenty years. I want out. I want to convert."

"The Seven will explode! They won't have anything to do with us anymore. They'll blame us." Selfishly, he added, "We'll be blinded."

Consent was not offended. "That will come eventually anyway, Captain-General. The Elders are beginning to question the benefit of continuing an alliance put together for the Calziran Crusade. Nor does the Patriarch see any need to keep on getting along with Deves or Dainshaus."

"Shortsighted of him."

"Indeed. Our moneylenders are the main financiers of his adventures. The Seven won't lend Sublime a copper for a crusade against the Connec. We don't have that many people there. The Seven think it will be easier and cheaper to protect them by just fixing it so the Patriarch can't afford to hire soldiers.

"I think they have blinders on. Sublime isn't worried about money. Not nearly so much as he should be. He has something going, under the sheets. But the Elders won't hear that. Apparently, the Elect is supposed to be seen but not heard."

Hecht was lost. "You mean it? This conversion?"

"Of course. I don't want to be anything special. I just want to take care of my family and do my job. Which is perfect for me. I love it and I'm good at it."

"I'm confused."

"I'm sorry. My fault for not being clear. You have no idea how stressful this is. This is the biggest thing I'm ever likely to face."

"Tabill Talab. How will he respond? His father . . ."

"Is one of the Seven. Yes. That does worry me. But you're going to lose him before long, anyway."

Not good, Hecht thought. Not good at all. The Devedian connection had made him look good.

Honed by three decades lived in a city and land that had been old in the wiles of conspiracy before the beginning of time, Hecht started sniffing for a whiff of what Consent was really up to.

They resumed moving because Titus was too nervous to stand still.

An arrow, presumably from a longbow, removed Hecht's hat. The shaft came from amongst the monuments. It missed Consent by a scant inch, too. It ricocheted off the pavements into the cold brown of the Teragi River. Bystanders yelled and scattered. Ten thousand pigeons took wing in a flapping roar.

"You see where that came from?" Hecht demanded.

"No." They crouched at the pediments of a small memorial arch. Consent held a dagger with a long, slim blade. Hecht had not realized that the Deve carried any weapon. He carried a short sword himself, more emblematic of his office than useful in a fight. "Only generally, that way. Because of where it went."

"Yeah. Who's Galinis Andul?" Hecht tapped the inscription beside his head, so ancient that it was almost illegible.

Startled, Consent said, "The man who designed the arch. Those guys grabbed the chance to make their names last. The memorial proclamation is up top. This one looks like it predates the Old Empire. Meaning it was moved here by Arember the Hairy."

Hecht wanted to ease Consent's tension, not listen to a lecture. "Work from cover to cover and flank him from the left. I'll move in from the right."

He did not expect to find the sniper. There had been no second shaft. Not that a lone archer could expect to take out a distant target who was alert.

And the would-be assassin *was* gone. No one had seen an archer. There was no physical evidence. A sorcerer of exceptional weight might have found a trail. Hecht did not have one handy.

His amulet had not warned him. The assassin would be nothing but a skilled archer.

"It was a pretty good shot," Hecht admitted. "At least a hundred fifty yards. On a breezy day. From in here where the wind would swirl."

"Yes." There was no admiration in Consent's tone. "Who was he after? Or would it matter, as long as he got someone from Central Staff?"

"Sure you want to convert?"

"Yes."

"If there's a plot, wouldn't Deves be more likely to ferret it out?"

"No. The underworld doesn't intersect with the Devedian."

"That archer wouldn't belong to the underworld. He's a soldier after fast money." Nor did he swallow Consent's protest. Thieves had a cautiously close relationship with the men who purchased the goods they appropriated in their struggle to redistribute Brothen wealth. But Hecht seldom challenged known falsehoods. People became defensive. They clammed up. He believed in paying rope out and watching.

Consent would understand. He and Talab did the watching.

Hecht said, "We're accomplishing nothing." He brushed his left forearm. Yes. The amulet was there. Which reaffirmed that there was no sorcery active nearby.

Someone was keeping track of him somehow, though.

HECHT AND PINKUS GHORT WERE AT THE WATERFRONT, WAITING TO BOARD *Lumberer*. Hecht asked, "What are you into on the side, Pinkus?"

"Huh?"

"If I didn't have your word for this being a fast coaster I'd suspect her of being a smuggler." The crewmen looked shifty.

"I'm not involved in anything. But do note that smuggling and trading are a matter of viewpoint."

"No doubt every smuggler ever born makes that argument. And princes send them to the galleys anyway."

"You're probably right. You always are. So what? They're handy people to know. What the hell is this?" A couple of black crow Brotherhood types were headed their way, on horseback, in a hurry. They slowed to an easier pace when they saw that Hecht and Ghort had not yet shoved off.

"Seems like everybody knows where to find me, these days."

"You told Bechter?"

"I did."

Hecht did not recognize either rider. A handsome man with salt-and-pepper hair and beard dismounted. "Captain-General?"

"Me."

"I bring messages." He presented a large leather courier's wallet. It bore no seal. "And our wishes for your success. Prayers will be offered."

"Thank you. Do keep us in your prayers." A formula he was just now learning to use automatically.

"And the Brotherhood in yours." The man bowed his head slightly, in the manner of those who grew up inside the Grail Empire.

"And so shall it be." Hecht returned the nod. He took the Brotherhood deadly serious. They were scarce in Firaldia but wielded power beyond their numbers.

There were few checks on the Brotherhood. They accepted none. They did not hesitate to enforce their prejudices.

"How and where to deliver that is all in here." The Brother handed Hecht another smaller case, then returned to his mount.

Hecht considered the anonymous courier's wallet. He began rubbing his left wrist.

Ghort muttered, "There's a Special Office thug if I ever saw one. He don't even try to cover the smell."

"You're right."

"So's the other one."

The Special Office was a sub-cult inside the warrior order made up of sorcerers sworn to destroy the Instrumentalities of the Night. Using the Instrumentalities as their principal tool.

"So what did he bring you, Pipe?"

"Let's wait till we're moving."

"Gotcha." Ghort stared after the two riders in black. "I think I know who the other one was."

"Uhm?"

"Parthen Lorica. The Witchfinder."

Hecht started. Parthen Lorica? Not possible. Parthen Lorica was dead. "I don't think so. Unless there's more than one Parthen Lorica. Him and Bugo Armiene died in our hospital camp at al-Khazen. Special Office guys came in and snatched the bodies."

"I missed all that. I heard, but not the names. But them two was definitely Special Office. And that one was definitely a Witchfinder. So. Hey. Time to go." A smuggler—or coastal trader—beckoned them. Two others began casting off.

Hecht hoisted his bag to his shoulder. "I wonder what they really wanted."

"To give you a courier packet. Unless they were looking for witches." In the context of the Special Office a witch would be anybody who consorted with the Instrumentalities of the Night absent the blessing of the Church.

That troubled Hecht. It was vague. The Special Office could make anyone fit. Even the most devout Episcopal Chaldareans bought small charms and invocations against the malice of the Night.

"WHAT YOU GOT?" GHORT ASKED AS LUMBERER CLEARED THE MOUTH OF the Teragi, after creeping past dredges valiantly trying to keep the channel navigable. The craft rode the evening ebb tide. Lights in Remale-on-Teragi shone to their left. Hecht was, at last, allowing himself to examine the contents of the anonymous courier wallet by the light of a storm lantern. A crewman stood by lest the landlubbers did something stupid and set the ship on fire.

Fire was the fiercest terror of sailors.

"What've we got, Pipe?"

"Other than this letter telling me to take the big packet to somebody named Montes Alina, who'll be using the name Beomond, and how to find the guy, there's nothing here."

"Turning us into mail carriers, eh?"

"Possibly." Paranoia suggested the possibility that the packet would finger him for another assassin.

The Special Office owed him some pain. But they should not know that. He hoped they did not know that.

Ghort said, "That's right. They got their fanatic asses roasted and kicked out up there, a couple years ago. That's where Drocker got himself all crippled."

"Yes. Something about them trying to wipe out the Sonsan Deves."

"You ask me, they were just gonna rob them. But the damned Unbelievers had the balls to fight back."

"So then the ruling families got their tails all twisted because that would cost them their clerical class."

"Yep. Ran the Brotherhood out of town. Too late, the way I heard. The Deves packed up and left."

Hecht knew that story from the inside.

Only Anna Mozilla and a few Deves knew.

"We should be careful," Ghort said. "Till we know who wants to kill you."

"I plan on that. I'm going to hang around just long enough to steal enough to set myself up with a commercial farm. So Anna and I can spend our old age raising grapes and making babies." He was half serious. He did not expect to return to Dreanger while er-Rashal al-Dhulquarnen remained the power behind Gordimer the Lion, who was the power behind the Kaif.

That *Lumberer* did not always operate inside the law was born out by the skills of her crew. After crossing the bar they turned north and sailed on into the night, navigating by the light of a quarter moon. In often treacherous seas. There were a million little islands out there. More shoals appeared regularly as sea levels fell.

Near as Hecht could tell, more permanent ice lingering in the high mountain regions meant less water in the rivers feeding into the Mother Sea.

THERE WERE DREDGES WORKING THE CHANNEL OF THE SAWN RIVER, UP TO Sonsa. *Lumberer* had a shallow draft and, of course, rode in on a flood tide. That was basic, common sense seamanship, old as the trade itself.

Hecht was surprised by Sonsa's quays. Today's highest high water was three feet lower than at his last arrival.

He said, "I want out of Sonsa as fast as possible. So we deliver the courier case and scoot." Though he had no reason to think anyone would recognize him now.

"I'm with you. This place is so quiet, it's creepy."

The waterfront was unnaturally sedate. Two dozen large ships tied up at the family quays looked like they had not moved in a long time. The rigging on some had gone ragged.

"The place is dying," Hecht said. He slung his bag, stepped up to the quay from *Lumberer*'s rail, using a main stay for leverage.

A dozen men and boys surrounded him. Each tried to outshout the others. All offered to help carry his possessions, to guide him wherever he wanted to go, to take him to a willing sister or daughter. There had been none of this desperation last time Hecht came through.

"This is worse than back home," Ghort murmured. "Except around where the squatters are. You." Ghort grabbed a little weasel with a swift, bright smile, maybe eight or nine. "Where we headed, Matt?"

At the moment Piper Hecht was Mathis Schlink from Schonthal and Ghort was Buck Fantil.

"It's a great name," he had told Hecht aboard *Lumberer*. "I always wished I had one of them names like Dirk or Steele or Rock. Pinkus Ghort. My momma ought to be spanked. What the hell kind of name is Pinkus Ghort?"

"You tell me," Hecht had responded. "You made it up."

"You want to know the sick, sad truth, my friend? I didn't. It really is the one my momma hung on me. Though nobody never believes me when I tell them."

Hecht remained firmly established in that class. He was sure that Pinkus Ghort would be wanted in more than one principality farther north, under other names.

About the boy, he asked, "What are you doing, Buck?"

"You know your way around this dump? I don't. Besides, the kid reminds me of me in my better days. What's your handle, Shorty?"

"Pella, Your Honor. Pella Versulius."

Pella's competitors laughed. One advised, "Don't turn your back on the little turd, Outlander. He'll steal the hair off your ass."

"He's got shorter legs than me. I can run him down and break his neck."

Hecht caught a flicker of admiration from the urchin. "We need to come to a place called the House of the Ten Gallons in Karagos Middle Street. You know where that is?"

The boy lied easily and glibly. "Absolutely, Your Honors. My own mam was born in Cuttlebone Close an' that's practically next door. Just follow me, Your Honors."

Ghort murmured, "As long as he's out front my butt hairs are safe."

"I'd still keep an eye on our back trail. And not follow him into any place that's narrow or dark."

"You don't need to teach me how to dance. I told you, I used to be this kid. Watch how he gets just far ahead enough so we can't hear him ask people how to get to Karagos Middle Street."

"And how they eyeball us before they decide to help him fleece us."

"Yeah. You feel like there ain't much love for foreigners going on here?"

There was anger under Sonsa's thick despair. The waterfront was moribund. Many of its warehouses appeared abandoned.

Hecht shuddered suddenly.

"What?"

"I don't know. I got one of those feelings like you get when some night creature is watching you."

The truth, though, was that the boy had led him past a site where two friends had been killed by sorcery during his previous visit.

"Yeah? What did you think of the kid's name?"

"Sounds a little classical."

"A little, huh? He insulted us, you know."

"How so?"

"Basically, he told us we're too damned unlettered to recognize the name of the poet who wrote *The Lay of Ihrian.*"

"You know what? He's right. In my case."

"You are ignorant and unlettered up there in the Grand Marshes, aren't you?"

"I never denied it. That's why I left."

"There's a damned lie if I ever heard one. Nobody runs away from home on account of . . . Anyways, if I was honest, I'd admit that the only reason I know is because life around Doneto's dump is so damned dull there that there ain't nothing else to do but read. Because you got me hooked on that shit when we was locked up in Plemenza."

"You don't need to make excuses. Reading isn't a bad thing."

"Now you sound like the Principaté. Hey! Kid! Pellapront. How's Alma?"

The boy froze in place, eyes big. He stared at Ghort, bewildered. "Your Honor?"

"Never mind. Go on. And stay on the paved streets. I don't care if it is longer that way." To Hecht, he said, "*The Lay of Ihrian* is this long-ass comic poem about a guy who goes on a tour of the Holy Lands. But only in his dreams. Guided by a ghost who lies about his name all the time."

"I can see where you'd be amused by that." Hecht eyed his surroundings uneasily. This was a different Sonsa. Too many surly men stood around doing nothing. Blaming their ill fortune on anybody but themselves.

"Ain't we all? Anyway, all the names the ghost gives are names of gods that had something to do with the Wells of Ihrian. Very blasphemous. Toward the end, this guy—whose name in the story is the same as the name of the poet—he gets into a big romp with a whore who turns out to be his sister, Alma. It's pretty funny. But *The Lay of Ihrian* was banned by the Church. Though nobody probably pays any attention except in Brothe. Principaté Doneto says there's probably only four or five copies in the city but the story is famous up north. Like around here, I guess."

"I think we're close."

"Keep an eye out. This could be the tricky part."

Pella let them catch up. "That's Karagos Middle Street up ahead, Your Honors. Cutting across. But I never heard of no House of the Ten Gallons."

"Ask around," Hecht suggested.

"Yes, Your Honors. Right away. What did you mean about Alma, Your Honor?" he asked Ghort.

"Nothing, really. There's a poem with a Pellapront Versulius in it. He has a sister named Alma."

The boy gulped some air.

"Shit," Ghort said. "*You* got a sister named Alma?"

Pella nodded. He was a gaunt little thing, small for his age. His eyes seemed exaggeratedly large.

"Find out about the house," Hecht urged.

"That's spooky," Ghort said when the boy was out of earshot.

"It is unusual," Hecht conceded. "But not a mystery we need to solve."

"No. Hey. Somebody knows where the place is."

"Good. It's late. We need to get off the street."

Pella came back. "Your Honors didn't have it right. It's the House of the Ten Galleons."

"That makes more sense. Here."

"My sister would make you a better deal."

Hecht recalled the boy offering his sister on the quayside. "Another tie to the poem. I take it the House of the Ten Galleons is a sporting house."

Pella nodded, not conceding the possibility that his charges would be unaware of that fact.

Ghort observed, "An interesting place to find our friend."

"Indeed." Members of the Brotherhood took the same vow of celibacy as less warlike priests. But the Brotherhood tried to observe its vows. All of them. Which was a source of frequent and abiding friction with the rest of the Church.

"We'll think about your sister later," Hecht said. "We need to see a man who lives at the House of the Ten Galleons."

"Really? He must be a eunuch, Your Honor."

"Show us where."

Pella showed. Ghort gave him a coin and told him to wait. "We'll be right back out. We'll need you some more." Once they were away, he asked, "We will be right back out, won't we? You didn't get any special instructions in that mess, did you?"

"Just to give the packet to a man named Beomond. Using a set of signs and countersigns."

"What's he look like?"

"Six and a half feet tall, almost as wide, with a big scar on his face. Plus a wine stain birthmark that starts on his left cheek and runs down his throat and under his shirt."

"Sounds like a beauty. Good evening, sir," Ghort told the man who responded to their knock.

Hecht offered, "We came from Heber," which was the formula included in his instructions.

"Confuckinggratulations. Show me some silver."

That was not the appropriate response.

A small, high voice piped, "Out of the way, Tiny."

Tiny moved. A truly tiny, wrinkled old woman whose coloring suggested origins far to the east stepped forward. "Where are you from?" Her Firaldian was flawless, with a Sonsan accent. She must be a Chaldarean refugee from the Kaifate of Qasr al-Zed. There were countless pockets of non-Episcopal Chaldareans scattered around the Realm of Peace.

"Heber."

"Welcome, countrymen. Come in. Can I offer you refreshments?"

"Coffee, perhaps." All part of the sign-countersign, but here the old woman broke the rhythm. "We can't afford coffee anymore. Business has been bad lately."

"I'm sorry to hear that." Hecht knew that was the sort of complaint an eavesdropper would expect to hear. "Whatever's convenient, then."

"Wine would hit the spot," Ghort said.

Hecht scowled. Ghort was far too fond of wine. But to say so would be dangerous. All westerners drank wine, many to excess.

Hecht asked, "Is my cousin Beomond here? My uncle wanted us to bring him his birthday gift."

Tiny held out a hand. Hecht ignored it. The old woman told him, "Go wake him up." She continued a frank examination of the visitors. "You're finally catching on how to look like regular people."

Hecht did not understand. Ghort replied, "It's a gift. Some got it. Some don't. Me an' Matt, we're natural-born talents. In fact, Matt really was regular people, once upon a time."

A great, sloppy, jiggling mountain of a man appeared, rubbing sleep out of his eyes. He was naked to the waist. The wine stain birthmark extended down his chest to the level of his heart.

Ghort said, "Cousin Beo has been living large since we seen him last."

Hecht released a blurt of nervous laughter. Because what Ghort said was true. The man had gotten fatter since last Hecht had seen him, in Runch, working as a porter in the Sonsan factor house. He had lacked the scar, then. And the birthmark had not been obvious in the poor light of the factor house. His name was Goydar back then.

He was drunk. He squinted at Hecht. "I seen you somewhere before."

"I'm your cousin, Mathis. Matt. I brought a birthday present from your father. I wanted to hand it over. We're in kind of a hurry. We have other business."

Mention of a present pierced the fog in the giant's mind. "Dad remembered? I was beginning to wonder. You have any trouble out there? In the street?"

Puzzled, Hecht said, "No. We hired a boy off the quay. He brought us straight here." He indicated the possessions they had dropped after being admitted. "The city almost seems deserted."

The fat man asked, "You didn't get stopped by any Family patrols?"

"No."

"You will. There'll be rumors about strangers out by now. That'll turn into spies from the Brotherhood or agents of the Deves. They really want to get even with somebody. Sonsa is dying. And they claim it's all our fault. Not the damned Deves. They're gonna need passes. Good ones. Brothers, when they stop you, forget who you are. Just show your passes. Do what they say. Don't give them any excuse to strip you down. They do, you'll be lucky to end up just having your stuff taken and your ass seriously kicked. They killed a Deve last week. And he was under the protection of Don Alsano."

Ghort chirped, "Matt, you want to remind me why I had to come with you?"

"Stupidity?"

"Yeah. That's the one."

Tiny offered what was, likely, the only profound statement ever to escape his mouth. "You can't fix stupid."

"Shit. Man. I like that," Ghort said. "I'm gonna use that."

The old woman yelled in from the next room, "Will you see who the hell is at the door, Tiny? Hey! You girls get back where you belong." Hecht spotted several girls trying to get a look at the visitors. They seemed awfully young for denizens of a joy house. "You two from Heber. Come in here. That should be a customer. I don't like my customers to see each other."

"Really?"

Voices at the door. Ghort said, "That's Pella. I better see what's up." He went.

Beomond asked Hecht, "You been involved for long?"

"Only a few years."

"Been to Runch?"

Hecht considered admitting that he had. But that might start Ghort asking questions.

He was doing fine with his Duarnenian past. "I hope to go someday. To the Holy Lands, too. To walk the roads the Founders walked, among the Wells of Ihrian . . . I have to make the pilgrimage. But the traffic all seems to be headed this way these days. Those who sent the packet were Special Office."

"You talk too much. These walls have ears."

"Point taken. Apologies." He had let too much thought leak through while he concentrated on Ghort's conversation with Pella.

Old Bit had gone into a corner. She rummaged through a pile of what looked like refuse, came up with passes bearing the Durandanti family crest. "These will do. As long as you stay away from Durandanti patrols. If you don't act like what you are and piss somebody off. These make you agents of Don Alsano Durandanti. The Three Families are trying to get along. Them against the world. Don Alsano has a plan to bring Sonsa back."

"Hey, Matt! Granny!" Ghort yelled. "The kid says somebody's staking the place out. There's four of them. Another one ran off like he was going after reinforcements."

"That's not good," Bit said. "Not if they think you're the ones who came in on the smuggler. They'll want to know why you didn't go straight to the Don's palace. I know what. The girls don't have anything to do. We'll make up families for you. Beomond, get your damned birthday present put away. Tiny! Look around. Make sure there ain't nothing laying out that we don't want to answer questions about."

In ten minutes Hecht and Ghort left the House of the Ten Galleons accompanied by their wives, Ghort's son, and Hecht's brace of prepubescent daughters. He had a real daughter in al-Qarn older than these apprentice prostitutes. The purported wives managed to look surprisingly respectable.

Bit had had practice showing witnesses what they wanted to see.

The thugs in the street evidently did not find it remarkable that men would take their families along on a visit to a brothel. There were no challenges. Hecht wondered how they meant to catch spies with no more information than they had.

Once clear, Ghort said, "I get the chance, I'm having me a chat with my sailor friends. They sold us out."

"Not completely. Those men didn't have good descriptions of us."

"Yeah. So my guys gave up what they had to in order to keep from getting their own nuts in a clamp. But they didn't volunteer anything useful. Good on them. What say we get out of town, now? Suddenlike."

"That's always been my plan. We made this side trip because I didn't have guts enough to tell the Special Office no."

"You never get to where you can say no anytime you want, do you?"

"You're turning into a philosopher in your dotage."

"What do we do with the wives and kids?"

The families were quieter than good, obedient Praman families. The women wore the black expected of rural wives even here in this land of idolaters. The daughters were clad poorly and plainly. Both had been among those who had tried to spy on Bit and her visitors.

"I'm sure they have instructions already. Right, ladies?"

Exactly. Except that Hecht and Ghort soon found themselves equipped with children who refused to go away. Pella Versulius thought he had a good thing going. He insisted they still needed his help. The girl, one of the supposed daughters . . . She grabbed hold of Ghort and refused to be returned to the joy house. She was, probably, clever enough to see that these men would not be long on respect for the claims of a whoremaster.

Madness, Hecht thought, watching the two women try to pry the girl off Pinkus Ghort. What did she face back there that was more terrible than running off with men she knew nothing about?

The older prostitutes cursed and shouted, their fear mounting. Big trouble awaited them if they did not bring this child back to the brothel. They did not give a damn what became of the other girl.

That child sidled up to Hecht. She whispered, "Her name is Vali Dumaine, Mr. Soldier of God. Her father is important. They stole her to punish him. And to blackmail him. They're going to auction off her virginity. If her father don't do what they want. There'll be a really big reward if you take her home."

"She talks?" The stubborn child had been stone silent, the women treating her like a deaf-mute.

The girl nodded. "Nobody knows. The whores don't know who she is, either. They'd probably steal her for the reward if they did."

"What would we do with her?" Loud and physical as the prostitutes became, they could not separate the girl from Pinkus Ghort. Ghort did not help them. Neither did he fend them off. He was waiting for more evidence to develop.

"Take her home, Mr. Soldier of God. Ransom her."

"You're trying to help her?"

"Yes."

"What about you?"

"It's too late for me, Mr. Soldier of God."

Hecht chose not to pursue that. "Won't you get in trouble?"

"Not me. Bit is my granny. She won't believe I fixed it up. I cain't do no wrong. Them bitches are gonna pay for every time they slapped or pinched me when Bit wasn't looking. Now."

So. Helping the other girl's escape attempt was not a selfless act.

Vali Dumaine kept her death grip on Ghort's belt.

"Ladies!" Hecht snapped. "If this doesn't stop we all end up in chains." The uproar had begun to attract attention.

The women shut up. They stared at each other, murmured, tried one more time to pull the girl off Ghort, then grabbed Bit's granddaughter and fled. Cursing all the way.

Pella said, "Your Honors, we need to get out of here. This kind of racket always brings investigators."

"Just another reason for us to get out of town now." He felt hidden eyes watching.

Pella said, "You can't leave before the gates open. The guards don't bribe."

"Lead on, Pella." Hecht related the story the girl had whispered during the squabble. As they followed Pella.

"Hey, Pipe, we can't go dragging a kid around."

"I'm open to suggestions. Including what to do about the fact that we've attracted the attention of the Night." His amulet had begun to offer a faint warning.

"The street's full of kids. Give her to Pella." Ghort glanced round, sensing the stirring of shadows.

Hecht's wrist tingled. The warning was unnecessary. Somebody was coming. In a hurry. A lot of somebodies, considering the racket.

Ghort said, "I thought them whores gave up awful easy."

Hecht grunted. "They'd know their city. They'd know how long they could raise hell before they had to run for it."

"I don't like this. These guys have torches."

"The Special Office won't forgive us if we get caught and questioned."

"No shit. Not to mention me. Pella, little buddy, I'm thinking we ought to get us up on a roof somewhere. Unless you got a better idea."

"That's what I'd do, Your Honor. But not here. People here are on the lookout on account of the noise them stupid whores made."

"Pipe, I tell you, this kid reminds me of me. Smart as a whip."

"Make up your mind. Which is it? Like you? Or smart?"

"Huh?"

"I'll bet he can remember names. Even when he's excited."

"Oh. Good point. Sorry. Get on, boy. Find us a place."

"This ain't my part of town. But come on."

Hecht kept an eye on the shadows.

THE CHILDREN WERE MORE CONVINCING THAN FALSE PASSES. THOUGH THEY did leave early, while the guards were still yawning and barely able to stumble through their routine questions. Hecht lied liberally. The guards failed to recognize them as dangerous foreign agents making a desperate getaway.

Hecht and Ghort muttered about what were they going to do with two kids who would not go away. Pella, not even for money. And Vali . . . Well, Vali Dumaine steadfastly refused to talk. How could they ransom her without finding out anything, were they so inclined?

"She ain't stupid . . . Matt. Keeping hope alive. In our black hearts. So we'll take good care of her."

"She must remind you of you, too, then."

"Yeah. You know, I'm thinking we should've broke down and brought Bo and some of his crew. I'm thinking that bunch back there might not have been the most dedicated bunch of Brotherhood types we ever run into."

"You think? When they use a brothel for a chapter house? And an old woman for a castellan?"

"I'm thinking we shoulda read them letters. Might be handy to know what they're up to."

"Had we done, they wouldn't have believed we were Brothers, too. Which means this morning would've found us less happy than we are now. Maybe even swimming in the Sawn."

"Another good point. You bring much specie?"

"You're zigging when I'm zagging. For the thousandth time since I've known you."

"We got families, now. I'm thinking we'll have a hard time getting there on time. With the girl. I don't figure she's done a lot of walking before. So we might want to hire a cart and driver."

Hecht eyed the girl. And thought he could read the story of her kidnapping. "She'll handle it. They made her walk to Sonsa. And they weren't kind about it, either. Right, Vali?"

That did not crack any barriers. Hecht had hoped for a nod or a headshake.

Ghort asked, "How long you figure it'll be till they send somebody out here to look for us?"

"Bit and Beomond?"

"Whoever. Somebody had a whole lot invested in this kid."

Hecht wished he did know what was in those letters, now. "The other girl said they were trying to blackmail her father into doing something."

"Two things going on in the same place?" Ghort wondered. "Maybe. But most people are like me. Narrow focused as me. I have trouble walking and talking at the same time."

Not that Hecht had noticed. Ghort could talk in his sleep.

"We'd better not use the passes anymore. I wish we could put different clothes on the kids."

"There's some woods up there. We get off the road. You and me, we dig out a clean outfit. We put the girl in the boy's clothes. Bingo! We got two boys."

"One of them naked."

"No. Put him in my dirty shirt. Be huge on him but street kids live like that all the time."

Pella observed, "She's too clean, Your Honors. She looks like a rich kid in disguise."

Hecht told him, "Help her look less prosperous, then. Once we get off the road."

They were just inside the tree line when six horsemen raced in from the west. "Shit, Pipe, Fortune's grinning at us today. We'd been on the road, we'd never have got off in time."

"They're killing their horses. And that's why." He eyed Vali Dumaine. "Who's this bony chit's daddy? Who does the Brotherhood hate that much?"

"You really asking? Or is that one of your rhetorical type questions? Them riders wasn't Brotherhood guys, anyway."

"I'm pleased to listen if you have answers. And I know they weren't Brotherhood. They couldn't have that many hidden around town. But they might have men working for them who don't know who they really work for."

Ghort shrugged. "I got nothing, then. The girl is fair. She maybe better pass as your kid. I'll take the other one. We need to get out of here. Those guys will start working their way back after a while."

"We'll stick to the woods till we see them go back."

"You been away from the wilds a while, Pipe. You able to handle the woods? To cover a trail?"

"I think so. If they do catch us here it'll be where their bodies won't be found for a while."

"I like your confidence. What if we get stopped?"

"I'll leave that to you. You're a natural. Me, I have the same problem as my daughter. Runs in the family."

"Thought she was gonna be your son, Your Honor."

"My son. Yes, Pella."

"Oh, hell, yeah. They're gonna take one look at you and want me to tell how you got some woman to get that close if you didn't fog her mind with bullshit."

"Do Your Honors go on like this all the time?"

"He does," Hecht got in first. "I'm the responsible one."

"O Responsible One. How're we gonna make any bodies to leave in the woods?" Pretending to be poor travelers, they carried no weapons heavier than knives. "We can't be looking for mercenary work if we're on this road. Headed away from Sonsa? Not if Sonsans ask."

"They'll give up when they don't find any sign of us." Hecht felt slightly rattled. Why was he even out here? His choices recently seemed slightly unreal.

"Child of Fortune."

"What?"

"That's what they call orphans where I come from, Pipe. In general. And me, specifically. That was my only name for a long time."

Hecht grunted. Really? Not that long ago Ghort had blamed an assassination attempt on men recommended to the City Regiment by relatives. And, farther back, he had told a story about his father being murdered in Clearenza.

In the language of Hecht's youth, Child of Fortune meant someone touched by the gods. One who had become a tool of the Instrumentalities of the Night. One who became a prophet. Or a raging lunatic.

Which might explain aspects of his life he could not understand in any other context.

Frightening.

You were in trouble if you started thinking you had been singled out by the Night.

"We're ready to go, Your Honors."

"Oh. Good." Hecht had paid little attention to the children changing.

"Hey!" Pella said. "Where's your tattoo?"

"What? I likes my wine, boy, but I ain't never been drunk enough to let no failed torturer's apprentice use me for no art board."

Pella studied Hecht. "You don't got one neither, do you? You guys lied. You ain't Brotherhood of War, are you?"

Ghort said, "We never said we was."

Hecht asked, "Members of the Brotherhood have an identifying tattoo?"

"That's what I heard."

"Did you? It's news to me. Buck?"

"I never heard that before. Don't mean it ain't true."

What were the chances a Child of Fortune off Sonsa's streets would know something the Brotherhood had hidden successfully from men who were around them every day?

"Everybody knows that!" Pella insisted.

"How?"

"When there was all that fighting with the Brotherhood chapter house and the Deves, when I was little. When people stripped the bodies the Brothers all had tattoos. The same one. Back here." He tried to slap his own back behind his heart. "It was only about this big." He indicated his left thumbnail. "It looked like an acorn. With a leaf coming out."

"From this seed shall a mighty oak rise," Ghort mused. "Aaron of Chaldar. Talking about Domino. Who became a disciple when Aaron was dying. And he was right. Domino preached all along the southern coast of the Mother Sea. There are tribes in the mountains down there that still haven't bought the Praman evil."

They were worms in the belly of a dog. . . . Hecht said, "You never cease to amaze me, Buck. How would you know something like that?"

The Founder Domino was not well known to Episcopal Chaldareans. He had not evangelized in the west. The Brotherhood of War, however, considered Domino their patron. Before his conversion Domino had been the Imperial general, Anelos Andul Gallatin, Dominius, Dominius being a title reserved to commanders who had celebrated several significant successes.

Hecht suspected that, as would be the case with Josephus Alegiant a generation later, Domino had been successful mainly because of his willingness to make converts at spear's point.

"I was a divinity student. For about two years, one week. They threw me out on account of somebody drank all the teaching brothers' wine and they needed somebody to blame it on."

"Don't you hate it when people scapegoat?"

They resumed traveling, but stayed in the woods, which snaked along the banks of a creek that, headed the other direction, eventually emptied into the Sawn. Sometime later Hecht sensed the drum of distant horses. "They're coming."

The riders did return, not racing now, looking into the woods, sometimes darting in to look for sign. They missed Hecht and his companions. They continued on westward.

"I feel better, now," Ghort said. "Though they should've been smart enough to have some minor mage with them."

"They're criminals. But if they did have one, how would we know?"

"You're just all the time the incarnation of optimism, Pipe."

"How come he calls you Pipe when your name is Mathis?" Pella wanted to know.

"Because he's an idiot?"

"Because he used to smoke a ton of *kuf* when we was in the Holy Lands."

Pella sneered. He had established his disbelief in their holy calling already.

Hecht said, "We have to get back on the road and start making time. We ought to get to Alicea before dark." The town was a long way off. He could remember nowhere to get in out of the night anywhere closer. And the sooner they established themselves at the Knight of Wands the more they would be part of the background when their quarry arrived.

Ghort launched a fanciful account of his adventures in the Holy Lands with his good pal Mathis Schlink. Because he wove in commonplace fairy tale, tall tale, and legendary elements, Pella knew he was lying from the start.

Hecht said, "Think I'll range ahead. You two stick with Buck."

Ghort nodded. "Be careful." By which Hecht understood that he, too, had noted that one fewer rider had returned than had gone east.

Pella betrayed his own quick eye. "Let me do it. They ain't looking to ambush me. Whoever they are."

Ghort told him, "Go to it, kid."

With Pella out of earshot, Hecht asked, "And what would you do now, Child of Fortune?"

"Play it straight. He don't see any obvious way to cash in. He knows they'll just rob him if he tries to cut himself a share of whatever Vali is worth." A bit later, Ghort added, "He's making a long-term investment. That's what I did. It worked for me. He'll probably end up brokenhearted."

Ahead, Pella rounded a verge of the woods and disappeared. Whistling.

"He has nerve."

"You need that to survive when you're on your own."

This sounded more like the real Pinkus Ghort than most of the stories he told. "I'll stroll ahead, now. Vali, stay by Buck."

Hecht rounded the trees and found Pella in a brisk argument with a tall, bony, skinny man whose natural posture made him lean forward. His hands swooped and flew as he talked. His horse was tied to a bush beside the road, on a long tether, busy grazing and ignoring its rider. Its saddle, loosened, bore a Sonsan household crest.

Hecht stalked closer. Durandanti. The Durandanti family had an old relationship with the Brotherhood of War. That broke down when the Brotherhood tried to plunder the Devedian quarter of Sonsa, but, evidently, peace had been made, under the table. The Durandanti plan for reviving Sonsa must require becoming intimate with the ambitions of Sublime V and the Brotherhood.

Where did Vali fit?

That depended on who she was.

Pella demonstrated his street bona fides by maneuvering the bony man round to present his back to eastbound traffic. He remained unaware of Hecht until his horse became restless.

The Durandanti spun. His face was unnaturally pale. He had one of those lantern-jawed faces that looked like the planners forgot to put meat on over the bone.

"Hi!" Hecht smacked the man solidly between the eyes. "Ow! Damn! I forgot how much that hurts!" He shook his fingers vigorously. "My guess is, this fellow doesn't do this sort of thing for a living." His victim staggered two steps, cross-eyed, then went down on one knee.

"You're probably right, Your Honor. He was only trying to sound tough."

Hecht breathed on his knuckles. "I'm a Your Honor again, eh?"

"Just being careful, Your Honor. You've started smacking people."

Hecht chuckled. "You are like Buck. Help me move him over by that tree." The bony man had both knees and a hand down in the dust now.

Ghort and Vali arrived. The Durandanti, his back against a sapling, groggily worked on a leaky nose. Ghort asked, "What did you do that for?"

"Seemed like the most direct way. Get that mare ready. We'll put him back aboard. Vali can ride pillion. That'll let us pick up the pace."

"You think they won't miss him?"

"I expect they will. We'll talk to him while we walk. He'll let us know what we need to do."

"Uhm." Ghort got it. In his own way.

They would pump the Durandanti full of false information while draining him of what he knew.

Hecht shared his theory about the Durandanti and Brotherhood getting into bed. Ghort readied the mare, then examined the Durandanti's nose. "Not broken. Not even bloody. Just running bad. Got some tears going, too."

"You knocked the snot out of him, Your Honor." Pella giggled.

THEY MADE GOOD TIME, NOW, AND PASSED THROUGH ALICEA WITHOUT attracting attention an hour before sunset. They saw no other travelers till they neared the town. The area was busier than last time Hecht passed through. Ragged tents and shanties had appeared. Beggars came out. He had seen none of those before.

Hecht released the Durandanti two miles past Alicea, up the West Way, tied to a willow tree. With his horse tethered nearby, contentedly grazing. Master Stain Hamil had been cooperative. "You don't do a lot of yelling, you can get those ropes off pretty quick. You do yell, chances are you'll get robbed. Maybe even murdered."

Ghort and the children had dropped off just east of Alicea, turning back to get established at the Knight of Wands. Master Stain Hamil of House Durandanti was led to believe that they would scrounge supplies, catch up, and trek on east to Plemenza. Having been prisoners there Hecht and Ghort were able to talk about Plemenza convincingly.

Hecht entered the Knight of Wands carefully. It proved uncrowded. He spotted Ghort, joined him. Ghort asked, "It go all right?"

"Tied him to a tree. Left him his horse. He'll be home tomorrow night. If the boogies don't get him."

"We might be sorry. If they got balls enough to come after us on somebody else's turf. But I'm glad you didn't do the hard thing."

"He was a worker bee. He didn't even know why they were chasing us. Did you get us in here?" The Knight of Wands was a sprawling derelict of a building, mostly one story high, that had been added to a dozen times. The older parts looked like they would just fall down and be abandoned once they did. When Hecht arrived a boy younger than Pella was outside plugging holes leaking smoke using the contents of a bucket of mud. The smoke came from a fireplace in the common room that needed its chimney cleaned. The up side of the smoke was that it helped quell the stench of the place.

"Sure. Room and board. Fleas, lice, and bedbugs on the house."

"Only because they don't have the imagination to charge. Where are the kids?"

"Out running around. They get along. Vali has problems, Pipe. I'm wondering if maybe somebody didn't rape her. Pella's trying to show her how to be a kid."

"Why doesn't she run away?"

"Not in her nature. If she was raised in a castle somewhere, with somebody doing everything for her but shit, it wouldn't occur to her to run. Biggest thing she ever did on her own was latch on to us, probably. Which took some major guts."

"Or absolute certainty that going with us couldn't possibly be more horrible than staying where she was. How long you figure it'll be before your cousins show up?"

"I'm not gonna argue about that no more. You want them to be my family, so be it." Ghort pretended to count on his fingers. "We had good winds. We probably made twice as many miles a day as them. But they came almost straight north while we went the long way around."

"How about a straight answer?" Ghort sometimes created drama where there was none.

"They could turn up tomorrow. If they ran all the way. Which would depend on whether they think you got killed or not."

"How does that make a difference?"

"Just brainstorming. If they got you, a shitload of people would be pissed off and looking for somebody to burn at the stake. If they didn't, they'd figure us to be a little more relaxed. Here come the kids. Must be getting scary dark out."

Pella and Vali dodged a scruffy one-eyed man who tried to keep them out because they were obvious refugee trash. They zipped to the table, seated themselves. Vali did not appear particularly remote or frightened. Pella announced, "We're hungry."

Hecht said, "I'm not surprised. It's been a long day."

The one-eyed man arrived. "These yer brats?"

"Right. And they'll be in and out for the next several days. Till the rest of our people get here."

Ghort told the children, "Let's see what they've got in the pot."

"Just checking. We got problems with thieves, anymore."

"Of course." Hecht told the children, "You two be on your best behavior while we're here."

"Yes, sir, Uncle Matt," Pella said, struggling to keep a straight face. Vali managed a nod. It took an effort.

"They're good kids," Hecht told the one-eyed man. "But they are kids. Full of energy. Hey. Where can we go to church?"

Later, with the children in bed, Hecht and Ghort relocated to a shadowed corner, unoccupied because it was so far from the fire. They observed the clientele, watching for anyone who might be waiting to meet their quarry.

"Cold back here," Ghort muttered.

"Lonely, too. And so dark hardly anybody . . . Well. Look here. Master Hamil figured out my knots."

The Durandanti rider had stumbled into the Knight of Wands, paler than ever, deeply frightened. With a big bruise on his forehead. Ghort observed, "That's a man what ain't used to being out in the country after dark."

"Sshh. Let's don't make him stop thinking we're headed for Plemenza."

The one-eyed man braced Hamil. Hamil could not show him coin or anything else of value.

"You robbed him?" Ghort asked.

"Sure did. Didn't want him thinking we're honest folks on a mission."

"Good for you. There he goes."

With help from the one-eyed man, who shoved the pallid Sonsan back into the darkness. Hamil protested all the way, invoking Don Alsano Durandanti.

"Think One-eye just made a booboo?" Ghort asked.

"Depends on how much the Don backs his troops. Uh-oh. Here's real trouble."

"What?"

"That dark corner over there. There's a guy in there. He wasn't there when we moved over here. I didn't see him slide in. He's wearing a pilgrim's robe. Catch him when the scullery boy throws the next load of wood on the fire."

Silent minutes passed. The boy who had been caulking earlier brought firewood to beat back the chill of the night. The fire flared briefly.

"Well," Ghort murmured, "was I a betting man, an' I been known to lay one down now an' then, I'd put money on that fellow being Ferris Renfrow's ugly twin."

"Maybe his evil twin?"

"I'd say Renfrow is the evil twin. Interesting, though. You think he's involved?"

"My guess? Only obliquely, if at all." Ferris Renfrow and his masters in the Grail Empire had no cause to murder the Patriarch's Captain-General. "I'd guess it's coincidental. This would be a natural gathering place for conspirators."

Ferris Renfrow did as they did. Sat in the shadows and watched. Hecht and Ghort picked out three men they felt deserved closer scrutiny.

Time rolled on. And on. Ghort muttered, "I wish that asshole would give up and go to bed. It was a long fuckin' day. I need some shut-eye."

"Uhm." Renfrow seemed to be paying them no heed. Hecht did not believe he was unaware of them. Their shadows were deeper than his, though.

Hecht began to feel the weariness, too.

"What're you doing, Pipe?"

"Going to see what he does when he recognizes me."

"Is that smart?"

Hecht shrugged. He crossed the room, stepping over and around sleeping men and men who had enjoyed too much of the heavy, dark, foul beer brewed by the Knight of Wands. Renfrow appeared disinterested at first, then started and swore, "Eis's bloody ass boils! What the hell are you doing here?"

Hecht settled beside the Imperial. "The very question I asked myself about you."

"I'm here on my lord's business."

"And I as well. With an added touch of the personal."

Renfrow contained his shock. "You're outside your home territories."

"Outside the Emperor's, too. Might be Sonsan."

"The Counts of Aloya, theoretically. But they haven't been seen since you and I were pups. Nobody's moved in because that would be more trouble than leaving the territory to rot."

Which would lead to banditry and chaos, eventually. Of course.

"I've had a long day. I just wanted you to know I'm here." Hecht headed for his quarters before Renfrow could respond. Ghort stayed where he was.

He left right after you did," Ghort reported. "He looked like he'd had a major shock. I don't think he recognized me."

"I wouldn't count on it. Who's always around when I'm somewhere?"

"Go teach granny to suck eggs. Put the kids on him. He won't expect them."

Hecht nodded. "Warn them. So he doesn't see the connection right away."

Ferris Renfrow did not turn up next morning. Hecht asked a few questions but soon stopped. Questions about fellow guests were not well received. He assumed questions about himself would find equally small favor.

Renfrow did not reappear till the ownership opened the evening pot.

Prepared meals could be had any time but cost extra. Budget-minded guests lived out of the bottomless porridge and goulash pots. The ingredients of the latter varied according to what leftovers from custom cookery were available. One had to beware small bones.

Renfrow drew a portion and retreated into the same shadows as the night before.

Hecht had assumed his place in his own dark clot a half hour earlier. His day had been unproductive. The children had discovered nothing—though they did feed his suspicions of the men he and Ghort had tagged as probable villains. They were from farther north or west, by their accents. They had horses stabled behind the inn. The stable boys had been paid to keep their tack ready for instant use. They prayed a lot. Pella considered that the most damning thing about them.

Hecht told Pella to arrange for some of that tack to disappear.

The suspects did not seem unusually wary.

Sometime during their second morning there the Knight of Wands began to buzz. A Grolsacher mercenary force, supposedly armed with letters of marque from Sublime V, had come to a bad end in the Connec. Only a handful survived—by running faster than Count Raymone Garete could chase. One survivor was a dastardly coward of a bishop, Morcant Farfog of Strang. The band's captain, Haiden Backe, had been among the first to fall. Prisoners willingly betrayed the Patriarch's role in their bad behavior. Documentary evidence had been thin in the Grolsachers' camp, however. The actual letters of marque had vanished. Of course, they were extremely valuable instruments.

Ghort whispered, "Your boss is a raving madman, Pipe. What the hell was he thinking? That Raymone Garete was one of the guys who made the Calziran Crusade work. What kind of gratitude is that?"

"Typical gratitude. The gratitude of kings. Sublime has never been out of Brothe. He's never been outside his tiny little clique of family and associates. He only hears what they think he wants to hear. He honestly believes that most of the world thinks just like he does. That they're longing for a champion who'll lead them into the fray. He thinks big things will go his way because little things have ever since he was in diapers. He's absolutely convinced of his divine right and of Patriarchal Infallibility. I don't think there's any way to scrape the scales off his eyes. I've tried. Though I never get close enough to actually talk to him."

"People like that mostly end up prematurely dead."

"Now we know why Sublime and his gang weren't worried about money."

"Plundering the heretics was always part of his plan."

"It won't work out any better in the Connec than it did in Calzir. There's a lot of wealth there. That country has been peaceful for so long. But most of the wealth will get destroyed or disappear during the getting."

"Shit," Ghort murmured. "This news is gonna get back to Brothe before we do. Our asses are gonna be in a sling when they can't find us."

Hecht thought so, too. There would be a lot of running in circles, screaming and shouting, once this news reached the Mother City. Though it should not have much practical impact. "We might've made a bad career move, sneaking off."

"Maybe this guy will give us a job." He meant Ferris Renfrow, who was headed their way.

Renfrow said, "You've heard the news from the Connec."

Hecht nodded.

"You should know that while the results delight me, neither the Emperor nor I contributed to Haiden Backe's embarrassment."

"That makes it all right, then."

Renfrow grinned. Hecht had not seen that before. "Sublime . . . No. Mustn't show disrespect to the Father of the Church. But I have to wonder about a man who'd hire Grolsachers—and Backe in particular—after all the disasters involving those people the last ten years. It'll be a fearsome hard winter in Grolsach, for sure."

Ghort said, "He hired Haiden Backe because he couldn't find anybody else stupid enough. Never minding Sublime's genius. Grolsach is terrible. Not so bad to be from, though, on account of nobody expects a lot from you." More to himself, Ghort muttered, "Any Grolsacher tries to change their luck, he screws up and it just gets worse."

"Spoken like a man who knows whereof he speaks."

"Smart guys get out and find work somewhere else. Which helps them and Grolsach both because then there's fewer mouths to fill."

"If the smartest people emigrate, what does that say about those who don't?"

Ghort shrugged. He did not know Ferris Renfrow. He did know the man's reputation. The Imperial fancied himself the cleverest man around. And liked to show it in pointless debates.

Renfrow turned to Hecht. "You've got a couple of kids you're towing around. How come?"

"Cover. Plus, somebody has a soft streak." He nodded at Ghort. "Says one of them reminds him of him."

"Ugly kid?"

"First shot. They have their uses. Eyes and ears. Though the smaller boy is a mute."

"You came from Sonsa." Not a question.

Hecht nodded. Renfrow knew.

"What's going on there?"

"We weren't there long."

But long enough to collect a couple of street urchins, Renfrow said with his calculating gray eyes.

Ghort said, "The dump's a ghost town. I expected more people and more business. Guess they ain't never recovered from the Deve uprising."

"Perhaps."

Hecht knew Renfrow wanted to keep talking, but every question he asked revealed information as well. Which was why, in turn, Hecht did not ask about Vali Dumaine.

If anyone did know that story, Renfrow would.

So Hecht asked, "How much support will Lothar give the Duke of Clearenza?"

Renfrow chuckled. "What will the Patriarch do in response to fon Dreasser coming to his senses?"

Hecht smiled back.

Renfrow saw something that interested him. Startled and disturbed him, perhaps. For a flickering instant. "He wouldn't have delusions of . . ."

"Plenty," Ghort said. "Illusions, too. He's loony as a band of rock apes on fermented fruit."

What did that mean? Hecht said, "We wouldn't be here if he was serious about that, would we?"

Renfrow grunted, headed out the front door.

A man went out after him. Hecht said, "That would be the man he hoped we wouldn't notice."

Ghort agreed. "Yes. And now I'm curious. Because that was Lyse Tanner."

"Don't know the name."

"He's from Santerin. One of the ones who ran out after their last succession squabble. He tried to get a commission from the Patriarch. His brother is a bishop. He didn't get the job."

"So he went to work for the Emperor?"

"He was probably on Renfrow's payroll first. Let's keep an eye on him. See who his associates are. If he brought any. Think Renfrow knows we caught it?"

"He won't assume we didn't, I expect."

"Pipe, I'm getting a little anxious. Things are going on around us. And we ain't got a clue what they are."

"That's the story of my life. I'd be worried if I thought I was getting on top of everything."

HECHT AND GHORT WERE EATING SUPPER WITH THE CHILDREN WHEN THE deserters arrived. "That's them," Ghort whispered. He handed his bowl down to Vali, who pushed it under the bench. She was more relaxed but had not yet spoken. Ghort stared at the floor, letting the shadows disguise him.

Hecht whispered, "Pella. The men who just came in. Go outside and wait for them to come back out. Keep track. Don't be obvious." He glanced over. Ferris Renfrow had not yet crept into his evening shadow.

The children headed out the back way, Pella blathering about outhouses. Nobody paid attention. The brats had become furniture already.

"And now?" Ghort asked.

"And now I wish I'd had Pella go eavesdrop." The newcomers had begun by questioning the one-eyed man. If he had a name Hecht had yet to hear it. One-eye indicated one of the men Hecht had picked out earlier. The newcomers interrupted his before meal prayer.

The seated man was not pleased.

Hecht said, "He didn't want them to find him in here."

Ghort asked, "You dug out anything that you haven't told me yet?"

"They pray a lot. That one told the redhead serving girl that he's a priest. From Ormienden. He didn't say from where." Sublime's backers in parts of Ormienden were savage fanatics. Immaculate's were less determined but more numerous.

"Your basic godshouter is a shifty weasel, whatever his spiritual poison. But that guy and his pals look a little more so than usual."

Hecht thought so himself. But he had found no way to learn more about them.

"Here comes another one." Another supposed priest. "There's one more, right?"

The newcomer seemed nervous. The deserters paid no attention.

Ghort related what he imagined was happening. "My boys want their money. They're anxious to get on down the road. The paymaster is saying, relax. Don't attract attention. Anyway, it wouldn't be smart to get back out there on the road. There's some bad Night things prowling around north of here."

Which was true. A blood-drained corpse had been found only miles away just that morning.

"My boys don't care. They've worked themselves into a lather, worrying about how awful their lives will get if Iron Bottom Ghort ever gets hold of them."

"I'd be nervous myself."

"You'd have reason . . . Uh-oh."

"What?"

"The prayer brothers just sold them some snake oil. The money is hidden outside. The stable, probably. Some kind of crap like that. They're going to let the priests take them outside." The deserters and their interlocutors rose.

"Can they be that stupid?"

"They signed on to set you up."

"There is that." That seemed more like overweening optimism, though. "Let's don't let them get too far ahead."

Ghort muttered, "Shit. Timing. Here's your Imperial pal."

Ferris Renfrow drifted into his habitual shadow. What had passed between him and Lyse Tanner? Why was he still hanging around? Did he have regular connections at the Knight of Wands?

"They are going out back. The stable or the outhouses."

"Or the woods behind, if they're up to any real wickedness." He thought Renfrow showed a flicker of interest in the four men. Then glanced from them to him.

Of course. Renfrow would want to penetrate his business if he could.

"No help for it," Ghort muttered. "Let's go. I wish it was busier tonight."

The deserters were not complete fools. Both made sure of hidden weapons when their paymasters were not looking. Hecht saw Renfrow become more alert.

"You're right. Nothing for it."

The path to the outhouses led through the kitchen area, dark, smoky, and filthy enough to silence hunger for days. A greasy, heavily furred fat man was loafing, dispiritedly chatting up a bored serving girl who had no interest in a game of slap and tickle. She was not more than three years older than Vali. The cook demanded, "What's this damned parade to the jakes? Ain't nobody drunk enough to need a piss between them. You." He pointed a sausage finger at Hecht. "You ain't had a drink since you been here. That's unnatural."

Ghort countered, "It ain't the beer, brother. It's the rotten food all in a gassy hurry to get out the shit chute."

The cook considered taking umbrage. It was not worth the energy. He would save himself for the serving girl.

Hecht said, "She's probably his daughter."

"Even so, can't say as I blame him for trying. She's got an interesting look."

Pella materialized outside the back door. He whispered, "They headed for the stables, Your Honors. With two other men. Ones that was staying here already."

"Where's Vali?"

"Watching them."

"Show us where they are. Then you and Vali get back inside. Go to bed. You'll need the rest. We'll be on the road again tomorrow."

"This what you been waiting for?"

"Yes. Get moving."

Pella led off like he could see in the dark. Hecht and Ghort eased along behind, Hecht wondering what had become of the third priest.

The stables were quiet. The stable boys were asleep and the animals snoozing. Even the rats seemed to have taken the night off. An utter lack of response from his amulet told Hecht that no supernatural threat was afoot. Meaning none had an interest in what was happening here.

Their quarry proved not to have gone to the stable itself but into the attached feed shed. A lantern burned there. Light leaked through un-sealed walls. Ghort used touch and gesture to tell Pella to collect Vali and head back inside. To Hecht, he breathed, "Keep alert. There's another one around somewhere."

Hecht nodded. He eased up to peek through an uncaulked crack between horizontal logs.

The missing man was inside. He helped his friends move sacks of oats. The would-be assassins were more wary than the men paying off.

Interesting, Hecht thought. The holy men seemed inclined to play it straight. The deserters must have convinced them that everything had gone well.

Ghort breathed, "I don't buy it. Those two aren't even the ones that were sent down there."

Hecht squeezed Ghort's arm. They could talk later.

The three counted out silver to the two. There was a brief argument about whether or not the wages of dead conspirators ought to be paid. The deserters argued that the dead men had left families behind.

The paymasters offered half the agreed sum. Or nothing.

The deserters took what they could get. Hecht got the sense that their concern about the families of relatives now fatherless and husbandless was genuine. The plot may have been an extended family enterprise.

There was little talk, though the deserters did offer an account of the attack that failed to match what Hecht recalled.

Why were the paymasters so amenable?

Well, the deserters were no real threat since they could not know anything about these three.

The deserters pocketed their money and took off for the stable. They roused the stable boys and ordered their mounts readied. One boy protested. "Them nags is plumb worn out. Yer killin' them. And yer don't want ter go ridin' round in the night, nohow. On account a they's banes on the road up north. An' thank 'e, Yer Honors!" The boy stopped having opinions. Hecht guessed that he had received a nice tip.

Hecht peeked through the feed-shed wall. All three priests were seated on sacks. After a joint prayer, one produced a *kuf* pipe. As he packed it, he asked, "Coyne is ready?"

"I sent word. He'll handle it."

Hecht became aware of Pella's continued presence. Irked, he said nothing. He did not want the boy to argue and give them away. He pulled Ghort closer, breathed, "What do you think?"

"We need to move now. Never gonna get a better chance. They're cornered."

But there were three of them, complete unknowns.

GHORT WENT FIRST. HE WANTED TO SEE THEIR SHOCK. WHEN HECHT FOLlowed the three had just begun to rise in a cloud of *kuf* smoke, confused. Ghort said, "Just a social visit, guys. We smelled the pipe. Hoped you'd share."

Pella slid in behind Hecht, armed with a piece of kindling he considered a worthy truncheon.

Ghort continued. "My name is Pinkus Ghort. My friend is Piper Hecht. The short guy is a famous literary character. You know who we are, now. We'll talk while we're passing the pipe."

The trio did recognize at least one of the names.

Pella looked at them, back and forth. He did not know those names but was pleased to hear what might be real ones.

Ghort warned, "Don't be that way. You aren't killers. We're professionals. You pull a knife, you get hurt."

One man did not listen.

Ghort moved so fast he startled Hecht as much as the man he disarmed. "So, what we're going to do here is, we're going to share a pipe and talk about assassinations."

Ghort collected the fallen knife. "Pipe? Want to throw anything in here?"

"You're doing fine. But let's not dawdle."

Ghort flipped the knife. It stuck in the throat of the man farthest from him. "You," he told the next farthest. "Take care of him. He'll live if you pay attention. Unless you all want to be stubborn. Then none of you will. And you'll ruin a lot of good oats before you stink enough for them to dig you out."

"Sit," Hecht told the man Ghort had disarmed. "Talk to us. Who are you?"

After a brief consultation with his courage, the man said, "We're priests. Lay brothers, actually."

"Priests don't murder people."

"They do it all the time, Pipe. They just dress it up in mumbo jumbo. Do go on. This could get fascinating. Our own Church is trying to stab us in the back."

"Not the Church. Not your Church. Not the Usurper."

"She-it! Viscesment! *Immaculate?*"

Hecht found that hard to swallow. It was a given that the Anti-Patriarch was weak and ineffectual, little more than a joke. The consensus was that Immaculate II would drink himself to death and the dual Patriarchy would fade into history with him. Immaculate's line, though it had sound legal footing, would end.

"That will take some explaining," Hecht said.

"Are you really the Captain-General?"

"Yes. Why?"

"The Advisory concluded that you are the most dangerous weapon the Usurper has in his arsenal. If you're removed Sublime will never pull together forces able to impose his will outside his own territories. Especially once the Emperor dies."

The Empire was expected to weaken and become chaotic when Lothar died. His sister Katrin would succeed. And she would have to deal with scores of Electors and lesser nobility who would chafe under the rule of a woman.

"Explains the incompetence of the whole thing," Ghort muttered. "The Anti-Patriarch. Who'd of thought he even had a hair, let alone a complete set of balls?"

"Supposing anyone is telling the truth," Hecht observed. "I can think of several men who have the nerve, supposing there's any real point to killing me." There must be. Attempts had been made regularly.

He watched the other two pray over the wounded man. He pushed Pella back out into the darkness. "Take care of Vali. You don't want these men to know you're with us, anyway. They're not nice people."

The fight had gone out of the three, though. Ghort asked, "What now, Pipe? I didn't expect no priests from Viscesment."

"Nor did I." Where to? Race the news from the Connec to Brothe with no hope of beating it?

"We didn't give this enough thought before we hared off on an adventure."

"A young man's game," Ghort philosophized. "A game for men who don't got nothing to lose."

"Yes. Gentlemen. Priests. This is an important question. The fools you just paid. What did you send them into?"

"They're going to run into robbers. If they don't fight, all that will happen is, they'll lose the money."

"It isn't supposed to turn lethal?"

The priest acted offended. "We don't murder people . . . All right. Yes. There's no need to harm them. They'll disappear into Grolsach's population. They don't know anything, really. But we can't afford to let them keep the money. It'd ruin Immaculate's treasury."

Meaning the conspirators were never meant to be paid. "Why?"

"Because we have almost no income anymore. The Usurper's . . ."

"I mean, why kill me?"

"I told you. You're the only . . ."

"Not true." There was no sense whatsoever in that claim. He was *not* that important. He was *not* irreplaceable. Ghort could do what he did.

Ghort said, "He believes it, Pipe. Somebody sold him."

Hecht growled. "Stupid."

"Can't fix stupid. Hey, Pipe! You know you've made it big when people you don't even know think they got to kill you."

"Jealous?"

"Not quite. Brother, I don't need nobody wanting to cut my throat. Unless maybe a jealous husband. Sometime next century."

"You say that only because your faith is weak," one of the priests said.

"Weak ain't the word, godshouter. I been around damn near forty years. I ain't yet run into an Instrumentality what's out to improve my life."

Hecht interrupted. "No religious debates. It's the middle of the night. I'm tired. I'm crabby. This is what's going to happen. You're going back to Viscesment. With a message. Anyone tries this again, I take it personal. The men I'll send won't be incompetents like Sublime's. There won't be any warning ahead of time from the Empire's spies." Osa Stile's espionage had thwarted an attempt on Immaculate II by Sublime's agents.

Ghort eased past the wounded man. He moved a few sacks of oats, came up with a leather money bag that was almost empty. "This is sad. It looks like they did give it all to Aubero and Ogier."

Hecht said, "We'll take their horses, then. You don't mind walking in order to stay alive."

One priest responded with a sullen nod.

Ghort offered battlefield medical advice for the care of the injured man. "Keep the wound clean. He'll be fine if it don't get infected. Find a healing witch. Have her make a poultice."

"Let's call it a night, Pinkus."

"What? You don't want to find out who handed these guys the job in the first place? You guys didn't make this up yourselves, did you? Neither did your hero, Immaculate. You set up for something like this, you do a lot of spying and recruiting and training and rehearsing. You guys are just paymasters. Maybe with different sets of instructions, depending on what happened in Brothe. Right?"

Both uninjured men grew more frightened.

"You see?" Ghort said. "You need to ask the right questions. Who sent you guys?"

A short course of vigorous, nonphysical interrogation produced a name. Rudenes Schneidel.

Rudenes Schneidel had managed everything. Planning. Personnel. Scouting the target. Paying bribes. Recruiting the paymasters, who were otherwise unemployed lay brothers. Offered easy money, in hard times, they had no problem signing on.

Ghort asked, "Rudenes Schneidel? That somebody from back home with a big-ass grudge, Pipe? You ruin his sister?"

"Never heard of him before."

"Sounds like it comes from those parts, though."

"It does. I admit it. Any of you deal with Schneidel directly?"

The spokesman shook his head. Feeling bad for talking too much. "He used an interlocutor."

"Can you describe him?"

Of course not. Not well. The spokesman volunteered, "I asked the go-between about Schneidel. He said he only saw him once. If it was really him. He had a foreign accent so thick you could hardly understand him." The physical description suited every typical short fat thin tall dark brown white man you could run into on any Firaldian street.

"I've been here before," Hecht said, recalling trying to get a useful description of the witch Starkden, who had been behind a scheme meant to facilitate the premature demise of Else Tage of the Sha-lug, then pretending to be the Episcopal Chaldarean crusader Sir Aelford daSkees. "He wouldn't be a sorcerer in addition to his other transgressions, would he?"

Ghort leaned in. "We got a name. I can give it to Bo. Right now we need to get back into executive mode."

Hecht nodded. "Enough, then. Good night, gentlemen. Brothers. We'll include you in our prayers."

Pella wakened Hecht an hour before first light. "Sir, them priests are stealing their horses and running away."

"How do you know?"

"Vali saw them. She woke me up."

"I see." Before he finished getting his trousers on he heard horses crossing the rude pavements out front. "They have the moon, don't they?"

"Yes, sir."

"I'm a sir, now?"

"Yes, sir."

Hecht was amused but had no time to explore the workings of Pella's mind.

He might as well have taken time. The men from Viscesment got away easily.

There seemed little reason to hurry. Without horses the journey to Brothe could not be hastened much.

Ghort said, "Let's just be folks headed south looking for work. So stop looking prosperous."

Ferris Renfrow materialized. Hecht wondered how close the man had followed events last night. He seemed satisfied to watch them go. Pinkus Ghort's paranoid side wakened. "He might plan to have us snatched out in the country somewhere."

"Would there be a point?"

"Hell, yeah. He'd ruin Sublime's hopes for decades. Where would that fool find two more men like us?"

"A telling point. But I doubt he rates us as highly as we rate ourselves. But to reassure you, I'll just go ask."

"What? Are you out of your bean?"

Hecht approached the Imperial. "The name Rudenes Schneidel mean anything? Especially in connection with Viscesment?"

Renfrow raised an eyebrow. "It's turned up inside a few unpleasant rumors. Evidently a sorcerer. Of some attainment. But a complete blank otherwise. Why?"

"There was an assassination attempt in Brothe. You'll be hearing about it. Schneidel was behind the play. If that's something you can use."

"Probably not. The folks at Viscesment have grown increasingly independent. Tell your friend I'm going to let him get away. This time."

Hecht laughed. "Is his act that obvious?"

"It is."

"I'll pass the word. One more name I want to toss up. Dumaine."

"Dumaine?"

"That's all I've got. I heard it in Sonsa. Overheard it. Someone who's part of a plot involving the Durandanti family."

"The only Dumaines I know are minor Arnhander nobility. The current Viscount Dumaine is an enemy of Anne of Menand. With the enmity mostly on her side. Dumaine is a minor marcher, unimportant in Arnhander affairs, except as a scapegoat when Anne's plans go bad. Although he spends all his time at home, fending off his cousins who are enfiefed to the King of Santerin. He evidently had the bad judgment to turn down an offer Anne made. Doing so publicly."

Anne of Menand was the mistress of King Charlve of Arnhand, who was mentally incompetent. She wanted her son Regard to succeed. Charlve had no legitimate children. Her physical appetites were legendary. As was her malevolence toward those who crossed her.

"That wouldn't fit. I don't think. I must've heard wrong."

"Ah. This doesn't look good."

A rider was coming down the West Way astride a mount so blown it could barely keep moving. The beast would be ruined forever. Yet the rider's was not the will driving it. He was unconscious. He had tied himself into the saddle.

Ghort jogged out and intercepted the animal. It did not resist his guidance. It had no spirit left.

Hecht and Renfrow followed Ghort. Something bad had happened. Horse and rider alike were covered with dried blood, not all of it their own.

Ghort said, "It's Ogier. Three-fourths dead."

"They lied to us," Hecht said.

"Priests? Tell lies? You must be joking. But, no. That's not it. Look at these wounds."

Hecht and the Imperial walked round man and beast. The horse's nose practically dragged on the pavements. Hecht untied Ogier. Ghort and Renfrow lowered him to the ground. Hecht said, "He might've run into a rabid bear. Or a hungry lion."

"Lion? Excuse me, Pipe. There ain't been no fuckin' lions in these parts since Old Brothen Imperial times."

Renfrow agreed. "The ancients used them up in their blood games. Once in a while one would cross the Escarp Gibr al-Tar back then, maybe, but they were even hunted out on the far coast of the Mother Sea by the time of the Praman Conquest."

"More than I needed to know." Hecht's amulet was responding to the residual shadow clinging to the deserter and his steed. They had fallen foul of something powerful.

Gawkers from the Knight of Wands began to gather. Hecht and Renfrow kept them back while Ghort tried to question the deserter.

Ogier was not hurt as badly as all the blood made it seem. But he would need luck to survive. Claw wounds always festered.

One client of the Knight of Wands confessed to having some small skills as a healer. Once he was satisfied that no one would denounce him to the Church he went to work on the deserter.

The Episcopal Chaldarean Church suffered from a schizophrenic attitude toward powers derived from the Instrumentalities of the Night. It railed against congress with sorcerers and witches, yet some of its greatest dignitaries were among the most powerful mages known. Talented folks not on the inside frequently suffered persecution. Particularly where the Witchfinders of the Special Office roamed.

"Well?" Hecht asked when Ghort finally came away. "Did he have a story?"

"Fraught with irony."

"I'm surprised you even know two of those three words."

"All right. Hang on. I'm going to do this all in one long blast. Then we need to get on down the road."

"So, go."

"Ogier and Aubero ran into robbers. Who robbed them. While the robbers were arguing over whether they should kill them it suddenly got icy cold. A mist closed in. The moonlight faded away. Men started screaming. Something with claws and rotten breath mauled him but got distracted before it finished him off. He passed out. He woke up at daybreak. Some of the horses were missing. The rest, along with his brother and all the robbers, were dead, some torn to pieces. He headed here because it was the only place he could think of. He kept passing out. He hid out whenever he felt that coming on. He remembers our three priests charging past. He tried to warn them but they didn't hear him. A while later screaming broke out back the way he had come. He kept moving. He found a saddled horse grazing in a field. He caught it and calmed it, mounted up and tied himself on in case he passed out again. Something in the woods roared and started crashing toward them. The horse panicked. It ran till it couldn't run anymore. Then it kept walking. And here he is."

"What happened to the money?" Some things of the Night had an abiding loathing for silver. Iron bothered a lot more, though those daunted by the ignoble metal were mainly minor entities.

"Whoever had the coins would've stood the best chance of surviving." He went back to Ogier briefly, then returned to Hecht looking puzzled. "He had some silver on him that the robbers didn't find. Their captain took the money. But he and the rest all ended up dead. The money must still be there. Somewhere."

Though Ghort kept his voice down, he was overheard. Members of the crowd began to find interests elsewhere. Despite complete ignorance of how much might be involved.

"Ain't that amazing?" Ghort beckoned the one-eyed man, whispered briefly, then said, "We got to get on the road, Pipe. Trouble ain't gonna wait on us down there."

And so they did, turning their backs to a sudden flow northward. Hecht muttered, "They're idiots. Eight or ten men have just been killed by a monster and all they can think about is there might be money on the corpses. What were you whispering about, there at the end?"

"About him taking care of Ogier till he can get on his feet again. I explained about the money Ogier has. And how things will turn nasty for the Knight of Wands if he don't do right by Ogier."

"I see." And saw more than Ghort perhaps intended.

Ogier and Aubero might have been family after all.

3. Alten Weinberg, Heart of the New Brothen Empire

Princess Helspeth, Grafina fon Supfer, Marquesa of Runjan, and so forth, had come to Alten Weinberg thinking the Emperor meant to celebrate her twentieth birthday. She went to her knees three times before her little brother, Lothar, Emperor of the Grail Empire. In the presence, now, she suspected his summons had nothing to do with her birthday. The hall was filled with the ravens and vultures who orbited Lothar these days. And Katrin had come, too.

But not Ferris Renfrow. She would have been more comfortable if Renfrow were visible. You could call Ferris Renfrow the conscience of the Empire.

Helspeth did not like bending the knee but her brother was acting in his official capacity tonight. Probably reluctantly. In front of Omro va Still-Patter, Grand Duke of Hilandle, first among equals in the Council Advisory, styled the Protector. Accompanying Hilandle, interposing themselves between the Emperor and the lesser lights in the hall, were the Master of the Wardrobe, the Master of the Privy Purse, and the Lord Admiral Vondo fon Tyre, whose fleet was almost entirely imaginary. These men had gotten their claws into the Imperial power simply because Lothar was still five years short of his majority.

Helspeth's older sister Katrin, Grafina fon Kretien and Gordon, Princess Apparent, also knelt. She did not disguise her irritation, nor her loathing, for Hilandle and his cronies. Lothar was her baby brother, her beloved "Mushin." She had pampered him through countless illnesses, spoiling him terribly. Helspeth did not like or think well of her sister but she could not deny that Katrin loved, nurtured, and indulged her brother selflessly. And, like Helspeth, she loathed the grasping old men who had seized control of the boy.

Tall, lean, blond, and beautiful, clad simply in dark clothing, Katrin Ege seemed cold and remote. She had her father's stubborn will but little of the magnetism that had served him so well. That lack, her sex, and the ambition of so many nobles put her in a weaker position than she liked. But the Protector and his cronies were blinding themselves willfully, seeing either of the Ege daughters as a weakling.

All the children of the Ferocious Little Hans were in weaker positions than they liked.

Johannes had compelled the Electors to fashion an Act of Will and Succession that enacted, published, and ratified by the Patriarch and Collegium would withstand every possible challenge. But Johannes Blackboots had not anticipated his own death in battle. He had expected to outlive his sickly son and see the Imperial throne passed on through Katrin and her sons. He had hoped to forge powerful alliances through both daughters.

Negotiations had come and gone before Johannes fell at al-Khazen. No arrangements had been finalized.

Helspeth had been included in the succession almost as an afterthought. Johannes was thorough in everything. After Helspeth, the sons of his sister Anies were named in the Act.

It would take a major Ege family disaster to put the succession back into the hands of the Electors.

Lothar stated, "The Council Advisory has cautioned us, and we are in agreement, that the world today presents our reign with unprecedented challenges."

This was the first time Helspeth heard Mushin use the royal "we." It took her aback. She was not accustomed to her little brother being anything else. And, studying him closely, she suspected that this Emperor Lothar was a creation of the Grand Duke and his cronies. An eventuality she had feared increasingly as Hilandle and his flock circled more closely round the Emperor and isolated him ever more from his family and the world.

Lothar understood what was happening. A minor, he had little hope of halting the process. He had to remain strong and play one Councilor off against another. He managed that with some success.

"It has been demonstrated that our present style of life is inappropriate for a family of Imperial dignity. The daughters of our father should not be inviting scandal and disaster by roving like common men-at-arms."

Helspeth glared at Lothar. Half the nobility had spent the past ten years appalled and scandalized because the old Emperor not only permitted but encouraged his maiden daughters to accompany him to the field, to risk the life of the camp, and to come into regular contact with coarse, crude common soldiers.

So the Council was about to end all that.

The boy Emperor wilted under Helspeth's glare. And was no happier when he turned to his older sister.

Katrin was less inclined to the scandalous life. Helspeth had taken up arms and armor during the Calziran Crusade, getting into desperate straits under al-Khazen's wall. Katrin was more willful, more determined to preserve her prerogatives and independence.

Lothar was strong of mind, if not of flesh. He did not remain cowed. "We have decided that our princess sisters shall withdraw into their households till suitable marriages can be negotiated. Silence! Both of you." Helspeth had been about to explode. She did not see Katrin's reaction because her own focus had become so narrow. She was sure her sister was equally outraged.

The Grand Duke all but sneered behind his short, gray-tinged beard. His eyes were icy. "It's the Emperor's will." Meaning Lothar had been bullied until he gave in.

Helspeth reminded herself that Hilandle, till Johannes forced his Act of Will and Succession upon the Electors, had counted himself the leading candidate to succeed.

The boy Emperor then demonstrated that his advisers did not have him as neatly under thumb as they might want to believe. "Katrin, we convey to you the Imperial holdings at Grumbrag, with all the rights of Eathered and Arnmagil."

Members of the Council were so aghast they failed to sputter. There were snickers amongst the lesser lights.

The boy continued. "To our sister Helspeth we convey the City of Plemenza and its dependencies and trust that she will take the opportunity to further her education."

Plemenza was much the lesser prize. Eathered and Arnmagil, now unified into a single Imperial province, had been kingdoms in their own rights scarcely a century gone. But Plemenza had been Johannes's favorite city. He would have shifted his capital there from Alten Weinberg had the Firaldian city not been so far from the heart of the Grail Empire. He had spent a lot of time in Plemenza, often for his own pleasure, not just because Imperial policy focused on Firaldia and the difficult behaviors of Sublime V and the Church. Johannes's daughters had enjoyed much of their schooling there.

Helspeth flashed a grin. Lothar flashed right back.

Hilandle had been outmaneuvered. Two score witnesses, few congenial to the Grand Duke, had seen the Emperor convey Imperial holdings to members of his family. If Lothar was clever indeed, the patents were ready now, prepared by someone he knew was not Hilandle's tool.

The Grand Duke's face turned stony. He would never underestimate the boy Emperor again.

Helspeth glanced sideways. Katrin seemed pleased. Eathered and Arnmagil was a plum, a fine, fruitful country—and Grumbrag was known for its craftsmen and ingenious artificers. A suitable city and province for the Crown Princess of the New Brothen Empire.

The fleeting look Katrin sent Helspeth's way was only slightly less venomous than the one she had given Hilandle.

She was jealous! Of Plemenza! Because her time there was filled with happy memories, too. Perhaps the only such memories she had accumulated in her twenty-three years.

Johannes Ege—variously known as Johannes Blackboots, Hansel Blackboots ("Little Hans" because he was not a man of great physical stature), or Hansel the Ferocious—had been elected Emperor of the New Brothen Empire before the birth of any of his children. Katrin's mother, Hildegrun of Machen, had just turned nineteen when she married the new Emperor. She was tall, blond, and beautiful. Gossip at the time suggested she had caught Johannes's eyes when she was just fifteen. The Imperial nuptials antedated the birth of the Princess Katrin by a scant five months.

The alliance with Hildegrun's family solidified Johannes's hold on the Grail Empire. She was a devoted wife with numerous knightly brothers who served the Emperor faithfully all his years, remaining friends and allies through several bouts with misfortune. Hildegrun often accompanied Hansel on his progresses through the Empire. She made herself beloved immediately everywhere, even by the wives of the Emperor's enemies.

When Katrin was four months old, while her father was campaigning amongst the countless states of Firaldia, Hildegrun died in a riding accident.

An accomplished equestrian, Hildegrun loved to gallop with the bolder women of her household. On the evil day her mount stumbled as she raced along the bank of a canal. The Empress was unable to leap clear. The horse fell on her. The animal thrashed its way down the bank into the water, rider unconscious and still entangled in harness. Horse and rider drowned before they could be dragged out.

Patriarch Clemency III, the Collegium, and the Five Families of Brothe sent up praises to God. The Patriarch's forces had been defeated in detail everywhere that summer. The Emperor was marching on the Mother City itself when the news reached him.

Hildegrun was not in her tomb many months when Hansel wed Helspeth's mother, the Dowager Princess of Nietzchau. The Princess Terezia was his senior by ten years. The alliance further strengthened Johannes's position among the Electors. The Dowager Princess, at thirty-four, had been a woman possessed of considerable carnal appetites. Her new husband satisfied them sufficiently to subject her to two miscarriages, a son, Willem, born live but who died within two weeks, and, finally, Helspeth. Who never knew her mother.

The Dowager Princess died of childbed fever three days after Helspeth's birth. She was interred beside Willem in the family tomb of her first husband in Wortburg, in Nietzchau.

Before her death the Dowager Princess transferred all her family honors and obligations to the Emperor. Leaving him, in his twenty-seventh year, the third most powerful man in the Chaldarean world, exceeded only by the Brothen Patriarch and the overlord of the Eastern Empire. Among the tasks she left him was the humbling of the worldly power of Brothe. That he prosecuted with skill and success.

But never again did he come as close to breaking the temporal power of the Church as he had before Hildegrun's death. In part, that was due to despondency over his own losses, in part because he had to cope with pro-Brothen sentiment among his own nobility. He did not show much vigor in the field for nine years after Terezia's passing. By then bribery and treachery had undone half his earlier successes.

Then a stubborn new Patriarch, Sublime V, assumed the mantle of the Brothen Episcopal Church.

Eighteen months after the death of the Dowager Princess, Johannes wed Margaret of Eathered in an alliance arranged by Hildegrun's father. Margaret, the spinster daughter of Johannes's predecessor, was a devout woman he respected but never loved. She worshiped him. The marriage brought Johannes the territories endowed upon Katrin by her brother. It joined the Ege line with that of the family that had provided the majority of past Grail emperors.

Margaret of Eathered was never a well woman. Nor was the one son she bore her beloved Hansel. Nevertheless, Margaret survived longer than either of Johannes's previous wives. But when Lothar was seven a plague swept through the Empire. It carried off most of the elderly and sickly. The Crown Prince himself was preserved by being sent into ferociously enforced isolation at the first hint of the outbreak.

When Margaret died Johannes swore he would not marry again. He contented himself with courtly romances ever after.

Each of the Emperor's children favored their mothers in appearance and their father in intellect. Katrin might have been Hildegrun at twenty-three had she lived. Helspeth, everyone said, was the image of Terezia in her youth. Katrin had a bevy of uncles who doted on her and still bore their love and admiration for her father. Because of those five hardened warlords, and the families of Johannes's subsequent wives, the Council Advisory of the New Brothen Empire would not dare dispute Lothar's gifts to his sisters.

Lothar failed to win one point. Johannes's daughters would not be permitted to behave as though they were his sons. They had come into vast new estates. Now they would have to go to them and behave like other women of their stature and time.

Helspeth was not pleased. But she was dutiful.

Katrin, she could tell, was going to cause trouble.

THE GRAND DUKE'S FACTION HAD A POWERFUL BOLT IN ITS QUIVER. Marriage.

Lothar could not ignore marriage indefinitely. Neither his own, nor those of his sisters. It was his bounden duty to provide an heir, despite the past Imperial tradition of election. And his sisters . . .

Marriage would clip their claws. Though they would not lose their places in the succession till Lothar produced a son who survived, any husbands they took would have strong legal rights to control them.

Helspeth sneered. Law and character could come into conflict.

She knew of no man with a will more powerful than her own.

She had no desire to wed but if circumstances so compelled, she would make sure the gentleman involved regretted his ambitions.

Anyone who wed Katrin would be even unhappier.

Still, the daughters of Johannes Blackboots were among the greatest prizes in the marriage market of the Chaldarean world. Because every month that Lothar Ege survived was another amazement to that world.

Lothar could not possibly live long enough to provide an heir.

After what he had done tonight, Helspeth wondered if Mushin was not at risk. The Grand Duke sometimes acted before he thought things through. Action against Lothar would not be bright. Katrin had less love for Hilandle than did Lothar. And she had attained her majority.

She should be a terror to the Grand Duke's faction.

Unless she failed to win the allegiance of Ferris Renfrow.

Katrin did not like Renfrow. Helspeth did not know what Renfrow's feelings might be. Ferris Renfrow never revealed himself.

Sometimes Helspeth thought Renfrow was like the Night: a fact of existence. A force of nature. Part of the weather. Always to be reckoned in any strategy.

Ferris Renfrow might be the most important man in the Grail Empire.

And no one knew where he was.

Helspeth Ege stared at the back of the Grand Duke's head, willing him to fall down dead.

As so often happened, the object of her anger failed to respond to her will.

The universe was stubborn that way.

The Emperor dismissed his sisters with the direction that they claim their new possessions immediately. He assigned a small company of Braunsknechts, the Imperial lifeguards, to each. Helspeth thanked God for small favors.

Her captain would be Algres Drear, long close to her father and well known to her. Johannes had entrusted Drear not only with his life but with special missions outside the competence of Ferris Renfrow. Drear was intimately familiar with Plemenza.

Even so, Helspeth wished she could sit down with Renfrow. Renfrow would restore her courage and confidence.

Helsepth tried to talk to Katrin as they returned to their quarters. Katrin refused to speak. Katrin had changed. Katrin was no longer her friend.

Katrin was afraid.

Katrin was a heartbeat away from the throne of the Grail Empire. Katrin was caught in the eye of a growing cyclone of intrigue. Everyone wanted to manipulate or control her. She trusted no one. Not even the little sister who might someday want to replace her.

Where, oh where, was Ferris Renfrow when Johannes Blackboots's girls were in desperate need?

4. Winds of Despair

Brother Candle followed Count Raymone Garete from Caron ande Lette down to Antieux. The Count gave him no choice. He was suspicious of the Perfect Master. He was suspicious of Maysaleans in general, though he had Seekers After Light in his own family. The Count was not a warrior of faith, he was a devout Connecten nationalist who refused to permit outsider mischief in his motherland.

Count Raymone's determination animated Antieux as well. Despite disasters wrought by a succession of corrupt Brothen Episcopal bishops and two invading armies, the city was busy, defiant, and increasingly prosperous. Much of the destruction wrought by the more successful siege had been undone. The cathedral remained as the invaders had left it, ruined by fire, with a thousand dead women, children, old people, and innocents entombed inside. Count Raymone had decreed that the cathedral would become a monument, "Sanctified to the Usurper Patriarch by the blood of those he claimed are his flock."

That massacre would undermine the Church in the Connec for centuries to come.

No one who had not been there ever fully understood how deeply the massacre scarred the survivors.

It was burned black on their emotional bones. And on Count Raymone more than most because he had been unable to prevent it.

He had powerful support throughout the End of Connec.

Duke Tormond failed to understand how much the hearts of the people of Antieux had been darkened.

Brother Candle said, "I've known Tormond since we were boys. He's not a bad man. He means well. He's just disconnected from everyday reality. Despite his daily opportunities and a suite of advisers." Brother Candle became one of those whenever he visited Khaurene.

Count Raymone snapped, "He's a fool. As well meaning as Aaron of Chaldar himself, possibly, but a blind fool."

The discussion of the Duke's capacities had been occasioned by a letter ordering Count Raymone to appear before the Duke to explain his bad behavior. There had been complaints from Sublime V and Bishop Morcant Farfog of Strang.

Brother Candle did not argue. "Sometimes Tormond does act like a man with a sorcerous caul across his eyes."

"I believe it. I'm not going. He wants me, he can send Dunn to arrest me." Sir Eardale Dunn was Duke Tormond's military chieftain, a refugee from Santerin who had not returned when the latest shift in succession fortunes there had made that possible. "I'm sitting right here."

"You sure you want to do that?" Brother Candle meant defying the Duke.

Count Raymone answered a different question. "You're right. I need to get back into the field. My spy in Salpeno says Anne of Menand has started trying to raise another invasion force. She hasn't gotten much support. Yet. Because of the confusion in Salpeno, Santerin is pressing its claims all along the marches. Too many nobles are protecting their own towns and castles to come steal ours."

Brother Candle nodded. He had visited Arnhand last spring. And remained healthy only because local Seekers warned him whenever the Church sent men to arrest him. "True. And they still send their third and fourth sons, and too much treasure, to the Crusader states in the Holy Lands."

Past crusaders had carved a half-dozen small kingdoms and principalities out of the Holy Lands. Those always needed more men and money to keep going. They were not natural entities and were under continuous pressure from the neighboring Praman kaifates.

In Arnhand the crusades were considered a religious obligation. Knights and nobles from elsewhere did try to make an armed pilgrimage once during life, but Arnhanders often went with no intention of returning.

"You need to think in longer terms, young man." Brother Candle was old and respected. He would be given the opportunity to speak. Getting Raymone to listen would be the real challenge. "You have to consider what consequences your choices might visit on you and Antieux both tomorrow and far into the future. Right now, just as a mental exercise, forecast for me some possible consequences of you refusing to see the Duke."

The question did slither into Count Raymone's mind. It began to turn over clods of wishful thinking.

Brother Candle said, "Suppose Anne of Menand assembles another gang of adventurers and, by some misfortune, she recruits a competent captain. Perhaps someone honed on the harsh battlefields of the Holy Lands. Say Antieux is besieged and that Captain is smart enough to expect competent resistance."

"Enough! I get your point, old man. If I refuse the Duke, he could refuse me later." That would not set a precedent. All feudal rights and obligations ran both directions. "Considering that's a situation where he might actually do something. I must be getting old." Count Raymone was on the cusp of thirty. "I have to admit you're probably right."

When Brother Candle departed, dismissed, Count Raymone sent for the Rault family. He had dragged them back to Antieux, too. Brother Candle suspected he had taken a fancy to Socia.

Brock Rault had been included in the Duke's summons.

"THIS IS WHERE I LEAVE YOU," BROTHER CANDLE TOLD HIS TRAVELING companions. Count Raymone scowled, ever suspicious. The Perfect feared the Count's dark outlook was ripening.

Brock Rault grinned. He was excited. This was his first visit to Khaurene. "See you at the castle, Brother." Then his face darkened, too. He liked to point out that Raymone Garete had reason to be suspicious. His city had been attacked. More than once. He had been attacked himself. The Brothen Church kept sending priests to foment trouble in his territories. Hanging them did not dissuade others from coming. And, more than once, he had caught someone close to him conspiring with Sublime's agents.

Brother Candle watched the column wend deeper into the city, destination Metrelieux, castle of the Dukes of Khaurene.

Brother Candle went to the home of Raulet Archimbault, a leader in Khaurene's Seeker community. His eyes watered. He was surrounded by tanneries. Archimbault was a leader in that community, too.

The tanner's daughter, Kedle, admitted him.

"You've certainly grown, child."

She reddened, lowered her gaze. He remembered her bolder, holding her own when Seekers After Light gathered.

"I didn't mean to upset you."

He did not understand that he was a demigod to Kedle. The Perfect were rare, even here in the heartland of the Maysalean Heresy. Brother Candle thought of himself only as a wandering teacher.

"We didn't know you were coming."

"I had no way to send word."

"You're always welcome, Master."

"Brother Candle. Just Brother Candle. Or Teacher, if you must. Ah. I sense a but. You're here instead of at the tanning shed. I expected your little brother. He can't possibly be working yet. Can he?"

"Yes, he can. I'm not working because we're getting ready for the wedding."

"Whose wedding?"

"Mine."

"But you're just . . . Well."

"Time does pass, Teacher."

The child always did have a philosophical bent.

"Evidently faster when you're not around to keep an eye on it."

"Well, come in, Master. We'll manage something."

The Maysalean Heresy retained a concept of communal responsibility that had been forgotten by the Brothen Episcopal Church. The same philosophy had animated the Founders but faded as the Brothen rite of the Chaldarean creed aged and became increasingly hierarchical, reflecting the culture around it. When the Old Empire collapsed the Church assumed most of the old Imperial palaces, dignities, and trappings. The Old Empire's ghost lived on—inside the Church bureaucracy.

KEDLE'S WEDDING TOOK PLACE ON TIME. ASKED TO SPEAK, BROTHER CANDLE did so briefly, his themes optimism, spiritual vigilance, and tolerance. Afterward, he arranged to spend his nights in rotation between several Seeker families. He did not want to add to the strain on the Archimbaults. The Maysaleans of Khaurene were eager for the status conferred by having him as a houseguest.

Days passed. He heard nothing from Metrelieux.

Evening meetings continued to be held at the Archimbault establishment. Only they had room to accommodate those who turned out to see the Perfect Master.

Ten minutes into the first gathering, Brother Candle knew that Khaurene's Maysalean community had changed.

People were afraid. They had no confidence in the future.

Maysaleans should not fear tomorrow. Tomorrow would come. There was no need to dread it, however harsh.

"What's happened?" Brother Candle asked. "Have you all lost faith?"

Kedle Archimbault stepped in when her elders failed to explain. "The trouble is the Duke, Master."

"Brother," he corrected automatically.

"The Duke is old. And tired. And weak. He's done nothing to keep the Connec from falling apart. His orders seldom make sense and usually make things worse. No one outside Khaurene pays much attention anymore. He won't enforce his will."

Similar complaints could be heard everywhere. The lesser nobility no longer feared their Duke, nor had much confidence in his protection.

Raulet Archimbault found his tongue. "That's the surface of it, Master. There's also the uncertainty caused by the Duke's bad health and lack of a designated successor."

That was a huge point. Brother Candle hoped Tormond's sister would succeed.

It did not matter what religion you were, nor what class. The passing of Tormond IV would have a profound impact. Because someone would replace him. And that someone's religious views would be crucial. The struggle for the souls of the Connec grew more heated daily.

"Gangs roam the streets," Amis Hainteau said. "Brothen Episcopals, whipped up by monks from the Society for the Suppression of Sacrilege and Heresy. The Duke does nothing. Chaldareans sworn to Viscesment outnumber the Brothen thugs but hardly ever fight back. The gangs mostly attack Seekers. And Deves and Dainshaus when they find them."

"They looted the Praman church last month," Kedle kicked in. "The only one in Khaurene. They tried to burn it, too. Twenty-two people were killed."

Her mother, with fat arms folded across her chest, said, "And the Duke did nothing. Again. He ignored it entirely."

Brother Candle was baffled. How could the situation have deteriorated so?

Archimbault said, "We're about two outrages short of civil war."

Someone mentioned priests being murdered. Somebody had begun picking off priests who favored Sublime or any of his works.

Someone observed, "War is unavoidable. The Brothens intend to force it."

That fit the common prejudice, Brother Candle was sure. "I should see Duke Tormond soon. I'll prick his conscience." He had little real hope of that, though. The man seemed blind to everything, trapped in a world spun from his own wishful thinking.

Agents of the Brothen Church causing chaos? Why? They were a minority in Khaurene. And across the End of Connec. The border counts whose faith more closely aligned them with Sublime than Immaculate had defected to Navaya, the Santerin dukedom of Tramaine, or Arnhand, already. Navaya's influence continued to wax along the Terliagan Littoral. King Peter did not permit disorder in his realm. Order was what people wanted most.

"We wish you all grace and good fortune, Master," Archimbault said. "But we'll continue to prepare for the worst."

Madam Archimbault said, "My cousin Lettie's son Milias is a varlet at Metrelieux. He sees the Duke all the time. He thinks Tormond is demented. The way really old people get."

Amis Hainteau said, "It isn't badly behaved Brothen Episcopals or the Duke's apathy that worries me. It's the Night I'm scared of."

Brother Candle asked, "There's more bad news?"

Raulet Archimbault nodded. "The Night has begun to stir. It started with mischief. That turned to malice. And now it's getting dangerous to go out after sunset."

"There have been murders." Kedle's manner made it sound like wholesale butchery started up with every sundown.

"Two," her father said. "Blamed on the Night because there wasn't any more obvious explanation."

"Only two," Kedle admitted. "But they were awful. The people were torn to pieces. And parts were missing."

Grim. But ordinary little men, tradesmen, artisans, shopkeepers, were capable of such evil. There were monsters behind a lot of smiling eyes. Quite possibly some of the agents of the Society for the Suppression of Sacrilege and Heresy.

Brother Candle promised, "I'll find out what's being done."

"Ain't nothing being done!" someone grumbled. An angry murmur followed.

"That may be," Brother Candle said. "But Tormond and I have known each other since childhood. Sometimes he listens to me when nobody else can get his attention."

Prayers for his success broke out immediately.

METRELIEUX, HOME OF THE DUKES OF KHAURENE, STOOD ON A BLUFF overlooking a bend in the Vierses River. Brother Candle had been in and out many times in his three score plus years. Each time he approached it he thought the place seemed that much nearer surrendering to the seduction of gravity. The old gates would not close anymore. And the same few guards were on duty, now, daily less capable of offering any real resistance to an incursion. No one was there to meet him. He made his way to the privy audience, where he found a dozen others also waiting.

Count Raymone asked, "You take a look at the outside of this place, Brother? The disease has gotten to the stone itself."

Time's bite was even more obvious here inside.

The Raults had not visited before. All they saw was old. Socia Rault was angry and exasperated. She had received strict instructions to hold her tongue, both from her brothers and Count Raymone. The Count had enjoyed Socia's company for several days now and had learned to dread the bite of her sarcasm.

She was too young to be concerned by considerations of consequence.

Count Raymone had developed an interest, in part, Brother Candle suspected, because Socia made it ever more clear that she could not be won through flattery and romantic ballads.

The Count was a fair lutist and managed a workmanlike baritone. For a poet and composer, though, he made an outstanding soldier and indifferent administrator.

Still, he tried, demonstrating the same ferocious determination he had shown in dealing both with Haiden Backe and those Arnhanders he had butchered during the Black Mountain Massacre.

Socia did appreciate his effort. She understood determination. She was determined herself.

Or just bone stubborn if you consulted her brothers.

Brother Candle socialized and observed for half an hour before Tormond's chief herald, Bicot Hodier, materialized, embarrassed. "My apologies, Master. I didn't think you'd arrive on time. Come with me, please."

Hodier led Brother Candle to a small, chilly sitting room with no proper furnishings and no refreshments. It was unpleasant and lonely, not unlike the anchorite's cell it resembled. Moisture collected on the cold walls, then dribbled down to puddle on the floor. The chill was too deep for mold or mildew.

He waited an hour, pacing more than sitting on the room's one damp stone bench. Shivering. His patience waned, a weakness he had not suffered since his ascension to Perfect status.

"Is it getting to you, too, Brother?"

He turned, confessing with a nod, though unsure what "it" might be. "Sir Eardale?" He pronounced it "Ey-air-da-lay," which was nearer the Santerin than most managed.

"Yes. And you want to know why me and why this."

Brother Candle exercised his nod again. Sir Eardale Dunn was not the man he expected to see. Dunn was Duke Tormond's top soldier and adviser. The Perfect Master wondered why he did not return to Santerin. He must like his life here, despite Duke Tormond's tendency to ignore his advice.

Sir Eardale said, "This room is proof against sorcery. The stone came from the Holy Lands, quarried near one of the wells of power. You waited so long because I wanted to make sure nobody noticed me."

"I see." Though he did not.

"No, you don't. Not yet. But I'll explain."

"Please do."

"Something bad is happening here. The Duke hasn't been himself. Not for a long time. Lately, though, he's been getting worse. It's like a wasting disease of the spirit."

"He isn't young anymore." Tormond was just weeks older than Brother Candle.

"He has those problems, of course. Complicated by his diet. All meat and wine. But this is something else. It exaggerates those tendencies that make him ineffective."

"Has anyone new moved into Metrelieux?" Having summed the evidence, Brother Candle suspected malign sorcery. But by whom?

"No one significant. There's always turnover in staff and pages. None of them suspicious. It's someone we know. Someone who's been here all along. Who found a new talent recently. Or a new calling."

"Uhm. And this secretive interview is because?"

"Because you have stature and respect and haven't been here to become part of any faction. You're neutral. You care about the Duke and you care about the End of Connec. You might see something the rest of us can't."

"I see." More, probably, than Sir Eardale thought.

The knight from Santerin would not be alone in reaching the conclusions he had presented. Everyone not guilty would be watching everyone else, hoping to finger a villain. The paranoia would be thick.

"I misspoke," Dunn said. "There is one new face. Father Rinpoché, representing our friends in Salpeno."

"That idiot? I thought he was dead."

"Unfortunately, no. Or, maybe, fortunately. He's too stupid and blindered to be a real danger."

"Why would they send him? Of all people?"

"He's a favorite of Anne of Menand. And Anne is in the ascendant, these days. She's real chummy with the Brothen Church lately, too."

"She always was." The mistress of Arnhand's King Charlve once raised her own band of crusaders to punish the Connec on the Church's behalf. The force fell apart before it did anything but that hadn't been Anne's fault.

"More so, now. I hear she bought the letters of marque that belonged to Haiden Backe. From Bishop Farfog, who managed to salvage them when he got away from Count Raymone. The Bishop, by the way, is now the Brothen Patriarch's chief agent in the Church's effort to tame the Connec."

Sublime seemed to dump all his dimmest and most corrupt agents on the Connec.

Dunn added, "I don't think Rinpoché is here as a true ambassador. He's really a spy, looking for weaknesses. Finding collaborators. And probably not doing well at that. He's too stupid."

Brother Candle was not so sure. Rinpoché might be a clever man posing as a fool.

The Perfect nodded as though everything in this world was perfectly clear. "Do you people have any idea what's really going on outside Metrelieux?"

Sir Eardale sighed. "No, Brother. Most of us don't. Most of us apparently don't want to know. Or don't care." He paused a moment. When Brother Candle said nothing he continued. "I myself am aware of the creeping chaos. Incompletely, no doubt."

"Creeping chaos is putting it too optimistically, sir. The Connec is dying. It's falling apart. So fast it makes the head spin. If you travel more than twenty miles from Khaurene, you stand an excellent chance of wandering into a local war or falling foul of brigands. Half the counts and knights out there, especially in the north and west, are feuding. Half of those can't explain why. It's just something they have to do. A matter of honor. If it weren't for Count Raymone and a few men like him, I'm afraid the collapse would be complete in another year."

"I hadn't thought it that bad. Not yet. I thought we still had some time."

"The time is all used up. The Duke has wasted it for far too long already."

"Tormond is obsessed with the state of his soul. When he's rational at all."

"While all the southwest and the Terliagan Littoral defects to Peter of Navaya."

"Not a stupid move for those people, eh?"

Brother Candle frowned.

"I'm being rational, not disloyal. I understand what's happening. I'm powerless to do much. I'm allowed to send letters to this noble or that ordering him to stop burning his neighbor's corn but they don't listen. I have no teeth. They know they can go right on murdering sheep. The only power capable of staying them will be the owner of the sheep. Or maybe the sheep themselves once they've had enough. I can't raise the levies. I can't send ducal troops out. And superior force is the only answer. Everyone else has to pile on whenever anybody acts up. So I can't blame people for switching fealty to Peter, or even Charlve, if that's what they have to do to secure themselves against anarchy."

Brother Candle said, "Of course. On that one level. Strictly speaking."

"I am worried, though, by all the mercenaries coming into . . ." Dunn shut up, cocked his head, laid a forefinger across his lips. He eased toward the doorway, making a series of signs Brother Candle took to mean that Dunn thought someone was eavesdropping.

Dunn made a production of drawing the short sword that symbolized both his station and the level of trust the Duke invested in him. The sound echoed in the barren room.

Footsteps hastened away.

Dunn said, "I've stayed too long. Can you find your way back to the privy audience? Bicot Hodier will find you there. He'll show you your quarters."

"Quarters? I'm staying down in the town."

"No. The Duke wants you here. But he can't see you today. Probably tomorrow." Dunn leaned out the doorway. Seeing no one, he departed. Swiftly.

BROTHER CANDLE'S PARTY COOLED THEIR HEELS SEVERAL MORE DAYS. THE Perfect had not spent that much time there ever before.

Metrelieux was typical of its time and kind. Large, badly furnished, and cold. Cold even for the time of year. For the climate.

Last winter there had been snow for the first time in modern memory. Snow that accumulated and stayed, not just the occasional scatter of random flakes that vanished in the morning sun.

Spring had been late arriving.

THE SUMMONS TO THE PRESENCE CAME AT LAST.

Tormond IV, Grand Duke of Khaurene, Duke of Sheavenalle, Count of Flor and Welb, and so forth, looked like he had enjoyed a sleepless night and had not yet pulled himself together. He had aged severely. He had lost a lot of hair, in no regular fashion. His beard had gone white and was patchy, too. His gray eyes, once steel and as penetrating as death, were dull and hollow. He seemed confused about where or when he was and what he was doing.

Nevertheless, he recognized Brother Candle. "Charde! Charde ande Clairs. Welcome. At last, a friendly face among all these shrieking blue jays."

"It's Brother Candle now, Your Lordship. But a pleasure to see you again, too."

The Duke slid his right arm across Brother Candle's shoulder, letting the Perfect take some of his weight without being obvious. Tormond was tall and lean. What little hair he retained was white and wild. His clothing showed no care, either. He had not changed in days. Residue from several meals decorated his shirtfront.

Tormond murmured, "Help me, Charde. I can't tolerate this much longer."

"Your Lordship?"

"I think I'm going mad. It's like there's more than one man inside me. And none of them are any good at being the Duke."

"You're too critical. You've done some wonderful things."

"Wonderful things," Duke Tormond said, and sighed. "Wonderful things, Charde. Did you know they call me the Great Vacillator?"

The entire Connec knew. Little children knew, though no one would call him that to his face. At his best Tormond IV was so deliberate that crises usually resolved themselves before he responded. "I've heard that. Don't let it bother you." Brother Candle looked around to see if anyone was particularly interested in their conversation.

Everyone fell into that category.

The Duke made a feeble gesture. Pages began seating people. Tormond asked Brother Candle to sit beside him, in the seat his sister Isabeth occupied when she visited Khaurene. She, much younger than

Tormond, was in confinement in far Oranja, about to present King Peter with an heir. If she had not done so already.

News moved slowly. Unless it was bad. Ill tidings had wings.

Servants brought coffee, a rare treat. No one refused. Brother Candle smiled into his cup as Socia and Thurm Rault enjoyed their first encounter with the dark beverage.

After coffee the Duke seemed collected and animated. "Thank you all for coming. Count Raymone. Seuir Brock. Brother Candle. My apologies for keeping you waiting so long. I didn't know you'd arrived."

Really? Odd indeed.

The group was the same council Tormond always assembled. Sir Eardale seemed as tired as his Duke. Michael Carhart was a renowned Devedian religious scholar. Bishop Clayto was the senior Brothen Episcopal in Khaurene. Brother Candle's friend Bishop LeCroes's allegiance went to Viscesment. LeCroes liked Sublime better than Clayto did. Bishop Clayto viewed the Brothen Patriarch with open contempt.

Tember Sirht had replaced his father, Tember Remak, as spokesman for the Dainshaukin. Hanak el-Mira represented the Connec's small surviving Praman population, on the Terliagan Littoral. Brother Candle recalled el-Mira from the Calziran Crusade. Terliagan slingers had been an important part of the Connecten contingent. El-Mira was younger than Brock Rault but belonged to a proud old family. Only in recent years had his people become active participants in the broader Connecten civilization.

Since Isabeth's marriage to Peter of Navaya, in fact. Though committed to a relentless reconquest of Praman Direcia, Peter won numerous friends and allies among the Pramans. He did not destroy their religious places nor force his own beliefs on them, being content to let time and the superiority of the Chaldarean vision hasten the false religion into yesterday's dust. Peter's most devoted allies were the Pramans of Platadura, a city-state of traders. Platadura's fleets engaged in continuous, bitter, and often deadly competition with those of the Firaldian mercantile republics, Aparion, Dateon, and Sonsa.

An unknown Praman accompanied Hanak el-Mira. Brother Candle thought his dress looked Plataduran. No one introduced him. Duke Tormond was in what was, for him, a hasty mood.

The Arnhander, Father Rinpoché, was there, too, in the background, alone, shunned. He seemed frightened, unhappy, lonely, and out of his depth. Brother Candle judged him a lute with just one string. More would be too much for his circumscribed intellect.

Brother Candle concentrated on Tormond. The Duke was involved in a visible struggle to retain control of himself.

More than one man inside, he had said.

Was it possible that Tormond's problems might not be of his own making? The hair loss, the distraction, the odd cast of his skin, suggested poison. Or truly wicked sorcery.

But, who? Someone right here, right now, if Sir Eardale was right. Someone who saw the Duke as an obstacle, not an enemy. Duke Tormond had no enemies. By doing nothing he offended no one. Not to the point where they sneaked around dripping dark ichors into his wine or gruel.

Anne of Menand could contort her conscience enough to order a murder. But someone would have to do the dirty work.

Brother Candle studied Bishop Clayto. Not long ago he had been Father Clayto, assigned to the worst parish in Khaurene because he would not keep quiet about Sublime's bad behavior. Now, he was a bishop, in good odor with Brothe. At a time when the Brothen Episcopal sees of the Connec received nothing but scoundrels.

Clayto met his speculating eye, raised an eyebrow.

Maybe not. They had been chaplains together during the Calziran Crusade. Father Clayto had trouble clinging to his faith but Brother Candle never saw any indication that he had the moral agility to justify great wickedness.

And yet, he had been made bishop.

The Duke said, "Let's get started." He gestured at Brother Candle, then Count Raymone, and such Connecten nobility as lurked round the fringes, hoping to vent complaints. Counting pages and serving folk, more than fifty people stopped doing anything but breathe.

Brother Candle continued to survey the gathering. The fate of the Connec would be decided by people in this crowd. They would keep it alive. Or let it die. It was time for the Great Vacillator, despite all, to do what he had been born to do.

Brother Candle chuckled suddenly.

Tormond had managed to create this situation in spite of conspiracies simmering around him. Possibly even despite malevolent espionage by the Instrumentalities of the Night.

The Duke said, "Seuir Brock Rault. Tell us what happened at Caron ande Lette."

The youngster looked to Count Raymone, to his siblings, to Brother Candle, for reassurance, then grasped his nerve by the throat and told it.

"Well done," Brother Candle whispered when Rault finished. "Exactly as it happened."

Duke Tormond nodded, still focused, the businesslike personality firmly in charge. "Count Raymone?"

The Count told his tale, somewhat less humble in admiring his own role, but without fabricating.

"Sir Eardale?" the Duke said. "A comment?" Tormond having some trouble, now.

"What I find interesting is that before the villain's feet were dry we received news from Brothe that Morcant Farfog has been appointed Chief Inquestor of the Patriarchal Office for the Suppression of False Dogma and Heretical Doctrine. With a new order of monks being created to support the office."

Brother Candle was not surprised to hear it. "Farfog's first job will be to root out heresy and dogmatic diversion in the Connec."

Count Raymone could not restrain himself. "I recall this being tried before. Eight thousand people died. Because of the meddling of one man who didn't have the right."

Bishop Clayto said, "Complain to Immaculate. He'll cover you."

Count Raymone glared. "The men responsible . . ." He controlled his emotions. Brother Candle nodded approval. Raymone Garete was maturing.

Sir Eardale continued. "Our options aren't broad. Our mission to the Mother City, a while back, in effect recognized the Brothen Patriarch as legitimate."

Bishop LeCroes opined, "Treat that with a respect equaling what Sublime has shown our contribution to his war on Calzir."

"Grumbling won't change the man. And he now has a Captain-General who's building a real Patriarchal army. The man seems to be competent."

"And he pays for men and arms with what?"

Sir Eardale said, "Just a minute. Perit. Bring our other guests."

One of the pages departed. Murmurs started but did not last. The page returned quickly.

Dunn said, "I'll let these gentlemen answer that." He indicated two men who entered behind the page, Perit. "Tell these people what you told me earlier."

"Yes, sir," the elder newcomer said, amused. Brother Candle thought the pair looked a little frail for the hardships of travel. Though they could have come to Khaurene by boat, up the Vierses from Tramaine.

Sir Eardale said, "Gade and Aude Learner. On behalf of King Brill of Santerin." Dunn's tone was neutral. Brill's father had been the winner in the succession war that caused his exile. "They aren't official ambassadors, just men with a message."

One Learner took a seat. The other leaned on the back of a tall chair that had seen generations of service. "Our holdings are in Argony, near the Pail of Arnhand. We have cousins over there. They keep us posted. What's been happening since the Black Mountain Massacre is scary."

Learner had his audience's full attention. "Anne has widened her web, nursing the anger of those who lost men. The fact that they asked for it doesn't matter."

Brother Candle stepped in. "Why has King Brill sent you?" And felt dim immediately. Any problem Arnhand suffered benefited Santerin.

"We have our own troubles with Arnhand. The more troubles they have, the better. Especially now, when the Crown is ineffectual and the strongest voice in the kingdom belongs to a whore."

That was extreme. Anne was of high birth. She just had a huge appetite for pleasures of the flesh. And for power. She wanted her son Regard, by King Charlve, to succeed him despite the boy's illegitimacy.

"And Anne's problem lies at the heart of what you're here to tell us?"

Both outlanders started.

"When you're my age you'll read minds, too."

The talking Learner grinned. He had a decade on Brother Candle. "Yes. Anne has pulled most of the key folk of Salpeno into her camp by telling them she's building a war chest to raise armies to punish the Connec. She's making all manner of secret deals. Now she thinks she's invulnerable. She's raised enough."

He had his audience enrapt. Even the serving staff.

Nothing said here would stay secret longer than it took these people to get home to their families. Even the churchmen would gossip.

"Enough?" Sir Eardale demanded. "Get to it, man. Never mind the drama."

"Enough money to buy the Patriarch, sir. Not to raise the army that she's been promising."

That caused a stir, of course, but more of confusion than consternation.

"Please expand," Sir Eardale ordered. "Again, dispensing with the drama." A whip crack edged his voice, the soldier in the old knight blazing through.

"Yes, sir. Sublime has huge money troubles. Anne has problems getting her claws on Arnhand's throne. Should Charlve die." Anne had two sons by Charlve the Dim, Regard and Anselin. Only Regard interested her. "She's also raising money by selling royal treasures. Altogether it's enough to see that Sublime will discover Charlve's marriage to Queen Alisor not to be valid because he's actually been married to Anne for two decades. Making Regard and Anselin legitimate and placing them at the head of the succession. With enough money extra to put together a small army."

Terrible news, Brother Candle thought. Unless Anne's obsessions had led her to pick Arnhand's fiscal bones so clean that there was no way Arnhand could sustain more than a brief incursion into the Connec.

But now, perhaps, the Brothen Patriarchy could afford an invasion of its own.

Clever, clever Sublime, Brother Candle thought. Exploiting the Arnhander woman's avarice. Probably leaving her convinced that she had gotten the better of the deal.

Only the Brothen Patriarchy stood to profit from a crusade against the Maysalean Heresy.

Brother Candle shook his head sadly. He had prophesied disaster for years. Circumstance had beaten him down every time. But now everything was falling into place for the Adversary. At last.

"Is it true? The rumor about the Queen of Arnhand?" Kedle Archimbault asked. No. Kedle Richeut, now.

Brother Candle was staying with the Archimbault family, essentially in hiding from those who haunted Metrelieux. He used all the resources of the Maysalean community to collect information about everyone close to the Duke. Those who did the scut work in Metrelieux were especially useful. People full of themselves generally failed to notice the worker bees.

"What rumor is that?" Brother Candle asked.

"That she's bribed the Brothen apostate . . . I'm sorry."

"No need. If you've heard that, news got out faster than usual." Brother Candle stated the facts as he knew them, feeling no need to keep any secrets.

"I hope you don't mind," Raulet Archimbault said. "I've invited the members of our circle in tonight."

"Not at all. An evening of talk and debate with your circle is what I need. They're intelligent people, open to the old ways. The ways of Aaron and Eis and the others." And they might turn up a few useful facts.

"Good. Though we'll be serious and practical for a while."

"Raulet?"

"We have worldly matters to discuss. We're having trouble refurbishing the works on the Reindau Spine."

"That would be?"

"The height overlooking Lake Trauen. Almost vertical, with a knife edge top. The stoneworks up there date from the bad times after the fall of the Old Empire. We're refurbishing them and laying in stores. Because someday the Adversary will make himself known in the End of Connec."

"I don't know the place but I understand what you're doing."

"Students everywhere have been getting ready since the Black Mountain Massacre."

"When did Student come into use here?" Brother Candle asked. The usage was common in the dualist communities of the Grail Empire and the Lowland Duchies north of Arnhand, but not among the Connec's Maysaleans.

Raulet said, "I don't know. A year ago I wouldn't have understood that a believer who isn't yet Perfect could be considered a student. Now everybody knows."

"So. What's the trouble with your illegal fortification?"

"The cold. And ice. Everything is covered with ice up there. It's almost impossible to get there without falling and breaking something."

"Then don't go."

Raulet would have no congress with common sense. He shook his head, sorrowing at the Perfect Master's uninformed attitude.

"Ice?"

"The rain all turns to ice up there. When it does melt it drains down into places where it'll freeze and be more treacherous. Even the cisterns freeze over."

"They say the whole world is getting colder."

"Yeah. I don't remember it being nearly so cold when I was a kid."

"I don't know what to tell you. Except don't attract the Duke's attention. He has strong opinions about people who build their own forts."

Raulet sneered. "He may have strong opinions but it'd be ten years before he actually got around to actually doing anything. By then he'll be back for another go round the Wheel of Life."

THE LEARNERS' NEWS SWEPT ACROSS THE END OF CONNEC AS SWIFTLY AS ever bad news does.

The Counts of Robuchon and Doy repudiated their oaths to the Dukes of Khaurene. They shifted their allegiances to Tramaine and Arnhand, respectively. Which allowed them to continue being enemies while aligning themselves with strong, decisive protectors. Jancar, Herve, Carbonel, and Terliaga formally took their allegiances southward, to Peter of Navaya, sheltering under the skirts of the day's strongest sovereign. A king not the least cowed by Sublime V.

Respect for Duke Tormond continued to wane. More local leaders hired more mercenaries, most of them Grolsachers. Which meant more refugees coming into the Connec in hopes of finding similar work. Neighbor fought neighbor. It became increasingly difficult to sustain the armed bands. Their to and fro destroyed resources. Travel grew ever more dangerous. Mercenaries who had not been paid indulged in fits of banditry. Then people who had lost everything fled to the wilds and became brigands themselves. In the very shadow and embrace of the Instrumentalities of the Night.

Those who could afford to recruited more mercenaries to guard what they had. While mercenaries who did not get paid not only robbed travelers, they turned on their employers and ate them alive.

THE CHIEF INQUESTOR OF THE PATRIARCHAL OFFICE FOR THE SUPPRESSION of Sacrilege and Heresy began to filter operatives of the Society for the Protection of the Faith into the eastern Connec. Many were retired members of the Brotherhood of War, come over from their island of Staklirhod. They were hard men accustomed to employing harsh methods.

Brother Galon Breul and a team twelve strong, confident of the righteousness of their cause, established themselves in Antieux while Count Raymone Garete continued to dally at court in Khaurene.

5. The Mother City: Sublime's Revenge

Hecht left the children with Anna Mozilla. Vali had not spoken yet. To an adult. She had Pella wrapped around her finger.

Anna was not pleased. "I don't know anything about children. Except that they're loud and dirty." She kept house obsessively.

"They're people. Just not as polished as you. Treat them like people. Pella's been through the survival wars. He's probably more grown up than you."

Not the best thing to say. But Anna had a knack for getting what he intended to say. Which saved a few blowups.

"What do I do with them?"

"Clean them up. Get some decent clothes on them. Put them to work around here. Pella will go stay with Pinkus as soon as he gets it worked out with Principaté Doneto."

Anna's look made it plain she considered Ghort a long shot. "When will you tell me the whole story?"

"Soon as I get back. I hope. I missed you."

"You missed me? You have things to occupy you?" As near as ever she came to lamenting her lot.

"It was a long, mostly unpleasant journey." He would not share the more gruesome details. Like most warriors, he spared the innocent the worst.

PRINCIPATÉ DONETO SAID, "AS USUAL, YOU TWO HAVE MANAGED TO AVOID getting fired. By the expedient of having produced useful results. My cousin was thrilled to hear that Immaculate is desperate enough to try assassins."

Ghort asked, "How thrilled was he to hear about what happened to Haiden Backe?"

"Not at all. As you must know. He's summoned Bishop Morcant. We'll have to suffer Morcant's version of events before we're allowed to reach conclusions."

Meaning, Hecht supposed, that the conclusions had been concluded already and history would be hammered and polished till it fit. Because Sublime would want the official version to be one that served his purposes.

It was not a situation Hecht liked. Nor did Ghort. But their scruples would not be consulted.

Ghort had a miserable habit of spouting what he thought. "Easy to see where this is headed. That godsdamned thief will tell the world his victim is the villain because he had the effrontery to defend himself." He did not make clear whether he meant the Bishop of Strang or the Patriarch.

Doneto assumed the latter. "You may express that opinion with me, Colonel Ghort, but don't let me hear you say anything where people outside the family might hear."

"Heh? Why the hell? Is there anybody out there who doesn't know what kind of a dick he is?" So he did mean the Patriarch.

Anna Mozilla was psychic. Principaté Bronte Doneto did not opt to find room for Pella in his household.

"WHY DID YOU SEE DONETO BEFORE YOU CAME TO FAMILY?" PRINCIPATÉ Delari asked Hecht. He asked similarly uncomfortable questions often. "I was disappointed, Piper."

"I went there first because Doneto is the man who can deflect the Holy Father's displeasure from Ghort and me. He won't gain any advantage from what I reported. Nor did Pinkus give him everything that he could have."

"I'm pleased to hear that."

"He could get me fired if he wanted. Who'd stand up for me? If he wanted Pinkus's job, though, three of the Five Families would get in the way as a matter of political principle."

"So. What will you share with me that you didn't let Doneto have?"

Hecht glanced around. "Where's Armand? I don't like telling you things in front of him. He makes me uncomfortable."

That irked the old man. "He's a boy, Piper. He cares about nothing but clothing and baubles."

"Even so, despite all, he makes me uncomfortable. I don't apologize for that." He would not tell the old man that his toy was an agent for both the Grail Emperor and Gordimer the Lion.

Delari did something that seemed trivial, said, "Go ahead. No one will hear what you say but me. If you like, I can add a veil to make it impossible for someone to read your lips."

"That won't be necessary." Hecht told his guardian angel the whole story. Including his suspicions about Sonsa.

The old man said, "That bothers me. The Brotherhood giving up their inflexible rectitude. That's the problem with the Special Office. They want to conquer the darkness by drowning it with darkness."

Hecht did not raise the question of the elderly Principaté's own devotion to powers drawn from the Night.

Delari went on. "I'm equally troubled by the monster on the West Road. Might it be a bogon? Possibly the one you ran into crossing the Ownvidian Knot?"

"I never was close enough to get a feel for it. Principaté Doneto would be the man to ask. He handled the thing in the Knot."

Principaté Delari shrugged. "I doubt he'd cooperate. His cousin won't let him."

When Hecht did not comment, Delari added, "Sublime really believes most people are cattle put on earth to enrich the Church. And the rest of us are here to help make Honario Benedocto's dreams and schemes come to pass."

Then he said, "He's decided not to punish Duke fon Dreasser. Not right now. You haring off gave time for cooler heads to prevail. So to speak."

"Oh?"

"There was time for word of what happened in the Connec to get here. The Collegium was outraged. Sublime did that without consulting anyone. He fell into a deep despair. He was counting on Backe and the Bishop of Strang to generate a flood of money. Instead, he's worse off than ever. His debtors are clamoring to be paid. No one will loan him another copper. Not just because of his poor prospects but because of the bad judgment he's shown in his efforts to acquire funds."

"They'd have given him an old-fashioned triumph if his scheme had worked," Hecht opined. His regard for those who facilitated the Patriarch's lunacies was low. There was no morality among them at all.

"Probably. Success erases all moral failure and defects. However . . . We can expect a period of uproar and outrage when the news gets around. Maybe a riot or two. Then life will go on as it always does. You may have noticed that assumption of the Patriarchal throne endows its occupant with considerable insulation."

"I have noticed." Hecht chuckled. "The way donning the Imperial vestments insulated the old emperors from everyone but their own families and palace guards."

Delari raised an eyebrow.

"No. I'm not floating a suggestion."

"Good. I'm much more interested in that powerful Instrumentality near Alicea. And in what may be afoot in Sonsa. The Sonsans have done well, concealing their troubles from the rest of us. Give them credit for clever."

Hecht did. The raging capitalists of the Firaldian and Direcian mercantile republics ran rings around more traditional states. They were possessed of an amazing energy.

How much more dangerous might they be were they not ones to waste resources fighting each other over markets and themselves for family supremacy inside the several republics?

Delari said, "An aside. Your man Consent's conversion. Is it heartfelt? Or a ploy?"

"I don't think it's a ploy the way we Chaldareans would see it. Deves don't suffer that much, here. Has he discovered the verities in the preachings of Aaron and the Founders? Maybe. But I think the passion driving him is his own need to escape the expectations of the Deve Elders. He just wants to be Titus Consent, one part in a machine, peerless at what he does, well rewarded for it—then able to go home to his family at night."

"You're friends?"

"No. But we're around each other a lot. We talk about life. I talk with everyone. Sometimes I learn something. From him. From you. Or even from Pinkus Ghort."

"I imagine Colonel Ghort is a fountain of low information and possibly a plebeian sort of wisdom."

"He's a good man to have at your back."

If Delari harbored reservations he did not relate them. "The girl's name. What was it?"

"Vali Dumaine."

"There's no important family in Firaldia with that name."

"There is one in Arnhand. Minor nobility. The current count is in bad odor with Anne of Menand. He wouldn't make the beast with two backs when she offered the opportunity."

"That wouldn't make sense. What would the Brotherhood hope to gain from a minor Arnhander?"

"Consider this, too. The girl doesn't talk but she understands Firaldian perfectly. Vulgar and High, both. At her age I doubt she would if she'd been kidnapped from north and west of Salpeno."

"I'll make inquiries. When you're Principaté Muniero Delari of the Collegium you can ask for any damned thing you want. You get it without much question."

"Naturally."

"Again, I'm especially intrigued by that monster up there. Except for the thing you ran into crossing the Ownvidian Knot, there hasn't been anything like that seen since the dawn of history. Not since Eru Itutmu came over from Dreanger with his elephants and armies and crew of tame monsters."

The Kaif of al-Minphet and those who recognized him as the Living Voice of the Founding Family discouraged interest in anything that happened before the Revelations and Conquest. Despite his decades in Dreanger Piper Hecht knew little about the priest-king general who tormented and terrified the young Old Brothen Empire for a generation. Pramans rejected the glories of their pagan ancestors.

"I won't speculate. That's your area of expertise."

"So it is. Once more about the villain from Viscesment, Rudenes Schneidel."

Hecht told it. "I think Schneidel is another enigma dragged up out of the shadows, like Starkden and Masant al-Seyhan when Calzir went crazy."

Delari nodded. "An interesting notion. Although I have heard of Schneidel. As a rumor out of the High Athaphile, and that only recently."

"I don't know that geography."

"The High Athaphile is the central mountain range on Artecipea, the big island in the Mother Sea between Firaldia and Direcia, southeast of the Connec. It's claimed by the Patriarchy, the Empire, and Peter of Navaya by his recognition of Calzir's claim, since much of Calzir passed to him by right of conquest. Peter and his Plataduran allies have made inroads. Neither we nor the Emperor can do anything but bark. We've got more immediate problems."

Hecht knew little about the islands of the western half of the Mother Sea. Vaguely, he recalled having seen Artecipea on a map. "Is that a Praman realm, then?"

"The Kaif of al-Halambra reckons it part of his kaifate. But in name only. He's occupied elsewhere, too. Sonsa and Platadura are the leading players there. No one else cares. There isn't much of value there."

"Except to sorcerers, apparently."

"True. It's a throwback land. The pagan presence is strong. It's been ages since anyone bothered to slaughter them so the survivors turn to the Church for salvation."

Piper Hecht enjoyed Principaté Delari's cynical attitude. But he made a face. His own purported homeland had a long history of murdering the pagans of the Grand Marshes.

Delari ignored that. "We'll try to dig out the connection between Rudenes Schneidel and the attacks on you."

"Colonel Ghort plans to send a man to Viscesment."

"Tell him to be careful. Pagan sorcerers have cruel habits."

"I know the man he'll send. He served with us in the Connec. He'll treasure caution like it's his secret name."

"Good. See Consent. Arrange his rebirthing ceremony. We're coming up on Heron's Day. That evening would be perfect for it." Heron had been a fanatic Dainshau religious monitor, fierce in his suppression of the Chaldarean sacrilege—and barely tolerant of the Devedian—before suffering a dramatic, overnight conversion. Heron credited the Apparition of the Well of Atonement for showing him the way.

The Apparitions of the Wells were critical, if minor, entities in the narrow Dainshau pantheon.

"That should do. I'll let him know."

Delari smiled a small smile that Hecht would not understand until later. He said, "That's enough of that. Come walk with me, Piper."

HECHT THOUGHT THEY WERE HEADED FOR THE BATHS. HE DID NOT MIND, after being on the road—though he resented spending the time. Chasing adventure just left him that much farther down the unconquerable mountain of his work as a military bureaucrat.

Delari forged on through the baths and regions beyond, which Hecht had not known existed. Delari took flights of stairs downward and down, into depths known only in rumor even inside the Palace.

Brothens were sure that the Chiaro Palace sat atop catacombs that descended a mile into the earth. They believed that all the major structures associated with the Patriarchy were connected by tunnels, including those on islands in the Teragi River, the Krois Palace and the Castella dollas Pontellas of the Brotherhood of War.

The Principatés Hecht dealt with regularly never confirmed nor denied the rumors. The Collegium savored the mystery surrounding them. Even the outright lies. They left rivals and enemies unsure.

Hecht asked no questions. If Delari meant to confuse him so he could not find his way again, he would fail. Sha-lug were trained to remember under much more distracted and stressful conditions.

"Just in through here."

Hecht took three steps, halted, astounded. He faced an empty space as vast as the basilica where the Patriarch celebrated holy days with the Collegium and bishops. The ceiling arched eighty feet above the floor. There were no pillars other than those supporting the balcony on which Hecht stood, twenty feet above the chamber floor. Wooden catwalks crisscrossed the chamber, at the level of the balcony. The vast chamber appeared to have been carved out of limestone bedrock.

The Collegium was supposed to be a conglomeration of powerful sorcerers. Piper Hecht had seen little evidence of that, though the old men of the Church had made a small effort during the Calziran pirate incursion a few years ago. Here, though, he saw proof enough for him.

The hall was round. It was three hundred feet across. It was lighted bright as day by some witch light that made his amulet turn icy cold.

There were a dozen monks and nuns on the floor. The monks belonged to one of the orders sworn to silence. Hecht knew little about nuns.

They moved along narrow aisles between long, wide tables. Delari explained, "This is a relief map of the known world sliced into strips so the geographers can make adjustments when new information comes in."

When Hecht moved thirty yards to his left the map came together. It had to be the most accurate map ever, at least within a thousand miles of Brothe. "This must have taken ages to put together."

"I was a boy the first time I saw it. That was sixty-four years ago. I was apprenticed to Cloven Februaran, about to move up to probationary journeyman." Cloven Februaran was a legendary Collegium sorcerer, renowned as a recluse. So reclusive did he become in later years that it was not commonly known when he died. If he did. He would be over a hundred twenty now.

"*The* Cloven Februaran?" Hecht murmured. Awed. "The Ninth Unknown?" Despite his withdrawn, secretive nature, Februaran was rumored to have stalked the worst of Brothe by night. Which might have been true. No one knew what the man looked like.

"He was called that sometimes. Because he was the ninth man chosen to manage this project. Each Unknown was handpicked by his predecessor. Each kept his role secret. Well, mostly. I haven't done that well. You could call me the Eleventh Unknown. I may be the last. I haven't found a worthy successor. Grade would have done. But neither Clemency nor Concordia were interested in adding another apolitical member to the Collegium. And Sublime is beyond hope."

Muniero Delari felt unappreciated amongst his own kind. He continued. "New Principatés include fewer and fewer scholars. They're either political animals or cretins who buy their robes. Or both. None of this will matter after I go, anyway. Probably. The end of the world won't dally once I do."

Hecht admitted, "I have no idea what you're talking about. Or what's going on down there."

"It's a map of the world. Ever less exact as you stray farther from Brothe. Our priests, legates, and missionaries send news of changes in their areas. Those people down there translate the reports into physical representations. So we track what's happening in the physical world."

"Which would be?"

"What everyone is talking about, now. What the First Unknown suspected when he started the project two hundred years ago. The world is turning colder. The wells of power are drying up. Even the Wells of Ihrian have slowed. Sea levels are falling. The ice is advancing. Both of those are happening fast.

"In my lifetime the Mother Sea has fallen nine feet. It's fallen thirteen since the project began. Beyond Hypraxium and the Antal Land Bridges the Negrine has fallen even more. The inland seas farther east are shrinking, too. While ice piles up in the mountains beyond." Delari pointed as he spoke.

"A thousand years ago the Old Brothen Empire had a hundred thousand slaves permanently raising and reinforcing the Escarp Gibr al-Tar because the storms on Ocean were throwing up waves that topped it sometimes and threatened a breakthrough. Imagine the disaster that would be."

The surface of the Mother Sea lay hundreds of feet below that of Ocean. If Ocean broke the Escarp thousands of cities and towns, with millions of people and countless acres of farmland, vineyards, and orchards, would be obliterated. And the water would, no doubt, then overtop the Antal Land Bridges and flood the Negrine basin, too. And the surface level of the Negrine lay a hundred feet below that of the Mother Sea.

It would be the end of civilization.

Delari shrugged. "They succeeded. So now, instead of drowning, civilization appears destined to freeze. Come."

The old man shuffled onto the nearest catwalk. From overhead the layout looked more like a map. Except that it was three-dimensional. Delari said, "The vertical dimension is exaggerated. Otherwise, the contrast wouldn't be obvious."

"This is all hugely impressive, sir, but I don't see the point."

"Planning was the point, originally. So our people could survive. If we had forward-looking leaders able to see the true long term."

The progression of change was not obvious to Hecht. The despair harrying the edges of the world required no trained eye, however. The entire north, down to the Shallow Sea, was buried under ice. The Shallow Sea itself showed only scattered pools of open water, suggesting leaks of power from the underwater wells common there and in the Andorayan Sea. The Ormo Strait, despite vicious tidal bores, had become an icy bridge. Elsewhere, wherever there were mountains, there were permanent accumulations of snow. Areas exposed by the dropping sea levels were a sickly gray in color. Some, along the northwest coast, were extensive.

Delari said, "Overall, they're way behind reports. This represents the situation at the end of last winter."

"Planning, you say?"

"The advancing ice is pushing whole peoples ahead of it. The ice might explain Tsistimed the Golden and the Hu'n-tai At. When their grasslands could no longer support their herds they had to move somewhere else."

"So you're trying to predict where problems will pop up in time to do something useful."

"Yes. Though there doesn't seem to be much point to the project, now. Sublime isn't interested in anything but his own delusions. He'll still be ranting about crusades when the ice comes over the city wall."

"It can't happen that fast, can it?"

"No. It won't get here for generations. Which is good, Sublime being mortal. My hopes aren't high, though. My predecessors couldn't interest the Patriarchs much, either."

"Some of that isn't natural. Are they markers of some kind?"

"Yes. Supernatural phenomena are part of the landscape. So are power leaks. And anything else somebody wanted to track."

Hecht looked south of the Mother Sea, at the Realm of Peace. The Praman Conquest. The Principaté's project had not gotten perfect reports out of the Praman world. But the details were better than anyone over there would like.

Changes were smaller there. So far. There were no fields of ice or snow. But the deserts were shrinking because of increased rainfalls.

"Enough for now," Delari said. "I just wanted you to know this resource is here."

Hecht knew he had missed something important to the old man. To do with the map? With the Night? Or had he hoped to find Hecht armed with some talent he was unaware of himself?

"We'll revisit later. You must be behind in your work."

The Principaté took a stairwell directly to his own apartment. And made the climb without killing himself.

Hecht headed for the Castella dollas Pontellas. Principaté Delari still looked mildly disappointed.

ANNA BROUGHT THE CHILDREN TO TITUS CONSENT'S CONVERSION CEREmony. Over Hecht's objections. Pella might behave like the street creature he was. Vali would irritate people by not responding when they told her how pretty she was.

His dread was misplaced. Anna had tamed the boy. She cleaned and polished and dressed Pella till he whimpered. She had him convinced that the end of the world would taste sweeter than what would come down if he embarrassed the Captain-General.

His final assignment was to stick with Vali and explain that she was mute. Vali was expected to bow and curtsy at appropriate moments.

"You stop fussing, Piper," Anna told Hecht in the coach. "They'll be fine. Worry about yourself. What do you have to do?"

Hecht had only a vague notion of his part in the ceremony.

"How come they's all them soldiers?" Pella wanted to know as they neared the Delari family's city residence. It was modest by the standards of the Principaté's class. Contingents from the Brotherhood of War, the City Regiment, and Hecht's own small in-town Patriarchal guards company filled the street. Most wore formal parade costume. But a few remained in mufti, there for trouble instead of show.

"In case the Deves try to keep Titus from converting."

"They won't commit murder over it," Anna said. "One more time. What do you do?"

Until only a short time ago Hecht had had no idea how a conversion ceremony went. It was similar to a child's confirmation.

He rehearsed it aloud as the coach came to a stop.

Anna said, "You've got it." She told the children, "He's never done this before."

Hecht grunted. "Where I come from they baptize babies when they're born because so many die. And conversions usually happen at sword's point, blessed by the nearest sober priest."

Pella said, "I don't think I'd like Duarnenia, sir."

"Me neither. That's why I left. Watch that puddle. Those shoes cost a fortune."

"Piper!"

"I can't help it, honey. I grew up poor."

Anna's schooling proved adequate. Principaté Delari, as Consent's sponsor, required nothing of Hecht but a ritual attest to the excellent character of the candidate.

There was little pomp and circumstance. A few questions and responses, a "Who presents this man?" and the remarks about what a good fellow he was, followed by a ritual laying on of hands by the Bruglioni and Arniena Principatés, then Bronte Doneto, and Titus Consent became an Episcopal Chaldarean of considerable stature.

Consent seemed appropriately excited. Hecht did note that Noë and the children did not go through the ceremony. Though, as Consent's wife, Noë would be whatever Titus decided. The children were not old enough for baptism and confirmation, the way those were handled locally.

Hecht shook Consent's hand. "I admire your courage, Lieutenant." He presented the customary baptismal gift of a coin. For children that was usually a small silver piece. Hecht turned over a gold solidus, or five-ducat piece, which bore the bust and crest of a long-dead, obscure Patriarch named Boniface. The senior military men, including Colonel

Smolens, Clej Sedlakova, Hagan Brokke, and members of their staffs, were equally generous. Consent had to start a new life. His situation would be difficult. His skills were crucial.

Despite his background, Consent was well liked.

"Thank you, sir. Courage isn't as important as knowing what you want, though."

Principaté Delari was more generous than Piper Hecht. After amenities, the old man said, "If I can borrow you for a moment, Piper, I need a word in private."

"Or course, sir. If you'll excuse me, Lieutenant?"

This time the official rank and title sank in. Hecht watched Consent's face light up. He had been welcomed to the tribe he had chosen over his old.

"Sir?"

"When we're in private."

The Principaté led the way upstairs, away from the public rooms. Hecht had deemed those austere, even by his own standards. The private quarters were more so.

Here Principaté Muniero Delari had no congress with decadence or sinful luxury. Hecht considered a man who chose to live that way one worthy of respect. But only here. His Chiaro Palace apartment lacked no comfort desired by his boy.

Delari took Hecht into a room with four unpainted plaster walls, furnished with one rude table, three rude chairs, and two clay lamps burning cheap, unscented oil. Hecht's amulet tingled.

Delari sat, said, "I've examined the matter of Rudenes Schneidel. He is in Viscesment." Delari pulled a cord. A bell tinkled somewhere, muted.

"You have? So soon? How?"

"I'm a member of the Collegium, Piper. And not one of the hacks. There is some basis to the rumors about us. Which, I'm pleased to see, are the subject of public disparagement lately."

"Oh."

"Occasionally, I worry about your powers of observation, Piper. I fear that my son overestimated you."

"I worry about that, too. I never understood why he chose to mentor me. So, did you find out anything useful about Schneidel?"

"Very little. But enough to caution you against sending someone after him. Unless there's someone you want to dispose of without taking the blame."

A woman came in. Hecht had seen her downstairs, looking vaguely out of place. She was tall, faded blond, and worn down by life. She brought coffee and cups. Hecht pulled the aroma into his lungs. Coffee was his biggest vice. "Ah. The best Ambonypsgan beans." He sighed. "You're much too good to me, sir."

"Quite possibly true. Time will tell. This is my granddaughter. Brewing good coffee is one of her special talents."

Hecht exchanged nods with the woman as she presented a cup.

Delari continued. "The sorcerer has set up shop not far from the Palace of Kings. But there's no obvious connection with Immaculate. He may want it thought that there's a hidden connection. He seems to have much too exalted an estimate of himself. A fault he may be granted the opportunity to regret."

"Thank you," Hecht told the woman. The beverage was rare and rich. Frowning, he eyed her more closely. Had he seen her before? There was something remotely familiar there. Then he concentrated on Delari.

The Principaté said, "Rudenes Schneidel can't possibly have any feud with you personally. He may have wanted to eliminate the Captain-General. My own feeling is, the attack was meant to frame Immaculate." Delari frowned as he spoke, possibly questioning his own reasoning. At the same time, he again seemed disappointed in Piper Hecht.

"A stretch, sir. That would mean he knew how things would go before they happened."

"It is a stretch, isn't it?"

"Did you find out anything else?"

"No. Rudenes Schneidel is an accomplished sorcerer. He has no trouble covering himself."

The woman refilled Hecht's cup, then left. Hecht said, "She doesn't look much like her father."

"You knew him only as a dying cripple. And none of Grade's children took after him. She's the image of her mother."

"How many kids did he have?"

"Four. Two sons, two daughters. All on the wrong side of the blanket. While he was overseas. By a woman he freed from Praman captivity. She'd been captured by pirates as a child and purchased by a merchant in Aselin who treated her badly. Grade was in the field for the first time. The Brotherhood and the Gisela Frakier had taken Aselin by surprise. Grade saved the woman from the Frakier when he recognized her rusty Old Brothen. She came from a family of education and standing."

Though key words had been butchered in transition from Peqaad to Firaldian, Hecht understood the Principaté. Gisela was a transliteration of a tribal name. Frakier, roundabout, came from a phrase meaning "beloved traitor." In common usage in the Holy Lands, Frakier were Pramans who allied themselves with the crusaders.

"I apologize if I've made you uncomfortable, sir."

"You haven't. I'm at peace with all that. I'm guilty of the same indiscretion. I did do a better job of seeing my son to his maturity. I never had to leave him behind because of my martial obligations."

"You didn't want him to be a soldier."

"Nor a priest. But he was of age. He chose. When he created a family he did the best he could. But three of the four were lost."

Hecht could think of no appropriate response. That was the way of the world. As the world had been, always.

Harsh. Cruel. Unforgiving. Merciless. That was the world Piper Hecht knew. Happiness and pleasure were fleeting. Each moment had to be seized. The positive constants he had known were the brotherhood of the Sha-lug and the loyalties soldiers shared. Which, with limited success, he had been trying to recapture in exile.

"You seem troubled, Piper."

"My faith has been shaken lately, sir. I'm troubled in spirit."

"What more can you ask than what you have?"

"I don't know. That's part of the problem. A higher purpose? I owned one, once."

Principaté Delari looked disappointed yet again. "We'd better get back downstairs. Leave the cup. Heris will take care of it."

"WHO WAS THAT WOMAN YOU KEPT STARING AT?" ANNA DEMANDED AS they left Delari's house.

"Delari's granddaughter. Drocker was her father. He wanted me to see her for some reason. Maybe to show how he takes care of family. Drocker kind of adopted me. I kept thinking I'd seen her before. I was trying to remember where."

He was not concentrating, though. There was something not right. He beckoned a soldier from the City Regiment. "Where did the rest of the men go?" He saw none of his own guards, nor anyone from the Brotherhood of War.

"Sir. Armed men were spotted up that way. Where the coaches would pass. Maybe setting an ambush. So the Brothers and the Patriarchals decided to ambush them back."

A distant tumult began on cue, metal rattling on metal. Anna heard it, too. She dropped her nag immediately. "There may be problems bigger than my insecurities."

"Huh?" Piper Hecht was not a man who caught things unspoken by women. Till Anna he had spent very little time around them.

"Let's get the children home. By a different route."

This was something Hecht did understand. "No. We'll go the way we know what the situation is. Somebody may want people to go another direction."

"You're the expert." She began harrying the children into the coach.

The kids were excited. Hecht thought that Vali might break down and talk. But Pella would not shut up long enough for anyone else to get a word in edgewise.

Hecht had the coach stop at the scene of ambush. A young officer hurried over.

"We got them all, Captain-General."

"Indeed? Any prisoners, Mr. Studio?"

"Uh . . . No, sir. The Brotherhood guys killed everything that moved. They were seriously angry."

Hecht sighed. "Claim some of the bodies. Maybe somebody interesting will come looking for their dead." At a glance, in the poor light, he saw nothing unusual about the bodies. "We might yet come up with a clue about who to hunt." Damnit, prisoners should have been taken! "And see that any wounds get taken care of right away."

Hecht's amulet gave him a series of tweaks, none of any weight. Things of the Night were about, drawn by pain and fierce emotion. As he was about to climb back into his coach, he asked, "Was this a diversion or the main attraction?"

"The Brothers say this was it."

"Interesting. Drive on," he told the coachman, then considered his improvised family. Vali was pale as paper. She stared at him fixedly. Pella, suddenly, was as quiet as Vali. Anna had grabbed hold of his arm, so tight it hurt. "I had a good time. Really. Everyone treated me better than I expected."

She started shivering. The night was not that cool.

"Maybe because the only married man who brought his wife was Titus." Other than Consent's whelps, Vali and Pella had been the only children, too. They had milked all the spoiling possible from celebrants in their cups, Pella selling the tragedy of the poor little mute girl. "Why wouldn't they fawn over you? They're all goats. And you were the most beautiful woman there. I'd have been worried about leaving you alone with the Principaté. Poor little Armand."

"Piper!" But Anna liked it. She had seized the day, shipping a cargo of fine wine. "Where did you and the old man disappear to? Or is that too secret for girls?"

"We had coffee. Fresh roasted Ambonypsgan. Maybe he didn't want to share with the whole mob." Hecht shuddered suddenly.

"What?"

"Creepy feeling. Like something we might not want to meet just started following us around."

"The women in the square talk like that happens all the time. A lot of people won't go out after dark anymore."

Not an entirely remarkable state of affairs. Brothe was dangerous at the best of times. A glance outside revealed nothing unusual. The street was empty except for one man in tattered brown who staggered along without showing any interest in the coach.

Piper Hecht and Anna Mozilla moved in distinct circles when they were apart. His life was all studies of companies and regiments and how to feed, arm, pay, transport, and keep happy the troops who formed them. He had to outthink the ambitious warlords of the Grail Empire, his employer's lesser enemies, and Sublime himself. The latter was his biggest headache. He never saw the man. There was little reason to his decisions, which were subject to whimsical shifts. Too many, like letters of marque granted to Haiden Backe, originated deep inside a circle of cronies so intimate that even Sublime's cousin, Bronte Doneto, seldom knew what would happen next.

Hecht said, "I get the feeling that I keep disappointing Principaté Delari. But I can't figure out how."

"You'll have to tell me more than you have. Unless it involves your super-secret Collegium business."

He described recent visits with Muniero Delari. Anna asked questions. Good questions.

"Obviously, there's more than a big map down there. Just having it buried like that, all secret, means you have to think that it's a powerful magic artifact. Or will be when they finish it. It sounds like they're still building it."

"We're home. Let me look around first." He still had that sense of a presence close by. Though his amulet remained dormant. "You kids need to get right to bed." That would not be a hard sell. Vali was groggy, all reserves exhausted, and would have to be carried. Pella was dragging.

Hecht saw nothing unusual. He paid the coachman, adding a generous gratuity. The man fawned. Times were hard.

The coach team clip-clopped away, on damp cobblestones. A light sprinkle had begun. Hecht entered the house last, backing in, like a rearguard covering a desperate retreat. There was no light outside once the coach and its lamps turned a corner, the driver in a hurry to get away.

Hecht made sure of the locks and shutters while Anna put the children to bed. Vali had to be carried.

In bed, still nervously alert, Hecht remarked, "What you said about the Principaté's map. That's why I love you. I never thought of that." Could his blindness be the cause of Principaté Delari's disappointment?

"Talk to me about that ambush, Piper. Were they after you?"

"I don't think so."

"What did you and the old man talk about? When you were having coffee."

"Rudenes Schneidel."

"Does he think you know something you're not telling?" Plainly, she thought he was holding out on her.

"Honey, I never heard of Rudenes Schneidel till a couple weeks ago."

"So maybe he never heard of Piper Hecht, either. Or you might know each other by different names. There's a lot of that going around."

Worth reflection, Hecht thought.

He was about to say he knew no one from Artecipea, nor had he heard of the High Athaphile or Artecipea before hearing that Schneidel called them home. He stopped as his mouth opened. He had had a thought about Vali. Which should have occurred to him long ago. One that meant a visit with the newest Episcopal Chaldarean before Consent's information sources dried up.

Anna continued. "There's been some fibbing about where people really come from, too. But forget that. It's time to find out if I drank too much to enjoy anything else."

THE NIGHTMARE WAS SO REAL IT REMAINED CONVINCING AFTER HECHT awakened. Anna demanded, "What was it? You're shaking."

"Nightmare. Haven't had it for a long time."

"The one about your mother?"

Hecht frowned. He did not believe Anna was psychic. She made no such claims. But she surprised him sometimes.

"It started there. Same as always." The same as memories he had had when he had cried himself to sleep in the Vibrant Spring School, back when they took the new slave boy in. He doubted he would recognize his mother today, even as she had been then, if she walked up and boxed his ears.

"Must be awful, being little and having no family."

"You make your own family there. Or you don't survive. That's the whole point." The Sha-lug schools produced hard men who disdained anyone who was not Sha-lug.

Piper Hecht feared he had softened during his sojourn amongst the Infidel, but his core remained adamantine Sha-lug. The Sha-lug were still his brothers, his family.

"It started out?"

"Huh? Oh. Yeah. Then it turned dark. There was a monster I couldn't see but I knew what it was. If I could catch it I could kill it. But I couldn't catch it. It kept doing awful things to people I cared about. And getting closer and closer to ambushing me. Meaning I wasn't really the hunter."

"That's ugly, Piper, but it sounds like standard dream fare."

Hecht grunted. He agreed. But . . . "It had more than a dream flavor. Like my mind was trying to create images it could understand."

"Think you can lay down and go back to sleep?"

"Probably not. But I'll try."

Sleep came more swiftly than he expected, though that sense of the nearness of horror never went all the way away.

ANNA LET HIM SLEEP IN. SHE WAKENED HIM, THOUGH, WHEN NEIGHBORS came looking for someone who could act in an official capacity. "They don't know where else to turn," she told him as he pulled himself together.

Grumbling, he stumbled out into the cold to see the body some children had found. Pella and Vali ducked around Anna, tagged along, though not so close that Hecht would notice and send them home.

Hecht stiffened when he saw the corpse. Not because of the atrocities he had suffered but because he knew the man. Who had no business being anywhere within a thousand miles of the Mother City.

"You know him, Your Honor?"

"Sorry. No. It's the wounds."

One gawker said, "This ain't the first one that's been chewed up like that."

Another agreed. "And this one, he's got a foreign look to him."

Hecht nodded. The dead man looked like someone pretending to be Brothen without knowing the nuances.

Alive, he had been Hagid, son of Nassim Alizarin al-Jebal, a soldier in Else Tage's company. He had been placed there by his father, for seasoning in the field. Nassim Alizarin, called the Mountain, was a crony of Gordimer the Lion. A classmate from his old school. Nassim had sent Hagid out with the unstated understanding that the boy would come home if everyone else had to die to make it so.

Back in the house, with the kids still outside, Hecht told Anna, "He was a good kid. He tried hard. But he started fifteen years behind the rest of the company. I can't imagine him ever leaving al-Qarn once I got him home alive."

"You're sure it isn't somebody who looks like the boy?"

"I'm sure!" He was angry. "Here's another mystery I don't have time to solve. And I can't hand it off to anyone else."

"We'll see."

"Honey! Before you get any ideas, go look at what happened to . . ."

Pella burst in. "Anna, you shoulda seen! Part of his skin was gone and his stomach was cut open. They said they pulled out his heart and his liver."

Hecht's glower shut him off. "I want you to remember that there's someone out there who does that to people."

Pella was suitably cowed. For maybe thirty seconds.

"At least Vali has sense enough to be scared," Anna said as the children raced off to the kitchen. "I'd better keep an eye on them." But the children, excited, returned eating seed cakes and scattering crumbs. "They're hopeless!" Anna complained. "Freke will quit on me." Freke (pronounced Freck-ie) Blagowidow was Anna's part-time maid and housekeeper. A desperate refugee, she would not quit no matter what.

"I'll talk to Herrin and Vernal next time I visit the baths."

"Oh, no. This is my house. You won't bring any of your toys in here."

Hecht leapt into the squabble happily. It distracted Anna from thoughts of Hagid.

A CAPTAIN-GENERAL WAS SELDOM ALONE. ESPECIALLY SINCE THE ATTEMPTS on Hecht's life. He wanted to vanish into the confusion of the Mother City, to sneak off to the Dreangerean embassy or the hideout of a spy from the Kaifate of al-Minphet, but the opportunity never arose.

Principaté Delari asked, "Did you collect this body, too?"

"I did, sir. I thought you'd want to examine it."

"We're developing quite a collection. Though we've started releasing those from the other night. People are claiming them. We buried the ones that attacked you. Nobody wanted them."

Hecht was surprised. "People are claiming them?"

"They were all city residents. Disgruntled Brothens who wanted to bash whoever was in charge for being in charge when they're disgruntled. If you follow."

Hecht did not and said so.

"There's an upwelling of revolutionary sentiment out there. Which doesn't seem to have caught any official attention yet."

Hecht understood that. "The Deves haven't bothered to warn us?"

"Say, rather, that a man in my position can't logically trust the cooperation and faithful support of people who follow false gods."

Hecht considered reminding the Principaté that Aaron of Chaldar never declared his god a deity different from that of the Devedians. What Aaron and the Founders set forth bore only passing resemblance to its Episcopal descendant.

"Were there Deves among the dead?"

"No. Mostly unemployed Episcopals, according to relatives—who had fallen in with a crowd that blames Sublime for all the world's ills."

"Interesting. After centuries of being told that the Holy Father is infallible. Would the ambush be part of a broader conspiracy?"

"My sense is that it was, yes, but it was just slapped together, on the spur of the moment, by drunks in a winehouse egging each other on. They didn't mean it to go as far as it did. It wouldn't have if the Brotherhood hadn't been there."

"No half measures there. For them it's all black and white."

"A certain kind of man likes everything inscribed in absolutes. He gravitates to the Brotherhood naturally."

Pinkus Ghort had inherited the problem of the dead. He had arrested none of the claimants of the corpses. He hoped to find out who was connected to whom, and how.

"Maybe Pinkus organized it so he can keep his job. No, sir. I'm joking. It doesn't look like the Five Families see much point to maintaining the City Regiment."

"Oh. I have trouble recognizing it when you aren't being serious."

"You aren't unique, sir."

"Yes. So. Let's go examine your corpse."

HECHT STAYED OUT OF THE OLD MAN'S WAY. DELARI MUTTERED TO HIMSELF. Hecht worried that the body might betray its origins.

The Principaté observed, "A Calziran, presumably. A Praman, certainly. His one true God didn't protect him from this horror, though."

"Sir?"

"We have a problem, Piper. Of a sort I've only read about."

"Sir?"

"There's a necromancer among us. A sorcerer who kills people in order to effect his sorcery. And he's thrown it in our faces. He's daring us to come after him. Possibly to draw us out."

"Really?" Hecht did not want to believe it. Firaldia was civilized. That sort of thing had not happened since the black heart emperors of the Old Empire had indulged their egos. "If some human monster did this for sorcerous reasons, wouldn't that mean that there are Night things around strong enough to need rough handling?"

"It does. We should've anticipated this. It could become a real crisis."

"What can I do?"

They were headed for Principaté Delari's apartment now.

"Nothing. Pretend you haven't noticed. This animal won't watch his back if he thinks he hasn't gotten our attention."

"All right."

"You seem rattled."

"I am. This is outside my experience. Outside my imagination."

"Then loosen your mind up. Because horror and madness is coming."

"Sir?"

"I'm not supposed to know. Sublime's party lumps me with Hugo Mongoz. Failing to realize that Mongoz is more than he seems, too."

Hecht stirred impatiently. Which made Delari smile. "In that case, you get to enjoy a short lecture before I give you the bad news."

Piper set his expression in stone. The Principaté could ramble endlessly if so inclined.

"Don't throw yourself on your sword, Piper. I'll keep it short. Here in the Chiaro Palace we not only fall into pro- and anti-Benedocto parties—siding with the high bidder—we also form factions according to our talents for manipulating the Instrumentalities of the Night. And our inclinations to use those talents. So while Doneto and I are at odds over Sublime's idiot ambitions, we're in lockstep about harnessing the powers of the Collegium."

"I thought. You and Principaté Doneto don't squabble nearly as much as you should."

That thin old man smile again. "Good. You didn't ask for it. So you shall receive. Sublime wants to punish Duke Germa fon Dreasser and Clearenza after all. He's heard that Lothar is sick and not expected to recover. The Imperial Court is distracted by succession concerns."

Hecht kept his opinion behind his teeth. Even Principaté Delari operated under serious misapprehensions about the Imperial court. Other than Pinkus Ghort, nobody Hecht knew took Ferris Renfrow seriously. In Delari's case it was obvious why. Osa Stile would have put a swarm of bugs in the old man's ears. And would report everything Delari learned as soon as he learned it.

Ferris Renfrow would know about Sublime's shift in attitude toward Clearenza before official word came out here.

"Would it do me any good to protest the stupidity of it all?"

"If you argue with Sublime he just gets more stubborn."

"I know the type. My sister . . . Sir?"

"Piper? Oh. Nothing. Just surprised. You never talk about your family."

"I don't think about them much. And wouldn't mention them at all around anybody I didn't trust." He hoped he sounded suitably mysterious. He dared not stop not being who he really was.

They reached the Principaté's apartment. The old man halted a few steps inside. "You need to get to work. You'll get your orders in the morning. I'll start sniffing around for this necromancer."

Hecht glimpsed Osa Stile. The boy had a talent for lurking. If there were a curtain or tapestry nearby Osa Stile might be closer than you hoped.

Hecht said, "Don't count Lothar out. He's always sick. But he always comes through."

Delari frowned. He did not want to hear that any more than Sublime did. Probably not for the same reasons.

HECHT RAN INTO PINKUS GHORT BEFORE HE LEFT THE PALACE. GHORT said, "I see you've heard. My boss would be interested to know how."

"How come you know?" Not asking what Ghort meant.

"My boss is a crony of your boss. And I have friends who get on the eary with anything he says. He talks to himself, you know. When he thinks he's alone."

"As long as he doesn't answer."

"But he does. He really does. It's kind of spooky."

"Must be because of all that time he spent locked up with you and me in Plemenza."

Ghort chuckled.

"So what did you want?"

"To let you in on what was coming."

"Thank you, then. I appreciate the thought."

"And to ask about last night. Bad?"

"Worse than you think." Hecht explained about the dead man found near Anna's house.

"Crap. Sounds like big-time shit. Black fairy-tale stuff."

"Don't talk it up. We don't want this monster to find out that we've caught on."

"No problem, buddy. I'm staying far away from that shit. This other stuff with people who want to stir up shit, though. I'm all over that. If I don't see you before you go off to your war, good fucking luck."

"I'll need it." He was being paid well not to think but to execute the Patriarch's will, however ill-conceived. If the man distracted himself from his ambitions in the Holy Lands, then the diversionary insanities needed to be nurtured.

Hecht often wondered about Sublime's mental state. He did not know the man. Had been in his presence rarely. Might have exchanged words with him once, on demand. Did not think Sublime would recognize him without an introduction, though he was the Church's top soldier.

He did not expect a more intimate relationship to develop. Orders would be relayed by Bronte Doneto or another of Sublime's cronies, mostly relatives less public than Principaté Doneto.

TITUS CONSENT SEEMED GLUM. HECHT ASKED, "SECOND THOUGHTS?"

"Not exactly."

"Really? Then you know yourself better than I know me. Isn't every Devedian in Brothe trying to make you miserable?"

Consent donned a strange expression. "Sir, who is the last Deve you know of who converted?"

Hecht could not recall one. "A lot must have. Once upon a time there weren't any Pramans or Chaldareans."

"That's true. The Founders converted. *Some* of the Founders. Those who weren't Devedian to start. Those who started out Devedian never considered themselves anything else."

"Your point being?"

"That conversion may not be unknown, but it's rare. Brothen Deves can't remember the last time it happened here. So they're sure that it hasn't happened this time, either."

"I see. That'll be handy." He placed no faith in Consent's conversion himself. "That will make my life easier." Maybe.

From Piper's viewpoint, unfortunately, there was too good a chance that Consent knew all about his shortcomings as a Chaldarean.

"How so?"

"I feared your connections might suddenly dry up. Just when we need them most."

Consent nodded. "That probably wouldn't happen even if the Deves did believe I'd converted. It's a tit for tat game, information moving both ways. They really want to know what the Patriarch is thinking."

Hecht understood. Everyone wanted to know that.

"Why are they staying cooperative? The war is over." Deve espionage efforts during the Calziran Crusade had bought them immunity from the fury of the invaders there.

"Because they know there'll be more crusades. One after another while Sublime is Patriarch. Maybe longer if his peculiar brain disease transmits itself to his successors. There'll always be Deves who need shielding."

"I have two things for you. Clearenza is the most pressing. We're going to get orders to march. Maybe within a few hours."

"I've been on that since right after Duke Germa had his political stroke. You're in good shape. Move fast. The Emperor's people can't react right now. They're tied up with internal politics."

But Osa Stile was sitting in Principaté Delari's lap. "They'll know as soon as we pull our boots on."

Consent nodded. Brothe was awash in Imperial spies and sympathizers. "And the other thing?"

"Somewhere there's a man who really interests the Brotherhood of War. Probably the Special Office. I don't know who he is. His child has gone missing. The bad guys took her because they want to twist his arm until he helps them with some underhanded plot. I want to know who he is."

"And that's all you can give me?"

"That's all I've got. I was hiding in a shadow in Sonsa when I got it. Sonsa is where the plot is headquartered."

"We're out of Sonsa. You must know that. There's been enough crying about how unfair it is that Deves should stand up for themselves."

Hecht nodded but did not believe Consent. "At least one of the Three Families, the Durandanti, is involved. They had a relationship with the Brotherhood before. The plotters may be getting orders from the Castella dollas Pontellas. When Ghort and I went up they had us take a courier pouch."

"If it's underhanded and involves the Castella, then the Patriarch is probably involved, too."

"The notion has occurred to me."

Consent bowed slightly. "I'll do what I can, Captain-General."

CAPTAIN-GENERAL PIPER HECHT, WITH TWO HUNDRED MEN AND TWO small brass cannons, camped a half mile outside Clearenza's east gate. Two hundred men could not impose a siege. They did interfere with traffic to and from the city, known for its embroidered linens and its exquisitely colored glassware.

Duke Germa chose not to fight. His family were devout Episcopals. He did not want to provoke the Patriarch to the point where he issued Writs of Anathema and Excommunication. But fon Dreasser made no attempt to treat with Sublime's Captain-General. His disdain for the Patriarchals was palpable.

Piper Hecht sat under a canvas awning. It was a miserable winter day. Another in a parade of cold, gloomy, drizzly days. He and Redfearn Bechter shivered and stared at Clearenza. The city was a gigantic gray boar shape behind the misty rainfall.

Bechter said, "We could occupy the estate houses south of town."

"Make it happen. I miscalculated. I thought the hardship of living under canvas would make the men bond. It's been more miserable than I expected."

"I like an officer who's flexible," Bechter said. "It would've taken Drocker longer to see the light." He went on to opine, "Bonded men aren't much use if they're dying of pneumonia."

Hecht grunted. That was an iron truth of warfare. Likely, more lives would be lost to disease than to any enemy effort. Thus had it been during the Calziran Crusade. Most conflicts operated at a low level of violence. The last big western battle had taken place at Themes, eight years ago.

Though Sergeant Bechter was the Captain-General's aide, he had acquired his own assistant, Drago Prosek. The youngster hailed from

Creveldia, a province of the Eastern Empire that more closely resembled Firaldia in religion and culture. Prosek was an apprentice member of the Brotherhood of War. For generations most Brotherhood recruits had come from Episcopal Chaldarean enclaves inside the Eastern Empire.

Though never treated as badly as Devedians and Dainshaus, Episcopals were a persecuted minority.

Prosek appeared. "Permission to approach, Sergeant."

Bechter waved him closer. Drago leaned down, spoke swiftly and softly. Piper Hecht did not catch what he said. Prosek whispered for nearly a minute. Bechter nodded occasionally. Drago finished, stepped away. He did not volunteer to abandon the shelter of the awning.

Bechter said, "A courier just came from the Castella. He brought the usual sack—and some news. There's been rioting in Brothe. About food shortages and inadequate shelter. Somebody is provoking them. And the first chest of money from Arnhand has arrived."

Would that render the action against Clearenza obsolete? Sublime could buy back Duke Germa's love.

Drago Prosek brought the courier. He presented the document bag to the Captain-General. Verbally, he related more news. "Nobody knows how much Anne pledged but it looks like Sublime will retire all his debts. Even those left over from his election. With money enough extra to finance new mischief."

Not good, Hecht thought. Sublime could start lining up a whole new clutch of creditors. Getting ready to make more people die.

"Sergeant, I fear we'll be visiting the Connec again, before long."

"Sir, I wish I could say you're wrong. And I'm not looking forward to it. Our next visit isn't going to be nearly as sweet as the last one."

"It was sweet last time?"

"It should've been. And would've been. If the black side of the Night hadn't taken hold of Bishop Serifs."

"The man did do everything he could to make people hate him."

"The guys in there now are probably even worse."

"No doubt. Where's Sedlakova? I haven't seen him all morning. I need to know if we can make those hounds bark." He meant the cannons. Devedian artisans had cast and crafted them, based on a design he recalled from the east. The Sha-lug falcon was supposed to be a secret weapon. The Deves of Firaldia, though, had turned out to know more about firepowder weapons than ever he had, and understood them better.

Bechter said, "He's having trouble keeping his firepowder dry enough to go bang."

True. Sedlakova would handle that by baking the powder at a low heat, carefully keeping it away from any flame.

Hecht opened the courier packet. "Messenger. You see any of the rioting yourself?"

"No, sir. The Castella did go on alert. So did the Patriarchal Guard. But the City Regiment handled it."

"And they still won't keep Pinkus on," Hecht muttered. The Five Families wanted to shed the costs of the City Regiment, finding it not worth the price if they could not use it against one another. "Go ahead," he told the courier. "I'm listening." He read while the man talked.

Titus Consent was right about his former co-religionists. They remained cooperative.

Consent had joined the expedition. He was inside Clearenza now. No siege had been set. Hecht was mounting a demonstration meant to intimidate Duke Germa. If fon Dreasser remained stubborn, and his Imperial friends lent no more support than they had to this point, he would summon additional troops and lay a real siege.

The other side knew the plan as well as he did.

Word of Sublime's financial windfall would be spreading. The troops would be more cooperative.

Hecht's natural cynicism made him wonder if Sublime hadn't planted the story.

How could Sublime be thwarted if the Anne of Menand story was true?

How would that much specie be moved from Salpeno to Brothe? Any number of people might be tempted to interfere. Grolsach, in particular, would be dangerous. Those people were hungry enough to dare holding up the Church itself.

A roll of thunder off toward Clearenza got his attention. Sergeant Bechter, Drago Prosek, and the courier started, suddenly frightened.

They had not heard the hounds bark before.

Hecht said, "I hope that stone comes down somewhere that will impress the Duke." He had no real hope, though. The hounds threw a stone that weighed about ten pounds. That would not do the damage caused by traditional stone-casters. But the hounds were impressively loud and smoky and could hurl their missiles a lot farther.

"Unless we have a spot of luck they'll put holes in a few roofs and let in the drizzle," Bechter said.

"Tell you the truth, I'd as soon go home and get out of the weather."

"Sir, if I had a woman like yours I wouldn't ever have left."

"I'll mention your appreciation, Sergeant. I'm sure she'll agree."

Bechter reddened.

"And here's a note from the boss himself. Wants us to be quick and wrap this up on account of he's got other work for us. Are you sneering at our master, Sergeant?"

"Not me, sir. He's the Infallible Voice of God."

Drago Prosek was appalled. Hecht said, "Prosek, go check out the houses south of the city. Find us a place. Duke Germa's would be good, if we fit. You. Courier. There's a mess tent about thirty yards back there. Go get warmed up. Get some sleep. I won't have anything for you to take back till tomorrow."

After a moment, Bechter asked, "Why did you get rid of them?"

"You were giving them apoplexy. They both really believe the Patriarch is the Living Voice of God."

"They'll get older. What else?"

Bechter was getting to know him. "Titus Consent is headed this way. He shouldn't be back this soon."

There was another boom. Different. Louder. Less directed. Hecht sighed. "I hope they were behind something before they matched that fuse. Because that sounded like it blew up." Which had been a big problem during the development of the weapons in Dreanger.

Titus Consent slipped in through the closed back of the tent, looking for eavesdroppers hiding in corners that were not there.

"You found out something special?" Hecht asked. "I didn't expect you for a few more days."

"Plans have to adapt to circumstance."

"Good news? Or bad?"

"Depends on what you want to do and who you are."

"You going to play games with me?"

"No. I came back because I thought we could . . . Shit!"

"Language, young man. Language."

Consent grinned, showing bright, perfect teeth. "What was that?"

"One of the hounds barking. I didn't think you'd be surprised." A second boom followed a moment later. Which meant that there had not been a blowup, after all. Hecht told Bechter, "Go check that out. Find out what that odd bang was before."

Sergeant Bechter nodded. "Of course, sir. Of course."

A moment later, Consent said, "You didn't need to send him away."

"That wasn't the point. I do want to know what happened. There was an explosion. It sounded like one of the hounds blew up. Those things are expensive. And almost as dangerous to their crews as to their targets. So. Why are you back already?"

"They aren't taking us serious. It's business as usual over there. The Duke's men and some advisers from the Grail Empire have been looking at the defenses and talking about reinforcing the gates, but they aren't in any hurry. Two hundred men don't scare them. They don't expect us to get help from our garrisons. And they expect reinforcements of their own."

"How soon?"

"I don't know. Because they didn't. But Lothar promised to send a company of Braunsknechts."

"Not good, that. But the first shipment of money from Anne of Menand has arrived. That should alter the balance of power."

Consent looked skeptical. "In that case, I recommend we move right now."

"Tell me what you're thinking."

Titus Consent had in mind jumping on Clearenza with both feet before anybody thought there was the least chance that the Captain-General would do anything but show the flag.

The night sky began to clear as the Patriarchals stole toward the city. They made very little noise, except by snarling at one another to keep quiet. A fragment of moon kept trying to peek through cold clouds that promised snow.

Clearenza's north gate was a minor one. It served agricultural traffic. The gate was shut, but not so the sally port built into it. That was not secured because illicit traffic, avoiding tariffs and customs duties, moved in and out by night. Titus Consent and several obvious Devedians took point. Those who were not Episcopal Chaldareans were subject to a weighty head tax by day.

The guards were not alert. So much not so that all the sneaking went to waste. The only guard awake enough to demand bribes was so focused on a jug of wine that he found himself tied up before he understood what was happening. His only comment was, "Oh, shit!"

Piper Hecht muttered, "Is this a trap? Can they possibly be this lax with an enemy outside?" Though he saw the same loose attitude every day, everywhere. There was no professional tradition amongst Firaldian soldiers. Maybe because they did not get into many real fights. "Please tell me this isn't a trap."

"They've been setting it up for ten years if it is."

"Really?" Did Pinkus Ghort's adventure here predate that time? Or was his story about service here another tall tale?

"This was the easy part," Consent said. "Now we have to reach the citadel without raising an alarm. If they lock us out . . ."

"Thought the Duke goes whoring every night."

"Not *every* night. He's not as young as he used to be. But a lot."

"None of us are as young as we used to be. Send your lead teams."

Three teams of three men each headed for sporting houses Duke Germa was known to frequent. They would do nothing but find out if the man was there. That would be obvious. He dragged a retinue everywhere he went. A runner would carry word from each location to Consent. He would be waiting outside the citadel. If fon Dreasser was out, they would try to capture the citadel gate. The Duke always left it open when he went out on the prowl. Or such had been his custom since the advent of the Patriarchals had forced him to abandon his manor outside the wall.

Hecht told Bechter, "If we don't bring this off, I'll make him hurt by using his manor for our headquarters."

"Aren't we supposed to respect his properties? Sublime wants him back in the fold."

"I must've misunderstood my instructions."

Bechter grunted. He was recovering from the hike from camp. He was in shape for his age, but he was his age, trying to keep up with men mostly younger than the Captain-General.

Hecht said, "That's enough head start." Consent's band was five minutes gone. "Move out by squads. Quietly." The group leaders had been briefed by Titus Consent but Hecht was sure somebody would get lost. Clearenza was not vast but it was old and had grown organically. Streets meandered and were not marked.

Confusion was the natural state of combat. Hecht hoped to cause more of that on the other side than plagued his own. His men supposedly knew what to do even if they got turned around.

Hecht offered an encouraging word to each departing team leader. He did not want anyone getting killed.

He shuddered suddenly, touched by an unexpected chill. It was not the weather. Maybe it was his imagination.

Or maybe not. Sergeant Bechter murmured, "You felt that, sir?"

"Sergeant?"

"You shivered. It was a cold presence. I don't know how else to put it. Like there's something here. Right behind you. Looking over your shoulder."

"And there's nothing there when you look."

"Yes, sir." That almost defined the Instrumentalities of the Night. "I've been feeling that a lot, lately."

"As have I." But that just puzzled him more. If there was something of the Night out there, close by, of the magnitude suggested by the creeps he and Bechter felt, his wrist ought to be hurting so bad that he would be thinking about cutting his amulet off.

"Stay alert," Hecht told the men who would stay at the gate. "Let those guys tied up in the guardroom be your inspiration. Sergeant, let's go."

In the dark street, headed for the citadel, Hecht concluded that there was only one way his amulet would not function in the presence of the

Instrumentalities of the Night. Because er-Rashal al-Dhulquarnen, the man who had created it, did not want it to work.

Only Gordimer the Lion and the Rascal knew the amulet existed. Gordimer would not know how to get around it.

But why would the sorcerer want to kill Else Tage?

Hecht had not been able to work that out. He was sure er-Rashal had been trying from the moment he had left Dreanger. And possibly from even earlier.

Someone had raised that bogon in Esther's Wood, near the Well of Calamity, beside the Plain of Judgment. He had slain it. And by doing so had demonstrated a hitherto unsuspected vulnerability of the Instrumentalities of the Night.

Death had stalked him ever since.

There was fighting at the citadel entrance. There were occasional pops inside, suggesting that the men were discharging their handheld firearms in spite of orders to save them for something supernatural. Hecht understood why. Those weapons could bring an enemy down while he was still too far away to hurt you back.

One of his subalterns reported, "We surprised them, sir. But we had some bad luck. They surprised us back."

"How?"

"There are Braunsknecht guards in there. We don't know how many, but they aren't staying neutral."

"What about that, Titus? You didn't know they were here?"

"I knew there were advisers. I told you. I thought there were only a few. That's what people outside thought. We don't have to take the citadel, though. The Duke is holed up in a sporting house. I've sent men to dig him out."

Rapid popping inside signaled a counterattack by the defenders.

"Good." Hecht gathered his officers. "We don't push back unless Lieutenant Consent has his signals crossed. But we'll hang on here till we have the Duke. Titus. Don't wander off. Bechter. I need stuff to start a fire." That ought to win Sublime a new crop of hatred.

A fresh chill made him shudder. He looked around. Spectators had begun to gather in the moonlight, at a distance. They twitched every time there was a pop inside the fortress. "Bechter. Break that crowd up before it gets tempted to turn into a mob."

"Yes, sir." Bechter grabbed several men who had nothing else to do.

Consent reported, "There's word, sir. They've got him. They're headed for the gate. We should think about going."

"Excellent. You men. Get that fire started." That would make it hard for the Duke's men to come to his rescue.

Bechter fell in beside Hecht as they left the city. "Sir, there was a man in that crowd back there that we've seen before."

"Uhm?"

"In Brothe. He's a little under average height, average frame, hair well trimmed. Beard likewise. No hair on the cheeks. Head and chin both brown, so he's probably not a native. Salted with gray. Gray eyes. Forty to fifty years old. He looks pretty much like Grade Drocker did at the same age. Make that like Drocker would've looked if he didn't get mutilated."

"Really?" He would have to consult Principaté Delari about that.

He thought he had seen the man Bechter meant. Without noting any resemblance to Drocker. Whom he had not known unmutilated. He had had only a few glimpses of the sorcerer earlier. "Was he wearing brown?"

"Yes, sir. And every time I've noticed him it's been right after that creepy feeling came on."

"Worth remembering. Keep an eye out once we're back in Brothe. I'll see if I can't get the Collegium after him."

THE PATRIARCH HIMSELF CAME OUT FOR PIPER HECHT'S REPORT ON THE Clearenza operation, though the Captain-General never spoke to him directly. By the time the Collegium assembled Sublime had accepted Germa fon Dreasser's ransom and the Duke was headed home. The soldiers were not pleased. They had received no share of the ransom. There had been casualties, though just a few and only two of those fatalities.

Hecht told Anna, "I can't fathom this man's mind. He doesn't understand people at all. Next week he'll tell my men to go break up one of those riots. And he won't be able to figure out why they just stand around watching."

"It's getting scary here, Piper."

Her tone got his attention. "Yes?"

"It isn't just the riots. I don't feel safe outside anymore. I don't like the kids going out. Not since that man was killed. I always feel like somebody is watching me. Even stalking me. The kids feel it, too."

"I'll talk to Pella. He understands the streets better than you or I do."

Anna was not impressed. He needed to make a better showing. "There's an advantage to being the Captain-General of the Armies of the Faith."

"Other than being able to fling around an overweight title?"

"Yes. I can tell people to do things. And they do them. Even if they think it's crazy to hold exercises in a neighborhood like this. They'll do what I say because they're afraid they won't get paid."

"And what does all that mean?"

"That I can come around here and turn the whole neighborhood over. And claim it's business. I'd be hunting heretics."

Heretics were about to become big business. There was a lot of talk about heresy in the Collegium, mostly among Sublime's cronies. Preparing minds for what they hoped would come.

"Bring that idiot Morcant Farfog. Maybe the boogeyman will get him."

Hecht had not met Bishop Farfog. He knew little about the man other than that he headed the Patriarchal Office for the Suppression of Sacrilege and Heresy, with the title of Chief Inquestor. Rumor had the monasteries emptying out as monks signed up to help.

What little Hecht knew about Farfog suggested that he was more foul than Bishop Serifs of Antieux had been.

Why did Sublime favor such men?

"CLEVER WORK IN CLEARENZA," PRINCIPATÉ DELARI TOLD HECHT, joining him in the baths. Osa Stile smirked from behind the Principaté.

"Thank you, sir. Lieutenant Consent deserves most of the credit."

"And you used his information to sculpt a plan. You made the decision to go."

"Uh . . ."

"You took a chance. It paid off. Most men would have dithered like Tormond IV, never confident enough to jump. We suffer from an absence of decisiveness. Everyone wants a sure thing."

"We sure got a surprise when we discovered those Braunsknechts." Though the Imperials had gotten a big surprise themselves.

Delari chuckled.

Herren and Vernal seemed a little starstruck this morning. And unusually friendly. "Stop that!" Hecht told Vernal.

Delari chuckled again. "Everybody loves a winner."

"There's a problem, sir."

"I don't like the sound of that. What?"

"I thought it was my imagination till Sergeant Bechter mentioned having the same problem."

The Principaté listened. Hecht described the creepy feelings he sometimes got and that Bechter sometimes saw a particular man when that feeling got to him.

"I may have seen this man myself, once or twice. Bechter says he looks a lot like Grade Drocker a few years before his misfortune. Though shorter."

Delari frowned. Drocker's passing still pained him.

Hecht preferred to avoid the subject, too. Because Drocker's unhealing wounds, that claimed him eventually, had been his fault.

"Sir, I'm just reporting hearsay. I didn't know Grade Drocker before his misfortune."

"What happened to my son still troubles me, Piper. A lot. You can't imagine how much. But talking around the sides of it doesn't help. Say what you mean if you have something to say."

"Yes, sir. Though there isn't anything else to say, now."

"How is your Anna doing?"

"She's worried." Hecht explained.

"We haven't learned anything more from the man who was butchered. No one claimed his body. Other than the usual sailors and embassy people, there aren't many Pramans around. The dead man doesn't seem to have any local connections. If we had anyone capable, I'd try raising his shade."

"Sir!" That lurked at the edge of the blackest of sins imaginable.

Osa Stile looked shaken, too.

Might Hagid bin Nassim have known Osa Stile, back in Dreanger?

Possibly. Hagid's father might have been in on the planning. But had Osa seen the corpse?

"Only thinking out loud. Tell Anna not to worry. We'll arrange for her to feel more comfortable." The old man might have been decreeing a new law of nature.

Chip by chip, glacially, another face emerged from the facade of the doddering Principaté Muniero Delari. Was this the real Eleventh Unknown? Hecht was certain, now, that Muniero Delari *was* the heavyweight sorcerer far peoples believed members of the Collegium to be.

"Herren, stop that!"

"You don't like it, Captain-General?"

"I like it altogether too much. Stop it."

Osa Stile snickered. So did both girls. But Herren desisted.

Delari made a tiny gesture. Osa's amusement stopped instantly.

Osa might not be as much in control as he wanted.

"THERE ARE TWO WORLDS, PIPER. THIS IS PARTICULARLY TRUE IN THE Church," Principaté Delari said. They were under the Chiaro Palace, overlooking the huge map. Hecht saw no obvious changes. "But it's true everywhere, everywhen. There's the raucous old world of everyday passion, pain, and corruption. The one where we come of age, basically. Then there's the world few touch but which most are sure exists. That's the world of secret powers and secret masters. The silent kingdom. The silent kingdom shapes the raucous world without revealing itself. Just as surely as do the Instrumentalities of the Night, though with more direction and purpose. The silent kingdom hides in the secret spaces between mankind and the Night."

Hecht asked, "This is a common belief amongst men of talent?"

Delari peered at him intently, sniffing after the thought behind the question.

"Some of us have a foot in the world between. Knowing about it only because we've been shown. Others, like our Special Office brethren, are too ideological to contribute."

"And get shown for no obvious reason? Because of the murky motives of those already inside?"

The curtain had been opened enough for one day. The Principaté changed topic. "Has the girl spoken yet?"

"Uh . . . Vali?"

"Yes."

"Not where any adult can hear. She talks to Pella. Occasionally. Sometimes Pella deigns to tell us what's on her mind. Mainly, she's worried about what's going to happen to her. You find out anything about her?"

"No. There is a Vali Dumaine but she's Countess of Bleus. The wife of the Count who got into it with Anne of Menand. They don't have children. She's twenty-nine. Rumor says evil sorcery keeps her from conceiving. It also says Anne means to buy the Archbishop of Salpeno with the Dumaine honors."

"She's giving everything away."

"She's a determined woman."

"With everything to gain. I see that."

Hecht could not understand how one harlot could become so influential.

Delari mused, "She must be quite something in private."

"Curious?"

"Intellectually. I'd like to meet her."

"Uhm. But you can't hazard even a guess about where my Vali fits?"

"Beyond stipulating that circumstantial evidence suggests that she does, no."

"But if the Brotherhood of War was interested . . . Sir! I just had an unpleasant thought. A connection I didn't see before."

"Yes?"

The old man reminded Hecht of the pensioner instructors at the Vibrant Spring School, waiting for him to state a conclusion he had had trouble reaching.

"Sir, the people holding Vali were conspiring with the Special Office. Who sent me to the House of the Ten Galleons in the first place."

"So you've just realized that they must know where the girl is?"

"I'm a little dim sometimes, sir. I'm a fighting soldier, remember."

"Can you take it another step? Or two?"

"Sir?"

"Have they decided that it's better for Vali to be with you, out of sight, safe from people whose loyalties are commercial? Did they set you up to spirit the girl out of Sonsa?"

"I couldn't guess, sir. My thinking tends to be more linear."

"I understand. It's one of your charms. Quite possibly the main reason that Bronte Doneto recommended you to his cousin. You're a sharp blade that looks like it can be used with little danger of cutting both ways."

Hecht wished Gordimer the Lion believed that. "Maybe. But he also thinks he can manipulate me if he wants."

Delari grunted. "There's still another possibility, Piper. And it seems the most obvious and likely to me."

"Sir?"

"Did the girl just make up a story to win help getting out of an awful situation? Creating fictitious personal histories isn't exactly unheard of, Piper."

"Uh . . . I'll ask Pella about that."

"Good. Do. There's nothing new here. Just more of the same, worsening at a frightening rate. Will all the water in all the seas end up part of the ice? Will even Firaldia go under?"

Hecht thought Firaldia would drown in refugees first.

The great map did show that there would be no quick, direct confrontation over Clearenza. The passes to the heart of the Grail Empire were closed. A courier might make his way out of the continental heartland, but no armed force could make the transit for months yet.

Hecht asked, "Do we know where Lothar and his sisters are?" Johannes Blackboots had preferred the Imperial cities of Firaldia, Plemenza in particular. He liked to stay close enough to tweak Sublime's nose when the mood took him.

"Hogwasser. In Lothar's case."

"Sir?"

"Sorry. Bad joke. Hochwasser. Means 'high water,' literally, but generally translates as 'flood.' The name goes back to antiquity. When it was called something else that meant the same thing."

Hecht knew a little about Hochwasser because he claimed to have passed through during his journey south from Duarnenia. It was a military city, of sorts, and had been since old Imperial times. Today it served as the headquarters for the Grail Emperor's lifeguard, the Braunsknechts.

The concept of even that limited a standing force found little favor among the Imperial nobility. Anything that strengthened the Emperor necessarily weakened the noble class.

Delari said, "Lothar is at Hochwasser. Katrin is either there or at Grumbrag. There's some doubt about Helspeth." The Principaté gestured at the grand map. "Don't let that lull you. If Lothar decides something needs doing he has people here who can make our lives miserable. Follow me."

Hecht did so, down to the main floor, passing monks and nuns engrossed in their work. One of the latter appeared to be extremely gravid.

Principaté Delari approached a heavy wooden door. Ancient, bound in spell-wrought iron, it looked capable of withstanding assault from barbarian or Night. A shelf in the stone to its right bore several old-time brass lanterns of the sort once carried by Imperial night couriers. They even had an Imperial seal on the adjustable shutter that controlled the amount of light emitted. Delari chose one, checked its fuel level, lighted it from a candle at the end of the shelf. Tallow spills showed that a candle burned there all the time.

"Open the door, Piper."

The door was not locked, latched, or barred. Hecht pulled. It opened.

Cold, damp air greeted him. It smelled of raw sewage and very old death.

"The catacombs?"

"Exactly." Delari nodded. "They're real. Take a lantern yourself. Never come down here without one."

"I don't want to be down here at all. Not if half the stories are true."

"They aren't. But the reality can be worse. The light from these lanterns repels things of the Night."

Hecht sorted through the lanterns. They all seemed fully fueled. He took the heaviest on the theory that it would last the longest. He lighted it, tried to look ready. If go he must.

Delari chuckled. "Remember, down here, as in the world above, the worst monsters go on two legs and have mothers who love them."

"Why would *we* want to be down here?"

"Sometimes a man needs to move around without being seen." That sounded too pat. "What about your mother?"

The Principaté had moved into the tunnel, which was lined in stone set without mortar, using an Old Brothen technique. The question caught Hecht off guard. "Sir?"

"I was curious about your mother."

Hecht temporized, trying to recall anything he had told anyone about the woman. "I expect she'd agree with most mothers. Piper is a good boy. He didn't mean any harm. He couldn't possibly do anything bad. I didn't know her, though, sir. She died when I was quite young. Childbed fever."

"And your father?"

"He was a good Chaldarean. In Duarnenia that means he got to heaven early. I don't remember him at all. They say he came home just often enough to keep my mother pregnant."

Delari seemed amused. He did not pursue the subject. "The catacombs here belong to us." He did not define "us." "They're safe. Most of the time. There are wards. And watchers. Not much gets past. But you can't count on being safe. *Always* carry your own lantern."

The footing grew damper. The stone had been plastered at one time. The plaster had fallen into the muck underfoot.

The Principaté said, "We're near the Teragi, but deeper down. We could visit the Castella or Krois. Or cross over to the north side, if we wanted. But that isn't something you need to know how to do yet."

Hecht muttered, "This is real silent kingdom country." He saw no evidence of life. No rats. No spiders. No vermin whatsoever.

"You're uncomfortable."

"I don't like tight places. Tight places underground are worse."

Delari chuckled.

Evidently he found everything humorous today.

Hecht asked, "Where are the vermin?"

"Cruel things roam down here. They don't care what they eat. Including you and me if they could catch us."

"That's no help."

Delari chuckled yet again. "You're in the underworld now, Piper. Like in the old mythology."

"I'll keep an eye out for black rivers and blind boatmen."

"If he was down here for real he'd get knocked in the head and robbed of the passage money."

"You're so reassuring. Where are we going?"

"Nowhere in particular. I'm suffering from an inclination to share Collegium secrets." Delari turned left into a cross tunnel. That led to a huge chamber. The lanterns revealed no farther walls, only ranks of ancient colonnades marching off into the darkness. It looked like an abandoned cathedral at midnight. A cathedral abandoned for ages. Debris lay everywhere. The lantern light took on a blue-white hue. Everything appeared in shades of bluish gray. Dust was thick and cobwebs ubiquitous.

And there were bones. Bones great and small, everywhere. Ugly bones, some of them. Bones that Hecht did not find familiar. Perhaps bones not human. There was little odor of decay.

Delari said, "Flesh doesn't last long enough to putrefy down here."

Some larger bones had been broken, presumably to expose the marrow.

"Another silent kingdom."

"Not always. Though it is now. Bats sometimes establish colonies that don't last. Sometimes pagans celebrate demonic rituals. Which is an ironic twist. This is where the earliest Chaldareans got together to worship and to hide their dead. Now the demon worshipers use the far end, over there. And break into the crypts to get bodies to use in their wicked rites."

"Really? How do they do that?"

"Excuse me?"

"What do they do with the bodies? There was a story I heard when I was little. Overheard, actually, and only part of it, because I was supposed to be asleep. The storyteller claimed it came out of the Grand Marshes and every word was true. It was colorful. But he only got to the part where the three brothers who were the heroes were coming home with the mummies of some old-time sorcerers when I started sneezing. I got whipped and sent to bed and never did find out why they wanted the mummies in the first place."

Delari's frown was obvious, despite the lighting. "This was a story?"

"Up north we have traveling storytellers. Like jongleurs down here. Only they don't usually sing. And they don't tell love stories. They're really grim hero stories, mostly. They always claim the stories are true, but mostly you know better. This storyteller—I can't remember his name—was famous for scary stories. This one about stealing mummies sounded real."

"Mummified sorcerers, you say?"

"Yes, sir." Had he said too much?

"Interesting. Tell me more."

"Sir?"

"Who were the heroes? Where did they go for their mummies? Who were the dead men?"

"I was five years old, sir. Pybus. That was the name of the brother who was in charge. I remember that. It was all his idea. And there was a . . . Flogni? Something like that. He was the one who said they shouldn't disturb the dead. But he went along because brothers have to stick together. The place they were looking for was in the mountains way off to the east. It was a secret tomb. I don't know how they knew where to find it. One of the old-time horse people conquerors was buried there. One of the ones that those people still worship. The sorcerers in the story were murdered and buried at the points of the winds so their spirits would protect the tomb. They'd be in such a rage about what happened to them, they'd destroy anybody who got close enough to notice. The one buried in the south was a woman who was also the conqueror's lover. She laid some kind of curse on his tribe when she found out what they were going to do to her."

"Good story. I wouldn't mind hearing the original." Principaté Delari never stopped moving, staying close to the wall, going round to their right. Hecht suspected they were making a long, slow circle, the Principaté operating with no specific destination. Delari said, "I've heard a story something like it, only this one happened in Lucidia."

"Sir?"

"There's a hidden fortress in the Idium desert in Lucidia called Andesqueluz. Carved out of the living rock of a mountain. A long time ago an ugly, murderous cult operated out of there. They were exterminated by the rest of the world. Which always happens when that kind of people gets too ambitious. A few years back the great mage of Dreanger, er-Rashal al-Dhulquarnen, sent a band of Sha-lug warriors to Andesqueluz to steal the mummies of the slain sorcerers."

"Er-Rashal al-Dhulquarnen?" He mispronounced it. "Wasn't that the one . . . ?"

"He was at al-Khazen. Yes. We distracted him while you and the Emperor eliminated his associates. We couldn't keep him from getting away. I expect he's back home and up to some other mischief."

"So what would he want with dead bodies? Well, you said mummies. That's not quite the same thing."

"Specifically, mummified sorcerers who were of the first water when they were alive. Some of the worst ever. More than one lord of Andesqueluz ascended before death dragged the rest down."

"Uh . . . Ascended?" Hecht knew next to nothing about sorcery. He would have been damned if he did.

"They worked sorceries powerful enough to make themselves over into Instrumentalities of the Night. Demons, if you will. The djinn of the east were all human once. The cruel immortality was once much less difficult to achieve, and the more so near the Wells of Ihrian. One would suspect that the Dreangerean has a scheme to transform himself." Delari took careful steps sideways. Hecht followed, round a skeleton wrapped in scraps of rotted linen. The skull had wisps of hair attached. The empty eye sockets seemed to track him.

There were dozens of skeletons, then. Someone had ripped open countless crypts. "No jewelry," Hecht noted. "Grave robbers."

"No. These are the earliest Brothen Chaldareans. They didn't believe in jewelry. They took nothing to the grave but what they brought into the world when they were born."

"Times have changed."

"Human nature will prevail."

"If this sorcerer can turn himself into a god . . . Well, what's he likely to do if he does?"

"The conventional wisdom says ascendants lose interest in their old lives. They get busy doing the same old things inside the Night, going after more and more power. But that's really just speculation. Nobody really knows. They don't come back to chat about what it's like on the other side. And there hasn't been a lot of it happening in recent centuries. Stop!"

Delari's voice fell to a whisper. "Say nothing. Do nothing."

The old man turned his head slowly, side to side, listening intently. Eyes shut, he sniffed the air. He breathed, "It's time to go." He began to retrace their path carefully, straining for silence.

Hecht asked no questions. His amulet had suddenly turned bitter cold.

Something extremely unpleasant had begun to stir out in the darkness.

The old man relaxed visibly once they entered the tunnel to the Chiaro Palace.

"What happened?" Hecht finally asked.

"We almost walked right into something very dark and very powerful. It was asleep, but suddenly restless. I didn't want to waken it." Soon afterward, he added, "It may be the thing responsible for those grotesque murders. Now we know where it dens up, we can go after it."

"Why not now?"

"Because I'm one old man, by myself, all alone, and worn out from showing you this tiny slice of the world below." A chuckle. "And because I'm unarmed and it felt like it might be nastier than anyone guessed before."

6. The Princess in Plemenza

Princess Helspeth started angry. Algres Drear kept dragging his heels. She stayed angry. Drear persisted in his claim that waiting a few weeks would make for a dramatically easier journey. Weather was Drear's determined ally in thwarting her desires. Her most fervent desire.

She wanted to be in her city of Plemenza. *Now.*

Weather be damned, just days after Lothar bestowed the Plemenza honors, Helspeth and those of her household hardy enough moved from Alten Weinberg to Hochwasser, on the Bleune. Hochwasser was a ghost town just beginning to show signs of life because the Emperor was expected. The Bleune was wide, filthy, and speckled with floes of ice, some the size of warships.

The serious delays came at Hochwasser.

Couriers reported only one pass even remotely usable. This was the worst winter on record. Only the toughest, most determined travelers had any hope of getting through. Helspeth was determined to try. And did, accompanied only by Captain Drear and two Braunsknechts who felt the eyes of Johannes Blackboots's ghost crisping the backs of their necks. They refused to let Hansel's baby girl go alone once it was clear she could not be dissuaded.

Helspeth demonstrated a stubbornness the Braunsknechts found disturbing. Weather did not stop her. Cold did not stop her. The threat of frostbite did not intimidate her. The presence in the mountains of something abidingly awful did not frighten her into turning back, though it stalked them for days, singing in the wind. Algres Drear was both impressed and deeply concerned.

That was a prince of the Night out there. Something remarkably wicked and cruel, a near god. You needed no mystic talent to sense it. Yet, this time, it was content to stay its evil. And the folk below the mountains were amazed and disturbed.

This dread spirit had sown terror liberally for close to a year, its predations worsening dramatically with the weather. Those who claimed expertise in the forms assumed by the Night believed it must be some wind-stalking demon-thing somehow displaced from the realms of permanent ice now advancing from the north.

Ignorant folk concluded that the Princess was favored by God. Or was about to become a bride of the Night. Each conclusion led to its special set of fears.

HELSPETH REACHED PLEMENZA TWO .WEEKS BEFORE SPRING OFFICIALLY commenced. In a punishing sleet storm that coated men and animals with ice and left the footing so treacherous she thought she might die on the cobblestone street after having survived the worst handed her by the high Jagos.

Other Braunsknechts and hangers-on dribbled in throughout the following month. Following an annoyingly dramatic change of weather that began almost as soon as she reached the Dimmel Palace. Ten days later there was no snow or ice to be seen on the Firaldian side of the Jago Mountains. Traffic through the range normalized quickly.

Algres Drear never said a word.

Which made Helspeth want to cane him with a bamboo flail till he puked up the smug "Told you so!" smiling behind his calm gray eyes.

More galling still was an illness that claimed her for several weeks. Her cough became frighteningly fierce.

Ferris Renfrow reentered Helspeth's life at the height of her fever. She lay in bed, curtains drawn. She was always too hot or too cold, always exhausted from continuous coughing. She pretended sleep to evade her fussing women. Worst were Lady Chevra diNatale and Lady Delta va Kelgerberg. The former was an unpleasant old cow related to the former Counts of Plemenza. Lady Delta was just four years Helspeth's senior but ancient in her perception of the way an Imperial Princess should comport herself. Lady Chevra was a devoted Brothen Episcopal and, probably, a tool of the Council Advisory. Va Kelgerberg was a devoted companion but tedious to the point of excruciation.

The true, deep horror was that both women believed they knew best what was best for Princess Helspeth Ege.

When Helspeth first heard Renfrow she thought it was the fever talking. Purely wishful thinking. He would not enter her personal quarters.

Renfrow asked about her health.

"She brought this on herself," Lady Delta opined, with a superior sniff. "She's a spoiled, willful child. Much too selfish and far too stubborn. She will have what she will, when she wills it, never mind the cost of her self-indulgence to others. It's a miracle Algres Drear and those two sergeants . . ."

Chuckling, Renfrow interjected, "It runs in the family."

"Johannes was willful but never petty. Nor was he particularly selfish. His stubbornness wasn't about himself or his pleasures. It was always about what was best for the Empire. Sir, this child could become our Empress. In a moment, if God has a bad afternoon. Where will we be if she won't grow up?"

"She's bright. She'll learn."

"She hasn't given us any reason to hope."

"Algres Drear is a good man."

"Who would make a lot more headway if he'd paddle her when she wants to do something as stupid as crossing the Jagos during the winter."

"I'll talk to her. She took risks that make no sense. I suspect that she didn't understand the dangers, then got lucky. There's a baron of the Night on the prowl up there. Nothing as terrible has been seen since the early days of the Old Empire. Maybe she caught it napping. Maybe the cold slowed it down. It wasn't as nasty as it should have been. I'm no expert. I can't consult the people who are. They're all Sublime's lackeys. But I saw the monster's handiwork. We can only thank God that it took no interest in the child."

Helspeth wanted to be angry with Delta. She did not indulge. Renfrow was much more critical. Renfrow had always been a demi-god, the iron hammer that forged the Emperor's finished will. If Renfrow found her lacking, then she needed to do some serious self-examination.

Helspeth Ege's circumstances compelled her to live inside herself but she did not do much introspection.

Lady Delta's remarks touched home. Renfrow's criticism kicked the door of her soul wide open.

She did not believe she would become Empress so saw no need to prepare. Others obviously did not concur.

Eges seldom died of the complications of old age. And Lothar, of course, was not expected to survive the year again this year.

Ferris Renfrow asked to be summoned when the Princess could see him. He did not hint that she might not be so inclined.

Helspeth was not so inclined. Who did Renfrow think he was, talking like that?

It took time to sink in.

Those nearest to her did not like her much. Her own behavior was the cause.

She did get it. Katrin would not have done.

IT WAS NOT SEEMLY THAT THE PRINCESS SHOULD ENTERTAIN A MAN ALONE. There could be no hint of a possibility of a chance of a stain on her reputation. Not when she was on the marriage market. But she did not want the usual ladies there, eavesdropping for the Council Advisory, the Patriarch, her brother or sister, or anyone else.

She was sure her women were all spies.

She told Renfrow as much.

He nodded. "Of course. You're an object of considerable value." The Imperial spymaster accepted tea from one of the younger girls attending Helspeth this morning. She hoped these vacuous daughters and granddaughters would garble whatever they overheard. "You have no friends."

Helspeth crushed an angry retort. What others thought should not matter. But it did. Renfrow's conversation with Delta and Chevra hurt.

Renfrow revealed striking white teeth, smiling. He was enamored of the eastern custom of cleaning his teeth.

Helspeth halfheartedly cared for her own teeth, only because it was fashionable.

"You're right. I have no friends. I'm more alone than I imagined it was possible to be when I came here." Hurrying because most all of her happy memories included Plemenza.

"You're surrounded by people who could become your friends. If you'd let them. Most of these people do want the best for you."

She did not respond. She did not know what to say. Until, "My world ended when my father died. Before that, even though I never saw him much, I belonged. I had my place. Not much was demanded of me. Katrin and I spoiled Mushin. We played at being girl soldiers. Papa indulged us. Especially me."

"Because you were so much like him. It was a fantasy. Which he recognized for what it was. But he enjoyed letting you be the son that Lothar couldn't. A cruel jest on God's part."

Helspeth sipped her tea. "Must be a side-splitter. Look around. All the strong rulers have weak successors behind them."

"There are succession problems, here and there. But King Peter's son—as much as can be told from an infant—should be a worthy successor. And Anne of Menand will, likely, prove forceful after she becomes King of Arnhand."

Helspeth overlooked the sharpness. "I wish my father hadn't charged into al-Khazen like that."

"Excepting Grand Duke Omro and his cronies, most everyone would agree. We may never recover from the loss. But the Grail Empire doesn't run on 'what if?' and wishful thinking. Most of the time."

"If he was alive I wouldn't be here like this."

"Or you might be. With the same household. Your father was greatly concerned about what he started, letting you girls play at being boys. You in particular worried him. You kept throwing on armor and trying to get into fights. Al-Khazen would've been the last straw. You might've ended up in a nunnery."

"No."

"He considered it."

Helspeth was stunned. "But I thought . . . I thought that's what he wanted. I thought he'd be hugely proud."

"He would've been, in his secret heart. But he was the Emperor. He had to consider appearances. And your welfare. And you did get into a situation where you had to be rescued by Patriarchals."

Again Helspeth stifled a sharp rejoinder. He was right.

"All right. I did. The Captain-General himself saved me."

A small smile from Renfrow. "I saw him a few months ago."

She failed to mask her interest.

He said, "He's well."

"And?"

"And ready to become a serious burr under the Imperial saddle.

Clearenzas could keep happening now that Sublime can afford to build up his forces."

"What would Papa do?"

"Probably summon the levies and march on Brothe. Stop it before it can get going."

"But that won't happen."

"No. Lothar is a minor. And the people on the Council didn't approve of Johannes's policies when he was alive."

"What about Katrin?"

"What will she do? I don't know. No one does. Including Katrin."

"How much trouble will she have being Empress? She isn't a man."

"Less than most people think. She'll have the Braunsknechts."

"And you?"

"Some. Yes." The hard Renfrow shone through briefly. Helspeth shuddered. That was the Ferris Renfrow who had caused nightmares amongst Hansel's enemies.

"What?"

"You aren't going to just vacation here."

"Uh . . ."

"Did you think you would? You're the Emperor's daughter. You're on this side of the mountains."

"I didn't . . ."

"I know. Those people up at Alten Weinberg and Hochwasser didn't think about that, either. But you'll be the Empire's proconsul in Firaldia. What with the mountain crossings being closed for half the year, now." And the only way around required an overland journey through the Eastern Empire or Arnhand.

Like it or not, Helspeth Ege had to be an adult. With responsibilities.

"You'll do fine," Renfrow told her. "You are your father's daughter. And you have Algres Drear. It's no accident he was assigned to you. Your father chose him. Trust him." Renfrow started to leave his seat, remembered he was in the presence of an Imperial princess.

"You have something else to do?"

"Always. I'm always behind and always running late."

"Maybe you need your own Algres Drear."

"I have a few. But you hit the mark. I could use more. Since your father died I'm a one-armed juggler with twelve balls in the air. It's necessary to let some things slide. I sometimes decide wrong."

RENFROW FADED OUT OF PLEMENZA AS THOUGH HE HAD BEEN BUT A WISP of imagination. Helspeth consciously tried to stop feeling sorry for herself. She had to concentrate on improving the standing of the Empire in northern Firaldia.

She was less effective than Renfrow hoped. The Council Advisory sabotaged most of her efforts.

She accepted what befell. She could do nothing else. But behind her cold, neutral eyes lurked the troubling, certain knowledge that Mushin's frailties would take him soon and she would become second in succession.

She wrote Katrin frequently, saying little of substance, trying to nurture and rebuild a family relationship. Katrin seldom replied. She was unpredictable when she did. She could be angry, petty, scolding, or demonstrate the warmest expressions of sisterly love. Helspeth suspected Katrin's attitude shifted with the moods of those around her. Which did not augur well for the reign of the Empress Katrin.

Every letter, however grim or cheerful, left Helspeth more frightened.

During her appearance at a religious procession, in the course of one of Plemenza's festivals, Algres Drear warned, "It's time to take more care what you say and who hears you say it." He chose a moment when no one would overhear.

"What do you mean?"

"I get letters from north of the Jagos, too. Be careful, Princess."

He had no chance to say anything more.

Helspeth worried for hours. The Council Advisory must be poisoning Lothar's mind. She could not defend herself. She had to shut up and make sure she offended no one.

Being an Imperial princess, even in her wonderful city of Plemenza, held no joy now that Johannes was gone.

7. A Fire in the End of Connec

Tormond IV, being the Great Vacillator, kept Count Raymone Garete, Seuir Brock Rault, Brother Candle, and their companions in Khaurene all winter. And a hard winter it was, out where the nobility squabbled. Hungry peasants flooded Khaurene. Serfs deserted estates where men were bonded to the soil. Their masters were too busy to hunt them down. They joined the bandits in the hills, became low-grade mercenaries, or drifted into the cities where they lived by their wits. Meaning many became wood to be hewn by the headsman's ax.

Count Raymone chafed. He pleaded. He received letters almost daily begging him to come home. The best he could do in the face of Tormond's intransigence was issue a patent to his cousin Bernardin Amberchelle authorizing him to take all steps necessary to maintain order and defend Antieux.

Brother Candle was appalled. Bernardin Amberchelle was an animal.

He was stupid, vicious, and a stranger to conscience. "Your Lordship! You can't . . . Anyone but Bernardin!"

"Because he's an atheist? Or because he's a murderous lunatic?"

"Yes. That."

"But that makes him perfect."

"What?"

"He'll only kill people he doesn't like."

"Your Lordship, it isn't a joke."

"He'll be savage but he'll do more good than harm. And I'll look grand by comparison when I get back. Even my enemies will be glad to see me."

Brother Candle shook his head at the sheer cruel cynicism of the man.

"Bernardin won't be out of control. He has a certain low craft. And he does listen when I explain clearly. Nobody will take it in the neck who didn't ask for it."

Brother Candle was not mollified.

BROTHER CANDLE MET SIR EARDALE IN THE SILENCING ROOM THE DAY BE-fore he left Khaurene. The knight from Santerin did nothing to hide this meeting. "It doesn't matter anymore," he explained. "The cause is lost."

"No cause is lost while we don't despair."

"Despair has found a roost, Brother. With all its brothers and sisters."

"Then go home."

"I am home. I want your final thoughts before you leave."

Tormond had been adamant. Brother Candle was to stick to Count Raymone Garete like a rash. A rash of conscience.

"You've heard them, Sir Eardale. The Duke won't listen. There isn't much more that can be done."

The old knight grunted. "And our traitor?"

"Excuse me?" Stalling.

"Sublime's inside man. Who is he?"

The answer placed the Perfect Master squarely in the jaws of a fierce quandary. He had wrestled it for months. Pursuing the example set by the Great Vacillator.

Any action meant making a choice between friends.

Sir Eardale observed, "There are issues larger than the fates of a few men, Brother."

"Intellectually, yes." Emotionally, it remained a choice between men.

"The entire Connec . . ."

"I know, Sir Eardale. Poisoning the Duke is the moral equivalent to poisoning the End of Connec."

True. Both were almost moribund.

Dunn said, "Bries LeCroes is the villain. He's decided to ride the Brothen pony. He's been promised that he'll be Bishop of Khaurene if he keeps the Duke under control."

Brother Candle agreed. Bishop Clayto would be smashed for his long criticism of Sublime.

But Bries LeCroes was a friend. They had been through the Calziran Crusade together.

"I won't kill him," Dunn said. "Unless he finds it too difficult to relocate his conscience."

"You're going to turn him again?" Further admitting that the accusation was sound.

"I see an opportunity to castrate Rinpoché. And to plant an eye inside the local Society." The Society for Suppression of Sacrilege and Heresy had become just "the Society," already. It had had little impact, locally. There were plenty of pro-Viscesment bullies to bust pro-Brothen skulls. "And to sabotage Sublime's Connecten ambitions."

Brother Candle continued to keep his own counsel.

Dunn said, "As you will, Brother. Though you must know what LeCroes's villainy might mean to you Maysaleans."

There was that, too.

"I can't fault your conclusion," he admitted. "But I couldn't work out the practical side. How was he getting the poison to the Duke?"

Dunn started to speak, thought better of it. He had his suspicions but did not want to share them. "God speed you safely to Antieux, Brother." He walked out.

SPRING THREATENED ITS EXPLOSION OF GREEN. COUNT RAYMONE'S PARTY straggled into Antieux under the empty eyes of a dozen severed heads. Cousin Bernardin had done his work well.

Crowds came out, of course. The first folk seen were not as demonstrative as the Count might like. Among them, though, were men of such harsh countenance that they could only be Society hacks.

Brother Candle saw despair everywhere. Hope was not dead here, but ravens cast deep shadows as they circled down on its quivering body. Count Raymone's long absence had given misery time to breed.

Bries LeCroes had a larger, darker stain on his soul than Brother Candle had imagined.

Inside Antieux, near the citadel, the crowds were warmer. They cheered. The dark, cold fish of the Society were scarce. A chant began. It demanded Brothen Episcopal scalps. Youths set fire to straw effigies wearing signs identifying them as Sublime V, Morcant Farfog, Mathe Richenau, and Helton Jael.

"Who is Helton Jael?" Brock Rault asked.

Jael was the current senior brother of the Society locally. He had just arrived, to replace Icaté Dermot, who had gone missing. Dermot himself had replaced someone else not long ago.

"I don't like this," Brother Candle told Rault. "It means big trouble."

"The fact that there's gonna be big trouble just blindsided you, eh, Brother?" Socia sneered. "Came at you right out of the blue?"

"I try to be optimistic, girl. I don't abandon hope. I keep praying that disaster can be averted. If men of goodwill want it so, it can be so."

"Name two. Not counting you."

Socia had a point, possibly without realizing it.

Everyone was crazy.

Everyone subscribed to an apocalyptic vision.

Was this one of those ages when mankind needed the purification of a holocaust?

Bernardin Amberchelle met his cousin amongst the flaming effigies. He grinned an idiot's grin. He was proud of his achievements. He expected praise.

THE RAULTS LEFT ANTIEUX SHORTLY. THEY DID NOT EXPECT TO BE GONE long. There was to be a midsummer wedding for Count Raymone and Socia Rault.

Brother Candle left with the Raults but did not accompany them. He spent a few weeks finding the temper of the countryside. He was amazed. Bernardin Amberchelle's savagery *had* done more good than harm. Though those whose heads decorated Antieux's gates might disagree.

The Society no longer indulged in persecutions inside Antieux's wall. But Bernardin had felt little obligation to the rural folk. Maysaleans, in particular, were being persecuted. And so, as Brother Candle feared, neighbor turned against neighbor. Families who had been friendly for generations became estranged. In St. Jeules ande Neuis, Jhean the carpenter told him, "People are too frightened of those black crows. They're almost supernaturally scary."

Brother Candle got no chance to see that for himself. Whenever he came near crossing paths with the Society the rustic folk hustled him out of the way. Even local Brothen Episcopals had no use for Sublime's crows.

COUNT RAYMONE HAD MATURED INDEED. HE EXAMINED THE SITUATION BEfore acting. He consulted his knights and leading men. Once he was certain where everything stood he sent for the Brothen Episcopal Archbishop of Antieux.

Antieux had been elevated to an archbishopric. One Persico Parthini had assumed the new mantle, replacing Bishop Mathe Richenau. A disease acquired whoring had driven Richenau into drooling madness.

Brother Candle returned in time to witness the first encounter between Count Raymone and the new regional lord of the Church. Parthini, technically, outranked Raymone. However, according to Raymone, he lacked the swords to make that stick.

The Archbishop arrived full of arrogant bluster. Count Raymone ignored him till the bluster faltered in the face of rising uneasiness. Bernardin Amberchelle's relentless, mad, hungry stare wore Parthini down.

Raymone stared through Parthini, hard. "Who is this barking dog? Why is he here, annoying me?"

Though Parthini had been announced, Raymone's chief herald said, "This is Persico Parthini, who styles himself Archbishop of Antieux."

"He's the Usurper's hound?"

"Yes, Your Lordship."

"You. False priest. You violate both canon and civil law by masquerading as a man of the cloth. But you have a guardian angel. A Maysalean Perfect has prevailed upon me to overlook your transgressions. For the moment. So I'll be merciful. You have until sundown, day after tomorrow, to remove yourself from Antieux. Your fellow brigands must accompany you. Those who don't leave the Connec will suffer those penalties faced by all thieves and robbers."

The Archbishop was both livid and speechless. And frightened. There was no doubt Count Raymone meant every word. And had a ferocious presence.

On the up side, Antieux's criminals served their sentences in their home city, helping with reconstruction. They were not sold down to Sheavenalle for service in the galleys. Nor to overseas mines.

Few prisoners survived the mines.

Count Raymone waved a hand. Functionaries surrounded Parthini, hustled him away.

Brother Candle asked, "Wasn't that a little harsh? Not to mention disrespectful?"

"You asked me not to kill him. I gave you what you wanted. Don't go all woman on me and keep asking for more and more."

Brother Candle opened his mouth to argue. He shut it. He had vexed Raymone enough.

The Count smiled slyly as he turned to the next item on his calendar.

BROTHER CANDLE UNDERSTOOD THAT SMILE THE MOMENT HE LEFT THE citadel.

Cousin Bernardin and a dozen henchmen were putting up whipping posts in front of the ruined cathedral. They had two customers ready to serve. Both wore the austere black of the Society. Brother Candle sidled over.

"What did these men do?"

"They took possession of property that didn't belong to them. After the Count ordered them to leave Antieux."

Definitely Society, then. Who would have had no chance to hear about Raymone's order to Archbishop Parthini. To whom they did not report directly, anyway.

Thus Raymone's wicked smile.

It took only a small investment of imagination to fathom Raymone's scheme. While Brother Candle roamed the countryside the Count had been gathering trustworthy men. Now he was ready to assert himself.

The prisoners received a dozen lashes and orders to quit Antieux instantly. Whatever they claimed to own was forfeit.

Raymone's partisans launched a sweep that collected both mundane villains and Society crows. Few got the chance to defend themselves. The more hated crows received hard labor sentences.

The latest chief of the Society mission had more confidence and courage than was good for him. But he was new, too.

Inwood Bente had replaced Helton Jael after the latter's sudden and mysterious disappearance or desertion. He refused to believe these provincials would dare defy the Brothen Church, or that most of them considered that Church a foreign criminal conspiracy. So when his followers began to suffer, he went looking for the Count, all filled with fury and bluster, having failed to understand the lessons of his predecessor's disappearance and the Archbishop's humiliation.

Brother Candle tried to warn him. Bente's associates would not let the Perfect near. They threw stones. They called him, "Damned!" and, "Heretic!" In front of witnesses who exaggerated considerably when Count Raymone took their testimony only minutes later.

Inwood Bente caught the Count at a particularly bad time. He had just received his first letter from Socia Rault. It had not said anything he wanted to hear.

Caron ande Lette had suffered severely during Seuir Brock's extended absence. An immediate turnaround and reunion was out of the question. There was too much work to do. The nuptials might have to be postponed.

Raymone knew who to blame.

Inwood Bente, who might have been an honest man, received thirty lashes for failing to control his underlings. With eight lashes to go he suffered a massive seizure.

"You're going to kill him," Brother Candle protested.

Count Raymone would not listen. "Brother, I want these vultures to shit themselves if Sublime even hints that he'll send them to the Connec. I want them absolutely convinced that even if their God is holding their hands, they're going to die. Badly. If they're lucky. If they're not, they'll suffer more cruelly here than they will in their Hell after Judgment Day."

Brother Candle shook his head sadly.

"You disagree?" Raymone gestured. His men cut Bente down. After the man received his final eight lashes.

"They're just as sure of their righteousness as you are, Your Lordship. Individuals can be intimidated. The movement can't."

"Then they'll be exterminated like any other vermin. We'll throw their carcasses to the hogs."

It was a harsh world. Yet that appalled Brother Candle.

Still, only men like Raymone Garete, with their backbones of iron, created history.

Count Raymone was not concentrating on what was happening in front of him.

"Brother, I would beg a boon." There was a conciliatory edge to the Count's voice.

"Your Lordship?"

"I want you to go to Caron ande Lette."

Duke Tormond wanted Brother Candle's breath kept hot on the back of Count Raymone's neck. To be his conscience. A pointless, hopeless enterprise.

The old pilgrim had sworn no oath to execute the Duke's wish.

"You've got it bad, don't you?"

"I've never met a woman like Socia."

"I fail to see what good I can do by being there. But the Seekers in that part of the Connec need encouragement." He had decided that the Connecten Perfect must combat national despair. If hope could not be nurtured—kept alive in hidden places if need be—darkness would swamp the world.

"You'll go?"

"I'll go. But not really to press your suit. I can't play the lute or carry a tune, let alone put together a seductive song."

The Count grinned. The sudden light in his face made him look like a different man. "If that was how Socia had to be wooed I'd have no hope. My main musical talent is, I'm loud."

"I noticed."

"As most people have. I just want a voice on the scene, Master. To remind the Raults."

"Of course." Brother Candle suspected the brothers Rault were celebrating their coup still. Finding a prospective husband who did not flee as soon as he met the bride. And one of superior status at that.

"I hope you'll behave while I'm gone."

"I'll be no more disrespectful to my Duke than his other vassals are."

"Scary thought." Brother Candle wanted to caution Raymone against further irritating the Brothen Church but knew his breath would go to waste if he did.

That evening, during his meditations, Brother Candle wondered what great forces were moving him. Why did Providence want him back in that unhappy land on the verges of the Connec?

He was, he feared, being made over into a sort of historical apparition, something like a supernatural eyewitness to the last days of the Connecten idyll.

8. Long Winter, Short Spring

Piper Hecht was enjoying a rare evening with Anna and the kids. And Pinkus Ghort, who had brought a couple of newly discovered vintages that he wanted to share. Not uninvited. Ghort being as near a friend as Hecht had—though he did get on well with his staff. But his staff were all married men disinclined to spend their free time with the people they saw all day every day at work. Nor was it appropriate for the Captain-General of All the Patriarchal Armies to become too familiar with men he expected to send into harm's way.

Pella showed off how much he had learned since entering Anna's house. He could read now, slowly. And was all excited about it. For someone of his class literacy was akin to magic.

Anna and Pinkus played chess while Pella stumbled through his reading. Hecht looked over the boy's shoulder. Vali looked over Pella's other shoulder. She was all polished and dressed like a doll. Her own doing. She was impatient with Pella's pace.

Hecht asked, "Can you do better?" And chuckled. Vali was in complete control. You could not trick her into talking. Though she did, occasionally, relay messages through Pella. Hecht now believed she was just a clever chit who had created the perfect legend to weasel herself out of a terrible situation. A stubborn pretense to muteness saved her having to explain.

Ghort moved a piece, said, "Kid already reads twice as better than I do. Maybe he's gonna jump back in time and be the Pella that wrote that damned play."

Anna asked, "You sure that's what you want to do?" But only after Pinkus took his finger off his piece.

Ghort protested, "I don't see anything."

Hecht said, "She's trying to rattle your confidence."

"I don't have no confidence to rattle. I seen what she done to you. You ever beat her?"

"No. I can't even beat Vali." In fact, Vali was the superior player. She thought far ahead and easily developed long-range strategies. "Pella, I'm impressed. You're learning faster than I did. Would you put more wood on the fire?"

Pella was cooperative in all things. He knew when he had it good. It had been a hard winter on Brothe's streets.

Anna did nothing dramatic in response to Ghort's move. He sighed, asked, "Anna, our raids got your neighbors pissed off yet?"

Anna replied, "They haven't tried to burn me out."

The City Regiment made regular sweeps through the quarter. What was left of the force.

Anna went on, "They like having me here. You looking out for me gets them looked out for, too."

Pinkus Ghort now referred to his command as the City Platoon, though five hundred men remained on his payroll. Hecht kept cherry-picking the best for his expanding Patriarchal force. He was trying to create a unified command for all the Patriarchal garrisons.

Sublime was amenable—according to Principaté Doneto. Sublime was optimistic now that he had his arrangement with Anne of Menand. He was positioning himself for a future of his own design. He would need an effective, efficient military. He expected to be able to afford the best.

Hecht noted that little of Anne's money had reached Brothe yet. Delivery arrangements remained confused.

Hecht asked, "Did you come up with anything? Ever?"

"Nothing useful to me. But we've got two or three Principatés underfoot all the time. Having more fun than we were."

Anna said, "I heard you arrested some people."

"Sure. There's always bad people dumb enough to tell you their real names. With the Man in Black standing right behind you."

The Man in Black, the public executioner, was not missing many meals for lack of work. Folks who behaved badly were being hunted vigorously.

Ghort's men wanted to seem useful.

Ghort moved a piece. Anna wasted no time. "Check."

Ghort tipped his king. "I know when I'm outclassed. What do you figure is going on, Pipe? Besides me getting my ass whipped again, here."

"Where? When? Who?"

"All good questions, Pipe. I mean here, in Brothe. Ain't all these riots something less than spontaneous?"

"You think? My gut says you can thank Ferris Renfrow. But I'm not sure we ought to trust my gut."

"Uhm. I can think of a couple people who'd get more out of civil unrest here."

"That Duke out there in the Connec?"

"Absolutely."

"Not his style. He'll just wait for Sublime to die."

Anna asked, "Is that why they call him the Great Vacillator?"

"It is. I'd look at Immaculate first."

"No. Not Immaculate," Ghort said. "But maybe somebody in Viscesment who thinks that's the way Immaculate would want it if only he had enough goddamn sense. And don't write off the Connec just because of Duke Tormond. He ain't hardly in charge out there no more. That Count Raymone in Antieux, the one that squashed Haiden Backe, he's getting tough with them Society monks Sublime keeps sending."

Hecht scowled. Pinkus had better intelligence than he did. "I don't like the sound of that. Sublime might want me to go protect them. And won't believe me when I tell him I can't do it."

Anna asked, "What makes you think the riots are being provoked?"

Ghort said, "They're always drunk. Somebody keeps filling them up with wine, then giving them reasons to be mad. The wine costs money. The bullshit is cheaper than air."

"You can't claim they don't already have reasons, can you?"

"Sure, I can. They didn't need to come here without no prospects. Don't nobody here owe them nothing."

"You and Piper came here with no more prospects."

Which was true in Ghort's case. "We didn't expect nobody to give us nothing, though."

Anna rose. "Pella. Vali. Go get dinner started." She made little use of hired help, now. There were too many secrets around. "You may be rounding up a few bad men, Pinkus, but people are still worried about mystery men and night stalkers who chop out people's livers."

"There hasn't been another killing."

"Not the point. There will be. And you know it. You're catching common criminals. The real evil is laughing at you."

Hecht interjected, "That's hardly kind. Even Principaté Delari says Pinkus is working miracles with half a kit of flawed tools. A remedy for that might be on the way, Pinkus, but I can't tell you about it yet. We have to get Sublime's go-ahead."

Anna snapped, "And Delari has been doing so good? He may be the great bull ape of the Collegium, but I notice that even him and his cronies have only slowed down whatever it is out there."

"She's got that right, Pipe. There ain't no concrete proof, but I'm pretty sure all we've managed is to chase him, or it, farther underground."

Hecht knew. Delari was unhappy about it, too. In the extreme. And, after a fruitless winter, was beginning to worry. Saying just what Ghort had.

In a city teeming with refugees it was impossible even to guess how many people were disappearing. Or why.

There were people willing to buy bodies, living and freshly dead. And others willing to supply them.

"It's almost . . . It's like there's another one of those bogon monsters. Here. A clever one. Historically, they haven't done a good job avoiding people."

"Not a bogon," Ghort countered. "Not possible. That would be something the Collegium can handle. It's what they were created for."

More or less. Though it was now the senate of the Church, the consistory of its high priests, in pagan times the Collegium had been a parliament of sorcerers created to beat back the Instrumentalities of the Night.

"That was then. They're mostly hacks today."

"Then maybe it's time to call in the Special Office."

Hecht did not say so, but the Special Office was involved already. He was not supposed to know. But he had recognized several faces amongst recent visitors to the Chiaro Palace. One was the man who had given him the courier wallet to take to Sonsa.

Muniero Delari was not happy. He loathed the Special Office. He hated Witchfinders. He had little love for the Brotherhood as a whole. He blamed them for the death of his only son.

"We don't want to have to deal with that. They're too powerful already."

"And getting more powerful fast," Anna said. "Rumor says the top Witchfinders have come over from the Castella Anjela dolla Picolena. They want to take control of the Society for the Suppression of Heresy and Sacrilege."

Hecht said, "It does look that way. And it's making a lot of people unhappy."

Everyone in the Church, excepting the Brotherhood of War, were certain that the Brotherhood enjoyed too much power and influence already. The Brotherhood believed it ought to rule a Church Militant. A Church far more aggressive toward Unbelievers and the Instrumentalities of the Night. Honario Benedocto's commitment was too feeble for them.

Pella announced, "There's food, people."

"I swear," Anna grumbled, "I can't teach him manners at knife point."

"He does fine in public," Ghort said.

"Kind of like you," said Hecht.

"A lot like me. I'm slick as a weasel when I got a audience. The lad must be my spiritual offspring."

Anna said, "He doesn't tell as many tall tales."

"Give him time. He's only a kid. So what's on the table, Pella?"

"Lamb pie. Piper always wants mutton something whenever he's here. Like he was a Deve, or something."

"I just like mutton. And you don't get it around here much." He started to pull a seat away from Anna's low dining table.

The world began to shake.

"What the hell?"

"Earthquake!" Anna squealed.

Pella's jaw dropped. Nothing came out of his mouth. Vali shrieked, the first sound Hecht ever heard from her. She flung herself at Anna, buried herself in the woman's skirts. Terrified.

"I don't think it's a quake," Ghort gasped. "It's going on way too long." The earth did go on shaking. A deep-throated, distant, ongoing roar, punctuated by screams, came from outside.

"I don't think so, either," Hecht said. He was aware of no historical instance of an earthquake in Brothe. He headed for the front door.

Anna barked, "You don't want to go out there!"

The racket outside suggested rising panic.

Something fell in the kitchen.

"I want to see . . ."

"Every one of those idiots will expect you to know what's happening. And what to do about it."

The woman might have a point. She knew her neighbors. "You check it out, then. I'll see what happened in the kitchen."

Anna went outside. The kids followed her, too quick and elusive to be stayed.

Ghort said, "We're gonna got to go out there anyhow, Pipe. 'Cause whatever that is, it's big and it's our job to get in the middle of it."

PINKUS GHORT WAS NOT PSYCHIC. ANYONE ABLE TO WALK AND TALK AT THE same time could have made that call. They had made themselves critical cogs in the Brothen machine.

They got away without attracting attention. People were all focused on a vast, thick, dense boiling cloud rising to the north-northwest.

"What the hell?" Ghort muttered, awed.

"That doesn't look like smoke." But Hecht could not imagine how so much dust could be thrown up.

The ground still trembled occasionally, but no longer continuously. Lightning crackled inside the roiling gray cloud.

"Sorcery," Ghort murmured. "I've never seen lightning with that greenish tint."

"I'm getting a bad feeling, Pinkus."

The lightning flashed more emphatically. The cloud lit up from inside, a flickering lilac glow that waxed and waned like a slow heartbeat. Thunder burped.

"That's got to be up by the hippodrome, Pipe. Maybe the part they're working on fell down."

The racing stadium was fourteen hundred years old. In ancient times it had been the scene of gladiatorial contests and other blood games. Renovations had been under way since the close of the autumn racing season because a small collapse had taken place during the pounding excitement of a late-season chariot race featuring champions from Firaldian cities against several from the Eastern Empire.

"It'd have to be a big part."

They were afoot, pushing upstream against a current of fugitives whose panicky reports made no sense.

The lightning in the cloud grew more excited. The cloud itself was ferociously active but contained. It was not spreading. It did rise higher with every flash. The waxing/waning light sent glowing globs climbing the vast trunk, fading as they slowed.

"It's definitely dust," Hecht said. "I can smell it already."

"Maybe we better not get any closer, then. That much stuff could drown you without water."

Particularly vicious lightning ripped through the cloud. And sustained itself.

The cloud burst.

"Shit! Look at that!"

The cloud collapsed. Moments later a churning flood swept around a turn a quarter mile ahead. It charged them faster than a man could run. Ghort swore. "Aaron's Hairy Balls!"

Hecht hoisted his shirt over his face, almost panicky.

Ghort pulled him into a tenement doorway a moment before the flood arrived. Ghort pounded on the door. "City Regiment! Emergency! Open up!"

To Hecht's amazement, that worked. A stooped crone stared at them from behind a preteen boy armed with a broken board. Her cataracted eyes were open amazingly wide.

"We ain't spooks, Granny. Get your ass in there, Pipe! You want to drown in this shit?"

Ghort slammed the door. Dust swirled in through cracks. Ghort brushed himself off enough to reveal his City Regiment officer's jacket. Which he wore mostly because of the perks it could command.

The boy recognized him. "It's the Commandant his own self, Nana. Really."

The old woman remained suspicious. Which seemed a sound strategy to Hecht.

Ghort told her, "Don't open up again before the dust settles. It'll choke you right now. Boy, is there any way to reach the roof from inside?" The tenement stood four stories tall.

The boy said, "Follow me, Commandant."

Hecht raised an eyebrow. Ghort had the title but nobody used it. Strange as it might sound, this looked like a case of hero worship.

Disturbing thought.

The roof did raise them above the worst of the dust. But did them no good when it came to betraying the source of the dust.

The boy chattered away. He had followed Ghort's career. He wanted to be a regular city soldier when he grew up.

Hecht shook his head and tried to discover the source of the dust. He could see nothing but a sinking, flattening dome of gray that hid the city immediately north. The high points of Krois, the Castella, the Chiaro Palace, various obelisks in the Memorium, distant hills, and so forth could just be distinguished beyond.

"It was the hippodrome," Hecht guessed. "But how?"

"Sorcery."

IT WAS THE HIPPODROME. AND MORE. AS GHORT AND HECHT DISCOVERED after the dust subsided enough to let them approach the scene of the disaster.

"Sorcery," Ghort said again, looking down into the vast hole full of rubble that had swallowed the racing stadium.

"Sorcery," Hecht agreed. He would rather have blamed the collapse on time and failure of strength in the catacombs below, but had seen what he had seen earlier.

"Ever see anything like this?"

"Never." And, as an afterthought, "You were there every time I've ever had any run-in with the things of the Night."

"Hey! Don't go blaming it on me."

"This is probably something you should handle." Some of Ghort's soldiers were there already, standing around looking dazed. Along with hundreds of gawkers. "We don't want a lot of people getting hurt."

"Too late for that, Pipe. There's gonna be plenty of bodies in that mess, you can bet." Looking down into the pit.

No doubt. Craftsmen would have been doing renovations. And there were always squatters hiding in the great stadium.

Hecht could see corpses and parts of corpses already. "There may be survivors down there, too, Pinkus. You get to it. I'll muster my troops and send them over to help."

There was a brilliant flash beneath the rubble. Crackling, muted thunder followed. Then the earth shifted.

They retreated. The pavements where they had stood tilted, slowly slid into the pit. On the far side the last surviving wall of the hippodrome sank majestically into the earth. More dust roared up, less dense than before. A breeze from the south pushed it away from Hecht and Ghort. "Later," Hecht said. "And be careful."

"Careful is my new family name. You see anything around here worth stealing?"

"Huh?"

"I'm thinking my guys might have to worry more about looters than rescue and cleanup."

Hecht grunted agreement, then headed for the Castella.

HECHT FOUND HIS STAFF IN PLACE, AT WORK, WHEN HE ENTERED THE SUITE provided by the Brotherhood. "Have you all heard what's happened?"

"Some kind of disaster," Colonel Smolens said. "I sent people out to investigate. So did the Brothers."

"A disaster. Yes. The hippodrome fell down. Because the catacombs caved in. Sorcery was involved. I saw it happening. It's a huge mess. I expect we'll need to help keep order."

Everyone asked questions at once.

"That's all I know. Except that there'll be casualties. Call out the soldiers. Assemble them in the Closed Ground. Weapons and kit. Do we have enough messengers?"

"We can borrow from the Brotherhood. They've got a lot of extra mouths around here lately."

"Good. Go. Titus. Who owns the hippodrome?"

"The Church. Why?"

"That's what I thought. Meaning the Church will have to clean up and rebuild."

"Sir?"

"If Sublime has to do that, he'll have less to invest in us and his ambitions."

"Oh. My. Are you talking about sabotage? A scheme to disarm Sublime?"

"No. We know people who are ruthless enough. But not smart enough to recognize the opportunity. Actually, I think the disaster could be the by-product of something much darker."

Everyone stopped work and turned.

"The sorcery involved was huge. You won't believe the eyewitnesses."

HECHT, WITH TITUS CONSENT IN TOW, WENT TO REVIEW THE TROOPS. THE few seemed lost in the expanse of the Closed Ground. Colonel Smolens reported, "This is all we could pull together. So far."

Hecht guessed he was looking at a hundred twenty men. "Something we'll have to work on."

"Sir?" Consent asked.

"Responding to the unexpected more quickly."

Colonel Smolens observed, "They'll come as soon as they get the word. We need a signal. A horn, maybe."

Hecht grunted. The slow response was his fault. He had not wanted his married soldiers living separate from their families. He had suffered too much of that when he was Sha-lug. The trouble with the horn notion was that the city was too big.

Titus Consent said, "Company coming. Looks like Principaté Doneto."

Doneto, Donel Madisetti, and several lesser lights of the Collegium. Doneto demanded, "What are you doing, Captain-General?"

"Assembling my troops in order to help keep public order around the collapse."

It would be dark soon. The looters would bloom by moonlight.

"Admirable," Doneto said. "Exactly the responsible sort of action we expect of you, Captain-General. But I have to change your plans."

"Sir?" Insanity. The Brothen people would be outraged if the Church did nothing. Loving Mother Church with her infinite charity.

Principaté Doneto did one of those disconcerting mind-reading tricks Collegium sorts enjoyed so much. "We won't deliberately withhold assistance, Captain-General." He jerked his head sideways. He wanted a private word.

Hecht joined him. "Sir?"

"There's an uprising coming tonight. Possibly connected to what happened at the hippodrome."

"There hasn't been much disorder since Colonel Ghort got aggressive."

"A change of strategy by those who would misbehave, I expect."

"What am I supposed to do?"

"Back up the Palace guard. The mob is supposed to hit us here."

Principaté Doneto was an accomplished liar, hard to read. But Hecht thought he was being sincere but not entirely forthcoming. "This is what His Holiness wants?"

"Desperately."

Oh? The response suggested some special interest by the Patriarch's cousin.

Men continued to assemble. Smolens and the staff kept order while Hecht conferred with Doneto. The Drumm brothers arrived filthy, sweaty, and minus their tunics. The elder, gasping, reported, "There's a huge mob in the Memorium, sir. They chased us. Because of our uniforms. We almost didn't get away."

The mob could be heard outside, getting louder.

The Chiaro Palace had been built at the height of the Old Brothen Empire, when the frontiers were a thousand miles away and whole legions quartered in the city, capable of suppressing disorder instantly. There had been no need to make the Palace defensible. A bastion of bureaucracy, it remained untouched during even the ferocious Imperial civil wars.

Whoever crowned himself Emperor needed the tax rolls and a means of extorting money from the citizenry.

THE MOB POURED INTO THE CLOSED GROUND. BROTHENS HAD BEEN ACcustomed to do so for two score generations. These pilgrims were drunk. Some carried torches. Weapons were makeshift, cudgels, bricks, tools, knives, and, rarely, a rusty keepsake military sword purloined by an ancestor.

"Looks like mainly refugees," Titus Consent told Hecht. "I've heard several languages already that aren't native to Firaldia.

"They don't seem eager for a confrontation, though."

Some sobering up was taking place out there.

Someone whose job it was to stir trouble threw a stone. Hecht told his staff, "I don't want anyone doing anything unless they actually break in. They'll go home if they just stand around long enough for their heads to start hurting."

Voices exhorted the mob. It was not necessary to understand to get the gist.

Hecht said, "They'll be too tired and hungover to become obnoxious if we don't respond."

Captain-General Piper Hecht's Patriarchal soldiers were combat veterans. He was able to cherry-pick the very best available. Having seen the elephant up close and smelled her foul breath, his men were not eager for a bloodletting contest.

The Palace guards did not suffer a comparable level of basic sense.

"That damned fool will get us all killed," Colonel Smolens said, indicating a guard officer who was headed out with three uniformed footmen.

"Must think the livery makes him invulnerable," Hecht said. "Principaté Doneto, how about you . . . Where did he go?" Doneto, Madisetti, and the others had vanished. "Doneto could have ordered him back." He could not. He might be Captain-General but there were a thousand exceptions to his being in charge.

Titus Consent observed, "They might deal with him too fast to get the mob fired up. Here! What are you doing?"

Hecht had started to go out. Consent's outburst stopped him.

A waving torch had revealed two familiar faces. One belonged to Pinkus Ghort's man Bo Biogna. Biogna would be right at home in a seditious mob, identifying ringleaders. It was the man next to Bo whose appearance froze Hecht's heart.

He was a little older, a little grayer, showed a hitherto unsuspected bald spot, and was less enthusiastically bearded, but there was no doubt. Hecht would know Bone anywhere, if all that was left was his skeleton. Bo and Bone. Bone and his bones. What the hell was Bone doing on this side of the Mother Sea? Let alone being here, in the front rank of a mob quickly losing all enthusiasm for an assault on the beating heart of western religion?

Hagid.

There must be a connection.

Bone, known by no other name insofar as Hecht knew, had been the leading sergeant in the special company commanded by the Sha-lug captain, Else Tage.

"Sir?"

"Bechter. There you are."

Sergeant Bechter had been forced to take a long way around. Accompanying him were the newly minted Bruglioni Principaté, Gervase Saluda, and old Hugo Mongoz. Principaté Mongoz appeared to be having a good day. Hecht told Saluda, "Congratulations. Finally." Paludan Bruglioni, the chieftain of the Bruglioni family, had nominated Saluda long ago, after Principaté Divino Bruglioni had been discovered dead on the battlefield outside al-Khazan, scant hours before the conclusion of the Calziran Crusade.

There had been fierce opposition to Saluda. The man had not been inside a church since his christening. He had no supernatural talents. He was a strong personality. He was dedicated to the Bruglioni family fortunes. And, from Hecht's point of view, he was dangerously smart. He had held the Bruglioni together for the last ten years.

"The right always triumphs," Saluda replied, in a sarcastic tone. He was amoral, and cynical in the extreme.

"Pardon me. We have a situation here."

More than one, possibly. Osa Stile materialized back in the shadows, behind the soldiers. The catamite tried to get Hecht's attention.

Studying the crowd again, Hecht could not find Bone or Bo Biogna. The mob was dispersing, the provocateurs first to go. Those who stayed were content to taunt the Palace guards.

Hecht shuddered suddenly.

"Sergeant Bechter."

"Sir?"

"To the left, there. In the second rank. Behind the guy with the huge beard. Wearing brown."

"Got him, sir. That's the man I've been talking about. And I got the chill a minute ago."

"Cloven Februaren," Hugo Mongoz said, peering between Hecht and Bechter, hanging on to their shoulders, leaning forward and squinting. "That would be Cloven Februaren. No doubt about it. The Ninth Unknown himself."

Only Hecht understood. "The Ninth Unknown, Your Grace? But he's been dead for fifty years."

"Yes," the old man said, musingly. "He should have been. So you'd think." Mongoz looked resentful for a moment, then a shadow stirred behind his eyes. He slumped, his grip weakening. Hecht and Bechter caught his arms. He turned panicky, suddenly lost.

Gervase Saluda said, "Let me take him, Captain-General. Biggio. A hand, if you will."

The quick change was a dramatic reminder of human frailty. Hecht said, "Sergeant Bechter. Where's the man in brown?" Ninth Unknown or mundane rioter, he was gone.

Hecht nodded to Osa Stile, to let the catamite know he had been seen. He was being ignored only because of the more pressing situation.

It would be important, though. Osa did not appear in public without his protector.

The new Bruglioni Principaté, about to depart with Principaté Mongoz, said, "I need a few minutes in private when you get time, Captain-General. A family matter. Of some importance to Paludan."

"Of course. Sergeant Bechter can work out something that fits our schedules." In the Name of God, the All-Knowing and Merciful! What was this? He could not have imagined himself saying that a year ago. "Bechter?"

"I understand, sir."

Hecht moved to check the situation in the Closed Ground. "That idiot will talk himself into thinking he's a hero."

The mob was a third of what it had been. The deadenders had a tail-between-the-knees look and were hanging on mostly because they did not want to desert the friends with whom they had come.

Hecht remarked, "The professional agitators have taken off. Nothing but inertia keeping it going now. It's over unless somebody suffers a last-second stroke of idiocy. People. Gather round. Let's make *sure* there's no plague of stupidity. Feel free to deal with anybody, even on our side."

Colonel Smolens asked, "You won't be here?"

"I won't. I have another problem that needs immediate attention."

"Sir?"

He did not explain. "Once those morons clear out take the troops to the hippodrome to help Colonel Ghort."

"Yes, sir."

Hecht glanced around. The Mongoz party had gone. He was the senior man present. He could do what he wanted.

He wanted to find the catamite.

"ARMAND." HECHT OVERTOOK THE BOY HALFWAY TO PRINCIPATÉ DELARI'S Palace apartment. The catamite beckoned and increased his pace. He wanted to be inside the safety of the Principaté's apartment when he talked.

"What is it?" Hecht asked as soon as it was safe. Osa was too professional to take a risk unless there was a greater risk in not acting.

"He's trapped down there."

"What? Who? Start at the beginning."

"The Principaté. Our Principaté. Delari. He's down in the catacombs. He was supposed to come back a long time ago."

"You're still not at the beginning. Did he have anything to do with the cave-in at the hippodrome?"

Osa was puzzled. "What cave-in?"

"The catacombs under the hippodrome collapsed. The stadium fell into the hole. It's a huge mess. A lot of people got killed."

Osa turned pale. "I thought it was just another riot. We have to do something."

Hecht ground his teeth. "He's really down there?"

The boy nodded.

"Oh, damn! That is bad. We need that old man to get by. You and me both. You're absolutely sure?"

"He went this morning. He got up way early. He said he'd figured out how to deal with what was down there. Whatever that meant. He doesn't tell me nearly as much as you think. He left right after breakfast. Whistling. Said he should be back in time for a late lunch."

Hecht considered his options. And saw only one. Get Delari out.

Osa said, "I'm going, too." Before Hecht could demur, he whispered, "I am Sha-lug."

He was. Yes. Before all else. And from the Vibrant Spring School.

"All right. Wear something that doesn't make you look like a whore."

"I'll go change."

Osa did so. And looked nothing like the rouged, perfumed bed bunny who shared Muniero Delari's nights. Nor did he smell like it.

This Osa would have no trouble fading into the Brothen mob. His threadbare apparel suggested that he did so occasionally.

Osa smiled. "Part of the job, Captain. You know where we have to go. Lead on."

Hecht wondered if Stile was taking the opportunity to unearth secrets never shared by his keeper.

THEY ENCOUNTERED TRACES OF GRAY DUST AS THEY APPROACHED THE baths. Inside, the staff were cleaning everything and skimming the pools.

Herrin intercepted them. "It blew in from back where nobody is supposed to go," she explained. "Along with a lot of cold, stinky air. We can't bathe you today."

"Not a problem. We're just passing through."

Herrin's eyes widened.

"We're going back where nobody is supposed to go."

"Be careful, sir. Something's really wrong there."

THE MAP ROOM WAS A DISASTER. THE DUST HAD NOT YET ALL SETTLED there.

Osa asked, "What is this place?"

"You don't need to know. Don't ask questions."

The priests and nuns had begun a halfhearted cleanup. Some just sat or stood, eyes glazed over. One sitting woman rocked steadily, hiding out in her own secret universe.

One senior priest intercepted Hecht. He spoke slowly, coughed a lot, and sniffled continuously. "You going after the Unknown?"

"Yes."

The priest hacked. "He went through the Old Door. He hasn't come back. We need his direction. This is a disaster. Three brothers didn't survive."

Not good. Hecht said, "We'll find him. Meantime, do what he'd want done."

"But . . ."

"What more, brother? Look around. What needs doing?" Hecht remained perpetually amazed that so many people would not pick up a stick unless somebody told them to do it. "You're in charge. Get to work." He pulled Osa along.

He could not make the speed he wanted. Hurrying raised dust, made breathing a pain. Breathing through cloth helped a little.

Hecht repeated the lamp instructions he had gotten from Principaté Delari. "I've only done this once." He ought to be alone this time. Osa Stile did not need to know about the underworld. "The Principaté was adamant about these lamps. I'm sure he knew what he was talking about. We almost ran into something that had *him* shaking."

"Probably what he came down here hunting, then."

"What did he tell you?" Hecht examined the massive door. It had been left unbolted. Naturally. Delari wanted to come back through. A huge wind, carrying tons of dust, had blasted it wide open. It had not closed all the way again.

"Almost nothing. I couldn't work him for anything he didn't want to talk about."

"Did he suspect you?"

"No. It just wasn't any of my business."

"Ah?"

"I've been less effective with Delari than you think. The association is useful, though. It opens doors." He grinned his winning grin.

"Let's go. Slowly. This dust may be dangerous." Slowly was mandatory. Just stumbling on tricky footing raised choking clouds.

"This probably isn't the smart way to do this," Hecht said. But did not turn back.

He was surprised that he had so much emotion invested in Principaté Delari.

Avoiding deep breathing, Osa asked, "What was that place? With the old priests and nuns."

"Ask Delari. He'll tell you if he wants you to know."

"You going to keep it from our masters in al-Qarn?"

"My masters in al-Qarn have abandoned me, brother."

"I don't understand."

"Neither do I. But since I left Dreanger there have been at least seven attempts to kill me. Those that I could trace all led back to the Rascal."

Osa stopped. By lamplight his wide eyes were strange, almost inhuman. "Truth?"

"Truth. And I can't get my questions or messages through to Gordimer. So how can I help thinking that I've been discarded? That I keep on breaking hearts by not lying down to die?"

"But . . ." Osa Stile shook his head. He seemed baffled.

"There's something bigger than me going on, too." He told Osa about Hagid's brutal murder. And that he had seen Bone in the Closed Ground only a few hours earlier.

"Hagid? Nassim Alizarin's son?"

"The same."

"That's definitely a major mystery."

"You really think?"

"Sarcasm isn't necessary. That news could cause a major power shift back home. Nassim Alizarin al-Jebal had his whole soul wrapped up in his son. He hoped Hagid would become the next Marshal of the Sha-lug."

"Knowing that, I feel more lost. There's no way the Mountain would have sent Hagid to Calzir with the whole Chaldarean west swarming over the kingdom."

"Calzir?"

"I saw some of my old company in al-Khazen. My guess is, they weren't able to escape with the other Sha-lug and Lucidians."

They were approaching the great underground cathedral. Something crashed in the darkness ahead. Rubble surrendering to the blandishments of gravity? Or something stirring?

Both men shut up. Talking was dangerous. Who might be listening? *What* might be? The Night itself might be eavesdropping down here.

"It gets lonely," Osa said. He said nothing more and did not need to. Hecht understood perfectly.

And Osa had been this side of the Mother Sea longer than he had.

HECHT HAD ASSUMED THE COLLAPSE HAD BEEN INTO THE SUBTERRANEAN cathedral. There could be no other voids that huge under Brothe. Could there?

Must be.

Moonlight leaked into the hall through a new gap in the overhead. Rubble lay scattered across the vast tiled floor. Bones were everywhere. A dense animal musk overlaid the odor of ancient death and modern sewage. Hecht's earlier visit had not prepared him for what he could see even by the scant light of a partial moon.

Osa murmured, "Where did all the bones come from?"

"Ancient times. Brothe used to be a lot bigger. The early Chaldareans brought their dead down here. For centuries."

"Some of them had some pretty weird bones." Osa pointed at bones that were humanoid but unlike the rest. "This can't be the right place."

"Yes." Hecht stared at a clot of darkness. It had been just about there that he had sensed the something awful before. He felt nothing, now.

His amulet offered no warning. It was never inactive in the Chiaro Palace. He no longer noticed that low-level tickle.

Osa said, "We headed away from the hippodrome when we took that second turn. We should've gone the other way."

"How could you know that? You've never been down here."

"True. This is all folklore to me. But I have a perfect sense of direction."

"Oh?" Something to keep in mind. "Lead on, then."

Osa did so, returning to the cross passage where, he believed, they had gone astray. "The dust gets worse going this way."

That dust made breathing miserable. The lanterns had trouble reaching far ahead. Hecht's amulet remained quiescent, but—

He pointed, directing the strongest lamplight.

Footprints. People had passed this way.

"You good on fuel, Osa?"

"I'm fine." Whispering. Following the tracks.

"Shall I take point?"

"I'm all right. I'll bite them in the balls."

Hecht let it ride. For the moment. He did draw the short sword that served as a mark of his status. It was not much of a weapon. But it was the tool he had.

His amulet began to respond to the proximity of power. Feebly. "Stop," he whispered.

Osa froze.

"Where would we be if we were upstairs?"

"At a guess, roughly, somewhere just north of the hippodrome. Within a few hundred yards."

A squeaky creak came from up ahead. It sounded like a huge stone sliding across other stone.

Hecht focused on his amulet.

No change there.

"What?" Osa asked.

"I'm listening." True at a figurative level.

Principaté Delari had come down here hunting something big and wicked. Something at least as terrible as a bogon. Maybe something darker, considering his fear last time around.

That power would be wide awake and angry if Delari had stirred it up.

"I'm point, now. I insist." Hecht eased past Stile. And wished he had a falcon rolling along behind, charged with silver and iron. "Oh."

"What?"

"Something just occurred to me. Something I knew without fully understanding what it meant. I'm going to follow these tracks."

He did so slowly. The stone sound came again. A chill crawled his spine. His amulet responded mildly. There was something there, but . . . They came to a pile of rubble, loose stone from the passage wall. Ages passed. The advance grew slower and slower. The dust became as much as an inch deep. Then, in a few yards, almost vanished, all blown outward.

Hecht spied a glimmer, a sliver of silvery light. It proved to be a spot of moonlight, come through a small gap high overhead. Rubble nearly blocked his path. A chamber lay beyond, dimensions indeterminate because of the collapse and lack of sufficient light.

"Obviously not the main cave-in," Osa said.

"No. We'll need to make a huge effort to find all the places like this. Otherwise, the city will keep falling in under us."

"Principaté Delari," Osa said. To keep him on task.

"Yes." He was tired. It was past his bedtime.

He was getting old. And soft.

Life in the west was damnably seductive.

He heard that noise again. Closer. "What does that sound like?"

"Stone on stone. Or the lids of those big terra-cotta jars for grain storage."

"You're right. That does sound like one of those being dragged off the mouth of a jar." Those huge pottery containers forestalled mice and rats.

"Sshh." Hecht heard voices.

"I hear them." In a breathless soldier's whisper.

Hecht adjusted the shutter on his lantern till it shed almost no light. Osa did the same.

Hecht went on, thinking that he must have an affinity for the world underground. Here, now. Al-Khazen, during the Calziran Crusade. And Andesqueluz. That had been terrible. Despite there having been no living thing inside the holy mountain of the extinct cult.

His amulet tickled him as the terra-cotta on stone sound recurred.

The rattle of a small rubble slide followed.

"My point," Osa breathed. "I'm shorter."

Hecht yielded. Light flickered ahead, limning hip-high flows of rubble. Those had washed into what resembled a deep mine where large blocks of material had been left to support the earth overhead. There was almost no dust here. The little still in the air gave the light a pumpkin hue.

The voices were clearer but no words stood out. Hecht decided he was hearing a foreign language. Two men were arguing. A third added a tired whine while a fourth rambled through a "Why me?" soliloquy.

What were they doing? They could be up to no good. Not down here.

Osa stopped him with a touch. The boy set his lantern down, crept forward.

Hecht breathed hard, heart hammering. He sweated. His exposed skin grew muddy.

Stile had not lost his Sha-lug skills. Which meant there was hope for a Sha-lug captain seduced by western decadence.

Osa sank down behind a rubble sprawl. Hecht joined him, looked at six men on what might have been a tiled floor as expansive as that of the underground cathedral. Most of which was now buried. All six wore monk's robes. Their hoods were up and their faces were concealed by cloth—because of the dust, not any desire to be sinister. Though that effect resulted.

The argument continued between two of the six. Another two kicked in randomly while a silent pair stood on the far edge of the light cast by six earthenware lamps. Those two seemed obsessively intent on something in the darkness beyond them.

Now that he could hear them clearly Hecht felt he ought to be able to understand what was being said. He had heard that language before.

He thought he should know the voices, too.

The grinding returned. It came from beyond the silent watchers. Grumbling, the whole band surged that way, into the darkness.

"I don't understand," Hecht breathed to Osa. "I don't like this."

"They have a prisoner. It keeps trying to get away. They're waiting for instructions. They've sent two messengers. There's been no answer. The argument is over whether to send another."

"You understand them?"

"They're speaking a Creveldian dialect. Hard to follow but what they're saying is pretty basic. They can't go but they're afraid of what will happen if they stay."

Another heavy groan of terra-cotta.

Osa finished, "They're Witchfinders. And they've caught something that won't let them go."

The two who entertained themselves arguing returned to the light. Which was like none Hecht had seen before. It was not just the dust that made the lamps burn an odd color.

They must do the same work as Principaté Delari's lanterns.

And the more so when one Witchfinder removed his face covering to clear his nose by blocking one nostril while blowing through the other.

He was the man who had given Hecht dispatches for Sonsa when he and Ghort were about to sneak out of Brothe.

Osa squeezed his left arm fiercely, cautioning him against sudden movement.

Time passed.

The argument resumed. The whiners became more involved. They were all tired and thirsty and hungry. And nothing useful was happening.

Hecht did not need to speak the language. He had been a soldier all his life.

What to do? There was no obvious way to bypass this bottleneck. This was a fool's errand. They had no plan and no intelligence. Pure storyteller's heroic nonsense.

The argument peaked in a furious exchange.

One of the silent pair threw his hands up, frustrated, then stamped away into the darkness. The others did not catch on immediately. Then the argument became much more heated.

Osa breathed, "These five believe that six Witchfinders is the minimum needed to control it."

"It?"

Stile shrugged. "Or him. Those two want to get out of here while they still can without being recognized."

Hecht now caught the occasional phrase. He could not disagree with the catamite's interpretation.

He did not like being at the mercy of someone he trusted so little.

He smiled. Chances were, Osa did not like being at the mercy of Piper Hecht, either.

Earthenware ground against stone. The Witchfinders shut up. The one Hecht had identified took charge.

The sound grew louder and more malignant. The Witchfinders reacted with the speed of those who knew they had just one desperate chance. To the sound. Fearfully. As a babble of Old Brothen echoed all round.

For an instant Hecht thought his left hand was being ripped off his wrist.

"What?" Osa asked, startled.

"Smacked my knuckles against a rock." He had, in fact, done just that, responding to the sudden pain.

"That was dumb."

The pain faded to a throb, like a wound an hour old. Hecht had lived with that before.

Shouts of anger and fear. Groan of terra-cotta ground against stone. Shouts of triumph. Hecht's pain faded.

Osa had been about to cross the lighted area when the self-congratulations started. He dove back into shadow just in time. Two Witchfinders supported a third who was unable to work his legs. They settled in the center of the light.

The injured man passed out as soon as his associates set him down. One said something like, "We've got to get out of here! We just used up our luck."

The last two men stumbled into the light.

The Witchfinder in charge gave orders. Three men hurried back into the darkness. They began making noise.

The senior Witchfinder opened his unconscious associate's robe. The man wore little underneath. Hecht saw no obvious wounds or traumas.

"They're piling stones onto something so it can't move," Osa said.

One of the three leapt back into the light, babbling.

Osa translated: "The other two just ran away. He wants this guy to haul ass with him. This guy says they can't leave their buddy behind."

Hecht breathed, "Maybe we shouldn't be here, either."

Nobody got the chance to run.

The terra-cotta grind had a triumphant ring. The Witchfinders grabbed their unconscious comrade . . .

Stone flew.

Hecht and Stile embraced the cracked tile floor. Stones up to the size of a fist hurtled around, smashing into rubble and pillars. All three Witchfinders got hit.

The air filled with dust. Hecht's eyes began drying out. He fought down a sneeze. Osa did sneeze, then blew his nose desperately, but only Hecht noticed. The Witchfinders had been pounded into unconsciousness.

A little voice called, "Help." It seemed familiar.

None of the lamps suffered till the final moment of the stone storm. Then one shattered, scattering burning oil in a spray eight feet long. One Witchfinder caught fire. He leapt up and took off blindly, screaming.

"Help!" A little louder. Followed by a weak terra-cotta grind and a rattle of disturbed rubble.

Osa blurted, "That sounded like the Principaté!"

Hecht thought so, too, but was suspicious of anything that happened easily.

"This is easy?" Stile asked.

"We'll check it out." Easy or not. "But there're men out there that we don't want to see us."

"Cut their throats."

"Let's see if we can't find something less savage and final."

"They're Brotherhood of War. Special Office. The worst of the worst."

"We aren't in the Holy Lands. Our work isn't tactical. Let the Principaté decide what to do. If we find him."

"Help!" Louder, now.

"He knows we're here."

"Get busy."

Stile produced a wicked little knife with a slight bend at its end. He sliced strips from the cassock of the man who had handed Hecht that courier wallet, back when.

"Yes. Him first.. He's the dangerous one."

Both men recovered during the binding. Hecht was not pleased. But he stuck to his decision to leave them to the mercy of Principaté Delari.

His left wrist ached.

A HALF-DOZEN GRAIN JARS HAD BEEN SET INTO THE FLOOR. THREE WERE occupied by corpses. They had not been dead long. Another held Principaté Muniero Delari. Its lid lay at an angle in the opening. Tumbled blocks lay scattered all round. The lid made that characteristic groan as they dragged it aside.

The old man was weak but in good spirits and game.

"Looks like there's been some sorcery here," Osa said. "They used no sorcery themselves, though. They just tried to keep the lid on."

Hecht hoisted the old man. "Thank you," Delari breathed. "I thought I'd made a fatal mistake this time. How did you find me?"

"Chance and reason. Armand knew you'd gone hunting down here. I guessed that would be where the hippodrome fell down."

"Fell down?"

"Collapsed. Into a big hole in the ground."

"I thought some of the roof fell in when . . . Oh, drat! I miscalculated seriously, didn't I?"

"I don't know. What did you do?"

"I brought a keg of firepowder . . ." He coughed. "Laced with silver and iron pellets. It worked. The monster charged into the trap. I fired the powder. The explosion killed the thing."

Hecht sighed. The man was being disingenuous, to say the least.

Delari continued. "Firepowder is new to me. The explosion was more violent than I expected. I set the keg against a pillar so the force would all blow toward the monster."

"It doesn't work that way."

"So I found out."

"How did you get down in that hole?" Stile asked.

"They put me there. The servants of the beast. They found me unconscious and put me down there."

"The Witchfinders?"

"Witchfinders?"

"The men keeping you here were Special Office," Hecht said. "One of them was involved with what they were doing in Sonsa, too."

"Where are they now? How did you get past them?"

"We didn't."

Stile said, "Most of them ran away. We have two of them tied up."

"Take me there." The old man was coming back.

Even so, Hecht scooped Delari up and carried him to where the Witchfinders were trying to wriggle free.

"Put me down, Piper. Turn them around so I can look them in the eye. Ah! Gryphen Pledcyk." That was the man Hecht had met on the wharf. "Explain yourself."

Pledcyk avoided the old man's eye.

Osa said, "The rest claimed they were going for help."

"Let help come. In the form of the man behind this." Delari considered the other captive. "I don't recognize this one. Show me his bare back."

Hecht did as instructed. Delari grunted.

"Sir?"

"He has the tattoo. That means this is a Brotherhood operation."

The nameless man started to protest. He shut up as Pledcyk gave him an ugly look.

Delari said, "Kill Pledcyk. It'll take too long to break him. The other one will talk to save his own skin."

Hecht hesitated. Osa slid behind Pledcyk, grabbed the man's hair, yanked his head back. Pledcyk did not struggle.

Delari nodded.

Stile did it. Using that nasty little knife.

Hecht jumped, surprised.

No one was more surprised than Gryphen Pledcyk.

Delari asked the other, "Can you walk?"

The Witchfinder nodded, thoroughly cowed.

"Armand. Take him to my apartment. Kill him if he gives you any trouble. Don't attract attention. I'll question him after we clean up here."

Osa beckoned the captive. "Come."

Hecht asked, "Are you sure, sir?"

"You mean, can I handle this?"

"Exactly."

"I'll manage. But if I do run dry, carry me."

"If I can find the way."

Pledcyk continued to bleed out, his eyes filled with terror.

Hecht suspected the Principaté was making statements on several levels. Delari said, "I'll stay awake."

Hecht had nothing more to say. He watched Osa herd the captive into the darkness. And worried that Delari might not be as blind about the catamite as might be hoped.

"Was I too harsh, Piper?"

"About Pledcyk? I think so. Yes."

"He knew you were down here. His bunch shouldn't have been. There'd be no explaining why they threw me in that hole. Which I wasn't intended to survive."

"We found dead men in three of the others. I don't know who they were. Yes. I understand the rationale for killing Pledcyk. I'm a soldier. But he might have told us something interesting."

"He might have. Yes. That's sound soldier's thinking. But a sorcerer can follow other paths to the truth. A fact you should keep in mind. I'm going to nap, now. Wake me when company comes."

"Sir?"

The old man went out like a snuffed candle.

Hecht supposed he was right. Someone would come. If for no other reason than to get rid of the evidence.

The monster Delari claimed to have slain. What was it? Truly an Instrumentality of the Night? In Brothe? Why? How did it get here? Was it really responsible for all those horrible killings?

Whatever the facts, Delari had thought the danger sufficient that he had visited the catacombs personally to eliminate it.

HECHT JOSTLED THE PRINCIPATÉ. "SOMEONE COMING, SIR."

"Get out of sight. Jump in if it's too much for me to handle."

"You know who it'll be?"

"I have a suspicion. It's likely to get out of hand if you're seen. Go on!"

Hecht drifted back to where he and Osa had crouched earlier. He felt more positive once he reclaimed his lantern. Osa, he noted, had taken his.

Delari slumped, a man too exhausted to do anything but breathe.

Hecht crouched, lantern and blade ready, and hoped for the best. Those who were coming would not be starving refugees armed with rusty tools.

The first entered the light warily, weapon hand demonstratively empty. He considered Delari and Gryphen Pledcyk. He wore a cloth across his face to help with the dust.

Sudden concern. Tracks. They would point like an arrow . . . But something had erased them. The dust appeared undisturbed.

Delari had managed it with barely a tickle from Hecht's amulet.

A lesson? Certainly another point worth remembering.

A second man entered the light. Gryphen Pledcyk had more impact. Two more arrived, men who had fled earlier.

Principaté Delari transformed. A tired, slumping wreck of an ancient metamorphosed into a thing of power. He seemed taller than normal and much younger. His voice was stronger than ever Hecht had heard. "Come on into the light."

Nothing happened.

"Time to come in out of the darkness. You may not surrender to the Will of the Night."

Hecht felt a presence beyond the range of the lamps. And a man did come forward a moment later. Another Witchfinder who had fled earlier. He pretended Gryphen Pledcyk was invisible. He asked, "Where are Tomaz and Chollanzc?"

Delari gestured at the darkness. "Out there. You. There. Come in out of the darkness. It's not too late. The beast is dead. But another will come. Sooner or later, the Night will creep in. Come into the light. While you can."

Bronte Doneto stepped forward. He wore a monkish cassock like the others. He had his face covered. But Hecht recognized him even before he said, "You knew it was me."

"I suspected Honario, actually. No one else is so desperate to rewrite the world to conform to his own fantasies. Have *you* convinced yourself that you can manipulate the Instrumentalities of the Night with impunity?"

Doneto did not answer the question. "My cousin has a scheme. He'll destroy the Church before he's done."

"You surrender to the Will of the Night to rescue Mother Church from Sublime's insanity?"

How the devil had he made that leap? But Hecht was too stunned by Doneto's appearance to work that out—considering the fact that Delari would have observed Doneto all his life.

Delari said, "Don't be thinking what you're thinking, Bronte. You tell yourself, 'He's a thousand years old. He's got to be worn out after everything he's been through. There's six of us and one of him.' But the one of him is the Unknown. You have a touch of talent. But that's all you have. Come back into the light."

"Your own son . . ."

"Was a lord of the Brotherhood. And powerful before his mishap. But even in his deepest despair he never surrendered to the Will of the Night."

Hecht was not sure Delari was right about that.

"Come back into the light, Bronte Doneto. Explain what you were up to in Sonsa. Do what you need to do so you and your Witchfinders don't end up like Gryphen Pledcyk."

"You seem to have it all figured out."

"But I could have you all wrong, too. I'm thinking there might be an effort to keep Sublime from collecting his payoff from Anne of Menand.

Or just to steal it. You've always been closer to Honario than you pretend to the rest of us. And you've always been less loyal than you pretend to him. Again, let me caution you against giving in to temptation. You aren't strong enough."

Hecht could see Doneto weighing his chances.

Muniero Delari made two sudden gestures. The man nearest him shrieked and collapsed into a violent seizure. A second shriek came from the rubbled darkness, from over Delari's right shoulder. A crossbow twanged. A bolt rattled around, never seen.

Everyone ducked. Except Principaté Muniero Delari. He did something. Two more Witchfinders collapsed. Quietly, this time.

The old man said, "And then there were three. Come back to the light, Bronte Doneto."

Principaté Doneto bowed his head in submission. Hecht considered that suspect. Principaté Delari would do so, too. And Doneto would understand that perfectly.

Pretense all the way round.

Delari asked, "What have you been doing, young Bronte?"

"You figured it out. We meant to scuttle Honario's plan."

That might be, Hecht thought. But there would be more.

Doneto's feigned surrender was a fiction that would bring this confrontation to an end with no harm done. Where it went later would hinge on how committed Doneto was to his schemes. And how clever he thought he was.

Delari said, "A thousand eyes will be watching, Bronte. Now that it's no secret who to watch."

Doneto stilled a surge of rage. He knew he was at a serious disadvantage.

"Better, sir," the old man said. "Invest some time in reflection on the quality of mercy. And on the prospect of its withdrawal. Sabotage your cousin if you will. But do it without invoking the Instrumentalities of the Night."

Doneto held his tongue.

Delari continued. "One thing more. Who is Vali Dumaine? How does she fit into your plot?"

Doneto seemed honestly baffled. "Do you mean the urchin your pet general adopted last fall?"

Principaté Delari stared at Doneto coldly. The power he exuded was palpable.

Doneto shook his head. "I have no idea who she is. She isn't involved."

That was not what Hecht hoped to hear but it was what he expected. Ghort would have mentioned Vali to Doneto. No doubt, Doneto had Ghort keep track of what was happening inside his life. Because he felt that Piper Hecht owed him. Maybe without Ghort knowing how he was being used.

Maybe. Hecht trusted no one completely. Not even Anna. Anna had had other loyalties before she led him to her bed.

"You may go," Principaté Delari said. "We'll enjoy opportunities to consult further in the world above."

"The wounded? It won't be safe for them down here."

"Those two are recovering now. The others won't. If you feel a need to take them out you'll have to carry them."

Hecht squeezed down into shadow to avoid being spotted by two men headed out to collect the fallen crossbowman. He was drifting off when Delari called, "You can come out now, Piper."

Hecht shook off the drowsiness, shuffled forward. The Witchfinders had left their dead.

Delari saw him staring at Pledcyk. "They'll come get him. I'm exhausted, Piper. If they had tried again they would've had me."

"You were bluffing?"

"I used myself up early so they'd expect the worst. You'll have to carry me."

"Where's your lantern?"

"No idea. Lost. Worry about it some other time. Work out how to do this. We need to be gone before Doneto realizes how weak I must be."

"Back the way I came?"

"Of course. They'll set ambushes on their route of retreat." Question time ended. The old man slumped into genuine unconsciousness.

SERGEANT BECHTER WAKENED HECHT. IT WAS MIDMORNING. HE HAD managed a scant three hours of sleep. "You going to lie in all day, sir?"

"I was out all night. Because of the disaster."

Bechter raised an eyebrow. He had not seen his Captain-General out there. But he did not challenge Hecht. "The Bruglioni Principaté is here. He wants to see you. He's insistent. He talked to you about getting together last night. I suggested this morning would be good. He's been waiting for a while already."

Hecht grunted. "What else is on the table today? What else am I late for?"

"We have a go-ahead for your joint unification proposal. The staff wants to get started. We have forty-three city militias used to doing things their own way. They need to be integrated into the overarching structure."

"That's a challenge I'm looking forward to." He believed he could ameliorate problems of ego and local chauvinism. "Bring Saluda in. I'll talk to him while I'm getting ready. By the way, how is Polo? Do we know?" The servant had had a long, difficult struggle with the wound he had suffered in the assassination attempt.

"I hear he's going home soon. To the Bruglioni. You and Colonel Ghort won a lot of goodwill, standing up for him."

It was a world of disposable people. But Sha-lug did not abandon their brothers, crippled or no.

Faith had to be kept both ways.

So long as that was not inconvenient for some fellow of lordly status, evidently. For Gordimer the Lion, say.

In the west they threw people away everywhere, every day.

"Remind Saluda that I can't give him much time."

The Bruglioni Principaté came in quickly. "Interesting times, eh?"

"A lot's happening. The new job seems to agree with you."

"I'm enjoying it. Paludan isn't. Several of his cousins insist that they're more qualified."

"That's unlikely."

"I heard you mention Polo. He came home two days ago. Singing your praises."

"Good. But is he welcome? He won't be much use with one hand."

"He'll be taken care of. There's work he can do."

"Good. But Polo isn't why you're here."

"Before you moved to the Chiaro Palace Divino gave you a bag of coins."

"He did. Yes. It got me through an uncomfortable transition."

"Was there a ring in the bag?"

Hecht frowned. The truth was, yes. What looked like a simple gold band till you held it to the light. "Odd question. Divino asked me the same thing. But there were only some old coins. All foreign or odd. I took the bag to a goldsmith and exchanged them for modern coinage. He probably robbed me. But it saved me having to deal with a different kind of coin every time I wanted to buy something."

"There was no ring?"

"I didn't see a ring. Why is it important?"

"It's a magic ring. So Divino believed. And Paludan still does. It's been in the family for ages. It's disappeared. All anyone can figure is, it must have been in that sack."

"I didn't see it."

"Neither did Hanfelder. So what became of it?"

"Who's Hanfelder?"

"The goldsmith. We tracked him down. A slimy Deve. He didn't seem to be lying."

"Now I'm nervous. You going to all that trouble. Over an heirloom."

"It's a magic ring."

"I got that. But what does it do that makes it important?"

"I don't know. I'm not sure Paludan does. Divino probably knew. But he died before he could tell anyone. We do know, though, that one of its qualities is to make you forget it."

"Forget it?"

"More like overlook. Then not be there when you remember and start looking."

"All right," Hecht said in a slow, skeptical drawl.

Saluda flashed a charming smile, not something he did frequently. "I know. I know. But I have to do what they ask. Even if it makes no sense to me."

"If this ring knows how to hide I'd find me a sorcerer I could trust and start hunting in Divino's apartment in the Bruglioni compound. It's probably hidden under his mattress."

Scowling, Saluda responded, "I'll pass that suggestion on to Paludan. I'm sure he hasn't thought of that."

"Just trying to be helpful, Principaté. Sergeant Bechter. What's on the schedule?"

"The consolidation program. There'll be local resistance."

"I think I know how to avoid some of the problems."

"Sir?"

"We pander. To the local egos. If the Patriarch approves. If I sell Principaté Doneto he'll convince his cousin. There. I'm ready. Was there anything besides the missing ring, Principaté?"

"Call me Gervase, Hecht. No. But that was important enough."

"I'm sorry I couldn't be more help, Gervase."

"A little clumsy, eh?"

"It is. Wait. You never told me what the ring looks like. Something big, gaudy, and ugly, right? If it's got a charge of sorcery on it?"

Saluda shrugged. "I've never seen it. Paludan says it's just a plain gold band."

"That doesn't sound like much. Not very impressive."

"There's stuff engraved on it."

Hecht waited. Saluda did not expand.

"Spells? Family history?"

"I don't know. I wasn't told. I'm not family."

"Really? From where I stood you looked more Bruglioni than anyone born to the name."

Saluda grunted. Hecht had touched a sore spot. He asked, "The old place still holding together? Madam Ristoti managing all right?"

"You done real good while you were there, Mr. Captain-General. It hasn't fallen apart yet."

"Good. I gave value for money."

"More than that, really. Paludan does take an interest nowadays. You sure you can't help with the ring?"

"You're a Prince of the Church, now. Bully some low-level witch doctor into hunting for it. It's got to be in the house somewhere. Unless it was pinched by somebody I fired."

"That doesn't seem likely."

"Is that it? There isn't anything more critical?"

"Just the ring."

"Then it must be more important than I suspected."

Saluda considered a moment before admitting, "Could be. Paludan didn't tell me why he's so interested, suddenly. Maybe he found a note he wrote to himself and decided to get after it before he forgot again."

"I see. Let me know if anything turns up." Hecht made a small gesture to Bechter. "We have work to do at the Castella. Oh. Gervase. Did the disaster yesterday hurt the Bruglioni?"

Saluda flashed a smile. "Not much. The Madisetti and Arniena took the brunt. And Cologni. A fortune in racing tackle went down with the hippodrome."

"I see. As I said, keep me posted. Sergeant, those papers you wanted me to read. Bring them once you show the Principaté out."

Redfearn Bechter did as instructed. Hecht scanned reports during the walk to the Castella dollas Pontellas. Half dealt with recent events in Brothe. They were more properly Pinkus Ghort's responsibility. "Give me an opinion, Bechter. How should we deal with this disaster?" The human cost was greater than he had expected. The hippodrome had been infested with squatters.

"That's been determined already, sir. The Patriarch announced a subscription effort. As donations are made the money will be used to clean up and rebuild."

"Not going to spend any of his own, eh?"

"Hardly. Not that he has much. Most of the Arnhander bribe still hasn't arrived."

The plan was to pay unemployed refugees in food for labor.

PRINCIPATÉ DELARI ASKED, "DID DONETO SHOW UP AT YOUR STAFF MEETing?"

"Yes. And showed no sign that he thinks I might suspect him. But maybe he was too tired to play around. I know I was."

"Good. I was concerned." The old man poured white wine into sparkling scarlet Clearenzan stemware, pushed that across a walnut tabletop polished smoother than a sheet of glass. Muniero Delari lived an austere life but did not disdain presents when someone wanted to butter him up. "Did you present your case?"

"I did. He told me it was ingenious. That Sublime should go along. I should get a Patriarchal Bull before the end of the week."

"I was afraid of that."

"Sir?"

"That tells me they've been looking for the kind of tool you've just given them."

"All right. I give. How did I mess up?"

"You didn't. You're doing your job. I'm in a political place where that disappoints me. Do you want to see our captive?"

"Not unless I need to. Did you get anything?"

"Of course. He wasn't at the center of the conspiracy but he knew where the Witchfinders want to go. Which is to gain direct control of the Patriarchy."

"They're not happy with Sublime? The man is obsessed with the Holy Lands and heretics and unbelievers."

"They're not happy at all. Sublime isn't at war with the Night. The Witchfinders don't care about the Connec. They don't care about reclaiming the Holy Lands, either. They believe all that will follow automatically from a triumph over the Night."

"So they're up to what?"

"Thwarting Sublime. Breaking Sublime. Positioning themselves to seize control of the Patriarchy by naming Sublime's successor. Who will forget the Connec and Dreanger and preach a crusade against the Night itself."

Hecht shook his head. "I don't understand your world. This makes no sense to me."

"Better start trying to get it. Suppose Sublime does stumble?"

"I understand that. Can I change the subject?"

"Of course."

"Look at this." Hecht produced the Bruglioni ring. "I understand it's magic."

Delari took the ring into a better light. "Where did you get this?"

"In a bag of old foreign coins I got hold of, back when we were fighting the Calziran pirates."

Delari's glance said he did not believe a word.

"If you hold it to the light at different angles you can see different lines of writing. On the inside. I've been studying them. This is what I wrote down." He pulled a strip of paper out of his sleeve.

Four lines, printed with painstaking care, had been recorded one above another. The result of hours of eye-straining work. "One must be

Classical Brothen. Most of the words resemble Church Brothen. But not all of them. Plus some of the characters are different."

"You're right. It's a spell. Meant to disorient. If you spoke it while wearing the ring everyone nearby would become confused. They would forget what they were trying to do."

"That's scary."

"And useful if you spend much time around people who want to hurt you."

"I don't recognize any of the other writing."

"It's all in alphabets older than Old Brothen. The second line is Philean, a language common in the Holy Lands in antiquity. Ancestral to languages spoken there today. I know scholars who can translate it. I don't think anyone speaks it properly anymore."

"Would that be a spell, too?"

"Undoubtedly. This third line uses Archaic Agean characters but the language isn't Agean. My guess is, the spoken line would be a Dreangerean dialect. Just guessing, though, based on the distribution of consonants."

"Could the ring really be that old?"

A brief-lived Agean empire had ruled the littorals of the eastern Mother Sea when Brothe was still a modest town under the dominion of the Felscian Confederation.

"I do get a sense of great age, Piper."

"What about the last line?"

"I don't know. I've seen characters like those before but I don't remember where. I'll need to do some research. Looking for mention of the ring itself, too. If it's important at all it will have left a trail across time. Likely mile-marked by unpleasantries."

Hecht nodded. That had been his guess, based on stories about magical artifacts he had heard.

The Principaté said, "One wonders how such an item falls into the hands of someone like yourself."

"Exactly the way I explained it."

"Oh, I believe that. I'm curious about the mind that made it happen. That singled you out. The way you were singled out for the attention of the soultaken, before? Who? Why? Did he have good intentions? Or is this a booby trap?"

"I have no idea. And I don't intend to dig into it, either. I'm leaving the damned thing with you."

"Piper. You never want to give up something with so much potential value."

"Why not? It's no use to me. It wouldn't be like I was turning out my pockets and tossing my money into the Teragi. All I could do is sell it for the gold."

"Or to a sorcerer for its power."

"Which you can't even tell me what it is. So even for you it's only a chunk of gold with potential."

Delari shrugged. "Life is that way. For me. Trying to winkle potential out of stubborn nuggets."

Hecht did not respond. Delari had to become more forthcoming if he was going to tap the potential in this particular nugget.

Delari seemed more amused than frustrated. "Patience is my great virtue, Piper. All right, I'll study this beast. In my copious spare time. And let you know as soon as I find out anything interesting. Who can guess? It might turn out such a dud that you can just give it back to the Bruglioni."

The old man startled him. And he let it show.

"It's common knowledge, among those who pay attention, that the Bruglioni are looking for a talisman that belonged to Principaté Divino. And they suspect that said talisman passed through the hands of one-time employee Piper Hecht."

Delari, as always, was better informed than he ought to be. Which was frightening.

Piper Hecht had secrets he did not want known by even the friendliest member of the Collegium.

The old man smiled like he knew exactly what was going on inside Hecht's head.

DESPITE REPEATED ASSASSINATION ATTEMPTS, HECHT DID NOT TRAVEL WITH A klatch of bodyguards. He hoped anonymity would protect him. He never dressed his station. That offended some at the Chiaro Palace but left him indistinguishable from other outlanders in the streets.

He headed for Anna Mozilla's place, by way of the hippodrome, where he visited Pinkus Ghort. Ghort had set up a military camp right there in the plaza. Hecht told him, "You look terrible. You need to get some sleep."

"I love you, too. Yeah, mom. I'm gonna get on that real soon. Seriously, we've got a handle on it. I can take some time, now. There ain't much chance we'll find anyone alive anymore. Thanks for sending your guys."

"No problem. I'll get some grief but they won't fire me."

"They worried about the mob? I heard you almost had an incident."

"Yes. One of your boys was right in the middle of it, too."

"Bo? He's doing good work. We get done with this shit here, I'm gonna make some moves on them rabble-rousers."

"You need him desperately?"

"Bo? Why?"

"I want to borrow him. There was another man in that crowd that shouldn't have been there. Shouldn't even be alive. I want to track him down."

"Important?"

"It might be. I want to know for sure."

"He's around somewhere. I'll talk to him after my nap."

"I'll be at Anna's house."

THE NEARER HECHT GOT TO ANNA'S HOUSE THE MORE UNCOMFORTABLE he became. He could not shake the feeling that he was being watched. He tried to catch a stalker but had no luck. There were too many people in the streets.

"You look like hell," Anna said as she let him in.

He gave her an edited version of recent events. She asked, "How can you expect to get along with Principaté Doneto, now?"

"He doesn't know I know what he's up to."

"Don't bet your life on that. And what about Pinkus?"

He had been examining that question from every angle he could imagine. "What about him?"

"Where does he stand? He's never pretended to be anything but Doneto's man. What'll he do in a pissing contest?"

"I don't know. I doubt that he does. That's the kind of question you can't answer until you have to. I'm not even sure about me. I think I'm Principaté Delari's man. I *want* to think I am. But the Church pays my wages. Doneto, at least publicly, will go right on being Sublime's biggest supporter."

"Just be careful."

"I will. I promise. You been out much lately?"

"Only to get water. With the children. Why?"

"What're they saying around the fountain?" As everywhere, the neighborhood women took their time getting water, indulging in gossip.

"Today they were more relaxed. And they all knew it. But not why."

"That isn't hard. The bad thing is dead."

The children entered the room, Vali carrying the tea service. Pella had a book. He wanted to show off his reading skills. Hecht allowed him to do so, certain he could not have improved much in just a few days. He had not. "Good job with the tea, Vali."

Vali did not stumble. She shot him a look that said he would have to be more clever than that.

He smiled and winked.

Vali winked right back.

Hecht told Anna, "I'm worried about what Delari is up to."

"Meaning?"

"When we found him he told me he caused the cave-in by exploding a keg of firepowder. Which he blew up in order to kill the monster."

"And? You don't think he could carry a powder keg? Or that one keg wouldn't cause that much damage?"

"It could do the damage. The stuff is amazing. When it's made right, by skilled artificers. No. My problem is what he didn't explain. Which is all that sorcery we saw happen. *After* the hippodrome fell down."

"Oh. I see."

"If the explosion killed the beast, then why was there a lot of sorcery?"

Hecht glanced at Vali. The girl looked like she was about to explode. She grabbed the tea service and headed for the kitchen, dragging Pella.

Anna chuckled. "You're about to hear an interesting theory."

So. Maybe the way to lure the girl out was to engage her intellect.

Someone knocked on the front door. Hecht asked, "You expecting somebody?"

Anna shook her head. "It'll be for you. Or the kids." Even so, she went to see who was there. Pella returned from the kitchen and leaned on the back of the chair Anna had just quit.

The boy said, "The thing that died in the underworld would've been almost a god. Right?"

"A seriously powerful Instrumentality, yes. But a demon. There is only one God."

"So what you saw happening coulda just been it dying? Right?"

Death throes? All that? "Maybe." Impressed.

He tried to recall what had happened with the Old God who died outside al-Khazen. And found a hole in his memory. One that made itself evident by the fact that he knew it was missing when it ought to be there. But there remained a vague recollection of a dramatic conclusion.

Was that what happened when gods died? Even their memory fled the world? But there were a lot of ancient gods still around, lurking in myth and old stories.

Maybe remembered because they were not yet dead.

Anna called, "Piper. This must be for you."

Hecht had been easing toward the door already. He peered out the gap allowed by the heavy security chains. "It's all right. I know him."

Bo Biogna stood on the stoop, short, wide, dirty, and a bit scary.

Anna whispered, "I'm not sure I want that man inside my house."

"It's important." Though why Biogna would turn up here was a puzzle. "I'll see him in the kitchen."

"You can't take care of it outside?"

"No, darling. There might be eyes out there. I'll make sure he doesn't put anything in his pockets."

Anna was not amused.

"In," Hecht told Ghort's man. "Follow me." He led the way to the kitchen. "Pella. Find us a couple of stools. Vali. Get Mr. Biogna a cup. Assuming you'd like tea, Bo."

"Tea is fine. But I didn't come to socialize."

Anna joined them. She took over the tea preparation. While keeping a wary eye on the visitor. Biogna sensed her discomfort and suspicion. He seemed more amused than offended.

"What's up?" Hecht asked.

"Colonel Ghort sent me. Said you need my help. That you need me to get on something right away."

"It isn't that critical. You can work on it while you're doing what you're doing already. There's a man I need found and identified. He was out there in the Closed Ground right by you." Hecht described the man he had seen in the mob.

"I know the one you mean. Surprisingly enough. I noticed him because he was creepy. And he smelled bad."

"Find out whatever you can. Who he is. Where he lives. That sort of thing."

Biogna studied him from beneath shaggy brows. He had grown stocky. He looked much more like a prosperous thug than the starving refugee Hecht had met on the road to Brothe. "You got somewhere for me to start? Brothe covers a lot of ground."

"I don't. I've only noticed him a few times. At a guess, spying. My man Bechter noticed him before I did. He seems to be keeping an eye on me and my staff."

"Imperial?"

"That would be my first guess. If not that, then Connecten. Or possibly Arnhander."

"Or maybe our big boss is keeping an eye on you?"

"He has people on the inside to handle that."

"Probably. You asked for me on account of you want to keep this quiet. Right?"

"Yes."

Biogna nodded. "You got it. Good tea, ma'am. Thank you. I'll be shoving off."

Hecht did not argue. He accompanied Biogna to the door. As the man stepped out, Hecht asked, "You still see Just Plain Joe?"

"All the time. He's easy to be around."

That was true, Hecht remembered. Just Plain Joe was not much smarter than the animals he cared for but he was a comfortable companion. "Sure is. Next time you see him, tell him hello from me. And ask if he's happy where he is."

"Hell, Pipe. Of course he is. He's Just Plain Joe. Joe is happy. Wherever he's at, that's the best possible place to be."

"I could use a man who's good with animals."

"He'll be looking for a job before long. We all will. Unless something scares the Five Families so bad they figure they've got to keep us on."

"You find yourself out of work, come see me."

Biogna bobbed his head, glanced around to see who might notice him leaving, then took off.

Hecht watched him go. How much could he be trusted?

The better positioned he became the more vulnerable he felt.

"We are being watched," Hecht said when he returned to the kitchen. Where Anna seemed to be taking inventory in case Bo was a thief with illusionist's skills. "And I won't ask Biogna in again if he makes you that uncomfortable."

"Good. And next time one of your henchmen turns up, *ask* me before you let them in."

There it was. The root of it all.

"Absolutely."

"What about us being watched?"

He had seen a familiar face on a man lounging against a wall a hundred yards toward the sunset. A face he had not seen in years. The man's name was al-Azer er-Selim. He had been the Master of Ghosts of the special company once commanded by the Sha-lug captain Else Tage. Az was an old hand. He would not be spotted easily unless he wanted spotting.

Az wanted to make contact.

Later, though. When there would be fewer witnesses. "There's a man out there who doesn't have any business around here."

"Who sent him?"

"That would be the grand question. That's the off side of being Captain-General. Everyone—including the man paying my salary—wants to track what I'm doing."

Anna nodded. She had completed her inventory. Now she dug amongst her pots and pans as she got ready to cook. "I'd as soon they stayed away from here. All of them." Her wealth in utensils declared her status in her own mind. A new pan was always a welcome gift.

"Even Pinkus?"

"Pinkus I can suffer. Barely. Titus is acceptable. If he was willing to socialize and would bring Noë and their kids. But not as business. I've got a good life here, Piper. I'd as soon forget the past."

"Little pitchers."

Pella and Vali seemed very interested.

Anna said, "Don't you two go telling any of your . . . Any of Piper's friends that I don't like them." She was wide-eyed when she looked at Hecht again.

No one missed the fact that she had come near calling Hecht their father. Which betrayed much of what was going on inside her head.

The uncomfortable moment was shattered by another knock at the door. This one seemed urgent.

Hecht said, "Pella, you go."

He stepped forward and caught Anna by the elbows, stared down into her coffee and amber eyes. He did not know what to say. She seemed unable, or unwilling, to offer any cues.

He did not get the chance to work it out.

"Captain-General. A moment."

Pella said, "I'm sorry, Anna. I couldn't stop him."

Hecht gaped momentarily, reflecting on the old saw, "Speak of the Adversary."

"Titus? What the hell are you doing here?"

"We have a situation."

"Well?"

"A world-altering situation, sir. A courier killed two horses bringing the news."

"And?" Dread crept into the back of Hecht's mind.

"Here, sir?"

"Yes. Here. Now. In front of everyone. Spit it out."

"As you will. The Emperor is dead."

"Lothar?"

"That one. Yes. Right now we're the only ones who know."

And the Devedian community, of course. And all the Instrumentalities of the Night. And anyone who had congress with them.

Hecht turned to Anna. Before he could speak, she said, "It's time to go. And waste no time. The whole world just changed."

9. Hochwasser: Ceremonies of Death and Life

Princess Helspeth, Grafina fon Supfer, Marquesa va Runjan, Contessa di Plemenza, and so forth, thought she had herself under control. She had known it would come. She had had time to become intimate with the truth during the bone-breaking rush from Plemenza to Hochwasser, where Lothar had been gathering a small army for a limited campaign in northern Firaldia. But seeing Mushin in a coffin, in a room lined with blocks of ice, took it out of the realm of the intellectual, into that of the intimately painful and real.

She threw herself onto the boy's pale, still form.

Mushin was so cold. And so much smaller than he was inside her memory.

She lost control.

A hand squeezed her shoulder. She looked up. Katrin stood over her. Katrin's eyes were red and hollow. The pain had razor-slashed her soul.

The sisters fell into one another's arms. They wept together under the scowls of Katrin's women and several of the Empire's leading men. The majority and most powerful of the Council Advisory, however, had not yet arrived. They seemed in no hurry to present themselves for Emperor Lothar's final ritual obligation to the Grail Empire.

Helspeth pulled herself together before Katrin did. To the surprise of the younger sister, Katrin was the one they called the ice maiden. Katrin was the one who concealed everything happening inside. But Katrin was the one who had focused all her strained and stilted emotion on her beloved Mushin.

Katrin said, "My world has ended, Helspeth."

Helspeth wondered why Katrin had no pet name for her.

"This is worse than when Papa died. Though we've always known that it would happen."

"Father was hard to live with," Helspeth said. Parroting Katrin explaining her lack of distress after Johannes's fall at al-Khazen. Helspeth was too rattled to engage her own wit. "Who are those men?" She indicated three priests who seemed intent on remaining unnoticed.

"Father Volker. My confessor. I don't know the other two. Father introduced me but I was too distracted to remember. One of them is a bishop. He's going to preside at the funeral and my first vows."

"Oh."

"I don't want to be Empress, Helspeth. I don't want to deal with Omro va Still-Patter and all those coldhearted vultures. Help me, Helspeth."

"Always, dear sister. I am your most faithful and devoted subject. Whatever you ask of me, I'll do it. Just tell me."

A flicker of cold suspicion crossed Katrin's features.

KATRIN EGE ASSUMED THE IMPERIAL HONORS THE DAY FOLLOWING HELspeth's arrival at Hochwasser. She did so in the absence of the Council Advisory, with the blessing of Bishop Hrobjart of Carbon. The Bishop administered a preliminary oath in the interest of state continuity. The official coronation was set for late summer, during the Feast of Kramas. The

Feast was an ancient celebration, the reasons for which were lost in time. Grail Emperors were elevated officially on that date. They had been since the New Brothen Empire was imagined by the Patriarch Pacific II. Some who indulged an interest in matters historical believed Kramas commemorated a victory by tribesmen over invading Old Brothen legions.

The Battle of Carmue, in Brothen history, had had an impact so great that the emperors never again tried to conquer the heart of the continent.

There were arguments. Those of the Council Advisory already on hand insisted on delays. The full Council was needed.

Unsaid, but understood, was that the full Council had less trouble bullying Katrin.

Helspeth was careful to say nothing negative about those ugly old men.

Privately, Algres Drear suggested, "If you want the Empress to know anything special you'd better deliver the message before Hilandle shows. Once he does Katrin will be hard to reach. He'll make sure access to the Empress is strictly managed."

Helspeth was impressed. That was the most the man had said since Lothar placed her under his protection. His advice was sound, too. "Captain, I need you more than ever. How do I assure your loyalty?"

"My loyalty is assured, Princess. It was the will of the emperors, your father and your brother. Only death can separate us. I'll be closer to you than I am to my wife."

Literally. Drear's wife refused to travel to Plemenza.

"I wasn't made for this, Algres."

"No one is till it's thrust upon them."

"But . . ."

"You are the daughter of Johannes Ege and Terezia of Nietzchau."

Helspeth wanted to argue but was too tired and too depressed. She hated her life. And it was unlikely to get better. Even Plemenza was losing its charm.

"I'm not sure that will be sufficient."

Drear turned grim. "You have enough on your mind. Get some rest. But see your sister as soon as you can."

Katrin did not answer Helspeth's message. She had gone into seclusion with her confessor and the other churchmen.

FERRIS RENFROW ARRIVED BEFORE THE GRAND DUKE, IN TIME FOR THE INterment and a hasty succession ceremony performed by Bishop Hrobjart. Just materializing behind Helspeth's left shoulder. She knew he was there without looking. The overcast began to clear from her emotional skies. The slump went out of her shoulders.

She felt guilty.

Algres Drear was supposed to make her feel this way. That was his mission. She could not manage without Captain Drear and his Braunsknechts, but he never inspired her the way Renfrow did.

Sad, too, because Ferris Renfrow's first loyalty was always the Grail Empire, not the sad second daughter of its penultimate Emperor.

Katrin sank to her knees before Bishop Hrobjart. After a murmured exchange, Hrobjart turned to his left and accepted a coronet from the nameless churchman who accompanied him everywhere. Father Volker swung a censor with one hand and sprinkled holy water with the other.

All three priests wore white. Father Volker's robes were simple. The unknown priest's were austere. Bishop Hrobjart's, though, had lace, uncut gems, and seed pearls all over it. The last time Helspeth saw priests in white was at Lothar's coronation. Normally, they wore gray or brown. Or black.

Helspeth loathed the new crows in black. They served the harsh orders: the Patriarchal Society for the Suppression of Sacrilege and Heresy; the Brotherhood of War; the Knights of the Grail Order. And the former two grew more powerful by the day across the Jagos.

Grail Empire disdain kept the Society and Brotherhood from developing much power north of the Jagos. But the Grail Order—a sort of northern Brotherhood—was immensely influential where the Episcopal faith collided with the pagan world.

Ferris Renfrow summoned her from her reverie. Time for the witnesses to take a knee before the new Empress. Then both knees while the Bishop of Carbon invoked the blessing. A long responsorial followed. She did not need to pay attention to keep up. It was standard back and forth in Church Brothen. A five-year-old could keep up and have attention left over for mischief.

AS THEY LEFT THE CHURCH, RENFROW SAID, "YOU MAY FACE DRAMATIC challenges on your return to Plemenza, Princess." He seemed not to care if someone overheard. "The Patriarch is sure to test the new order."

"Sublime will find the Ege daughters no less formidable than their father." She thought of the Captain-General. Their paths might not cross again.

"That is fondly to be hoped," Renfrow said. "Unfortunately, the reality may not be so promising."

"Meaning?"

Renfrow glanced at Algres Drear. As always on public and ceremonial occasions, Drear was within arm's reach of Helspeth. "Time will tell, Princess. I have to leave. Take care of her, Captain."

In an eye's blink Renfrow vanished. Look away, look back, the man was gone. "How does he do that?" Helspeth asked.

"And at his age. Sorcery? Or is he even human?" Drear respected Renfrow but did not like the man. Points he had striven to impress upon his charge.

"What do you mean, at his age?"

"Just that he's been around forever. Doing the same work. Steering the Empire. Subtly. Some think he engineered your father's election. And the Act of Succession, too."

"Father did say that Renfrow knows all the secrets. And isn't reluctant to use them."

"Lucky you're too young to have secrets."

"Lucky me. Like I've ever had a chance to do something I'd want to hide." Her women were closing in, to separate her from her desperado chief bodyguard. Reputations were at risk.

KATRIN'S COURT WAS UNDISMAYED WHEN THE EMPRESS CLOSETED HERSELF with three priests, without benefit of chaperone. When priests had worse reputations than any other variety of man. Their opinions shifted dramatically when Katrin announced that she would rectify her father's error by shifting the Empire's support from Viscesment to Brothe.

If that was not enough to poleax the Imperial aristocracy, Katrin then announced a pilgrimage to the Mother City. Where she would be crowned by the Patriarch himself.

Algres Drear observed, "The Grand Duke must be apoplectic." While packing.

"I can't see Hilandle having that much imagination. This was his fault. He could have been here. But he wanted us to think the Empire can't function except at his pleasure. He thought an Ege daughter would swoon. Katrin's as clever as Mushin was. More so, maybe. She isn't shy about revealing her contempt for those people. But she shouldn't have shown her independence that way."

Drear grunted. Helspeth's women were close by. As always. Eavesdropping. Some would report to the Empress. Others would inform the Council Advisory.

The Imperial nobility included a pro-Sublime faction. Sentiment against Sublime appealed to a larger bloc of folk more exalted and emotionally committed.

When her household was ready Helspeth sent for permission to return to Plemenza.

Lady Chevra approached nervously. Her expression would not remain fixed. One moment it was worried, the next sheepish, after that maliciously triumphant.

"Yes?" No doubt the old cow brought bad news. She wanted to do right but could not help taking joy in the misery of others.

"Her Majesty denies your request. You are to join her pilgrimage to the Mother City."

"We're enjoying a change of plan, Captain Drear."

Drear nodded.

"Coordinate with the Empress's people. We can reduce costs if we make the progress through the Imperial cities of Firaldia."

Lady Chevra was unhappy. The girl she wanted to torment had taken disappointment without a whimper.

Helspeth Ege would not whimper or whine. Ever. Not for Grand Duke Hilandle, not for the Empress Katrin Ege.

There was a positive side. To assert his influence the Grand Duke would have to follow Hansel's girls into the heart of Firaldia. Which he loathed. In that land no one knew who he was. Nor cared.

In that land, she reflected, lay Brothe. Where the Captain-General of the false Patriarch's armies made his headquarters.

She felt a rush of excitement.

This might not be so bad after all.

"Are you all right, Princess?" Lady Delta va Kelgerberg asked. "You just turned red as a beet."

Her breath had gone shallow and wheezy, too.

THE GRAND DUKE DID NOT GIVE THE NEW SITUATION ADEQUATE THOUGHT. He favored himself too highly to accept defeat by the Ege bitch.

He plunged into an intemperate rush south from Alten Weinberg. He should reach Firaldia in time to quell the chit's insanity. She would *not* get down on her knees in front of that pox-ridden Brothen boy-lover, Sublime V.

Hilandle's party numbered forty-three to start. It began to dwindle almost immediately. A half dozen disappeared at Hochwasser. Swearing, he drove on into the Jagos range. Into a fierce, unseasonable snowstorm.

Some wanted to den up and wait. But the band did not have enough provisions. They had to turn back or press on.

Several turned back.

Thirty-two pressed on.

One day of biting cold cracked the sense of obligation of more of the Grand Duke's companions, who turned back to Hochwasser. Where the troops Lothar had begun to gather still awaited instructions. While they lived off Imperial stores.

In the deep night, with snow swirling like sudden ivory embers in the light of small fires, the camp wakened to screaming.

Four men had sentry duty. Three could not be found. The other had seen and heard nothing but the screams.

No one got any more sleep.

The snow stopped next afternoon. The accumulation showed no sign of melting. The Grand Duke's party climbed above the tree line. They had only what firewood they could carry.

There were no inns, hostels, or way stations. Those had been abandoned. Even the Imperial post remount stations stood empty. A couple of small castles held out, supporting the post. They would not open their gates. The Empress's party had picked their bones already.

Another night brought more screams.

Wrapped in blankets, shaking in the cold, his sword bared upon his lap, the Grand Duke crowded the only fire and fought to stay awake.

Omro va Still-Patter, the Protector, was a loathsome old man today. In his youth he had been bold and fearless. He had spent three years in the Holy Lands and two with the Grail Order knights converting the savages of the Grand Marshes. Age might be gnawing his bones and his tolerance for discomfort, but it had not stolen his capacity for staying calm in the face of terror.

Screams startled Hilandle awake.

They came from just a dozen feet away.

He jumped up, both hands gripping his sword.

Something came at him. Something he saw only for a moment. Something huge. Something carrying a bleeding man. Something insectile, like the biggest walking stick that could be imagined, with more legs. Its bulbous eyes seemed filled with fire.

It thrust a claw at Hilandle. The Grand Duke met the thrust. The grasper separated from the limb and fell. A second tore at his blankets, his armor, and left shoulder. The collision flung him aside.

In the instant of contact torrents of thought smashed into Hilandle's brain. A fraction seemed quite rational. Almost philosophical. From a mind that observed and cataloged. But overriding that was madness, founded in hatred, bloodlust, and a compulsion toward revenge unending, with a thousand images of murders past and hoped to come.

Then it was gone, still dragging its prey.

Sprawled in half a foot of bloody snow, stunned, trying to push the cruel visions away, the Grand Duke banged his nose on the severed grasper, which continued flexing.

"Hartwell," he gasped at the first man to arrive. "Find something to put this in. I want to take it along."

"Your Lordship?"

"I didn't stutter, man. That may tell us something about that thing."

The monster did not return. Not then.

To Hilandle it seemed he lay there for hours, mind ensnared in the thing's blood madness. In truth, it was minutes. One of his grooms began cleaning his wound. "Did you see that thing?" he asked the man.

"What thing, sir?" Hilandle did not insist on formality in the field. Which surprised his enemies. They considered him a pompous, self-important stiff.

"The monster."

"No, sir."

"It was like . . ." A vengeful god. But he could not say that. There was only one God. And He was not a gigantic, ugly carnivorous bug. "It was one of the Instrumentalities of the Night. One of the Great Devils, surely."

The groom, Horace, appeared unconvinced. Despite the screams, the bloody snow, and the absent companions.

Twenty-three men moved on next morning. The missing left little evidence that they ever existed. Except equipment and possessions abandoned because there was no one to carry them.

The Grand Duke and his men pressed on, often cutting the day's travel short where there was no certainty of reaching a defensible campsite before nightfall. He was furious all the time, in constant pain from his wound. He was falling farther and farther behind the Ege chits. And he continued to lose men.

Twelve men, one the Grand Duke, reached the friendly foothills of northern Firaldia. Hilandle told his closest surviving associate, "Remind me, after we recover. The most pressing problem facing the Empire today is the thing we just survived." He winced. Any thought of the monster made him tense up. And his wound hurt worse than its constant ache.

Discovering that the Ege bitch had not suffered at all crossing the Jagos did nothing to improve his temper.

Nor was he cheered by the news from the Connec.

10. Caron ande Lette: Flood Tide

News seldom reached Caron ande Lette in a timely manner. Few travelers came through. The little the Raults knew of the world came to them courtesy of messengers jogging up from Antieux.

For Raymone Garete the saw about absence and hearts grown fonder was an understatement.

Socia alternated between excitement at so much attention and fright because Raymone was so intense.

Emperor Lothar had been dead a month before word came.

"This isn't good," Brock said seconds after a courier delivered the news. Brother Candle suspected Brock had reflected on the possibilities from the moment that sickly boy took the ermine.

All the west had.

"I can't see any good coming of it," Brother Candle confessed. "This news will trigger all kinds of mischief." Because no one, anywhere, believed that Johannes's daughter could pull on the black boots and show the iron hand.

Brother Candle knew nothing about the girl. Catherine? Something like that. But he had roamed the world long enough to grasp the essence of human nature.

All those people starting to wind the engines of conspiracy eyed reality through a fog of wishful thinking. Expecting the world to conform to their imaginings.

Reality enjoys harpooning self-delusion.

Usually silent, Thurm Rault observed, "Interesting times are sure gonna get more interesting."

Brock said, "We need to put out more patrols. Trouble out of Grolsach is a sure thing once they hear the news. Thurm. Spread the word to the hamlets. The peasants need time to get ready. And we need to get their provisions safely in here."

"Will they go for that?"

"I hope they still trust me." Chaos had come close to prevailing during his absence. "I should've left you here." The people did not understand why he should be so completely subject to the whims of Tormond IV. The Mad Duke was almost mythological at this remove from Khaurene. Count Raymone was more real. Mainly because he had helped destroy Haiden Backe.

A less traveled, more ignorant and inflexible people Brother Candle could not imagine. That the Maysalean Heresy had taken root in a single generation was an amazement.

The Path did present a vision sharply at odds with the routine despair of everyday life.

The Raults prepared. The people joined in reluctantly. The threat had to be exaggerated. But what harm in making ready?

"Your layabouts are grumbling," Brother Candle said one morning, on the parapet. Facetiously. "If it didn't take so much effort, the peasants would revolt."

Almost true. The Connec was generous, even here. People did not have to drudge and scratch from dawn to dusk every day of the year to barely subsist. Human nature being what it was they thought being asked to do anything extra was grossly unfair.

"Here comes Socia, riding like all the Instrumentalities of the Night are after her."

They might be. The gentler sort. The peasants kept reporting strange lights and odors.

Socia always rushed when she rode. Brother Candle thought she was overdoing it this time. Feeling compassion for the horse.

The girl joined them, puffing from the climb. She reported all in a gush. "It's starting, Brock. We ambushed some Grolsachers up by Little Thysoup. They were scouting."

Brock said, "Little Thysoup would be a waste of time. What have they got out there? A few scrawny chickens and a three-legged dog?"

Socia resumed, "There were four of them. A family, I guess. There was a fight. They wanted to get away. We didn't let them."

Brock started to ask about prisoners. Brother Candle said, "There's one. A child."

Several peasants, all women, drove the prisoner toward the stronghold gate. They had ropes around his neck. And were not being kind.

Peasants seldom were when given a chance to express anger normally kept in check.

The prisoner *was* a child. A boy. Eleven at the oldest. He was injured, terrified, pale, and shaking. Tear tracks streaked his dirty face. He had just witnessed the brutal killings of his father, his grandfather, and his uncle.

"Show a little gentleness," Brother Candle suggested, iron in his voice. Socia nodded, thumped back downstairs. Brock and the Perfect followed at a pace in keeping with the capacities of an older man.

Socia was not all blood and ferocity. When Brother Candle reached the forecourt behind the gate he found that she had separated the prisoner from his captors. She was examining his wound. The boy shook so badly he could barely stand.

Brother Candle said, "Get some soup into him. Just broth, to start." Signs of starvation were there, though not advanced. "Move him somewhere warmer. Give him some wine and wrap him in blankets."

Brock said, "Put salve on those rope burns, too. How bad is he, otherwise?"

Socia replied, "One shallow cut, shouldn't need sewing. A lot of bruises and scrapes. They beat him."

Brock turned to the cowed peasant women. "Good work, ladies. But this is only the beginning. You need to do two things more. Make the dead out there disappear. Then warn all the farms to prepare hiding places. And let me know immediately if anything else happens."

Brock had no worries about being able to handle the raiders if he knew where they were. His people were a match for ten times their weight in hungry Grolsachers worn down by travel.

"How do you suppose they got here?" Brother Candle wondered.

"They walked, Brother. If they had horses they would've eaten them."

"I meant their route, Seuir. The direct way would be across Imp or Manu. That would raise alarums."

"Then I expect they're taking the long way, around the west end of Ormienden. Through Arnhand, with the connivance of the Arnhander nobility."

"It could be a plan that kicked in when the Emperor died."

"Could be. We'll ask. Socia. How soon can our guest talk?"

"Depends on how much you care about his health."

"Let him worry about his health. He won't stay healthy if he doesn't talk to me."

Brother Candle murmured, "You can't scare him, Brock. He's already too terrified to think. And he can't see anything left to lose."

"Do you ever get tired of always being right?"

"Not often. Though that's a very Count Raymone thing to ask."

"Socia. Mother the boy. Sweet-talk him. Bring him around so we can open him up."

A SECOND SKIRMISH OCCURRED FOUR MILES WEST OF LITTLE THYSOUP, IN the evening. It involved an indeterminate number of Grolsachers, who suffered only because the alert from Caron ande Lette had reached the area shortly before. Peasants, armed no better than the invaders, fought back. Four Connectens died. The raiders left four of their own behind. Those who escaped were all injured.

BROTHER CANDLE AND SOCIA RAULT TOOK TURNS SITTING WITH THE BOY. He called himself Gres Refello. His terror never faded completely but he believed a Perfect Master when Brother Candle promised no further harm would touch him. He had Seekers After Light in his own family. Nor did he possess the guile to lie to save countrymen he did not know.

When questioned, he answered. Mumbling.

"MUST BE A LOT OF THEM COMING," BROCK RAULT SAID OVER SUPPER. There had been several more incidents.

The grand hall of Caron ande Lette contained leading men from the surrounding country, the Raults, Brother Candle, a courier from Antieux, and Seuir Lanne Tuldse, who had brought up a handful of fighters after hearing that there were Grolsacher raiders north of him. These men were eating whatever they could grab. Free food was not common.

The grand hall was not large. Caron ande Lette was not large. The grandest thing about it was its wall.

"I need a little quiet," Brock bellowed. "The Perfect Master spent the morning with the boy we caught yesterday. You need to hear what he has to say."

Wearied by life, tempted by despair, Brother Candle abandoned his cluttered platter and rose. He was not in the mood for roast hare.

"The Seuir is correct. A lot of them are coming. But not in any organized fashion. Most are bringing their families." Which meant having women and children underfoot when the bloodshed started. "They've been promised land and plunder by Anne of Menand. Arnhanders, in general, have decided that, religion aside, the Connec is properly part of Arnhand. Sublime has encouraged this belief. Arnhand is letting the Grolsachers pass through. They're providing supplies to any Grolsachers who swear allegiance to Anne and to the Brothen Church.

"The boy isn't sophisticated enough to understand any of that, except on a personal level. But there are broad implications for everyone in the west." Brother Candle did not tell them he thought Anne of Menand was positioning herself to be the mother behind what she hoped to make the most powerful monarch in the Episcopal world.

"The invaders will come down the Sadew Valley. There's game and water. They think we won't expect them to come that way."

Haiden Backe and Bishop Farfog had arrived using the easier route farther east.

Brock Rault said, "I'd assume that, after the recent skirmishes, they'll pile up somewhere till numbers force them to come on. We can deal with that. Our real problem is what comes along behind. Brother?"

"The boy doesn't actually know anything more than your children do about your plans. But he does believe that an Arnhander army is going to come in behind them, to protect them. And to restore order." That excuse had been used to justify previous Arnhander incursions.

Brock said, "Ralph, take the boy to Antieux with you. I'll have a letter for the Count, too. The rest of you, bring your men to the Catna Calci spring before sunrise tomorrow."

Brother Candle was not pleased. He feared Brock wanted to repeat the Black Mountain Massacre.

He would argue but knew that was a waste of breath. Grolsachers entering the Rault demesne arrived under sentence of death.

SOCIA RAULT, IN ILL-FITTING BOILED LEATHER ARMOR, TURNED UP ONCE IT was too late to make a scene about the impropriety. Brother Candle strained to hide his amusement. Brock Rault was too young to have forehead veins stand out like that.

Had he truly expected that confiscating the mail she had worn before would hinder her?

It was chilly for the time of year. Teeth chattered. Mist lay in patchlets in the hollows along the creek in the Sadew Valley. As had been the case three mornings running, a trickle of invaders passed without hindrance. They would be dealt with a few miles farther on. Some would be allowed to go back to report that the folk of the Connec were making no organized effort to defend themselves.

Three days of waiting left Brock's followers impatient.

Everyone kept quiet while three men passed, arguing bitterly. Once they were out of earshot, Brock asked, "What language was that, Brother?"

Brother Candle had to admit, "I don't know. That's the second group that talked like that." And that made the incursion more disturbing. Fugitives from the advancing ice would grace the Connec's enemies with more power to destroy.

After quelling a belated response to Socia's arrival, Seuir Brock told his family, "I can't keep these men restrained much longer."

The force numbered thirty-five. Thirty-three armed men, a woman, and one Maysalean Perfect Master. Some were from neighboring holdings and felt little need to defer to Seuir Brock's leadership.

There was an invader camp up the valley, in a marshy meadow. And someone was in control. There were pickets. They were not well posted or alert, but they were there. They made scouting the camp difficult. Scores of women and children were among the several hundred people there.

For differing reasons Seuir Brock and Brother Candle each wanted a closer look at that camp.

Thurm said, "That ground is too boggy for a decent camp. There's springs all over. You can sink in up to your hips some places. There's a million mosquitoes. If they stay there very long they'll all come down with dysentery or malaria or something."

Brock replied, "I only pray there's that much stupid among them."

Brother Candle muttered, "So do I."

"God should take the stain from our souls before we smear it on ourselves?" Brock chuckled. "Yes. I'm starting to see how your mind works."

There was no opportunity to debate the rights and wrongs and costs, of defending today's Connec. How many times round the Wheel of Life would it take to expiate the evil that would happen here?

One of the scouts came scooting down the hillside. The needle-strewn slope was steep. "Seuir, some people showed up at the Grolsacher camp. Better clothes, horses, twenty to twenty-five of them. At least eight are knights. Their pennons weren't recognizable."

"Arnhanders," Thurm said. Socia spat to her left like a man sealing a curse.

Brock said, "I didn't expect them to turn up yet. What was that?"

A roar had come rolling down the valley.

"Just guessing," Brother Candle said. "The raiders have been turned loose."

"All in a mob, you think?"

Socia said, "The healthiest will be the first ones here. And the most dangerous."

Brock was not pleased. "The Arnhanders won't be part of the first rush." Meaning the ambush could not be as successful as he wanted. He made a decision. "Put the barricades up." He had kept his men gathering brush and deadwood to create a barrier across the valley. It would not stop the invaders but would create a chokepoint where archers would be more effective.

THE GROLSACHERS CAME IN A RACING FLOOD. THERE WERE OTHER FOR-eigners among them. Cruel poverty was the commonality of the horde.

A dozen archers went to work. Ten men with shields and spears pro-tected them. The archers seldom missed.

Those invaders who escaped climbed the steep far slope, then fled downstream. Very few broke through the barrier.

The other Connectens struck farther up the valley, hitting the tail-enders of the mob. They pushed downstream. Brother Candle and Socia Rault were tasked with guarding their backs.

There was but one incident involving the two. Brother Candle avoided getting blood on his hands or soul.

"Booga-booga?" Socia demanded in a mocking tone. "What the hell was that?"

"He ran away, didn't he?"

"Right back to the meadow. Where he'll complain that he ran into a ferocious sorcerer."

"Foo."

"You think he'll admit he ran away from a Maysalean Perfect?"

"The thing is done. Don't!"

Too late. Socia had stabbed the moaning, wounded old woman. The lives of these desperate intruders meant no more to her than did those of roaches or rats.

"What?"

"Never mind."

"We need to get back to Caron ande Lette. Fast." Only women, children, and a few old men were there to defend the fortress.

Brock Rault had a different idea.

The butchery was over. The Sadew Valley was now a vale of the dead. Brother Candle knew the mind exaggerated horrors but still thought there were at least a hundred dead. Moans and whimpers came from hiding places in the undergrowth. Brock ignored them. After excusing six men who had been injured, he murmured, "I'm going after the men behind this."

"Oh. No," Brother Candle muttered. "That'll only make it worse."

"Brother, nothing will make it worse. They mean to kill us, take everything we own, and make the Connec part of Arnhand. With no leftover heretics. Self-defense is not a sin. Your own Synod of St. Jeules so ruled."

The Perfect bowed his head. That was true.

And he no longer deserved the title Perfect. His thinking had become dominated by emotion.

Rault continued. "We aren't asking you to cut throats. Just get out of the way." Irked.

"That I can do." But he did not stay behind when the healthy and willing headed for the meadow camp.

THE CAMP WAS A SPRAWL OF PATHETIC SHELTERS BUILT OF DEADWOOD, brush, reeds, and ragged blankets. A nest for misery unimaginable.

The new arrivals were not alone. Scores of sick, elderly, women, children, and even healthy men had not joined the rush down the Sadew Valley. The camp was in an uproar.

Socia glared at Brother Candle. "Booga booga."

"What?" Brock asked.

"Private joke."

Brock looked at her askance but addressed Thurm. "You know this ground. Can mounted, armored men operate on it?"

"Not most places. Not well."

After consultation, Brock chose a direction from which to attack the camp. He approached boldly. His archers launched fire arrows, starting several blazes. Some Grolsachers came out, angry. They accomplished nothing. Several got killed for their trouble.

Brock let fly a few more fire arrows, then began a slow withdrawal.

"Ah. Here they come."

A parade of horsemen left the camp, spread out abreast. Knights, squires, and mounted sergeants, they numbered eighteen. Thurm said, "They don't look much more prosperous than the Grolsachers."

"Paid fighters," Brock said.

"Most likely." Meaning they would be clever and cruel.

Changes were going on in Arnhand and the Empire. Younger brothers with nothing to inherit traditionally went to the Holy Lands or joined the Grail Knights in their wars to convert the pagans of the east. But those journeys into a brief, brutal, lethal exile had lost their emotional appeal. Still, one had to make a living. Having been raised up to follow only one trade.

Thurm said, "They plan to carve out chunks of the Connec for themselves."

"Let's see if we can't disappoint them."

The Connectens kept backing away. The day was near its end. The sun's lower limb settled into the pines behind them.

Brock had his archers launch a flight at the Arnhanders. Most of the shafts fell short. The few that did not miss or, in one instance, strike a shield, shifted to intercept it.

Socia complained, "These damned mosquitoes are driving me crazy!"

Swallows ripped the air overhead. Soon bats would come to the feast. But not ravens, Brother Candle hoped. Ravens lived on both sides of the boundary with the Night. Human faith had endowed the birds with vast symbolic and oracular power.

The horsemen began their advance. In no hurry. Measured. Which was not what Brock wanted. "Loose another flight, then run for the trees. But watch where you put your feet down."

The horsemen were closer. Most of the arrows reached. Only one found a living target, however, and that a horse when a shaft ricocheted off a shield.

Several Arnhanders spurred their mounts, knowing the woods were too dense for a successful pursuit there.

Others followed.

Within a minute two-thirds of the animals had bogged down in the narrow, sluggish streams meandering under masking surface vegetation.

Those hazards were obvious enough in a good light, when one was unhurried and watching.

Brock ordered, "Archers, turn and loose. Concentrate on the horses."

There was grumbling. The animals were more valuable than the men riding them. But there would be no prizes taken here.

Rault's order was sound tactically but difficult practically. The archers had scarcely a dozen arrows left amongst them.

Brock swore. "Damn! I was hoping more would go down. And that some would drown. That we could finish them off while they were tangled in their harness, in the peat and the mud."

The Arnhanders did not let that happen.

One man and four horses did suffer. Those Arnhanders who remained mounted declined further pursuit.

"At least their damned camp will burn down," Socia grumbled.

BROCK RAULT INSISTED ON TRAVELING THROUGH THE NIGHT. PROGRESS was slow and exhausting. And often painful. In the wee hours Brother Candle told Seuir Brock, "Leave me. I can't keep up. I'll be all right. They won't harm a holy man."

"You're whistling in the night, old man. You're exactly what they're hunting. The only way you'd survive is if they sent you to Salpeno for a show trial."

Rault ordered an hour's rest. While he and Thurm scouted ahead.

The break gave Brother Candle a chance to become so stiff he could hardly move. Nor did he have the energy to swat mosquitoes. "They're going to suck me dry," he muttered to no one in particular.

Despair threatened him. He thought about Margete, began suffering worldly regrets about the choices they had made. Margete was now Sister Probity in the Maysalean convent at Fleaumont. He had not seen her for years. Had she seen any of the children lately? He had not. One of his sons, the wholly materialistic Aiméchiel, refused to acknowledge him because he had given his wealth to support the Seekers.

He was ashamed. He no longer knew where to find any of his children.

The Perfect jerked out of his reverie, smitten by sudden fear.

There was a huge absence in the night.

The mosquitoes were gone.

The Sadew Valley lay in the embrace of a silence as absolute as that of a crypt. As the darkness grew deeper.

No insects buzzed. No owls gossiped about where to find the fattest mice. Nothing scurried through the leaves and needles, trying to find a meal without becoming a meal.

And the darkness deepened.

Leaves crunched, then, as Brock and Thurm returned. Brock whispered, "We're two hundred yards from the edge of the woods. We'll be home before dawn, easy. Even if we have to carry our chaplain. What?"

Brock froze, finally sensing the horror. The deep horror. Which came without accompanying menace.

It did not come near enough to be seen. It wore darkness like a disguise. But darkness did not mask its smell, nor the soft sounds it brought along when it came close.

The stink was that of summertime death a week old. The sound was the hum of ten thousand flies.

Brother Candle shook his head violently, as though to fling the stench out of his nostrils while rejecting the power of ancient Night. Those old gods were gone! Rook had been disarmed, dismembered, *constrained*, in the very earliest days of the Old Empire. Not even another god could shatter the mystic shackles holding defeated Instrumentalities.

Those harsh old gods had been conquered by men. Only human instruments could loose them again.

The stench drifted onward, following the trail of corpses down into the Connec. The darkness faded back to normal. Sound returned.

The Connectens resumed travel. Not one of them believed the real Rook had passed by, dripping maggots on the forest floor. They would rather believe their priests than their senses. To them that Instrumentality was too awful to bear thought. Someday they could garner the notice of the Lord of Flies. Unless they prayed very hard to their own greater god.

The Arnhanders did not believe, either, though something so terrified their horses that most fled despite the darkness. The surviving camp folk, now without shelter, had less trouble believing. Quietly, beneath Grolsach's placid Chaldarean surface, some recollection of the old gods soldiered on. In circumstances as woefully reduced as those of the Grolsachers themselves.

The mosquitoes returned. As they did, Brock Rault insisted, "Get up, Master. We don't have far to go. And the worst is behind us. You'll be asleep in a feather bed before the sun comes up."

BROTHER CANDLE CLAMBERED TO THE PARAPET OVERLOOKING CARON ande Lette's gateway. The sun was going down. He had slept eleven hours. Every joint still ached. As did every muscle. He was too old for adventures.

Before coming topside he had eaten till he was ready to burst. Now, content despite his discomfort, he stood in twilight considering the besieging mass pathetic despite its numbers.

There were hundreds of Grolsachers out there. More were off foraging, finding neither food nor plunder. Those on hand were not in a bellicose mood. They were the tailenders. Yesterday's survivors. There were not a lot of healthy adult males among them.

Wailing broke out whenever a corpse was found and identified. Though how they recognized their dead after Rook's passage was beyond Brother Candle.

He had not seen a corpse touched by the Instrumentality. He had heard a description. While eating. The Great Demon left only a dried husk so desiccated that it could be hoisted with one hand.

Brock Rault was on post. As always. The Perfect asked, "You've decided to live up here, now?"

"I can see from here, Master. Not a lot, but enough to follow what's happening right around here."

"Which would appear to be not much."

"Correct. Pretending, but nothing of substance. We broke their spirit."

Thurm and Socia arrived, Thurm teasing crumbs out of the red brush at the corners of his mouth.

"And the Arnhanders?" Brother Candle acknowledged Socia with a nod.

"Trying to forage. Having no luck. If they work in small parties they get attacked. If they go in number they only find people too stupid or stubborn to go hide in the woods."

"So someone deluded the Grolsachers into thinking they'd just stroll into milk and honey. And the Arnhanders into believing that there would be no resistance."

"That isn't wrong. We can't do much but sit here."

Brother Candle did not believe him. Sitting was not in keeping with the Rault character.

Socia said, "You've got plenty of initiative left, big brother." She gestured. Barely discernible in the failing light were earthworks the invaders had begun that day, without enthusiasm or urgency. Only a fraction of the foreigners had pitched in. The more hale had gone looking for food and plunder.

Many foragers failed to return to their loved ones.

"Yes?" Brock asked.

"If the Arnhanders go foraging, sortie. Destroy their camp. Steal or kill their extra horses. And their grooms and servants."

Thurm grunted. "Only, why take risks? If we just wait . . . How long before Count Raymone rescues his precious Socia?"

Socia punched him. An argument ensued. Socia was full of blood-lust. Ready to fling one-woman sallies at the Grolsachers. "To keep the weeds down. So they don't get too numerous to handle."

Brother Candle feared the truth of her central argument. What they saw was the first lapping wave of a flood. The Sadew Valley could become a river of desperate humanity that would come till they overwhelmed the Connec.

Providence knew, the province could not mount an organized effort to defend itself. The central authority remained confused and irresolute, if not moribund. Foiling the poison plot had not paid off in a ducal resurrection. Many lesser lights remained interested only in making their neighbors miserable. Those who did retain a sense of responsibility mostly were content to wait for trouble to come to them. Only Count Raymone Garete, because of past successes, could rally many followers. But he had no legal power to raise levees or give orders outside his own county.

Count Raymone was the most dangerous man in the Connec, from the viewpoint of the Brothen Church. Which explained why Antieux attracted so much attention from the Society.

Campfires appeared as darkness deepened, all round Caron ande Lette. They were too few to establish a blockade.

That could change.

Brock had no intention of letting an investiture develop. He collected a volunteer force of five. He and they went down ropes on the south side of the fortress, where the wall was shortest. Rault explained, "They should be watching for a sally from the gate."

Brother Candle spent hours, waiting, listening, watching. There was nothing to hear. And only lightning bugs to see. Brock was working with admirable stealth.

The old man wore out before midnight. His body still had a thousand repairs to make.

THE PERFECT WAKENED ONCE, ROUND WHAT WAS CALLED THE WITCHING hour. He had felt something terrible in the night. But it was gone before he wakened fully. He drained his bladder, returned to bed. He shivered like it was the heart of a cold, damp winter till sleep returned.

BROTHER CANDLE ROSE WITH THE SUN. DESPITE ALL THE SLEEP, HE WAS weak and groggy and inclined to lie down again.

Thurm and Socia joined him for breakfast. That included fresh bread, preserves, and bacon in quantity. Brother Candle felt compassion for the Grolsacher families outside.

Thurm said, "That thing was out there again last night."

"Thing?"

"From before. Up the valley. The Lord of Maggots."

Socia said, "Oh, stop pussyfooting and say it. Rook! Rook! Rook was out there, following Brock around while he exterminated the vermin."

As Brother Candle opened his mouth, Socia barked, "Don't even bother. You might be more clever than the average Episcopal priest but you just aren't gonna twist things around so you can say that that wasn't Rook."

Brother Candle responded, "The Instrumentality we call Rook can't exist in today's world."

"Go tell it that, dipshit. I'm sure it'll be embarrassed and go lie down again."

Thurm slugged his little sister on the upper arm. "A little respect there, girl child."

Brother Candle said, "I'm not saying that something big isn't crawling around in the dark. And it does present similarities to the old pagan god of corruption. But that god doesn't exist anymore."

Socia sneered. "If it looks like a turd, smells like a turd, and draws flies like a turd, I'm gonna call it a turd."

Thurm said, "Maybe not all of Rook got bound. Or maybe part of him got loose. Something weird happened in the White Hills when the Arnhanders came down on Antieux that time. The ones that ended up getting killed in the Black Mountain Massacre. They say a bunch of old graves opened up and evil things came out."

Could be, Brother Candle thought. The White Hills, on the northeast edge of the Altai, were also called the Haunted Hills. For all its stench and psychic impact, the thing did not seem particularly powerful. Could it be just a tiny shard of a god, driven by its original instinct?

Would it try to grow? Was that even possible? Would it hunt for scattered bits of itself? Would it free other old terrors from its youth?

"I'll stop wishful thinking and defer to my own ignorance at this point," the Perfect said. Though he despaired of the answer, he asked, "Did Brock enjoy any success last night?"

Thurm showed fresh excitement. "He did. He got into the Arnhanders' paddock and stole some of their horses. Which he killed where the Grolsachers could grab them and eat them."

That ought to sow seeds of distrust.

Thurm's face closed down. The Perfect sensed that there was more, of a nature so dark he did not want to share it with a holy man.

"I see. Maybe that's all I need to know."

BROTHER CANDLE MADE HIS WAY TO THE PARAPET OVER THE GATE. THE INvaders were digging a trench around Caron ande Lette. Piling the earth on its far side. If the siege lasted long a palisade would be raised atop that earth. Others worked on what, even from afar, was obviously a cemetery. And a few Arnhanders were adding to the defenses of their camp.

Horsemen gathered in the small court behind the fortress gate. To the east, near the river, a file of ragged people trudged southward, ignoring Caron ande Lette.

The gate swung open. Socia Rault and a dozen youths burst out. They ignored besiegers. They galloped over and scattered the people by the river, killing the men, then ran away before the Arnhanders could ready themselves for a fight. Socia committed atrocities along the developing trench until the Arnhanders did come after her.

Keeping low so as not to be seen, archers jostled Brother Candle as they took position. Others came to operate the ballistae.

Socia tried to lure the Arnhanders into range. They would not come.

Seuir Brock showed up. Livid. When Socia arrived, grinning wildly, he told her, "You won't do that again. Am I understood? Brother Candle.

Would you be violating Count Raymone's instructions if you were to escort my sister out of here?"

Socia shut Brock out the instant he started telling her what she would not be doing anymore.

"Would that be wise? With all these lawless folk roving the countryside?"

Softly, Brock said, "They'll be the lesser risk."

"Seuir?"

"We can't survive here. Not if this keeps on. They're disorganized and incompetent. I'll kill thousands. But I'll lose a man sometimes. And get no replacement. They'll wear me down. Like a riverbank devoured by a never-ending stream. They'll find the hiding places in the woods. I don't want Socia here when that happens."

Brother Candle opined, "If I take her to Antieux and you fall, don't doubt that you'll be avenged." Socia struck him as the sort who would slash and burn all Arnhand if Charlve the Dim or Anne of Menand irritated her sufficiently. "She'll find a way."

"You might be right."

"What are you two muttering about over there?" Socia demanded. "Are you talking about me?"

"In a way. I'm trying to get the Perfect to leave while he still can."

"That's a big puff of wind, brother. What are you really saying?"

"Every minute. She has to be contrary. Every minute of every day."

Brother Candle nodded. That would be the way to get the girl to do the necessary.

Seuir Brock said, "Little sister, come share a bowl of wine. I need you to do something. Maybe the most important thing you'll ever do."

THE HEIGHTS OF ARTLAN ANDE BRITH FELL BEHIND. BROTHER CANDLE ADmired Seuir Brock Rault's manipulative skills. Rault had sold him on saving Socia. Then he had sold Socia the notion that Brother Candle was too important a Maysalean philosopher to lose. He was a moral giant, to be preserved at all cost. Only she had influence enough with Count Raymone to see that he was protected.

Letters each carried to Seuir Lanne had convinced that worthy to send them on, disguised, accompanied by a pair of Tuldse nieces and two donkeys. Their horses remained at Artlan ande Brith.

Socia's war gear, however, was in the packs on one of the donkeys.

The girl and nieces were disguised as peasant boys. Brother Candle wore what he had for years. All Perfect wore the same gray robe.

Care was necessary even south of Artlan ande Brith. Grolsachers had gotten past the Tuldse stronghold.

Seuir Lanne was every bit as pessimistic as Seuir Brock Rault.

*   *   *

COUNT RAYMONE WAS PLEASED TO SEE SOCIA BUT NOT THE PERFECT MAS-
ter. The Tuldse nieces did not enter the equation. Those had been delivered to local relatives.

Count Raymone was almost obsequious toward Socia while apolo-
gizing for having sent no troops north.

The man was smitten.

Then, "Nobody's listening, Master. Tell me the truth. What happened? What's really going on up there?"

Brother Candle left out nothing.

Count Raymone goggled at Socia's behavior but asked only, "Rook?
Really?"

"Some part of him, possibly. Or something that wants him remembered. Maybe something meant to spread fear and chaos by wakening
our dread of the old evils."

"I think it's the real thing. A sliver of the real thing."

"But . . ."

"I get news from a hundred sources, Brother. This tale of an awak-
ening Instrumentality isn't unique. It's happening all over, wherever
there are old stories about hauntings. I think there must be some truth in
all the reports."

Brother Candle asked, "Why didn't you send troops to Caron ande
Lette?"

"Because Sublime's villains have kept me too busy here. These are
some nasty churchmen. They adapt every day, finding ways to be irritating without offending temporal law to the point where I can round them
up. And more and more keep turning up. I don't know where they find
them all."

"The monastic orders are turning applicants away. You don't go
hungry when you belong to the Church. And a certain sort enjoys having petty power over the rest of us."

"Not what I want to hear, Master. But I don't get the good much
anymore. Just yesterday I heard that the new Empress, Katrin, was
crowned by Sublime himself. In return, she bent the knee to the Brothen
Patriarchy."

"That could mean civil war inside the Empire."

"It could. It definitely means that the Empire won't shield the Connec anymore. Which leads to the other bad news. Sublime is ready to
preach a crusade against the Maysalean Heresy."

Brother Candle shuddered and sighed. Seekers could be found everywhere but the Connec was where they were most open, numerous, and
in control. The Connec would be where the main blow fell.

"One way or another, the false Patriarch will plunder our land."

The Count said, "He'd better hurry. Before it's all eaten up in our little country wars."

THE SOCIETY RECEIVED INSTRUCTIONS FROM BROTHE. THE LATEST BROTHEN Episcopal Bishop of Antieux issued an order for Count Raymone to present himself. But the Bishop's messengers could not find him. And several messengers failed to return.

Count Raymone had handled two problems with one quick sidle, summoning those who were willing to join a small army he took north. Bernardin Amberchelle and his betrothed stayed to deal with the importunities and expanding arrogance of Brothe's agents. Then Amberchelle, in turn, disappeared. But rumor saw his savage hand behind the killings and disappearances that continued to plague Antieux. Fewer and fewer Society brothers came to the city. Those already there began wearing disguises and moving around in groups.

And still there were casualties. Some quite gruesome.

Amazing how much Church blood could be let when those doing the bloodletting were neither afraid of excommunication nor intimidated by their own consciences.

Socia caught Brother Candle several weeks into what she called her regency with her in charge. "It's all a big damned conspiracy, Master! These people tell me I'm the lady of the city, now! They go through all the motions, asking me for orders. Then they go do whatever they want!"

"Raymone set it up that way, dear girl. So he can't be blamed for the wickedness. He isn't here to stop it. And, of course, you can't because you're only a woman."

After a pause during which she fought her anger, Socia said, "I can honestly say I understand that. It's clever enough. What I can't get a handle on is all the foreigners involved in the struggle with the Society."

That baffled the old man. Count Raymone had hired no mercenaries. "Foreigners? You lost me, child. What foreigners?"

"Being a girl I guess I'm supposed to be too dim to notice. Before he disappeared Bernardin was chummy with some outlanders who spoke a dialect harder to follow than Firaldian. Men who looked like they'd butcher and roast their own mothers if they missed a meal. Bernardin disappeared but those men are still around."

"I haven't been paying close enough attention, obviously. I haven't noticed them."

Naturally, when Socia tried to point them out not a one could be found.

But the war on Sublime's running dogs never abated.

11. Brothen Homecoming

Well?" Anna Mozilla asked as Piper Hecht collapsed onto a couch. "How bad is it?"

"It's awful. It's beyond awful. Sublime is a raving lunatic. The whole west will go up in flames if he has his way. He's determined to invade the Connec. Anne of Menand seems to be in complete control in Salpeno. She takes the crusade idea seriously. She has people in the Connec already. She's so focused on the south, you *know* Santerin's surrogates will get busy elsewhere. If it goes badly for Arnhand in the Connec, King Brill might invade the Pail itself. To press his claim to the Arnhander throne."

"No more politics, Piper."

"How are the kids?"

"Getting fat. And in bed. Bechter sent word you were coming."

"I don't know what I'd do without him."

"What was the coronation like?" With a sharp edge there. The Captain-General's mistress had not been invited.

Hecht said, "That was weeks ago."

"And you haven't been home since."

"Uhn? I didn't realize . . . We really are working hard."

"You're the man in charge, Piper."

He sighed. He would not be able to keep much from Anna, anymore. Titus Consent had had to leave the Devedian quarter. He had moved in not far away. Noë and Anna were getting chummy.

Neither woman had an extended family to give her support.

Anna had become uncomfortably domestic. She was older than Hecht. Maybe the adventure had gone out of her.

She did have plenty of domestic adventure left.

Lying in the post-prandial glow, half asleep, Hecht tried to get the coronation out of his head. It was stuck like a song that would not go away. Like the latest love song from some Connecten jongleur. Princess Helspeth had stared at him throughout the ceremony. It was so obvious that several people asked about it. He explained that he had saved her life at al-Khazen.

He hoped he was more subtle than she.

The girl fascinated him.

But it was only a fancy. Helspeth Ege was Princess Apparent of the New Brothen Empire. He was a sword in the pay of her father's favorite enemy.

The Imperial party still had not left Brothe. But the Captain-General had seen nothing of those people since the ceremonies.

Nor would he have had time.

Sublime wanted to send an army through Ormienden into the End of Connec. He had more backing than Hecht had thought possible. Many supporters, disappointed by the Calziran Crusade, were willing to throw more wealth down another rathole hoping they could fatten up in the Connec.

Titus's reports made it sound as though there would be little left to take. Bad things were happening out there.

Sublime still had received only a quarter of the money promised by Anne of Menand. As much more was supposed to have disappeared in transit. And there were rumors that Anne was financing Arnhander incursions to the Connec using the rest of Sublime's bribe as security for loans for her own warmaking.

Brothen moneylenders had become reluctant to deal with the Patriarchy.

Sleep came. Helspeth haunted his dreams. She did so every night. He had gotten no chance to speak with her. Then, or since. The Imperial party would leave soon. The Empress Katrin wanted to cross the Jago Mountains while the passes were in their best possible state.

Anna rolled over and buried her face in his chest. Her hot breath wakened him. "Can't you relax?" she murmured. "Can't you just push it all out of your head for one night?"

He could not. When not obsessing about Helspeth Ege he worried about Principaté Delari, Osa Stile, recruiting troubles, the next assassination attempt, and what had become of al-Azer er-Selim. He wanted a long talk with his onetime Master of Ghosts. But Az had not revealed himself again.

He had not had news from Bo Biogna yet, either. No one had seen Bo for a long time.

Piper Hecht was worried.

Dangers circled like impatient vultures.

"I'm trying, darling. Truly, I am. But . . ."

Sleep finally returned. Almost that suddenly.

PELLA AND VALI MADE BREAKFAST. AND DID A CREDITABLE JOB. THEY brought it in to Hecht and Anna, still lying entangled. Neither child was troubled. Privacy was not that common.

Hecht was not comfortable with the situation although, intellectually, he knew that here in the west, even among nobles, whole families slept in the same room, often in the same bed. The usual business between men and women proceeded anyway.

Hecht asked, "Has our little girl said anything yet?"

"No. But her motives have changed. It isn't about hiding anymore. Now she's just being stubborn." Anna leaned in to whisper, "I heard her talking to Pella. She didn't know I was in the next room."

"She'll come around." After a few minutes lying there, fed, enjoying the holding and being held, Hecht said, "They're good kids."

"Amazingly so, considering their backgrounds. Yes."

"Aren't we all? Pella ever show signs of homesickness? Does Vali?"

"Pella? Not that I've ever seen."

"He knows when he's got it good."

"He mentioned his sister once."

"The prostitute?"

"He's asked if he can read the book that has him and her in it. I don't know what he means."

Hecht explained. "Bronte Doneto has a copy. According to Pinkus. Who claims to have read it. I doubt that Doneto would let us see it. It's banned in the Patriarchal States. It pokes fun at the Church. Supposedly."

"You haven't found out anything about Vali?"

"Only that her real name can't be Vali Dumaine. Titus can't find Dumaines anywhere who are missing a daughter. Nor are there any girls named Vali missing anywhere, at least at a level where there would be any notoriety."

"So she's just a clever con artist."

"Probably. But I still have trouble swallowing the coincidence of her being a prisoner in a sporting house that fronts for the Witchfinder side of the Special Office. For a Brotherhood cabal set on scuttling Sublime's deal with the secret mistress of Arnhand."

"If you didn't have to be here, if you could just retire and go live your own life, where would you go? What would you do?"

Anna was tense, suddenly. His answer mattered. She was not just chattering in bed. "I don't know. I've never thought about it." Dreanger's call was fading, even ignoring its unfriendly attitude since he had been on this side of the Mother Sea. "I do tell people I want to get rich enough to buy one of those big latifundia farming operations, but I don't mean it. Farming is too much work. Even for owners."

"You ever done any farming?"

"No."

"Then definitely don't start. The farmer is at the mercy of everything and everyone. Bugs. Rodents. Moneylenders. Weather. Disease. Peace. War. The whims of God and Man. If it wasn't for forced tenancy, the people who do all the real work would quit."

"Voice of experience?"

"I had the great good fortune to have good skin, big eyes, a pretty face, and excellent tits when I was young. Those bought me out of the rustic life."

Hecht knew little about Anna's life before he met her. He never tempted fortune by prying. She seldom shared what she had survived or seen before she opened her door that night in Sonsa. That simple act marked the start of new lives for both of them.

He said only, "Uhm?"

"You should've seen me when I was sixteen, Piper. I can't believe any girl ever looked that good."

"I'm sorry I missed you. Though I can't imagine you being more desirable than you are right now."

"You do have a knack for slinging the bull, Piper Hecht. And a woman of my years does need to hear that sort of thing occasionally." She grabbed. "Is this thing interested in another adventure?"

Anna Mozilla made it entirely impossible for Piper Hecht to remember that there were children in the next room.

PELLA AND VALI WERE YOUNG BUT NOT IGNORANT OF THE WAY OF MEN AND women. In fact, but for Hecht rescuing her, Vali would by now have had considerable direct knowledge.

Young girls were very marketable.

Boys were, too, though to a smaller pool of eager consumers.

Hecht was half-awake, thinking about Principaté Muniero Delari. He had not seen the old man for weeks. Delari was preoccupied with refurbishing his underground world. While striving to avoid exposure to the machinations of Principaté Doneto.

Anna snuggled closer, murmuring, "We should probably think about getting up."

Hecht had just finished dressing when the world seemed to end.

HECHT WAKENED ABOARD A LITTER. THE AIR WAS THICK WITH SMOKE AND the stench of spent firepowder. Men from the City Regiment carried the litter's four corners. They wore the padded leather shirts and hard leather caps of the new militia patrol, the constabulari. They jogged up the steps of a church. Other constabularii jostled them, carrying other litters.

As the City Regiment dwindled it was being replaced by unpaid citizens performing duties defined by laws newly promulgated by the city senate and approved by the Church and Brothe's leading families. All able-bodied were now obligated to work a shift of fire watch and street patrol once each ten days, inside their native quarter, the shifts set by the crafts guilds and neighborhood social associations.

Although called quarters, there were nine military districts in Brothe. The patrols had had a dramatic effect on crime.

Hecht wondered where Pinkus Ghort had found the model. The Eastern Empire?

The constabularii lowered the litter. They eased Hecht onto a pallet. One called, "Father Capricio! This one might be important." Then they were gone, back for another customer.

Hecht stared at the high ceiling. Angels had been painted between supporting beams. A priest dropped to one knee beside him. "Ah. You're conscious." His cassock was that of one of the healing orders. "Can you tell me how badly you're hurt?"

"Concussion. I think there was an explosion."

"A huge one. A dozen buildings were damaged."

"Anna. The kids . . ." He tried to get up.

"Lie still. The constabulari will deal with it. Injured women and children would be here already. One of the deacons or altar boys can help you look. If you don't need me?"

"I don't know if I do. I'm having trouble feeling things."

"I don't see anything external. And I do have seriously wounded people here."

"Go."

Where *had* Ghort harvested his three-branched militia idea?

Every Patriarchal city now had to organize a militia. The Captain-General's idea. Pinkus Ghort, overseeing the Brothen militia, built the local force to his own standards, dividing it into the constabulari, the guardi, and the equestri. The guardi manned permanent watch stations on the city wall and manned the several gates. They came from a more prosperous class than the constabulari. Already, some were pooling resources to hire individuals to fulfill their obligations for them. All of those hirelings were veterans of the City Regiment. And now, more than ever, beholden to the man who found them their jobs, Colonel Pinkus Ghort.

The third group was drawn from the richest families. The equestrian order. The men who could afford horses. Mimicking antiquity.

That puffed wealthy egos. Though there was resistance to actually going into the field.

The Brothen militia, as were those being organized in all the other Patriarchal cities, was expected to make some of its number available for service outside the home city.

Since ancient times the overlord had had the right to call out the entire male population. In the developing system a militiaman could expect to do forty days of active field service about once every six years.

Even the least enthusiastic cities would tolerate a ten percent call-up. Or, Hecht hoped, they would contribute money. That would let him hire experienced troops from amongst the refugees.

One of Anna's neighbors, a widow named Urgent, found him. "There you are. Anna is beside herself. You should treat her better."

"You could be right. Is she hurt? Are the children all right?"

"They're fine. The girl is covered with blood but it was just a nosebleed."

"Good. Would you tell them where you found me?"

"Why don't you?"

"Madam, I'm here for a reason. Not because I need a nap."

The Urgent woman was the busybody sort. Nevertheless, she nodded once, sharply, and went away.

He passed out moments later, while trying to get up.

"PINKUS?"

"The one and only. How come you're loafing around in here?" Ghort settled cross-legged, part of him on Hecht's pallet and part on that of a man who had arrived while Hecht was unconscious. The other man would not mind. He was dead.

"Last time I tried to get up I passed out."

"What I heard. I'll have a couple guys hang around. In case they try again."

"What?"

Ghort reflected. "That's right. You wouldn't know."

"Know what?"

"The big boom. We think it was meant for you. Only it went off early."

"Uhm?"

"All right. From the beginning. There was a donkey cart loaded with kegs of firepowder. Made a hell of a bang. It was supposed to go off in front of Anna's house."

Impossible that he should be so lucky, Hecht thought. He suspected that Ghort agreed. Ghort said, "We caught two men. Which is how we know what was supposed to happen. We'll backtrack it. From them and from the source of the firepowder."

"Sounds like you got it all under control."

"I think so. Tell me something, Pipe."

"What's that?"

"How come people keep trying to waste your ass? You might be the fucking Captain-General but it still don't make sense that somebody keeps coming after you."

"Pinkus, I wish I knew. If I did, you can bet your mother's reputation I'd be on top of it. But I don't have a clue. It can't be the past catching up. I don't have that interesting a past."

"Freaky."

"Absolutely. This scares me more than if I did know why. Because then I'd know who. Are you *sure* somebody was after me?"

"As sure as I can be of anything. And they were so eager that they didn't care how many people got hurt as long as they killed you."

"You have prisoners who were involved, I'd be thrilled to visit with them myself. Or, if you don't have anything special in mind for them, turn them over to Principaté Delari."

"I might be able to arrange that."

"Good. Help me get up, here."

Earth-turning dizziness overwhelmed him before he could get his feet under him. "I'm not ready. Put me back down."

Hecht slipped into unconsciousness again.

HE WAKENED. HIS HEAD WAS POUNDING. HE THOUGHT ANNA MUST BE RE-sponsible. He worried about the concussion . . . No Anna. No Pella or Vali. Nor anyone else who was part of his current life. But on the pallet formerly occupied by the dead man was a face from another life.

"Az?"

Al-Azer er-Selim, Master of Ghosts. Almost unrecognizable in western clothing, wearing no facial hair. His eyes gave him away. Those eyes had looked into the heart of the Night, yet remained amused by the folly rampant in Man and all of God's creation.

"Captain." Softly. Breathlessly.

"What are you doing?"

"I haven't been able to see you any other way. You seem to be avoiding us."

"Not so. Fate itself is determined to distract me."

"Fate, Captain?" Though Az had regular congress with the Night he remained a faithful Praman.

"Poor choice of words. Hard not to pick up bad habits here. Especially when you have to fit in."

Az took no position in response. But he would be familiar with the problem.

Hecht asked, "See anybody paying attention to us?"

Headshake.

"How did you get in here?"

"Had myself carried in. They're still finding people out there."

Hecht levered himself into a sitting position. He was feeling better, now. He would be doing no running, though.

"You were the target, you know."

"What?" As though he had not heard it already, from Pinkus Ghort.

"The explosion was supposed to destroy you and the woman's house. They've been waiting for weeks for the chance."

"How do you know?"

"We know some of the people. We know who's paying them."

"Excellent. Why are you here?"

"To talk with my captain."

"Here in Brothe? You don't belong."

"We weren't given a choice, Captain. They wouldn't let us on the boats that took the Sha-lug and Lucidians out of Calzir. Men we knew, some from our own schools, showed us the edge of their weapons and made us stay. We weren't supposed to survive al-Khazen. Your attack, the Emperor's, the Instrumentalities that appeared, and the intercession by the Collegium, all those kept us from being slaughtered. Evidently it was extremely inconvenient that we survived. People have been hunting us ever since."

"Pretty much what I've suspected. But I can't get it to make sense. Gordimer's paranoia doesn't explain it."

"It isn't Gordimer. It's the Rascal. We're sure. For some reason we can't figure he's afraid of everybody who got him his mummies from Andesqueluz. He's determined to see us all dead. And you in particular."

Hecht shook his head slowly, checking to see if anyone was interested. "How bad has it been?"

"We lost Agban, Norts, and Falaq. And Hagid. Which could be a huge mistake. For the Rascal."

"I knew about Hagid. It happened . . ."

"He wanted to get to you. Some big secret. So big that he sneaked out of al-Qarn and came all the way here to tell you. You made an impression on that boy."

"And er-Rashal killed him."

"Not personally. He made it happen."

"You know for sure? You're not just speculating?"

"Half and half. The Rascal has a long, strong reach on the Night side."

"What's he up to?"

"I don't know. I don't want to speculate. Maybe he's just trying to conceal the facts."

"That we plundered Andesqueluz? He's wasting his time. It's common knowledge in the Collegium. That it was done. Not who did it, specifically."

"What?"

"I heard them talk about it. They know a lot we didn't suspect they knew. You saw the firepowder weapons at al-Khazen."

"I blamed that on you. I think everyone did."

"They already had them when I got there. Why are you here in Brothe?"

"To watch over you. Here comes your woman."

Charitable of Az. And he said it with no hint of disapproval.

Anna was paler than Hecht had ever seen. And looked immensely relieved. "I've been everywhere looking for you."

"I've been right here."

"Smart-ass."

"Really, Pinkus was supposed to tell you. And the Urgent woman was supposed to, too. She said I should be ashamed, worrying you the way I was. But I passed out when I tried to get up to go find you. The kids. What about the kids?"

To the side, where Anna would not see, Az made a tiny gesture when Hecht mentioned the widow Urgent. One little finger motion that meant, "Enemy."

"They're fine. Rattled at first. But now it's an adventure. Vali even started to say something but shut up after a couple of words. They're at the house. Making sure nobody helps themselves to my things. Two of Pinkus's men are there, too. But they didn't say anything about you. Except that I should come here to see if you were with the wounded."

"Pinkus was here. He thinks the firepowder was meant for me but exploded before they could get it up against the house."

Anna's eyes became smoldering pools of dread. "No."

"I'm sorry. That's what he thinks. I don't know why anyone would do that."

"Can you get up?"

"I think so, now. You might have to help." He did get his feet under him. He did not sway much. "It was a pleasure talking to you, Mr. Suppor. I'll keep your advice in mind." Ten steps away, he muttered to Anna, "Everyone wants to tell me a better way to do my job."

"He looked foreign."

"A Calziran Deve. Came to Brothe after the Crusade because he has family here. Told me all the ways I screwed up down there and how I could have done everything better. Give the Regiment credit. They're taking care of everyone equally." He stumbled. Anna caught hold before his legs went out from under him.

"You sure you're ready to go?" The healing brother was staring their way.

"I'll be all right. Let's just go." There were things he had to do because of this. Being Captain-General included huge symbolic obligations.

HECHT FELT WELL ENOUGH UNTIL HE SAW THE DAMAGE CAUSED BY THE EXplosion. That was disheartening.

Part of the brick facing had fallen off Anna's house. The shock had powdered the mortar between bricks. Another half-dozen buildings had suffered as much. Or worse. Amongst those, in the center of the street, there was a hole as deep as Hecht was tall. "Wow!"

He barely had imagination big enough to grasp the implications of that crater. That would require hundreds of pounds of firepowder, probably not the finest because the stuff was so hard to make.

That much firepowder represented a huge investment.

Much less firepowder had brought the hippodrome down.

His own stores, for use by all his forces, amounted to half a ton. His alchemists worked ten hours a day, six days a week. Finding the saltpeter was their biggest challenge.

There was a line of wagons in front of Anna's house. "What's this?" Hecht asked.

Anna said, "I don't know."

The teamsters were not there to help everyone in the neighborhood. They leaned against their vehicles, waiting. Looking disgruntled.

"Six of them. Ho. There's a familiar face."

Sourly, Anna asked, "Isn't that the woman who was at Titus's conversion shindig?"

The blond woman stood beside the first wagon, in front of the steps to Anna's house. "Looks like her." He was not sure, though. Osa Stile's was the face he had recognized. Osa moved over beside the woman. "It is her. Herros? I'm not sure about the name."

Osa wore his go-out-into-the-city disguise. Which made him look like a street kid of about Pella's age. This street kid was enjoying life. His rags were not completely awful. And were almost clean.

Up close, Hecht asked, "What's going on?"

The woman said, "Grandfather wants you to move to his town house." She was not happy about that.

Osa Stile added, "Captain-General, Principaté Delari hopes you and your lady will accept his offer of assistance." He paused, beckoned. "Come here, sir." Out of earshot of women, he said, "Here's the deal. Load up everything and move it over to the town house. He doesn't use it. You can move back after this place is fixed up."

Hecht did not respond. He was disoriented. He considered Anna's house. Pella and Vali stood where the front door had been. He glanced at the guards Ghort had assigned. He knew both. They would do their job.

"All right. I understand." He went back to Anna. "The Principaté says to use his town house till we get your place restored. The wagons are supposed to take away anything that you don't want stolen."

Anna betrayed several emotions, including anger, annoyance, and gratitude. She was not happy. But the situation was what it was. Pinkus Ghort could not protect the house forever. After fuming silently, she grumbled, "I'm grateful that the Principaté is so thoughtful and generous. All right."

Hecht reported her acquiescence. The blond woman told him, "Have her show the teamsters what she wants taken away."

Hecht shuddered. Her voice raised his hackles. But it was not a fight reflex. It was more like a reaction to the proximity of some unseen element of the Night.

He stepped back. Why should she disturb him? Was he sensing some subtle threat? His amulet was quiet. Nothing dark was stirring nearby.

He returned to Anna. Osa Stile regarded him closely.

PINKUS GHORT MATERIALIZED. "WHAT'S WITH THE WAGONS, PIPE?"

"Delari sent them. He's moving us to his town house."

"Sweet deal. You really got yourself an angel."

"Yes. I'm lucky. And it worries me."

"Afraid he'll bend you over in the bath?"

"No. That I could handle." He realized Ghort was ribbing him. "Good luck makes me nervous. I never had much."

"Good. Because you don't worry enough. About the right things." Shifting topic, he said, "We've made some arrests."

"Already?"

"Already. A little luck, a lot of good old stupid, and a hundred men to find out where the firepowder came from, all help you move fast. Toss in a lot more stupid and you come up with people you can slap into chains."

"A little more detail would help me understand." He watched Anna confer with the blonde. Both seemed unusually wary.

"It took ten minutes to figure out that there's only one private firepowder maker in Brothe. Wiggin Pinnska Sons in the Devedian quarter. It took them ten minutes to convince us that they hadn't sold what went bang over here. They could account for every ounce they ever made. They sold it all to you. I looked at their facility. If they manufactured anything secretly, it couldn't have been more than a few pounds. They have a hard time getting saltpeter. They get it from Shippen or Artecipea.

"Now, according to Wiggin Junior, two months ago somebody wanted to buy five kegs. The Pinnskas sent them to the Graumachi brothers. Apothecaries. They had some saltpeter. We visited them. They said they would've gone ahead and made some firepowder except for one technical problem. They didn't know how."

Interesting. Though firepowder weaponry had begun to proliferate, the secret of the powder's manufacture remained closely held by those who had acquired it.

"So now it starts to get interesting," Ghort said. "Hello, Lieutenant."

Titus Consent joined them, as did Anna soon afterward. "Good afternoon, Colonel. Captain-General."

"Titus. Go ahead, Pinkus. Interesting how?"

"The buyers told the Graumachis that they had to get permission from Artecipea to hand over the formula and instructions. They didn't know how you make firepowder."

"Artecipea?"

"Where Rudenes Schneidel supposedly hides out."

"I thought he was in Viscesment."

"Not anymore," Ghort said. "I've been trying to hunt him down."

"So have I," Titus Consent said. "Anyone who knows anything says he went back to his home island. I've had no luck finding out anything there. Sonsans and Navayans keep getting in the way."

"Anyhow," Ghort said, "I've got men working the waterfront now. They've already swept up some Artecipeans connected to the people we arrested here."

"Impressive speed. Very impressive."

"Not so much when you realize that all these people were too stupid to understand that there would be a big-ass manhunt after something like this happened. Who go around bragging that they were involved. Titus, my man, you had something for Pipe?"

"Nothing helpful with this. I'm off early because Colonel Smolens wants me to find out what's happening. We're behind schedule. He doesn't want to fall farther back because he didn't know the Captain-General was hurt too bad to work. The Patriarch seems serious about an expedition to punish Count Raymone Garete for his persistent defiance."

Hecht blurted, "Stupid! Stupid! Can't anybody make him listen?"

"No. He hears what he wants to hear. His cronies tell him what he wants to hear. And right now he wants to hear about disasters happening in the Connec."

"This something new? More of his bandits get themselves butchered?"

"There's that. And more. A chest of Arnhander specie arrived this week. Another chest vanished en route last month. He blames the Connectens. Rumors say the men moving the gold decided they needed it more than Sublime does. A more sinister rumor says Anne of Menand arranged the disappearance to finance her own mad ambitions."

"Insanity," Hecht said. "I hope they get into it with each other."

"I don't think you'd like it if they did. We might have to fight Arnhand."

"I don't want to think about it right now." He needed to stop talking sedition.

"Another reason I'm here. I've found workmen to do restorations. They'll start in the morning. If that's all right with you, Anna?"

"Oh, it's fine. Thank God everybody is so thoughtful and practical. All I've done is worry about Piper and the children."

"You really moving to Delari's town house?" Ghort asked.

"Looks like."

"Lucky shit. My angel is a goddamned tightwad."

"What's he say about Delari? Especially lately?"

"He don't like him much. So what? None of them like each other. Hugo Mongoz, whenever he wakes up long enough, hates the whole goddamned world. But you don't see him in no hurry to leave it."

"I heard them arguing a while back. It got pretty hot. Something about Doneto trying to sabotage Sublime."

Ghort looked like someone had slapped him with a board. "That's nuts."

"Maybe I heard wrong."

"You must have. Look. I'm gonna have those guys cover Anna's place. What I want to tell them . . . Here's the thing. I've got to let a bunch more guys go come the end of the month. They'll be a lot happier if they can get on with you than if they've got to wait for a spot to come up with the militia."

"Sounds like I'm hiring, want to or not. Fine. Tell them. But they need to look out for all these houses, not just Anna's."

Anna rushed off to bark at a teamster for not being careful enough with her furniture.

Hecht looked for the blond woman and Osa Stile. He did not see her but Osa was in tripping range, eavesdropping. Unabashedly.

Ghort noticed him, too. "Isn't that . . . ?" He backed away, holding Hecht's arm, then turned his back to Stile. "I just twenty minutes ago heard from Bo. He's got a report for you."

"Really? I'd about given up, it's been so long."

"He had a rough, slow go of it. What do you want him to do?"

"He can come to the town house. I'll stay there till Anna and the kids get settled."

"And then?"

"Then it's likely we'll get to take a trip to the Connec."

"God help us all."

"I don't think anyone else can."

DARKNESS WAS NEAR. PRINCIPATÉ DELARI'S STAFF—ALL THREE—HELPED the teamsters carry things into the house, without enthusiasm. Piper Hecht stood halfway between the wagons and the doorway, not watching the teamsters so much as the surrounding night. He never, never trusted the night.

There were people out there who wanted to kill him. There was the malice of the night itself.

He scratched his left wrist. There was some faint sorcery going on somewhere close by. Maybe inside the town house. The Principaté might be in there.

Scratching, he reflected that there had been no warning before the firepowder cart exploded. Again, the attack had been straightforward.

Because the mastermind knew he would be forewarned about any sorcery?

Probably not. Somebody was using the tools at hand.

Somebody kept failing. But the sad fact was, somebody only had to get it right once.

The blond woman joined him. She said nothing immediately. He told her, "We'll do our best not to inconvenience you."

She grunted like a man. "I won't be the best housemate. I don't know how. I live like a hermit. I seldom leave. The only people I see are Turking and Felske. And Mrs. Creedon. And Grandfather, when he comes around."

Her voice lacked animation. That chilled Hecht. "Turking and Felske?"

"The servants. They're married. Mrs. Creedon cooks and does what she can to help the other two. She's a widow."

"You were here first. You set the rules. Within reason. I don't want the children sleeping in the garden."

The woman weakly laughed. "I'm not used to the little beasts but I think I can cope."

"They're calm for their age."

"Your woman, though. She doesn't like me."

"She feels threatened. I don't know why."

"Does she enjoy coffee?"

"I couldn't say. We haven't shared any since we've been together."

"I'll go brew some." Little smile. "It's one thing I do well." She strode away, forcefully while slightly bent, as though expecting a blow. She was focused and alive, suddenly. Hecht wondered what her story was.

Anna materialized. Hecht was startled, noting how short she was, compared to the other woman. She was much bigger in his mind. "What was that all about?"

"Trying to work out how to get along. I gather she isn't used to people. Especially kids. But she wants to get along. Because the Principaté wants it."

"And he's her free ride."

"Ours, too, right now."

Anna did not respond but seemed determined to be sour.

"You have a problem with her? Do you know her from somewhere?"

"Never saw her before Titus's conversion. And I can't explain why she bothers me. She just does."

"Know something? She bothers me, too. And I don't know why, either. But I don't feel threatened."

The last wagon pulled away. Anna said, "I'll make the best of it. We probably ought to go inside."

"I'm waiting for somebody."

"They can knock."

THE BLONDE'S COFFEE IMPROVED ANNA'S ATTITUDE DRAMATICALLY. "OH. I haven't had coffee since my wedding. I'd forgotten how wonderful it is."

The blonde said, "It's useful, having a grandfather who belongs to the Collegium." Which startled Hecht.

That sounded like an attempt at a joke.

Turking appeared. "There is a person to see you, Captain-General." Someone he disapproved.

"Where?"

"At the door."

Hecht turned to the woman. "This will be business. A spy. Where can I interview him without disturbing the household?"

"The room where you spoke to Grandfather before. That's what it's for."

Hecht left the women chatting.

BO BIOGNA WAS SKITTISH. HE KEPT LOOKING INTO CORNERS. HE WOULDN'T sit in one of the rude chairs. He prowled incessantly.

"What the hell, Bo? What's got you like this?" Biogna was cool, irreverent, and sarcastic, normally. "What did you find out?"

"The guy in brown . . . I don't know . . . I couldn't . . . He may be a ghost. He pops up and disappears like one. Nobody knows who he is. But . . ."

Hecht pressed. "Why does that make you so nervous right now?"

"I did track him down, Pipe. I'm good enough to track a ghost to his lair. Given time."

"And?"

"This is where he lives, Pipe."

Hecht started. He began looking into corners himself. "You're sure?"

"Yeah. And you're looking for ghosts now, too."

"I am." Because he believed Hugo Mongoz. The man in brown was Cloven Februaren. The Ninth Unknown. Principaté Delari's predecessor, who should have been dead a long time ago. And who might be, but who continued to walk the earth, even in daylight.

He suffered an instant of panic. Felt the walls closing in. Felt the stress of his position, which he did not ordinarily. Much. Mostly he was who he was believed to be, doing the best he could. Piper Hecht was everything Sublime V could demand in a Captain-General, except mindlessly passionate about his principal's ambitions.

"You know Titus Consent?"

"The Deve who converted? I know who he is. The spy guy. He lives over where your woman does."

"How do you know that?"

"I seen him when I was tracking the brown ghost. Who's always watching you when I catch up with him."

Hecht put more effort into studying empty corners. There might be a wholly unexpected reason for the tingle in his wrist. "See Consent. Go to his house. I'll give you a note. Tell him to write your story down. Every detail. But not to share it with anyone but me."

"All right." Biogna sounded puzzled.

"You need to get out of here. We'll talk somewhere else." Hecht had hoped to ask Biogna about his visit to Viscesment, though that was old news.

Biogna said, "You don't need to convince me." He had not stopped prowling.

Hecht scribbled a note, then saw Biogna to the street. "I appreciate what you did, Bo. I'll see you're repaid."

"Find me a job. The City Regiment won't last out the summer."

"Goes without saying. See how you get along with Titus Consent. There's a good chance he can use you."

"WHAT'S THE MATTER?" ANNA ASKED, DEEP IN THE NIGHT.

"Can't sleep."

"Really? Just because somebody tried to kill you today?"

It was not that. To his surprise. That he had put out of mind. Instead, he was obsessing about the man in brown.

"Not really. I put that aside once the threat went away. You have to. Or you can't function."

"Must you? Function? We could . . ." She fell silent. Knowing that asking was a waste of time. Instead, she distracted him as only a woman could.

He had no trouble falling asleep afterward.

*   *   *

HECHT LEFT THE TOWN HOUSE EARLY. SIX ARMED HORSEMEN AWAITED HIM. With an extra animal. All six were men he knew. Men who could be trusted.

He did not argue. The choice was no longer his. He was too valuable an asset.

He might never be alone again. His whole life might have to be structured to fit the convenience of bodyguards.

He spent six hours at the Castella dollas Pontellas. The development of the militias of the Patriarchal Estates was going well, except in the area of armaments acquisition. There had been no official word from Krois, yet, but his staff were all confident that orders would not be delayed much longer. Action would be taken to tame the Connec.

Sublime felt free to move. He no longer dreaded what the Empire would do if he turned his back. Empress Katrin had chosen to support the Brothen Patriarchy. In defiance of tradition, the Electors, and the Imperial nobility.

Hecht said, "Gentlemen, I congratulate myself on my ability to pick good men." The jest came out sounding pompous. "I mean, I'm just plain thrilled by the job you're all doing. And doing so fast."

Colonel Smolens asked, "This your way of sneaking up on you going to leave us to our own devices again?" He wore a big smile. Hecht had grown to like the man.

"That, too. For a while. I have to see Principaté Delari. But I wanted you all to know that I see the long hours paying off. We just might be able to do some of the things we're likely to be asked to do. So. Carry on."

Titus Consent caught Hecht as he was about to leave. He carried a courier pouch. "I didn't get much sleep last night. Noë is ready to put a curse on you. Despite your misfortune."

The man did look drained.

"I appreciate it. Tell Noë. Anna will treat you to a fat dinner once she gets her house back."

"I couldn't pick up the gist of what your man was talking about when I was recording what he had to say."

Hecht shrugged. "That was part of the point." Clej Sedlakova approached. With parts missing he moved more like a collection of limbs than one man. "I don't know what it means, Lieutenant. But I'm sure it's important. Mr. Sedlakova?"

"A personal word, sir. On behalf of the Brotherhood. We intend to use all our power and influence to root out the people who attacked you."

"Really?" What a startling notion. "Why?"

"Sir? I don't . . ."

"Excuse me. I just mean, I guess, that I'd rather they didn't." Although he had been forced to admit a Brotherhood observer to his staff

Hecht had given the man a real job and used him. The idea being to make Sedlakova critical to the success of the object of his espionage.

Clej Sedlakova handled most personnel matters and developed uniform standards for training and equipment for city militias. He had a reputation as a siege engineer, too. He was intent on participating in planned field exercises despite his physical shortcomings.

Sedlakova appeared displeased by Hecht's response.

"It's generous. And I do appreciate the thinking. Seriously. But I'm suddenly buried in people who want to protect me. And ever since I recovered consciousness yesterday people have been telling me they're going to hunt down whoever did it. So add on the Brotherhood . . . Wait a minute. Wait a minute. You do have other resources, don't you?"

"Sir?" Puzzled.

"A name came up when Colonel Ghort and I chased down the men who ambushed us. Rudenes Schneidel."

"I've heard it." And it had meaning, apparently. "A sorcerer."

"Schneidel was supposedly associated with Immaculate. Ghort sent people to Viscesment. They couldn't make that connection. And couldn't find Schneidel. He'd gone to Artecipea."

"Another one from the mystery nest. Like Starkden."

"Exactly. And Starkden was big on the Brotherhood's list before I ever heard of her."

"The Special Office's list. The Witchfinders."

"Maybe Schneidel is on their list, too. Maybe they could tell me something useful about him."

Sedlakova shrugged. "I can try to find out. But I may need a Witchfinder finder to manage it. Those people have become damned scarce lately." He went away, the parts inharmoniously headed the same general direction.

Consent murmured, "You almost made a mistake, there. You don't want to offend any part of the Brotherhood."

"I'm learning. I do have to see Principaté Delari. Thank you." He thumped the courier wallet.

PRINCIPATÉ DELARI HAD SEVERAL PEOPLE WHO CAME IN TO WORK, SELDOM more than one at a time. All were retainers of long standing. An ancient answered his knock. Hecht did not know his name. He cooked for the Principaté.

The old man said, "Good evening, sir. I'll announce you to Master Armand."

"Thank you." So he was expected. But why bring in the boy?

Osa Stile appeared shortly. "He's not here right now. He's down in one of his secret places. He shouldn't be long. He said you should wait."

"He did, did he? How did he know . . . ?"

"It's a logical assumption."

"I suppose. I'll wait."

"You hungry?"

"Yes. But don't go to any trouble. I don't need entertaining, either. I brought work."

"As you will. I have work to do, too."

Hecht concealed his surprise. He made himself comfortable. The old man brought wine and cakes, cheese and sausage. Always, there was sausage in this part of the world. He ate. And read what Bo Biogna had reported to Titus Consent.

Clever Bo. He had related everything Piper Hecht needed to know using words that Consent could misunderstand. Too bad Titus was clever himself and likely to see through Bo's efforts.

"PIPER."

Startled, Hecht scrambled to his feet. "Your Grace. I'm sorry. I was reviewing some documents. I fell asleep."

"Bad night last night? Not much sleep?"

"That's true. That's partly why I'm here."

"I haven't identified the responsible party but I've eliminated the obvious suspects."

"The responsible party is an Artecipean sorcerer named Rudenes Schneidel. I have no idea why he wants me dead. He's walking the trail blazed by Starkden and Masant el-Seyhan. I'm out of patience. He shouldn't be trying to kill Anna and the kids. Or my neighbors, just to get me."

"Calm down."

"Sorry, Your Grace. Rudenes Schneidel isn't why I'm here. That would be Cloven Februaren."

Startled, Delari said, "The Ninth Unknown? What brought that on?"

"First, tell me what happened to him."

"As far as I know, he's dead. Why?"

"Did you see the body?"

"I didn't. Why?"

"A man keeps turning up wherever there's some excitement. I've seen him half a dozen times. The night of Lieutenant Consent's conversion. In Anna's neighborhood. In the Closed Ground the day the hippodrome came down. Among the spectators watching when we captured the Duke of Clearenza. Redfearn Bechter has seen him more than I have. He's the one who pointed him out. Colonel Ghort has seen him, too. I expect Anna and the kids will have, as well."

Delari frowned. Puzzled. "I don't see where you're going."

"Just laying groundwork. When the man showed up in the Closed Ground Hugo Mongoz took a squint and said he was Cloven Februaren. He was certain."

"Principaté Mongoz is older than most Brothen monuments. And his mind is more weathered."

"Stipulated. But the man does fit the only description of Cloven Februaren I ever heard. I borrowed a man from Ghort. I told him to find out about the man. Giving him not much more than that to start with. His report is in this case. It's illuminating. The key point being, the man lives in your town house."

Delari looked frightened. For an instant so brief Hecht was not sure he saw it. "No."

"What?"

"If it's a ghost . . . Cloven Februaren owned the house. Long ago."

"Really? I thought it belonged to your family. That they built it."

"They did. Cloven Februaren was my grandfather."

"Oh." Why was he surprised? He was, though.

"This bears thought. And investigation. Are you getting along with Heris?"

"Who? Oh. The blond woman."

"Yes. Her. Heris. My granddaughter. As I've mentioned more than once. Are you getting along? Have you talked?"

There was an odd, added level of distress in the old man's voice. He was looking for something. Hecht was not providing it.

"We talked about how to avoid getting on each other's nerves. She isn't comfortable having us there. She seems reclusive. Anna didn't like her until she made coffee. That helped."

That was not what the old man wanted to hear. "Do you have more work to do here, Piper? Or at the Castella?"

"There's always work. But nothing that has to be handled tonight."

"Then we'll deal with this directly, right now. Otherwise . . . A reliable source tells me you won't be here much longer. Sublime has made a decision about the Connec."

Though unsurprised, Hecht swore. Delari said, "You're right. It's stupid. But he's the Infallible Voice of God. And God will shut Sublime up when He doesn't agree with what he says."

"And if someone takes exception and tries to silence the Voice?"

"That would be the Hand of God in motion, wouldn't it? The outcome would be in accordance with God's Will, wouldn't it?"

Almost a Praman way of looking at the world. A way of justifying almost anything, however wicked.

"Armand!"

Osa Stile appeared almost magically. He had been eavesdropping. Or trying to do so. "Your Grace?"

"We're moving to the town house. Make the arrangements."

The boy bowed his head slightly. He seemed puzzled. He had not overheard.

"Go! It's time you made yourself useful around here."

Hecht caught the Principaté's wink from the corner of his eye.

"Of course, Your Grace."

When the boy left, Hecht asked, "You found out anything more about my ring?"

Delari frowned. "Ring?"

"I gave you a ring to study." He had begun remembering things about the ring. For example, that he had shown it to Polo the day Divino Bruglioni gave it to him. Had Polo mentioned that to Paludan or Gervase Saluda? Would they remember? Hecht even recalled admitting having received the ring to Principaté Divino. Had the dead man mentioned that to anyone?

"Oh." Delari frowned again. "You did. What did I do with that thing?"

"It supposedly makes you forget it. But could that turn around on you? Could you suddenly remember all about it?" Was that why Gervase Saluda was interested, suddenly?

"I remember, now. I wanted to fix it so you'd keep it with you even when you forget it. Because it would make you seem unworthy of notice. Not invisible, like the rings and cloaks in stories, just somebody nobody remembers seeing."

"That wouldn't be such a good idea. I'm supposed to be the Captain-General."

They discussed the ring several minutes more. Delari opined, "The shock of the explosion is the most likely reason that you're remembering. You should write it all down. Now. So the information is there if you forget it again."

Hecht grunted, thought for a moment. "That might be a good idea."

"Over here."

Time fled.

Osa Stile came to report, "Everything is set, Your Grace. When you're ready to go."

"We'll be a few minutes yet, Armand."

ANNA AND PRINCIPATÉ DELARI'S GRANDDAUGHTER HAD REACHED AN ACcommodation. They came out to meet the arrivals together. It was late.

The children and household staff had retired. Anna was not shy about showing affection, though she did seem upset.

Armand and the coachmen got busy carrying the Principaté's necessaries inside.

Anna demanded, "Where are your lifeguards, Piper?" So. That was her problem.

"Ah . . . Oops? I forgot them."

Anna shot a look of appeal at Delari, then glared at Hecht in a way that said there would be no more forgetting.

Principaté Delari took his granddaughter aside. They spoke, he heatedly, she slowly and frowning. She bowed her head in submission, departed.

Anna said, "He shouldn't be that hard on her. She lived a terrible life till Grade Drocker found her a few years ago."

"Oh?"

"We talked a lot. I have a whole new appreciation of how good I've had it."

"And?"

"Her mother and her and her whole family were taken by slavers when she was five years old."

Hecht recalled Delari saying the woman's mother had been a slave liberated by Grade Drocker in the Holy Lands. So she had been dragged back into slavery.

Anna said, "The slavers sold them to different buyers. Drocker was big enough in the Brotherhood to use it to look for them. She was the only one he found again. Isn't that awful?"

It was, but that was the way of the world. That story repeated itself every day.

Anna shut up. Principaté Delari was approaching. He said, "Piper, join me in the quiet room as soon as you can."

"Your Grace?"

"The room we used during Consent's confirmation."

"Oh. I understand."

"I doubt that sincerely. But do come. Heris will make coffee. Using Ambonypsgan beans."

"Yes, Your Grace."

"Don't dally." Delari went off to bark at his catamite and coachmen.

Hecht glanced at Anna. He frowned. She responded with a shrug. She had no clue, either.

PRINCIPATÉ DELARI SAID, "I DON'T WANT TO INJURE YOUR FEELINGS, Madam Mozilla, but this doesn't concern you. Please join your children."

Hecht was astonished. That bordered on being rude. Was that one of the perquisites of surviving long enough to become an antique? He told Anna, "It's private, dear. Apparently." And, "It's his house."

"Of course."

Principaté Delari strolled the bounds of the room, scowling. He reminded Hecht, "The plaster conceals stone from a quarry in the Holy Lands, near where Aaron was born. One tradition says Aaron's father worked in that quarry."

The woman arrived with coffee. Hecht's mouth watered.

Delari mused, "This house has been in the family for ages. Settle somewhere, Heris. And relax."

She served the coffee before seating herself. Overlooking the admonition to relax. She sipped coffee and waited tensely.

Hecht grunted. She seemed oddly familiar when she drank.

"Piper?"

"Nothing, Your Grace. A vagrant recollection that got away before I could get hold of it."

"Ah. About this house, then. As I was about to explain. In the family for ages. Passed down, father to son. The usual. Except that we've all become members of the Collegium."

"How does that work if the clergy can't marry and illegitimate children aren't supposed to inherit?"

"Power and money, Piper. Those always trump the most ironbound rules. This family is always long on the former. They'd rather have us in the Collegium than running around loose. Sorcerers not on the inside cause too many problems. Our member of the Collegium is usually the bull sorcerer of the club. That definitely helps people come up with workarounds."

"Of course." Power and money did shout. Wherever you were.

Delari turned to the woman. "There's a problem, Heris. It has to do with the family and the house."

"Yes?" Evidently this was not what troubled her.

"Reliable witnesses have seen Cloven Februaren coming and going."

"What?"

"A man, so tall, always wears brown. Very much in the image of your father. Before his misfortune in Sonsa." Delari's voice hardened. "He looks how old, Piper?"

"Forty-five. Roughly. Definitely not his real age."

The woman shrugged. "I haven't seen anyone like that. Anyway, isn't Cloven Februaren dead? You said he was already old when you were born."

"You're right. He should be long gone. But someone identified as Cloven Februaren has been coming and going here. We need to look at that. It could be profoundly important."

"Turking or Felske might know something. Or Mrs. Creedon. Most of what happens here goes right past me. I've never visited most of the house."

"We'll correct that shortly. We three will go over it intimately. Piper?"

"It's been a long day. Piled atop yesterday."

"You're a thousand years younger than I am, Piper. But the hunt comes later. Right now, I want to know, what do you remember about your earliest childhood?"

"I was cold a lot." Which was true. Memories of cold were his most vital connection with the time when he was little. "Even then three out of four seasons in Duarnenia were winter. I remember wanting to hurry and grow up so I could have ice crystals in my beard like Papa when he came in out of the cold. Mama used to cry . . . She'd bury her face in his beard to hide her tears. She was so happy when he came back. When he was gone she spent a lot of time staring at the door. She was terrified that he wouldn't come through it again. And then he didn't. His brother Tindeman did. And we all started bawling before he could say a word.

"That's when I knew there was no way I'd ever be a good enough Chaldarean to follow the trail blazed by Rother Hecht.

"Mama died of a broken heart. The day we buried her my brothers went east to avenge Papa. They made me stay home because I was too young. An hour after they left I took a rusty old Sheard long knife, a leather helmet, and three pounds of cheese and headed south and west. I broke the knife before the day was over, so I had no way to defend myself when they beat me and took my cheese. The helmet saved me. I kept it till they made us prisoners in Plemenza. It was my good-luck talisman. They didn't give it back."

Principaté Delari and the woman stared in amazement.

He was amazed himself. He had come near believing every word when he spoke it.

Delari asked, "Any chance your father was mistaken, Heris? Any chance at all?"

"No, Grandfather. He consulted the Instrumentalities themselves."

"I see. You did that quite well, then, Piper," Delari said. "What do you remember about your earliest childhood, Heris?"

The woman looked at Hecht oddly. "It was almost like he said. Mother worried so much. Father was always away somewhere fighting. When he did come home he never stayed long. We cried when he came home because we were happy to see him. Then we cried when he left because we didn't want him to go. Mother always begged him to stay. He wouldn't. He couldn't. The time he spent with us was time stolen from the great work of his life."

Delari said, "She romanticizes somewhat but that's the truth. My son—call him Grade Drocker because that was the name he preferred—had a mission. You saw him. Even at the end . . . He denied his heritage and he denied himself so he could war against the Night. And, in the end, it gained him nothing."

The woman said, "He was hunting a monster in the Holy Lands when the slavers came. In the night. Surprising everyone. There hadn't been any ships sighted. Mother said so. That it couldn't be. That there hadn't been any raids for years. Aparion and Dateon kept them away. She kept saying that all the way down to the ship. That's almost the only thing I remember about that night."

The earth fell away beneath Piper Hecht.

His earliest fixed recollection was of being dragged aboard ship by foul-smelling men who spoke a foreign language. The ship had pretended to be a trader. The slavers took only younger women, girls, and small children. By the score.

Earlier memories visited his dreams, too. He never remembered when he woke up. He had spent thirty years forcing all that to go away.

Principaté Delari and the woman studied him intently. Delari said, "You seem disturbed."

"I'm thinking about what she said. We live in a harsh world."

"Warm his coffee, Heris. Piper, I may have to practice a small sorcery on you."

Hecht had regained control. Despite his internal turmoil.

Memories. He had had a sister named Heris. An older sister.

Delari once said that this Heris was the image of her mother.

She matched those fleeting images tormenting him now.

"I think you have already. What's in the coffee?" His amulet itched only faintly, though.

Delari asked, "Again, are you *sure* your father was right, Heris?"

"Absolutely. He spent a fortune and most of his last year making sure. Hidden somewhere here, or at the Castella, are copies of his records. Before that, all the way back to when he first heard about us being taken, he looked for us and hunted down the men who took us. Almost every man who was on that ship. They died knowing why, too. Excepting the last few. Starkden, who planned everything, and some Deves who financed the expedition. Wherever Father is now, I'm sure he's glad about what happened to Starkden. But not about the Deves. They still haven't been found."

Delari grunted. Then turned his stare on Hecht.

Hecht could feel the earth shifting. He was not ready for anything like this.

The Principaté said, "I've been trying to nudge you toward the truth gently, hoping you'd figure it out for yourself. But you're exceptionally, persistently, stubbornly blind."

The blond woman sighed wearily. She came to stand in front of him. "Don't you remember anything, Gisors?"

"Gisors?" he asked.

"The name my son gave you. I'm not sure why. It's an eastern name. As is Heris. We'll still call you Piper. You're comfortable with that and it's the name everyone knows. So there'll be no slipups. It's much too late to have you emerge as the long-lost child."

Hecht wanted to argue. To deny. To go back to his stories about Duarnenia. He had done an inspired job of selling. These people just were not buying.

So he went silent. He would admit nothing. No matter what. However great the shock. He was Sha-lug. He was the most promising product of the Vibrant Spring School.

Heris said, "The slavers were Deves. That's how they got a ship with so many men aboard into the harbor. That's why Father hated Deves. That's why he was in Sonsa. Everybody thinks it was because the Brotherhood wanted to plunder the Deves. He let them think that. He exploited their greed. But he came over from Runch because he'd heard that some Deves who financed that raid were in Sonsa.

"He was cruel and clever. And devious. He used the Brotherhood of War to engineer his revenge. And no one ever saw that. Because he gave them what they wanted."

Hecht betrayed no emotion. It was too absurd to be true.

They thought they knew who he was. Some Devedian who did know must have betrayed him. Or Anna had. Or Titus Consent. This would be a trick to get him to open up.

"Once he realized who you must be, your father . . . He forgave you the hurt you did him."

Could the Sha-lug Else Tage have fired the blast that crippled and slowly killed Grade Drocker had he suspected that the Special Office sorcerer was his natural father?

He could have. Knowing no more than that. He had had no reason to love Grade Drocker. Nor had Drocker had any reason to love him. The man had tried to kill him only days earlier.

"He insisted on directing the Calziran campaign. He wanted to shield you and bring you along."

Hecht had a hundred questions. He did not mouth a one.

He would not anger anyone by arguing. Neither would he concede anything.

"He failed. Once it became obvious that he wouldn't last long enough, I came down and took over. I've tried to bring you along. I've celebrated a few successes. But never those I hoped to enjoy. My grandson has become the most important soldier in the Chaldarean world. But he won't admit that he's part of my family. And, after generations of breeding the most powerful sorcerers in the Episcopal Chaldarean realm, the line has burped up children with less grasp of the power than your average pig farmer."

Hecht took a calming breath. "I thought we were going to investigate the mystery of the unexpectedly healthy Cloven Februaren."

Delari and his granddaughter exchanged exasperated glances. Delari said, "As you wish, Piper. As you wish. You can't be forced. But you'd better assess the risks of persevering in refusing to admit the truth."

Was that a threat? Or just a statement of fact? Or both?

He began to catalog everyone who might know that in his once upon a time he had been Captain Else Tage of the Sha-lug.

The possible number was dishearteningly large.

He said, "If it is necessary, I'll be Gisors. I've learned that sometimes I have to be what others want me to be."

That had worked when he was a prisoner of the Grail Emperor. That had worked when he was employed by Bronte Doneto. To a lesser extent, it had worked with the Arniena, the Bruglioni, and when he had commanded the City Regiment during the Calziran Crusade. The trick was to make people see what they wanted to see while he got what needed doing done.

Principaté Muniero Delari wanted no illusions. He wanted what he wanted. His intensity made that clear. "Heris. Assemble the staff. In the kitchen. We'll start there."

THE STAFFERS WERE NOT HAPPY. THE COOK WAS IN HER NIGHTDRESS, RUB-bing sleep out of her eyes. She was not afraid to demand, "Will this take long? I start my days early."

"How long it takes is up to you."

Turking and Felske were locals of middle age. Felske was graying and Turking would soon be bald. Service in the town house was all they had ever known. Unlike Mrs. Creedon, they had not been wakened.

The Principaté asked, "Is there anyone living here that I haven't been told about?"

The staff exchanged appropriately puzzled glances.

"Well?"

Mrs. Creedon said, "I'm not sure I understand what you're asking."

"I didn't stammer. Nor did I obfuscate. Who is living in my house without my knowledge or permission?"

The cook shook her head. The couple looked at one another, shrugged. Turking said, "No one, Your Grace. We wouldn't presume."

"Yet a man of medium stature, resembling my son, middle forties to fifty, always wearing brown, has been seen coming and going here."

The servants wilted under Delari's glare. Mrs. Creedon managed, "Could it possibly *be* young master Drocker, Your Grace?"

"It could not. I supervised the execution of his final wishes. I watched his cremation." The Principaté glanced back. "Ideas, you two?"

Heris asked, "Has anything unusual happened? Unexplained noises? Food gone missing? Has anyone seen a ghost?"

The servants looked worried. More worried, and a little trapped.

Delari observed, "We seem to be onto something, now. Mrs. Creedon. Tell me your ghost story. Turking, Felske, don't interrupt. But signal me if you have something to add. Start, woman."

She did not have much, after all. Unexplained noises. Footsteps heard. Nothing there when she looked. A feeling she was being watched. The usual. But no poltergeist activity. No intrusion into the realm of the living.

"Felske?"

"The ghost don't seem malicious. Not like you hear they can be. It's like it just don't care."

"I see. I suppose that fits."

Hecht asked, "Could it be a ghost?"

"No. Mrs. Creedon. Where did you sense the spirit?"

Hecht became unsettled. There might be some sizable Instrumentality of the Night afoot. His encounters with that side of reality were never pleasant. But his amulet was no more active than usual around Principaté Delari. His most improbable grandfather.

Delari consulted the others. Then, "You, too, Heris?"

"I don't know that part of the house. But I've felt the watching eyes."

The old man met Hecht's gaze. "Let's go see."

Out of earshot of the staff, Hecht said, "Your Grace, I could never publicly be the man you want."

"That's why you'll always be Piper Hecht. Soldier with an angel."

As was common with the homes of the Brothen rich, the Principaté's town house surrounded a central garden. The establishment was smaller than those of the Five Families. It lacked a curtain wall to mask it from the street. The garden had not been maintained—except for the cook's herb bed. Though not much could be told by the light of the earthenware lamps everyone carried.

Delari said, "I need to invest in some upkeep."

The wing they entered definitely needed the kiss of mop and broom. Delari volunteered, "If we have a squatter he'll be here. This wing hasn't been used in ages."

Heris observed, "They wouldn't come here if they thought it was haunted."

Not only was cleaning needed, so was plaster restoration and paintwork.

The dust on the floor showed signs of regular traffic.

Delari said, "The staff still ought to be doing more. This ghost hasn't bitten anyone yet."

Heris said, "They don't have permission to spend your money. Or to bring workmen in."

"You do. Now. Take charge. Piper? What?"

"Back there."

Something clicked. Lamplight glittered off disturbed dust.

"A door," Hecht said. "It must have been open a crack. I didn't catch that." His amulet had begun to itch. The itch turned to pain momentarily.

Delari asked, "Are you all right, Piper?"

"Stomach spasm. I have them sometimes."

The Principaté frowned. Before he followed up, Heris asked, "Do we want to open this, Grandfather?" Her voice squeaked. She was terrified.

"Huh? Oh. Yes. Go ahead. I just said he hasn't bitten anybody."

Bright light blasted into the corridor when she pulled on the door.

Hecht leapt past her, into a small, square room. He heard soft laughter. "How come the light went away?"

"It was supposed to startle and distract us." But it had not prevented Hecht from seeing a man duck out.

"Did you see that? Was that him? Is he real?"

"Real, or one vigorous ghost. Either way, definitely the Lord of the Silent Kingdom."

"Cloven Februaren."

"Yes."

"Your grandfather?"

"Your great-great-grandfather."

"Still alive. Looking younger than Grade Drocker when I met him."

"I don't understand, either."

Hecht said, "I thought you were Lord of the Silent Kingdom."

"I was. Never comfortably. But I'm not it if he's still here. He was the original. He was the one who charged the Construct."

"Uhm?"

"I don't have the flare. My father or me. We weren't dramatic enough. The program is largely forgotten now."

The program might be, but not the dread. The entire Collegium feared Muniero Delari.

"Come, Heris." Delari scanned the little room. It had a door in each wall. Floor and walls were a polished marble that, by lamplight, appeared to be the shade called flesh. Veined with gray, like cheese.

Principaté Delari began to chuckle. "Definitely his sense of humor at work here. This door opens onto the street. On the west side of the house. Which he could use whenever he wanted without being noticed. This door, that he just went out, will put us in a hallway behind the outer face of the house. Designed with defense in mind, a long time ago, and entirely impractical today. It will have little glazed windows that, at noon, let in only enough light to prove that the staff don't keep the place up."

Hecht and Heris awaited instructions. The Principaté eyed them, then chuckled again. "I can be a right bastard sometimes, can't I?"

"You said it, Grandfather," Heris said. "I won't repeat it."

"Ouch! Clever girl. He went that way so we'll check the outside hallway. He'll have left whatever clues he thinks we need."

"Your Grace?" Hecht asked.

"Oh, do dispense with all that, Piper. Go. I'm right behind you. For what good that will do if the Ninth Unknown is in a bad mood."

Hecht pushed through the doorway. The hallway beyond met Principaté Delari's gloomy expectations. He asked, "Is there still some point to this? He can stay ahead as long as he wants. We have to be careful. He doesn't. You have sorcerer's skills. This would be a time to tap them."

The itch under his amulet and the unease he felt when he peered into the clotted darkness led him to suggest that.

"He's the superior practitioner, Piper. He'd spank me."

"Do something, Grandfather. Piper is right. We'll be at this all night, otherwise."

The old man turned grim. And pale.

The hallway lit up suddenly, bright as day.

The man in brown, hair standing straight out, eyes bulging, lunged out of a doorway a dozen feet ahead. He croaked, "What have you done?"

Delari said, "Come meet my grandchildren."

The man in brown regained his aplomb. "Took you long enough."

From distress to calm to seriously irritated took scarcely a dozen seconds. Hecht growled, "Don't do that!" when he thought the man in brown was likely to respond unpleasantly. The man stopped, startled. Hecht asked, "Is this really Februaren?"

"It is. Looking pretty much the way he did the day I became his apprentice. I thought you were dead, Grandfather."

"You were supposed to, Muno. Along with everyone else."

"Why?"

"It's easier to roam around and stick your nose in when people think you're gone. So. You've found me out. Come on in. We'll talk about what needs doing."

Hecht said, "Not everyone thinks you're dead. Principaté Mongoz recognized you in the mob in the Closed Ground."

"Hugo was born a pain in the ass. He was half the reason I went missing. He built his career on trying to reduce my funding. And it was all personal. He stopped being an asshole as soon as Humberto took over."

"My father," Delari clarified. "His son."

If there was any truth to the lineage proclaimed tonight, Hecht was just the latest in a long line of bastards.

At least he had avoided becoming an Episcopal priest. And a sorcerer. Thanks be to God and his mother, he supposed.

Cloven Februaren led them into small but comfortable quarters with a lived-in look. There were no seats. "I don't have company," he explained without being asked. "And you wouldn't have caught on, Muno, if this boy didn't make it so damned hard to protect him. When some seriously deadly people want him dead."

"Name two," Hecht challenged. "And tell me why."

"Er-Rashal al-Dhulquarnen. Why isn't clear, even with my insight. Something dark is stirring in Dreanger. Something neither Gordimer nor the Kaif are aware of."

Hecht did not demur. That fit his own suspicions.

"Then you have Immaculate II, Anne of Menand, Duke Tormond in the Connec, and everyone else who'd prefer a Patriarchy with no power to enforce the Patriarchal will. You frighten people everywhere.

"Finally, there would be Rudenes Schneidel in Artecipea. Whose motives are as opaque as those of er-Rashal. He's hiding deep in the High Athaphile, at Arn Bedu, in country never completely tamed by the emperors. It's impossible to spy on him. While Schneidel's motives may be opaque, recall that sorcerers like Masant el-Seyhan and the woman Starkden also tried to dispatch you."

"All right. I'm not sure I buy all that. . . ."

"There are more. The queue seems endless. And none of the would-be killers know why you're needed dead." Februaren added, "For every attack that came close enough for you to notice I've foiled a dozen."

"Why?"

"You're family."

"Don't start . . ."

"Stop! That isn't all of it. But it's a big part. And none of your fabrications change a whit who you are."

Principaté Delari asked, "You're certain, Grandfather?"

"There is no doubt. Excepting in his own mind, possibly. Because he doesn't want it to be true."

Delari asked, "Did they know who he was when they sent him over?"

"No. They still don't. They sent him because they wanted shut of him. Gordimer feared his popularity with the soldiers. Er-Rashal feared him because of what he knows. He couldn't silence him there because questions would be asked."

Hecht didn't argue. "The world is full of fools."

"One named Piper Hecht," the Principaté said. "I can figure it out third hand. It would be about the truth concerning the brothers who raided the haunted burial ground."

The man in brown said, "Young Piper, you need not fear betrayal. We three alone know who you really are."

"Really? You just mentioned the Rascal. What about a half-dozen Deves who helped me early on? Or Anna? Or Ferris Renfrow, the Imperial spymaster?" He chose not to mention Osa Stile or Bone and his band of the betrayed.

Cloven Februaren stared. He wore a small, knowing smile. "I was the Ninth Unknown, Piper. More powerful than the Patriarch. I gave that up so I could study the world through naked eyes instead of the lens of the Construct. Thus, I've wasted the best part of fifty years. Mostly trying to deflect inimical fortune. The raid that ushered you children into slavery was a complete surprise. Had there been the least likelihood of slavers striking so far from the usual places, neither of you would have been taken. But even the gods themselves don't post guardians against the impossible."

The man seemed much less than Collegium legend declared. He did not stand nine feet tall and fart lightning. He was just a middle-aged man so used to power that he could not imagine being disobeyed. Nothing about him suggested any supernatural power or congress with the Night.

Nothing suggested that Muniero Delari was a big bull sorcerer, either. But Hecht had seen what he could do. And he, in his seventies, was still intimidated by his grandfather.

The man in brown said, "Muno, you and Heris can go, now. You've solved your mystery. I'll join you for breakfast."

Delari started to say something.

"In the morning, Muno. Right now I need to talk to Piper privately."

Heris was a biddable child, though a grown woman who was Hecht's senior. She went to the doorway, her eyes unfocused.

"Use the other door, please. Over there, Muno. In the interests of efficiency. That opens onto the interior hallway. Easier for you."

"As ever, I must defer to your judgment."

*   *   *

"HE DOESN'T LIKE THAT," FEBRUAREN SAID AFTER HERIS AND DELARI LEFT.

"And you'd be pleased if you were in his shoes?"

"I wouldn't be thrilled. Stipulated. I went through it with my own grandfather. He wouldn't lie down and stay dead, either. But there's a method to my madness, to dust off a cliché. First, get Muno out of here. There's work to do. Now. The emotionalism and long explanations would just get in the way."

"Let me confess to complete ignorance of whatever the hell it is you're talking about."

"Clever. Excellent. Borrowing your attitude from your friend Pinkus Ghort."

"If there's something so time-critical that the Principaté has to be hustled out . . ."

"Where was I an hour ago? Right here. But undiscovered. Just the fact that you're onto me changes the equation. Now I can't be the ghost in the walls who's your guardian angel. You knowing I'm real and here, and Muno doing the same, changes your attitude toward everything. I'm about to be hauled out of the realm of legend into a world where somebody besides that asshole Hugo Mongoz can see me."

Hecht did not understand. He was disinclined to pursue enlightenment.

Februaren said, "We've failed to examine one whole class of would-be assassins. The Instrumentalities of the Night."

"What?"

"The soultaken you defeated at al-Khazen were neither the beginning nor the end of your war with the Night. Their reasoning is fallacious. It's too late to stuff the djinn back into the bottle. But the Night doesn't see time the way we do. They think in centuries. They don't often recognize individuals. But you they know. You're a threat. You're the Godslayer. You have to be stopped. Despite the obvious fact, from our viewpoint, that a lot of other people have figured it out, too, by now. Because you're the spark who sparked bright enough for them to see."

"One who hasn't figured it out being Piper Hecht."

Cloven Februaren told him, "A while ago you decided to go along. You'd stop insisting that you're Piper Hecht from Duarnenia. You'd let us define what we want you to be. As once you promised Ferris Renfrow you'd let him. As you've done with everyone since you arrived in Firaldia.

"Right here, right now, I'm telling you—between you and me, boy— the age of bullshit is over. I know every detail of your life. The most critical is that you stumbled on a way to kill the Instrumentalities of the Night. They don't know how you did and they don't know why it works, but they saw you spark. And your entire life since has been shaped by that night in Esther's Wood.

"And your life is only one of thousands. On either side of the curtain between the world and the Night. More so, probably, on the other side. They're slow to learn but they can smell a threat before it arises. The soultaken meant to destroy you began their journey two hundred years before you were born. And though they've failed so far, they haven't failed yet.

"You've shown the world that there's a way to free itself from the Tyranny of the Night. Unfortunately, those dedicated to that end are captained by a lunatic named Sublime who is the slave of his own obsessions. And who is continuously manipulated by people who make sure he never comes into contact with any taint of reality."

"I'm no messiah."

"Of course not. You can't crusade against the Instrumentalities of the Night. You have neither the will, the skill, nor the temperament. You're a talisman. A totem of the living. While you live, the Night feels threatened."

"Wouldn't it be threatened anyway, if the knowledge is loose?"

"Of course. But the Night is constrained by its own mythical thinking. You need to understand that. You can't reason with the Night any more than you can with a crocodile. But you can figure out what goes on behind the curtain by studying the shadows cast."

"I'm lost. I always am around this kind of talk."

Februaren said, "The wells of power are weakening everywhere. The same thing happened in antiquity. Which is partly why those people were able to tame that generation of Instrumentalities. The wells came back that time. Hopefully, they will again. Meanwhile, though, we suffer the consequences. Sea levels are falling. The ice is coming south. And building up in the high mountains. Fast. Populations are running ahead of the ice. The Instrumentalities of the Night as well as humans and animals."

"Animals?"

"It shouldn't be many years before we see species formerly found only in the north. They shouldn't be a problem. Refugees will. They are already. But worst will be the hidden things. As they flee the ice they'll be forced into closer contact. The predators will get stronger. The confined, constrained, and shattered monsters of the past will grab the imaginations of fools, offering a lie. 'Free me. I will be your God, before all others, and you shall reign over all the nations.' That sort of thing."

"Resurrecting the old devils."

"As you wish. What they're called doesn't matter. What does is, it's already happening along the edges of the ice. And in the other cold places. They've smelled the essence of Rook in the End of Connec. The ghost of the Windwalker has been seen up where your imaginary forbears battled the pagan horde. On the steppe . . ."

"Hang on. Kharoulke the Windwalker isn't a Sheard god. He belongs to a pantheon displaced by the northern Old Ones."

"You're right. And those Old Ones have fallen, blessings be upon you. Some of their strengths have been taken by the monster in the Jago Mountains. The survivors are locked inside a pocket reality that is, itself, trapped inside a closed realm they created for themselves long, long ago. Meaning they can't constrain the terrors they conquered when they arose anymore. More are sure to reemerge after the Windwalker."

"There are worse things to come?"

"It will happen, Piper. Everywhere. But this time we can fight."

"Uhm?"

Irked, Februaren snapped, "Because of your damned toy cannon! What was it called? A falcon? A silver and iron blast from one of those will stop the most powerful Instrumentality."

"Even God Himself?"

Februaren missed only one beat. "Most likely. If He assumes a corporeal form."

Hecht shuddered. It was true. Godslayer.

"Like it or not, the God of the Chaldareans, and the God of the Pramans, is just a glorified brownie."

"Excuse me?"

"Brownie, Piper. Pay attention. A little bitty Instrumentality. The difference between a grain of sand and a mountain is the size of the rock. A brownie is a God who hasn't grown up yet."

"There is no God but God."

"You can't possibly be that blind ignorant. Take five minutes when you have five free. Use them to *think*. Then use the next five to think some more."

Hecht started to say something underpinned by a foundation of his faith. The faith on which his life had been built since his earliest days in the Vibrant Spring School.

"Stop it, Piper. You're over that nonsense."

In a way, Hecht realized, he was. But dogma was a shield against reason. Faith was the way you defended yourself against real world evidence.

"It's hard."

"It's hard for everyone, boy. You spend three decades being fed half-truths and untruths by trusted elders who have an abiding interest in having those who come up behind them swallow the same nonsense that they imbibed when they were young. Then you begin to discover details of the landscape and horizon that faith just doesn't explain. You begin to grow suspicious. But you're part of a culture that just can't survive and prosper if it becomes infected by a widespread disbelief in the absurd."

Hecht could not restrain himself. "What in the hell are you babbling about, Your Grace?"

"I'm saying it's all bullshit, boy. The Episcopal Chaldarean Revelation. Everything Praman. Any other belief system you want to toss in. Every religion. The truth is, there are the Instrumentalities of the Night. As huge as God. As tiny as a water sprite. All neutral in fact. All wicked in declaration by true believers of other religions. The believers shape the Instrumentalities by believing. They create reality with their faith. Change the minds of the true believers and you change the face of God. That's what the first Pramans did. And the first Chaldareans. Before Aaron and the Founders, the Devedians found that they could no longer honor the harsh God of the Dainshaukin."

"You're saying it doesn't matter what I believe? That God wears whatever face I want? That any belief, however heretical, is as valid as any other?"

"An uncomfortable way of stating it. But nearer the truth than most of my profession would admit."

Hecht was honest. "I need the foundation."

"Most people do. It's essential to their spiritual well-being. They need to be a brick in a great edifice to feel like they have any meaning."

"I'm happy the way I am."

"Fine. Don't let it blind you when the claws of the Night are pulling you down. Remember: Neither your God nor mine showed up at al-Khazen. But gods were there."

The Godslayer reflected: Who but the God Who Is God could have inspired him to load that falcon with silver that night in Esther's Wood?

Cloven Februaren revealed another thin smile suggesting he knew what Hecht was thinking. He said, "I'm not shilling for the Adversary, Piper. I'm trying to waken what small spark of reason you have, somewhere. You need to keep a watch for things that aren't what they seem."

"Yes." With a touch of sarcasm.

"For example. The amulet you wear. Useful, yes? Saved your life several times, no doubt. But a huge frustration, now, to your great enemy. Who no doubt curses himself daily for having given it to you. In the form that he did."

"Sir?"

"Relax. No one else has the skills to detect it. Though Bronte Doneto and Muno surely suspect there's more to you than meets the eye."

Hecht said nothing. He pursed his lips. He would gut it out.

"I think er-Rashal discovered something distressing after he armed you with the amulet and sent you our way. Maybe from the mummies. Maybe because of what happened in Esther's Wood. Suddenly, you were more valuable dead than alive. But he can't strike directly because of the amulet. His hirelings failed the straightforward attempt in Runch . . ."

The old man was thinking out loud, now. "Failure in Sonsa. Not er-Rashal's fault. Grade had been warned there might be a person of interest aboard ship, but that wasn't why he was traveling. Failure in the Ownvidian Knot. Substantial failure by Starkden and al-Seyhan, here and at al-Khazen. Failures by the soultaken and even by He Who Harkens to the Sound. And numerous failures since. It's almost as if you have a guardian Instrumentality."

"Thank you."

"I nearly failed with the firepowder cart. Can I be lucky forever? The amulet. I know what a boon it's been. But it's coming time for it to go. It's how they track you."

Hecht had begun to nod. Exhaustion was wearing him down.

The old man told him, "I'll replace it with something better. As soon as I can. Does it cause much pain?"

He was too tired to dissemble. "When something big gets close, it's bad."

"I'll fix that. Er-Rashal isn't half the sorcerer he thinks he is. Sit back down. Let me see your wrist." Februaren dropped down cross-legged, took Hecht's left hand, ran fingers lightly over his wrist. "The madman was cleverer than I thought. This is difficult to sense, even knowing it's there."

"Ouch!"

"Cleverer. That stung me, too. And here's the problem. He'll know the instant it comes off. And he'll know where. That offers us a strategic opportunity to switch it out in the right place, at the right time, and panic someone."

"Sir, I don't feel like being clever. I feel like cutting throats to get a message out. Leave my people alone."

"I understand your anger. Your frustration. How many of my family have I seen victimized? But people who behave that way aren't often persuaded. They haven't yet gotten the message when you start shoveling dirt into their faces."

"I'm in a mood to fill a big hole."

"If we must, we will. There's one more thing. The ring."

"Uh . . . Ring?"

"The ring accidentally given you by Principaté Bruglioni. The ring of forgetfulness. Where is it?"

Wow. He had forgotten it. That quickly. "I gave it to Principaté Delari to study. Why?"

"It's of no consequence right now. But it could be, someday. If it's the ring I think it is."

"Grinling?"

"Excuse me?"

"A ferociously nasty and treacherous magical ring in northern mythology. Shares some characteristics with this one."

"Not that ring. Which probably does exist. Buried under the ice, one hopes. That sort of artifact can be crafted only with the connivance of the Instrumentalities of the Night. But it exists independently afterward. If Grinling, or any number of mystic swords, hammers, lassos, runespears, and whatnot, failed to get folded up inside the pocket reality forged by the rebel soultaken, we'll have to deal with them as soon as they seduce a suitably foul character."

Hecht stared.

"All real, remember. There is no God but God. And ten thousand other beings equally wicked." Sarcastically.

"Your Grace!"

"Spend another century on this vale. Or just one decade inside the Construct. You'll see this world through new eyes. If you retain any religious inclinations at all, it'll be to buy into the dualist heresies of the Maysaleans and their theological cousins."

"I know nothing about the Maysalean Heresy, Your Grace. But I'm sure it won't be long before I get to see some heretics up close."

"It won't be long, no. Get that ring back. And keep it close."

GROGGY, DRAINED, HECHT WENT DOWN TO THE STREET. ONE OF HIS LIFE-guards helped him mount the horse they had brought. The sergeant in charge glowered but did not chide him for wandering off yesterday.

The Castella was in a ferment. Hecht did not notice. Colonel Smolens observed, "You seem distracted."

"Uh. To put it mildly."

"Anything you want to talk about?"

"It's family."

"Woman trouble." Buhle Smolens had off days related to conflicts with his wife.

"Yeah." That was good enough. "What's on the table?"

"Rumors running hot and heavy this morning."

"Worse than usual?"

"Way. And Consent says Dominagua, Stiluri, Vangelis, and some others mean to try to slide out from under their obligations if we call up their field contingents."

"We knew there'd be problems with Dromedan and the Patriarchal

States in Ormienden. The heretics have a strong influence there. Brother Sedlakova. Good morning."

Clej Sedlakova observed, "Convenient as the dualists are, blame really comes from a deep disinclination to do the Patriarch's bidding."

"Meaning?"

"Meaning they think Sublime is out of his head. Meaning the Maysalean Heresy doesn't bother them enough to make them kill their cousins and neighbors over it."

Titus Consent invited himself into the conversation. "The Patriarch *is* the problem. In any choice you can count on him to pick the stupider option."

"Excuse me?" Bronte Doneto snapped. "What did you say?"

How had Doneto managed to sneak up? Hecht said, "The man stated a plain fact, Your Grace. Reporting what people in the Patriarchal States are thinking. And elsewhere, as well, I expect."

Sedlakova's credentials as an Episcopal Chaldarean were beyond challenge. "There are hundreds of bishops and princes who pray daily that God will call His infallible servant home, Your Grace. That's truth. It won't go away if we just wish hard enough."

The Principaté scowled but dropped it. He was not blind to his cousin's ever-expanding unpopularity. "Captain-General, I need you to come with me."

Two of Hecht's bodyguards had followed him into the planning center. They were not about to let him get away again. They closed in. Hecht said, "We can trust His Grace." And what good could they do if that were untrue?

Doneto started walking. Hecht followed. The Principaté asked, "Are they all so disdainful of my cousin? Are you?"

"They are, in the main. I try to reserve judgment. I've seen the man only a few times, never to talk to."

"Not that you know. Keep up. There isn't much time."

"I'm still suffering the effects of that explosion."

Doneto went into regions of the Castella Hecht had not seen before. Down and into passageways obviously seldom used: cold, damp, creepy, and lighted only by clay lamps carried by the visitors. Doneto said, "This isn't pleasant down here. I always expect to bump into a minotaur or some other monster out of the old myths."

"It's the kind of place where I'd expect to meet all the Instrumentalities of the Night," Hecht puffed. "Where are we going?"

"Krois."

Hecht said no more. He made sure he could see Principaté Doneto all the time. Not that he expected anything. Not here and now.

Underground. Again. This time under the Teragi. Imagining all that water overhead dampened his spirit.

"Oppressive, isn't it?" Doneto asked as he started up a long stairway. It curved away to the right, opposite the direction customary inside fortresses. Meaning the architects had been thinking about retreat downward rather than up.

Hecht's thoughts seldom wandered from his calling. He could not look at a hill and appreciate it as a hill. His mind instantly began working out how to both defend and assault that particular piece of ground. The same with any building, inside or out. And this one, so safe on its island, was vulnerable through its escape routes.

He did not mention that.

There were sentries. Two Patriarchal lifeguards posted at the archway where the stairwell debouched in a hidden alcove. Hecht did not disdain Sublime's protectors as soldiers. They had performed well when the Calziran pirates attacked the Mother City.

They expected Principaté Doneto. They greeted him by name but did not let him past without examination. The Captain-General suffered an even closer search. Meanwhile, additional lifeguards arrived, summoned in no obvious way.

Hecht carried one weapon, a sixteen-inch blade. The Patriarchals did not take it. As he and Doneto followed an escort onward, Hecht asked, "What was the point of that?"

"To make sure we aren't smuggling some Night-inspired piece of mischief in."

Hecht scratched his left wrist. They had missed his amulet.

Er-Rashal al-Dhulquarnen was skilled indeed.

HECHT WAS STARTLED. HONARIO BENEDOCTO, USING THE REIGN NAME Sublime V, appeared to be suffering from a wasting disease. He was pale, sweating, and shaky. His clothing appeared unchanged for days. He smelled bad. He was barely recognizable as Honario Benedocto. And his hangers-on did not appear to care.

Hecht had seen the man several times, even exchanging a few words informally. This man was a shadow of the one he recalled.

Was he dying?

Hecht went to his knees, touched his head to the cold stone floor. Doneto had rehearsed him. The forms were little different from those one showed before the Kaif of al-Minphet. Doneto repeated it all, in a more restrained style.

The Patriarch's cronies circled like flies round a cow patty. The Captain-General did not recognize any of them.

"Get up," Sublime barked. "I'm not having a good day. I don't want to waste time on frivolities."

The flies stopped circling, startled.

Hecht rose but kept his head bowed. "At your service, Father."

"Can you do it?"

"Do what, Your Worship?"

"Scour the End of Connec. Rid me of this heretical pestilence calling themselves Seekers After Light. I'm in torment. I'm in hell on earth. I can't sleep. I can't keep food down. These cackling old hens stall and delay and put me off . . . It's time God's Will was done." The little man shuddered, as though stricken by a sudden chill.

Hecht signed himself, eyes still downcast. "God's Will be done."

Sublime half stumbled backward. He settled into a massive chair that seemed to swallow him. The awe of his position did not illuminate him whatsoever.

After a half minute of silence, Sublime shouted, "All of you! Leave us! I wish to consult the Captain-General privately."

Sublime's cronies and handlers and Principaté Doneto alike protested.

"You will leave us!" Screeching like a whore cheated of her fee.

The hangers-on went, Bronte Doneto last. Giving Hecht his hardest scowl.

Sublime observed, "They hate to leave me alone."

Hecht nodded. That was obvious.

"They're afraid an unapproved thought might creep from your mind to mine."

"Your Worship?"

"Forget my title. I'm Honario Benedocto for the next few minutes. Tell me what you really think about the crusade against the Connecten heretics. Your Patriarch is about to preach it."

Right. He was going to shoot the bull with this man like they were private soldiers at a campfire dissecting the shortcomings of those who made decisions for them. He had been through this before. The friendship would wither the instant he said one word honestly.

"I think it's risky. I haven't gotten any solid intelligence out of the Connec. What little I do get suggests a stronger local strain of nationalism than outsiders perceive."

"Meaning?"

"That even the most devout adherents of the Church don't like outside meddlers. Due mainly to a plague of incompetent, corrupt, foreign bishops."

Honario Benedocto scowled fiercely. The air was filled with noise that he did not want to hear. He heard his judgment being questioned.

Hecht said, "When the command comes I'll do everything I can to turn the Maysalean Heresy into an odd memory. But you have to understand that Connectens are stubborn people. They're fiercely resentful of foreign intrusion. My spies say Connectens of every philosophical camp are fighting the refugees and Arnhander freebooters plaguing the province right now."

"I hear the same. While my legates are treated with scorn and dishonor. I don't understand it."

"Your Worship, only your advisers ever see you. The lies of your enemies take root because Chaldarean folk never see you. They don't know the real Sublime."

Hecht spouted nonsense in order to avoid being critical. Leaving the Patriarch with room to assume that all shortcomings had to be someone else's fault.

Hecht had no interest in giving Sublime tools that would make him a more realistic leader. In an actual campaign in the Connec he would be only as successful as he must to continue directing the Patriarchal armed forces. If Sublime survived to proclaim it, Hecht wanted to be in command when the crusade against Dreanger and the Holy Lands began.

"Can you expunge the Maysalean Heresy, Captain-General?" Sublime asked again.

"I will. It'll be difficult, though. King Peter found pagans still active on Shippen during the Calziran Crusade. After a thousand years of Chaldarean and Praman rule."

The Patriarch considered him in silence so long Hecht began to grow nervous. "May God forgive me," Sublime said. "But if they resist, kill them all. Without exception. God will know his own."

"Is this the time we've awaited? Are you directing me to act?"

"The wait is over. I have decided. I have no more patience with the Connec. Rid it of heresy. Bring the rebellious Episcopals to heel. I'll arm you with all the warrants, documents, and powers you require."

"As you command, Your Worship, so shall it be done. But the tool I need most desperately is specie."

"Come here, Captain-General. Pray with me."

Hecht followed instructions. And wondered what the Sha-lug would think, could they see him kneeling beside the Adversary's very viceroy in the Realm of War.

As he mumbled the rote formulas he focused on what needed doing before he took Sublime's army into the field.

CRASH PREPARATION CONSUMED TWENTY-TWO DAYS. HECHT GOT LITTLE sleep. And enjoyed more disappointments than successes. Despite Patriarchal promises.

There was little crusade enthusiasm outside Krois.

"You had a private audience?" Pinkus Ghort asked. Ghort was underfoot all the time, now. He had been appointed commander of the field brigade Brothe would contribute to the Patriarchal army. Principaté Doneto insisted.

"I sure did. We prayed together, shared a meal, talked and talked and talked."

"What did you think? What's he really like?"

"He's crazy." They were outside and alone. He could speak freely. Within limits. "It was like being with three people who live inside the same body. He's inconstant. Excited for a while, then depressed. Convinced he wants a complete bloodbath of a war—till he decides thinking it's all a horrible idea foisted on him by his cronies. Only he won't name names."

"What I figured. Fits the rumors. Guess what? Bronte Doneto invited himself along."

Unsurprised, Hecht asked, "Think he misses the Connec?"

"Could be. He had such a wonderful time last time he went."

"I'm not thrilled." An impossible and stupid war was bad enough. Having the Patriarch's cousin perched on his shoulder could only make it worse.

Particularly if, as Principaté Delari believed, that cousin was up to his nostrils in some grand scheme of his own.

Hecht scratched his left wrist and wondered how deeply Pinkus was involved in Principaté Doneto's machinations.

12. Plemenza: The Plot to Clear the Jagos

Inspired letters and personal pleas to Katrin, before the Empress finally left Brothe, won Helspeth permission to go home to Plemenza instead of having to recross the Jagos to Alten Weinberg, where Katrin could keep her under thumb. Helspeth was determined to be the best younger princess she could. She wanted Katrin to have no excuse to deepen her misery.

Katrin had miseries of her own. The Council Advisory worked at creating them. Grand Duke Hilandle was especially unpleasant. Because of events during his desperate attempt to catch up with the Imperial procession before it reached Brothe, especially. Helspeth could not believe the stories the survivors told. They sounded like tales cooked up to conceal the wickedness of human monsters.

On reaching the Dimmel Palace Helspeth slept. For ten hours. Then she got up for a few, removed the road and ate, then slept some more.

Then she dragged herself out. She had duties. She had been away a long time.

Those left behind had done well. Only a few whiners showed for the summary assizes. Their petitions were easily handled. Helspeth retreated to her quarters.

There had been changes among her women. Gruff Lady Chevra di-Natale had gone home. Lady Delta va Kelgerberg had wheedled her way into Katrin's entourage. She had been replaced by Lady Hilda Daedal of Averange. Helspeth was glad to have her.

Lady Hilda was only a little older than she. Helspeth knew her from the Imperial court. Her husband's father had been a favorite of Johannes Blackboots.

Lady Hilda was a tall, slim blonde, in the mold of Katrin Ege. At twenty-three she had been married nearly nine years. She saw her husband Strumwulf just often enough to become pregnant regularly. She had given birth five times. Two of her children survived.

Lady Hilda's life appalled Helspeth. Yet it was typical of a woman of her class and time.

Despite all those pregnancies she remained attractive.

There were rumors. Lady Hilda might not be one hundred percent faithful to the Landgraf fon Averange. One suspected lover was her husband's father, Sternhelm, the Graf fon Sonderberg. Averange was a walled town inside Sternhelm's barony.

Other names mentioned all belonged to older men.

Lady Hilda was a Brothen Episcopal. "And I won't hide the truth, Princess," she told Helspeth. "I'm supposed to keep an eye on your religious practices. Though I'm not a fanatic myself."

"I don't understand. Katrin never showed any religious interest before Father died."

"It was there. Secretly. Because her mother was religious. What she's doing now is more about prying the fingers of the Grand Duke and Council Advisory off her throat. She'll be less devoted to Sublime once she rids herself of those foul old men."

"The men she's allying with aren't much better."

"They'll follow the Council. Katrin wants to be as powerful as your father was. Without having to give what he did on behalf of the Empire."

Helspeth doubted Lady Hilda. She had seen her sister regularly in Brothe. Not once had Katrin changed in private, in her suite in the Penital, when there were no witnesses.

Helspeth would not disagree with Lady Hilda. There was much she wanted to learn from the more experienced woman.

"What is that you keep fussing with?" Lady Hilda asked.

Helspeth had been reading a letter when Lady Hilda joined her. Searching for any missed nuance.

She dared all. Took a huge risk. Trusted a woman whose mind she did not know, for no better reason than that she liked her. "It's a letter."

"From the way you say that, and from the way you're coloring, it has to be from a man. About whom you've had unchaste thoughts."

Helspeth felt the heat rise to her cheeks.

Lady Hilda laughed softly.

"It's not funny."

"I wasn't . . . Never mind. You poor girl. Your age and never been touched. Too valuable a counter in the game of empire." She extended a hand. "Let me see what he says."

Helspeth felt like she was caught in a trance.

Lady Hilda was not impressed. "Plainly, he isn't any more practiced at this than you are. And he doesn't get carried away saying anything romantic or concrete. Does he?"

"You don't understand. The important thing is, he replied. I almost died of anxiety waiting to see if he would."

"You wrote to him? First?"

Heat in the cheeks again. "Yes. Several times. I . . ."

"Not the way the jongleurs sing it."

"I can't help it. I'm fascinated. Like the mouse in stories about mice and snakes."

"This snake doesn't sound eager to catch a mouse. He sounds wary. He's afraid you're a living pitfall."

Helspeth grimaced. Princess Apparent Helspeth Ege, lethal pitfall.

Had she truly pelted the Captain-General with letters while she was in Brothe? She had gotten no opportunity to do anything but exchange glances with him, otherwise. The one time they might have met, he had gotten caught in an explosion beforehand.

The big thing was, he had answered her. Twice.

The second letter she would share with no one. Ever. It contained hints that fed her imagination. And might be enough to betray their author.

"Are you going to report this?"

"Of course not. I'm supposed to protect your soul, not your chastity. You do have sense enough to know you need to remain a virgin, don't you? Anyway, this can't go anywhere."

"I'm not . . . It isn't a matter of . . ."

"Calm down. I know what you're going through. Though I didn't go through it till I'd been married a while. I was just ready to turn seventeen. I was pregnant. For the third time. I'm pregnant a lot. The first two times I miscarried. And that one would be stillborn, later. Strumwulf was off to the Holy Lands. He'd be gone for two years. I'm saying things I shouldn't."

Helspeth took her letter back. She folded it and slipped it into the hiding place it occupied when the other women were around. "Are you ashamed?"

Lady Hilda seemed surprised. Like that had not occurred to her. "No. The flesh has its hungers. Some endure them more easily than others. Can you imagine a dragon like Lady Chevra engaged in passionate congress? The victim of her appetites?"

"You can't control yours?"

"I can. I don't want to. You can't possibly understand, now. You may not even after you're married. If you fail to marry a man who shows you the best of that."

Lady Hilda's sour tone suggested direct knowledge. She continued. "The final, ugly truth is, your husband will end up more interested in some pliant peasant slut . . . Never mind. I have no room to be bitter. Providence fashions some of us to be rutting animals, Princess, with little more self-control than coupling dogs."

"You aren't helping me, Lady Hilda. You make me ache for a lover to show me the pleasures hinted at in the songs of the jongleurs."

"I apologize, Princess. I don't intend to make you regret your virginity. Ignore me. Your innocence is priceless on the marriage market."

"I'm sure." Sourly. Though she understood her value to the Empire. Of Johannes Blackboots's children she was most like the Ferocious Little Hans.

"I doubt you'll bear the burden long, Princess. The factions at Alten Weinberg are shopping for husbands for you and Katrin, both. If your sister had her choice she'd take Peter of Navaya."

"But . . ."

"He's taken. And all she knows about him is a painting she saw in Brothe. She was taken with his beard."

"Really?"

"Really. Katrin feels the fire but doesn't know what it is. Or doesn't want to acknowledge it."

"She always scorned that when we were younger."

"The court would like to make a match for her in Arnhand, with Regard of Menand or the son of the Count of Earistnei, a cousin of Charlve some want to succeed Charlve."

"Wouldn't marriage to the Empress decide the succession?"

"Probably. For you the leading candidate is the Duke of Brandecast."

"Who? Uh . . . Shouldn't your betrothed be somebody you've heard of?"

"Errol, first Duke of Brandecast. The oldest son of King Brill of San-terin. The Crown Prince. You'd be queen, someday."

"And forever at war with my sister if she was Queen of Arnhand. But your smirk tells me there's a joke here somewhere."

"Errol is eleven years old."

Helspeth sputtered. Ridiculous! But similar arrangements happened all the time.

Lady Hilda said, "There's also talk about Jaime of Castauriga, in Direcia. Your sister wants a Direcian connection. Jaime is younger than you, too, but he's seventeen. And will be king—unless Navaya swallows Castauriga. Jaime is both handsome and a seasoned rakehell."

"Considering those options, I don't think I'll marry. The Empire will survive."

"The Empire may, Princess. But will the Empress?"

"Excuse me?"

"There's disaffection already. Katrin's rapprochement with Sublime is unpopular. Her granting the Society the right to operate inside the Empire is unpopular. Her decree that churches in the Empire must for-ward twelve percent of their incomes to Brothe to finance the war on heresy is unpopular. She's won no friends at all."

"She overstepped herself. Even my father wouldn't have dared tell the Church how to distribute its monies. Even if Defender of the Faith has been added to the Imperial titles. What is it, Claire?"

Claire was a fair-haired wisp of ten, the daughter of one of Hel-speth's new attendants.

"I'm to tell you that a man named Ferris Renfrow is here. Captain Drear said to tell you."

"I'll be there shortly. Lady Hilda. Help me make myself presentable."

"Can we dispense with the formalities in private, Princess? Just call me Hilda. You're excited. Is this him? The spymaster? Or is it the Braunsknechts captain?"

"Neither. Ferris Renfrow was my father's friend. He's like a second father to me. I like having him around. He makes me feel safe."

Lady Hilda accompanied Helsepth to her audience. "Most of the Council Advisory don't want you here, on your own, with the Jagos be-tween you and them, Princess. Playing at being a man again. The Grand Duke and the Lord Admiral both have volunteered to take you into their households."

"I envy the peasants their freedom from such nonsense."

"You wouldn't envy them anything else."

AS USUAL, FERRIS RENFROW WAS TIRED AND ALGRES DREAR WAS WORRIED. Neither said anything substantial till Claire and Lady Hilda cleared off.

Renfrow asked, "Did you enjoy your stay in the Mother City?"

"Not especially." Startled. She had forgotten how informal Ferris Renfrow was in private. "I got few chances to see the famous places or monuments."

"Or anyone."

She scowled. "What? I don't know anyone there."

Renfrow's smile was enough. He knew she had tried to see the Captain-General. Algres Drear did not. Though he might suspect.

Renfrow said, "War is coming. Chaos is coming. This may be the last summer we can cross the Jagos safely. You have choices to make, Princess."

After a pause, she said, "You've lost me."

"Sublime has unleashed his Captain-General. Told him to tame the heretics of the Connec. The Patriarchal forces gather strength from the Patriarchal States as they travel. Two of the most intimidating members of the Collegium are with them. The Captain-General and his staff have justified our fears. They've worked wonders. They've changed the way things are done in Firaldia. He may collect twenty thousand men, mainly well-equipped and properly trained veterans. Forming what may be the most professional army seen since the Old Empire.

"Arnhand's factions have put together several smaller armies. Once they're engaged, Santerin is sure to take advantage. King Brill has been raising troops, too, since last winter. None of the Arnhander factions have seen fit to buy a truce. King Peter of Direcia will get involved somehow, too, for Isabeth's sake. And to his own advantage.

"Once the Patriarchal forces get bogged down in sieges the independent Firaldian republics and principalities are sure to act up. Some of them supposedly subject to the Empire. If you see what I mean."

She did. The perceived weakness of the Imperial proconsul in Plemenza would encourage misbehavior. What could a mere girl do? Especially a mere girl who had only her lifeguard and a rabble of a city militia?

"Not just because you're a woman but because the Empire is fragmenting. Most of our nobility disagree with the Empress about her surrender to wicked Sublime.

"I take no position on that. I just point out the obvious. Someday soon I'll say the same in Alten Weinberg. I serve the Empire. I hope Katrin will listen."

Not wanting to hear the answer she expected, Helspeth asked, "What do you mean, this may be the last summer we can cross the Jagos?"

"That might qualify as hyperbole. Between the worsening weather and growing threat of some insane Instrumentality, the Remayne Pass will be unusable."

"Alternatives are available."

"If people up north stop fussing about religion and pay attention. We need to secure the east and west routes. Then we need to deal with the monster in the Jagos."

Reports from the survivors of the Grand Duke's party, unfortunately, did not seem exaggerated. Helspeth said, "If something needs doing, please do it."

That startled Drear and Renfrow alike.

Helspeth put on a big-eyed little-girl expression, smiled cutely.

She had employed the formula used by Johannes Blackboots to urge actions for which he preferred not to be seen as responsible.

Helspeth said, "What about the monster? How do we destroy it?"

"Destroy it? That's impossible, Princess. We may still be able to constrain . . ."

"Destroy it! That's *not* impossible. I saw what became of an older and far more powerful entity at al-Khazen." She would not call Ordan a god, though he had been a mighty one in his time. "The Instrumentalities of the Night are no longer invulnerable."

"They never were, Princess."

"I'm not talking about tricking them into an idol that you shatter into a thousand pieces and broadcast across the continent. I'm talking about destruction. About what happened to the Gray Walker at al-Khazen. I'm talking about *killing* the Dark Gods." She gasped. She had not meant to state it quite that bluntly.

Algres Drear observed, "That would be extremely risky, Princess. We don't know how it happened. It might have been magical happenstance."

"Ferris?" Renfrow was certain to be better informed.

"I've had reports. I must say, I don't find them particularly plausible."

"Why not?"

"The method is too simple. A mix of silver and iron flung at an Instrumentality. And it dies? Silver and iron have been around forever. The Instrumentalities of the Night never liked them, of course. All kinds of charms use iron and silver to stave off the malice of the Night. Why would the gods themselves suddenly be mortally vulnerable?"

"You're missing something."

"I can't imagine what. But you're right. There's something. Without knowing what that is I wouldn't attack a water sprite."

"Find out. Isn't that what you do?"

"It's what I try to do. I'm less successful than any of us like."

"Where is the Patriarchal army now?"

"Princess?"

"Where is it? Right now. You know that, don't you?"

"Roughly. In northwest Firaldia. Or eastern Ormienden. Probably at Dominagua, resting and waiting to hear from Sublime. There may be some sort of subsidiary campaign involving Sonsa. Aparion or Dateon might have bribed Sublime to finish them off. Or I might have missed something."

Helspeth did not recall Ferris Renfrow being ambiguous when she was younger. "They'd be just the other side of the Ownvidian Knot, then, wouldn't they?"

Narrow of eye, Renfrow admitted, "Yes. They would be. Why?"

"The Captain-General is the authority on godslaying. One of you, named Algres Drear because he knows the way, should volunteer to toddle through the Knot and find out how it's done."

"No," said Renfrow.

"I can't leave," Drear insisted. "I promised your father."

"My father is dead. I give the orders now."

Renfrow argued. "The Captain-General won't just turn the secret over. It's too valuable."

Drear said, "He wouldn't want the pass open behind him. That would make sure the Empire got up to mischief."

"The Empire is already up to mischief. My sister supports the Patriarch. And you, Ferris, were just saying I'm going to be cut off on this side of the Jagos if nothing is done. I won't let you have it two ways."

After brief silence, Drear observed, "She is her father's daughter."

Renfrow nodded. "I heard the echo of his bark that time."

Helspeth asked, "Captain, what do you need to make this happen?"

13. The Connec: First Despair and First Flight

Black despair blanketed the End of Connec. Even Count Raymone Garete had shed his optimism. The eastern counties were carpeted with corpses. The soil of a thousand farms had been enriched with the blood of Grolsacher starvelings and Arnhander soldiery. And still they came. Seldom in any organized fashion.

The Arnhanders came anarchically because there was no central authority behind their invasion. Anne of Menand's friends and enemies were in a race to see who could steal what the fastest. Both were paying a harsh price.

Caron ande Lette had fallen. Likewise, Artlan ande Brith. No word of the fates of the Rault brothers or the Tuldse family had reached Antieux. Brother Candle and Socia feared the worst.

Count Raymone remained aggressive but he was like an old woman chasing chickens, trying to stem the tide.

Brother Candle joined Socia Rault for dinner. The fierce Rault daughter said, "Raymone wrote. He's having trouble getting his men to do what needs doing. They're tired of killing and getting nowhere."

The Perfect Master shuddered. He knew Count Raymone's men. Few were less hard than Bernardin Amberchelle. It was difficult to imagine the magnitude of the slaughter that would put them off their enthusiasm for murder.

"We're all at the mercy of our consciences."

"Conscience isn't the problem," Socia countered. "It's that, if you're even a little bit sane, there's only so much bloodletting you can stand."

"I understand." Most men could resist armed invaders with little soul searching, but butchering the endless stream of refugees . . .

Socia said, "I'm sure Raymone exaggerates when he says he's killed more than ten thousand. But . . ."

Brother Candle feared the converse was true. That Raymone had reported smaller numbers because of the horrific scale of the killing.

Count Raymone's vigorously optimistic nature made him overlook the earthy, harsh character of his beloved.

Make that his vigorously self-delusional nature. The invaders now beginning to benefit from the moral exhaustion of the Connec's sons ought to thank their God that they did not have to face this daughter of the land.

The girl surprised him. "I've sent letters, in Raymone's name, to Tormond, Peter, Jerriaux, Huntar of Biorgras, Deitrich of Cienioune, and a dozen others. I asked for the loan of troops. Strictly to support Antieux's defenses. Raymone can afford to pay them."

Brother Candle scowled. This girl-child was even more dark and wickedly clever than he had thought. Each of those nobles had been feeding mercenaries into the private and local armies of the Connec.

The feuding had fallen off dramatically, lately, in those counties where raiders from Arnhand had appeared. The hunchback Rinpoché, now a bishop paid for by and owned by Anne of Menand, had his own little army of eight hundred men. By dint of speed and fury he had captured Tomacadour and Firác. Now he was stalled on the Dog River across from Calour. His troops, foraging or being too enthusiastic in their search for heretics, had strayed into Tramaine. Which garnered them no friends amongst a nobility subject to Santerin and already eager to do mischief to all persons Arnhander.

Socia asked, "Where do you think the Patriarch's army will attack?"

Good question. It seemed disinclined to move at all, now that it was in Ormienden. "Here. If Duke Tormond fails in Salpeno. The enemies of the Connec have suffered too many embarrassments at Antieux."

Duke Tormond had gone to Arnhand to plead with his second cousin,

King Charlve. A fool's errand, most thought. Charlve was a lap dog of that whore, Anne of Menand. But a good sign, to others. The Duke was doing *something*. The poison no longer held him in thrall.

Brother Candle mused, "The Captain-General, once loosed, will come here. Then to Sheavenalle and Castreresone. Then Khaurene itself. And the Connec will lie at Sublime's feet."

"And you don't think we can stop him."

He did not. The Patriarch's army was large, well trained, well equipped, paid, and competently led. It lacked the internal conflicts of a gathering of Connectens. "I'm telling you how I think they'll see it. It may not work out that way. There'll be resistance. But it won't be effective if our soldiers are busy with Arnhanders and Grolsachers."

"It's all so awful. So frightening."

"But you're the famously ferocious Socia Rault, fearless fiancée of Count Raymone Garete."

"Count Raymone. I'm beginning to wonder. Why won't he get back here and cure me of virginity?"

"Well?"

"All right. I know. Even though we share some sacraments with the Church, including marriage, Maysaleans aren't supposed to be interested in pleasures of the flesh."

"True."

"So where do you get new Seekers After Light? Suppose you convert everybody? Wouldn't you run out of people pretty soon?"

"No need to worry on that score, child. Sin is eternal. There'll always be sinners. Which assures us an endless supply of students."

"Can it work out? Without war, I mean."

"War is like sin, child. It's always with us."

"It could be a lot more harsh."

"It could. But Sublime's demands are tolerable. Especially since he doesn't have the Emperor behind him, ready to stab him in the back."

"Can't you give a straight answer?"

Brother Candle thought he had. "Negotiations are going on. Everyone but the Society wants to avoid a holocaust. But nobody is ready to ante up the full price of peace."

Connectens were proud, stubborn, unruly, and particularly averse to outside meddling. Devout Brothen Episcopals rode with Count Raymone, despite the Writs of Excommunication and Anathema issued against him. Despite the publication of letters proclaiming plenary indulgences, erasing the accumulated sins of anyone who joined the battle against heresy, accompanied by a decretal formalizing the Holy Father's permission for those who fought on God's behalf to confiscate the properties of heretics, Sublime had yet to issue the final order declaring a Maysalean Crusade.

Forces inside the Brothen Church still strove to forestall the insanity. So rumor said.

Socia Rault was cynical. "Those rumors are just wishful thinking." She was sure that any priest who became a bishop was as corrupt as Morcant Farfog of Strang or Bishop Serifs of Antieux—and all of Serifs's successors. "It's just a matter of time till everything starts to unravel."

Brother Candle thought the unraveling was well under way.

"The price of peace . . . It's simpler than you old farts make out."

"Really?" Amused.

"The problem is, you old-timers just want to talk. But the real solution is, kill all the Brothen Episcopal bishops." There were eighteen to twenty-four of those assigned to the End of Connec. The number fell into a range because the bounds of the Connec were largely a matter of viewpoint. "Along with anyone who has anything to do with the Society."

The Society had begun to adopt the conversion tactics of the Perfects of the Seekers After Light. Monks roamed the countryside, trying to convince common folk that the Brothen Church had a monopoly on spiritual Truth. In cities the missionaries debated leaders of the local Maysalean communities.

Those leaders usually accepted the challenge. Not smart, in Brother Candle's eye. Thoughtful, articulate Seekers normally bested the missionaries, who quoted dogma rather than presenting reasoned arguments. They almost always claimed to have won, though.

"That might be effective. Temporarily."

He was being sarcastic. She did not get that. Another divide between generations. The young were literal, linear, and ferociously direct.

DUKE TORMOND, IN SALPENO, SENT MESSENGERS FLYING IN EVERY DIRECtion. He would do anything to keep the peace, now. A serious army was poised to force what he had put off so long. He sent ambassadors to Brothe to plead with the Patriarch. He begged his nobility to restrain themselves, to disband their private armies, to restore properties they had taken from the Brothen Church. He told them to make peace with the Brothen bishops and to stop interfering with the Patriarchal Society for the Suppression of Heresy and Sacrilege. Count Raymone he directed to withdraw from the field. He should prepare Antieux to be purged of heretics and unbelievers.

Socia Rault said, "As far back as I can remember people complained because Duke Tormond wouldn't take a stand. Wouldn't make a decision. Wouldn't act. Looks like they got what they wished for."

Tormond won no sympathy in the Connec or Brothe. Count Raymone never bothered to acknowledge his letters. His answer was to ambush a company of Arnhander knights and slaughter them more savagely than he had the enemy at the Black Mountain Massacre.

Tormond's cousin Charlve could do nothing for him. Though he did evade Sublime's demand that Arnhand immediately hurl its full might into the wicked province. Charlve might be dim but did understand that throwing the full resources of his kingdom at his cousin would leave him naked in the rain if King Brill or the Grail Empress decided to take advantage. And Santerin was probing already.

Charlve temporized. Adopting the habit of his kinsman. He did not deny anyone who chose to take the Crusader mantle, though. There would be stay-at-homes who could be called up if the neighbors got pushy.

Duke Tormond changed his itinerary. He abandoned plans to visit the Empire. News from home made him want to hurry back to Khaurene.

The conspiracies round Charlve worried Tormond. He slipped out of Salpeno in the middle of the night. He and a handful of supporters raced for territory held by Santerin, just thirty miles west of the Arnhander capital.

Sixty hours later Duke Tormond found himself in the presence of the lord of the island kingdom. Whose presence on the mainland was not yet suspected in Arnhand. King Brill was waiting for the right moment to stab Arnhand's heart. His encouragement and promises to Tormond were entirely transparent.

Brill did gift the Duke with a regiment of four hundred Celebritan crossbowmen whose wages he paid a year in advance. Celebritans were renowned for their deadliness on the battlefield. More than one Patriarch had threatened to place their home city under interdict if they continued using their evil weapons against fellow Chaldareans.

That interdict never quite went into effect.

NEWS ABOUT THE CAPTURE OF SONSA SWEPT ACROSS THE END OF CONNEC. No one could figure out what the Patriarch was doing. Sublime's enemies were sure some foul scheme lay behind that action.

Not long after the news about Sonsa, word came that Brothen soldiers had surprised Viscesment and had captured the city against minimal opposition.

"I HEARD AN INTERESTING STORY TODAY, MASTER," SOCIA RAULT TOLD Brother Candle as they settled down to a late, simple supper.

"Yes?" Sure it would involve bloody behavior somehow.

"You remember Father Rinpoché? He was at Khaurene when we were there. That hideous little hunchback."

"I remember. There aren't many men more arrogant or obnoxious. What about Rinpoché?"

"They made him an auxiliary bishop. And gave him permission to raise his own force to deal with the Maysalean Heresy."

"Hard to believe how much stupidity can be loose in the world at one time."

"Not for me. Anyway, Rinpoché's gang have been plundering the far northwest part of the Connec. He nearly got killed for his trouble, too."

"Due to his own stupidity, no doubt." Brother Candle's exposure to Rinpoché had been limited. But a man did not need to pigeonhole the hunchback. Rinpoché did that for himself. "You're bursting. So tell me."

"He was on the wrong side of the Dog River to attack Calour. There are a lot of Seekers there."

Brother Candle knew. He had visited Calour. That was wild country.

Socia continued. "The local men of substance got Rinpoché talking. They stalled him for almost a month, keeping him thinking he might get what he wanted without fighting. That they'd turn over the local Seekers if he treated everybody else all right. But they used the time to bring in two hundred Sevanphaxi darters."

"I think I see what's coming."

Sevanphax was a remote mountain principality between Direcia and Tramaine. Several neighbors claimed suzerainty. The Sevanphaxi acknowledged none. They fought anyone who tried to tame them. And hired out as mercenaries.

Their reputation far exceeded that of the Grolsachers. They were exceedingly professional. They favored a short throwing spear, or dart, smaller than a javelin but longer and heavier than an arrow. Those darts would penetrate all but the thickest plate. And Bishop Rinpoché had only a handful of destitute knights backing him.

"The darters dropped the Arnhanders by the score when they tried to ford the Dog. The Sevanphaxi captain, named something like Ghaitre, let them force the crossing, though. He fell back to the town. Crossbowmen on the wall covered them till they got inside. The Arnhanders were tired and wet and cold after forcing the river crossing. They didn't press the attack against the town."

"So . . ."

"So while all that was going on townsmen who swam the river the night before attacked Rinpoché's camp. They destroyed his stores, killed his animals, scattered his camp followers. Rinpoché nearly drowned in the rush to get back over the Dog to salvage what he could. And he might've been killed later, when the darters came out to finish his mob off."

So now there would be leaderless bands plaguing that part of the Connec. Hopefully, trying to get home to Arnhand.

Defenders of the Connec would do their damnedest to keep them from making it, no doubt.

THE NEWS BECAME LESS GRIM AFTER RINPOCHÉ'S EMBARRASSMENT. THE flood of refugees began to dry up. Brock Rault got a message through to Antieux. Caron ande Lette's occupants had escaped to Ormienden. Now they were with Count Raymone. Several small encounter engagements against disorganized Arnhander forces had gone well.

Socia told Brother Candle, "It's coming together. The villains will be defeated."

Pessimistic of late, the Perfect observed, "There's still a fat Patriarchal army waiting in Ormienden."

That was the great puzzle. The Patriarch had launched his might out of Firaldia with apparent gleeful anticipation of the damage it would do. But now all those soldiers were just sitting there.

Rumor suggested ongoing diplomacy. But with whom? Negotiating what?

The fighting tailed off. Count Raymone managed to protect almost all agriculture south of Yperi, the town that marked the southernmost advance of the Arnhander invaders. Raymone's jubilant but exhausted followers began to arrive in Antieux. Most tarried only briefly before heading home.

Brother Candle remained pessimistic. He predicted, "Next time the Arnhanders will have a strategy. And they'll have someone in charge who'll see that things get done. If the Patriarch leaves anything to attack." He looked northeastward, toward Sublime's Captain-General and his Collegium accomplices, poised like vultures waiting for the body of the Connec to expire.

There were a thousand dark rumors about the upsurge in activities of things of the Night. Every outsider brought tales about old wickednesses resurfacing. Especially where there was fighting.

Brother Candle reminded anyone who would listen, "None of those people have seen anything themselves. You realize that, don't you? Every single tale-teller is retelling something he heard from somebody who heard it from his cousin, who wouldn't ever lie about anything."

Socia never failed to remind him, "You were there when Rook went by so close you ended up squishing maggots in the morning."

He would growl some nonsense back but could not dispute the truth.

BERNARDIN AMBERCHELLE SLIPPED INTO ANTIEUX WITH A GROUP OF PILgrims headed west, to the shrines in Khaurene and thence to the waters at St. Overdret. He had put his ferocious nature aside. He seemed a reasonable middle-aged gentleman, typical of the wealthier quarter of any Connecten city. He was portly, dark of hair and eye, and had bee-stung lips. More immediately, he stank, was dirty, and was clad in rags.

He insisted on seeing the Perfect Master and his cousin's fiancée immediately.

Neither knew Bernardin well. Count Raymone's local staff assured them that the man was devoted to form and ceremony. Yet he insisted on seeing them without taking a day to recuperate and prepare for the courtly behavior he loved. Socia observed, "He does come from Raymone."

Amberchelle met them in Raymone's room lined with stone from the Holy Lands. He could not suppress his fearful excitement. He told them, "Count Raymone has a plan. You two are critical to it. The first step is to prepare Antieux for an extended, harsh siege."

They frowned, puzzled.

"Raymone has discovered unexpected friends. He knows our enemies' plans. And what some unanticipated allies are up to, too."

Deeper frowns from the old man and girl.

"The Society has planted agents here. They aren't supposed to reveal themselves until Antieux is under siege. Then they'll seize the gate in the night and open it. The enemy will rush in and kill everyone, Maysaleans, Deves, and Dainshaus first."

"Dainshaus?" Brother Candle asked. "I've never seen a Dainshau here."

"They're here, Master. Several families. The Society plans to exterminate them. Here and everywhere. Deves and Maysaleans, too. And here in Antieux they plan to kill everyone else, too. Even their own. As an example to the lesser cities that owe fealty to Count Raymone. So they'll surrender without a fight."

Socia said, "That's the insane rationality you find only in the gods . . ."

Brother Candle squeezed her arm.

Amberchelle said, "Its sanity is irrelevant. I've been told to ready the city for a long siege. Your job is to lead the Deves, Dainshaukin, Seekers After Light, and Immaculate's adherents out of here while that can still be done. The Unbelievers need to go to Sheavenalle. The Seekers should go to Castreresone or farther west. Or into the White Hills."

Socia took one deep breath, then another, getting ready to argue. Amberchelle forestalled her. "There'll be some surprises. I haven't been told all about them myself. I do know we all need to do our parts according to Raymone's design, without question or debate, as fast as we can, if we want to see another summer."

Bernardin leaned in close to Brother Candle. "Machinations are afoot. We'll win the victory yet. But you really do have to make the needful moves. Now."

Brother Candle understood. Without grasping specifics. He silenced Socia before she could get her back up. Then he asked for what specifics and directions Amberchelle could provide.

THE MINORITY PEOPLES OF ANTIEUX SHOWED NO RELUCTANCE TO LEAVE. Which surprised Brother Candle. He was puzzled, too, by the fact that Count Raymone would send away people with the fiercest reasons to resist Brothen Episcopal invaders.

The Count's lady and her spiritual adviser, accompanied by the Perfect of Antieux, led the way. The column stretched for miles. Many of Antieux's leading families were sending their children to relatives in Sheavenalle or Castreresone, or safety even farther away.

Moving the children made sense. They were mouths that would need feeding. The bodies attached would not contribute much to the city's defense.

Country folk were preparing for war, too. Valuables and edibles were being moved into the city or fortifications nearby. Or into hiding in the hills. This county had been invaded several times in recent years. These survivors would not make it easy for the next wave.

Brother Candle could not convince himself that resistance made sense. Despite all the disorder, members of the Society continued to filter into the Connec, pressing the cause of the Brothen Church. They grew increasingly extreme as they failed to whip the land into line. Duke Tormond issued regular proclamations favoring Sublime's cause, now, but no one paid attention. The assumption was that he would change his mind the instant the Brothen Church stopped twisting his arm.

Even agents of the Society doubted Duke Tormond's sincerity.

Beyond his failure to suppress heresy, the Society found fault in his failure to suppress the followers of Immaculate II. His failure to persecute those who attacked or defended themselves against Brothen Episcopal agents. Not that that mattered much, anymore. News out of Viscesment made it pretty clear that Sublime had brought the long struggle with the legitimate line of Patriarchs to a conclusion favorable to the Brothen house. But there was still his failure to return properties seized from corrupt clerics, his fortification of churches, and his employment of Deves and heretics in the instrumentalities of the state. On and on and on. No genius was needed to see that the Duke would never fulfill the demands placed upon him.

The Socia Rault solution might be Tormond IV's only salvation.

The Devedian and Dainshau families left the column not far west of

Antieux. They headed south for Sheavenalle. The Chaldarean refugees continued eastward on the ancient road, toward Castreresone. That road made plain how heavily age lay on the Connec. Brothen legionaries had built it fifteen hundred years ago. The bridges dated from that era, too, yet needed little maintenance even now. As the name implied, Castreresone was once the site of an Imperial regional military headquarters. Its walls rested on foundations laid down by legionary engineers.

"Time lies heavy in this land," the Perfect told Socia.

She was not impressed. She was too young for the deeps of time to mean anything. Whatever happened before she was born was ancient history. But she did admit, "It is kind of creepy out here." She looked back at Bernardin Amberchelle, whose party followed close behind. Some uncomfortable people were traveling with the Count's cousin.

Brother Candle felt uneasy when he considered Amberchelle's band, too. He did not know those men. Had not seen them around Antieux. Bernardin said they were lesser nobles, like the Raults, who had been driven out of their homes up near Viscesment. None were Seekers After Light. And they used a dialect that did not sound Connecten.

Socia added, "I'll be glad when we get out of the country." Which seemed a remarkable thing for a country girl to say.

Her comment crystallized the unease the Perfect had felt for days. This southern Connecten countryside was distinctly uncomfortable. For no reason that was obvious. And that was new. He had wandered this land for decades without feeling anything like this.

His thoughts drifted back to the woods above Caron ande Lette. Rook. There were rumors suggesting the return of other ancient Instrumentalities. Something in the sea. Things of the Night in the darkness. But always hearsay.

Still, the sheer number of reports suggested that the hideous and horrible were creeping forth from the graves that had held them so long.

A city seemed a good place to be, then.

The road west followed the north bank of the Laur, which ran east, back whence they had come, then southeast to Sheavenalle and the Mother Sea. Traffic had passed this way, on riverbank and water, since before men learned to remember by writing things down.

The Laur, navigable to Castreresone and beyond, boasted dozens of boats and barges of shallow draft, some under sail, some driven by sweeps. Brother Candle told Socia, "I've often thought if my life had gone different I might've become a barger."

"Didn't you have tummy troubles going over to Shippen and back?"

"The open sea is something else entirely. Only a lunatic would subject himself to that as a way of life."

"I learn something weird about you every day."

"You should be learning something new and weird and wonderful about something every day, child."

Their path to Khaurene last year had passed thirty miles north of Castreresone. That storied city had been the seat of the governors of the Old Imperial province of Closer Endonensis. Khaurene had been the capital of Nether Endonensis.

Closer Endonensis had been fruitful and pacific and therefore much favored by the Brothen emperors.

Castreresone was an impressive sight. Some called it the White City. The limestone sheathing its walls was nearly as pale as marble. And those walls, though set on ancient foundations, were the most modern and best maintained in the Connec. Improvements were under way now, the outer curtain being heightened, machicolations being added at key points, roofing being installed over the wall walks. New curtain walls with D-shape mural towers were under construction around two wealthy suburbs that had come into being during the last century.

Castreresone held an odd place in the feudal order of the End of Connec. Its overlord could claim suzerainty over most all Connecten coastal territories from Terliaga to the delta of the Dechear River, excepting those fiefs belonging directly to the Dukes of Khaurene. Such as Sheavenalle. But there was no fixed family of lords in Castreresone. Traditionally, the city belonged to the Duke of Khaurene's heir. Tormond IV had no declared successor. So Castreresone was held by an uncle, Roger Shale, who was actually younger than Tormond. A Maysalean who never married, Roger Shale had no legal heirs. His niece Isabeth was his designated successor.

Roger Shale was nothing like Tormond. He was energetic, efficient, and organized. He had kept order locally during the recent troubles. But he had no power in the broader affairs of the Connec. He spent his energies making Castreresone the best protected city in the End of Connec.

Brother Candle said, "Weird and wonderful. I don't know about that. But I can say this: This quiet, beautiful city is much nearer being the soul of the Connecten nation than is Khaurene, Antieux, or the Altai." The Altai being that part of the Connec, center north, that was most mountainous and most inclined toward heresy. Many Seekers had taken refuge there already. The Altaien population as a whole were convinced that they were the only "true Connectens."

The column from the east first spied Castreresone in the early morning light. The white walls shone. The road went down to a bridge over the Laur wide enough for eight men to march abreast. On the south bank the road traversed half a mile and rose a hundred feet to approach the acre of flat, open killing ground in front of the huge, complicated barbican that guarded the main entrance to the White City. Black wreaths hung on the wall, sad memorial to events in Viscesment.

It was there, as they waited to be let into the city, that the news about the god worm caught up.

"What does it mean?" Socia asked, absent all her usual spiteful spirit. She was subdued because the old man was so obviously deeply shaken.

"I don't know. Except as a signal that the Instrumentalities of the Night have begun to move into a whole new level of involvement with the world."

"The gods will walk among us again?"

"It may be. It may be. And that terrifies me."

14. Crusaders: Wolves on the Border

The movement north and east went too smoothly for the Captain-General. "I worry when things go right," he told his staff as the army settled in to rest near the monastery complex at Dominagua. "You people can't be that good at what you do."

The backhanded compliment sparked smiles.

The high excitement soon faded.

Principaté Doneto brought news from his cousin as Hecht was about to resume movement. "His Holiness is involved in delicate negotiations, Captain-General. He wants you to hold off a few weeks."

"Why? He's been so keen to get on with it for so long."

"I'm baffled, too. I'm not part of the inner circle, cousin or not."

"Does this mean stay here? Can I position myself better for when he turns me loose? Are there any other new constraints?"

Principaté Doneto seemed disconcerted. He glanced round as though displeased by the presence of so many witnesses. "You just shouldn't take the campaign into the Connec. Yet."

Hecht surveyed his staff. He and they never stopped working. During the rest several notions had gotten schemed out. The professionals wanted to get the maximum return from the city militias during the short time they would be available.

Legally, they could be kept in the field only forty days. The sands were racing through that hourglass. There were ways to balance that. Pay to those willing to serve longer and rotate replacements in at different times.

Hecht asked, "He does realize that in a month this army will start shrinking? And that bad weather will be along soon?"

"I'm reporting, Captain-General. That's all. I can send a letter voicing your concerns, but I can't make him read it. I can't make him pay attention if he does."

"I want to move up to the frontier."

Doneto shrugged. "You're the military commander."

Hecht turned to Titus Consent. "Are those scouts back yet?"

"One party. The ferry crossing will be tough with this many men. It could take a week."

"It took us all day last time with just a few hundred. But we need to secure it. Even if we can't go over we can control traffic. Colonel Ghort. Let's take a walk. I want to pick your brain."

Hecht paid Doneto no more heed, which probably irked the Principaté. He did not care. He had his own personal Principaté. Muniero Delari traveled slowly but he traveled. His presence assured Doneto's best behavior.

There was no sign of trouble between them.

How long could that continue?

Of more immediate concern was the depth of Pinkus Ghort's commitment to his sponsor.

Doneto thought he owned Pinkus Ghort. Pinkus might not agree but would still feel indebted. It was no secret that he still lived in the Principaté's town house.

"What's up?" Ghort asked once they were safe from eavesdroppers. Hecht's lifeguards maintained an acceptable separation but were close enough to intervene if evil showed its face.

"Recall what we talked about during the ride up? Just tossing things around?"

"We talked about a lot of stuff. Gad, it's nice. I like it cool like this."

It was windy, almost cloudless, and unseasonably cool. "Might affect the vintage."

"Yeah. Probably. What do you think?"

"I have no idea. I don't understand wine. The Sonsan nation is what I'm thinking about. Check the map. It's barely seventy miles from here."

A Bronte Doneto involved in a scheme with the Special Office would not find a raid on Sonsa to his taste. If Ghort was in tight . . .

"You thinking just a raid? Or a general chastisement of the city for being unfriendly?"

"I'm thinking, make Sublime love us by forcing the Three Families to bend the knee."

"And maybe get a closer look at Bit and her crew, too?"

"Absolutely. I do still want the real story on Vali."

They stopped walking, looked across slopes and hills covered with vines. It was beautiful country. Ghort said so. "The Connec is, too. What we saw of it."

"We'll get to see that part again. Sublime is close to obsessed with taming Raymone Garete."

"Lot of that infecting the Society, too. I'd as soon not. It won't be close to easy. Even with a pair of heavyweight sorcerers tagging along."

"One sorcerer. Principaté Delari isn't here to participate. He's here to keep an eye on your boss."

"On my boss? On you? I thought he'd, like, adopted you."

"On Doneto."

"Doneto? What do you mean, Doneto? I don't work for him. I work for the City. What do you mean, Delari wants to keep an eye on him?"

"You still live in his house, Pinkus. And he thinks you're his man. He still tries to lay claim on me, sometimes. I don't know what the problem is between him and Delari. Maybe it's all just Delari. But there is bad blood."

"He hides it pretty well."

"He does. I wouldn't know about it at all if it weren't for the boy."

"Armand? There's something weird about that one, Pipe."

"Wow! Can't get anything past you."

"What I mean is . . . Can it. The demon himself." Bronte Doneto had come out for a stroll. Not unusual. But his constitutional kept bringing him closer.

Hecht said, "Go snatch Sonsa. If you need more than the Brothen contingent . . ."

"They should be plenty. How soon?"

"I'm done telling. It's your mission, now. Do what you need to do and go when you're ready. Your Grace."

"Gentlemen."

Ghort said, "I was just telling Pipe that this looks like the place I want to retire, I get lucky and round up enough booty. Go into the wine-making business."

Hecht said, "You'd probably suck down all the profits."

GHORT'S MAN BO BIOGNA LEFT CAMP WITH A PICKED TEAM THAT SAME night. Next morning the entire Brothen contingent departed. Hecht told the morning staff meeting, "I've given Pinkus a special mission. If our master unleashes us, he'll catch up."

There were questions. Hecht did not answer them. These men did not need to know.

Principaté Bronte Doneto was among those asking. Maybe Pinkus *had* moved beyond a sense of obligation to him.

Maybe.

"Forget Ghort," he said. "We need to move up to the Dechear. Colonel Smolens, I suggested a feasibility study to you and Lieutenant Consent. Mainly to keep you out of trouble. Did you follow up?"

Smolens admitted, "We did. It should be easy. Sir." The honorific added only because members of the Collegium were present.

Titus Consent said, "There is no plan for stopping you. Assassination is their only worry."

Hecht considered Muniero Delari from the corner of his eye. The old man showed no special interest. He hoped that meant this would not get to Osa Stile. "Good. Get out warning orders to prepare to move up. Smolens, you get the other job."

"Is that an execute, sir?" Smolens asked. He was eager.

"Put it together and do it."

Delari was paying attention, now. And suddenly suspicious.

Whatever anyone thought, Piper Hecht was still his own man.

THE PATRIARCHAL ARMY DRIFTED WESTWARD, COVERING BARELY A HUNdred miles in ten days. Forward elements reached the Dechear and staked out camps at likely crossing points. The nearest surviving bridge was way upstream, at Viscesment. The Captain-General divided his forces, the better to reduce the strain on Ormienden and to remain tactically prepared. Principaté Doneto chose to accompany the southernmost division. The same favored by the Captain-General himself. This was the largest division that would strike toward Antieux. Doneto had begun to smell blood. He had a score to settle.

There was work aplenty even for Principatés, including turns watching over the bridgehead the Captain-General established on the west bank. Doneto and Delari alike spent hours interviewing locals and itinerant members of the Society, trying to gather solid facts about the strange events plaguing the Connec.

Smugly, Piper Hecht noted that neither Principaté had missed Colonel Smolens. They assumed him to be with one of the other divisions.

Smolens would do to Viscesment what Pinkus Ghort meant to do to Sonsa.

Only Hecht's immediate staff knew. Enough of a bond had formed that even Clej Sedlakova enjoyed belonging to an inner circle putting something over.

HECHT WAS WITH SEDLAKOVA, REVIEWING RECOLLECTIONS OF THE COUNTRY round Antieux. "They won't make the same mistakes. They'll have built more cisterns and those will be full. Titus says they've reengineered the main gate, adding machicolations and a second portcullis operated from a second guardroom in order to make treachery more difficult."

"I wasn't putting much faith in the Society's secret friends, anyway."

"That may still work."

"What's the ground like? Is mining an option?"

"I think it's on bedrock. That and a height advantage are why it's sited a little back from the river. We'll see something similar, on a larger scale, when we get to Castreresone."

"How high are the walls? There'll be a lot of deep topsoil around if winemaking is serious business."

"You lost me there."

"Something we don't do much anymore, that they did a lot in ancient times. Build a ramp to the top of the wall. Raise it higher than the wall if you can, so you can attack downhill."

Clever members of the Brotherhood of War had done that in the Holy Lands in the early crusades. Praman castles were no longer sited where that would be possible.

Titus Consent entered the room, which was on the second level in an old windmill. The mill had not worked in years. There was no obvious reason for it having been abandoned.

Hecht said, "Something?"

"Several. All hitting at once."

"And?"

"Smolens has done his job. Had a little problem with Immaculate's guards, though."

"They didn't back down?"

"Not soon enough. Smolens got the bad end of the casualty equation."

"I was afraid of that. But why were they still there if the Empress went over to Sublime?"

"I don't know. But Braunsknechts do take themselves seriously. Which could be a problem."

"Meaning?"

"We've got one downstairs. He wants to see you."

"Smolens took prisoners?"

"This one came from Plemenza. He doesn't know what happened in Viscesment. Yet."

It would not be long before the news reached the ends of the Chaldarean world.

That world now knew that Patriarchal troops had occupied Sonsa. Already there were rumors that Sublime had attacked the city because of a deal he had made with Dateon or Aparion. Or possibly Peter of Navaya, whose Plataduran allies wanted the Sonsan holdings on Artecipea.

This Braunsknecht came from Plemenza? That meant from the Princess Helspeth.

This had to be handled carefully.

"This Braunsknecht say why he's here?"

"Because he wants to talk to you. He thinks you'll want to talk to him."

"I don't get it."

"He did say it has to do with the monster in the Jago Mountains."

"Ah." That was much less dangerous. "There was something else?"

"Colonel Ghort is ready to leave Sonsa. The Three Families have sworn allegiance to Sublime. They've promised the use of their fleets come time for a new crusade into the Holy Lands, hoping that comes soon. They have sailors starving and ships rotting at the quayside while Platadura is taking control all over the western Mother Sea."

Hecht nodded. The real message was that Pinkus had taken prisoners and had dug out all the information he could. "That's good news. Anything else?"

"One more thing. Colonel Smolens says there were some weird people in Viscesment when he got there. They took off before he could catch them. Into the Connec. Just a creepy feeling, he says, but he wants you to stick close to your lifeguards."

Hecht shivered. His bodyguards were all down below. He did not like having them so he tended to keep them at a distance. "All right. Tell Madouc I need to see him, soon as you're done here."

"Yes, sir. One more thing."

"You said that already."

"I almost forgot this."

"Well?"

"Count Raymone may be more clever than we've credited."

"What's he done now?"

"It's what it looks like he's ready to do. He's telling all the Connecten Devedians and Dainshaus that they should emigrate somewhere where Sublime and the Society are powerless."

"Does that make sense? He'd deprive himself of his educated class."

"It does if he thinks they're spying. Which they've been reluctant to do. The Society has won us no friends. It makes even more sense if he expects to lose his war. We won't have anyone to keep records. Or any records, either, probably."

"Strategic thinking, not tactical. Interesting. So. Unless you have another one more thing, bring the Braunsknecht, then fill Madouc in on the warning from Smolens."

Hecht met the Braunsknecht outside the mill. He frowned. "I should know you, shouldn't I?"

"Algres Drear, sir. I commanded the company that took you prisoner when you were withdrawing from your previous Connecten adventure."

"Ah. Yes. The Plemenzan captivity. I hope you didn't offend Bronte Doneto too much, back then. He's a member of the Collegium, now. And he's here with us. Again."

Hecht studied Drear while he talked. The man was in his middle thirties, looking older. Gray speckled his beard and temples. His brown eyes were almost soullessly without emotion. This was a hard man used to the hardships of the field. Who found himself in too comfortable cir-cumstances in his current assignment. And who was not troubled in the least by the possibility of enduring the displeasure of a member of the Collegium.

Stupidity? Or ignorance?

Hecht said, "You asked to see me. I'm giving you time. In deference to the family you serve. But I do have a war to get ready for. So what do you want?" He stifled any hope that Drear had brought some special message from Princess Helspeth.

"The Princess Apparent has a request. I don't know why she thinks you'd grant it. But it isn't my place to think."

"Anything within reason. And politically feasible."

"She wants to know how to kill a god."

Not much could have been a bigger surprise. "Kill a god?"

"An Instrumentality. A demon, if you will."

"I don't understand." How much had Ferris Renfrow told Princess Helspeth?

"You do. You killed the Gray Walker. At al-Khazen. Deliberately and methodically. The Princess needs the know-how."

"I'll bite. Why?"

Drear talked about the monster preying on travelers in the Jago Mountains.

"It's a giant bug?"

"Not many people have survived to describe it. The Grand Duke Omro va Still-Patter is the best known and most reliable. He managed to cut a claw off it. He kept the claw. He describes the monster as a huge praying mantis with a lot of extra legs."

"I know the thing. It was at al-Khazen. If I understand right, it used to be a man. Now it's an insane Instrumentality. I didn't make the con-nection then but I think it was active just north of Alicea last year."

"How do we kill it?"

He did not want to admit that he had an answer. He was not sure why. The secret was spreading, if slowly. But no one understood why it worked.

Captain Drear read him well. "How do I reassure you?"

"I don't know. I'm not sure why I'm worried."

"Is it because you don't know how?"

"It's easy. You didn't need to come to me. The Princess saw the Gray Walker destroyed."

"Not strictly true, sir. Not strictly true." Drear removed a doeskin wallet from inside his shirt. "The Princess's personal appeal, sir."

Hecht accepted the letter. He read. The contents underscored just how much the girl trusted this man. Otherwise, she would never have dared commit such thoughts to paper. "She trusts you more than I could ever trust anyone. I suspect with reason, because your mission is to protect her. Why should *I* trust you, though?"

Drear understood him. "True. I serve the Grail Empire. I *can't* make you trust me. Maybe you can explain why it's important to you not to let anyone know how to dispatch the Instrumentalities of the Night."

"But . . ." Yes. Everyone did know. Iron and silver. The metals that had afforded some protection for thousands of years. But . . .

He had not worked it out himself until just a short time ago, despite countless hours spent on the puzzle.

His response in Esther's Wood had been sheer panicky inspiration, silver sprayed out in a blast too wide for the bogon to avoid. He had been lucky. That particular bogon had been especially sensitive to silver. Any iron in the blast would have been there by happenstance.

Now his artillerists nurtured secret charges for their falcons. Three charges of godshot for each of the twelve weapons he now possessed.

Reason eventually led him to the conclusion that it wasn't the fact of the charge that had slain the bogon in the Holy Lands. Nor the Gray Walker at al-Khazen. Instrumentalities of the Night had coped with iron and silver from earliest times.

So what was different now?

Firepowder.

Firepowder weapons, falcons or the light tubes employed by the Devedian fusiliers at al-Khazen, flung their missiles at a velocity too extreme to track and evade.

He read portions of the letter again, amazed that the girl could write such things, then trust anyone to bring them to him unread.

He went to the mill doorway. "Titus. You still in there? Yes? Find Bechter. I need to borrow Drago Prosek." He told Drear, "It'll take a while to organize."

Drear just nodded.

Hecht led the way inside the mill and upstairs. "Find yourself a seat." He collected quill and paper and began to write. Drear waited quietly. Hecht sanded the finished product. He was folding it when Sergeant Bechter arrived, huffing and puffing.

Bechter said, "Prosek's on his way. What's up?" He spent one glance on Algres Drear. And took the man's measure.

"Our new good friends in the Empire have a problem. Only we can solve it. I want Prosek to go with Captain Drear and handle it."

Bechter nodded. He gave Drear another glance. "Braunsknecht?"

"I am. Brotherhood of War?"

"Retired."

"Of course."

Drago Prosek arrived. "Permission to enter, sir?"

"Get in here," Hecht said. "Prosek. This gentleman is Captain Drear of the Braunsknecht lifeguard of the Princess Apparent of the Empire. He's brought an appeal for assistance. I've decided to accede to the Princess's request. Her friendship could serve us well."

"Yes sir." Without any suggestion of a reservation about his superior's thinking.

"I'm going to give you a chance to show us what you can do."

"Yes sir. What would that be, sir?"

"Take two falcons to Plemenza. With their crews. I'd recommend Varley and Stern, but the choice is yours. Take two special loads for each falcon."

Prosek's eyebrows jumped. His eyes widened. "Sir . . ."

"There's something ugly in the Jago Mountains. Something of the Night. You were at al-Khazen. Captain Drear tells me this is the monster that got away from us there."

Prosek's eyes got bigger. Even Bechter showed some reaction.

Hecht continued. "Go figure out how to ambush it, or trap it, then kill it. Do whatever you have to do. Then get yourself back here because by that time we'll probably be besieging Antieux and we'll want you there to starve with us."

"Yes sir." Ignoring his Captain-General's tone. Prosek turned to Drear. "Drago Prosek, sir." He extended a hand. Drear seemed surprised.

Hecht met Drear's eye. "That's what I can do."

"Good enough. I think. Thank you, sir."

"Take this letter to the Princess." He passed the doeskin wallet back. "Prosek."

"Sir?"

"Don't let these people tell you what to do. Not even the Princess herself. Make *them* support *you.* You're smart enough to know what needs doing. And bright enough to figure out how to do it."

"Yes sir."

"All right. Everyone go. I have thinking to do."

Once the last man left, Hecht read Helspeth's letter for the fourth time. And still could not believe the girl trusted Drear that much. Although, mainly, it revolved around her plea for help ridding the Jagos of the monster.

*   *   *

TITUS CONSENT TOLD HECHT, "THERE'S A PROBLEM GETTING INTELLI-gence out of the Connec."

Hecht was tired. The less the army did the more work there was for him. He did not want to hear more bad news. He wanted to go to bed. Maybe to dream about Anna. Or Helspeth Ege. Who was an infatuation he did not yet understand. He sighed. "Tell me."

"The Society is killing us. Their attitude toward Devedians is black and white. Not Chaldarean? Bad. Kill. So the Connecten Deves won't deal. And they're all going away anyway."

"Explain that."

"The Devedian and Dainshau minorities are emigrating. The Society is so obnoxious that even Maysaleans and some Chaldareans are going with them, some places."

"Really?" His preconception was that he would face raving fanatics who considered yielding to Sublime worse than martyrdom.

"At the best of times the Connec is a loosely structured realm. Anarchy is one tomorrow away. Connectens have enjoyed a comfortable life since Imperial times. They'd tolerate anything as long as people tolerated them. Until Sublime decided to stick his nose in."

"So . . . Oh-oh." Principaté Delari had appeared.

Some people felt no need to get permission to drop in on the Captain-General. All of them were members of the Collegium.

"See you later," Consent said. He was not comfortable around Principaté Delari. Despite the man's sponsorship.

Delari watched Consent scamper downstairs. "That man is awfully timid for a soldier."

"You have no idea how much you terrify ordinary people, do you?"

Puzzled, Delari asked, "Why would he be afraid of me?"

"To ordinary folks you're like Cloven Februaren is to you." Who was in Hecht's thoughts because Redfearn Bechter had seen him yesterday. "Only more so."

Delari was not pleased. But he brushed it aside. "I hear Colonel Ghort is coming back to us."

"He will be. I'm glad you came. Saves me looking for you. Pinkus should have prisoners who may explain what we saw there before. Who may tell us who Vali is. But Principaté Doneto might want to keep us away from them."

Delari had not mentioned his conflict with Doneto since that fierce encounter in the catacombs.

"And you're afraid Colonel Ghort is still beholden to Doneto."

"Yes."

"Doneto doesn't know what Ghort was doing. Besides taming a re-public that wasn't friendly to the Patriarch. He hasn't bothered to find out. That tells me he has no interest in Sonsa."

"Why is he here?"

"Sublime sent him."

"But . . ."

"All very complicated, right?"

"I don't know how you people live the way you do."

"You're talking? Never mind. I'm sure Bronte Doneto has motives for being here that aren't those of his cousin. Nor those of any conspiracy to thwart Sublime. Doneto has an abiding hatred for Antieux. Bad things happened to him there."

"He asked for them."

"That isn't relevant, Piper. If an enemy is so arrogant as to defend himself and defeat you . . ."

Titus Consent returned without being invited. He was pale and confused. "Sir, there's a message from Colonel Smolens. Somebody assassinated Immaculate."

"What? Damnit! Damnit! I wish I could swear like Pinkus. Get in here, Titus. Talk to us."

"That's it. Somebody got into the Palace of the Kings. The Braunsknechts weren't on duty anymore. There wasn't any reason for a heavy guard. Immaculate had been overthrown."

"I understand."

Consent continued. "He's made arrests. The assassins were clever getting to Immaculate but not clever getting away."

"The news isn't a hundred percent bad, then, is it?"

"The men they caught were all members of the Society, Captain-General. They were defiling and destroying symbols of the Viscesment reign when they were captured."

"That isn't good," Principaté Delari observed. "We've just gotten us thousands of new enemies."

Hecht shook his head. "What were they thinking? Never mind. I know. The human capacity for stupidity is infinite. Instead of a crusade against the Night, how about we exterminate stupidity? Titus. Send a courier right now. Smolens should question those assassins publicly. Then execute them publicly. And fast. I won't condone evil even in God's Name. What do you want?"

Principaté Doneto had appeared, also uninvited.

Principaté Delari said, "Deep breaths, Piper. No matter how angry you are, you can't address a member of the Collegium that way."

"My apologies, Your Grace. You've heard the news that has me so distressed?"

"I overheard your instructions to Lieutenant Consent. They're a bit draconian. A response that dramatic is sure to blunt the initiative of Society members."

Principaté Delari caught Hecht's elbow and squeezed with surprising force. "Stifle it, Piper. Bronte, anything less will provoke a firestorm."

"Well. Yes. You could be right. Those people are becoming too full of their mission. Lieutenant, forget your orders."

Delari squeezed till Hecht ground his teeth.

Doneto continued. "I'll go to Viscesment. The trial and executions will have more impact if the Patriarch's cousin presides."

Hecht growled, "If the executions are of somebody besides some poor spear carrier."

Doneto glared at him, for the first time in his recollection directly angry.

Principaté Delari squeezed his elbow again.

"Titus, that's how we'll do it." He bowed slightly to Doneto. "It's in your hands, Your Grace. Please move swiftly, lest the wound fester."

It might be useful to have Bronte Doneto far from the main camp, too.

"I do understand that, Captain-General. I'll be on the road within the hour." Doneto turned and left.

Give the man his due. He traveled without an entourage. He could move fast when he decided to do so.

Hecht waited fifteen seconds to ask, "You think he was behind it?"

Delari said, "No. His anger was genuine. The Society is fast becoming more curse than sword. They win no friends for the Church."

Hecht mused, "So how long do I have to sit here while they make our future more difficult? Sublime has become as wishy-washy as Duke Tormond."

Consent said, "We could get lucky. Tormond and the Patriarch could just sit there waiting for the other guy to die."

"A vision likely prayed for by millions."

Principaté Delari opined, "The news from Viscesment should inspire Sublime. He'll think the murder was a good thing. He'll convince himself that the collapse of the Viscesment Episcopals will follow. That all he needs to do now is exterminate heretics. Who, being inhuman minions of the Adversary, will just line up for execution."

Heartbeat normal again, Hecht said, "Titus, Colonel Ghort is bringing prisoners from Sonsa. Meet him. Take charge of them. Bring them to Principaté Delari. Any couriers going to Viscesment are not to say anything about Ghort or Sonsa."

Hecht tried to get back to the work of the day. He was too restless. He told Delari, "I need to get out in the air. Walk some of this energy off."

"I understand."

*   *   *

SERGEANT BECHTER FOLLOWED HECHT OUT OF THE MILL. SEVERAL LIFE-guards did the same. Hecht wanted to tell them all to go away. He did not waste his breath. They would not go. Bechter said, "Sir, I saw that man in brown again this morning."

"If he's being that obvious he must want to talk."

"Sir?"

"I know who he is, now. He's all right."

"Who is he?"

"You wouldn't believe me if I told you. An Instrumentality in his own mind. But he's no danger. Except to the fool who gets in his way."

"A sorcerer?"

"Of the first water. Let's walk down to those meadows south of camp. Where they pasture most of the animals. We'll watch traffic on the river." He felt like a stress-free conversation about mules or oxen with Just Plain Joe. Joe and his mule Pig Iron were completely comfortable with their lives. What a wonderful peaceful, prosperous world it would be if everybody in it was like Pig Iron and Joe.

Six lifeguards tagged along. They remained at a distance once Hecht left the confines of the camp. They knew where he was headed.

A breeze stirred the meadow. It carried the perfume of late season flowers. There were few trees this side of the river, and only scattered shrubs. The hillsides to the east bore splashes of yellow, carmine, and violet, and several shades of green. The army's animals had not yet stripped the land of fodder. In the distance a bleak gray ruin of a castle watched over the river. Hecht did not know its name or story. The river itself was a sluggish band of olive drab syrup, showing no hint of current. On the Connecten bank Patriarchal troops had raised a palisade round the hamlet of the ferrymen. There was plenty of timber over there. Hecht had work parties harvesting some to build rafts. He had a few more men cross over every day. A casual, slow invasion.

This appeared to be fertile land. Some calamity must have befallen it. Else these meadows would be wine country or farmland like the rest of Ormienden.

Curious. That river down there, the Dechear, was one of the great traffic ways of the continent. Traders had been sailing it before the rise of the Old Brothen Empire.

He did not see Just Plain Joe. Pig Iron, the unmistakable mule, stood out, lording it over the cavalry mounts.

Hecht asked, "Does it feel like the wind is getting cooler?"

No response. He looked around. He was alone. He had wandered away from his protectors. Who didn't seem to have noticed.

His amulet itched something fierce.

He started toward the lifeguards.

"Wait."

Cloven Februaren stood a dozen feet away, having materialized out of nowhere.

"Ah. Ah?"

"Enunciation, Piper. Enunciation. Don't make people think you're a lackwit."

"I'd heard you were lurking around. What is it?"

"You did? How can that be? I've used the strongest sorceries to remain unseen."

"What is it?" The man in brown frightened him. Little else did. He was testy because he considered that a failing.

"I want to caution you. There are schemes afoot with you as their target."

"Not really news."

"True. But arrows are in flight. I don't know what. Or where. But it's coming. Also, it's time to rid you of that amulet. I've created a replacement that will do everything it does, including cloud men's minds when they start asking you about your background. And it may polish up your personality besides."

Februaren laughed outright at Hecht's expression. "That's not true. But, face it, Piper. You're a bit of a stick."

"Why are you here?"

"To swap your amulet for a new and improved version that won't let your great enemy track you. And for the same reason I'm always nearby. To be your guardian angel."

Hecht prepared to quarrel.

"How many times have they tried to kill you?"

Hecht counted off, starting with the effort by Benatar Piola, in Runch, on the Brotherhood island of Staklirhod.

"Very good. At least you do recall the ones you were aware of at the time."

"Meaning?"

"Meaning, you thickheaded and ungrateful excuse for a descendant, that you've survived another two attempts for every one you know about. Thanks mainly to your great-great-grandpa. Since the end of the Calziran Crusade, you've become the focus of an assassination industry."

The old man made no sense. He never had. Hecht said so.

"You're right, Piper. Insofar as your argument goes. You're a talented military personality. You've had some luck. You've had support from some hidden sorceries. But there's no reason to think you're likely to reshape the world. Easier to assume you've triggered a lethal obsession in someone of immense power."

"That's easy. The Rascal. I've never been close to anyone else who has his connections with the Instrumentalities of the Night."

"The Rascal?"

"Er-Rashal el-Dhulquarnen. The great . . ."

"I know who he is. From the little I've been able to find out, he seems the most likely candidate for being your great enemy. And he's completely mad."

"Really?"

"Sarcasm doesn't become you, Piper. Let's get this amulet change done. Your bodyguards have begun to develop a vague notion that something is going on. Give me your left hand."

Whatever happened next, it did not stick in Hecht's mind. After some vague fumbling around his left wrist, there was a moment when he felt like he had been relieved of the weight of the world. Then he was standing in the middle of the meadow, alone. His left wrist itched horribly.

For an instant he thought he must be something more than just Piper Hecht, Captain-General of the Patriarchal armed forces. The word soul-taken came to mind. He drove it out.

He might be something wicked, after these years with the Unbeliever, but a tool of the Instrumentalities of the Night he was not, nor would he be.

Before he shook his disorientation completely disconcerted life-guards surrounded him again.

He had had enough fresh air.

"BECHTER! TITUS! WHAT IS THIS?" HECHT HAD FOUND FOUR SIMILAR RINGS on his map of the End of Connec. The map lay on its own crude table. It never got put away. Three rings were silver. The other was gold.

Bechter and Consent arrived. Consent said, "I don't know."

The rings were covered with symbols, none Chaldarean. Two lay atop sites where serious setbacks for Sublime's cause had occurred. Places where Arnhanders and Grolsachers, striving to do God's work, had suffered severe defeats.

Another ring lay on Viscesment. The last rested atop Antieux, eighty miles to the southwest in the End of Connec.

"Sergeant Bechter, see if you can't find the Principaté for me."

"Which one?"

"How many do we have? Did Doneto sneak back?"

"No. But two more showed up last night. The Bruglioni and Gorin Linczski from Aparion."

"Linczski? I don't know him. And that name doesn't sound Aparionese."

"I think he's from Creveldia, originally. Sedlakova could tell you about him."

"Why are they here?"

Bechter shrugged. "Aparion? Sonsa?"

"The old man is the one I want."

"On the way, then."

"Bechter, when people like that turn up I want to hear about it when they're still on the horizon. Not the next day. No exceptions. No excuses."

PRINCIPATÉ DELARI SAID, "THE MEANING WOULD BE BETWEEN YOU AND grandfather. You talked to him?"

Hecht nodded. "Mostly he talked about saving me from people who want me dead. You're sure it was him?"

"Yes. The rings may have belonged to someone who had you marked as a target. Though that's just a guess. I couldn't understand him half the time when he explained things face-to-face. Let me study the rings." Seconds later, "They all have the same symbol stamped inside." He indicated a trident that looked like a diving bird. "Piper?"

"Sorry. I was startled. I've seen that before. It's a pagan religious symbol. From antiquity."

"Eastern?"

"I saw it there. But I think it turned up everywhere before the Old Empire tamed the Instrumentalities of the Night."

"Let's look at the map again." After fifteen seconds' study, "Has anyone plotted the appearances of the revenants in the Connec?"

"Revenants?"

"Hilt. Rook. Weaver. Shade."

"Never heard of those last two."

"More of the same. Personifications. Discord. Crop disease."

"Saints?"

Delari chuckled. "You might say. Answer the question."

"I can't. Titus can, I'm sure." He called downstairs for Consent. When Titus arrived, Hecht said, "We need to know where all those weird things were seen. In the Connec."

"Sir?" Consent seemed unfocused.

"Rook. Hilt. Those things. I know you've heard the stories. We've talked about it."

"Oh. Yes. I kept a journal on that."

"Show us some whereats on the map."

"All over here. Where the Grolsachers first turned up. The Sadew Valley." Consent went on. Sightings had been grouped closely where two of the rings had lain. But the ande Lette area had produced the most sightings. No ring lay there.

"What about Antieux? Or Viscesment?"

"No reports there yet."

"Interesting," Delari said.

"Is something wrong, Titus?" Hecht asked.

"Sir?"

"You seem distracted."

"I just got a letter from Noë. Anna and the kids are fine. They've moved back to her house."

Hecht knew. As the Captain-General's woman Anna could take advantage of the courier service.

"She had bad news?"

"My uncle Shire. You met him. Shire Spereo. He died."

"I'm sorry."

"Thank you. But it isn't your problem. What I don't understand is, he committed suicide."

"Wow! That doesn't seem like him."

"You're right. But there have been several unlikely suicides since Gledius Stewpo went."

"Is something going on?"

"If there is I can't work it out. They were all old guys. Except for Stewpo and another refugee from Sonsa, they hadn't left the quarter in twenty years."

Principaté Delari asked, "Were they wealthy?"

"Sure. That's about all they had in common. Though they all knew each other."

Delari nodded to himself. "Bring me your notes about sightings of old Instrumentalities. On the other matter, ask how those men became wealthy. Could their consciences be catching up?"

Consent cocked his head slightly, mouth open. "That's an interesting thought." He shuddered. "I'll get the journal." He clumped down the stairs.

Before Hecht asked, Delari said, "No. Not me." Then, "But maybe Grade's mission didn't die when he did."

"Small world. If that's it."

"It is a small world when it comes to the people who shake it. And there are far fewer coincidences than we want to believe. The Instrumentalities of the Night weave schemes that arc across generations. We can't see ourselves caught in the web."

Hecht had created Piper Hecht so thoroughly that he was not tempted to challenge that heresy.

"You're amused?" Delari asked.

"The normal course of business here could put us on the Society's list. To do my job right I have to take into account the misbehavior of beings that I'm not supposed to believe exist."

"You can believe. You just can't call them gods." The old man chuckled. "We need to find out what unusual things have happened in the areas the rings marked."

"But . . ."

"Not just something that might be Rook scattering maggots. Any unusual, unexplained events. Any unusual histories. At this remove, even the most ancient folklore."

"Titus could send people to find out. But we can't twiddle our thumbs while he does." The Connec was growing less restive. The flood of Grolsacher refugees had begun to dry up. The disorganized bands of Arnhander crusaders had decided to wait on Sublime because it had begun to look like the Patriarch meant to let them do the dying before he swooped down on a province too exhausted to resist.

"Doneto's party must have the upper hand, now. That can't last. But I've had a thought about the ring business. Suppose those are places where someone liberated scattered bits of the Old Gods?"

"Deliberately?" Hecht asked.

"Deliberately."

"Why would anyone do that? The Night is bad enough now. Who'd want to bring back the Old Ones?"

"That would be the question, wouldn't it? Who and why. And is it real? Is it just a partisan campaign using fragments to create terror? Are the fragments themselves genuine? I could pull together an artificial monster able to ape the more blatant traits of one of the Old Gods."

"There was a god in the north. Who predated the Old Gods, even. Kharoulke the Windwalker. Who couldn't come past the edge of the ice. There's a Windwalker supposedly loose, now. Almost as bad as the original. That couldn't be a modern re-creation, could it?"

"Today's Kharoulke the Windwalker is an example of an unforeseen consequence."

"Your Grace?"

"Certain fading Old Gods sent soultaken to destroy someone they called the Godslayer. Because they did, several unwittingly positioned themselves to be slain. One of the soultaken, connected too intimately to divinity, ascended to become a Great Demon himself. The ascendant, lusting after revenge on those who conscripted him, went after those still surviving. He confined them in a pocket world he created inside the pocket universe they had created for themselves as their realm of the gods. That isolated them so completely that they couldn't constrain the monsters they put down in the dawn of their time. So things like the Windwalker can now come back."

Hecht stared. He realized his mouth was open. "Uh . . . How did you put all that together?"

"I pay attention. You can pick the trick up if you want."

Titus Consent rematerialized. "Here's the journal, Your Grace."

"Thank you, Lieutenant. Are we in imminent danger from a ferocious Connecten horde?"

"There may be ferocious Connectens, Your Grace, but those people couldn't put together a horde if they promised twenty gold pieces to every man who showed up."

"Then you can afford to take time to relax, Piper. That would be good for your soul."

PINKUS GHORT RETURNED. IN HIS TRAIN WERE PRISONERS, PLUS HOSTAGES given by the Three Families of Sonsa. The Captain-General arranged a meeting as soon as he could.

Ghort came in saying, "Shit, Pipe, that was exhilarating. Ain't nothing better than catching your target with his pants down."

"I'm glad you enjoyed yourself. I'll let you try your luck on Antieux next."

"I'll hang back and take notes on that one, you don't mind. Them folks won't get caught napping or stupid again in this lifetime."

"So what did you get?"

"I got Bit and Tiny but the Witchfinders was long gone. Bit thought they ran off to the Durandanti but we didn't find them there. It does look like they made that one gold shipment disappear, though. What's this I hear about Bronte Doneto running off to Viscesment?"

"We surprised them, too. He went to take charge of Immaculate."

"He didn't do so good, eh?"

"One wonders."

"Meaning?"

"Let's talk to Bit."

"Figured you wouldn't want to give her no more time to think. She's downstairs."

"Good. Two more Principatés turned up. They haven't come to see me yet. They're very interested in Sonsa, I hear. One is from Aparion. Keep him away from our newfound friends. If you can. Bring her up."

Ghort bellowed down the stairs.

Two men brought the woman. Titus Consent trailed them. Principaté Delari came along behind Consent.

Ghort whispered, "You all right with them?"

"They may be useful."

Bit remained uncowed. Not defiant, though. Just accepting. Fate had overtaken her. That happened in life.

She had chosen a hard profession.

She recognized Hecht immediately. "Mathis Schlink. I thought you were more than you seemed. Why drag an old whore all the way up here?"

"I have questions. I'm too busy to come to you."

She forced a smile. "Of course."

"Be seated, if you like."

The old woman settled into a canvas chair. She glanced around. Principaté Delari examined her intently, moving several times to get a different view. That troubled her, clearly. Maybe she feared recognition.

Hecht said, "You know Buck Fantil. The youngster is Titus. He's more dangerous than he looks. The other gentleman is an eye for the Collegium."

Bit was a practical sort. "What do you want to know?"

"You were involved with men from the Special Office of the Brotherhood. What were they up to?"

"Special Office? They didn't mention that. Some had been hiding at the Ten Galleons since the Deve riots."

Principaté Delari positioned himself behind Bit, out of her sight. He nodded. She was telling the truth.

"You had to think they were up to something, working out of your place all that time."

"Yes. But they paid well for the privilege."

"I'll turn you over to Titus eventually. Tell him the story from the beginning. Name any names you heard. And anything you overheard that seemed unusual."

"I . . . Of course."

"The reason being, those Witchfinders were working against the Patriarch and the rest of the Brotherhood. They may have been seduced by the Adversary."

Bit did not buy that.

Neither did Hecht. But it was a hypothesis fit to make people think.

"Tell me about Vali Dumaine, Bit."

The old woman frowned. "Give me more to go on. I don't know the name."

One of the staff assistants showed himself long enough to beckon Titus Consent, who went over, whispered, then followed the man downstairs.

"Buck and I came to the Ten Galleons. We did our business. You helped us disguise ourselves to get back out. So you wouldn't get burned out by the thugs then closing in. Women and children were part of our disguise."

"You're asking about the one who wouldn't come back."

"I am."

"What did she tell you?" ʼ

"That isn't the subject. The subject would be, who is she?"

"A natural-born liar. She convinced the other girls that she'd been kidnapped . . ."

Bit was a hard woman who had survived in a difficult trade for a long time. It took a lot to intimidate her.

Principaté Muniero Delari was a lot, however.

She stammered.

"Bit, cut through it. I want to know who the girl is."

"I said. A natural-born liar. A natural-born actor. I bought her from her mother. Doing the woman a favor. She needed the money. And I've been sorry ever since, haven't I?"

Hecht glanced at Delari, who shook his head. Bit hadn't gotten up close with the truth yet. Hecht said, "Real name, Bit. Mother's name."

This line of questioning was not what the old madam had prepared for. "I think it was Erika Xan."

Titus Consent came back to the head of the stairs. He waved for attention. Hecht nodded, held up a finger. "Your Grace, this woman is incapable of telling the truth. Why don't you work on her for a few days?" He went to see what Consent wanted.

Titus said, "Colonel Smolens wants to know if you want to keep control of the Viscesment bridges."

Surprised that Consent would interrupt with that, he said, "Yes. Even if we don't need them ourselves, we decide who does use them. Has he dealt with those assassins?"

"Three. He sent us the fourth. Who wants to buy his life by spinning tall tales."

"We can see about that after we're done here. Is that it?"

"No. There's news out of the Connec. Duke Tormond's uncle, who rules Castreresone on Tormond's behalf, has died."

"And that's important because?"

"Castreresone passes to Tormond's sister Isabeth. Who is the wife of Peter of Navaya. Meaning Peter now has cause to take offense if we attack Castreresone."

"I don't like it. That sounds contrived. Report as soon as you know anything for sure."

"I'm sure it was arranged. This might be why Sublime hasn't given the go order."

"Maybe. But this isn't critical. And I'm busy."

"I'm sorry, sir." Consent retreated downstairs.

"What was that?" Delari asked.

Hecht sketched the news.

"A scheme to keep Sublime preoccupied sounds likely. Sit down. The lady has been made cognizant of the implications of her situation."

"You ready to cooperate, Bit?"

"Your sorcerer convinced me. It makes more sense to fear the devil at hand than the one lurking in your imagination."

"Absolutely true. Tell me about the girl."

"Erika Xan brought her. She said she was the girl's mother. She wasn't. Erika Xan had dark hair, dark eyes, and dusky skin. The child doesn't. She speaks Firaldian with very little accent. Erika Xan had a heavy Artecipean accent. She paid me well to hide the girl. She never came back to reclaim her."

Hecht looked for Principaté Delari's opinion.

"She's telling the truth she believes."

"Artecipea again."

"Yes."

"Bit, why hear this Erika Xan's appeal in the first place?" Her scowl told him that was a question she had hoped she would not be asked.

"She was my cousin. On my mother's side. At one time she was in the life, too, but she found a sponsor. She was scared to death when she came to me. She was mixed up in something really wicked. She wouldn't talk about it."

"And she was Artecipean. Meaning you're Artecipean."

"Yes."

"I missed. I thought you sounded Creveldian."

Principaté Delari asked, "Where is your cousin today, madam?"

"I don't know. I assume that what scared her caught up with her."

"And she told you nothing about the girl?"

"No."

"Piper, I believe her. She didn't want to tell the truth and only sidled up to it, but she told it in the end. Madam, what is the child's real name?"

"I don't know."

Hecht asked, "Where did she come up with Vali Dumaine?"

"She never used that around me."

Delari said, "Yes, Piper. Ever more threads lead to Artecipea."

Hecht asked, "Bit, did your cousin mention where she'd come from? Or where she'd gotten the money she paid you?"

"She came from the island. I expect she stole the money."

"And she told you nothing about what was going on?"

With strained patience, "She was running. She didn't have time."

Principaté Delari stopped Hecht's interrogation. "Wait, Piper."

He waited. The old man meditated more than a minute, then said, "Other lives, other ways of thinking, Piper. You can understand that."

Hecht nodded. A brothel was foreign territory. How could he understand how things were done there? "Who else did Ghort bring back?"

"Mostly hostages from the Three Families, but some relatives of this woman as well."

"I want a girl Vali's age. This one's granddaughter. I don't remember the name."

"I think we have that one."

The old woman showed no reaction. A hard life had schooled her well. She said, "Interrogating the mistress of a sporting house is a waste of time, Captain-General. The essence of the profession is discretion. Clients expect you to fail to pay attention."

Delari responded, "That, madam, is first cousin to your earlier fabrications. Every whore or whoremaster who ever was looked for ways to squeeze their marks. You may not be able to provide the answers the Captain-General wants. But you will be honest when you answer him. Or this will be a long visit for you."

Hecht had the old woman returned to Ghort. "We have to explore this Artecipean connection. It just keeps coming up."

"Knowing my grandfather, that's already well under way."

"He's out there, you know. Sniffing around like a wolf scouting a sheep cote. Which reminds me. Mutton would be a nice change."

"Are you ready to question the Society assassin?"

"It never ends."

"If you'd stayed a spear carrier you'd be somewhere loafing right now, hoping your petty officer won't find you and make you dig a latrine or cut firewood."

"Meaning?"

"Meaning you made your choices. You said yes every time someone handed you more work. Oh!" Delari went white. He slammed both hands to his chest. For an instant Hecht thought it was his heart. Then—

The earth slammed up, fell down, shimmied like a belly dancer's bottom. There had been tiny, barely perceptible tremors for days. Nothing like this. Accumulated dust and dirt fell from higher up in the mill. Chunks followed. "Downstairs!" Hecht ordered. "Everybody out! Earthquake!" Hecht's left wrist itched cruelly. "It's sorcery, not . . ."

Principaté Delari, a ghastly pale, already starting down, said, "I know. Get out. Get the situation under control."

The panic faded. Hecht got down and out. He pushed through a mob of gawkers, all facing downriver. The ruined castle could not be seen. A cloud of dust, or fog, intervened. A breeze shredded that and carried it westward, over the river into the Connec.

Principaté Delari poked Hecht in the ribs. "Don't gawk, move."

Hecht moved. Toward the cloud. Which faded to a trace. His wrist continued to nag. He barked, "Colonel Sedlakova! Have the officers assemble on me immediately."

The earth continued trembling.

From the vantage of a hummock two hundred yards southeast of the mill Hecht could see that a quarter mile of hillside, sloping toward the river, had split like a rip in the seat of too-tight trousers. At several points he saw a pale bluish mother-of-pearl surface. Pulsing.

Puffing, Muniero Delari trudged past. "Come along, Piper. Come along." The old man's course angled uphill. He wanted a closer look at the crack.

The ground shivered. The pearlescent blue moved.

Pinkus Ghort caught up as Hecht and the old man climbed to where they could look down the length of the tear in the earth. He blurted, "Holy shit! It's a giant-ass fucking worm!"

"Grub," Delari corrected. "A larval stage." A wave of motion ran along the thing in the crack. Its downhill end moved forward slightly. The itching at Hecht's wrist amplified severely. "Piper! You should . . ."

Hecht had decided what he should. "Consent!" Puffing, Titus was catching up. Random officers followed, seriously confused. "Bring out the falcons! With special loads! I need them up here yesterday! Your Grace. Are we seeing what I think we're seeing?"

"The birth of a god. More or less."

"But what . . . ?"

"I don't know anything you don't. This could be the hatching of an egg left over from before mankind reached this part of the world. But we don't have the luxury of taking time to worry about who, what, where, and all that. We have to act."

True. That thing would be no friend of Piper Hecht's. Or anyone else round here.

It was Esther's Wood all over again. Another race against time. That thing was maturing. He could sense it nursing on what little free power was in circulation nearby. Soon it would want to feed in earnest.

A backward curved horn began to form atop the downhill end.

"That the head down there?" Hecht asked.

"It would seem," Delari replied.

"Pinkus, you aren't in the chain of command but you have a way with words. Go make those gawking fools take this seriously." The whole army wanted to see the monster. No one seemed smart enough to be scared. "Tell my idiot officers I want everyone moving upriver. With the animals. Except the artillerists."

The falcon crews were running round in confusion in the meadow where they had built bunkers to store their weapons and firepowder. Hecht hoped they would not try to tow the weapons. No. Here came Kait Rhuk and his gang, two men dragging the falcon and three lugging ammunition. The other crews seemed intent on following Rhuk's example.

Hecht told Principaté Delari, "I should go run this show. They know what to do only in theory. If you think of anything useful to do, don't hesitate." He stumbled down the slope. Several officers intercepted him. He repeated his orders to get everyone out of harm's way. "This thing is going to want to eat. Let's don't be its first meal."

Clej Sedlakova asked, "What're you going to do?" Hecht thought it worth noting that the handicapped officer was among the first actually to come for instructions.

"I'm going to kill it."

SEVEN FALCONS WERE IN POSITION. THE OTHER THREE CREWS WERE STILL getting organized. There would be personnel adjustments later. If there were survivors.

The god grub continued trying to shake the chains of the earth. Hecht moved down to the front end, which had come out of the ground a few dozen yards from the river. That end had developed obvious mouth parts and dark patches where eyes might appear.

Pinkus Ghort jogged up. Hecht demanded, "What're you doing back here?"

"I couldn't miss this."

"You could be as sorry as you've ever been. Rhuk! Weber! Stand by. Hell, Pinkus, we need to get behind those things."

Rhuk and Weber took his sudden movement for the signal to fire.

The simultaneous roar of both pieces, hurling sulfurous hot gases, felled Hecht and Ghort. Hecht rolled over in time to see hundreds of black spots appear on the grub's vast face. Three more falcons discharged, raking the monster's length.

The earth shook. Three-quarters of the grub rose into the air. It crashed back. Hecht, trying to get up, went down again.

The acne spots on the grub grew quickly. As did the spots that would become eyes.

"Get the eyes!" Hecht shouted. "Keep it blind!"

More falcons barked. The least competent crews were in place. Rhuk and Weber prepared their second shots.

Principaté Delari limped down to where Hecht had given up trying to get his feet under him, dropped to his knees. Shaking his head.

"There's no choice. I know there's no choice. I can't guess what spawned this . . . There's going to be a storm, Piper."

Hecht had no chance to ask what that meant. Falcons discharged. They ruined the face of the grub and tore smoldering black wounds along its length. Ten thousand tails of vapor, like feathers stirring in the breeze. The grub shook and screamed—inside every mind for miles.

Hecht's new amulet was not supposed to hurt. Good thing. He could not imagine how bad the pain would have been were he wearing er-Rashal's gift.

There was always ambient power in the world. It kept the ice at bay, made sorcery possible, fed the Instrumentalities of the Night. Like air, the power was always there. Like air, its presence went unnoticed. It became notable only when it was absent.

Rather than absorbed, the ambient power began to be sucked into the god grub. Its wounds stabilized.

Hecht made a whimpering noise.

Principaté Delari shouted.

The storm had arrived.

"This is too damned expensive!"

The falcons barked raggedly, voices nearly lost in the psychic roar. A power vortex began to form above the grub. It darkened and grew, spinning, streaked with threads of every imaginable color.

Delari said, "You *have* to get your men away from here. If the falcons don't work . . ."

"It's under way." The officers had gotten the rubberneckers moving at last.

Hecht spied Cloven Februaren back up the slope. Which had begun to shake with vigor.

The light grew feeble. Hecht barely made out Februaren falling. He headed for the old man, moving as though through waist-deep honey. Muniero Delari shouted something he did not understand.

The old man uphill tried to get his feet under him. He fell again and began to slide toward the tear where the grub had begun to thrash.

Two more charges ripped along its flank and back. And did not fade. And did not fade.

The black began to spread.

The deep honey drag weakened.

The grub's thrashing increased. Like the writhing of a broken snake. A sour, stink bug reek hit Hecht. His nose and eyes watered.

Cloven Februaren's slide toward catastrophe quickened.

The old man clawed at the grass. Hecht knew he would not get there in time.

The old man's left foot tangled in a ground-hugging vine. Hecht did get there as Februaren swung end for end. He snagged the old man's tangled ankle, ripped him loose, pulled him in, hoisted him onto his shoulder, and ran.

Instinct more than thought drove him. He had trouble staying upright. The grub kept punishing the earth around it. The stench punished the air.

He had staggered a hundred yards, gasping painfully, when he recalled the Gray Walker's death.

He pushed even harder, till the fire in his chest forced his collapse. He dragged himself into a low place, pulling Cloven Februaren. The ancient muttered some unintelligible warning.

Where was Muniero Delari?

Lightning filled the universe. The ground shook its worst yet. The earth itself rumbled but no thunder followed the ferocious flash.

Cloven Februaren moved feebly. He tried to say something. Hecht could not hear. The old man stabbed one weak finger.

Hecht looked.

A pillar of scarlet stood a thousand feet tall, its red deepening fast. A red and black ball churned atop it. It seemed to include a cherubic demon's face, looking for something it could never see because it was blind.

Hecht lay there a long time, watching. The pillar degenerated into smoke and soot. Some drifted on the wind. Most fell in a fine black snow.

The old man wanted him to do something.

Get up and take charge. Get up and find Muniero Delari. Get up and growl defiance at the Night.

Hecht got his feet under him. He had no strength left. He spotted a wooden shaft nearby. It had been part of a tool for swabbing the bore of a falcon. Now it was a broken stick but long enough to lean on.

He got the pole, then hoisted the old man. "Hang on. I can't carry you anymore. But I'll go slow."

Februaren grabbed hold, then tried to say something about pain in his side.

Hecht moved a dozen yards uphill, to a vantage from which he could see how fortunate he had been to get down when he had.

From that small eminence he could see that half the world had been toasted. Fires still burned where bushes and trees had stood. Smoke still rose from burnt grass. Yet patches and stripes of green spotted and wove through it all, fading into obscurity beneath falling soot.

A firepowder caisson exploded.

The falcon in a smoldering carriage nearby looked like wax left too long in the sun.

There were human shapes everywhere. Those in the black were charred, though a few still tried to move. Songs of pain rose all around. From the greens, though, healthier men appeared, all fascinated by the collapsing tower above the god grub pyre.

The black extended a quarter mile toward the mill. Which still stood, though its ruined sails had fallen and were burning. The black itself faded into the brown of dead grass, then the yellow-green of sick grass. A mile away the earth was normal.

The ruined castle had collapsed. A gray dust cloud still trailed downwind.

Februaren made a feeble gesture indicating direction. "Go. Help Muno."

Hecht set him down where he could be found easily, then shuffled off as fast as his body would allow.

He found the Principaté a hundred yards away, stirring weakly in a low place that had not been quite low enough. Delari's backside had been crisped. His behind had suffered local roasting. "Principaté? Can you understand me?"

Delari made funny noises. Hecht turned him gently. There was blood in the old man's nose and mouth. He wiped at it with his fingers, having nothing better to hand. Delari croaked, "Grandfather?"

"He's alive. Maybe a little bruised from me falling on him. I don't know about anyone else. I see a lot of bodies."

Another cask of firepowder exploded. The Patriarch would be livid about the waste.

"Anyone who . . . wasn't in a . . . direct line . . . should be all . . . right."

A racking cough seized him. It sounded like the cough that had dogged Grade Drocker when he was dying.

Was his conscience dredging up evils to haunt him?

Delari gasped, "I'm not broken . . . like Grade. I'll . . . recover." He tried to get onto his hands and knees. He managed, but not without a cry of pain. "What the hell?" He panted like a dog for twenty seconds, then tried to reach back behind him.

Hecht told him, "You didn't get all of you down out of the flash."

"How can I . . . ever go back . . . to the baths?"

Hecht chuckled. "I'm wondering how you're going to ride."

A voice suggested, "On a litter, face down." Cloven Februaren had arrived unnoticed. Much recovered. He wore a broad smile. "This should be amusing in the baths."

Delari snapped, "When did you ever visit the baths? And don't you think you ought to be a little less visible? I'm not the only member of the

Collegium here. The rest are going to come weaseling around trying to profit now the danger is past." He turned slightly, looked over Hecht's shoulder. "Here comes Ghort."

Pinkus, with stripes burned on his clothing, wobbled as he walked. He tripped, spent half a minute on hands and knees before getting his feet under him again. Hecht moved his way. When he glanced back Cloven Februaren was gone.

"How did he do that?"

Delari said, "I wish I knew. It would be handy in a few minutes."

Gervase Saluda and the Principaté from Aparion were leading the return of the curious. Carefully.

Hecht said, "Saluda is no coward."

"Nor is Gorin Linczski. He spent several years in the Holy Lands. Their caution is justified."

A recollection from Esther's Wood. "If you're able . . . Let's look in that crack." Titus Consent and other officers were headed his way, too. The falcon crews had begun to rematerialize.

Another keg of powder cooked off. Those approaching hit the ground.

Moving toward the crack, Hecht asked, "Can you manage?"

"Just don't ask me to run."

The ground nearer the grub gash was still hot. It hurt through Hecht's soles. Defunct sheep and goats spotted the slope. With their herd dog.

Delari gasped, "There's your mutton."

"We'll eat well tonight." He looked down. And saw what he expected. "There. The egg-shaped thing. Still glowing."

"Yes?"

He had to force it. "I've seen one before. In the Holy Lands. I don't know what happened to it." Which was as forthcoming as he could be. He glanced at the curious tide approaching. Most were distracted by distorted falcons, dead men and animals, and the gross impact of the god grub's demise.

From on high the devastation was appalling. Though mainly confined to nature. The abandoned castle was the only human construct to suffer extensive damage. The near countryside looked like the flank of a green and black zebra, the verdant stripes persisting wherever uneven ground provided protection. The breeze was removing the soot.

Hecht asked, "What do you think?"

"It's too hot down there. And we need to keep anyone else from acquiring it. Tell me what the other one was like."

"A big amber egg. With shot from the falcon trapped inside."

"Interesting."

"You know what it is? What it means?"

"No. Suppose I intercept those two Principatés and redirect their curiosity." Instead, though, he tipped his head slightly and scanned the blackened hillside.

"What?"

"Checking for Grandfather. These two should be too young to recognize him. But why take a chance?"

Hecht had the feeling things were happening that he could not see. Too often he felt like a blind beggar in the streets of intrigue. "All right. Here comes Kait Rhuk, too. I can't imagine how he survived." The engine of his mind was turning again, as though fresh lard had been thrown on its wooden roller bearings.

There would be a lot to do. First and foremost, a muster to see who had survived and who had not.

Principaté Delari headed toward his brethren from the Collegium. Hecht went to meet Rhuk.

"Mr. Rhuk. I can't say as I've ever seen such a demonstration of courage."

Rhuk had a heavy accent. His speech was hard to follow. "I don't know, sir. Meaning, I didn't know. Maybe did I before, I wouldn't a even come set up, let alone stood my ground and kept firing."

"Everyone probably feels that way."

"Yer old sorcerer, there. He have any idea what we just run into?"

"I'm not sure I believe him. A son of the Adversary. Trying to enter the world the way a butterfly does." Most people had observed the cycle of the butterfly as children.

"Interesting times," Rhuk understated.

"You all right?"

"Got a few splinters from a firepowder keg that went up. Otherwise, I'm fine. God loves me. I fell in a hole just in time."

"If you can operate, then, I declare you lord of the falcon artillery. You're in charge of finding out how bad we were hurt. How many weapons survived? How much ammunition? We need work parties to recover as much spent shot as we can."

Rhuk scowled.

"Success never goes unpunished in this army, Mr. Rhuk. I survived, too. So I get to do without sleep at all for the next few days."

Rhuk managed a weak grin before he bowed slightly and headed back downhill. Hecht was surprised to see how many artillerymen had survived.

That was the way, though, usually. Even the most horrific events turned out less terrible than the mind anticipated.

He thought he caught the Ninth Unknown in the corner of his eye but saw nothing when he looked. What was the old man up to now?

He had chosen his officers well. Despite the magnitude of the event, they had begun to restore order. The commanders of the smaller units seemed to be gathering their men for a head count—even before his order reached them.

What could he do about what might lie in the gash?

He moved a few steps farther into the black at the crack's rim. The soil crunched underfoot. A paper-thin layer had melted and hardened. The earth beneath was dryer than desert dust. And those few steps were all he could take before the residual heat became too intense.

He spied Madouc, a hundred yards toward the mill, in a ferocious sulk. "I forgot again. They'll have to kill me so I'll start staying where they can protect me." No excuse to avoid it, he marched down and apologized.

"I'm going to put bells on you. Sir."

The man was truly, richly angry.

Hecht was not contrite. If the bodyguards had been around he would not have gotten near the god grub.

OFFICERS' CALL WAS OVER. ORDER HAD BEEN RESTORED. BUT MORALE WAS severely stressed. None of the men believed the monster had appeared coincidentally. Even long-service professional soldiers did not want to face surprises of that sort.

Hecht could neither argue nor reassure. He feared he had been targeted again. And he had survived by using the weapon the Instrumentalities so feared.

Lessons learned. On all sides.

This had been a close run, with ten falcons barking. It would take bigger weapons to fell . . . Don't even think that. Pray, instead, for Drago Prosek, who would have only two weapons when he met the monster in the Jagos.

The staff meeting following officers' call was glum. No one had much to say. Titus tossed in, "The news from Brothe isn't good. Apparently we're not sitting still because of negotiations but because the Patriarch is deathly sick."

Hecht figured his staff began rooting for Death. "Who might replace him? How would that affect us?"

Not something anyone had thought about. Including the Collegium. Sublime was young.

"We're a forward-thinking lot, aren't we?" Hecht said. "Get some sleep. We're looking at long days ahead. Titus. Stay. You know you don't need to sleep. You're not old enough."

"Yes, sir." Resigned.

Once the others cleared off, excepting Principaté Delari, Hecht asked, "What became of our assassin from Viscesment? I didn't get to question him."

"Funny you should ask. He had the great misfortune to be the only rear echelon fellow to suffer a fatal event during the excitement."

"Titus."

"Somebody cut the asshole's throat."

"Principaté? Wasn't he in your keeping?"

"In theory." Delari was angry. "I'd better check on Bit and her daughter. And the hostages. You'll find them very useful soon."

Consent told Hecht, "You don't seem surprised."

"I don't have much capacity for surprise left, Titus."

THE PRINCIPATÉS ALL SHOWED UP NEXT MORNING, DELARI ARRIVING FIRST. He presented a heavy ring, its inside stamped with the birdlike trident. "Not much else to say. If he hadn't been beaten half to death I'd let Armand find some other benefactor."

"Bit and the others?"

"Bit is dead. The daughter is worse off than Armand. There was a lot of blood." After a pause, "The boy did put up a fight. He marked them. They'll be found and dealt with. The hostages weren't harmed."

Gorin Linczski and Gervase Saluda arrived. They brought messages from the Collegium. In a shaky hand Hugo Mongoz wanted to know what the hell Hecht was doing, attacking Sonsa? That was the oldest letter. Another, from the Patriarch himself, in a hand shakier still, was enthusiastic about the capture of Viscesment and the Pretender Patriarch, but otherwise lacked substance.

Letters from various Principatés ranged across a spectrum of attitudes. Hecht read them out of courtesy only.

Then Bronte Doneto appeared. "I didn't know you were back," Hecht said.

"I got in late. I should've left sooner. I missed the ruckus."

"Be happy you did. What happened with Immaculate?"

Doneto's story did not vary from what Hecht already knew. In the end, Immaculate II was dead. By the hand of someone not serving the interest of the Brothen Episcopal Church.

"I came back, though," Doneto explained, "because of a letter from my cousin. Spirited out of Krois, to me, because 'they' were censoring all his messages to you." Doneto handed Hecht a letter. The handwriting was less shaky than what he had seen earlier. It was dated before the missive about Viscesment.

"The sneaking out took a while."

"Yes. One of his sons finally managed."

"One of his sons."

"He has three. It isn't common knowledge."

For sure. Though Honario Benedocto had had a reputation for whoring around in his youth.

"I guess that's irrelevant."

"I'd say so."

"I'm supposed to have acted on this a month ago."

"It's never too late, Captain-General. My cousin understands that messages go astray. It's why we go redundant with important communiqués. When we can."

Hecht was in no mood for low-level philosophical musings.

The letter had included the orders he had been awaiting, hoping they would not come. Had they arrived in a timely manner Antieux would be invested now. Likewise, Sheavenalle. The main force would be giving Castreresone attention it did not want. And Antieux would not have had time to evacuate so many of its most valuable people.

Persons with skills were resources, too, and prize commodities for the successful conqueror. Which was why Devedians could be found all round the marges of the Mother Sea.

Hecht reflected briefly on the fact that even the children of slaves were not loath to participate in the slave trade.

And the grandfather of the grandfather of a slave was not loath to punish slavers for their daring cruelty. Nor cared that he himself must have slaves amongst his own ancestors. Everyone did. Somewhere, far enough back.

Piper Hecht was angry about the tardiness of the go order. He was excited about the challenges, real and potential. All but a tiny portion of him had *become* Piper Hecht, Captain-General of the Brothen Episcopal Chaldarean Church.

"Hecht?"

"Sorry, Your Grace. I was eye to eye with the fact that I'm going to make history. The kind remembered long after the misery ends."

Doneto paused. As though this unconsidered thought had an impact now that it hung there in front of his face. "Real history. You could be right. When this army crosses the Dechear it will step into the rolls of history as far more than a footnote about a skirmish. A successful Connecten Crusade will define the future of the west."

"True. But there's no time to speculate about futures quickened or aborted by what we do. I'm a month behind, now." He wondered if the timing of the belated war order had more to do with hidden agendas than with difficulties in transit.

Hecht shouted downstairs. He wanted a staff meeting immediately, with an officers' assembly to follow. And he wanted the ferrying of troops increased.

Despite having received no orders earlier, Hecht had sent three thousand men across already. Their presence yonder would simplify the crossing for the rest. There would be no resistance.

AN EMBARRASSED PINKUS GHORT ADMITTED, "THEY WERE MY MEN, PIPE. Again." He meant the murderers, who had been betrayed by wounds they could not explain, then identified by Osa Stile and Bit's daughter.

"I assume you'll protect them till they've been questioned?"

"Yes, Pipe. I'm doing it!"

Hecht's anger subsided. Some. "Have they said anything yet?"

"Only that they don't know anything. They got offered a good bounty. The guy who hired them took off when he saw that the killings hadn't taken. His name was Ingram Five. Him and his brother Anton crossed the river right after the attacks. They didn't report in over there. They just kept on going."

"This stuff keeps happening. And we keep reacting. How do we get ahead of it, Pinkus? These villains don't work in a vacuum. People have to notice them. How do we get them to warn us before somebody gets killed?"

"You're on your way. The soldiers are more loyal to you than to Sublime. Give them a victory and you'll have them. They'll winkle out the villains on their own."

Armies deified successful commanders. Too many commanders let that go to their heads.

"I want to take it back to the source. Smash some skulls there. Throw some people in a fire pit. Be an altogether unpleasant guest."

"We'd need to invade Artecipea first. The threads all lead there."

Pinkus Ghort seldom seemed thoughtful. This was one of those rare times. "That don't make sense, Pipe. None of us ever had nothing to do with nobody from out there. I don't think. You? So how come somebody from there is hot to put you under?"

"I ask myself all the time. All I can come up with is, the Instrumentalities of the Night don't love us."

"Sure you ain't getting a bit of a swelled head, there?"

"Just brainstorming. Based on what Principaté Delari has said. I might do something someday that will inconvenience the Instrumentalities of the Night. So they want to stamp me out before I can."

Hecht believed he had done what the Night feared already. He had turned up a tool that mortal men could use to end the Tyranny of the Night. Whatever the Night and its black agents did now would be throwing the bones with futility. The djinn was out of the lamp. And the lamp had melted down.

Hecht asked, "Has Bo finished?" Bo Biogna and his select thugs had been punished for their good work by being given the chance to collect materials of interest from the crack where the god grub surfaced. A gash vigorously sealed off by troops chosen by Titus Consent. Who were watched in turn by Brotherhood members supervised by Redfearn Bechter.

"He isn't finding any more amber pieces. His guys are still sifting pellets out of the dirt. They have to break the layer of glass to get it. They aren't finding enough silver to justify the work, though. Most of it burned up killing that thing."

Ghort drifted off into awed recollections. Then he shuddered. "Interesting times, Pipe. Interesting times."

Hecht sighed. "They are. But we're eating regular. I have a job for you. If you want it."

"You know me. A glutton for punishment. What?"

"Can you keep a secret?"

"It's possible. Just don't tell me anything I can sell for enough to retire on."

"This might be that."

"So. What've you got?"

"I want you to recruit men from the levies willing to stay on for pay."

"Not hard to come up with those. If you can pay them."

Hecht smiled tightly. "I can."

"How?"

"That's the secret you need to keep."

"You talked me into it, you sweet-talker."

"Smolens was in the right place at the right time. He picked off the latest specie shipment from Salpeno."

Ghort looked startled, then astonished. Then amused. "You're going to rob your own boss?"

"Isn't the money supposed to support this army? If I let it travel down to Brothe, then come back, how much will disappear along the way?"

"Most, probably."

"There you go. So, how about you take over the volunteer brigade?"

"We are going over the river, right?"

"Soon."

"I'm in. Bound to be something left worth stealing over yonder."

"Could be. You'll go to Antieux. You and Doneto. With Clej Sedlakova in charge. Keep Doneto from going totally berserk."

Ghort raised a questioning eyebrow. Hecht noted the gray there.

"I'd rather not be remembered for turning the Connec into a desert."

Ghort gave him a narrow look. "What'll you be doing?"

"I'm going to Castreresone. Smolens will try to take Sheavenalle."

"Castreresone? Even after Roger died?"

"Yes." It could not hurt to have Sublime V and King Peter nose to nose and fuming. "The confusion there should work to our advantage."

"Wish we'd gotten going sooner."

"So do I. So do I. Go on. You've got work to do."

As Ghort neared the head of the stairs, Hecht asked, "Is that daughter of Bit's still healthy?"

"She's recovering."

"Keep her safe. When you have trustworthy men going back to the city, send her along. I'll warn Anna that she's coming."

"You think you ought to ask her first?"

Hecht shrugged. "I should." But . . . "Principaté Delari will want his plaything to go back, too. If he can travel." He would love to have Osa Stile out of the way.

"That kid gives me the creeps, Pipe. They's something stone wrong with him."

"Then you better be careful he doesn't sneak into your tent."

"Not funny, Pipe."

Hecht did wonder, sometimes. Ghort seldom talked about women. That was not right in a soldier.

THE CAPTAIN-GENERAL WATCHED THE MARCHING TROOPS FROM A HILL-side that had been a vineyard once. "Pinkus would be disappointed if he knew," he told Cloven Februaren. The old man had turned up while Hecht was observing the force Sedlakova, Ghort, and Doneto were taking to Antieux. The Captain-General's lifeguards had yet to notice Februaren. The old man showed no sign of the pummeling he had suffered.

"The vines? Yes. I see. Those men seem healthy, trained, and modestly motivated. You've done well."

"Really? You walked up and none of these men noticed."

"Not to worry. They'll frustrate mundane dangers. I'll do the same to the Night."

"You weren't much help with that worm."

"You weren't paying attention, then. Why did it surface where it did, instead of under your mill?"

Hecht did not know. He shrugged.

"It surfaced where your old amulet was being worn by an unlucky goat. Somewhere, there's a very worried Dreangerean sorcerer." The old man chuckled.

Hecht did not know how to respond. Februaren had no reason to sidle round the truth.

The Ninth Unknown said, "You recall me saying that fools might ally with the elder Instrumentalities in hopes of gaining power and favor?" He surveyed Hecht's lifeguards. They were getting nervous.

"Yes."

"Those fools already exist. The trident ring is their emblem. Rudenes Schneidel is their western chieftain. Lieutenant to er-Rashal al-Dhulquarnen. Who seems to be dedicated to restoring the Dreangerean gods of antiquity."

Hecht was not surprised. "There was always a suspicion that the old religion hadn't been expunged. Er-Rashal was marginal in his devotions at best, but too useful to punish."

"Your brothers in the Sha-lug band have worked this out for themselves. The man Bone has returned to Dreanger. He hopes to warn Gordimer by going through Nassim Alizarin."

"If Bone convinces the Mountain I foresee a difficult life for the Rascal."

"Don't forget what er-Rashal is."

The bodyguards heard ghost voices. They talked about it. But they could not see the old man, nor did they note their charge holding a conversation with something invisible.

"No doubt. They're getting nervous. You need to go soon."

"Yes."

"What did er-Rashal want with those mummies?"

"I don't know. But no good will come of him having them. Maybe he wants to conjure the shades of the sorcerers they used to be. Though he'd have to be atop one of the Wells of Ihrian to have enough power. And he'd need the support of the Night. Unless he prepared with extreme discretion, then moved too fast for the Instrumentalities to notice."

"Not likely, if they see threats two hundred years ahead."

"He could be in for a painful surprise. If he hasn't made the right alliances inside the Night." But that was the story of most sorcerers, including those who had infested Andesqueluz. They began to overvalue themselves and underrate the Instrumentalities of the Night. Then the Night devoured them.

The lifeguards were thoroughly unsettled now. None could stand still. But none had yet discovered the ancient in brown.

Hecht said, "What changed when we crossed the Dechear?"

"What do you mean?"

"We had no trouble with the Night east of the river. Just the mischief you get anywhere. But once we crossed over we started getting pestered. Bad. Like the spirits of rock and brook and tree are more of-fended by our presence than Count Raymone and his friends. Principaté Delari seems indifferent. Or maybe he just can't explain."

"Might he be preoccupied with more pressing matters?"

"Sir?"

"The Night may be more active but it's still just a nuisance. Precau-tions you learned while you were crawling will head off most of the monkey business. Expect it to intensify. Yes. The land itself feels threat-ened. Because it *is*. And now it's time to go. Yon lad with the fine blond hair just caught something from the corner of his eye. He's going to mention it to someone."

The old man did a snappy about-face. And vanished as he finished.

"No," Hecht muttered. "You don't just disappear."

"Sir?" Madouc had crossed twenty yards of abandoned vineyard in a blink.

"Thought I saw something. Out of the corner of my eye. But it wasn't there when I looked. Are they coming out in the daytime? *Can* they?"

"I don't know, sir. You should ask the Principatés about that. But I think we should move you down where you'll be less exposed."

"Maybe so. Lead on." Hecht wondered why the Night would ha-rass Patriarchal invaders but not those from Arnhand or Grolsach.

"That isn't true," Principaté Delari said when Hecht made the point. "Arnhanders and Grolsachers alike have encountered a range of signifi-cant revenants. Rook and Hilt have been underfoot from the start. Weaver and Shade have turned up more than once. Others are stirring. Death. Skillen. Kint. Someone is freeing their bound fragments. Some may have pulled themselves together enough to start feeding on lesser spirits."

"I've never heard of those before. Death, Skillen, Kint?"

"Death is death. Personified. A reactive rather than a proactive. Not a claimer but a proclaimer."

"Huh?"

"Death shows up when it's time for somebody to die. Like a herald. Rook, Hilt, and the others come in to clean up."

"Skillen? Kint?"

"Misfortune. Despair."

"Did the ancients have any happy gods?"

"Does anyone? Today's gods range from unpleasant to psychotic. The God Who Is God, the All-Powerful and Merciful, when He bothers to show Himself—and note that He hasn't for several hundred years—only dispenses disasters, plagues, and pestilences. Likewise, the Deve-dian God and our Chaldarean deity, as currently edited. The Dainshaukin deity is a freak out of pre-history, always in an insane rage. None of them can fend for themselves. They need people like the Society to put words in their mouths and break bones in their names."

"I'm seeing a new side of you here."

"The Connec is upsetting my sense of discretion. God ought to be able to look out for Himself. If He doesn't like your heresy He can smack you down Himself."

"Pardon me. I'm going to move a few rods downrange so a stray lightning bolt don't pick me off by mistake."

"You just sealed your own doom, Piper. By definition, God can't make a mistake."

"He doesn't seem to mind sarcasm, either."

Madouc moved in and out of hearing as the road climbed, descended, and meandered. He seemed appalled by what he heard.

Delari suggested, "Those of His minions who feel He needs occasional assistance could be anywhere, Piper. Maybe even among the lifeguards of the Captain-General of His Living Voice."

Hecht wanted to protest the absurdity. But it was not absurd. He had not chosen the bodyguards. Surely one would belong to the Brotherhood of War. The Society might have placed a spy, as well.

He did not respond. Aloud.

Delari added, "We're never so invulnerable that there isn't one worm who can bring us down."

"Not even you?"

"Not even me. They haven't forgotten me, Piper. They're biding their time. There'll come a day."

There would. Of course. Those coals never burned out.

BUHLE SMOLENS CAME DOWN FROM THE NORTH. HE PASSED BEHIND THE main Patriarchal force. He turned over the captured Arnhander specie and records of all that he had done, investigated, and learned while in Viscesment. He picked up an additional two thousand men.

The material named and described several men he hoped to meet.

Witnesses in Viscesment believed them to be Artecipean. They fled into the End of Connec when Smolens arrived. Immaculate's more ardent supporters had done the same. Most were now in Antieux.

The Artecipeans had done nothing blatant while in Viscesment. Even so, the locals believed they were up to no good. Men with such ugly personal habits could only be villains.

THE NIGHT MADE ITSELF MORE FELT WITH EACH DARKFALL. THOUGH NEVER more than malicious mischief, the harassment sapped morale. Pinkus Ghort had trouble recruiting militiamen. When, despite their Chaldarean faith, every imaginable demon and malevolent sprite seemed possible, most wanted to relocate to where interaction with those entities was less likely.

There were few desertions from the Patriarchal force. And plenty of natives were willing to help the Church tame the heretics of the Connec.

The weather turned. Rains came. Not just the occasional shower whose misery faded in a few hours but frequent violent thunderstorms featuring high winds, massive lightning, and, often, accompanying barrages of hail. In calmer hours the sky remained overcast.

The wet did no good for equipment, clothing, boots, feet, or the hooves of the animals.

"It's natural," Principaté Delari assured Hecht when he asked if the gods themselves were conspiring to destroy the army with mildew, mold, foot rot, and rust. "There's just more of it this year than normal. So the locals assure me." The sky seldom shone through.

The weather was inhospitable the day they sighted Castreresone. Its walls were as dreary as the sky. The folk of city and surrounding countryside were astonished to find a crusader army going into camp astride the broad old bridge over the Laur. There was never any contact with enemy scouts or skirmishers. The vedettes met no one but startled peasants and amazed travelers.

Hecht kept asking, "How could they possibly not know we were coming? No infantry force moves faster than the news of its coming."

Titus Consent opined, "They heard. They didn't believe. It isn't possible. Peter of Navaya is their shield now. Not even Sublime V is crazy enough to offend King Peter."

The Captain-General set his main camp across the river from the White City, with a strong force beyond the broad bridge, fortifying the Inconje bridgehead. The bridge itself was a glaring reminder that war was alien to the Connec. It should have been fortified at both ends. Its main span should have been designed to be demolished easily.

The east end of the bridge was surrounded by the low buildings of an unfortified suburb, Inconje, inhabited by prosperous Deves, Dainshaus, and others who could not find a place inside the city or its attached, walled suburbs, the Burg and the New Town. The population had all fled. They had left little worth stealing.

"Those are some impressive walls," Hecht said. "We won't be going over them. And we don't have enough men to lock them in and starve them out." Half the army had gone to Antieux or Sheavenalle. The capture of the port city was critical to the success of the campaign. "We'll just harass them till we come up with a few traitors willing to help us get in. I should've kept Sedlakova. He might see something I couldn't."

Consent suggested, "Talk to Hagan Brokke. He works harder than anyone. And he's maybe a little disgruntled because a one-legged man got first chance at Antieux. He thinks you take him for granted."

Hagan Brokke had been close through most of Hecht's Brothen career, in the City Regiment for the Calziran Crusade and now with the Patriarchals for the Connecten Crusade. Hecht had, indeed, taken one of his more talented officers for granted. "Does he know anything about siege work?"

"Talk to him."

15. Plemenza: Tooth to Tooth with the Son of the Night

Princess Helspeth snapped, "You've been here six weeks, Mr. Prosek! When can we expect you to do something?"

Algres Drear caught her left elbow, squeezed, pulled.

Prosek had taken his orders to heart. "When I'm ready, ma'am." Always "ma'am," instead of honorifics due the Princess Apparent of the Grail Empire. "Or you can go try it yourself if you can't wait."

Helspeth fumed. Drear had trouble restraining his temper. He did so because he understood Prosek's response. The man was testy because he was being harassed.

Helspeth loathed Prosek because he failed to be impressed by her in any way—except as an annoyance.

Drear squeezed her elbow again. "Remember. Brotherhood of War."

Helspeth held her tongue. She watched Prosek's men make additions to a map of the high Jagos. Recon work had been slow and difficult. Few people were getting through to report and fewer were willing to go scout.

Something like a brown stain had been added to the crude chart.

Prosek tapped the map. He checked his team leaders, someone Varley and a man whose name Helspeth could not remember despite having been told a half-dozen times. Varley nodded unhappily. The other sighed hugely and unhappily. Forcing a smile, Prosek said, "This is why they pay us like princes. Buck up, Stern. We'll leave beautiful corpses."

Helspeth thought that might be a joke. Stern was the ugliest men she had ever seen.

"We've determined our ambush site, ma'am," Prosek said. "Captain Drear. Did you make up the charges I asked for?"

Helspeth ground her teeth. The man knew perfectly well that they were ready. He was reminding everyone of the professional pecking order. Unaware that what shielded him was not his expertise but his association with the Captain-General.

She would not ask the question Prosek was prodding her toward.

Drear touched her elbow again, lightly, to remind her he thought her problems with Drago Prosek were of her own manufacture and, probably, existed entirely inside her own imagination. Drear believed Prosek was so wed to his work that he was unaware of any conflict.

Drear said, "Six charges, prepared according to your specifications."

"Excellent. Then we're all set. We can leave in the morning. Weather, manpower, and drayage permitting."

Weather between the Ownvidian Knot and the Jagos was not benign lately, though good days still outnumbered the bad.

Prosek said, "Alert the people who'll go with me. Have everyone eat a big meal and get a good sleep. We're not likely to have either again soon."

Another annoying characteristic of the man. He believed he could better endure hardship than any effete Imperial. Drear would happily teach the man respect once his Princess had her use of him. But that pleasure would never be his. The girl would stray from her agreement not one inch.

"I'm sorry I'm giving you so many gray hairs, Captain," Helspeth told Drear. "Someday, perhaps, it will prove worth having endured my whimsy."

"I've endured worse servitude than here with you, Princess. It's the people around you who make the job difficult."

"In the morning, then, Captain."

She saw suspicion begin to cloud his thinking.

Stupid. She should not have given him that much warning.

DREAR WAS LIVID WHEN HE FOUND HELSPETH AMONG THE MEN ACCOMPAnying Prosek. She had donned the arms and armor she had demonstrated at al-Khazen. And wore a heavy cloak that concealed her sex and slight stature.

Weapons and armor had been confiscated during Lothar's reign but she had been clever and persistent and had gotten them back. The Empire enjoyed no shortage of corrupt functionaries willing to lose track of items in their care.

Lady Hilda joined the adventure, though she was supposed to keep the Princess Apparent under close control. She was bored to excruciation by the Dimmel Palace.

Captain Drear discovered them while taking a head count. There was truth in Prosek's notions about Imperials. Some were intimidated by the weather, which had turned cold and damp. It should get worse in the high Jagos.

Drear came up two long on his count. But by the time he isolated the ringers Drago Prosek was barking at the teamsters manning the wagons carrying the expedition's stores and equipment.

Helspeth told Drear, "I won't stay here voluntarily. If you force me, there'll be hell to pay."

"And yet, hell to pay if I don't. I should throw myself on my sword and save the Empress the cost of feeding me till she gets around to hanging me."

"So dramatic, Captain. I promise, I won't be any trouble."

"God, save me! Princess, you're trouble curdled just by being here."

"Lady Hilda will protect me."

"God, give me patience. Princess . . ."

"I'm going. Fix that in your head, Captain. Adjust to it. Console yourself with the knowledge that this will almost certainly be the last time I'll draw a deep breath without prior approval from my sister and the Council Advisory."

There might be a monster in the Jagos, interfering with traffic, but news did get through. There was strong sentiment in Alten Weinberg for cloistering the Princess Apparent somewhere where she could be controlled more completely. Not that she had done anything to offend anyone. No one complained about her efforts as the Empire's legate south of the mountains. But she was a valuable commodity. And a potential rallying point for those who disdained the Brothen Patriarchy.

Katrin was concerned. Her letters seldom demonstrated any warmth.

Helspeth repeated herself. "I'm going, Captain. We're wasting time and falling behind."

Algres Drear committed the sin for which he never forgave himself. He acquiesced. It was easier than fighting. He was tired of squabbling, especially with the girl. She never yielded.

It did not take long for others to figure it out. Helspeth knew little about the daily business of the march. Things had always been done for her. Lady Hilda was of only slightly more use.

Helspeth did work to win the men over. She convinced them they were about to perform wonders.

Drago Prosek was not restrained about forecasting disaster due to the presence of women.

Six days of cold misery and cold emotional truce brought the party to the point Prosek had chosen for his staging camp.

PROSEK AND HIS CREWS, ALGRES DREAR, AND PRINCESS HELSPETH crowded the larger campfire. Everyone wanted a look at the map that Prosek had prepared. "Here and here," Prosek said. "Perfect sites for the falcons. This lower one has a clear line of fire a hundred fifty yards long and is shielded by boulders. This other is under an overhang and has a cave behind it. It's thirty feet up the mountainside. You can tell it's been a lookout post since prehistoric times. Stern, you're up there because you aren't smart enough to get scared or nervous. You take the second shot, once Varley freezes the thing with his. If you have to take off, just fall back into the cave. It isn't big enough for the monster to get into."

Helspeth started to remind Prosek that the devil was a shapechanger. Algres Drear pinched his lips. Just to remind her that she had promised to keep her big mouth shut.

"We have one problem," Prosek said. "Other than this damned weather." It was cold. The heavens delivered infrequent but unpleasant bouts of freezing rain. "How do we lure this thing in?"

Helspeth wondered what drove her to put herself in her present position. She was miserable physically, at risk of life and soul, and the adventure would stain her marital value. It would leave her more disliked and distrusted in Alten Weinberg.

She was not disturbed by any potential collapse of her value as a commodity.

Prosek asked, "Anyone know anything about this beast that they haven't told me? Is it likely to know how many of us there are or the nature of our mission? It used to be human, according to the Captain-General. Does it still have a human ability to reason? Right. Nobody has anything. All sink or swim for Drago. Princess? You were at al-Khazen."

"I'm sorry, Mr. Prosek. I can't help you. I was occupied elsewhere when whatever happened to the man happened. I know less than you."

"Pity we don't have a wizard. But if wishes were fishes. The Captain-General told me I could handle this. Maybe he knows me better than I do. Drear. You look like a man who's done some hunting. How would you draw this thing?"

"I've only hunted deer and mountain goat. You go to them. Or ambush them."

Helspeth could not keep her mouth shut. "You've been to the Holy Lands, haven't you, Mr. Prosek?"

"I have. Five years. Actually saw Indala al-Sul Halaladin close enough to tell the color of his eyes. They're gray. Not what you'd expect. Your point?"

"The Sha-lug, the Peqaad tribesmen, Indala al-Sul Halaladin, even the H'un-tai At, all use the false flight tactic. And their enemies fall for it more often than not."

Reluctantly, Prosek granted, "Unfortunately true. A lot of Crusader commanders, new to the Holy Lands and eager to make a name, never believe the Unbeliever is as smart as they are. And veteran besides. So?"

"The man the monster was before he was soultaken lived in Andoray two hundred years ago. That will shape his thinking now. Won't it?"

"Seems likely. So?"

"Heroic individualism was a big thing back then. If somebody put on full armor and went up there like Red Hammer challenging the Midwynd Giant . . ."

Prosek's eyes glazed. He sucked spittle back and forth between his teeth. "Here's an idea. Why don't we . . ." He repeated Helspeth's suggestion word for word. As she neared the boiling point he winked at her, grinned. "Just one problem. Picking a hero. And I have a bad feeling about that. You're the only one here equipped for the role. Captain Drear, is anyone small enough to wear her armor?"

"There is no way . . ."

"I agree. But nobody else brought a convincing costume."

Lady Hilda volunteered, "I'm small enough . . ."

Helspeth said, "That isn't going to happen, either."

TWO DAYS OF DRIZZLING MISERY PASSED. BOTH FALCONS WERE POSITIONED, their crews rehearsed. Drear and Prosek had scouted the pass as far as the ruin of the next way station. They had felt the monster stirring. They planted small, standard wards to keep smaller Night things from scouting for the monster.

Three of Drear's Braunsknechts returned with armor fit for a grown man. They brought two long couch lances as well, complete with pennons.

There were no volunteers to don the armor and spring the trap.

Prosek grumbled, "It's too damned cold out here, anyway. Stern, Varley. Let's pack it up. These people aren't really interested."

DREAR TOOK THE LONGER LANCE. "WE'LL SEE IF I CAN STILL STAY ON A horse wearing all this plunder."

Helspeth kissed the knuckles of Drear's left glove. "Don't do anything stupid."

"You want me to do this? Or not?"

She stepped back, silent. He did not expect, or maybe even want, to survive this. He would suffer no end of grief if he did.

He had no business letting her be here. And no business leaving her to draw the monster into a position where it could be destroyed. That was not his job. That was not his mission.

Guilt pierced her down to the anklebones of her soul.

Drago Prosek followed Drear at a distance, still making measurements. Still making arcane preparations.

Helspeth pulled Lady Hilda close. "When we hear Drear coming back I want you to distract the other Braunsknechts."

"Princess?"

"Whatever it takes. Just get me a few seconds."

ALGRES DREAR WAS UP THE PASS, OUT OF SIGHT. THE WEATHER HAD TURNED more benign, though the wind still sounded like ghosts quarreling amongst the boulders and stunted trees. The falcon crews waited, ready.

Drago Prosek put no faith in matches or punks where there was no margin for failure. A charcoal fire burned near each weapon, warming the crew and heating an iron rod that could not be blown out by the wind nor extinguished by a raindrop. Prosek himself remained in constant motion between the weapon sites. He was nervous but not for the reasons everyone else was. He was worried about things working right when he needed them to work. The rest were worried about surviving.

The Braunsknechts had no familiarity with Prosek's weapons. They expected nothing good. The falcon crews did not know what to expect, either. They had yet to be in this position.

"Princess?" Lady Hilda whispered. "What are you doing?"

"I'm trying to pray. I'm not very good at it." Nor good at being a leader, either, she feared. This was what happened when you let personal desire overrule your need to be responsible. People got hurt.

A noise rolled down the pass, indefinable after battering back and forth between the canyon walls. It was loud.

Lady Hilda understood what was bothering her. "Like everybody else in the world, you're doing the right thing for the wrong reason."

Algres Drear appeared, low on the neck of his mount. The animal was fleeing but making no speed because it could not use its right hind leg. Drear no longer carried a lance. He had lost his sword, too.

A heaving something appeared behind him. It was the source of the echoing noises. Drear's broken lance protruded from what might be called a left shoulder. At eye height, as though the monster had dodged to avoid being blinded.

Helspeth started forward, meaning to snatch up the second lance. Drear's men seized her. She struggled weakly. As she did, she noted that the monster's lost claw had grown back.

The thing was in a mad rage. And gaining on Drear. Who was injured.

One of the Braunsknechts took the lance. He started forward. Prosek smacked him. "Let it unfold the way it was designed." But the man from the Brotherhood moved forward himself.

Drear's mount spied friendly folk ahead. She found some last reservoir of will and picked up the pace for the last fifty yards.

Drear's men swarmed round her once she passed between the last few boulders shielding the lower falcon.

The monster in pursuit sensed danger at the last instant. Limbs flailing, it stopped. Its hideous head rolled back and forth. Antennae waved, tasting the air. But the wind was blowing down the pass. The monster oozed forward, seeking a better taste of what had fired its suspicions.

Helspeth told the Braunsknechts to stop making a racket. Unaware that hearing was the monster's weakest sense.

Drago Prosek kept moving forward. He made no effort to avoid being seen. He carried a yard of burning slow match. The very thing he did not trust his falconeers to depend on.

The monster scooted forward a dozen yards, alert for danger. Had it not been excruciatingly wary it would be feasting already.

Its head rolled. Its antennae sampled the air.

It found something. It stiffened, then collected itself for flight.

Prosek stepped aside, between boulders.

The lower falcon discharged, hitting the monster's underside as it reared to turn. It rose yards higher, shedding noises describable only as painfully loud. It fell back and stumbled a few yards. Stunned.

The upper falcon discharged. Some of the thing's limbs flew away. Chunks of chitin flew out of the monster's back. Pale yellowish green liquid splattered the surrounding rock.

Then the thing's smaller wounds began shrinking. It began to regain control. Began to examine its surroundings. An antenna brushed the smoke trailing from under the overhang sheltering the second falcon.

The monster started to strike.

The lower falcon spat poison again. The impact shoved the monster back. The beast made horrible noises. Helspeth's thoughts entangled with its madness as it entered her mind briefly. Everyone experienced the phenomenon.

Now the beast rushed the lower falcon, all reason fled.

Sudden serpents of fire scurried along the walls of the narrows. First from the right, and two seconds later from the left, explosions savaged the monster's flanks.

What? Helspeth had seen Prosek fiddling around out there but . . . What was this?

The blasts near tore the monster in half. But it persevered.

The upper falcon barked again. Then the lower weapon exploded. Its crewmen shrieked.

Prosek materialized, running. He was pale, his face contorted by horror. He glanced back to see if the monster was gaining.

It no longer cared about anything but getting away. Its wounds were not healing. It had a huge problem turning without tearing itself in two. Steam the shade of its ichors rose from its injuries.

"It's not going to die," Helspeth murmured. "We did all that and it's still not going to die!"

Prosek stopped amidst the rocks piled round the lower falcon. He called for help. The higher falcon drowned him out. Its charge lashed the monster's side, destroying more legs but doing little more damage to the body proper. The thundering echoes faded. Prosek began yelling at Stern's crew.

A couple of Braunsknechts went to help the falconeers. Prosek zipped out of the position, staggering under the weight of a cask of powder and the charges Varley's weapon had not expended. He clambered up to the overhang.

Drear, though injured, managed to regain his aplomb. "Cheated death again," he muttered as he fumbled at the ties on a bent piece of shin armor, the name of which Helspeth could not recall. "But this leg may be broken. Somebody needs to run down to the teamsters' camp. Have them come take away the wounded." Braunsknechts brought Varley and his falconeers to the fireside. None were dead. Varley might prefer death, though. Only a massive growth of beard had kept the left side of his head from being torn off. That side of his face would become a mass of scars.

One of Varley's assistants explained, "We used a double charge of powder, second shot. It must've cracked the falcon, inside. Leaving a place for burning wad to hide. The next charge exploded when we were ramming it." He accepted water from Lady Hilda. "Get the falcon. We can't leave it."

Stern's weapon barked again, louder. The least injured gunner muttered, "Overcharged it. They'll be sorry."

Helspeth crept forward far enough to see the monster. It lay still, now, surrounded by pale green mist. Her bodyguards were not paying attention. She crept farther forward, to Varley's falcon. The blast had opened a break in its side. The stench of firepowder was strong. It would have been impossible to see had the wind not driven the smoke down the pass.

Pebbles rattled around a few yards out front. Prosek and Stern bringing the second falcon down. Cursing the thinness of the air, Prosek told Helspeth, "It's too far off, now. The charge scattered too much, last shot. We're going to go blow one up its . . . We're going to hit it point-blank."

"Mr. Prosek."

"Uh . . . Ma'am?"

"False flight. Watch out." She could not be sure because of the mist but thought the monster might have resumed healing.

"Good thinking," Prosek said. "Never take the Night at face value." He and his falconeers made sure the weapon was ready. Then they moved it toward the ascended Instrumentality.

Helspeth was right. It was less severely injured than it pretended. It would have destroyed Prosek, Stern, and the others had they not been ready.

Prosek had risked another overcharge. Some of the shot passed all the way through the monster.

Echoing thunder faded. Out of the ensuing silence came Drago Prosek's continuous cursing. He and his men came back down fast. "Time to leave, ma'am," he said as he reached Helspeth. "That last one did for this falcon, too."

The mouth of the tube had peeled back like the petals of a lily. "If that thing gets up again there ain't a lot more we can do." He did not keep running, though. He barked at his own men and co-opted two of Drear's. He got the damaged falcons moving downhill, then collected the remaining firepowder. "The thing knows the scent of its pain, now. It'll smell the powder and not want to get too close. That was why I planted those torpedoes. To teach it to fear unspent firepowder. Go back to your lifeguards. Get out of here. I couldn't forgive me if you got killed, now." He got busy with the powder. "Go, woman! Go."

Helspeth retreated. She found Algres Drear on his feet. "You said your leg was broken."

"I was insufficiently optimistic, Princess. It's just a bad bruise. Ouch!"

Helspeth had prodded his calf with her toe. "Be stubborn and manly all you want, Captain. But don't expect the rest of us to hang back because you can't keep the pace."

"In that case, I'll get a head start now."

The teamsters had arrived, bringing litters. The Braunsknechts sent the wounded down first. No one rode. Not even the Princess Apparent. Whose attitude scandalized some and made a lot more love her because she did not set herself beyond those who served her.

That news would not set well when it reached Alten Weinberg. "Hilda, my days of independence are definitely numbered. Even if this is a howling success."

"More probably, especially if this is a success. A girl your age conquers a monster none of the grand old farts of the Empire even dared attack? The daughter of Johannes Blackboots? Not good, Helspeth. Your sister will be afraid of you, now. So will the blackhearts who whisper wickedness in her ear. And her foes will all want to use you. Arguing that you're the truer daughter of the Ferocious Little Hans."

Algres Drear, injured leg in a splint despite his protests, observed, "No good deed goes unpunished, Princess. And the loftier your intentions, the worse the unintended consequences." He took another long drink of distilled painkiller.

Helspeth wanted to argue but was too tired and emotionally spent.

Brilliant light flashed above the pass they had recently deserted. Smoke or dust rose to be painted orange by the setting sun. Pale green threads wormed through it.

The roar of the explosion tumbled down the pass, arriving only after the light faded.

"Can we run?" Drear asked.

Helspeth said, "It's never come this far down."

Drear reminded, "It did on the other side of the Knot."

The teamsters were not too tired to run. And their teams were fed and rested. They loaded up and moved out, all the injured fighters riding.

"He'll catch up," Stern promised his fellow falconeers. But Drago Prosek never did.

Neither did the terrible ascendant Instrumentality.

That suited everyone perfectly.

TRAFFIC THROUGH THE JAGOS RESUMED ALMOST INSTANTLY.

16. Castreresone: Siege

I'm an observer," Brother Candle told Socia Rault. "I belong here, doing what I'm doing."

The ferocious young woman tried to glower but failed. She was in a good humor, confident the Patriarchals had made a fatal error by coming to besiege Castreresone.

As had become their custom, the two were atop a wall, watching the unfriendly folk outside. This time including the Captain-General of the Patriarchal armies himself. Accompanied by an impressive armed gang.

Impressed, Socia said, "There sure are a lot of them."

"The Captain-General has strong backing from Sublime and the Collegium."

"But those are forty-day men. Right? If we hold out for a month, they'll go away."

She was whistling in the dark. Wishful thinking. The backbone of Sublime's crusade were the professional, full-time soldiers raised and trained by the Captain-General. A huge anomaly in an age when army commanders were not professionals. Not in the Chaldarean world, outside the fighting orders.

"Some of them," Brother Candle said. "I'd guess some forty-day levies have cycled in and out already. But the majority of those men will stay till they starve or succumb to disease." Brother Candle was no fierce patriot, yet the notion of successfully besieging Castreresone was outside his Connecten conception. Roger Shale had rendered the White City proof against any attacker.

The Patriarchals arrived in a businesslike manner. They established their camp and saw to its safety before doing anything but put out patrols. No herald came to demand surrender, offer terms, or suggest any other interaction. The invaders began to dismantle the undefended Inconje suburb, using the lumber to build their engines and camp and the stone to erect towers at the ends of the bridge, and as ammunition.

The professionalism of the Patriarchals preyed on the imaginations of the Castreresonese. They went about their work like it was, indeed, just a job. They ignored the city until their first artillery pieces began lobbing stones at the outer wall—concentrating on exactly those points the Castreresonese knew were weakest. And on the carpenters belatedly trying to install hoardings.

Socia opined, "We should've kept on going to Khaurene. Or even into the Altai." She watched a siege engine loft a huge stone almost directly toward them. This crew were not yet expert in their craft. They had not scored a solid hit yet. This stone flew way long. When it landed it shattered like a thrown dirt clod.

Local field stone was soft and broke easily.

"You may be right," Brother Candle said. The absolute confidence of the besiegers troubled him. This was no mob of Grolsachers, nor an undisciplined mix of fanatics and adventurers like the Arnhanders who had come and gone. These men all had jobs, knew how to do them, and worked hard at them. And their efficiency and competence were being shown deliberately.

"They can't last," Socia decided. "There isn't enough food and fodder. We just need to hang on."

Food and fodder were likely to be problems inside Castreresone, too. Every refugee from farther east had been allowed into the city, where the Maysalean partiality for sharing was strong. Useless mouths would consume stores better reserved for fighting men.

Uncharitable of him, to think such things.

He should put the world aside and go into retreat. He was no longer Perfect. Not even close. The mundane had insinuated itself too deeply into his being.

The people of the White City mocked the Patriarchals. Their confidence in their walls remained high. And the enemy had not surrounded the city. For all his numbers, he was not that strong. Round to the northwest and southwest, where new suburbs had been added on, people came and went as they pleased. The enemy did not interfere. Both suburbs, the Burg in the northwest and the New Town down south, had their own walls, extending from the older main walls. Theirs were lower and thinner.

"They may not be entirely serious," the Perfect Master mused one afternoon. "This could be a show of strength meant to awe the city into giving up. They do say this Captain-General is niggardly with the lives of his men."

"They say he's pretty clever, too."

News of the extermination of the god grub on the Ormienden side of the Dechear River had reached Castreresone shortly before the Patriarchal vedettes. People did not want to believe that the Captain-General had faced down and destroyed a major Instrumentality. But he had captured Sonsa easily. Had taken Viscesment and Immaculate II by surprise, so quickly that Immaculate's bodyguards had offered only a token defense. His sub-commanders were at Antieux and Sheavenalle, now, the latter chieftain enjoying unanticipated success.

A week after the Patriarchal army arrived the White City's mood began to turn. The enemy had begun systematically capturing nearby towns and fortresses. The swiftness of their fall was frightening.

The mood blackened further when news spread that the darkest brethren of the Collegium accompanied the invaders.

Sorcery explained the failure of so many strongpoints.

Sorcery and treachery.

The Patriarchal Society for the Suppression of Sacrilege and Heresy had people planted everywhere. Those traitors worked their wickedness.

Bernardin Amberchelle was a crude, cruel man, not without cunning. His agents had penetrated the Society. On the eighth day of the siege one of those betrayed a plan to seize and open a hidden postern. Amberchelle's status ballooned after the traitors had been thrown off the taller barbican tower. Seventeen priests and lay brothers. Including an otherwise innocent Brothen Episcopal priest who had the nerve to beg mercy for the captives.

There was no central power in the city. Roger Shale had not been replaced. The magnates could agree on nothing. Isabeth was en route from Navaya with a hundred of Peter's knights and all their train. Having planned to land at Sheavenalle, then march up the Laur. But much of Sheavenalle was in the hands of the Patriarchals already. An attempt to land would be risky. So the ships were back at sea. They might put in at

Terliaga, two-thirds of the way back to Platadura, whence they had sailed.

Wind and rain returned. The bee-busy Patriarchals had created their own rude city by then, employing local labor. The Captain-General had done the same during the Calziran Crusade.

Though the Patriarchal army had arrived without a tail of camp followers, it was acquiring them now.

People did what they must to survive. And most country folk did not care who occupied the castles and cities. The ruling class were all the same, seen from a charcoal maker's hut.

Bernardin Amberchelle summoned Socia Rault and Brother Candle on the fifteenth day. Amberchelle seemed pensive. Unusual in a short, wide man best known for smashing his way through puzzles.

Several of Amberchelle's odd associates were in the background. Likewise, a dozen leading Castreresonese, including Berto Bertrand, Roger Shale's longtime companion and deputy, now castellan till Isabeth arrived. Brother Candle surveyed the assemblage with a jaundiced eye. There was not a leader among the locals, evidently. Else why defer to half-mad outsider Amberchelle? Simply because the man had the nerve to commit mass murder?

What about those lurking, dusky men with the odd accents, now believed to be Artecipean?

"Thanks for coming," Amberchelle said, proving he could find manners when he wanted.

"At your command," the old man replied. "Though I'm baffled. What can I possibly contribute?"

"Advice."

"If I'm able. Though you have more practical minds here than mine."

"Back to you in a moment, Master. We have a question for the Count's betrothed."

Socia was learning. She had not yet blurted something irrelevant just to establish her presence. She awaited Amberchelle's question.

"Miss . . . Did you get any replies to your requests for help?"

Socia sneered. "Not one. Though King Peter is sending Isabeth to assert his rights."

"We feared as much. Master. The enemy won't talk. They've ignored every proposal for negotiations."

"Sublime says there's nothing to negotiate."

"We have spies moving in and out of their camp. They don't seem interested in Sublime's opinions, either."

The Captain-General would expect his local laborers to include spies. Evidently he did not care what they learned. "And?"

"The enemy are confident that they can stay the winter—if the city refuses to yield. We may have to if they cut off communications completely. And they have started harassing anyone bringing in food or supplies."

The old man repeated, "And?"

"We're consuming food much faster than it can be brought in."

"That happens during a siege."

Socia said, "Turn out the people who don't contribute. Let the enemy have to deal with them."

Brother Candle said, "We'd better pack, then, hadn't we, girl?"

Socia glared.

The old man said, "She does have a point, though. Seeker refugees could slip out and go to Khaurene. Or into the Altai."

"Assuming the enemy lets them."

"Assuming that." The Captain-General might decide that overcrowding and starvation were useful weapons. Or he might want terrified refugees to carry panic to the rest of the Connec. "But you have something else on your mind, don't you? You don't need me to tell you that."

"The Night," Amberchelle murmured, like a boy caught doing something he should not. "The Night is . . . isn't . . . Whatever happened on the Dechear, the Night now seems to be *afraid* of those people. Despite being ten times as active as it was only a year ago."

Brother Candle frowned. What he knew about that event was limited to exaggerations heard in the street. Why was Amberchelle concerned? Or was it his odd friends who were? Those friends, he had learned, had taken flight from Viscesment after the surprise appearance of Patriarchal troops.

"I have no intercourse with the Night. I'm a philosopher, not a sorcerer or priest. If the Night shuns the Patriarchals, it stands to reason that they're afraid they could share the fate of the thing that perished on the Dechear."

Amberchelle sighed. "I didn't think you'd tell us much. But I hoped." He shook his head vigorously. That did no good. "They've got Principatés with them."

That was no secret. "They're substantially overrated, I suspect," Brother Candle said.

"He's right. We are."

The voice came out of nowhere. Socia squealed. The Connectens gaped and gabbled panicky questions. Some thought it was a practical joke. But Amberchelle's dusky friends panicked. Several produced weapons they should not have been carrying. They slashed empty air. Others fled the chamber.

"Master," Socia said in a scared little-girl voice. "Something just touched me. It put this in my hand." She held up a ring.

Brother Candle took the ring to the brightest lamp. Two outsiders nearby blanched when they saw it. The shorter staggered as though suddenly faint. "What is it?" the old man asked.

He got no reply. The chief foreigner herded his gang out of there. Berto Bertrand, Bernardin Amberchelle, and Socia crowded Brother Candle.

He said, "It's a signet ring. Like none I've ever seen. Uhn." That looked like specks of dried blood. "I've seen these symbols somewhere before." In the mountains north of Khaurene, the Altai, come to think. Back in the dark woods, where Eis, Aaron, and their fellows were come-lately and the Old Gods, though no longer worshiped, were not forgotten.

"Bernardin. Find out why your friends are upset." He wanted to quiz Socia about how it had come into her possession.

He did not want to accept her claim. Even he might panic if he believed there were invisible men afoot in Castreresone.

Amberchelle growled, no longer as pleased with his associates. Berto Bertrand said, "I'll spread the word that people who have somewhere else to go should do so."

BERNARDIN AMBERCHELLE WAS NOT IN CHARGE. THE CONSULS OF THE CITY, its magnates, and its urban nobility listened only because he was Count Raymone's cousin. They nodded politely, then did things their own way. Rejecting the presence of a large enemy army as any reason to create a strong central authority.

The sixteenth morning word spread that the enemy was doing something new. Several thousand forty-day men had arrived from Firaldia. The Captain-General meant to take full advantage. Later that same day a messenger from Sheavenalle brought word that the port city had surrendered.

Observing from the wall when he heard, Brother Candle mused, "That's what they've been waiting for. They can barge supplies up the Laur, now." He wondered about the fate of the Seekers of Sheavenalle. And of its Devedian and Dainshau minorities. The Captain-General's men were not fanatics, but the Society followed right behind them.

The seventeenth morning the invaders assaulted the Burg and the New Town, surprising defenders who had been warned that an attack was coming. The attackers got over the New Town wall and captured a gate immediately. Fighting spread across the suburb. The defense collapsed by nightfall. The Patriarchals immediately began using tall buildings as vantages from which to hurl missiles into the city.

In the northwestern suburb, the Burg, the defenders held the top of the wall but failed to prevent two breaches created by clever masons. The defenders recaptured those and closed the gaps under a hail of missiles from wooden towers the besiegers put up with astonishing speed. Heavy ballistae atop those flung blazing spears deep into the suburb.

BROTHER CANDLE TOLD BERTO BERTRAND, "I'M NO SOLDIER, BUT I DON'T think a sally would be wise." Small raids had been attempted almost daily. None had turned out well.

"We'll counterattack in the New Town tonight," Bertrand said. The consuls and magnates had decided. "And go after the towers bombarding the Burg, too."

Only light defensive artillery had been mounted on the walls of the suburbs. None of Castreresone's defensive weaponry had done any good yet. The stone throwers still lacked ammunition. Those who made decisions remained confident in the White City's wall.

Brother Candle feared Roger Shale's improvements would go to waste.

Bertrand added, "We'll hit their main camp tomorrow. They won't expect that. We'll push them back across the river and capture the towers they've built to control the bridge."

There was more. It was a grand and complex scheme. The enemy's unseasoned levees would be trapped this side of the river and destroyed. . . .

Beyond ignoring the certainty that any complicated plan will stumble, those who had created this one had forgotten that voice out of nowhere.

Brother Candle thought chances of surprising this enemy were nil. He did not stay awake to watch the disaster unfold. He did not want to live with the pain.

SOCIA COULD NOT CONTAIN HER EXCITEMENT. SHE BURST INTO BROTHER Candle's cell. She bounced up and down while he collected himself.

"It isn't seemly for a woman of your station to be here." Count Raymone had made little provision for her other than to trust her to the wisdom of the Perfect Master. "But you're here, now. Pull yourself together. Try to make sense."

"Everything is going the way they planned! They've retaken the New Town. They pulled those towers down that were shooting into the Burg." Her excitement faded. "They haven't put all the fires out, though."

Brother Candle slept on a reed mat. He sat there now, his ragged blanket pulled around him. It had turned cold during the night. "There was an actual surprise?"

"Completely!"

He was unprepared to believe that was not an enemy ploy. "Back out of here for a minute. Let me get dressed." Socia's life at Caron ande Lette had been rude, simple, and relaxed. That would not do in Castreresone. The Count of Antieux could not have his betrothed acquiring a tail of rumors.

"Come on!" Socia enthused as the old man left his cell. "I want to see!"

He refused to be hurried. He stopped to break his fast: bread smeared with a dark, heavy, almost bitter honey. By the time the girl chivvied him forth from the keep there was light in the east as well as the north, where the Burg continued to burn. "I suppose we should head for the eastern wall."

The streets were filled with nervous men, all under arms. The arsenals had been emptied out. These men were supposed to capture the Laur bridge and its defenses.

Brother Candle believed he was looking at walking dead men.

The families were out and underfoot as well. Their fear was thick. They knew some of these fathers and husbands would not be coming back.

Would any? Brother Candle dreaded the answer.

He offered a blessing when requested, for anyone who asked, Maysalean or otherwise. Most Episcopals were not unwilling to take what they could get where they could get it. Though priests loyal to Viscesment would be waiting near the gate, to bless the faithful as they streamed past.

Brother Candle doubted that Sublime's priests would reveal themselves, though devout Episcopals of the Brothen stripe were among those about to fight for their city.

They had their doubts and fears, as men do in the hour before battle. But they had faith in the righteousness of their cause.

Brother Candle suffered the doubts and fears while enjoying none of the confidence of unquestioning faith.

"Socia. Dear girl. Once we're done here I fear I must leave you."

"Don't be . . . What are you talking about?"

"I've forgotten what I am, child. I'm lost. I have to put the world aside and find myself again. I'm losing my soul."

Socia used his own past remarks to argue with him.

The soldiers began their sally before the pair reached a good vantage. The rush through the gate almost caught them up. Socia's lack of manners saved them that unexpected adventure.

They did not get a good place among the observers. The best spots had been occupied long since.

The Castreresonese descended the hill to the Inconje works in a roiling mob, tripping over one another. They were too numerous and disorganized to march. Brother Candle groaned. "What a waste! This city is run by idiots."

He did not care that several idiots were within earshot—instead of out with the men running to their deaths.

Soon it seemed the consuls and magnates were not fools after all. Something could be said for terrified enthusiasm and overwhelming numbers.

By sheer bodyweight the Castreresonese breached the palisade shielding the Inconje bridgehead. They drove the Patriarchals back. Cut a great many off. Some swam the Laur to get away. The raiders captured the unfinished guard tower at the western end of the bridge. They charged the tower at the eastern end.

That tower held out for two hours. The enemy used the time to bring up artillery and crossbowmen. They laid steady missile fire on the bridge. The artillery included something that made loud noises and belched sulfurous smoke. Despite their losses, though, the Castreresonese captured the second tower and prepared to defend it.

The Patriarchals did not counterattack.

They built wooden towers that, by day's end, let them lay plunging fire on the lost towers and anyone crossing the bridge.

The watchers on the walls cheered themselves hoarse.

Brother Candle did not join in. Nor did Socia Rault.

The girl understood. The Patriarchals had not suffered crippling reverses.

The day's work meant little in the long run. Especially if Castreresone's losses left it unable to defend its entire circumference against surprise attacks.

Only after night fell did the cost become apparent. The wailing inside the city had to hearten the enemy camp. The fallen numbered more than a thousand, the injured and wounded many times more. Some families had lost all their men. More would do so once sepsis had its way.

Brother Candle would have bet gold that the enemy had not suffered a tenth as badly as the bold fools of the White City.

He wept. And was not ashamed to be seen doing so while the city consuls proclaimed a triumph.

Brother Candle told Bernardin Amberchelle, "They haven't gone away. And, guaranteed, we'll hear back from them soon."

"Soon" came quicker than even the Perfect Master anticipated.

The counterstroke fell before sunrise. The Captain-General had men swim the Laur, and cross over on boats, above and below the bridge. No pickets had been posted to watch for that. The men who crossed upstream joined those already caught on the west bank. The downstream force attacked the Inconje defenses. They routed the poorly armed citizens, excepting those shut up inside the two towers. Dawn revealed the slope below the new barbican carpeted with newly fallen. No mercy had been shown.

Fugitives from nearby towns and castles all reported the same thing. The Patriarchals were merciless when they encountered resistance. So towns were falling as fast as the Captain-General's troops could accept surrenders. Few found the backbone to fight.

While the city was distracted by the slaughter on the fore slope, the enemy attacked the New Town again, bursting through the poorly repaired breaches. They drove the defenders out almost as fast as those could run. By midmorning the Patriarchals were undermining the main wall and building artillery towers so they could shoot down onto the ramparts.

Here the confidence and procrastination of the Castreresonese betrayed them again. Shelters had not been set up to protect defenders from plunging fire. Hoardings had not been installed, making it more difficult to counterattack the masons undermining the wall. It was no longer possible to counterattack through the posterns. The enemy knew where they were. He buried them systematically. The main gateway from the city into the New Town got heaped with brush and timber and set afire.

This living history was written under continuously heavy gray skies, often in drizzling rain. With the full attendance of the Night.

Brother Candle was deeply troubled. Even the most fanatic Brothen Episcopals feared the Night, now, as a thousand awful stories circulated. Rook's slime trails painted the fore slope, where so many had died. Death himself had been seen outside the barbican, tallying in his Book of Hours. A thousand people claimed their cousins or uncles had seen Hilt. Fragments of Kint lurked in every alleyway.

Brother Candle saw nothing. Nor did anyone else he spoke with. The reports were all hearsay. But their cumulative impact was potent.

Socia wanted to know, "Why would the Old Ones help the Brothen Usurper? The Church wants to destroy them." She asked over a weak noontime meal of hard cheese and harder bread, taken in a small room off the kitchen in the keep of the Counts of Castreresone.

"Only speculation, mind," Brother Candle replied. "But I'd bet those people out there are asking how come the Old Ones are helping us when nobody over here wants to see them back."

The girl started to say something but had a thought. She shut her mouth.

"The Night doesn't take sides. We only think it does because all we know is what we see and hear with our own eyes and ears." Considering events on the east bank of the Dechear, the Night might, indeed, have a definite preference in the current mortal squabble.

"They have members of the Collegium to help."

"They do," Brother Candle conceded. "Possibly some of the best." The enemy was not hiding that fact. Some of those Collegium members had no particular reputation. But Muniero Delari came wrapped in dread rumor. And Bronte Doneto, at Antieux, might be the most powerful Principaté of all. Doneto had spent his adult life hiding his real strength.

"We have no way to balance that."

"No. So all the advantages are on their side of the balance."

Bernardin Amberchelle showed up. He was depressed. "They've recaptured the tower on the far end of the bridge. And they've started building a floating bridge. We'll try to wreck it tonight. But I don't expect we'll have much luck. There aren't many citizens willing to go out there again."

There was more on Amberchelle's mind. Brother Candle made a little rolling hand gesture, inviting him to continue.

"The Patriarchals still can't manage a complete encirclement." With forty percent of their strength at Antieux or Sheavenalle and half the rest ravaging the countryside, the Patriarchals outside numbered no more than eight thousand. Still the largest concentration of troops seen in the Connec in generations. "We should consider leaving before the situation deteriorates any further."

"I thought Castreresone was impregnable." The Perfect was aware, though, that fugitives had been leaving since the Patriarchals appeared. Who were content to let them go. They would become an economic burden elsewhere.

"It could be. If it had leaders determined to defend it. The consuls and magnates aren't willing to deal with a real siege. Nobody wants his property demolished for stone and lumber. Let the other guy go first. And, of course, they'll get help from Khaurene and Navaya before it gets that bad."

Brother Candle nodded. He knew. He saw it all the time. People could not believe that Tormond IV could go on being the Great Vacillator, now. Nor that King Peter was unlikely to send more men than were with Isabeth already. If he weakened himself any more the princes of al-Halambra would seize the opportunity to blunt the Reconquest.

Nor would there be direct help from Santerin, despite any wishful thinking. Though King Brill's transgressions along Arnhand's borders did now have Charlve the Dim and Anne of Menand distracted.

With invaders just sixty miles away Duke Tormond began, for the first time, rehearsing his military options.

Brother Candle hoped Tormond would defer to Sir Eardale Dunn. "You're the man Count Raymone put in charge. I'm here to keep an eye on everybody."

Amberchelle was disappointed. Of course. He had hoped to be told what to do. "We'll wait and see, then. If the magnates here go on pretending the situation isn't desperate, we will act. Just be ready to go on short notice."

BROTHER CANDLE WENT UP ONTO THE WALL SOUTH OF THE BARBICAN TWO days later. A hundred fires burned outside, providing light for the Patriarchal artillerists. Their engines worked day and night. The troops manning them worked in shifts. Local people brought the stone and firewood.

Part of the barbican had collapsed a few hours ago. The main wall had begun to creak and groan and shift.

The Patriarchals had begun building floating wharves on the east side of the Laur, below their pontoon bridge. A dozen barges and boats were tied up already, unloading by night. Buildings were being erected to warehouse incoming cargo.

The besiegers were living far better than the besieged.

Though the siege might not go on much longer. The New Town had been lost. Now it looked like the crusaders meant to hit the Burg suburb again, soon.

Despair had found a home in the narrow, shadowed streets. Few people now believed this city, that had not been overcome in five centuries, would remain inviolate. They invested their hopes in Queen Isabeth and Duke Tormond.

Isabeth and her knights were twenty miles away. The Great Vacillator had sent out a call for volunteers to go help the Connec's second city.

Brother Candle suspected little would come of that.

A new, small hope came with news from Viscesment.

Immaculate's supporters had assembled after the departure of the Patriarchals. They had elected a successor to the murdered Anti-Patriarch. An unknown bishop, Rocklin Glas from Sellars in the Grail Empire, had accepted the ermine and assumed the inauspicious reign name Bellicose. He promised a vigorous campaign against the Pretenders of Brothe. Not the traditional resistance but an aggressive countercampaign. He had sent out a call for crusaders. Though he was not taken seriously outside Viscesment, the Society in those parts faced savage persecutions already. Reaping what they had sown.

Bellicose promised to execute a member of the Society every time a non-Brothen Episcopal suffered at its hands. He and Sublime were beebusy excommunicating and publishing Writs of Anathema against one another.

More insanity, Brother Candle thought.

Maybe the sides could exterminate each other. Leave the world to the Unbelievers, the Seekers, and those whose harsh old deities had begun slithering in out of muck and shadow.

The Perfect Master grew increasingly dismayed as he watched the besiegers. He realized he was looking at something unseen since the collapse of the Old Empire.

Professional soldiers led by professional officers, chosen for competence rather than noble lineage, veterans all, were going about their business with the dispassionate skill of butchers and bricklayers. However much the nobility on either side disdained them, they represented sudden, efficient death.

How would they stand up to a massed heavy cavalry charge?

Bernardin Amberchelle found him there, in his pessimism. "Brother? I just left another meeting of the consuls and magnates."

"Let me guess. They can't agree on a sensible course of action."

"You should be a professional gambler, Brother."

"I am, in a way, nowadays. Risking my soul chasing earthly illusions."

Amberchelle's short, wide frame shuddered. "I've decided. They won't do the needful things. The Patriarchals should go after the Burg in the morning. Tonight may be our last chance to get out."

"I feared as much. I am, of course, ready to go."

"Good. Good. There'll be enough moonlight. We should be well away before sunrise." Amberchelle sounded shaky. Frightened and trying to hide it.

"Something out there worries you?"

"Rumors. Horrible things in the dark."

Brother Candle nodded, though the horrible things he had heard of were awful mainly on an intellectual level. Rook. Hilt. The other revenants. They were disgusting but nothing he feared. Not at the strength they possessed now.

They barely qualified as ghosts of the gods they had been.

Brother Candle said, "Very well. I'll get my things and chivvy the girl."

"I've spoken to her already."

"Excellent. We might get out of here before sunrise."

IT WAS MIDNIGHT. SOCIA RAULT AND BROTHER CANDLE, ACCOMPANIED BY Bernardin Amberchelle and his associates, eased out a sally port in Castreresone's north end. They had waited half an hour for their turn. A human river was headed out.

Those Brother Candle made out by feeble moonlight were Seekers and other minorities. Those who had most to lose if Castreresone fell.

They made less than a mile before the clouds masked the moon permanently. The chill breeze picked up, growing colder. The darkness became oppressive.

A mile farther on the path rounded a hill. The darkness deepened. The fugitives now moved in a slow shuffle, feeling the way. There was talk of torches. Nobody had one. Then someone with a clear head observed that a torch would attract enemy pickets. Who were out there somewhere. Who would cheerfully rob and murder them all. The Patriarchal city levies did most of the scouring of the countryside. The Captain-General did little to restrain their greed.

It stood to reason that if they killed everyone who resisted soon enough few Connectens would show any inclination to fight.

This darkness was not friendly. It hid them but also blinded them. The path wound between rolling hills. Eventually, it split. The right-hand path led to the old Imperial highway, which could be followed easily even in darkness. Bernardin Amberchelle had hoped to be on it a dozen miles west of the White City by first light.

That did not happen.

First light came. They had not found the old road yet.

There were delays, not only because of the darkness.

Things moved in the night, pacing them. Things that stank. Things that laughed foully. Things that raced across the path, triggering screams, apparently just for the hell of scaring people.

Brother Candle's band never reached the Imperial road. Word came that it was occupied by Patriarchals moving west to keep an eye on Queen Isabeth. They thought she might do something when she heard about the new assault on the Burg.

The band joined the rest of the fugitives, heading back to find another way.

Snow began to fall.

"NO REST FOR THE WICKED," THE PERFECT MUTTERED TO SOCIA. HE HAD had no intention of joining the Queen's camp. He had gone there only because the road ran past Mohela ande Larges. And because the Navayans would make a nice block in the path of any pursuit. He followed the man who had recognized him among the refugees. "Michael Carhart, why must you do this to me?" He was amazed that the Devedian philosopher would be found outside Khaurene.

Carhart chuckled. "Relax. Isabeth just wants to talk about Castreresone. She's harmless."

"So is an adder. To those wise enough not to sup with serpents."

Michael Carhart did not like that. "Watch your tongue, old friend. The nobility have no patience for that sort of jest these days."

"Yes. I recall those times when the jongleurs roamed freely, like wild chickens, cackling that seditious nonsense to anyone who would listen."

"Make light if you like. But you know what I mean. Take care."

Brother Candle did understand. The mighty were not happy. They wanted someone else to hurt.

There were more familiar faces in the great hall of Mohela ande Larges, the little castle Isabeth had appropriated. She was accompanied by a half-dozen darkly handsome men, none of them her husband. King Peter must trust them indeed. Or the several women in shadow behind Isabeth were harsh enough chaperones to provoke Peter's absolute confidence.

Michael Carhart joined others whose presence startled Brother Candle: Hanak el-Mira and Bishop Clayto. Friends. Or as much so as could be amongst men of such diverse backgrounds. Only Bries LeCroes was missing.

What had become of LeCroes? He should ask. He had heard no final disposition of the poisoner's case.

The handsome men said nothing. They stared at the Perfect Master with a feigned indifference bordering on disdain. The Navayan nobility were dedicated Brothen Episcopals, their faith tempered by worldly convenience. King Peter had more allies among Direcia's Pramans than among rival Episcopal princes.

The Queen was courteous. "Be seated, Master. Your companions will be cared for. I understand they're rather ragged."

Brother Candle inclined his head. "Socia Rault and I have spent months staying ahead of Arnhanders, Grolsachers, revenant demons, and now the Usurper Patriarch's Captain-General."

"Tell me what you've seen since last our paths crossed."

Brother Candle did so. In detail. Duke Tormond's little sister was more patient than the child he remembered. The handsome men became restless long before he finished. She did not.

Isabeth observed, "The Night would seem to be more active in the east. We hear a thousand rumors from that direction but almost nothing from farther west."

"The things stirring are Instrumentalities associated with conflict and chaos. Peace seems to have settled in everywhere but around Antieux and Castreresone."

Isabeth nodded. Having known the child, Brother Candle found it hard to believe the rowdy storm of flying limbs had matured into someone regal. He wondered about her son. Where was the baby Prince? Was he well? Domestic gossip got little attention these days.

Isabeth asked, "Is Castreresone truly in danger?"

"Imminent."

"But those walls . . ."

"The walls are magnificent. The people behind them are the weakness. Half still believe there's no real danger. The Captain-General does what he wants, when he wants, where he wants. And those people won't do what they must to resist effectively. Their strategy is to wait for you and your brother to rescue them." He spent a few minutes cataloging the shortcomings of Castreresone's leading men. "Berto Bertrand drives himself to exhaustion but has no luck getting anyone to listen."

"God is a cruel practical joker. He could have left us Roger Shale for another half year."

Brother Candle did not respond. Their views of God need not clash just now.

Isabeth said, "The situation sounds bad. Count Alplicova." One of the handsome men stepped forward. "You know, in general, my thinking, and that of the King, in regard to our Connecten dependencies."

The handsome man bowed slightly. "I do, Your Majesty."

Brother Candle detected a hint of romantic worship. There would be nothing to it. Direcians, always at war and of necessity less relaxed than their Connecten cousins, did not indulge in the courtly love games promoted elsewhere by jongleurs.

The Perfect Master reflected. Count Alplicova. Could there be more than one? Diagres Alplicova was called Sword of the Unbeliever by the warlords of al-Halambra. His blade hammered out King Peter's great victories. Why was he here when there were Praman castles to conquer in Direcia?

"Your Majesty." Daringly, speaking unbidden. Though the Perfect often flouted such rules. "The gentleman you've named shouldn't be named aloud—if he's the gentleman famed for that name." He reminded Isabeth of the invisible intruder in Castreresone.

Isabeth replied, "I understand your concern. But we've made no secret of our cousin's presence. My husband believes it will give us additional leverage. As to your invisible man, you give the lie to his existence yourself when you report the successful attacks on the Laur bridge-works. You were the victim of a practical joke."

"Oh, he was. But not by me."

The voice seemed to come from amongst the smoke-blackened beams overhead.

Laughter followed. The Queen and her people began muttering about sorcery.

"Oh, yes. Sorcery in the highest. But not nearly so foul as that coming off the island of Artecipea."

Count Alplicova, Brother Candle noted, had shown no superstitious response. He and his companions studied the shadows while moving to control the exits.

Queen Isabeth yelped. She stared aghast at something in her lap.

The men surged toward her. Blades rang as they cleared scabbards.

Sidelong, Brother Candle caught a glimpse of someone in brown sliding out of the room. The man tossed him a mocking salute. And was not there when the Perfect turned for a better look.

He had seen that man before, in the streets of Castreresone and on its wall, among the watchers. "He just left." He described the man.

The others were not interested. They were focused on Isabeth.

The thing in her lap was a hand. With rock salt crusted on it.

"It's the ring," Brother Candle said. "The ring is the message."

"Explain," Count Alplicova said. With no stress in his voice.

The man had a reputation for being unshakable.

"The invisible man in Castreresone slipped a similar ring to Count Raymone's fiancée. Men from Artecipea were there at the time. They reacted as though they'd just gotten news of a disastrous defeat."

Isabeth recovered. "This hand isn't human."

It was an odd bluish black. The fingers were overly long, with less bluntly shaped nails. The flesh under the nails was yellow. The nails themselves were cracked and broken.

The Direcians were not convinced. One said, "The Pramans bring strange breeds of men across the Escarp Gebr al Thar."

Isabeth said, "It looks like an ape's hand."

Brother Candle asked, "Does it matter? It's more likely the hand of a demon incarnated. The invisible man is getting away." He described the man he had seen. "I've seen him before, always at the edge of crowds."

A frantic search enjoyed no success whatsoever.

ONCE ISABETH EXHAUSTED BROTHER CANDLE'S STORE OF INFORMATION, she told him, "We don't want you whispering any Maysalean nonsense in the camp. Take your charge to Khaurene. I'll give you letters to my brother. He'll see to your care. Nag him. His people are being murdered in the name of a God that most of them disdain."

He smiled gently. Isabeth's faith would not fill a thimble. Even leaned toward his own. But she could not show that to her husband's men. Politics trumped faith. As always.

Brother Candle observed every royal formality. Peter's men watched with faces of stone, fiercely disapproving.

The Perfect departed sure that he had missed something important. An argument started before he left the room. Some of the Navayans were concerned about the invisible man. Those who did not think it was all trickery by the devil-worshiping heretic.

The heretic left with letters to his Duke and a handful of silver to get him and his ward through the forty miles to Khaurene.

His small camp was in a turmoil when he arrived.

Socia babbled, "The Queen's men arrested Bernardin's foreign friends! They dragged them into the castle! They would've taken Bernardin, too, if one of them didn't recognize him from somewhere before. What's going on?"

"I don't know. We can ask Bernardin. After we're on the road to Khaurene. Which is where we've been ordered to go."

"Khaurene?" the girl whined. "Right now? We can't stay for even one day?"

"She wants us gone. From the looks of things back that way, it might be a good idea to give her what she wants."

Smoke rose to the east. Dark dots moved on the face of a distant hill.

The Captain-General was moving more troops closer.

Socia stared. She lost color. "You think . . ." She could not articulate her fear.

"No. Antieux won't fall till they've eaten each other. Until the last man left, Raymone Garete, goes down. Taking a dozen Patriarchals with him."

That was what she wanted to hear. And it might be true. Unless Raymone fell victim to treachery.

Socia started to say something. She let out a yelp of outrage instead. "Somebody just grabbed my bottom!"

From the edge of his eye Brother Candle saw that old man in brown. Grinning, the man saluted him, turned, and became invisible.

THE DAYS BECAME MORE TERRIFYING THAN THE NIGHTS. EVERY TOWN AND castle had been taken by the enemy. But the people themselves had not gone over. They would hide small parties from the invaders and the Night. But by day Brother Candle's band had to move. They covered little ground. Patriarchal soldiers and Society hounds were everywhere, patrolling every road. They broke up into smaller and smaller parties, till Brother Candle was accompanied only by Socia Rault and Bernardin Amberchelle.

The invaders changed behavior suddenly after abandoning Mohela ande Larges and suffering a severe reverse at the hands of Queen Isabeth's men. Travel became easier.

The Perfect surrendered to the girl's impatience. And had the opportunity to regret that before day's end.

17. A New Dawn and a New Night

Each day the staff selected two promising prisoners. The Captain-General took time to interview them while Madouc and his lifeguards hovered. "Titus. I'm suspicious."

"Sir? About what?"

"These prisoners. Are they being chosen to tell me what I want to hear?"

"You need more bad news? Or more defiance?"

"Never mind. How much longer will this take?"

"This being?"

"Castreresone."

"That's up to them. Isn't it? If you're determined to limit casualties and damage." The staff insisted that the White City could be taken whenever the Captain-General ordered it. But thousands would die and the city itself might be destroyed.

"I'm not in a hurry. Yet."

"You could offer terms. Sublime isn't here."

"Still no respect for our master?"

"Not in our lifetime."

"Don't be too public about it. Society types are everywhere. Popping up faster than these Connectens can murder them."

"I have trouble remembering that the rest of the world runs different than our little slice here."

"Don't. You have a family. Where's Bechter? I haven't seen him for days." Bechter was always underfoot when that was inconvenient.

"Making the rounds of the siege works. He has experience from the Holy Lands."

"Have you recruited any solid sources? Anywhere?"

Consent shook his head. Looked vaguely defeated. "The Devedian and Dainshau communities won't talk. They're getting out. Going to Terliaga, Platadura, anywhere where the Society won't be able to follow."

Hecht was baffled. Peter of Navaya, Lion of the Chaldarean Reconquest, openly accepted Unbelievers into his dependencies. And insisted that they be treated well.

Consent said, "Peter saw what you accomplished in Calzir."

"If so, he saw in it an affirmation of policies he had in place. He had a lot of Pramans with him in the Calziran Crusade. Now he's recruiting in Shippen and Calzir. And getting a good turnout." He heard that two thousand Pramans from Shippen had been ferried to Artecipea to further Peter's ambitions there.

Hecht felt a little thrill of apprehension. Bone and the company were on that island.

"I see Bechter. You still want him?"

"Yes."

Lifeguards orbiting him, Hecht moved a dozen yards, to gain a different perspective on the barbican protecting Castreresone's main gate, doing its job now as a mountain of rubble. Work gangs hauled the rubble off for use as ammunition.

Only the more ferocious of the expanding community of Society hangers-on dared complain about the Captain-General's efforts to reduce the White City. And they did. He tempered their fury by offering them weapons and the privilege of leading the assault wave.

No takers so far.

"Captain-General, you wanted to see me?"

"Sergeant. Yes. I've been wondering. The man in brown. Seen him lately?"

"Not in weeks, sir. Is it important?"

"No. I just hadn't seen him either, myself."

"Have you ever figured him out?"

"No. I do think I know who he is, now. Or was."

"Was, sir?"

"He might be a ghost." Or a minor ascendant. A notion Hecht was not ready to loose into the public domain.

Bechter frowned. That failed to conform to his Brotherhood vision of how the world should work.

"Yet another conflict between what we want to be true and what we have to suffer," Hecht said. Those conflicts tormented everyone but the Patriarchal Society for the Suppression of Sacrilege and Heresy, these days. Faith had begun to creak under the strain.

The Society thought God was testing faith by dealing contradictory evidence.

Piper Hecht wondered why God—anybody's God—would bother. The God of the World ought not to be so petty.

Bechter said, "Prosek is back."

"Tell me."

"He was just coming in when I heard you wanted me. I just had time to say hello. And make sure he didn't attract attention."

"I thought he was dead." There had been little communication with Plemenza. That little had not been optimistic. The falcons had been destroyed, their crews injured, and Prosek lost. The pass was open but the fate of the monster remained uncertain. It might be lying up somewhere, recovering.

Princess Helspeth's having opened the pass had generated a political storm inside the Grail Empire.

Hecht suffered troubled nights.

"I need to see him as soon as he's able."

GERVASE SALUDA AND THE PRINCIPATÉ FROM APARION, WITH MINIMAL courtesy, demanded an audience. After lurking in the background for weeks, acting as Collegium spies. Hecht expected an argument about access to Drago Prosek.

The Principatés surprised him.

Saluda, never warm since he had assumed the Bruglioni seat in the Collegium, said, "We've received a suggestion from Brothe that it may be time to be a little more aggressive toward Castreresone."

Not subtle, Gervase Saluda, hinting that Sublime had grown impatient. "Really? I think he'd let me know directly if he was. He hasn't been shy about that yet."

Saluda observed, "This siege can't go on forever."

"Nor will it. In fact, I'm authorizing you to go up there and talk them into giving up. Right now."

Both were startled. There had been no negotiations whatsoever, even sub rosa. "Terms?"

"I trust you to be sensible." He just wanted them gone. Bechter had Drago Prosek ready to report. Anyway, Hecht was sure that the White City did not yet despair enough to contemplate surrender.

Queen Isabeth remained poised just twenty miles away. And her brother had begun to stir behind her.

Gervase Saluda gave Hecht one long, penetrating look as he departed.

Hecht shrugged.

"Rough trip?" he asked Prosek.

"Yes, sir. Not attracting attention. Especially after I crossed the Dechear. We're not popular out there."

"Where anyone cares. Sit. Be comfortable. Sergeant, bring the man whatever he wants. So. Tell the tale."

Titus Consent entered as Bechter left. He made Prosek uncomfortable. But Prosek began after an encouraging gesture from his commander.

"Why didn't you go back to the others?"

"I didn't trust them. That Princess. She was probably straight. The ones around her . . . I figured they'd do what they did. Once we took care of their monster."

"That being?"

"They locked everybody up. Gonna force them to explain firepowder and how the falcons work. And how to make them."

"I see." Hecht smiled. "And you're the only one who could tell them anything."

"Pretty much, sir. Those guys aren't ignorant. They know the theory—just not the practical knowledge."

Typical of soldiers. Indifferent to why something worked, so long as it did when the arrows started flying.

Prosek continued. "On the up side, sir, they'll get decent medical care. Which most of them needed. Both falcons committed suicide. I made sure the firepowder was used up."

"The monster. The Instrumentality. What about it?"

"We didn't kill it. But I don't think it'll be a problem again. It can't be much more than what it was when it was still a man. And it's badly crippled. It could barely crawl."

"Good. Good. I'll ask Principaté Delari what it all means. Then we have to figure out how to make these confrontations go our way faster."

"I had a lot of time to think while I was traveling. I had some technical and tactical ideas."

Hecht listened patiently. Prosek amazed him. "Stunning. And expensive. Godawful expensive."

"Not my money, though. And worth it if you really want to break the Tyranny of the Night."

"Lieutenant Consent. Work some financial sorcery on these ideas. The rest . . . The way to speed the firing cycle . . . That'll have to go to the foundry people. Traps, though . . . We'll get to work on those. We can experiment right here. The Connec has become an Instrumentality-rich environment."

Consent said, "I don't have to do a lot of calculating to tell you there isn't enough silver in the world. So long as the wells of power keep producing. A vigorous push against the Night could even be counterproductive."

"Explain."

"The wells are fading. Which is cyclical. This time looks like the worst ever. For us, that means more people pushed into smaller territories having to survive on dwindling resources. Fighting over those makes things worse because much of the resources are destroyed in the fighting. Right here, we can see how that works. You see people worried about where food will come from—for the first time in centuries."

"And that connects with the Night how?"

"The wells of power produce the food and wine of the Night.

Again, dwindling resources. If we remove an entity from the competition, there'll be more resources for the rest."

"I think I see."

"I didn't make that as clear as I should have."

"Clear enough. Don't the big ones feed on the little ones? Like bugs and fish?"

"In a sense. I think."

"Would destroying the little ones starve the big ones?"

Consent shrugged.

Hecht said, "Prosek, stay out of the way. Get back in shape. And keep thinking. I may put you in charge of figuring out better ways."

Prosek looked to Redfearn Bechter for a cue. Bechter did not offer one.

DELARI ASKED, "HAVE YOU SEEN CLOVEN FEBRUAREN?"

"There was a rumor about an invisible man spying on the leadership inside Castreresone. If that was him, he hasn't bothered letting me know what they're saying."

"I'm worried."

"Oh?"

"Not by what he's doing. He's like the weather. All you can do is live with it. No. I think there's trouble in Brothe."

Politics. Certainly. Hecht wished he did not have to suffer that side of the human condition. But if people could get along he would be unemployed.

"Could that be why we've seen so little of Saluda, Linczski, and Doneto lately?" Pinkus Ghort had visited twice and was expected again. Principaté Doneto had not visited once.

"Could be," Delari admitted. "Doneto not wanting to draw notice. The other two are here mainly to keep an eye on us."

"I let them go up to the gates today. To offer Castreresone a chance. Evidently, the wealthy haven't suffered enough."

"And aren't sufficiently frightened."

"Letting the city levies run wild wasn't intimidation enough."

"They won't surrender while Isabeth is sitting there barely a day away. I know you don't want King Peter for an enemy. But to finish here you need to end any hope of relief. Before Church politics yanks the rug out from under you."

Engaging Queen Isabeth would support the mission he had been given in Dreanger. Particularly now that Sublime had an accommodation with the Grail Empire.

"I wanted a minimum of death and destruction."

Hecht was not unprepared to assume a more aggressive strategy.

Plans had been made. That was what he and his staff did while artillery pounded the walls, patrols kept the Burg and New Town cleared, and pickets harassed anyone trying to get in or out of the White City. While the engineers continued undermining and overtowering, trying to over-awe but preparing for an assault as well.

"I'll deal with Isabeth first, I suppose."

"Not going to be easy."

"I know. Peter won't have sent her without his best men to protect her. She has between eight hundred and a thousand men now, maybe half of them men Duke Tormond raised."

"Heavy cavalry."

Yes. He had to find a way to diminish that fierce advantage. Num-bers meant little if unprepared infantry had to face men in armor, atop warhorses running shoulder to shoulder.

"I know. We have ideas." Which would not work. These Navayans had survived all the traps and trickery of the Pramans of al-Halambra.

He wished he had Buhle Smolens and Pinkus Ghort with him. They managed to execute the strategies he chose to employ.

It was time to find the limit of Hagan Brokke's talents.

PROBING ATTACKS FOUND THE WHITE CITY IN A STATE OF EXCITEMENT. ITS defenders swarmed to every assault site and made themselves thoroughly obnoxious if the crusaders persisted.

Hecht did not sustain any assault for long. He was taxing the enemy. Wearing his will to rush hither and yon.

The artillery never stopped. Even the dimmest and most devoted Castreresonese could foresee the inevitable end to that.

One day the Captain-General would decide there were breaches enough and order a general assault. The Castreresonese could not resist everywhere at once.

But hope remained. Encouraging messages did get through.

"I know," Hecht told Consent. "There's no way to stop everything. Given time, though, those messengers will bring despair instead of hope."

Troops filtered out of camp after dark. For the benefit of spies they were sneaking off to reduce towns and fortresses to the northwest, where colonies of Maysaleans and adherents of the Viscesment Patri-archy were common. And they did make life miserable wherever the lo-cals had not yet yielded to Sublime's forces. But their mission was to collect on the upper Laur, along the northern road to Khaurene, two dozen miles from Duke Tormond's capital. Whence they could go for-ward against the Khaurenesaine or ease down behind Isabeth's position at Mohela ande Larges.

Hagan Brokke would command. He would make enough noise to be considered a clumsy sneaker. What he did later would depend on how Duke Tormond and Queen Isabeth responded to his presence.

Patriarchal forces east of Queen Isabeth would build up clumsily enough to be noticed, too.

Hecht told Consent, "These people have made a career of war. They're probably eager to teach us not to challenge our betters but smart enough to see the dangers. They won't charge into a trap."

"So you're doing what?"

"Creating options. Options they'll see clearly. If they sit, I'll gradually surround them. Their only hope will be Duke Tormond. Unless they fight."

"And Tormond does nothing but talk."

"He hasn't done anything else so far."

"They'll have the interior position. If they go after Brokke we won't know in time to help."

"We'll know. We have scouts camped in their saddlebags." He had a roster of the Navayans in Queen Isabeth's force.

"Where can you fight them? There's no good place out there."

"Too true. The best strategy looks like attrition. While waiting for them to do something stupid before I do."

"Is that likely?"

"Titus! Sarcasm? I like that. I think." Smile gone, Hecht said, "You could have a point. I'm feeling some time pressure. Things are happening in Brothe. And people there are trying to keep me from hearing about it."

"Did it occur to you to ask me?"

After a moment, "No. My spymaster? Why consult him? Because I've been too focused on what's in front of me? What do you know?"

"My contacts in the Devedian community aren't what they used to be. But some still think being friendly could pay dividends. They tell me when there's something they think we should know."

"And?"

"Most Brothens think Sublime is dying. The gang around him want to make sure they can name his replacement. The Fiducian, Joceran Cuito, looks like he'll be their candidate."

The Direcian. Peter of Navaya's man. That could lead to interesting times. "A Navayan? We're still not over the last non-Brothen who won a Patriarchal election."

Consent shrugged. "I'm just telling you what I hear. They say Peter wants it. And has the money to make it happen."

"I see. And I'm being kept isolated because?"

"Because you have an army. You could veto the outcome of an election. If you had the inclination. Like a general from Imperial times."

Hecht chuckled. What would Gordimer and er-Rashal think? Their throwaway agent was in a position to influence the selection of the next main enemy of the Kaifate of al-Minphet.

Consent asked, "You thought about who you'd rather have take over if Sublime went away?"

Hecht assayed tone and expression. Was he being felt out? He decided not. "Something else to worry about."

"Always plenty."

"Where is Principaté Delari? I don't see him around anymore."

"Nor do I. But he's out there. Maybe missing Armand."

"Maybe." Hecht did not miss Osa Stile even a little.

SEEING THE DIMINUTION OF THE BESIEGING FORCES, THE MAGNATES OF THE White City launched another desperate night sortie. The Captain-General saw it coming. Every sally had been presaged by the gathering of watchers on the city wall.

A lot of dead men decorated the slopes when the sun rose. Few were Patriarchals.

The revenant Instrumentalities were busy all night. There were numerous reports of encounters in the form of sound or stench, but only a few had seen anything.

Hecht asked his staff, "Are they rattled enough to fall apart if we attack?"

Consent said, "Our men are exhausted, too. Those who were away from the main action wore themselves out mounting diversionary attacks."

And had gained several footholds inside the main wall.

"I'll let the Principatés give them one more chance to surrender. What's this?"

A courier. With news that Queen Isabeth was moving. Her whole force was headed east, two hundred fifty knights, their associated sergeants, squires, and infantry, and nearly eight hundred Sevanphaxi and Terliagan mercenaries Tormond had conjured somehow. Nearly two thousand men, almost all veterans.

Hecht scanned the message again. "They're coming straight at us. To see what we'll do, I imagine. They're in no hurry. That's good for us." Otherwise, they'd be right behind the news. He sent messengers flying. To Hagan Brokke. To the scouts watching Isabeth. To those whose job it was to watch Mohela ande Larges.

An intricate dance began. It developed slowly. Each dancer waited for the other to misstep.

Isabeth halted after traveling twelve miles. She occupied the common farmland outside the town Homodel. Hecht's scouts reported the ground looked good for cavalry.

"Let them sit. Let them get colder." He thought it looked like there would be a more serious snowfall sometime soon. "Chase their scouts. Ambush their foragers. We'll let Brokke upset them."

While he waited, though, he kept on filtering men out of camp.

The bombardment of the White City went on.

HAGAN BROKKE FEINTED TOWARD MOHELA ANDE LARGES, THE ATTACK the Captain-General supposed the enemy expected. Once Brokke saw that the Queen's headquarters could not be taken quickly, he headed toward Khaurene. As always, his troops crushed resistance ferociously. In two days they captured six towns and fortresses and accepted the surrenders of three more.

The Patriarchals from around Castreresone established a camp three miles from Isabeth's. Making no offer of battle.

The nights became filled with the bark and chatter and numbing stench of the Night, worsening fast. The Connecten Instrumentalities were gathering, tormenting the sons of men not nearly so much as one another.

So said Principaté Muniero Delari, more in evidence now that a collision might be coming.

The old man assembled a team of falconeers whose weapons had been lost in the confrontation with the god grub. They built and tested traps, some as imagined by Drago Prosek, most designs handed down from early Old Empire times.

The smallest Instrumentalities were easily caught, often because they were desperate to escape larger predators. Delari hoped to use the small captives to lure the large.

"What kind of sorcerer are you?" Hecht asked. "I thought, as a class, that was your high purpose. To round up a bigger, nastier herd than anyone else has."

"You aren't sufficiently well informed." Delari said that deadpan. And did not explain. His sense of humor was hard to detect. "You need to spend more time with your grandfather."

The Navayans were patient. Hecht went out to the camp and took charge. It was an excuse to get away from Castreresone. He tried provoking the Navayans with nighttime harassments. His men could not penetrate their picket lines. He had his surviving falcons fire stone shot toward the fanciest pavilion. Their accuracy was foul, one exploded, and the noise frightened the crusaders' own animals. There was no evidence the Navayans were impressed.

Hecht began a process of encirclement, having his men pick off anyone who strayed from the enemy camp. His patrols watched for couriers.

Those from the White City were allowed to get through. Messages coming out were intercepted as often as possible. Those were in cipher. Even Titus Consent had no luck breaking the code. The couriers themselves, naturally, had no clue.

Hecht said, "I don't mind if they just sit there. Except that it's cold. We have food. They don't. Not enough to wait us out." While they sat, they would be hammered by increasingly desperate pleas from Castreresone.

The Captain-General refused to engage an enemy with such a heavy cavalry advantage.

Four days into the standoff news came that Patriarchal troops had gotten a solid foothold inside Castreresone. Several leading men had been captured.

It looked like the beginning of the end for the White City.

That same day word came that Hagan Brokke's men had shown themselves to watchers on the wall at Khaurene. They had burned villages and manors within sight of the city, concentrating on properties belonging to Duke Tormond. A huge, angry response from the city forced them to withdraw. But the message had been delivered.

TITUS CONSENT MATERIALIZED AT HECHT'S ELBOW AS THE CAPTAIN-General tried to pry advice out of Principaté Delari. The old man was depressed for no obvious reason. Hecht told him, "You don't have to be here. I can send you down to Sheavenalle. You could get passage across to Brothe. You could be back loafing in the Chiaro baths in a week."

"That won't change the future. Nor the past. Lieutenant Consent has something urgent. Spend your empathy on him."

"Titus?"

"The Navayans are up to something over there. Scouts are heading out."

Soon afterward the Navayans left camp. The knights headed toward the Patriarchal camp. The mercenary infantry marched out eastward. Their own infantry followed the horsemen. Knights, sergeants, senior squires, and whatnot, those numbered almost three hundred. More than Hecht had expected.

The horsemen stopped outside bowshot, dismounted, began an advance on foot, each armored man backed by two foot.

Hecht did not know what to do. Crossbowmen being at a premium, he had left his at Castreresone.

"We have to go. Now. Lay down some kind of harassing fire. Burn some firepowder for the smoke. The breeze is blowing their way."

It was close but the Patriarchals escaped. The Navayans evidently had no enthusiasm for their tactics and so did not move forcefully. Nor did they show any desire to enter the foul firepowder smoke.

Prosek caught up with Hecht. "You saw how the smoke bothered them? Sir?"

"Of course. It was my idea."

"Make some with more sulfur in it. For that purpose."

"Do it. Add captain of chemical warfare to your job description."

The Patriarchal forces reassembled farther east. Infantry there had been skirmishing with the mercenaries all afternoon. The mercenaries were waiting on their paymasters. Hecht did not press them.

The Navayans were not inclined to be drawn in, either.

Titus Consent opined, "This could be a long, nasty war if there are never any battles."

"It's long and nasty now. These people have been crippling each other by ruining one another's agriculture for several years."

"We can turn the country into a desert."

"And God will love us more. Apparently."

Redfearn Bechter scowled the whole time. He was a cynical old man himself, but this talk smacked of heresy. He sent a look of appeal to Madouc. The chief lifeguard shrugged. Doctrinal indiscretion was not his problem.

The Captain-General said, "Sergeant, disrespect for the intellect of the Patriarch isn't heresy. It isn't sacrilege, either. It's not even insubordination. We're doing what he tells us. We're just not sure he's hearing what God is whispering in his ear."

No explanation would comfort the old soldier. He had lived his life for God and the Church. He said, "The men we have hidden in the hills are having a lot of trouble with Night things."

"For example?"

"Just little things. So far. But always something wicked. Spoiling wine. Making beer go skunky. Stirring up hornets. Spooking horses."

"Where's Principaté Delari gotten to? He should've been here long before us. I started him off early."

Bechter said, "I kept him going back to Castreresone. Assuming you didn't want him exposed to misfortune out here."

"Of course. Damn! No, you did right. It's just inconvenient. I wanted to ask him why the Night is ganging up on us all of a sudden."

Consent asked, "Is it? I'd bet it's being just as obnoxious to those people back up the road."

The skirmishing ended at nightfall. The Navayans withdrew into a tight encampment. Which suggested that the Night was, indeed, being impartially obnoxious.

Something big came after midnight. Something that made Hecht's amulet burn his wrist. Something that reeked and birthed terror with its stench. The animals nearly revolted.

The Captain-General summoned Drago Prosek. "There's work for the falcons." The first weapon barked ten minutes later. There was no need for a second to comment.

Instantly there was an absence of any sense of supernatural presence. The falconeers reported a vast, panicky rustle a moment before the falcon spoke.

Then there was excitement to the west. Fires blazing up. Distance-muted shouting.

Nothing more happened. Hecht told Prosek, "Keep a crew standing by. They don't need permission to fire but they better not waste charges on their imaginations."

Prosek nodded, expression grim. Knowing perfectly well the nervous falconeers would fire first and worry about weathering the Captain-General's displeasure once they had survived.

Hecht headed for the shelter his lifeguards had thrown together. And discovered that he would be getting no sleep anytime soon.

Cloven Februaren sat in a corner, barely discernible. Hecht said, "I thought we'd lost you."

"I'm always around. Somewhere. You're getting comfortable with destroying Instrumentalities."

"It's easier than killing people. Emotionally."

"You should keep yourself inside a circle of ready falcons. From now on."

"Yes?"

"The Night sees you finding it easier than killing people, too. The Night doesn't understand that the djinn can't be shoved back into the lamp. It hasn't gotten over Man having gained the secret of fire."

Hecht nodded. He was exhausted. Dawn would come sooner than he liked. "You always turn up when something awful is about to happen. What will it be this time?"

"Not this time. Just passing through. Wanted to caution you to be careful with Isabeth. She's in a tight place. She has to be seen trying to do something. But neither she nor her captains know what. This war is nothing like what they're used to in Direcia, where they know who the enemy is. And people don't change sides when the whim strikes."

Hecht knew of no fickle, shifting allegiances, except during the little county wars that faded once the Grolsacher and Arnhander incursions began. "I haven't seen any of that."

"You will. All those towns and castles you're taking, that have sworn fealty to Sublime and the Church. They'll turn in an instant if they sense any weakness."

Hecht had not thought about that. It sounded true, though. Those people were not joining the Brothen cause for love of Sublime V. "Makes sense."

"I have further advice. Whatever you hope to accomplish here you'd best get done soon. Big changes are coming. And round up any Artecipeans you can. They're behind the resurgence of the Night. They're a third side in this war. They aren't friends of the Connecten factions but they're helping them because they're your worst enemies."

"Why?"

The old man bowed his head as though in contemplation. He said, "They want to destroy you for the reason they've always wanted to destroy you. A conviction on the part of certain Instrumentalities that you could become the mechanism of their destruction."

"Every encounter I've suffered has been initiated by the Night."

"Amusing, isn't it? Them bringing on what they dread by trying to get even first?"

"Isn't the same thing happening every day, somewhere? This prince, that duke, a random count, strikes before some enemy can carry out a potential attack?"

Februaren chuckled. "Every day. And half the time it's a damned good idea. Hitting them back before they can hit you back first."

"I'm tired. And, as usual, you're just being vague. So I'm going to sleep. You can get back to watching over me."

"Sarcasm? Interesting." The old man grinned. Despite his antiquity, he had a full set of teeth. "Go ahead. I'll hover like a guardian angel."

NEWS CAME EARLY. A FRESH CONTINGENT OF FORTY-DAY MEN FROM Firaldia, not told not to, had attacked the White City through breaches from the New Town. The defenders were unprepared for a heavy assault. The invaders were running wild in Castreresone's streets.

Hecht said, "We have to go get a bridle on this before the officers go loot-crazy, too."

Titus Consent asked, "What about those people over there?"

"They'll hear about it. They'll have to make a decision. Let Castreresone go? Or charge in where their prospects are grim?"

"We'd have the hammer by the handle if we caught Isabeth."

"We would. Yes. But don't expect it to happen."

Hecht withdrew toward the White City. The mercenary infantry remained in contact but avoided serious combat. The knights followed on, still looking for that opportunity to exploit their advantage. The wind picked up in the middle of the morning. A drizzle began soon after noon. That turned to freezing rain. Shortly afterward the Patriarchals reached hastily prepared defenses meant to break a cavalry charge.

The Navayans attacked, without enthusiasm, because the situation compelled them. Their appearance stiffened the resolve of the city's defenders.

Freezing rain turned to light, steady snow.

Come nightfall, the Queen's men withdrew. The Captain-General launched several nighttime counterattacks. He suffered the heavier losses. Come morning, though, the Navayans resumed moving toward Mohela ande Larges. Which they might find held against them, Hagan Brokke having taken the garrison by surprise the morning before.

Brokke would give the castle up uncontested, though. If instructions from his Captain-General got through.

Brokke reported taking prisoners that might be of interest to his commander.

CANNON FIRE WAKENED HECHT. THREE ROARS FROM THREE DIRECTIONS. The excitement was over before he caught up with Drago Prosek. Prosek's crews were digging up the muddy little eggs left by the deaths of the Instrumentalities.

"Changes coming fast," Hecht muttered. Using the falcons against the Night had become routine.

Prosek said, "Sorry we woke you, sir. Couldn't do it quietly." He brushed snow out of his hair.

"I thought they'd let us alone. After what we've done."

"You can't beat stupid, sir. I put some of the new traps out tonight. We'll see what good they do."

"Carry on, then. Make sure those eggs get to Principaté Delari." He turned to go back to his tent.

"Sir, we need more ammunition. We have nine rounds special left. Four of those I made myself from shot we'd already used once."

"We'll do something. Good work, by the way."

Hecht was halfway to his shelter when several blazing spears leapt off Castreresone's walls, barely discernible through the falling snow.

Excitement raced through the Patriarchal camp. Sleeping soldiers came out to see what the racket was this time. They added to it once they understood. Patriarchal forces had captured Castreresone's main gate from inside.

The soldiers raced off to sack the White City.

Hecht did not try to stem the tide. That could get him trampled. As dawn came, he told Titus Consent, "Sometimes you have to let chaos sort itself out."

"Not everyone has gone crazy. A few men stuck to their posts."
Consent indicated Hecht's lifeguards, all of whom looked like they were
constipated. Even lifelong members of the Brotherhood of War wanted a
share of the plunder.

"Good. Somebody needs to keep us from being caught with our
trousers down. What's this?" Riders were crossing the Laur bridge, looking around warily.

"Messengers."

"Gutsy guys, too, if they've been traveling in the dark."

"I'll get them."

PINKUS GHORT WAS ON HIS WAY FROM ANTIEUX. SOMETHING BIG WAS
afoot. Bronte Doneto had, with explosive suddenness, abandoned the
siege that had been the center of his life for months.

"Sergeant Bechter, we want to move into the Count's keep as soon
as possible. You need to figure out what we need for a permanent headquarters."

"Yes, sir. Colonel Ghort's party is on the down slope across the river
now."

"Hope he doesn't mind the mud."

"He'll be distracted by the damage to the vineyards."

Hecht laughed. "No doubt. Have you seen the Principaté?"

"Which? The Bruglioni and the Aparionese fellow are leaving, I
hear. Going to leave us to our fate."

"Delari. The only one who ever interests me."

"He's in the city. Keep an eye on the Bruglioni. Madouc tells me he
looks like a man nursing a secret grudge."

"Paludan Bruglioni and Gervase Saluda have never forgiven me for
abandoning them to go to work for the Patriarch."

Bechter scowled. He did not believe that for a moment.

Redfearn Bechter seldom said anything not involved with getting on
with work. But he had eyes and a brain. Hecht feared the man was picking up more than he needed to know. Which was why the Brotherhood
had him next to the Captain-General in the first place.

If Gervase Saluda had developed a true grudge, he might be putting
things together, too.

There were always people who knew uncomfortable things. Some
could not resist gossiping.

"It's time we went up there and saw this gem we've added to the
Church's crown. Right after I see Colonel Ghort."

Bechter was not pleased.

"There's a problem, Sergeant?"

"Madouc won't let you go without a full complement of lifeguards.

But that would tell the Castreresonese you're someone important. They might attack you."

"I doubt it. They've had enough. They don't want us to do the White City the way we did the lesser towns."

"Even where the troops were merciless we've had trouble with ambush and murder. The Society brethren won't go scourge the rustic heretics."

"Gosh, Sergeant. Imagine that. People who resist opportunities to be robbed and burned alive. How un-Chaldarean of them."

"Have a care, sir. The Society grows stronger every day. They might enjoy the opportunity to pull down somebody important, just to feed the fear surrounding them."

"Good point. Tell Madouc I intend to move into the keep." He should be safe there. That fortress within had been built to provide a refuge from the Castreresonese themselves, not as a place to make a last stand against invaders.

"As you will, sir." Bechter making his disapproval amply clear. "One point more. I saw that old man in brown. Be careful."

Once Bechter left, the Ninth Unknown asked, "How does he do that?"

Hecht squeaked. "How do *you* do that? Popping out of nowhere?"

"He shouldn't be able to see me."

"You have a special reason to scare the pants off me?"

"No. Except to reinforce what Bechter said. Don't irritate the Society. They'll get thick as flies now. There's been a battle on Artecipea between Pramans King Peter recruited in Calzir and some Artecipean mountain people. Your former associates participated. A great deal of sorcery was involved. Peter's forces were victorious. The point of it all, though, remains obscure."

Februaren seemed cocky. Like he had had a hand in assuring that outcome. But that could not be. Could it? The Lord of the Silent Kingdom must be powerful, but not so much so that he could cross long distances in no time. Could he?

Februaren revealed a small smile. Hecht suspected that the man knew his thoughts. Whereupon the smile became a smirk. Februaren startled him by asking, "Why would Gervase Saluda become your enemy? You did well by the Bruglioni when you worked for them. Set their feet solidly on the road toward restoring their glory."

"Principaté Divino Bruglioni. The only thing I can think of. Some rumor may have gotten out of the Arniena family. And the ring." A recollection of which took Hecht by surprise. He had not considered the Bruglioni ring for a long time.

"Ring?"

Even the Ninth Unknown could not resist the ring's power to elude memory.

"Polo knows I had it. I forgot that for a long time. He may have remembered and told somebody."

"Polo. That's the one who was your manservant when you were with the Bruglioni? Crippled in the ambush meant to kill you and Ghort."

Hecht nodded.

"Time to turn around. Bechter is back."

Februaren turned. And vanished. Leaving Hecht feeling that he was truly gone, not just hidden from the eye.

"Enter," he responded to Bechter's appeal.

The sergeant peered into shadows. He had heard something. "The lifeguard is assembling. Colonel Ghort should be here in time to join us. Apropos my earlier caution, Morcant Farfog is with Colonel Ghort's party."

It took Hecht a moment. "Bishop of Strang?"

"Archbishop, now. Head of the Society in the End of Connec. Convinced that he's the most powerful churchman after Sublime. I heard he may have one eye on the Patriarchy."

"You're kidding."

"Competence is seldom the leading qualification for succession."

"But . . ."

"Not to worry, Captain-General. He wouldn't get the votes."

PINKUS GHORT DID NOT LOOK WELL. "EXHAUSTION," HE EXPLAINED. Barely putting one foot in front of the other as he climbed the hill with Hecht. "That Raymone Garete is a stubborn bastard. Then I got Doneto barking in one ear and that pile of monkey shit Farfog howling in the other. That prick don't know how lucky he is to be alive."

"That could be more true than you realize."

"Eh?"

"The Brotherhood doesn't love him, either. Sooner or later, they'll butt heads. If Sublime doesn't rein them in."

"Man, you wrecked this place. It'll take years to fix these walls."

"How's your bombardment?"

"There's gotta be sorcery involved. Or something. We keep pounding away. And the rocks keep bouncing off."

"There must be a way."

"Starvation."

"What about mining?"

"Working on it. From half a dozen directions. Antieux is built on the hardest damned limestone I've ever seen. We'll get there eventually. If our bosses are patient enough."

"Principaté Doneto hasn't been any help?"

"Debatable. He's ferocious about tearing the place apart. But he never did anything useful. If he's really some heavyweight sorcerer, he does a damned good job of hiding it."

"Makes you wonder, doesn't it?"

"Uhm?"

"If he really is. You hear it all the time, he's one of the great bull sorcerers in the Collegium. But he never does anything." That fight under the hippodrome might be an exception. Though that had not been public and there should have been no survivors.

"Is he behind his own rumors?"

Hecht shrugged. "We're here." At the keep of the Counts of Castreresone. Madouc led them to a large, poorly lighted room where several dozen locals waited nervously. Hecht's most trusted soldiers lined the walls.

"The vultures didn't take long to gather." Black-robed Society brothers were much in evidence.

Hecht said, "Bechter, clear those crows out. This isn't religious business."

Ghort whispered, "Be careful. They have Sublime convinced that religious law trumps civil and martial law."

Hecht understood. The Church meant to follow his hammer strokes by insinuating its agents into every facet of Connecten life, intent on making everything subservient to the Brothen establishment. Soon enough, the Captain-General would have to be replaced with someone less competent but more ideologically dependable.

Bechter went to work with enthusiasm.

"Hope you see what I'm seeing," Ghort said.

"Which would be?"

"How much the Brotherhood resents the Society."

"Useful to know, down the road."

"I'm thinking so."

Ignoring the protesting Society brothers, Hecht assumed the role of Captain-General. "Let's have some order. Pay attention."

Silence. The Castreresonese were intensely interested in the victorious general's comments.

Hecht presented Sublime's directives, which had not changed. He presented a list of heretics and enumerated steps to be taken to suppress, convert, or evict Unbelievers. Their properties were forfeit to the Church. The city was expected to raise funds for repairs to its defenses and public works. Leading men were to be fined for their obdurate behavior.

Those fines would fall into Hecht's war chest.

Once Castreresone was settled he would move against Khaurene.

Castreresone, not Duke Tormond's home city, was the key to control of the Connec, in Hecht's estimation. He owned the key, now.

He took the seat reserved for the ruling count. His officers introduced locals of standing, starting with the consuls, the manager-senators who handled the daily business of city government. Castreresone retained many of the appurtenances of its youth as a city-state. With layers of feudal law and obligation laid on over the centuries.

The eight senators present were eager to please. Three more were absent, all on the Society's wanted list. Hecht asked. One supposedly died in the fighting. One had suffered a stroke. And one had fled the city.

Hecht picked names at random. "You three will speak for them to the Society."

The magnates were introduced next. They were the rich men of Castreresone. Many belonged to the urban nobility, disdained by traditional nobility because they were more interested in commerce than warfare.

Another round in the ancient contest between city and country.

The Captain-General found a total lack of defiance in the defeated. The excesses in the towns and villages had been useful. Once the introductions had been made and the oaths of fealty administered, Hecht made a brief speech. He would forgive the sins of the past. In return, he expected those oaths to be fulfilled absolutely. Rebellion would be dealt with harshly.

The Captain-General went through the motions, tired. But he studied the Castreresonese closely.

He did not identify a single potential troublemaker.

Titus Consent approached, grim as he weaved between Hecht's lifeguards. He whispered, "Bad news from Hagan Brokke."

"I'll finish as soon as I can."

Now that he had seen the human face of the city there was little more he wanted to do. Plans for the occupation had been made long since.

"HE WHAT?" HECHT ASKED.

"In the vernacular, he got his ass kicked," Consent said. "He slid out of Mohela ande Larges, as directed. He made a show of threatening Khaurene again, then headed east. And ran into Isabeth's mercenaries. An encounter engagement. Which escalated. Both sides seeing an opportunity that wasn't really there. Brokke had the advantage till the Navayans arrived."

Hecht said nothing. There was no point. Things happened. There were no guarantees. Genius was not infallible. And . . . things happened. Finally, "How bad?"

"Not sure yet. Pretty bad. But he didn't lose his prisoners."

"Good. Torturing them will make me feel better about losing those men."

"You're in a fine mood."

"I don't take misfortune well. As you see. And I want to go home. I haven't seen Anna or the kids in half a year."

"You are unique in your exaggerated pain, sir. Why is Colonel Ghort blessing us with his company?"

"I'm not sure. It must have to do with Principaté Doneto and Morcant Farfog. But he isn't as forthcoming as he once was."

"It couldn't be just that he needs to relax with someone he's known since before the responsibilities started piling on?"

The Captain-General closed his eyes. He drifted into a fantasy realm where he, Ghort, Bo Biogna, Just Plain Joe and the mule Pig Iron, and a few comfortable others surrounded a campfire, swapping tall tales. The good old days, when they were hungry but had the luxury of being able to relax.

"Could be, Titus. How scattered are we? How disorganized? How long to pull it all together to march on Khaurene?"

"I don't want to get above myself. But these guys need some rest. They need to relax. They need to get in out of the Night. Which won't get any better because we took Castreresone. Despite Prosek's efforts."

"What's that?"

"The racket? Probably Archbishop Farfog insisting on seeing you so he can give you your orders."

"Here are some orders for him. Go away. Stick to robbery and saving souls. I'll handle the war business."

"Sure you want to offend him?"

"I don't mind. Do you?"

"Sir?"

"They say he keeps records. On everyone. I'm sure you're one of his favorite suspects."

"I hadn't thought of that."

"It won't be a happy world if Farfog is running free. Maybe we ought to help him become Patriarch." He enjoyed Consent's startled response. "The Patriarch gets so isolated he has to drill through layers of hangers-on to have much impact outside Krois. Farfog isn't a leader. He's a pusher. He'd drown in the bureaucratic swamp."

Consent chuckled. "Interesting idea. Disarm the idiots by putting them in charge, then let their own incompetence destroy them."

"Something like that." Hecht did not think Farfog would destroy himself. But he was venal and corrupt enough to render the Church a cripple, incapable of undertaking another massive religious offensive. "When you tell him to go away, feel him out about how much the army's support might be worth to him."

Consent did not like that. But he did not question it.

PRINCIPATÉ DELARI WAKENED HECHT. WHO WONDERED HOW THE MAN HAD gotten past his bodyguards. "Problems in Brothe, Piper. I have to leave."

"What is it? Saluda and Linczski have gone already."

"And Doneto. He has a big lead."

"What is it?"

"Sublime is gone. Or going. His gang is trying to keep it secret."

"We've been hearing that for months."

"It's true, now. All the Principatés away from Brothe will be moving that direction. Like flies to a cow flop. Wanting to reach the Chiaro Palace in time to get in on the first vote."

Members of the Collegium not on hand for the initial vote could not participate in subsequent polls. The rule helped keep the Patriarchy in the hands of members of the Firaldian primates.

"You've been sharing wine with Pinkus Ghort."

"With my grandfather. I don't see him often enough." Nor sounded like this opportunity had gone that well.

"I'll miss you. I'll feel naked, having you go just when the Night has begun this escalation."

"You'll be protected. He'll be out there somewhere. Hovering. Trying to make the world run according to his own weird prejudices."

"I'm not worried about me. I'm worried about the other twenty thousand men . . ."

"Talk to him about that. I need to get busy. I'm way behind."

"Take a boat down to Sheavenalle. Then a ship across to Brothe. You'll get home weeks ahead of everybody. You can fix it up to be the next Patriarch yourself."

"I don't want it. Wouldn't take it if it was handed to me."

"If you get a chance, see Anna and the kids. I think that would mean a lot to them." He did not know what else he could do. "I'll give you a letter for them before you leave."

HECHT TOLD GHORT, "I LIKED IT BETTER DOWN IN INCONJE. THIS PLACE IS dark, dank, and smells bad." He exaggerated. The keep had not been built for comfort. The offending smell was the result of generations of cooking with unfamiliar spices.

They were alone except for a couple of lifeguards. Ghort was sampling local vintages.

Hecht asked, "What's really on your mind?"

"I don't know if we can take Antieux. An assault would just get a lot of people dead. They aren't getting hungry in there. They aren't getting thirsty. The walls won't come down. Winter is closing in. We're starting to see sickness in the camp. Probably brought in by all the hangers-on we've accumulated. And we're having trouble with Night things. Trouble that looks like it could get bad."

"We have that here, too. I've got a man, Drago Prosek, who seems to be on track to controlling it."

"I heard the falcons."

"That's for the big ones. I've got more falcons being cast, including a test kind that can be fired faster. But that's in Brothe. Which doesn't do us any good here. Where he is doing good, here, is with traps. You should see the things he's caught. A whole menagerie of stuff that should've been extinct since the Old Empire. Stuff no one's ever seen before."

"But not dangerous?"

Hecht shrugged. "I don't know. I'm short my adviser on those things."

"Delari? Yeah. Doneto was useful that way, too. When you figure on moving west?"

"It'll take a week to get organized. Then it depends on the weather. Much more snow and mud, I may just sit down here and keep warm. May just wait to see what happens in Brothe." If Sublime went, would all his lunatic drive to rid the Chaldarean world of heresy and Unbelievers go with him?

Should Sublime's successor be indifferent to goals set by the present Patriarch, what would become of the Captain-General and his army?

"My guys aren't going to like winter . . . Oh! This is awful!" Ghort shoved an earthenware bottle away.

"Have you been getting ready?" Pinkus Ghort, Hecht suspected, had let things slide on the assumption that long-term thinking was a waste of time for a soldier.

"Probably not enough," Ghort confessed. "Sedlakova, more than me."

"Then you know what you need to do."

"Winter is coming. We don't have a lot of stores. Count Raymone cleared the countryside."

"You're on a river, Pinkus. And there's a road to Sheavenalle. I have no trouble supplying my people." That Ghort was less than fully prepared was no surprise. He was not a born manager. Which was why Clej Sedlakova was in charge at Antieux. Sedlakova recognized his own weaknesses and chose under-officers to deal with them. "Is Sedlakova having trouble? Are you managing things separately?"

"I've got to, Pipe. Even working for pay, I'm City Regiment, not Patriarchal."

"Point. But the fact remains. You need to do the scut work. Or find yourself a Titus who can."

Admonished, Ghort nodded. Understanding the message behind the message. Friendship could not trump the welfare of the soldiers. Not with Piper Hecht. Who stared pointedly at the wine in front of his friend.

He had reason to believe that Pinkus spent too much time sampling the vintages at Antieux. Time better spent preparing for winter.

Ghort asked, "What do we do if Sublime does die?"

"We may have to look for work. If Joceran Cuito succeeds."

"The Fiducian? Why him?"

"I don't know. I've heard he's the front-runner. Backed by King Peter."

Madouc, the lifeguard captain, entered. "Hagan Brokke has arrived, Captain-General. You asked to be informed."

"Thanks. I'll see him as soon as he feels up to it."

"He isn't in good shape. He may need time with the healing brothers."

"Then I can go to him." He shifted to Ghort. "Any chance you'll take Farfog with you when you head back?"

"You don't have muscle enough to bully me into that, Pipe. That guy is the worst asshole I've ever met. He makes old Bishop Serifs look like a fairy-tale princess. It's too bad the Connectens didn't kill his ass when they had the chance."

"I've avoided him so far. I won't be able to forever."

"Something to look forward to, then. If we're lucky, the next Patriarch will get rid of him. Hell, if we could just get him up in front of the Collegium . . . He'd make such an ass of himself, they'd appoint him chief missionary to the Dreangereans. Or something bad. You got anything for me to take back when I go?"

"Just find Prosek. Have him tell you how to handle your Night things. If you need to, tell Sedlakova he should bring in people from the Special Office. I'm sure he knows a few."

"If he isn't one himself."

CLOVEN FEBRUAREN APPEARED AS HECHT WAS CRAWLING INTO BED. THE feather bed being the one thing he found positive about having moved into the keep. He groaned. "I was hoping to get an extra hour tonight."

"I'm only here to tell you I won't be around for a while. You'll need to stay closer to your lifeguards."

Hecht suspected that Februaren had a severely inflated notion of his own importance. Yet the old man might have stopped any number of attempts to assassinate the Captain-General. How would he know about attempts that failed? "I'll try to remember."

"They only need be successful once. It's important that they not be."

"I'm glad you share my viewpoint."

"I worry that you aren't serious enough about sharing mine. Very worried. It's important that you survive."

Hecht agreed. But he and the old man were not talking about the same thing. It was not personal with Februaren. Februaren was a man with a plan. And that plan hinged on a supposed remote descendant.

Again, "I won't be out there. So you *have* to think about your own safety whenever you choose to do something. Every single time."

"I've got it. Really."

Februaren did his turn-around thing. Hecht snuggled down into the warmth of the feather bed. He fell asleep wondering if he had it in him to be paranoid enough to satisfy the Ninth Unknown.

THREE THOUSAND OF THE BEST-RESTED TROOPS HEADED WEST. HECHT hoped to provoke Duke Tormond into doing something unwise now that he had invoked his feudal right to summon his dependents to war. Hecht was not eager for a fight. But a fight would stir the political cauldron. And he did want that kept bubbling, whether or not his most secret self remained faithful to the mission given him by his first master, Gordimer the Lion.

The review of the departing troops done, Hecht went to see Hagan Brokke. Brokke was apologetic about his failure to handle the Navayans. He had paid the price of failure, physically. He would not have survived long had he not come into the hands of the healing brothers.

From Brokke's bedside Hecht went to see the prisoners Brokke had brought in. He expected a handful. There were more than forty, the majority being knights and minor nobility. Those had been given comfortable quarters in Inconje. Those of more immediate interest, though, had been driven into a stock pen.

"Bo. I haven't seen you for an age."

"Been too busy to socialize. Sir." Biogna scowled at all the bodyguards. Madouc must have had a dream visit from Cloven Februaren. He had increased the protection significantly.

"Are you involved in this?"

"I was out there with Brokke. Being his Titus Consent. Keeping him convinced that we needed to take a few prisoners."

"Why such a mob?"

"Most of them can be ransomed. The men insisted. But there are some interesting ones, too."

"Them?" Hecht indicated the men in the pen.

"Artecipeans. Every one. Probably useless for anything but Society food."

"Uhm?"

"They're not just heretics, they're Unbelievers. Trying to bring back the Old Gods. Virulently dangerous. Unlike those ones back yonder in the other pens. That whole clutch there are Khaurenese we picked up at Mohela ande Larges. One of Immaculate's bishops, a Praman priest of some kind, and a Deve elder. A couple days later, we found a Perfect Master hiding in some brush. Wouldn't have known it. He wasn't in costume. But the ones from Khaurene knew him. One of them said something before his brain checked in."

Hecht considered the Artecipeans. They avoided his gaze. "I've seen some of these men before." One face, in fact, he recalled from the crowd of gawkers outside Anna's house the night they moved her to Principaté Delari's town house. "I'll work up a list of questions. Whoever answers them honestly won't get turned over to Archbishop Farfog. Show me what else you've got."

The captured soldiers were not impressive. Prisoners of war seldom were.

Biogna said, "This might be the best catch. Bernardin Amberchelle. Count Raymone's ugly cousin. In the top five on the Society's wanted list. He killed a bunch of their thugs. That's the Perfect Master over there, with the girl. He was traveling with Amberchelle. Says the girl is his daughter. He was trying to get her to safety in Khaurene. He's lying. She has a different accent. They're both very careful to protect her. She's got to be somebody important."

"Pity Ghort's gone. He might be able to use the cousin to get to Raymone."

"Send a messenger. He can use the information."

"Good work. Keep after these people. Use Farfog as leverage." Hecht considered the old man and the girl. The girl appeared to be about twenty, possibly not unattractive under the grime. She had a ferocious look.

"The Amberchelle person. Was he wearing or carrying anything we can send to Antieux? To prove we have him?"

"I'll find out." Skirting the certainty that the soldiers who caught him had relieved him of everything of value.

"Do that."

HECHT AVOIDED MORCANT FARFOG FOR TWO MORE DAYS. BY WHICH TIME he had Castreresone under control. It was not a pleasant interview. Those who had reported the Archbishop's failings had not exaggerated.

Hecht endured what he had to endure and gave the minimum in response to demands. The Archbishop went away thinking he had won several major points. In fact, Hecht had yielded little.

He told Titus Consent, "That man must be beloved of God. He's too stupid, venal, and opinionated to survive otherwise."

Farfog had been vigorously obnoxious from the moment he entered the White City. Local Brothen Episcopals fed him names where they wanted plunder or vengeance.

IT WAS ONE OF THE MOST INTERESTING DAYS PIPER HECHT EVER ENJOYED. In the morning, while reviewing a force of two thousand moving west to add to pressure on the Khaurenesaine, he received word that his troops had engaged enemy mercenaries in a series of skirmishes and small battles and had overcome them in almost every instance. Numerous towns and fortresses had sent surrender offers as a result.

More good news arrived early in the afternoon. Count Raymone Garete seemed inclined toward reason, suddenly. Having been apprised of his cousin's situation. He was now willing to talk, though apparently unwilling to yield.

Immediately afterward came news that Sublime V had gone to his reward. Brothe had begun the month-long series of ceremonies and rituals that would end with a conclave to choose a successor. Hecht ordered the appropriate shows of mourning—but instructed his officers to avoid allowing their opponents any advantage from the news. "I want our men seen everywhere. In bigger groups. They're to hit back hard at any provocation. I won't let Castreresone fall apart now."

Yet it almost did.

Archbishop Farfog responded to the news from Brothe by surrendering to his obsessions.

First reports were confusing. No one was sure what was happening. Violence had erupted but was not directed at the soldiers. First guesses suggested factional fighting between the two strains of Chaldarean Episcopals. Hecht kept sending small bands to establish order. Each conflict extinguished seemed to spark two more somewhere else.

Consent came to report. "It's Farfog. Out to do all the damage he can before a new Patriarch shuts him down."

"He foresees a shift in the direction of the Church? Does he know something we don't?"

"Inside his idiot mind, maybe. In the real world? Who knows?"

"It'll be a month before we get a new Patriarch."

"Then we have a month, ourselves. Not so?"

Hecht grinned. Exactly! He had that long to write whatever future he might inscribe.

Madouc arrived. "Sir, you might want to go up on the wall. See if you're inclined to intercede in what the Society is doing."

The view from the wall was a horror show. "How many?" Hecht demanded.

A junior officer said, "Over three hundred, sir."

Hecht stared. Some wore the yellow tabards the Society forced on convicted heretics. But not many. He recognized men he had met since taking control of the city. Men who had been perfectly cooperative. Men who happened to have had money left after Castreresone paid its fines.

"Madouc. Take Starven's company and break that up."

"Sir? The Archbishop . . ."

"I'll deal with the Archbishop. Bring him."

MADOUC DID NOT SAVE ALL THE PRISONERS. THE FIRST SCORE WERE GIVEN to the flames before the soldiers arrived. The more fanatic Society members resisted. The soldiers showed unprecedented restraint. Hecht watched Madouc and several of his lifeguards—all Brotherhood of War, the Captain-General suspected—take Archbishop Farfog into custody.

The soldiers did not release the prisoners back into the wild. Some might well deserve execution. But not by Farfog's brigands.

Hecht returned to the keep to await his confrontation with the Church's hellhound.

Time passed.

More time passed.

"Somebody! It's getting late. Where the devil is that idiot Farfog? Why isn't he in here? He's had time to go bald. Titus! Where are you, Titus Consent?"

Consent did not materialize. Nor did Redfearn Bechter, nor Drago Prosek, nor any of the others whose presence around him could be taken for granted. Nervous, he pulled his weapons within reach.

Madouc the lifeguard did materialize. Eventually. Twenty minutes after he should have done. He was bleeding. He had suffered a dozen wounds. More than one might qualify as mortal. He was going on by willpower and the insane sense of duty of a Brotherhood warrior.

"Sir. We were ambushed. By local partisans. They killed the Society brothers. They were after the Archbishop. They cut him to pieces. They took his head with them."

"This isn't good, Madouc. The Society . . ." But the Society might not be around much longer. Nor the crusader army and its Captain-General.

The course of history hinged on the choice of Sublime V's successor.

The uprising in Castreresone lasted one evening and night and focused entirely on the Society for the Suppression of Sacrilege and Heresy.

In a whisper next morning the Captain-General confided to his spy chief, "I'm not going to miss any of those villains."

"But Morcant Farfog's murder . . ."

"Will cause a lot of trouble. How much depends on our next Patriarch."

HAGAN BROKKE RECLAIMED HIS HONOR IN A SERIES OF FIERCE LITTLE ENgagements that stripped Queen Isabeth and Duke Tormond of their mercenary strength. His light cavalry harassed Isabeth's Direcians continuously, deliberately targeting one knight or noble at a time. Because they were who they were, each death or capture would have a significant impact in Direcia.

The Queen of Navaya withdrew to the shadow of her brother's capital city.

FROM ELATION ABOUT EVENTS IN THE WEST PIPER HECHT FELL INTO A DEpression over news from the east. Count Raymone Garete had resumed his stubborn defiance, with a more punishing daily cost now that Bronte Doneto had gone.

Piper Hecht reviewed the whys and wherefores. What strange, small change had reanimated the Count's stubborn insolence?

"Those prisoners Brokke brought in," Titus Consent said. "Some got away, probably with help, while we were running in circles because of Farfog's murder."

Hecht scowled. He grumbled a question about who he needed to have stoned or drowned.

"That would be a waste of time and emotion. Focus on those who didn't get away. Bernardin Amberchelle, for example."

"Tell me."

"Count Raymone's cousin. The man we thought he wanted back when he showed willing to talk. But he's gone back to being stubborn while Amberchelle is still down in the prison pens."

"Uhm? What changed?"

"The old man and the girl who came with Amberchelle," Consent said. "I'd bet she's the fiancée we've heard about. An upcountry girl who stole Raymone's heart. Socia something. Who is supposedly chaperoned by the Grand Masterest of all Maysalean Perfect Masters."

"And that would be the grayhair." The Captain-General did not finish. "You exult over little triumphs while big defeats sneak up."

Patriarchal crusaders now owned the eastern half of the End of Connec—excepting only Antieux. They threatened Khaurene from three directions. Lesser forces, featuring impassioned Society brethren determined to see Archbishop Farfog's great vision fulfilled, had begun probing the Altai, discovering the incredible mountaintop fortresses of the Maysalean heretics. And snow choked much of the rural world, not only in the Connec but in Tramaine, Ormienden, Grolsach, Arnhand, and even much of Firaldia. The Grail Empire was blanketed. Artecipea saw heavy, temporarily incapacitating snows for the first time since antiquity. The war there dwindled into the doldrums of winter. As did wars all round the Mother Sea.

WHEREVER SNOW FELL THERE AROSE DREADFUL RUMORS OF KHAROULKE the Windwalker, the god before gods from the age before antiquity. Kharoulke the Windwalker, before whom the great modern Instrumentalities must quail. But Kharoulke needed deep snow, deep ice, before he could supplant the gentler Instrumentalities of the present. Kharoulke needed millennial cold before he could rise above the vague lost deities who had supplanted his kind—before being shoved aside by the powers of today. Those vague lost deities beloved of secret cults devoted to resurrecting the lost lord Instrumentalities of antiquity.

18. Interlude at Runjan in the Reigenwald

The Marquesa va Runjan's sister the Empress insisted that she take up her rights in that remote town in the heart of the Empire's wildest, most remote hill country. Helspeth could not refuse.

The fury of the Council Advisory, of the Imperial court, of the Church, and especially of Empress Katrin herself could be described only as beyond reason. Nobody told the Princess Apparent how she had rendered herself criminal by opening that sealed mountain pass.

Almost no one would speak to her, let alone explain. She was a pariah and it might be catching. She was a prisoner now, in all but name, confined to the crumbling hilltop tower overlooking Runjan. The village, in its prime, had produced barely enough turnips, cabbage, and grain to sustain itself, with a small charcoal-burning industry taking advantage of the surrounding forest. Runjan was no longer in its prime. The iron industry had shrunk since Hansel's death, there being less demand for weapons metal. If the smelters were closed there was little demand for charcoal.

The tower had not been occupied since the last lord of Runjan passed on, childless, leaving the fief to his beloved Hansel. Its shutters were gone or broken. The drop gate could not be closed. Someone had taken the chain. There was no resident staff.

Helspeth came with a party of eight. Two were cruel old women who hated her. They were determined to punish her. Nothing Helspeth did could ingratiate her. Not that she tried to win them over. She had to work to mask her loathing.

The rest of the party were all one family. Harmer Schmitt. His wife Greta. Their daughter Grunhilde and three sons: Hansel, Fulk, and Fritz. The boys were named for Harmer's favorite emperors, the girl for Greta's great-aunt. Grunhilde was sixteen. And not attractive. The boys were sixteen, fourteen, and nine. Hansel was Grunhilde's twin. Not identical, of course, but every bit as homely as his sister.

The Schmitts were quietly sympathetic toward the Princess Apparent but dared not show it. It was a flawed sympathy, anyway, based more in dislike of the harpies assigned to be Helspeth's warders: the Dowager Grafina Ilse-Janna fon Wistrcz, the harridan mother of the Graf fon Wistrcz, and Dame Karelina fon Tyre, spouse of the Grand Admiral. Neither woman ever liked Helspeth. Both hated her now. It was her fault they had to chaperone her here in her rustic hell. The women hated one another as well, and had done for fifty years. Both were petty and spiteful and had been chosen because they could be counted on to take it out on Helspeth.

Each had her own small household follow her. Just people enough to maintain her in reduced misery. The Schmitts were supposed to maintain Helspeth but often worked for her keepers instead. They put in long hours but failed to make the tower fit for human habitation. Then the heavy snows came. Never warm, never properly fed, Helspeth became gaunt, subject to fits of the shakes and prolonged periods of withdrawal.

She did not expect to see the coming spring.

She wrote letters to the Empress but they came out almost illegible. Not that there was any point to pleading. There was no one to carry the letters away. Even had she been able to get them past Tooth and Fang, as she thought of those horrid old women.

She had felt alone and been afraid in Plemenza. But in Plemenza she had had Algres Drear. She had no bodyguards here, nor any patient ear to bend. Captain Drear had been sent east, to a garrison ever threatened by pagan savages. The other Braunsknechts had been scattered elsewhere. And the girl who was the author of their distress still did not grasp what she had done to earn such draconian retribution.

FERRIS RENFROW ARRIVED DURING A SNOWSTORM. HE DID NOTHING TO conceal his horror. Saying little, he went out again. He returned with the entire population of Runjan. He started giving orders.

Dame Karelina challenged him. "This isn't any business of yours!"

Voice heavy with scorn. Though her own antecedents were questionable.

Renfrow stared into her eyes. She wavered, but only momentarily. She was the wife of the Grand Admiral.

Renfrow said, "Pick up a tool and help. Or go away. If you insist on being part of the problem you'll be corrected with the rest of the problem."

Dowager Grafina fon Wistrcz got hold of the Dame's arm and dragged her away. Still within earshot, Ilse-Janna snarled, "Don't cross Ferris Renfrow! Ever! No good comes to anyone who does that! No telling why he's here. But he will go away."

Renfrow said, "He'll go away. But he won't forget what he's seen."

The villagers got a blazing fire going. Greta Schmitt brought a blanket. She placed it around Helspeth's shoulders, settled the girl close to the fire.

Renfrow stalked around, tossing off orders. Villagers went to work improving and weatherproofing. A single hour's work provided a dramatic improvement.

"Schmitt. Show me the account books." He knew exactly where the harridans would be vulnerable.

Warmth penetrated Helspeth deeply enough for her shakes to subside into an intermittent problem. She surfaced in the present reality for moments at a time. She recognized Ferris Renfrow. And experienced a flood of joy and hope so profound that she plunged into unstoppable crying.

"Schmitt's woman. Stay close to the Princess."

Elsewhere, Dame fon Tyre tried to bully her own small household into evicting Ferris Renfrow from the tower. She refused to hear warnings from the Dowager Grafina. Her people did not. They knew the Renfrow reputation. That had been dark and deadly since long before the accession of Emperor Johannes.

The Grand Admiral's wife had lived fifty-eight sheltered years. She had known little but her own indulgences until Empress Katrin, in a moment of high pique, rid herself of an annoyance by ordering the woman to Runjan to babysit her sister. Making Runjan a cauldron of rustic exile.

In one day's time Renfrow's will made the ground floor of the tower over into what it should have become with Helspeth's arrival. Helspeth stopped shaking before the villagers went away. She regained her composure. Softly voiced, she told Renfrow, "Thank you."

"You're welcome, Princess. You are the heir of empire. What they were doing is unconscionable." He said no more. Helspeth began to understand how deep her danger had been. And might be once Renfrow went away again.

Renfrow told her, "You won't be comfortable, here. You can't be the Helspeth Ege you were before your brother died. But no one will try to make you die by natural causes anymore, either."

Helspeth lost control of her bladder.

Renfrow told her, "I promised your father."

She pulled the blanket around her again and stared into the flames, wanting to go away again. Hansel Schmitt brought more wood. He seemed obsequious. The way people do who want not to be noticed by someone held in high terror.

"Helspeth. Listen. You *must* pay attention. Your life could depend on you actually hearing me."

Greta Schmitt brought hot broth. Helspeth responded to the aroma with more enthusiasm than she did Ferris Renfrow's voice. Renfrow said, "I'll take some of that myself."

The Schmitt woman's lips tightened and lost color but she held Ferris Renfrow in no less high terror than did her son. When she brought the broth for Renfrow he slipped her a small purse. "Tell no one. Use it on the Princess's behalf. And keep a close account. You may keep a fourth for yourself." He looked her straight in the eye. "Tell no one. Not either of those hags. Not your husband. Not the Princess herself. Understand?"

Greta nodded.

In a voice barely audible, Helspeth told Renfrow, "I'm listening. Thank you. For coming."

"I repay my debts. And I do what serves the Empire. Letting the heir to the ermine be murdered by neglect is not in that interest."

Helspeth eased her grip on her blanket. The ache went out of her fingers almost immediately. The fire had begun to have an effect. At last.

"Listen closely. Your life will improve going forward. But you must not attract attention. Be pliant. Do as you're told. Offer no offense, however unreasonable the dons at Alten Weinberg become. Be your sister's strongest supporter, regardless of your private opinion. Her reign won't be one of the memorable ones. Unless she surrenders to the Council Advisory or she goes completely mad. Which could happen."

She murmured, "Greta put something in the broth."

"Are you listening?"

"I'm listening."

"Good. I'm hoping you've learned something. The lesson being that a princess's actions directly impact many other people."

Tears slid from the corners of Helspeth's eyes as Renfrow reviewed the current situation of her Braunsknecht lifeguards and Lady Hilda Daedal, whose husband had required her to go into a convent. "This doesn't make sense. I didn't do anything wrong."

"Why are you here, then?"

"But . . ."

"You knew you'd irritate people in Alten Weinberg. Admit it. You could've saved everyone misery by staying in Plemenza while your hired men dealt with the monster. They would've censured you for employing foreigners but you'd still be there. However, you wanted to tweak their noses. In fact, you scared hell out of powerful people who saw way too much Johannes Blackboots in Hansel's youngest daughter."

"I know, Ferris. I know. I've thought about that so much."

"On the good news side, you won't be marrying anytime soon. If that's a positive."

"I'm not going to get married, ever."

Renfrow smiled. "As may be. But one more reason you're in bad odor is, your adventure cheapened you as marriage bait. Every court in the Chaldarean world was interested. Your portrait was making a progression from capital to capital. You were quickening hearts. Then word went out that you'd gone off into the wilderness for a month with a band of common soldiers."

Helspeth sighed and drew her blanket around her tighter. Renfrow was getting excited. She had not recovered enough to handle the pressure.

He eased up. "There is a humorous side. One court remained interested. Jaime of Castauriga himself came all the way to Alten Weinberg to meet you personally. Castauriga being under heavy pressure from Navaya, he's in desperate need of allies. When he presented himself to Katrin it was, for her, love at first sight. Despite the age difference."

Helspeth's brain began to move again. "And he wouldn't mind being the consort of the Empress of the Grail Empire."

"Especially after she has a few children."

"When will they marry?"

"Springtime. Ironically, after the Remayne Pass opens."

Helspeth sighed. "Have the crones heard?"

"They'll be told. The news will ease your situation. And the wedding should mark the end of your exile. Unless you do something else to frighten the councilors."

"I still don't understand all that."

"Certain people have elevated themselves dramatically by orbiting your sister closely, Princess. Most of them Brothen Episcopals. They know the majority inside the Empire are strongly indisposed toward the Brothen Patriarchy. When you show the initiative you did, even bringing in specialist operators, you remind them that you're Johannes's daughter. The Princess Apparent who could step in and change their world."

Helspeth began to get a glimmer. "But I'm not interested in any of that." She made a soft, squeaky noise as the Captain-General popped into mind.

"Yes?"

"Just a random thought. It startled me."

"I see. Tell me. Have you heard anything I've been saying?"

"Yes." Sigh.

"Katrin's marriage isn't set in stone. Negotiations are still going on. Jaime is making demands that no one on our end will meet."

"So I'm not off the hook?"

"Not till Katrin gives birth to a male heir who survives long enough to have sons of his own."

"God help me."

"As I said, it should get easier once I speak to your keepers. Then easier still after Katrin weds. That should end your rustication. Behave and you could be back in Plemenza before winter comes round again. In Alten Weinberg at the least."

Sadly, feeling shame, she asked, "And my Braunsknechts?"

"There'll be no pardon for them. They failed their trust."

Helspeth did not meet Renfrow's gaze. But at that moment she decided to rescue Algres Drear and the others. They did not deserve such cruel punishment for having been browbeaten into compliance by the daughter of the Ferocious Little Hans.

She awarded herself a small sneer. She was in a spot so weak she could not save herself. Her one hope was this mysterious Renfrow, who dashed around shoring up the creaking foundations of the Empire.

"Someday . . ."

"Yes?"

"Someday I'd like to find out who you really are."

Renfrow was startled. Then he smiled. "Your father said the same thing, once."

"And did he?"

"Sadly, Fate caught up first. Quiet. Listen. I've cautioned you. I've cautioned you again. I've changed your situation to one you can survive. If you think before you talk or act. If you avoid being your father's daughter."

"I get it, sir!"

"I hope. I sincerely hope. I have my doubts. Blood will out. I won't be here in the morning. I have to go to Brothe. *Please* take care."

"Why doesn't anybody . . . ? Why do you keep saying the same thing over and over?"

"Experience. It takes immense perseverance to get an idea through an Ege skull."

"But I . . ."

"You aren't who or what *you* think you are, Princess. You're what the world thinks you are. Your great task is to convince the world you are what it wants you to be. You have to be a chameleon. A timid, retiring chameleon. In the eyes of your enemies."

"Enemies? But . . ."

"You see? Not listening. Again."

A sharp pain of the soul. No one cared what she thought. She was a piece on a chessboard. Truly, she would have to wear masks to avoid sacrifice to the advantage of the Queen.

"I just grasped the full message, Ferris. Thank you."

"Excellent. When next we meet, then, it should be in better circumstances. Drink some more broth. Rest. The Schmitts will put you on a better diet tomorrow."

Helspeth wanted to ask something else. The question sort of slid out of her mind sideways. Renfrow shimmered.

She did not recall her dreams. They felt portentous. The Captain-General was there. Katrin was there. So were scores more, known and unknown, in a time of great stress.

She wakened feeling better than she had in months.

Ferris Renfrow was gone. He left the tower refurbished in plant and attitude. Helspeth had no more trouble with Tooth or Fang. She became perfectly pliant in turn.

19. Khaurene, in the Time of Bleakest Despair

Brother Candle and Socia Rault clung close for warmth. Also in the cluster were Michael Carhart, Hanak el-Mira, and Bishop Clayto. Above them were two ragged blankets taken from a dead man found alongside the road. No one knew which side he had served. No one cared.

The clump of misery huddled inside a stand of brush. The blankets had accumulated enough snow to conceal their color and keep body heat confined.

Though miserable and hungry, no one wanted to risk the road. There was a lot of traffic headed west. Ducking into hiding would leave tracks in the snow.

Brother Candle wondered if escape had been smart. Their captors had shown no inclination to abuse them, nor any to turn them over to the Society. They had been warm and fed regularly. Of course, their captors had recognized Bernardin Amberchelle. It would not have taken long for reason to lead them to Socia's identity.

There was a search on, prosecuted with minimal enthusiasm. It was cold out. Why be out in it when nobody really knew what they were hunting? Refugees? Those were everywhere, many young women trying to get somewhere safe from God's laborers. Many were Maysaleans desperate to escape territories where failure to acknowledge Brothe's primacy might become a capital crime.

Socia murmured, "We need to reach friendly territory before they realize who I was. There'll be a reward, then."

Brother Candle nodded, careful not to disturb the blankets. "But Patriarchals aren't the only danger. Duke Tormond's defeated mercenaries are out there, too."

Bishop Clayto muttered, "We have to move. This flesh is too infirm to withstand this for long." He was shaking. He could not stop. Fear, malnutrition, and cold all contributed.

El-Mira whispered, "Get a grip, Clayto. Brother Candle has a decade on you."

"He's used to this. I'm a bishop." Clayto snickered, still able to joke at his own expense.

THE WEATHER NEVER COOPERATED. ON THE OTHER HAND, THE NIGHT AND Patriarchal patrols proved harmless. Michael Carhart, el-Mira, and Clayto all claimed their success reflected the favor of their gods. Claimed without sharp conviction.

Like Brother Candle, they feared good fortune might be by the grace of Instrumentalities associated with the Adversary. Hard not to suspect special favor when Patriarchals were running wild during the interregnum in Brothe.

IT TOOK SIXTEEN DAYS TO REACH KHAURENE, A DISTANCE OF LESS THAN eighty crow-flight miles. That sixteenth dawn saw them still fifteen miles from the city itself. They fell in with a strong patrol led by Sir Eardale Dunn. Dunn put them onto borrowed cogs and hurried them westward. They could help steel the will of their respective religious communities.

Brother Candle clung desperately to his mount. He was no skilled rider. But he did have attention left for his surroundings. And did not like what he saw.

He saw devastation. The Patriarchals had decided to destroy the regional economy. But he was more troubled by what looked like preparations for a showdown battle. By his own side.

"You don't think that's a good idea?" Socia asked.

"I think it's insane. Any Connecten army will be a rabble with little prospect of success. Unless they outnumber the enemy badly. Or catch him unawares. Can our people manage that?"

"I think if Raymone Garete was in charge . . ."

"Yes. If Count Raymone was in charge the rivers would run red. The revenants would feast. And the Connec would become a desert. Because Count Raymone would burn it barren before he let it fall into the hands of Brothen invaders."

Socia had no problem with that, he knew. She would joyfully scour the earth to destroy her enemies.

What a horror it would be once she took her place in the shadows behind Count Raymone.

SIR EARDALE DID NOT LEAD BROTHER CANDLE UP TO METRELIEUX. "TOR-mond doesn't want to see you, Brother. He's made up his mind at last and doesn't want you whispering counterarguments in his ear."

The Perfect was surprised by the hurt he felt. Those few words declared a ripened disdain for the voice of reason. Henceforth, Duke Tormond IV would wear blinders.

"You blame me . . . ?"

Wrong approach.

"Not personally. Your faith. Two generations of passivity and pacifism . . . Decades of weak leadership . . . We have invaders among us by the tens of thousands. And haven't the skills or backbone to do what needs doing. Because we've been bedazzled by the Maysalean Heresy. Or whatever you want to call it."

"I suspect centuries of peace and prosperity have more to do with it." Brother Candle was startled by the strength of his emotions. He *had* to put the world aside and find his way back to the Path. He drifted farther from it by the minute.

The streets of Khaurene were crowded with Seekers from farther east. Some would go on to the strongholds in the Altai or to coastal provinces now under the protection of King Peter. Or even into Direcia itself. Peter welcomed Seekers. Most were tradesmen with useful skills.

They were welcome in Praman Platadura, too.

Tannery stench seemed thicker than ever, down where Raulet Archimbault lived. Socia observed, "I sure missed a lot, growing up in the country."

"Do I detect a note of sarcasm?"

"Each city we run to is bigger than the last. And is more crowded and smells worse."

"You'll like the Archimbaults." He hoped. But sparingly. Socia Rault remained deeply conscious of class and station. "If you don't, keep your mouth shut." She had had the chance to move into Metrelieux and had refused.

The streets were particularly crowded in this neighborhood, where local Seekers welcomed countless refugees into their homes.

Raulet's daughter Kedle answered Brother Candle's knock. He said, "Wow! That didn't take long." The girl was prominently pregnant.

"It can be difficult, trying to ignore the demands of the flesh." Kedle did not sound interested in denying the flesh. Nor was she pleased to find the Perfect on the family doorstep.

"You're not at work?"

"My work is here while this is going on." She patted her stomach. "The fumes at the tannery. Not good for the unborn. We don't have room here, Master. Soames and I have to live here. Because his father's brother's family are staying with them. See Scarre the Baker. His sons have gone to be soldiers."

Kedle stared at Socia but was too polite to ask.

"As you wish. Tell your father that I came by. He can trace me through Scarre's bakery."

Kedle donned a scowl worthy of the most guilt-ridden Episcopal or Devedian. Brother Candle turned away, pleased and shamed at having left the girl feeling bad about turning him away.

Socia asked, "What was that all about?"

"I've known Kedle since she was born. It's taken her longer than most young people, but she's in her rebellious stage."

"She's pregnant."

"Very. She was getting married last time I was here."

"She's younger than me."

"True. By several years."

"I thought you Seekers put sex aside."

"We Seekers?" The Raults were Seekers themselves. "Some manage. Once they get old."

"Weird. Where are we going?"

"Kedle is still too young. We're going to Scarre the Baker's."

Socia changed topic. "I don't believe in any of that stuff. Only in things that can bite me."

"The countryside is swarming with Instrumentalities wearing really big teeth."

Their little band had spent more time shivering in fear of the Night than from the cold during their flight. Out there, in the country, revenant Night prowled everywhere. And sometimes left pale, drained bodies alongside the roads.

Another reason for crowding in Khaurene.

Darkness was gathering as they entered Scarre's bakery. Scarre worked in a ferocious heat, sweat rolling off him as he scooped fresh loaves out of his huge oven. He was naked to the waist, like a blacksmith. His wife, wearing padded gloves, stacked the hot loaves. Scarre grunted a greeting.

Brother Candle observed, "There must be a huge demand for bread."

"You looking for a job? I can't keep up. I need somebody to work the dough."

"Not looking for work but we'll work for bed and board while we're here."

"Absolutely. But why aren't you staying with Raulet? You staying with him makes him feel like the big . . . Sorry. We're supposed to be beyond petty competitions."

"Kedle says there is no room there."

"Marriage hasn't agreed with that girl. She should've waited. Raulet should've waited. In one year she's gone from wide-eyed child of wonder to complete harpy. Raulet fears for her soul."

"I see. We can address that in our evening meetings. What is it?"

"We don't have many meetings, Brother. Society spies are everywhere. They keep records for after they take control."

"Once upon a time Seekers had the courage to stand behind their beliefs."

"Once upon a time they didn't used to burn us."

"They don't do that much, now. More members of the Society get killed, one way or another, than Seekers do."

Scarre shrugged. Plainly uninterested in the tribulations of Brothen Episcopals. "If you stay with me I'm going to expect some help. The girl can do the household cooking while you work in here."

Brother Candle chuckled. "I don't think so, Scarre. Not if you want to avoid being poisoned. She can help in here. Like an apprentice. Only, you'll have to keep your hands to yourself."

Scarre bobbed his head, getting the message.

Socia did not like being discussed. But the world outside Caron ande Lette had hammered her long enough to teach her to manage emotion. For minutes at a time.

"Long as she earns her keep."

"She will. She's a good woman. She just needs to be shown what to do."

Madam Scarre was not convinced.

SCARRE WAS NOT THE BEST HOST. HE WORKED HIS GUESTS HARD. WHICH explained why no refugees stayed with him. Most Maysalean households had a refugee family squeezed in. Brother Candle and Socia were exhausted when they joined the Archimbaults for their late meal.

Socia had complained just once. Brother Candle offered, "I'll take you up to the castle."

"No."

"No bread kneading. No Madam Scarre barking at you for being young and attractive."

"That woman is mad. Has she actually looked at him? All sweaty and covered with hair, like a bear? And fat? But I won't go up there. They'd use me to manipulate Raymone."

She had a point.

Which sparked a fresh worry.

The Society was strong in Khaurene. Those fanatics would have no reservations about using the girl as a weapon. And Raymone had shown weak that way already.

Brother Candle said little during supper, except to answer Kedle's questions about his adventures. Afterward, the leaders of the Seeker community began to arrive. Brother Candle found himself a place out of the light. He wanted to catch up. There had been changes. Despair and pessimism ruled.

Spiritual issues never arose. That was the most dramatic change.

Talk was iron-hard practical. Should the Seeker community emigrate now, before Patriarchal forces made escape impossible? Heading into winter, fleeing to fastnesses in the Altai that might not be adequately provisioned? Should they stay and hope that Patriarchal politics and Duke Tormond's stiffened backbone would make it possible to get through the winter here?

Brother Candle heard nothing to inspire faith in the Duke's steadfast determination to defy the invaders. Nor anything positive about the probable results. And little confidence in the friendship of Peter of Navaya.

"Peter needs the Brothen Church behind him to pursue his ambitions in Direcia," someone insisted when someone else suggested that Peter might send an army to enforce his rights in Castreresone.

Another someone said, "Peter can't turn his back on the princes of al-Halambra. And he has troops committed in Artecipea."

"Nothing will happen anywhere while there's no Patriarch in Brothe."

"The Captain-General isn't sitting on his hands."

"Duke Tormond will make all these worries moot."

"Excuse me," Brother Candle said. Silence fell. "These discussions remain speculative only until after the battle."

A puzzled Raulet Archimbault asked, "What battle, Master?"

"Sir Eardale Dunn is trying to engineer a decisive confrontation. Which, I think, the Patriarchals would rather avoid. They've done well with a pinprick strategy. But there *will* be a battle. And the passion of the Khaurenese won't be enough. My advice? Be ready to travel but wait on the result of the fight. If Sir Eardale is successful, there's no need to suffer winter in the mountains. If it's defeat, the Patriarchals will need time to pull themselves together and move against the city. That would be time enough to go."

A spirited discussion followed, a dozen people talking at once, all arguing with one another but all agreeing with Brother Candle. Though a few still heard the siren call of the Altai.

Brother Candle said, "I have carried the message through the Altai on occasion. I spent a winter there once. Not up in one of those drafty old ridgeline strongholds but down in a valley where the people know how to handle the weather. And it was still curdled misery."

More discussion. All the men had spent time in the Altai last summer, readying strongholds for the day when the failure of the weak Connecten state left Seekers at the mercy of a merciless, rapacious Brothen Episcopal Church. They were not ignorant of the harshness of the mountains. It was that harshness they had embraced when they chose the Altai as their final refuge.

"SO THAT WAS DEMOCRACY IN ACTION," SOCIA SAID AS SHE AND BROTHER Candle walked back to Scarre the Baker's.

"It was, yes."

"I see why it's an uncommon way of making decisions."

"Some would say that the fact that nothing gets done is the strength of the process. People get too busy arguing to go make trouble."

The girl expressed her opinion with a contemptuous snort.

DAY AFTER DAY THE MEN OF KHAURENE MARCHED OUT OF THE CITY. EVEN-tually, the streets seemed naked. Those who stayed behind remained in their homes, praying, suffering from escalating tension.

Brother Candle felt more tension than ever he had before. Duke Tormond had decided to do something. At last. And no one cared if it was the right thing. An entire country exulted because it was *something*.

He did not go out where he could hear rumors and misinformation from the field. He could imagine it. Inept bands of poorly trained men, under inexperienced captains, would rush around trying to catch enemy scouts and foragers and would get beat up in the process. Skirmishes between larger units would carpet the fields east of Khaurene with fallen heroes. The truth would not be seen because the little disasters would be scattered. At some point, the Khaurenese mob would force the

Captain-General to choose between withdrawal and showing Khaurene the truth about warfare.

Brother Candle was not without hope. Isabeth's knights could provide experienced leadership. The Connectens would enjoy a big advantage in heavy cavalry. Plus, Tormond had reenlisted thousands of mercenaries and had found knights willing to serve for pay. Numbers would not favor the Patriarchals.

SOCIA WAS DISTRACTED. SHE COULD NOT DO THE WORK SCARRE DEMANDED. Fortunately, there was less call for Scarre's product. But he anticipated a spike in demand when the hungry soldiers returned.

Brother Candle worked dough and roamed his memories, revisiting a thousand regrets. When the time came he knew there had been a battle before anyone brought the news. And he knew that it had not gone well. "Socia. Time to go. Get your things."

The streets were no longer empty. Everyone seemed to be pressing to the northeast, desperate to learn the fates of those they held dear. Wailing and panic were endemic. If the disaster was a tenth of what rumor claimed, Khaurene would never recover.

Those coming in now were men who ran before the fighting started. They had to tell stories that made their cowardice appear less foul. Rumor fed off that.

Though Brother Candle had spoken to no one but Socia he found himself at the head of a column of Seekers including all the regulars from the Archimbault meetings. The Archimbaults brought Kedle. They were not open to arguments about leaving her behind. In just days they had become convinced that Khaurene was doomed and the Society, backed by the Patriarchal army, would purge the city of heretics, Unbelievers, and adherents of the Viscesment Patriarchy.

Brother Candle told himself he was worried about the pregnant woman's welfare, not the chance that she would slow the party's flight. Told himself and wondered.

Fear stalked him. Gnawing, rationality-devouring fear. Partly because of his fall from Perfection. But just as much because of the presence of things of the Night.

They were always there, now. Always just round the corner, or just out of sight over the shoulder. For some, that was no problem. Those of a deeply superstitious nature lived in that reality always. But for those who wanted to live in a rational, orderly universe the waxing influence of the Night was an aggressive spiritual slime mold gnawing the mortar from between the foundation stones of existence.

Kedle's husband did not join the exodus. Soames was one of those excited thousands who had marched out confident that righteousness must prevail. Without being eager to go. He had gone because it was expected.

Kedle was sure she would not see him again. That if only one Khaurenese fell out there, that one would be her Soames.

Brother Candle told Socia, "Here's your chance to be a big sister. Help the girl handle this."

Raulet Archimbault's attitude was as bright as his daughter's was bleak. "The boy will catch up. He'll be fine. He knows the evacuation plan. Hell, he may get there before we do."

Getting there was an exercise in profound misery. More so than the flight from Patriarchal captivity. Though enemy patrols were fewer, the risk of butchery at their hands had worsened. The Khaurenesaine would suffer terribly for its defiance.

The band of Seekers was large enough to defend itself from brigands and small troops of Patriarchals. And had to several times. A third of the company perished on the road. Night things tracked them all the way, first to Albodiges beside frozen Lake Trauen, then onward along the precipitous trail up the Reindau Spine to the fortifications called Corpseour.

News overtaking the band was disheartening. Connectens in general had plunged to the bleakest, most hopeless deeps of despair.

Kedle's baby came early, while they were on the road. It was not an easy birth. The women feared she would not survive the bleeding. There was a worse fear among the men.

The birth drew the Night like a corpse draws flies. Even the learned, like Brother Candle, could not fathom why. He suspected, though, that it was just curiosity about intense pain and emotion.

The baby, named Raulet after his grandfather, was healthy enough. And arrived without birthmarks, a caul, deformities, teeth already developed, or other evil portent. To the great relief of the travelers.

CORPSEOUR HAD BEEN BUILT ALONG A KNIFE EDGE OF A RIDGE. NEAR VERtical drops fell away to both sides. The path up from Albodiges was the only approach. That was watched over by outworks capable of laying down heavy missile fires. Corpseour had existed as an ultimate refuge since before man learned to write. It had been used a hundred times across the ages, though not since the disorders following the collapse of the Old Empire. Maysaleans had been refurbishing the fortifications for some time. Defenses had been improved. Stores had been laid in. Most of all, cisterns had been deepened and expanded. Each time an Altaian stronghold had fallen in the past, the cause had been thirst or treachery. Little could be done to prevent treachery. That last tiny seed of lust, greed, or terror hidden deep inside a man's secret self, that made him willing to betray, just could not be known till it quickened. It might exist in every soul, awaiting the right conditions to sprout.

The overarching strategy of the Seekers was to outlast their enemies. Sublime V had passed away. Without a Patriarch of his obsession driving a Connecten Crusade the wider interest should fade. Arnhand and Santerin were preoccupied with one another. Santerin had the upper hand. Charlve the Dim was said to be in the early stages of dementia. Meaning there should be little threat from the north.

The Patriarchal Office for the Suppression of Sacrilege and Heresy ought to wither and die, too. It had no backers amongst the leading candidates for succession.

Cold and miserable as he might be, Brother Candle thought hope might return with the distant but inevitable spring.

PRACTICING HIS SECONDARY PROFESSION OF WATCHER ATOP THE WALL, Brother Candle stood in the highest lookout of Corpseour and surveyed his harsh new world. Mist filled the valley to the east. Snow clouds concealed everything beyond. That direction showed nothing but unreadable gray. Visibility was little better to the west. What was not covered by snow was weathered gray stone or scattered, weary green vegetation. A couple of villages lay partially obscured by wood smoke not moving because the air was deadly still.

Socia joined him. The girl looked tired and older than her years. Incessant dejection had ground her down. "What are you looking at?" There had been nothing different to see since they arrived. Just a little more snow every day.

"The future."

"Pardon?"

"All our tomorrows look like that."

"You do need to go off to one of your Masters' secret places for a spell."

"Want to know a secret, Socia? There are no secret places. Unless you count hideaways like this. They exist only in the imaginations of those who fear the Path."

"There's somebody down there."

Specks of humanity marked the trail. Maybe more refugees. Maybe someone bringing news. Maybe just the men who made the climb each day to clear the trail of ice and to bring yet more water up to the cisterns.

"There's still spring," the old man said. "A new year always holds promise."

There was the hardest part, these days. Encouraging others when he had so little optimism left himself.

20. Artecipea: The Unanticipated Crusade

The Captain-General was reviewing inventory lists and payrolls. Scut work was the biggest part of his job. "How the hell do one hundred fifty-eight crossbowmen use up eight barrels of bolts in one engagement?"

"They kill a lot of people," Titus Consent replied. Sounding mildly amused.

He was, Hecht knew. Consent thought he was becoming a miser.

"Sure. But you'd think they'd get more of the bolts back after the dust settled."

"They probably missed twenty times for every hit. Those bolts aren't going to be recovered. Unless you put a couple thousand men out to glean the battlefield."

"Phooey. I'll make the Khaurenese buy me fifty new barrels when we take the city."

Consent smiled without being amused. It was an open secret: The Connecten Crusade had run its course. Whoever got elected, the new Patriarch would discontinue the war against heresy.

Reports had the balloting deadlocked. None of the Five Families could muster even a significant minority backing for their Principaté. All they could agree on was unity against the non-Brothen candidates. Neither the Brotherhood of War nor the Society had backed a candidate yet.

Principaté Delari had garnered the second biggest plurality in the initial poll, to his complete consternation. Hugo Mongoz was the front-runner, a compromise candidate who could be counted on to die soon. An interim figurehead to fill a role while the Collegium worked out a real succession. The Five Families could stomach Hugo Mongoz for a year or two.

"Messenger from Antieux," one of Hecht's lifeguards announced.

"No doubt Ghort whining for more money. Send him in."

A road-weary, dirty, damp courier entered, accompanied by Redfearn Bechter. The room was the warmest in the fortress, Camden ande Gledes, which stood a scant twenty miles from Khaurene. It commanded both old roads from the east.

Bechter presented a one-sheet estimate of the damage suffered by the Khaurenese and their allies. The fallen numbered more than fifteen thousand. Thousands more had been captured. The fools had fielded an army with no centralized command. Hecht had given them no chance to overcome that disadvantage.

"Good, with the Navayans. Some important catches there."

Bechter nodded. Hecht turned to the courier. "Yes?" The man behind the mud was one of Ghort's most trusted.

"The Colonel wants you to know he's been recalled. The City Regiment has been ordered back to Brothe. Never mind that they're in pay. The orders came from the city senate but were signed by Bronte Doneto. Colonel Ghort says the senators are scared there'll be major disorders after the election."

Hecht surveyed his staff, saw raised eyebrows. "Does that mean they expect another foreign Patriarch?"

"Colonel Ghort said, 'When he asks if they're going to pick a non-Brothen, tell him the guy in Viscesment, Bellicose or whatever, is running a strong fourth. And he's excommunicate.'"

"I see." Hecht reflected. "How soon will he move?"

"He's already started. The orders gave him no wiggle room."

Doneto knew Ghort.

"Do the people inside Antieux know?"

"Of course."

"Any idea how much longer the election could take?"

"Maybe ages. There isn't much bribe money floating around. Extra funds got burned up financing the Calziran Crusade."

"Get some hot food and some rest. I'll have something for you to take back when you go."

Bechter led the courier out. Hecht asked the air, "What does this mean to us?"

Consent said, "You'll have to reinforce Sedlakova. Leaving us too thin here."

True. Losses had not been great and desertions refreshingly few but, still, there had been a sizable turnover. Hecht had little reason to trust the locals and defeated mercenaries who wanted to join up.

Consent said, "We have to decide what we want to get done before a new Patriarch comes in. Everything will change once he does. He won't share Sublime's obsessions. He may fire us all to save money so he can afford to commission monuments to himself."

That was the future Hecht feared and expected. Few in the Collegium shared Sublime's obsession with eradicating heresy and recapturing the Holy Lands.

Hecht said, "We've been on borrowed time since Sublime died. Being aggressive hasn't gained us much. Sure. A bloody triumph. Heroic in proportion. It'll be talked about for years. But it wasn't decisive. It just taught the Khaurenese to stay inside their walls. Send somebody over there tomorrow. Demand a huge fine and a commitment to root out the heretics. What we've been asking for all along. Tell them they have no time to talk about it. Start pulling in the patrols, foragers, and raiders, so it looks like we're going to attack. Let it out that we have Society friends inside waiting to help us."

"Your point being?"

"Maybe they'll bite. Maybe they'll bribe us to go away. But once we have everyone together we'll move back to Castreresone."

DUKE TORMOND DID NOT SURRENDER. DID NOT OFFER TO ACCEPT TERMS, despite Khaurene's suffering. The Captain-General was not surprised. Even the hotheads over there should see that their best course would be Duke Tormond's traditional strategy. Just sit and wait.

The Patriarchal army had exceeded the easy reach of its logistical support, in country desolated by fighting, in the midst of the worst winter the Connec had ever known. It lacked the backing of a distant, obsessed Patriarch. Its commanders were not driven by fanaticism, which was not lost on the snoops and note takers of the Society.

Khaurene had only one worry. Treachery.

Plots failed regularly. The plotters were, usually, outsiders who had entered Khaurene to escape the Patriarchals. So they claimed.

THE CAPTAIN-GENERAL FADED QUIETLY, TAKING VALUABLES BUT DOING NO great damage to homes or fortresses or public works.

Madouc asked, "You want something to happen to that asshole?"

He meant a Society bishop who had just left, after raging at the Captain-General for not furthering the Society's agenda.

"Not at all. I just turned it all over to him. He can do whatever he wants, any way he wants, now. I won't interfere."

"You figure he'll get shit on. Right?"

"The Connectens are a patient, long-suffering people. But they've passed the point where they'll tolerate him and his kind."

"Good. Those crows need a lesson in humiliation."

"You had a reason for seeing me?"

"I need to put more men around you and keep them closer."

"Please! I've already got men unlacing my trousers for me when I need to use the latrine. Why?"

"The last courier brought a letter from your uncle. He told me to be especially vigilant for the next two months. There will be a serious effort to destroy you."

"My uncle?"

"The author said. Lord Silent? Or is someone playing tricks?"

"Possibly. I'm never sure how to take him. He's actually more like a great-grand-uncle. If he says be more alert, though, we have to pay attention. Like it or not."

"I didn't know you had any family, sir." A hint of suspicion, there.

"I don't. In a blood sense. Lord Silent is a distant, secretive relative of Principaté Delari. He's part of that family's adoption of me."

"One must confess a certain curiosity about that."

"One must, mustn't one? I don't get it, myself. I think somebody saw something in a chicken's entrails."

HECHT HAD JUST SUNK INTO SLEEP, IN HIS DOWN BED IN THE KEEP OF THE Counts of Castreresone, first night back. Titus Consent burst in, accompanied by four of Madouc's lifeguards.

"What the hell? It can't wait till morning?"

"I don't think. The populace may have heard by then. It could cause trouble."

"All right. Let's have it."

"We have a new Patriarch. Pacificus Sublime."

"Huh?"

"I don't know why he chose that reign name. He used to be the Fiducian, Joceran Cuito."

"A front-runner before Sublime died but not a name we've heard much since. What happened?"

"King Peter showed up. And spread a lot of money around."

"The Five Families are fit to be tied, I'm sure."

"I don't know about that. There wasn't much more to the message. But this could mean trouble here. Castreresone belongs to King Peter."

Hecht avoided the obvious counterargument. "Put patrols out. Tell them not to start anything but to be ruthless if they're provoked."

"Letting that word out should do wonders."

Hecht treated everyone fairly, by his lights. But he was not merciful toward those who defied him. The Castreresonese would understand.

"Can I get some sleep, now?"

THERE WAS A DEFINITE CHANGE IN THE WHITE CITY. ANTICIPATION FILLED the air. Positively, not as a premonition or foreboding. The Castreresonese were willing to bide their time.

The officially sealed message wallet from the Patriarch arrived nine days later. His staff assembled while he reviewed the messages. "Nothing unexpected here. A formal announcement that the Connecten Crusade is over. A list of Connectens who are being restored to the bosom of the Church. Including Duke Tormond and Count Raymone Garete. The siege of Antieux is to be abandoned. Castreresone should be turned over to agents of its rightful master, who are on their way. We are to withdraw down the Laur and assemble at Sheavenalle for transport."

Redfearn Bechter said, "That makes no sense. Why wouldn't he just tell us we're fired? Just leave us where we are?"

"We aren't fired. Obviously. Maybe we're needed in Brothe. People there won't be happy having a Direcian Patriarch. It would be Ornis of Cedelete all over again."

There was more to the letters but little of immediate import. Hecht told the staff to make ready for movement. To finish getting ready. The order to abandon Castreresone was no surprise.

Titus Consent was last to leave. He observed, "Have you noticed who the big winner was in this crusade?"

"Navaya? King Peter?"

"Exactly. At small cost he's become the power in the Connec. He's been using his gains in the last crusade to take over Artecipea. Now he owns the Patriarchy. He's letting other people build him an empire."

"Clever."

INASMUCH AS THERE HAD BEEN NO PATRIARCHAL INSTRUCTION OTHERWISE, Hecht left a garrison in Castreresone's keep. They would guarantee access if he decided to come back. They would keep order. They received instructions not to resist Duke Tormond or Queen Isabeth.

BUHLE SMOLENS PREPARED QUARTERS. DESPITE LOSSES, DESERTIONS, AND the absence of the City Regiment the army numbered more than ten thousand. There were no forty-day men attached, either. The last of those had gone before the weather turned really ghastly. Hecht had won outside Khaurene with a third of the numbers he had had when crossing the Dechear, westbound.

Hecht assembled his senior officers and staffers.

"I wanted to thank everyone. We did well. Probably too well. The new people are afraid of us. Which leaves me suspicious of their gathering us here. They're up to something."

Sedlakova stood. His handicap lent no strength to his argument as he made an impassioned appeal for men of faith to enter the Brotherhood of War.

Hecht stopped listening. The others all talked about what they might do with their lives, now. The Connecten Crusade was over. Nothing had been concluded. They were not distraught, though. That was not a new experience. Castles and cities fell. Death and misery walked the earth. Little changed in the broader picture.

He sank into a reverie about Anna Mozilla and the children. Thoughts of home had had a powerful impact on him these past few months. Never had he been drawn that way back when he was Else Tage.

He had developed new dimensions here in the west.

*   *   *

EVERYONE WAS DISTRACTED BY CONCERNS ABOUT TOMORROW, FORGETTING that today still harbored dangers more deadly than the nuisance perils lately offered by the Night.

Hecht and some staff went to the harbor to watch the ships come in. Peter of Navaya's ships, mainly fat traders flying the banners of Platadura. A few lean triremes boasting Navayan colors larked around the flanks of the convoy. Hecht studied those ships and wished Pinkus Ghort was handy so they could brood over shared suspicions. He noted that several older, more weary-looking ships flew Sonsan standards and resembled vessels he had seen falling into ruin along the wharves of that city.

Shrieking birds wheeled and dove where the ships churned up the water. Though it was winter, the harbor reek was thick. The chill had reduced the insect population to a tolerable level.

Clej Sedlakova, seated on a cask, said, "Them tubs is riding high in the water. They must figure on really loading them down." Sedlakova was in a permanent foul temper lately. He was sure that, given just a few more weeks, maybe just a few more days, he could have reduced Antieux. Even absent Bronte Doneto and the City Regiment. People inside the city had begun to put out feelers, looking for rewards.

"Put Antieux behind you," Hecht told him. "We get paid the same sitting here as we do risking our behinds in the field."

Colonel Smolens said, "It isn't the risking that bothers me. It's the freezing and starving."

Sedlakova said, "Listen to that shit. What's he had going, this whole war? Hanging out in Viscesment. Then hanging out here. Check him out. He's gained fifteen pounds."

Smolens said, "I confess. The food is good. I'll miss it."

Hecht said, "You may not have to leave."

"What? What's this?"

"I haven't heard anything about us giving up Sheavenalle. If King Peter is running the new Patriarch, you can bet he won't give up control of a city this important. My guess is, they'll try to make it over into a free city, like Sonsa or Platadura. Allied to Navaya."

"What was that?"

"What was what?"

"Sounded like a giant bumblebee."

Twenty yards out on the mucky bay gulls dove to examine a small splash.

Madouc, always close by, still moving gingerly because of his wounds, said, "That was no bumblebee, sirs." Then he howled, flung back against Hecht, clawing at a crossbow bolt that had penetrated the left shoulder of his leather body armor.

Another bumblebee struck the cask that served Sedlakova as his throne. Sedlakova had vanished. Most everyone had. Madouc was down and trying to drag Hecht along.

Hecht refused to be dragged.

He headed for the source of the bolts. Not thinking, just reacting. With controlled anger. Grabbing half a broken oak stave abandoned by some dock walloper. The wood was old. Probably older than he was, Hecht thought, having one of those irrelevant thoughts that surface in times of stress, when everything seems to be happening in slowed motion.

People yelled behind him, telling him to get his dumb ass down.

Someone else yelled out front, right where the assassins ought to be. He jerked to the right. A bumblebee hummed on by, headed for the harbor.

He burst into a crowd of snipers. Two were desperately spanning crossbows. The third abandoned his weapon and took off. Which made no sense to Hecht.

He clubbed the first man he came to.

The second stopped wrestling his crossbow. He produced a short sword, then a dagger in his off hand.

Hecht drew his own blade. But kept the broken stave in his right hand.

He hit the man who was down several times so he would not help his associate.

Help arrived. "There's one more, headed that way. Dressed the same." He dropped onto a small bale of cotton that must have been smuggled out of Dreanger. Distracted by irrelevant thoughts again, he stared at his broken stave, imagining it being used to lever cargo before its mishap.

Buhle Smolens settled beside him. "What the hell was that, Piper? You could've gotten killed. Which was probably the point of the exercise."

"I didn't think. I just acted."

"Those boys are Artecipeans. You notice?"

"I'm not surprised. But how can you tell?"

Smolens said a blind man could see it.

"I didn't grow up around here, Colonel. Everybody from around the Mother Sea looks pretty much the same to me."

Smolens shook his head in disbelief. "Let me talk to these guys. They'll get cooperative once they understand the alternative."

Hecht began to shiver but not because he was cold.

"That was a stupid thing to do."

The words were a whisper so soft no one else heard. Hecht glanced aside. And saw Cloven Februaren. No one else noted the old man. Who said, "Something to worry about. Could someone else do the things I do?"

For sure.

"You have to be more alert, Piper. Those who want to destroy you never sleep."

"I can't live that way."

"Then you won't live at all." Februaren turned sideways.

Titus Consent asked, "Who were you talking to?"

"I said I can't stand to live this way. With somebody always after me."

"I heard another voice."

"I don't think so."

Consent did not believe him. But did not contradict him. "You don't want to keep on like this, find out who's sending the assassins. Deal with him. Or her."

"I know who's doing it. I wish I knew why."

"Who?" As Hagan Brokke wearily plunked himself down on a nearby bale, Hecht wondered why the bales were so small. Because of how they were smuggled out of Dreanger?

"Rudenes Schneidel. It's always been Rudenes Schneidel." He looked to Brokke. Brokke had not been there to watch the ships come in. Brokke was recovering from wounds suffered in the battle outside Khaurene, where his quick thinking had kept Queen Isabeth's Direcians from getting through the boggy ground to the unprepared troops on the Patriarchal left. "You feeling chipper enough to go back to work?"

"No. A courier boat brought some men in from the fleet. They want to see you."

"Some men?"

"A Principaté I don't know who speaks only Direcian and Church Brothen. Some functionaries from the Mother City. And a big wheel Direcian."

"And they want?"

"To talk to you."

"I figured that part out. What about?"

"They wouldn't say. They didn't seem very patient."

"Get your strength back. Then go tell them I'm tied up in another assassination attempt. As soon as I survive I'll hustle over there to see them. Where were we, Titus?"

"Rudenes Schneidel."

"Ah. So what have you found out about him, intelligence chief?"

"His name is Rudenes Schneidel. And he holes up in the High Athaphile, the mountains that form the spine of Artecipea. He has a castle up there. Arn Bedu. A legendary place on top of a mountain. He may be a pagan priest of some kind. His name comes up every time there's any serious talk about Weaver, Hilt, or any of those Instrumentalities trying to make a comeback."

"That's it?"

"Yes. He's a shadowy guy. And a scary one, according to his assassins."

Hecht's party had begun gathering before Hagan Brokke appeared. Madouc's men wanted to hurt some people. Hecht wished they would all go away so he could talk to Cloven Februaren. But he could not run them off. They would not go, now.

Buhle Smolens was last to rejoin. "I've made a few contacts here. I put out word that we're interested in Artecipeans. Dozens of them have shown up since Sublime died. And they have no friends here."

Hecht was not going to get a chance to talk to the old man in brown. "We came down to watch the ships come in. So let's watch the ships."

Everyone, of course, argued against taking the risk. And Titus Consent insisted on reminding him that there were important men who wanted to see him.

COLONEL SMOLENS HAD ESTABLISHED HIMSELF IN THE HOME OF A WEALTHY Praman who had fled Sheavenalle ahead of the approaching Patriarchals. Hecht felt a mild melancholy nostalgia there. The place showed strong Praman architectural influences. Entering, he spun off orders for dealing with prisoners and wounded. His visitors from the fleet heard the hubbub and came outside.

Redfearn Bechter had collected every man Hecht had ever suspected of being Brotherhood. They were arrayed around the newcomers suggestively, only a few of whom understood that they were surrounded.

Hecht read it fast.

These people had arrived with an attitude problem. And had failed to make themselves beloved. Someone had said something unflattering about the Brotherhood of War.

The Brotherhood did not care if you were a king. They were a kingdom unto themselves.

Hecht had seen only one of the newcomers before. He was a Witchfinder who knew his way around the Brothen catacombs. He was extremely uncomfortable right now.

The Principaté, too, understood and was thoroughly unhappy, but mainly because he was not in control.

The ingredients were there for a nasty pissing contest.

Hecht was tempted. He had reason. But the long game compelled him to be amenable. "Sergeant Bechter. Have these gentlemen been made comfortable?" He told the outsiders, "We're in a difficult situation, here. But we can protect you if you don't wander around. We've swept up a lot of villains since they tried to kill me this afternoon."

Hustle was the critical tool, here. Moving the outsiders around fast. Implying that a swift response, if not thoroughly effective, was better than any alternative.

Hecht asked, "What did you gentlemen want to bring to my attention, now that we're safe?"

Hecht kept moving, maneuvering the outsiders into the sprawling ground-floor space he had chosen for his center of operations in Sheavenalle.

He settled into a heavy oak chair. "Gentlemen. Again? You hurried in here, ahead of the fleet. You must have something you want to discuss before God's enemies find out that you're here."

The Witchfinder seemed ever more uncomfortable. He searched his surroundings constantly.

Cloven Februaren?

Sobering thought.

"Well?"

The Principaté took control. "I am Hernando Ernesto Ribiero de Herve, Patriarchal legate assigned to bring peace to the End of Connec. Too, I've been directed to crush paganism on Artecipea. Paçificus Sublime believes Rudenes Schneidel and his revenant Instrumentalities are a greater threat than the pacifist, dualist Connecten heretics."

Hecht exchanged glances with his staff.

De Herve noticed. "I see you agree."

"I never understood why Sublime was so adamant about exterminating them."

"Did you ask?"

"I did. I got a rambling answer that made no sense. But I'm not paid to ask questions. I'm paid to get things done."

The Witchfinder made a startled squeak and spun. Everyone stared. He said, "Must have been a flea." But he did not believe that.

"Knock it off, old man," Hecht said.

Now everyone stared at him, the Witchfinder with abiding suspicion.

De Herve said, "Pacificus Sublime wants the crusade shifted to Artecipea."

"Which explains the fleet."

"Yes."

"You can't manage Artecipea with the troops you have there now?"

The Principaté managed to appear baffled.

"King Peter has put several thousand soldiers in there. Sonsa is involved, too. And wasn't there a significant victory not long ago?"

"Each victory makes it more difficult to manage the survivors."

The Witchfinder said, "We're convinced that the chaos in the Connec has Artecipean influence behind it. That it was meant to be a diversion from what's going on over there. What we found in Calzir, especially at al-Khazen, has led some of us to believe there's a greater threat than Praman ambition. We first encountered the name Rudenes Schneidel there. We think that Schneidel developed his dread of the Captain-General after seeing what happened there. For some reason, the Night has decided that Piper Hecht is a walking, talking doom destined to destroy it. Unless he's destroyed first."

"What?"

De Herve nodded agreement. "Brother Jokai puts it plainly. All who commune with the Night know the Instrumentalities fear you irrationally and excessively."

Hecht felt a chill. Those who communed with the Night might learn more about the Godslayer than he wanted known. "I don't understand."

Jokai said, "You don't have to, Captain-General. None of us do. We accept what is and deal with that reality."

A man from the Special Office of the Brotherhood of War talking about accepting the Night as it really was?

De Herve said, "That's neither here nor there. The Patriarch wants to know if you'll stay on if the crusade shifts to Artecipea, Rudenes Schneidel, and his corpse birds, these Asparas of Seska."

That startled Hecht. Asparas were Sky Dancers. Minions of Kharoulke the Windwalker. Seska, the Endless, was an Instrumentality of the same ancient age and dark dominion, but from the pantheon that had preceded all other pantheons in Dreanger. "Seska? Asparas I understand. For the Windwalker they were like the ravens who brought rumors and whispers to Ordnan."

Jokai explained Seska. Great Old Gods must be his specialty. He concluded, "Seska is something like an older, darker Adversary. Some think Seska has survived into modern times, in reduced circumstance, hiding parts of himself in the devils of our age."

"All right," Hecht said. "I don't get it. But I don't have to. I'm a soldier. I get paid to get things done. Principaté, are we supposed to ship over to Artecipea right away?"

"Yes. Sorry. The campaign hasn't gone well, lately. The thinking . . ."

"Excuse me. Titus, see what that man wants."

The meeting would not be interrupted for trivialities.

Consent came back. "He didn't say how the information came. There's been some big sorcerous event in the catacombs in Brothe. Not as destructive as the one that destroyed the hippodrome, but Principaté Delari's house fell into a hole. The catacombs collapsed underneath it."

The temperature dropped suddenly and dramatically. Hecht's ears popped.

De Herve asked, "What just happened?"

Jokai said, "Something left us. I felt it before. Now I don't." He seemed more worried than ever.

Hecht asked, "Could that be connected with this?"

"What happened in Brothe?"

"Yes." Hecht watched closely. The Witchfinders were close to Bronte Doneto. Though Cloven Februaren claimed that Hecht and Principaté Delari had misinterpreted events in the catacombs badly. That those Witchfinders had not been in league with the monster Delari slew under the hippodrome. The animosity between Doneto and Delari was, however, real. And there had been congress between the Witchfinders and Rudenes Schneidel, the latter unaware that he was dealing with the former. Schneidel thought he was manipulating ordinary Special Office sorts, his goal the destruction of the Godslayer. The Witchfinders wanted to worm deeply enough into Schneidel's scheme to get at the man trying to resurrect the horrors of antiquity. Hecht's walk-through in Sonsa, with Pinkus Ghort, had started all that unraveling.

The Ninth Unknown had reported all that in snippets during the Connecten campaign. He had discovered no real significance to Vali Dumaine, however. He could not even confirm old Bit's claims about the girl's origins.

"Probably. The Artecipeans have been active there. As you know."

"Yes."

"You seem particularly disturbed by this news."

"I've been close to Principaté Delari. He's been especially kind to me and mine." In truth, though, what troubled him was confirmation that Cloven Februaren could move from one place to another without setting foot to the ground between.

There was much to learn about his guardian angel.

Principaté de Herve asked, "How long will you need to get ready for transport?"

"I could start some units loading tomorrow. But our animals might be a problem."

De Herve said, "Transport won't be any trouble. These crews know how to move troops and animals, both. Loading in this port could become an adventure, though. Sea levels have dropped so far that only smaller vessels can warp in to the wharves and still have water under their keels at low tide if they're loaded. The pilot who brought us in said the dredges can't take any more mud off the bottom. Sheavenalle's senate has talked about building new wharves farther out. But if the Mother Sea keeps getting shallower they'll have the same problem again in a few years."

"They should build floating wharves that can be pushed out as the shoreline moves." That seemed obvious enough.

"But they aren't there now. It's now that we need to load."

Hecht made himself unpopular by talking about loadmasters and cargo other than human. His force came with an immense amount of duffel, weaponry, equipment, and animals. A lot of technical, dull business stuff had to be managed so the men with sharp steel could show up where they were needed, with tents to sleep in, food to eat, and horses to ride.

His lifeguards and the Brothers were relaxed, now. They no longer expected a head-butting contest.

Once he had bored the newcomers cross-eyed with workaday details of army management, Hecht said, "Colonel Smolens, assemble the officers. Explain what we've been asked to do. Be clear. I want them to poll the troops. Find out how many will stick with us." There had been a lot of talk about seeing Brothe again, at all levels.

Smolens said, "I don't think many will drop out."

"We need hard numbers. We have ships to load. We have a new war to plan." In a land almost completely unknown.

THE CAPTAIN-GENERAL WAS TIRED. HE WAS SEEING DOUBLE. IT WAS DEEP IN the night. He was studying bad maps with men from the transport fleet, none of whom had been to Artecipea. They knew only that the new Patriarch wanted them to land on the west coast of Artecipea, near Homre, a fishing port on the north lobe of the island.

Artecipea consisted of two distinct land masses joined by an isthmus at one point only slightly more than a mile wide. The northern mass was a third the size of the southern. The northern people spoke a language not unintelligible to the folk of the End of Connec. Those from the south could make themselves understood to outsiders only with difficulty. According to Principaté de Herve Artecipea strongly preferred the Seska revivalists, other pagans, Pramans, and several varieties of primitive Chaldareans, to the Brothen Episcopal Church. Brothen Episcopals controlled only a few port cities. God and the Church had a more solid grip up north, though the mountain peoples there were all pagans, too, and lately devoted to Rudenes Schneidel.

All the fighting, so far, had occurred on the southern lobe.

Pacificus Sublime wanted to land an army behind an enemy focused south and east. A powerful, veteran army commanded by a man who had scores to settle with Rudenes Schneidel.

Hecht understood the thinking. He could not find fault with it. He could not imagine Schneidel having anticipated what was about to happen.

A change of Patriarchs changed the world.

Titus Consent, scarcely able to keep his eyes open, brought news Hecht would have waited, willingly, years to hear. "It's a day for harsh news, boss," Titus said.

"Give it to me. I'm numb enough to take anything, now."

"King Charlve suffered a massive stroke and died. It looks legitimate. Anne of Menand was nowhere around when it happened. But she was ready to go. She got hold of the instruments of power before anyone could catch their breath. That's just in from Salpeno."

"What's it mean for us?"

"Not much. It may mean a lot for Arnhand and the Connec. Despite her loose behavior, Anne is very religious. And ambitious. The Connec, with its heretics, has already given her excuses to express the one through the other."

Hecht frowned. "Oh? Which is which?"

"Write it yourself. It doesn't matter."

"We're out of it now, though, aren't we?"

"We should be."

"Are you going home? Or are you coming with me?"

"I'm going to Artecipea. Reluctantly. I have a child I've never seen."

"Noë deserves sainthood. On a throne in Heaven right beside Anna."

"Anna is more used to being her own mistress."

"Do you wonder about the Night determining times of drastic change? About what forces might be in motion?"

"You just lost me, Captain-General."

"In an historically minuscule time span we've lost a powerful Grail Emperor, a driven Patriarch, and the sovereign of the most militantly religious Episcopal Chaldarean kingdom. All harbingers of dramatic change. Especially considering the advance of the ice."

Titus grunted indifferently. He was too tired to worry about it. "I'm going to bed. Court-martial me if you want. Execution is starting to smell sweet."

"So waste your life on sleep, weakling." Hecht settled into a chair, out of the way, and tried to relax, rest, and recuperate while he eavesdropped on his deputies and the men from the fleet.

Hecht's ears hurt suddenly, briefly. For one instant the air seemed dense and oppressive. He did not care. He was too tired.

"False alarm," someone breathed into his ear. "Muniero is fine. Heris is fine. Anna and your children are fine. I've brought letters from all of them. There was some damage to the town house. Likewise, certain other properties. There is little likelihood of further problems. In the short run. Joceran Cuito has a new vision for the Church."

Piper Hecht pretended he heard the voices of distant ancestors, out of nowhere, all the time. "What will the new situation in Arnhand mean?" Hoping to catch the Ninth Unknown out.

He did not. "Misery for the End of Connec. In time. You'll be able to throw up your hands and say it wasn't your fault. You were gone before the real wretchedness started."

Hecht had no idea what the ancient was babbling about. He did have brainpower enough to realize that his mutterings were attracting attention. Jokai, in particular. The Witchfinder had that constipated look again. Hecht said, "Gentlemen, I need to go lie down. I've started talking to myself." His staff could see what needed doing and could get on it without detailed instructions.

Hecht removed his boots before lying down. Nothing more. "I mean what I said about resting. There's nothing that needs talking about so desperately that it can't wait till I'm able to uncross my eyes."

"I brought letters."

"They'll be there in the morning. Go away." He closed his eyes. Briefly, he wondered how Februaren accomplished so much in so little time. Then his lifeguards were rousting him out. One told him that Madouc would survive his wound. Again. "The man needs to retire. You can't win, you keep throwing the bones with Death."

That got him some looks.

DESPITE OBSTACLES AND CONFUSION, A DOZEN LOADED SHIPS WARPED OUT next day. To Hecht's surprise, most of the Patriarchal soldiers had chosen to stay. He blamed that on the harsh times.

Those who had become part of the army during its progress through the Connec were those most inclined to leave. Men with families did not want to leave them behind.

HECHT WAS ABOARD SHIP AND EXTREMELY UNCOMFORTABLE. HE DID NOT like travel by ship. And this ship in particular disturbed him.

Titus Consent joined him at the rail, in the waist of the vessel, where he stared back at Sheavenalle. "It's official, sir. The ships will have to make two trips. We're moving more people and animals and stuff than I would've thought possible."

"It's pretty impressive when you lump it all together." Hecht caught a glimpse of a man in brown trying to avoid notice on the crowded deck. That was good for a boost.

Consent asked, "Why the bleak look?"

"Ever been out on the Mother Sea?"

"No."

"You'll figure it out."

"When were you ever out?"

"When Ghort and I sneaked off to Sonsa." Sonsa? The wrongness about the ship hit him. He had been aboard her before, coming over from Staklirhod.

"What now?" Consent asked. "You look like you just saw a ghost."

"I just remembered how awful it got when we hit bad weather. Pray there aren't any storms. Are there storms at sea this time of year? Do you know?"

"No. Of course not."

Hecht caught a passing deckhand. "Are there storms out there this time of year? What's this ship's name?"

Head cocked, not quite sure about the Captain-General's sanity, the deckhand said, "Not so many storms this time of year, sir. In another month, month and a half, maybe. Her name is *Vivia Infante,* sir."

Consent asked, "Why does the name matter?"

"Where I come from people worry about the names of ships. Crewman, do we have a veteran crew? Men who have been aboard a long time?"

"Yes, sir. All experienced hands. We'll get you there safely, sir. I promise." He got away from the crazy man as fast as he could.

Consent said, "Sir, you'd better get hold of yourself. You're being watched. The men have never seen you show fear or a lack of confidence. Headed into a war with a sorcerer of the apparent stature of Rudenes Schneidel is no time to strain their faith."

"You're right. Of course. You always are." He had meant to mask his interest in the possibility that there might be someone aboard who could recall a down-on-his-luck, homeward-bound crusader named Sir Aelford daSkees. "But I can't help thinking about what's swimming around down there, waiting to eat me."

"It's good to see you have a human side, sir."

"Sarcasm duly noted, Lieutenant. In your intelligence capacity, find out why Sonsa is suddenly best pals with King Peter. They've been in a halfhearted war with Platadura for the last hundred years."

"That one's easy. Economics. Sonsa lost. They've joined the winners. It's their alternative to economic extinction."

Probably true, Hecht thought. But . . . was there still some hidden connection with the Brotherhood of War?

Good thing it was Pinkus Ghort and the City Regiment who occupied Sonsa. Otherwise, these sailors might see a chance to pay off a grudge.

THE CROSSING WAS NOT SUPPOSED TO TAKE LONG. A LITTLE VOICE IN Hecht's ear promised him good weather all the way. He stayed out from underfoot and, when opportunity afforded, dipped into the letters from

Anna and the kids. Over and over. Anna was stoically living the life of a woman whose man had a career that kept him away, a sort of benign, resigned, artificial widowhood. The children were living the excited lives of kids who had no wants and few fears. Pella's letter was, in the main, a vehicle for showing off his rapid grasp of learning. Hecht was impressed but thought Pella needed to improve his penmanship.

Vali's letter was brief and clearly a work of obligation. She was well. She hoped the war would be over soon so he could come home and make Anna smile more. Anna worried too much. There was a lot of rioting in the city, lately. She did not understand. She liked Lila, the girl he had sent.

And that was that. Except for the missive from Principaté Delari, which just told him to take care. To be prepared to undergo an intense educational experience once he returned to the Mother City.

HALF OF HECHT'S STAFF WAS ABOARD *VIVIA INFANTE.* COLONEL SMOLENS had been left behind. Hecht hoped to keep him in Sheavenalle, in control, indefinitely, as a logistical root for the Patriarchal forces in Artecipea. Rather than having that support come out of Brothe, at the mercy of whatever political wind happened to be blowing there.

Staff work proceeded, as best it could with limited information. Hecht could not find anyone who had visited the area where he was expected to land. Some genius in Brothe had picked it off a map because it looked like a handy place to get behind the pagans. Brother Jokai—full name Jokai Svlada, from Creveldia—assured him that a Brotherhood team had crossed over from the Castella dollas Pontellas to explore the region. Quietly. They would be waiting for the fleet.

"That's good thinking."

"The Brotherhood has a lot of experience at these things."

"What are the chances they'd be spotted by the enemy and captured? I wouldn't want to show up and find an army waiting for me."

"They're good. They're used to operating inside Praman territory in the Holy Lands. Those who don't learn how to do it don't live to try it again."

"I look forward to meeting these paragons."

Clej Sedlakova came round. "Stomach all right, boss? You don't seem as rattled as you were."

"I'm fine. Too busy obsessing about the deep trouble we could be in after we get there to worry about being seasick." Seasickness was troubling him not at all. Might Cloven Februaren be to blame?

He wished he could talk to the old man. But that could not happen. In his most private moments two lifeguards were within touching distance. Always. Even now. To them every Sonsan crewman was a potential assassin.

None of those men recognized Hecht. He wore his hair shorter now, affected a small goatee beard, and dressed like a Brothen noble. He bore no resemblance to the ragged, hirsute Sir Aelford daSkees. He did recognize several deckhands. None paid any attention to him.

Hecht consulted Drago Prosek often. Just three falcons remained functional. He wanted them instantly available for any confrontation with a major Instrumentality. He was sure something would come from the deeps to attack the fleet. There were old thalassic Instrumentalities uglier than any revenants stirring ashore.

A little voice told him he was wasting his worry. This enemy had no traffic with gods of the sea, nor with any lesser Night thing living on or under the water.

Hecht refused to be reassured.

THE FIRST DAY THE FLEET FOLLOWED THE CONNECTEN COAST EASTWARD, barely making headway. It was ninety miles from Sheavenalle to the mouth of the Dechear River. The fleet reached that around noon the second day. It hugged the coast thirty miles more, then turned directly south. The sailors expected to spy Artecipea before sundown the third day. Winds permitting. They would then follow Artecipea's western coast to the landing site.

PIPER HECHT EXPERIENCED IT AS A FAR LONGER JOURNEY THAN THE ACTUality. The first day was intense, the second more relaxed. There was nothing to do but talk. He pulled rank and forced himself on the ship's master. He wanted charts showing the land he had to invade.

Horatius Andrade was cooperative. So much so that Hecht became suspicious. But he trusted almost no one lately, Consent reminded him.

The charts were reliable, Andrade insisted, but concentrated on the waters off Artecipea, noting only those land features useful as navigational aids. Hecht asked, "Have you been this way before? Have you seen these coasts?"

"A long time ago. On another ship. It's never been a friendly coast."

"You know Homre?"

"Only by repute. It's a glorified fishing village at the mouth of the Sarlea River. I haven't been past in over twenty years. Sea levels have dropped. But even then we couldn't have brought any of these ships into that harbor."

"Are there beaches we can use?"

"Not there. Farther south. Do I know you? Your voice sounds familiar. Have you been aboard *Vivia Infante* before?"

"No. But I did sneak through Sonsa on a secret mission last year. Caused a big stir around a sporting house with galleons in the name."

"Maybe. Strange. I remember voices better than faces."

"I used to not have the beard and wore my hair in the Brotherhood style. Thanks for your help. I don't think we'll land at Homre."

CLEJ SEDLAKOVA JOINED HECHT LATE THE SECOND AFTERNOON, AFTER what little information anyone had about Artecipea had been talked to death. "Sir, I don't know how, why, when, where, any of those damn things, but when I dipped into my locker to dig out something for supper, I found these under my stuff. Sergeant Bechter says he thinks we have a guardian Instrumentality."

Vivia Infante had scores of lockers on her main deck, in places out of the way, there so travelers could stow their possessions.

"An interesting find, Colonel. An interesting find indeed. And so conveniently timed."

"Maybe Bechter is right. Maybe not all the Instrumentalities are our enemies."

"That occurred to me, too. Let's hope it's true."

Sedlakova had discovered copies of several ancient maps. The commentary on them was in Old Brothen. Not the Church version, either. They showed Artecipea as two islands. In modern times an isthmus joined them. Titus Consent said, "Sea levels have really dropped since classical times. Which means the changes in the world have been going on for a long time."

The Unknowns had been following the process for centuries.

There were too many secret things going on. And too many perfectly banal, openmouthed evils driven by ambition or fanaticism distracting everyone from the creeping apocalypse.

Hecht saw no man in brown that day. Februaren must have polished his turn sideways trick. Neither Jokai Svlada nor Redfearn Bechter was particularly uneasy, either, so it might be that the old man was no longer aboard.

The Ninth Unknown had skills more frightening than those boasted by er-Rashal al-Dhulquarnen. And the man was his ancestor? How deep did this madness run? What had he stumbled into?

"Who are you talking to?" Consent asked.

"Huh?"

"You're muttering. You do that a lot these days. How come?"

Hecht told the truth. "Trying to get advice from my grandfather's grandfather." Titus would not believe him.

"All right. That might be useful."

"Tell the captain I want to talk. We're definitely going on down the coast." Would the Direcian Principaté accept that? How would he get word to the other ships?

The sailors were more clever than Hecht expected. They used signals and fast boats to communicate between ships. They had done this before.

The Principaté did not object. He asked Hecht to explain his thinking. The Captain-General did so. Ships forced to lighter cargo ashore needed beaches more congenial than the dangerous, rocky coast around Homre, where sea levels had dropped a dozen feet since Andrade's most recent charts had been drawn. The boats would be too easily broken up in the pounding surf.

Landfall came the third day, just after noon. Soon pillars of smoke arose inland. Hecht said, "They were watching for us. So much for surprising them."

Brother Jokai observed, "Surprise shouldn't be necessary. There can't be two hundred thousand people on all Artecipea. A lot live in the cities and are good Brothen Episcopals."

"Or Deves, or Pramans, or Dainshaus, from what I hear. But I also hear that Rudenes Schneidel has found a lot of followers back in the mountains."

Another reason Hecht had moved the landing. The northern lobe of Artecipea featured an almost complete circle of mountains forming a vast natural fortress. Someone seemed to have thought he should fight through that and dispose of the Unbelievers there. Hecht saw no point. The soul and center of the problem lay inside Arn Bedu, in the western mountains of the larger southern lobe.

"Why are they fighting?" Hecht asked. "Any of them?"

"To restore Seska," the Witchfinder said, shuddering. "To resurrect one of the darkest, oldest Instrumentalities."

"I get that. But, why? The pagans in the mountains, maybe they've fallen under the spell of a glib talker. But what's in it for Rudenes Schneidel? What is he promising them? What does he get for opening the way?"

Jokai cocked his head, considered the coast. "Immortality? Power? The things that turn up in all the stories about wicked sorcerers? Ascension? That sort of went out of fashion after Chaldareanism and al-Prama began promising an eternal afterlife."

"I have no idea what you're talking about."

"In ancient times a clever, powerful man, unencumbered by any concern for his fellows, could ascend to Instrumentality status. Could become a god. Which explains those old Dreangerean gods with the heads of animals and bodies of men. They started out as real priests who elevated themselves by preying on the rest of Dreanger. Facilitating their own ascension through alliances with older Instrumentalities. Seska was a particular favorite."

"Is that what Rudenes Schneidel is up to?"

"I think so. The Special Office thinks so. We've had no luck convincing anyone else. This expedition isn't about that. This is Pacificus Sublime paying off King Peter for making him Patriarch. Peter wants Artecipea for its location and resources. And because it will make him lord of more lands than any Chaldarean but the two emperors."

"Things to think about."

The fleet raised Homre late in the afternoon. Too late to land. The shoreline was inhospitable. The bottom was muddy and not far down. The vessels closed up and anchored. The charts showed the mouth of a small river, the Sarlea, which was not obvious to the eye. There was none of the brown outflow common at the mouths of major rivers.

Brother Jokai went ashore to find his Brotherhood compatriots. He returned with six lean, hard men within hours. Only one was injured.

Jokai said, "You're right to move the landing site. There are thousands of pagans in the hills up there. They mean to swoop down while we're landing tomorrow."

"Ah. So not only did they know we were coming, they knew where we were supposed to come ashore."

Jokai's ripe henchmen nodded. They did most of their communicating by gesture. Their mouths were busy eating.

"Interesting. You have to ask yourself how they managed that."

"Their great sorcerer leader can spy on people from afar."

Hecht thought Rudenes Schneidel had agents spying for him.

Jokai continued. "They tell me the sorcerer is desperate and frightened. He believes that Piper Hecht is the only thing that can thwart his ambitions. He believes that powers greater than you are using you to block every effort he makes to relieve himself of your threat."

"Good to hear. Though every time I turn around, here comes another Artecipean assassin."

One of the recon brothers paused long enough to say, "That's how come the sorcerer thinks you got allies inside the Night. Clever things never get near you. Clumsy assassins do. Schneidel's followers were convinced that some great, grim sea Instrumentality would devour you during your crossing. It didn't happen. Nothing even tried. Now they're all terrified that you might be a revenant yourself. Maybe one of the old war gods who infested the lands around the Mother Sea in pagan times."

Hecht shook his head. "We've stumbled into a superstitious age, haven't we?"

Jokai and the recon brothers eyed him narrowly, themselves not entirely sure that he was not more than just a man.

Hecht said, "It's dark enough. Time to move on."

Men began making a racket all through the fleet, singing to mask the sounds of capstans hoisting anchors. Carefully, showing stern lights that could not be seen from ashore, ships drifted southward.

Silence returned. Though silence was never complete where wind moaned through rigging and timbers creaked as a vessel rose and fell upon the seas. Hecht rejoined Jokai. "On a completely different tack, do you know anything about people called the Unknowns?"

"Librarians for the Collegium, I think. I've heard that they keep a big map of the Chaldarean world. Why?"

"I'm not sure. I heard some talk when I was working at the Chiaro Palace. Principaté Delari had a connection with someone he called the Eleventh Unknown. I'm not sure why that got to nagging me right now. I never thought much about it before."

"A long time ago, the Special Office thought the Unknowns were an unholy cabal inside the Chiaro Palace. I suppose they found out differently. This is the first I've heard them mentioned since I was a student."

IT WAS A TENSE SEA PASSAGE, THAT NIGHT. THE MOVE WAS SUPPOSED TO DE-ceive people ashore. Would it?

Hecht slept only fitfully.

Dawn came. The right number of mastheads were visible. None had gone missing. Andrade guessed they had moved them thirty miles down the coast.

Signal smokes rose ashore. Hecht thought they seemed panicky.

He was thirty miles from where he was supposed to be. The rising breeze would push him along faster than his enemies could run.

Unloading began shortly after noon. Only a handful of men were ashore when friendly locals pointed out that just a mile back north the ships could move closer inshore and dramatically shorten the landing process. These people were Brothen Chaldareans. They had been perse-cuted lately. The arrival of the fleet had deluded them into believing that the Patriarch wanted to rescue them.

The Captain-General went ashore as soon as his lifeguards permit-ted. Earth underfoot, he sighed, said, "This is pure chaos. There must be a better way. If there was anyone here to resist us we'd be getting slaugh-tered." He spoke to no one in particular, though Redfearn Bechter, Drago Prosek, Titus Consent, and Jokai Svlada were all close by. "Titus, talk to these people. Get a feel for the ground. Hire some guides. I expect to have to fight off a major attack. Will we need to include the Night amongst the enemies we expect? Keep Prosek in the know."

By nightfall the ships were headed back to Sheavenalle. A solid camp had been established, in the Old Empire fashion. It had a timber wall with a ditch at its foot. Scouts with local guides crawled all over the surrounding countryside.

Two miles up the coast, on the south bank of a creek the locals called a river, was a fishing village cleverly named Porto. It had been called something else in Imperial times and had been bigger then, anchoring the north end of trade across the narrow strait that had existed at that time. The villagers were proud of their history, religion, and dialect, which resembled Old Brothen more closely than did modern Firaldian. They had suffered numerous turns for the bad since the fall of the Empire, as Artecipea passed through the hands of frequent conquerors. With, always, the hinterlands' pagan storm just over the horizon.

Piper Hecht spent his first night on Artecipea as a guest of the leading men of Porto. They insisted that he was a deliverer. He wasted no time disagreeing.

THE PEOPLE OF PORTO DELIVERED INTELLIGENCE ENOUGH TO SHOW HECHT what he must do to withstand the approaching pagan storm. In numbers that astonished everyone. Somehow, Rudenes Schneidel had gathered almost eight thousand men to throw the Patriarchals back into the Mother Sea.

The local chieftain's son, going by the unlikely name Pabo Bogo, told Hecht, "You destroy this bunch, you've won your whole war, Lord. There can't be many more down south. They say the Sonsans and Platadurans and King Peter's soldiers have cleared two-thirds of the High Athaphile. Only the evil sorcerer's witchcraft keeps them from complete success."

"I'll do what I can." Hecht hoped to use the lay of the land to get the better of an imbalance in numbers.

The transports were gone. Two Plataduran warships anchored close inshore, to be artillery platforms.

The first pagans arrived in the afternoon. They were a wild and ragged lot, reminding Hecht of Grolsacher refugees seen in the Connec. They were overheated from their rush south, and were tired, thirsty, and hungry. Hecht had positioned his visible force with the afternoon sun behind them. The pagans saw only a few men between themselves and the food and water inside the Patriarchal camp.

More and more pagans arrived, as families, clans, and tribes instead of as an army. Some tried rushing in to throw javelins. They met missiles from crossbowmen and archers. The crossbowmen, though few, were very good at what they did.

More pagans piled up. They made a disorganized charge. They suffered scores of casualties and enjoyed no success whatsoever. Even so, they tried again a quarter hour later.

Hecht watched in disbelief from inside the camp, atop a low tower infested by lifeguards. The pagans seemed compelled to do things his way.

"Looks like their big chiefs are arriving, Captain-General." The speaker pointed. A mob including standards and banners had appeared. Followed by a vast mass of pagan humanity. That settled down briefly after some horns blared. When the horns sounded again the pagans all roared and charged as though determined to see who could be first to die. Their sheer weight almost broke the Patriarchal line. Hecht muttered, "I didn't leave enough men out there." He had not anticipated such numbers, so soon.

His modest heavy cavalry force, hidden in some woods to the enemy right, saw the danger. They charged. The warships discharged their ballistae, an effect expected to be more psychological than actual.

The heavy cavalry were supposed to smash through, break free, then wheel for another charge. They lost their momentum instead. The pagans were too densely gathered.

Hecht's best infantry had hidden in ravines behind the heavy cavalry. They came out, in order, as the line protecting the camp did start to give.

Hecht ordered his infantry reserve out. He told his lifeguards, "The fools think they're winning. They don't see how badly they've been trapped. I'm being sarcastic!" he snapped at one puzzled bodyguard.

It looked like even the reserves would not suffice. Pagans kept arriving and rushing into the melee. But the later they showed, the more exhausted they were already.

An hour after the fighting began the pace of the struggle slowed. Hecht's fighters were tired, now, too.

The last of the Patriarchal infantry left cover south of the fighting, double-timing into blocking positions across the enemy's escape route. They went unnoticed till they set on a band of very late arrivals.

The pagan chieftains panicked. Not unexpectedly. Tribesmen were fierce, sturdy fighters individually but lacked team discipline. They did not train to fight as an army.

Hecht signaled light cavalry waiting inside the camp. The pursuit phase was about to begin.

Hecht left the tower. He had no desire to watch the slaughter.

More disaster awaited the pagans if they chose to flee to southern Artecipea. More Patriarchals awaited them where the land narrowed into that tiny, low isthmus.

"A FEW GOT AWAY," CLEJ SEDLAKOVA SAID. HE HAD GOTTEN INTO THE fight briefly, with the light cavalry, tied into a saddle. "They always do."

"Let's hope we took the fight out of them for this lifetime." The men had counted near five thousand dead. They were still finding bodies.

The chieftain of Porto was aghast at the magnitude. "It's going to be a hard winter in the mountains."

"It'll be a hard rest of their lives with so many hands not there to do the work anymore," Hecht said. "It's bound to be a better world once we get this Schneidel beast. I'm going to walk through the camp and talk to the men."

A lifeguard said, "That wouldn't be wise, sir. If there's a counterattack, there'd be no better time than tonight, when the men are worn out. You should stay here, with the falcons around you." He was worried about the Night.

"I'm going walking through the camp." He needed to burn off nervous energy.

"As you wish, sir." With great unhappiness.

"Yes."

Hecht visited the hospital tents first. The army's few surgeons were hard at work. So were any veterans who could manage minor field surgery. Hecht found everyone cheerful. Some of the wounded seemed grateful as puppies that he had come to visit.

"What are these men doing here?" He meant men from Porto who were being treated, but by gesture expanded the question to include a dozen pagan captives. Why waste resources on men who had been trying to kill him only hours before?

"The locals got hurt helping hunt down fugitives. The pagans are supposedly men of standing. They say they might be willing to change sides."

Hecht's inclination was to have them killed. But if northern Artecipea could be pacified . . . That would be useful. "Good for now. If they show willing, and aren't lying, we'll work something out. Has anyone seen the Principaté? I can't find him."

"The Direcian?" Redfearn Bechter asked.

"Preferably. If we have another one underfoot, he'd do."

"Principaté de Herve left with the fleet."

"He did, did he?"

"I assumed you knew."

"And the Witchfinder? Svlada? What about him?"

"Here, Captain-General," Svlada said from the far side of the tent. "Sewing men back together."

"Good. Tell me. Why did de Herve run away?"

"I don't know. Maybe he thought his work was done."

That matched Hecht's suspicions.

Minutes later he reached the area where the animals were tended. He heard a familiar voice. "Bo? That you?"

Biogna jumped as though ambushed by a ghost. "Oh! Sir." He looked at the bodyguards. "You startled me."

"What're you doing out here?"

"Helping Joe. This's when he needs a friend. It breaks him up when the animals get hurt."

"It bothers me, too." Beyond Bo Biogna's small fire Hecht saw Pig Iron, Just Plain Joe's signature mule. Strictly speaking, Joe had broken the rules by bringing the mule to Artecipea. Pig Iron did no work.

"Pipe." Just Plain Joe came into the light. He carried a big copper bowl full of surgical instruments and bloody water.

"Joe. How bad was it?"

"I'm only glad you're not a cavalry type. We haven't had to put too many of them down. But even one is cause for tears."

Hecht felt the sorrow rolling off Just Plain Joe, potent enough to make his own eyes water. He rested a hand on Joe's shoulder while the man cleaned his instruments. Items he had less business having than he did Pig Iron. There would be complaints. The Captain-General would ignore them when they came. "You keep on, Joe. You're the truest man I've got." He left the man to his calling.

Nowhere did Hecht find cause for complaint. The work of recovery was under way everywhere.

He climbed his observation tower, considered the moonless night. To seaward the stars shed just enough light to give hints of breakers rolling in. Elsewhere, torches floated through the woods like will-o'-the-wisps. A mortal shriek explained that. Chaldareans from Porto were sending their pagan countrymen to their rewards in order to grab loot not worth whatever they called their fractional copper here.

Fires burned in Porto. Were they celebrating?

He stared at the town. Something had come to mind during the fighting, a question he wanted to ask those people, but he could not now, for the life of him, remember what it was.

Another squeal from the woods sapped the last of his energy. Exhaustion hit like a boulder falling. "All right, men. I'm over it. I can sleep, now."

One of the falcons barked. Just once. "Must be a false alarm."

But one side of his shelter was smoldering when he arrived. Kait Rhuk looked him in the eye and made a dramatic showing of letting a little egg thing clunk into a small iron box. One of a dozen such that Drago Prosek had acquired in Sheavenalle.

Nobody said a word. Everybody looked at Hecht.

"I get the point. Everybody. Good night."

He refused to let the lifeguards inside.

HIS DREAMS WERE TERRIBLE.

SOMEONE SHOOK HECHT'S SHOULDER. "WAKE UP, BOY."

Hecht surged up, not quite aware that he was not in the grasp of the thing that had stalked him through his nightmare. He did not rise too high. The Ninth Unknown possessed surprising strength.

"Calm yourself."

Hecht did so. With an effort. "I was having a bad dream."

"Probably not. They know what happened. They're hunting you. They can't find you because of the amulet. And the ring. The thing they sent forgets what it's supposed to do when it gets close."

"They?"

"Rudenes Schneidel. And the thing he's trying to resurrect. Seska."

"Through my dreams?"

"They can't get to you in the wakening world, day or night."

"Then I should stay awake?"

"No. You're safe. I won't be far off. Trust the amulet, the ring, and me. And your lifeguards. You'll be all right. Your suspicions are on the mark, by the way."

"Which suspicions?"

"About you and your army being sent here mainly to keep you from intervening in Firaldia."

One candle burned inside the shelter. It was all the light and heat the Captain-General enjoyed. "I suspected that?"

"Or the like. The Patriarch expects you to be chasing Rudenes Schneidel for years. He doesn't know about me. He doesn't plan to bring you out of Artecipea once you do bring Schneidel down. Though King Peter might salvage you."

"He would? Why?"

"While we were preoccupied in the Connec, and while Brothe was getting a new Patriarch, al-Halambra gained a new Kaif. Not a Direcian Praman, this time, but an old-fashioned, hard-core Believer from beyond the Gebr al Thar. Something Sabuta Something al-Margrebi. Who's preaching a holy war to recover the lost provinces in Direcia. And more. Thousands of warriors have crossed the Gebr al Thar already. The news is spreading on our side of the Mother Sea. Pacificus will have to preach a real crusade, if he doesn't want Peter overrun."

"A big war in Direcia should show us just how grand a champion King Peter really is."

"And how strong his hold on his Praman allies is."

"And my part would be?"

"No part. You'll be here, trying to exterminate Rudenes Schneidel. But if things go bad for King Peter you can expect to see Direcia before long."

"I have family in Brothe. My men have families."

"Next time you see the Patriarch ask him how much he cares."

"Should I ask what his problem with us is?"

"You have the power to make kings. You have a large force of skilled, experienced soldiers who are loyal to you. He judges you by what he would do if he had what you have. It's a common weakness."

"What's your advice?"

"Send people to Brothe to see what's what. There are plenty of local boats. Finish Schneidel fast. Then cross over to the mainland yourself. You'll be safe. Pinkus Ghort still runs the City Regiment. Which has gotten a renewed lease on life and a fattened budget since a foreigner managed to become Patriarch. You'll have Muno and me behind you, too."

"Sounds good. You think Rudenes Schneidel might turn up tomorrow morning, ready to give up?"

"No. You'll have to lead these men into the High Athaphile and root him out of Arn Bedu. Which should be easier than it sounds. I'll be along."

"You. Yes. I've seriously begun to wonder. What are you, really, great-great-grandfather?"

"That. And the Ninth Unknown. Go back to sleep."

Hecht had an angry question but sleep snatched him quick as a shark's strike.

The dreamstalker did not get close again.

THE PAGANS LEARNED, FIRST DISASTER. NO MORE CONFRONTATIONS. THEIR guerrilla efforts were ineffectual, however. The Patriarchals had learned the cure while in the End of Connec. Any village or fastness that caused trouble ceased to exist. Villages and fastnesses that did not resist suffered nothing more than disarmament. In each such Hecht made it known that his sole target was the sorcerer Rudenes Schneidel.

The Captain-General's advance into the High Athaphile was inexorable. And grew stronger with the arrival of the rest of his troops from Sheavenalle.

Resistance faded. Schneidel's rebellion—if that was what it could be called—collapsed. Eighteen days after he landed near Porto Piper Hecht stood on a mountainside looking up at the sorcerer's final stronghold,

Arn Bedu. The Mother Sea was an amazing blue expanse behind him, stretching away forever. Looking east, he could just make out Pramans serving King Peter making camp at the far foot of the mountain. His successes had eased their difficulties dramatically.

"What's so amusing?" Redfearn Bechter asked.

"Look. Good Pramans out there. Men we fought not that long ago. And good Chaldareans here. All of us about to get together to go up there and exterminate that pagan who got all uppity."

"I don't see the joke. But I'm told I have no sense of humor."

"You won't get an argument from me. How about you let Brother Jokai know I'd be ever so appreciative if his scouts took a real good look at this mountain. Tell him they should be careful. Not just because of the pagans but because King Peter's troops will be scouting, too. Hell, we need to get together with them and coordinate. Work it out so they can get most of the glory by doing most of the dying."

"You're a cynical bastard. Sir." That was Clej Sedlakova.

"I am. I'm thinking, based on what we've seen in the towns and villages, that nothing up there will be worth plundering. So why not let somebody else get busted up getting there first to claim it?"

"Somebody heading this way from yonder camp," Bechter said.

Sedlakova observed, "Looks like Colonel Smolens is about to catch up, too," indicating people climbing the mountain from the west. Smolens had been evicted from Sheavenalle by Principaté de Herve.

Smolens arrived first. "Sorry I couldn't stand up to the Principaté, boss. I just didn't have the horses." He found himself a place to lie down. He surrendered to exhaustion instantly. Madouc was part of Smolens's party. He collapsed just feet from the Colonel. Hagan Brokke still labored up the slope with other invalids also expelled from Sheavenalle.

There would be regrets, someday.

The allied party halted, awaited a response. Hecht looked around for a flash of brown. He did not find it. "Prosek. One falcon team with me. Plus four lifeguards. And Brother Jokai."

Jokai started to protest. Hecht told him, "We're supposed to cooperate with them. For now. You're no good at disguising yourself. So it won't hurt to show you off. Let them know how serious we are. We need horses. Somebody. We can't meet them on foot. It wouldn't look right."

Moving at last. Two lifeguards out front. Two back behind Drago Prosek, Kait Rhuk, and another two falconeers. Jokai Svlada beside Hecht. Hecht wishing that Titus Consent were there instead of having sneaked into Brothe. Jokai asked, "Is us bringing the smaller party a statement?"

"No. I wanted to come alone. But the lifeguards would have revolted."

"You feel safe? You don't know these people?"

"I'm safe. As long as the man on top of the mountain is still up there."

"The wind's got a bite to it around here."

True. There was snow on the slope where shade lay most of the day. Local guides said snow was new this winter.

The other party resumed moving toward a grassy shelf not far away. Hecht caught the flash of brown he hoped to see. Cloven Februaren was the company he did want.

Hecht halted once his people were all onto the grassy shelf. The falcon team set up, trying not to look threatening as they did.

"Here's a ridiculous mix," Hecht whispered to Brother Jokai.

Ten men came forward. Four were Direcian. One of those was a Chaldarean bishop. Two were heralds or squires. The other looked to be a noble of standing. Hecht did not recognize his colors. Brother Jokai was no help.

Hecht was not interested in the Direcians. He focused on the Pramans behind them. Bone and Az watched from beyond the edge of the grass. Not so big a surprise. He had known they were over here trying to unravel the Rudenes Schneidel puzzle. But he had not expected to see Nassim Alizarin al-Jebal on this side of the Mother Sea. He locked gazes with the Mountain briefly.

The Direcian Bishop urged his mount closer. He scanned Hecht's companions, recognizing the lifeguards as Brotherhood of War but not comprehending Prosek and Rhuk at all. Brother Jokai rated barely a glance. Then he saw something behind Hecht that left him with his mouth open.

"Bishop?"

The man could not talk.

Wait! Everyone had frozen. As though time had stopped. But it had not. Yonder, birds swooped over the Direcian camp. To one side Cloven Februaren perched on a boulder like an anchorite on his pillar. The old man grinned, gave him the thumbs-up, then pointed.

The Mountain, baffled and disturbed, looked around carefully.

"Sorcery," Hecht said, trying his voice.

Nassim's gaze fixed on him. Confused.

Hecht got it. Februaren had frozen everyone but himself, Hecht, and the Mountain. But that would not last. "What are you doing here?"

"They killed Hagid. That word did get through. Thank you."

"You know who?"

"The one up there. Rudenes Schneidel."

"And?"

"Yes. I know that, too. The Rascal. His turn will come."

"They must be missing you in al-Qarn."

"They could be. And they may never understand. Neither Gordimer nor er-Rashal have sons. The Lion knows nothing but feeding his own vices, these days himself. The Rascal has some secret scheme going that only he understands."

"Gordimer is a puppet. And doesn't know it. Er-Rashal's scheme involves Seska and making himself immortal. He has no love for the Faith. There is no other explanation for the last several years."

"No other explanation that makes sense," Nassim agreed. "Why did he want those mummies?"

"I don't know. They must be part of his quest for ascension."

"What?"

"He's trying to turn himself into an Instrumentality. There's no time to explain. This spell won't last. We need to go up there and exterminate Rudenes Schneidel, who is the Rascal's partner."

"Looks likely to be difficult."

"I don't want to just sit here."

"You have somewhere else to be?"

"I do." Inasmuch as Sublime Pacificus meant him to perish on this island.

"Prisoners say they didn't expect a siege."

"We still might starve ourselves out first." Hecht explained his situation.

"There are ships here. Artecipea is an island. Not so?"

"Yes. The men behind you, though, are beholden to King Peter and the syndics of Platadura. And Peter made this Patriarch."

"I understand. The spell is starting to slip."

Hecht saw an eye blink slowly. "Anything more? Fast. We won't have this chance again."

"One thing. Rudenes Schneidel is mine. Whatever else he's done, I stake first claim."

"Done. But manage those others . . ."

Cloven Februaren made a warning sound.

The air shimmered. Everyone resumed moving. Universally adopting baffled expressions. Several, in lockstep, blurted, "What just happened?"

Brother Jokai said, "We were hit by a spell of some kind. Check yourselves. See how it affected you."

No one found anything unusual. Which only heightened the tension.

Hecht said, "You're our top sorcerer, Jokai. Guard against it happening again." He faced the Direcian party. "Gentlemen. I'm Piper Hecht, Captain-General for the Patriarch. His Holiness wants this fortress overcome and its tenants compelled to pay the penalty for apostasy. I assume King Peter wants the same. None of us gets to go home till we finish it. So why don't we figure out what we ought to do?"

"Hercule Jaume de Sedilla, Count of Arun Tetear," said the Direcian who was in charge. "King Peter's viceroy on Artecipea." The Count seemed to be having trouble with his eyes. Nevertheless, he forged ahead, naming his companions. Nassim he introduced as Shake Malik Nunhor al-Healtiki. Shake Malik was a survivor of the Calziran Crusade. Having no better prospects, al-Healtiki had raised a company of veterans to serve King Peter for pay.

Clever Nassim.

His company included Bone, Az, and the other survivors of Else Tage's special company.

Shake Malik was a minor captain amongst the Pramans. The overall commander was a surprisingly fat man from Shippen who used no name but Iskandar.

THE SIEGE OF ARN BEDU PROCEEDED TRADITIONALLY, THOUGH THE FASTness squatted atop one of the tallest and bleakest mountains in the High Athaphile. Iskandar and Count Hercule operated on the eastern slope. The Captain-General and Patriarchal forces operated on the less congenial western face. Each did what besiegers do—at a leisurely pace. They did not mind waiting. The pagan rebellion had fallen apart everywhere else.

Hecht worried about Titus Consent as the days and weeks turned into months. Where was the man?

The great monster sorcerer cornered inside Arn Bedu never deployed his vaunted power.

Hecht had Sedlakova try to undermine. The decomposed, soft stone on the surface gave way to hard, living stone too soon. Work went ahead anyway. The men had to be kept busy doing something.

Mining became an industry.

Hecht left that to his staff. He went down to the coast and hired ships to bring supplies over from Sheavenalle. He put spies aboard those ships. Those men brought back news of the broader world. Big changes were going on. The Church had abandoned the Connecten Crusade completely. Sublime Pacificus kept issuing bulls calling on all Episcopal Chaldareans to join King Peter in a crusade in Direcia. Anne of Menand had pledged the manhood and wealth of Arnhand to help repel the anticipated Praman offensive. Knights from Arnhand, Santerin, and Santerin's continental possessions were on the move. So were Brothen Episcopal knights from the Grail Empire, encouraged by Empress Katrin.

There were hints that Anne of Menand's men might give the Connec special attention returning home from obliterating the Unbeliever.

Other news was less exciting. The new Patriarch had subdued his enemies inside Brothe. Unlike Ornis of Cedelete before him. And managed without bringing home his Patriarchal army. Which said something about Pinkus Ghort's ability to work under pressure.

HECHT SELDOM GOT TO TALK TO THOSE HE KNEW IN THE OTHER CAMP.

Titus Consent finally returned. With a small fleet. "Thanks for sending me," he said. "I got to see my new son. Noë named him Avran. I wasn't there to remind her that we converted. So Avran he'll be." Consent handed over a case of letters. Some were from Anna and the children. Others were from Principaté Delari and several men of standing who wanted to get his ear.

"How were Anna and the kids?"

"I only got to see them once. I had to keep my head down. You're a lucky man. They miss you more than my bunch missed me."

"Did anyone notice you?" Dumb question. Of course they had. Otherwise, there would be no letters. "Did you get my new falcons and firepowder?"

"First instance, probably not till after I left. By anyone we worry about." He frowned, remembering something. "I did bring the stuff. All that I could lay hands on. Way more than you asked for. To keep anyone else from getting them. Those in the business kept working. They knew somebody would pay a lot for a more efficient way to kill people."

"It isn't people I want to kill. I can do that now. My concern is the Night."

"The Night is at our mercy. So let's see what we can do about its servant on the mountain."

Madouc, recovered enough to work now, and several other lifeguards all frowned over Consent's suggestion. They were quite willing to take it easy as long as there was food and drink and their pay came on time—though there was nothing to spend it on in the High Athaphile.

Hecht asked, "What about our situation here? Will there be problems if we try to come home?"

"Who could stop you? If you come up with the transport?"

"I don't know. I can't make sense of the political situation." He watched the men dragging up the new falcon batteries, kegs of firepowder, cases of ammunition, and other weaponry. Most of those men would rather be working the mines under Arn Bedu. That did not necessitate climbing the mountain carrying a hundred pounds. Men from the Direcian camp watched, too, obviously troubled. They suspected Hecht was about to pull something.

"There's more news."

Hecht caught the edge in Consent's voice. "Do we need to talk about it privately?"

"It wouldn't stay secret. I didn't make the trip alone. It's a question of caring, really."

"I'm likely to care more than most?"

"Precisely."

"Then get to it, since it won't matter to any of these dunderheads."

"Hey!" Madouc protested.

"Titus?"

"King Charlve is dead."

"And? We've known that for months."

"There have been a lot of changes in Arnhand because of it. And now it looks like Anne is trying to buy the new Patriarch, too."

"Meaning?"

"She has Sublime's letters of blessing. She's put Regard on the Arnhander throne."

Hecht chuckled. "She paid enough. To our profit."

"Now she wants something more. She's called out the entire feudal levy to help King Peter stop the Almanohides."

"The what?"

"The who. The Almanohides. Praman tribal fighters from the other side of the Escarp Gebr al Thar."

"Oh." Hecht had not heard that name for those people before.

"The new Kaif of al-Halambra summoned them."

That Hecht did know. The process had begun before their departure from the Connec.

"He's determined to crush Peter before he can be any more successful. He means to keep on moving north if he breaks King Peter. He sees nothing to stop him now that we've moved over here to Artecipea."

Hecht understood the hidden message.

A new storm was coming. It was time to keep an eye on their backs, in case the uneasy alliance here fell apart.

Hecht said, "Let's put the fear of God in our friends. We'll let them see the firepowder weapons at work. Speaking of which. You need to find Drago Prosek right away."

"The situation in Direcia had another interesting effect. The Patriarch himself postponed the marriage between Empress Katrin and Jaime of Castauriga."

Hecht had not thought much about events inside the Grail Empire. "Interesting."

"Want some more interesting? You were invited."

"Say what?"

"Anna showed me the letter. With the Imperial seal. Signed by the Empress herself. Requesting the presence of the Captain-General at the celebration mass. And so forth."

"I don't understand."

"Don't ask me to explain."

Was it Helspeth? "One more puzzle to keep me awake at night, then."

"Plenty of puzzles to keep me up."

Hecht frowned. Consent sounded unhappy. "How so?"

"There have been a couple more suicides amongst my Devedian relatives and acquaintances."

"And? I'm not understanding. Were they that upset about you converting?"

"No. None of them believed I meant it. I was the Chosen One. How could I run out? They're only now starting to believe it. But they're still cooperating. They still think they can profit from the connection."

"And I'm still confused, Titus."

"My problem is, these men who killed themselves, I've known them all my life. I can't believe any of them would become that hard a slave of despair. Devedians and despair are intimates. Life partners. Soul mates. They wouldn't kill themselves."

"So what's going on?"

"I don't know! That's the horrible part! Men who wouldn't kill themselves at the worst times did it in front of witnesses."

Hecht sighed. He sensed Consent's pain. But what could he do? "I can pray for them, Titus. That's all. I didn't know them. I don't know what drove them."

"Never mind me, Captain-General. The new falcons are here, including the ones Prosek designed. Along with tons of firepowder and ammunition. If you want to provoke the Night, now is the time."

"Which is why you need to get together with Drago Prosek."

THE PAGAN STRONGHOLD HAD NOT SUFFERED MUCH FROM TRADITIONAL artillery. The besiegers had not been able to build many engines. Lumber was scarce. What little there was had to be hauled a long, hard way before it could be used.

Ammunition was plentiful, though. There were rocks everywhere.

The falcons could do little damage, either. They did not have the power. But those that Prosek had redesigned could be fired faster than the others.

The powder and shot for the new generation were preloaded into a cast-iron pot that seated into a breech in the reinforced base of the falcon. A protruding thumb rotated into a notch, holding the pot in place. That rotation brought a drilled hole into view. Firepowder dribbled into the hole would be fired with a slow match. The pot could be replaced quickly. The spent pot could be reloaded at leisure while the weapon itself went through subsequent firing cycles.

Hecht now felt better about his chances for surviving the interest of the Night. But the new weapons and ammunition and firepowder had cost enough to leave the Patriarchal army strapped. Despite successes in the Connec and intercepted specie shipments from Salpeno, there would not be enough money to carry on past midsummer.

Hard work in the mines helped keep the soldiers out of trouble. And they needed distraction. Disaffection had begun to appear amongst the rank and file. Some thought their Captain-General was not forceful enough with Brothe. They thought their commander should have told the Patriarchal legate to use his new assignment for a suppository.

Titus Consent suggested, "A few bordellos down the mountain would be more useful than making these guys work fifteen hours a day on mines and approach curtains. Especially when those people around the other side aren't doing anything."

They were not working because Count Hercule and his Praman associates were as nervous about each other as they were about Arn Bedu. Both told the Captain-General, individually, that there was no reason to work. That time was the best weapon in their arsenal.

Hecht told them, individually, "I want to go home. And my men aren't in a patient mood."

The Mountain and Az, or Bone, were always close by when Hecht talked to Iskandar and Count Hercule. He got few chances to visit. Nor did the Ninth Unknown create many opportunities for communication. Yet the man in brown was often there, in the corner of Hecht's eye.

Redfearn Bechter reported sightings every day. Bechter was troubled. Bechter was no longer convinced by his Captain-General's protestations of ignorance.

CLOVEN FEBRUAREN DID MANAGE WHEN HE CARED ENOUGH. USUALLY DEEP in the night, when sleep was more precious than rubies. Employing one of those time-stopping spells. Freezing the lifeguards on duty. Who panicked when the spell wore off. They always knew that something had happened. They never came close to guessing the truth.

"Piper!" The old man spoke softly but insistently. "Wake up, Piper."

Piper Hecht grunted and rolled away. It seemed he had just gotten to sleep.

"Come on, boy. Wake up and listen. Or you're going to be dead. Real soon now."

That moved him. Some. He cracked an eye. And found himself nose to nose with Cloven Februaren. "What?"

"There's going to be an attack. By the Night. Soon. You need to get ready."

Hecht said something rude and tried to turn over.

A bee sting pain hit his right buttock. He almost cried out. Boyhood training stopped him.

Tears did flood his eyes.

"Are you listening?"

"Yes."

"The Night will come. Your great enemy has told it where to find you. That's always the Night's great challenge when it reaches into our world. Finding the right man in the right moment. The Night sees our world through nearsighted eyes."

"So I've heard." Tone suggesting that Februaren make his point.

"You must prepare."

Hecht believed he was prepared. "I'm listening."

"It's time to use the ring."

"Uh? Ring?" What was the man blathering about, now?

"The ring you appropriated from the Bruglioni. The one you forget about. The one you wear on a chain around your neck, along with your silver dove and iron pomegranate." Symbols from the earliest days of the Chaldarean faith—in metals the Night most despised.

Hecht rooted beneath his shirt and brought out his symbolic disguise. A gold ring hung between the pomegranate and dove. "Where did that come from?"

The Ninth Unknown was disinclined to waste time reeducating him. The old man touched his left temple. He remembered.

"Put the ring on."

"Uh?"

"Pick a finger. Any finger. The one that it fits tightest. Put it on. Then put this on behind it." Februaren extended a gaudy silver thing encrusted with small gems.

Hecht fumbled the gold band a couple times getting it off the chain and onto the middle finger of his left hand. It felt like the damned thing was trying to get away. Cloven Februaren helped herd it, then forced the garish bauble on after it.

"That's your safety lock. It won't come off till I release it. So the other will stay where you need it until I do."

Hecht did what he was told, thinking the ring could still get away. If it could get his finger amputated. He asked, "Why are we doing this?"

"We're denying the Night the focus that Rudenes Schneidel and er-Rashal have tried to give it. The nearer it comes to you the more distracted it will get. Distracted? That's not quite right. But I'm too tired to find the perfect word."

"You seem chipper enough to keep me awake all night."

"You've done what I came to get you to do. You have the ring on. You still wear the amulet. I can fade away and you can get back to wasting your life on sleep. All before these dedicated boys of yours can wake up and be terrified because they almost did something that might have put you at risk."

What in the name of the Adversary did he mean by that?

The old man touched him again.

Sleep came instantly.

SLEEP ENDED, SUDDEN AS THE MAN IN BLACK'S SWORD STROKE, SLAIN BY THE bark of falcons.

Waking with mind fuzzy, Piper Hecht tried to recall the name of the goddess of sleep. That seemed terribly important for a dozen seconds. Until he understood. That was not thunder, never heard up here anyway, but the crude speech of weapons designed to thwart the Will of the Night.

Drago Prosek and his henchmen were on the job, as alert and ready as they had been told to be.

The Captain-General shook off the slut sleep and got his feet under him. With the assistance of lifeguards who insisted they had to be right there beside his rude mattress even while he was unconscious. The same lifeguards who had failed to notice the earlier visit of the Ninth Unknown.

Sobering realization. They could be circumvented easily.

The moon was almost full. It splashed Arn Bedu with ghost light. And made it possible to see Drago Prosek's crews doing their cleanup while most of the Patriarchal force watched and babbled in awe.

The egg the falconeers came up with beggared the one found after the destruction of the bogon in Esther's Wood, a seeming eternity ago. What had died here, tonight, must have been a minor god. Eliminated quickly and efficiently by men just doing their jobs, using munitions designed for the task.

This was why the Night dreaded Piper Hecht. Destroying Instrumentalities was about to become no more special than any other death stroke.

Whole new realms of warfare would open up once men understood that they could butcher one another's gods.

The night lighted up when an immense flash appeared against the base of Arn Bedu's northwest mural tower. A roar like all the thunder in the world at once followed a moment later. That was so loud it deadened the ear. There was no hearing the crash and grind of stone as the tower and nearby wall surrendered to gravity and came down, but it felt like an earthquake.

Nearly a ton of new, refined, more potent firepowder had been packed into the mine under that tower. The fuse trail had been lit off by sentries with orders to do so whenever Rudenes Schneidel tried to use the Night against the besiegers.

The Captain-General stared up at the moonlighted pillar of dust leaning westward above the wreckage. He wished that he had had storm troops ready to go while the rubble was stabilizing.

Troops did push into Arn Bedu soon. Many carried portable firepowder weapons, after the fashion of the capture of the Duke of Clearenza. But this time the men were armed against the Night. Their attack was disorganized but they did know what needed doing.

Titus Consent asked, "Any idea how much this is costing?"

Hecht said, "I can't imagine. But I see ordinary guys like you and me grinning from ear to ear because we just murdered a midget god of some kind and we're about to take a fortress that's been considered invincible forever. And we hardly had to work at either one. Because we knew what we wanted to do and we worked hard to make sure everything was ready to make it happen when an opportunity popped up."

Exhaustion claimed Hecht before the sun rose. He left Arn Bedu to the mercies of his associates. His preparations had proven out. His veterans had done their work completely indifferent to the Will of the Night.

Hecht began to think that even he now had an inkling why he had gained the enmity of the Night.

He was sound asleep before his messengers reached the camp of his allies. They offered King Peter's partisans the opportunity to complete the capture of the pagan fortress.

That assault might be costly despite the horrible shocks already suffered by Arn Bedu's defenders.

The most shaken and enfeebled of those proved to be the dreaded sorcerer Rudenes Schneidel himself. The man offered no resistance whatsoever when discovered.

*   *   *

HECHT'S LIFEGUARDS CONVINCED HIM THAT IT WOULD BE POLITIC TO AP-
pear in full ceremonial dress to recognize his allies for having successfully cleansed Arn Bedu.

The Mountain passed him with a prisoner in tow, a man bound and
gagged in a way that made it clear he was important, powerful, and dangerous. The man's face was locked into an expression of utter, possibly
eternal disbelief. This could not be happening!

Iskandar, Shake Malik, and Count Hercule had conquered their disbelief. Publicly. But they kept glancing at Hecht as though certain he must
be more than what they could see, or that another shoe had yet to fall. He
wanted to yell at them. He had not done anything special. His sappers had
packed firepowder in under the wall. Drago Prosek's falconeers had overcome those Night things that tried to interfere with God's soldiers.

The same weapons lubricated the assault.

Arn Bedu's defenders were dead or captured. Including even Rudenes
Schneidel, whom Hecht had not expected to see in the flesh, ever. He had
assumed the man would escape in the final confusion, as er-Rashal had
done when al-Khazen's defense fell apart.

Titus Consent murmured, "Things have changed again. Reality definitely shifted when that wall came down."

Hecht understood. This time he saw the future as he had not after
destroying the bogon in Esther's Wood.

It should have taken months more, if not years, to reduce Arn Bedu.
He had brought it down in days once his new firepowder and weapons
arrived.

No fortress would be invulnerable ever again.

It would take time, though. He knew. People did not like change.

He started up the mountainside.

Madouc demanded, "Where are you going?"

"Up there to look around."

"You think you're suddenly safe?"

"I'm hoping." He glanced toward where an argument simmered between the Mountain, Iskander, and Count Hercule. Each wanted Schneidel. Hecht said, "See that Nassim gets the prize."

"What?"

"A random thought. The chief of that band from Calzir. He came
here because Schneidel was behind his son's murder. So I've heard."

"Schneidel tried to kill you and your family. Why don't you take
him?" Brother Jokai asked.

"Because I don't want the Special Office tempted by the evil that
surrounds him. And only the Special Office could manage him. So let
the Pramans punish him."

The Praman Nassim would put an edge on Schneidel and use him against er-Rashal. And right now er-Rashal al-Dhulquarnen was the most dangerous man in the world. In Piper Hecht's mind.

"You could be right. Unbelievers they may be. But they tolerate wickedness and truck with the Night less than do our own true believers."

Hecht knew better but did not say so. He was just a bright boy from the far north who got lucky.

He climbed the mountain. His lifeguards tagged along. Madouc complained all the way. Ahead, Prosek and the falcon crews warily re-covered shot expended during the assault. Several dark things flapped through the breach in the wall. Falcons dispatched them in seconds.

Prosek came to meet his Captain-General. "The loading pots worked perfectly, sir. As did the falcons. Not one blew up. You got to hand it to them Deves. They know what the hell they're doing when it comes to casting brass."

"That's why they got my contract."

"I hear there's some bad feelings about that."

"No doubt. Nobody likes an elitist."

Prosek frowned, puzzled.

Madouc told Prosek, "He's determined to go poke around. Get some of them damned thunder busters up there with us. He's got no fucking idea what the hell is still hiding inside that rock pile."

Hecht paused at Arn Bedu's open gate. He had not thought of that. And there was definitely a tingle round his left wrist.

All his thoughts had been focused on Cloven Februaren. What part had the old man played in Arn Bedu's fall?

There was no way it should have gone so smoothly and quickly. The Ninth Unknown was the only explanation for Rudenes Schneidel turning so meek in the end.

What the hell was that old man?

He said, "Arn Bedu was never meant to be anything but a refuge. This gate isn't big enough to launch a sortie."

Prosek said, "The guys found a lot more store than we expected. The pagans could've held out for ages. Except that their water went bad. The prisoners thought something in the stone used to line the cisterns was leeching out."

"What?"

"The captives say it was slow poison. Arsenic, or something. Guys sometimes suffered convulsions. Most of them didn't have much strength left. And nobody was thinking clearly. The guy in charge dealt with that by drinking nothing but wine."

Rudenes Schneidel was a drunk? That might have something to do with his passivity.

Bad water and too much wine might mean that the Ninth Unknown had not been the key.

Hecht was not ready to buy it. Not whole. The Ninth Unknown was huge in everything. He was totally sure.

Hecht did not move again until Drago Prosek brought up all his falcons.

Arn Bedu was a sad, barren shell. Evidence that it had been occupied by real, living human beings was limited. And there had been fewer prisoners taken than expected.

Arn Bedu was no standard castle. The wall did not shield inner courts. It was the outside wall of a building occupied by a rich, deep darkness. The interior was mazelike as well.

Piper Hecht lost his compulsion to prowl and investigate seconds after entering the fortress. The place was haunted by a bleak despair so deep it recalled the creeping fractions of fallen gods reawakened in the End of Connec. By a despair so deep it had become a part of Arn Bedu's stone.

Cloven Februaren's doing?

Was there *any* chance that old man was *that* powerful?

Just could not be. Had to be because of what Rudenes Schneidel had been trying to do.

Hecht really did not want that old man to be something that much more than an ordinary man.

The lifeguards gabbled suddenly. Drago Prosek and Kait Rhuk babbled, too. Firepowder exploded an instant later, in the darkness ahead. The flash illuminated a passage pretty much standard for the bowels of a stone-built fortress. But there was something in that passageway. It struck every mortal with a fear of the Night of the sort known so intimately when men huddled round campfires and willingly did whatever was necessary to push the terror away.

"Seska!" Hecht gasped.

The face he saw in that flash was the face of Seska portrayed on the most ancient bas-relief murals within the timeless structures of al-Qarn. That face could not be described nor be immortalized by mortal artisan, yet it could not be mistaken.

Godslayer. Come to your end.

A falcon barked. Light and smoke rolled down the passageway.

Another falcon spoke.

Pain. Stunned, uncomprehending, incredulous pain, accompanied by fear of a sort unknown for ages.

The first falcon reiterated its declaration.

The second barked again.

Prosek and Rhuk had brought weapons capable of rapid speech.

Godslayer. You have won nothing! Fading. *Surrender to the Will of the Night!*

The falcons spoke again. And again. Shot rattled and whined off the walls of the passage, searching for the mystical flesh of the Old One, Seska. The revenant, the Endless, who must be but a shadow of the original.

The insane, shrieking something surged forward, psychically far more powerful than any of the bogons that had crossed Hecht's path. But Drago Prosek's falcons grumbled their basso profundo aria, proclaiming the passing of an Instrumentality of the Night.

The tide of Night reached Hecht. It tried to devour him. His amulet burned. It froze. He cried out. The pain!

The revenant screamed inside minds, continuously, incoherently, its only discernible thought a driving need to destroy the Godslayer. It struck like a cobra, over and over, its aim never true.

The Bruglioni ring burned colder than the coldest ice. Hecht was sure he would lose the finger.

Hands grabbed him. He fought. Thunder rolled overhead. His cheek stung from the heat of a falcon's breath.

Darkness. Unconsciousness. A sojourn within the realm of the Night, hiding in plain sight amongst hunting Instrumentalities who snuffled through space and time alike in their search for the thing they were convinced could destroy them.

HE WAKENED INSIDE HIS OWN SHELTER. THE TRANSITION FROM DEEP DOWN in the darkness to waking came suddenly. He tried to jump up.

He could not. He had been placed in restraints.

His attempt to shout failed completely.

Reason set in. He noted that he was not alone. A priest from one of the healing orders hunched over a charcoal brazier. Madouc and Titus sat near the entrance, still as battered gargoyles.

"You made it." Cloven Februaren.

"I did."

"How deep did you go?" The voice came from behind him, from out of sight.

"I don't know. I don't know what you mean. I was out. I had nightmares. Now I'm awake."

"It never got its claws into you. Lucky you, you were wearing that ring."

"Why am I tied down?"

"So you can't hurt yourself. They'll cut you loose after I leave."

"What happened?"

"You found Seska. Then Seska found you."

"And?"

"You survived. Seska didn't. It might have done if everything hadn't been in place ahead of time."

"Everything? In place?"

"You with the proper amulet. You with the ring. You with the falcons behind you. And me behind the falcons. You need to leave this place, now. The Night is in chaos at the moment. But it does know where the Endless was before it was ended."

"It wasn't really the Endless, though. Was it? Wasn't Rudenes Schneidel building himself an imitation Seska?"

"It was Seska, Piper. *The* Seska. The real thing. Almost fully reborn. Almost ready to step back into the world where it was first imagined. Where it would have rewarded Schneidel and er-Rashal richly for having given it back its reality."

The old man had grown ferociously excited. "You definitely filled the role of Godslayer this time. You've won the attention of all the Instrumentalities of the Night, now. The human race is lucky that the wells of power have weakened so much."

Hecht had trouble following the old man. His mind had not yet fully cleared.

And his amulet had begun to itch. And more. "Something is coming."

"I feel it. I'll deal with it."

Time resumed as Hecht sank back down. He fell asleep vaguely aware that Madouc and Titus had begun a troubled analysis of why such a sudden chill had developed inside the boss's shelter.

THE CAPTAIN-GENERAL HAD NO STRENGTH IN HIS LEGS. HE WAS ON crutches. The healing brothers assured him he would recover. He needed to be patient.

Patience was not a virtue he had had to observe much since Sublime V loosed him on the End of Connec.

Jokai Svlada and some Special Office henchmen finished scourging Arn Bedu. Piper Hecht had come to the great hall there to witness the last Special Office purification ritual. That included Just Plain Joe and a big-ass sledgehammer. Drago Prosek placed an egg-shaped object the size of a toddler's head on an anvil captured with the fortress. The biggest man in the army swung his hammer. The shimmering egg shattered into a million fragments, most as fine as talc. Larger fragments returned to the anvil for further attention.

A voice in Hecht's ear whispered, "Once this dust washes down into the Mother Sea, there'll be no chance ever of pulling Seska together again." Which Hecht took to mean that there was no way to be rid of any Instrumentality eternally. That the Godslayer had not, really, slain the Endless. Not the way he left mortal men forever slain.

He murmured, "Seska is gone. Negated. The power it used to suck up is now available to Instrumentalities as yet undefeated."

"Clever boy."

Jokai Svlada and friends swept up dust, mixing it with acids or corrosives.

These Witchfinders definitely meant to end the rule of the Night.

Ceremonies done, Hecht commenced the long descent to the coast. On crutches, with lifeguards round about threatening to drive him crazy with their fussing. Wishing he had had more opportunities to talk to Nassim, Az, or Bone. But those men had gone as soon as they got hold of Rudenes Schneidel.

"If wishes were sheep."

"What?" Redfearn Bechter asked.

"Condemning myself for wasting time on wishful thinking. I know better."

"I see." Clearly meaning he had no idea.

The nearest usable port was Hotal Ans, a fishing town of fewer than four hundred souls. Hotal Ans meant something special in one of the old languages once used on Artecipea but nobody remembered what, now.

Piper Hecht arrived minutes after a ship from Sheavenalle tied up at the pier, bringing supplies and, more importantly, news.

A courier brought plenty of that and took the critical stuff directly to . . . Titus Consent. Who, minutes later, told his Captain-General, "Pacificus Sublime is dead. Of apoplexy, supposedly. He collapsed during a furious argument with members of the Collegium about his favoritism toward Peter of Navaya. He went red in the face, collapsed, and was gone before anyone with a healing talent could help. There were dozens of witnesses."

Buhle Smolens observed, "Sounds like God didn't approve the results of the last election." Invoking a timeless joke ascribing the final, definitive vote in any Patriarchal election to the Deity Himself.

Hecht asked, "What's our financial situation?"

Consent said, "There isn't a lot left in the war chest."

"Enough to get us off this island?"

"Some of us. What are you thinking?"

"That I'd like to have me and a convincing number of our hardest veterans in Brothe in time to monitor this new election." Having spoken,

Hecht ground his teeth. Anticipating unfriendly seas during any crossing to Firaldia.

MIRACULOUS STAFF WORK MADE IT POSSIBLE FOR THE CAPTAIN-GENERAL and a thousand picked men, with all the firepowder weaponry of the Patriarchal army, to land in a suburb of Brothe just below the most downriver of the chains across the Teragi. A vast sympathy for a successful Brothen general made that possible. Titus Consent acquired a crucial bit of information before anything inexcusable took place.

"Principaté Mongoz was elected Patriarch on the second ballot. My guess is, the main business of the Collegium right now is trying to decide who steps in after Hugo Mongoz."

Hecht asked, "How much did Peter of Navaya spend to get Joceran Cuito elected? He sure didn't get value for his money, did he?"

"He didn't? Think. Where does Peter stand today?"

Hecht could not refute the vast good fortune the Direcian King had enjoyed of late.

There was no resistance to the return of the Captain-General and his troops. Rather, the opposite. Crowds came out to cheer as they marched toward the heart of the Mother City. It could have been a triumphal procession in olden times.

"What is this?" Hecht asked his staffers, most of whom had accompanied him. "It isn't like we did anything for them. They won't benefit." Buhle Smolens and Jokai Svlada were the main left behinds. Hecht felt guilty about having left Smolens. His number two had family he wanted to see, also.

Clej Sedlakova said, "They're just thrilled to be associated with victories, boss. You had big successes in the Connec, then you wrapped the war in Artecipea practically overnight."

"Five months is overnight?"

"Compared to what the Patriarch counted on, sure."

On some thoroughfares the City Regiment held back the crowds. Pinkus Ghort's men did not seem pleased to have the Patriarchals home.

Hagan Brokke observed, "We've started losing men, boss." And that was true. A few were falling out when they spied families unseen since their departure for the Connec.

"Can't blame them. It's what I want to do. It's damn well what I plan to do before nightfall, too." But first he meant to present the troops in the Closed Ground. To force the new administration to show him its attitude toward its soldiers. "As long as a few hundred stick we'll be fine." The problems would all be on the Church's side until the new Patriarch came to an accommodation. The troops would not tolerate the machinations of another Pacificus Sublime. They would not let that happen under this regime.

Hecht would not be able to control them. Nor would he try to stay their righteous anger if it was baited.

Brothe had laws against garrisoning Patriarchal troops inside the city wall. Hecht intended to test those, though not to the point of conflict.

The majority of the men stuck, knowing their captains were as eager as they to see their families. They formed a fierce formation in the Closed Ground. The falcon batteries with their smoldering slow matches were particularly intimidating.

The balconies of the Chiaro Palace filled with nervous dignitaries and functionaries. Hecht spied Osa Stile's pale young face. He did not see Principaté Delari. Palace guards assumed the stations they occupied whenever there was a ceremonial observance in the Closed Ground. They seemed anxious.

Good.

Boniface VII—Hecht had just learned that Hugo Mongoz had taken that reign name—appeared on the high balcony reserved for the Patriarch. Younger priests supported him. The soldiers immediately saluted, then took a knee, the Captain-General included. The men stayed down. The Captain-General rose and advanced a few paces. "Your Holiness, we who serve Mother Church bring victories to shine on Her crown of glory."

Titus Consent, Hagan Brokke, and Clej Sedlakova then rose and stepped forward. They announced offerings like the keys to Castreresone's gates, to the gates of Sheavenalle, and a piece of hearthstone from Arn Bedu. They were replaced by men carrying trophies from lesser cities and fortresses, plus a banner listing the names of the pagan chieftains slain during the battle at Porto. Hecht had elected not to present a similar banner for the battle at Khaurene. Many key names belonged to men close to Boniface's predecessor and Peter of Navaya.

In a surprisingly strong voice, Boniface declared, "Well done, Soldiers of God. Well done indeed. Our blessings and those of Aaron and the Founders be upon you, and Our Lord's Favor also."

The soldiers responded, "And also upon you."

"You have performed well and honorably. For this you will be honored and rewarded. And for this, as must befall all who do well, you will be given further tasks on behalf of Mother Church. But not today. Go to your homes. See the ones you love. Visit your confessors. Square your souls with the Lord of All Things. Most of all, treat yourselves to a well-earned rest."

Not many remembered now because few were old enough. In his

youth Hugo Mongoz had spent five years in the Holy Lands, cleansing them of the Infidel. He had not forgotten what it meant to be a soldier.

Boniface's voice quavered toward the end. His hand and arm were shaky when he offered a last benediction. His companions helped him back inside the Chiaro Palace.

The Captain-General gave the sign to rise. "Sergeant Bechter. I want weapons turned in at the Castella. Keep them separate from those of the Brotherhood. Have any men who don't have somewhere to stay bunk at the Castella. Those who want can leave for their home garrisons tomorrow. I'll send word if we need to reassemble." The implication being that comrades still on Artecipea would not be allowed to languish.

He gave orders to everyone, those who needed them and those who did not. He shook hands with several intimates. Then, "Titus, ready to go home?"

"I am indeed, sir. I hope home is ready for us."

"Did you send word?"

"I'm trusting rumor. Anyway, I saw your kids in the crowd when we were coming up the old Chamblane Thoroughfare."

"Goddamnit, Madouc! What now?"

"We're your lifeguards, sir." Taken aback. The Captain-General never used blasphemous language.

"Don't you men have families?" He regretted asking immediately. Most of his lifeguards were Brotherhood. They had one another, and the Order.

"Those with that greater obligation have joined those going to the Castella dollas Pontellas, sir."

Hecht bit back what he was inclined to say. It would be a waste of venom. Madouc would do nothing but his best. And would cut no corners.

"All right. I understand. But I'm wondering, what will convince you that I'm in no more danger?"

"Us failing. You'd be dead. Then we wouldn't have to protect you anymore."

Hecht exchanged looks with Consent. Titus tried and failed to suppress a grin.

MADOUC BARKED. LIFEGUARDS SCURRIED. STEEL SANG LEAVING SCABBARDS. Hecht froze like a startled deer, taken so far off guard that he could have died right there if it had been another sniper attack.

"Easy! Stand easy!" Madouc ordered as Pinkus Ghort and two companion riders emerged from the late-afternoon gloom, hands far from their weapons.

"Damn, Pipe! Madouc. You scared the shit out of me."

"Don't jump out of the shadows like that."

Ghort had done no such thing but did not argue. His companions dismounted. Carefully. Making it clear they were doing nothing else. Ghort said, "I thought you might be tired of walking." Two lifeguards closed in, making sure he was not an assassin disguised as Pinkus Ghort.

Hecht said, "You shouldn't have changed your look so much. Why have you gone Brothen fop?" Ghort wore bright yellows and reds in the latest Firaldian courtly styles. He had a thin, Direcian style goatee, delicately trimmed and possibly colored. His hair hung straight, in bangs across the front, two inches below the ears on the sides and in back. The hair had been darkened for sure, and ironed. Nothing gray or curled remained. The silly hat up top made him look like a flaccid mushroom.

Ghort's companions handed him the reins of their mounts, carefully backed away.

"His nails are painted," Titus observed. "Can you believe that?"

"Not my choice," Ghort said. "Orders. These days I got to spend most of my time with the senators and consuls. Principaté Doneto nabbed him one of the consulships last month."

The senators were what civic bodies elsewhere might call aldermen or city councilmen. The two consuls were similar to mayors or burgomasters. The dual power sharing went back to beyond the beginnings of the Old Empire. One consul managed the city's business inside the wall while the other's mandate concerned business outside. Meaning, generally, seeing to the procurement of water and grain. And commanding the army during wartime. Not something the consuls had done in recent centuries. But might again, now, with Bronte Doneto in office.

The ancient Brothens dreaded personal ambition more than they honored skilled leadership. Consuls had to swap jobs every three months. Nor were they allowed to serve consecutive terms, one of which lasted just a year.

That, of course, changed under the emperors. Emperors derived much of their legitimacy by being consuls. And, initially, by being anointed dictator by their political cronies in the senate.

"Good for him. He always wanted to be the big cheese. What's he doing about the hippodrome?" Hecht had seen no obvious restoration work while passing the site, heading for the Chiaro Palace.

"Funny you should ask. The hippodrome was the issue he harped on the loudest, getting himself elected. If I've figured it out right, he managed to get hold of one of the specie shipments from Salpeno, too. He plans to use that to restore the hippodrome."

"Did any of Anne of Menand's bribe money get through to Sublime?"

"Quite a bit, actually. He got out from under his debts from the Calziran Crusade. He didn't get ahead. He didn't lose ground on the Connecten Crusade, though. Thanks to you."

Hecht allowed himself a smirk. "Yes. The hippodrome isn't why you ambushed me, though."

"No. It ain't. I wanted to see you. Before you get swamped."

"You could've come by Anna's house." His only immediate plans were to hole up with Anna for as long as he could.

Ghort chuckled. "Right. She'd rather set me on fire, then chase me off with a broom."

"You could be right. Unless you play chess with her. You aren't the most charming of my friends. And you haven't answered my questions."

"True. Not that I was evading. The fact is, folks a lot more important than me are going to be sucking up all your time, going forward. I wanted to sneak in ahead and give you some straight shit."

"I appreciate that. I'd do the same for you. So what do I need to know that everyone else is going to lie to me about?"

"One thing is, there's been all kinds of riots. I'm out there with my guys braiding ropes of sand every goddamned night. Every idiot in this damned burg thinks he's got a grievance and that entitles him to bash people and bust stuff up. About once a week some demagogue decides it's all the Deves' fault. A mob heads off to the Deve quarter. It gets mauled. Which all the rabid Deve haters claim is proof that they're in league with the Adversary. If they weren't they wouldn't fight back. And they especially wouldn't have all those loud weapons that cause such cruel, festering wounds."

Hecht glanced over at Titus, who was about to swing aboard the mount that Ghort had presented him. Consent shrugged. "I've been with you, boss. I'll get on it as soon as Noë lets me think about work again."

"What about Principaté Delari?" Hecht asked as he settled into a saddle. "He didn't show up when I presented the trophies to the Patriarch in the Closed Ground. I saw the boy, Armand. But not the old man."

"Delari and his pet aren't together anymore. I don't know why. They say the boy is playing night games with the new Patriarch, now."

Surprised, Hecht diverted himself by saying, "I heard that Principaté Delari's town house fell into a sinkhole. Because of some kind of confrontation down in the catacombs."

"That's crap. One corner of the place did collapse. But it wasn't because of anything like what happened with the hippodrome. Delari must be preoccupied with something. He hardly ever shows himself."

Mounted, Hecht walked his horse slowly in the direction of Anna Mozilla's house. Allowing Madouc and his lifeguards to keep up. He felt mild despair about the attention his passing caused.

"Things have really changed here, Pipe. But they've stayed the same, too."

"Good to know, Pinkus. But try to be a little less clever. What does that mean?"

"Never mind me, Pipe. I'm a walking cliché factory."

"That doesn't take us to any point, either."

"You are a hard, cruel man, Piper Hecht."

"The tasteful constraints of my faith won't let me say what you are, though it features the stern of a horse with tail upraised for the drop."

Ghort laughed. Then he got busy talking about everything he thought Hecht ought to know about the current situation in the Mother City. A situation unlikely to spark conflagrations of optimism.

The refugees just kept coming. There was nothing for them to do.

Ghort chattered all the way across town, from the Teragi right down to the street outside Anna Mozilla's house. He went right on chattering at Titus Consent when the Captain-General broke away. Hecht was grateful for Ghort's effort. The man had told him more than he had thought.

VALI AND PELLA WERE IN THE OPEN DOORWAY TO ANNA'S HOUSE, PELLA practically jumping up and down. They had known he was coming. They had been out scouting. Hecht had seen them dashing through the crowds, speeding ahead with news that he was coming.

Vali stepped in front of Pella and gave Hecht a huge hug, startling him totally. She did not say anything, though.

Pella had plenty to say for both of them. Questions. Reports. Brags about how he was doing with his studies.

Forcing a word in edgewise, Hecht asked Madouc to see Titus safely home, then told Pella, "You've grown about a foot. And Vali, too." Vali looked like she was starting to bud. He was thrilled to see the changes.

Pella continued to jabber. Vali was more restrained but did keep the fingers of her left hand touching his arm. "Anna! Anna Mozilla! Are you in there? Can you come rescue me from these wild monkeys?"

He was nervous about this. How had Anna dealt with their separation? Would she invite him in?

Anna came to the doorway because he had not been able to push past the children. His worries were unfounded. She was pleased to see him. Her embrace enveloped him, swamping him with hungry promise. But she said, "You smell like you haven't had a bath for a year."

"And I was just up at the Chiaro Palace. Why didn't I use the baths when I had the chance?"

"I refuse to say what I'm thinking. Pella! Calm down. Your father will be here. Piper. The other one, Lila, is too scared to come out."

"It's all right. I remember being the same way when my father came home from the marshes. You don't know how long it'll last. And you don't know if there'll be a next time. The Sheard are cruel and cunning."

Anna gave him the oddest look, as though wondering if he had started believing his own made-up back story.

No. But the children needed to believe it. Children talked.

Anna led him to the kitchen. She had bathwater heating. The precursors of a meal were cooking. Vali and Pella worked on that, Pella never easing up on the chatter. When his questions interested Anna, too, Hecht responded.

She asked few questions herself. But, "We heard a rumor about a giant worm attacking you beside the Dechear River."

"Sort of true. Whatever you heard would've been exaggerated. We destroyed it. Hardly anyone got hurt."

She gave him a hard look. "Principaté Delari was there, too. Wasn't he?"

"He was," Hecht admitted.

"I wonder if he exaggerated."

Hecht had no answer.

By the time he was clean he was so warm and relaxed he was inclined to head for bed. "Oh, how marvelous it will be to fall asleep with no worries to keep me up. Knowing there won't be interruptions all night."

Anna said, "I don't know about that."

Pella and Vali snickered.

Anna said, "Pella, set the table. Vali, keep an eye on the sauce. She planned the meal, Piper. I'm just a consultant."

"But I saw her out . . ."

"A working consultant. It's her project. And Lila's."

Hecht got the message. Though he never saw Bit's daughter.

As he settled in to work on the capon and sides, Hecht said, "Blessed Eis and Aaron, it feels good to be clean and wearing fresh clothing."

"Which, I see, hangs loosely. You lost weight."

"That happens. So now I'll get busy putting it back on."

"Aren't you forgetting something?"

"Hunh?"

"Prayer?"

"Oh. Got out of the habit out there. The only priests were Brotherhood of War types. Pella, unless Vali wants to do it, you go ahead."

Vali smirked. Pella managed a rather imaginative grace. Following the lead of his literary namesake, Hecht supposed.

Later, before the inevitable adult encounters, Anna whispered, "Vali is talking now. To Pella. To Lila all the time when she thinks I'm not listening. To me sometimes, when she's excited. She'll slip up with you, too. She feels secure enough, now. Did you find anything out over there?"

Piper Hecht had no worries about Vali Dumaine. But, "Nothing. No famous child disappeared anytime in the last few years. Titus's people found relatives of the Erika Xan who supposedly brought Vali to the sporting house in Sonsa. They knew nothing except that Erika Xan disappeared years ago."

His worries had faded mainly because Vali was getting older.

In the wee, paranoid dark hours in the camp, awash in the pervasive enmity of the Night, he had come to fear that Vali might be a planted living artifact. Like Osa Stile.

Anna Mozilla soon distracted him from all outside concerns.

21. Alten Weinberg: Hard News

Tension in the Imperial capital escalated daily. The Princess Apparent did not share it. She had no cock in the fight. Nor was she near the center.

The Empress had sent numerous knights and nobles to support King Peter against the Almanohides. All had volunteered. Most backed the Empress in her romance with Brothe. Her stay-behind supporters were afraid that those who were displeased by that romance might take advantage.

Katrin was frantic with fear for Jaime of Castauriga, who had summoned his full feudal levy to assist King Peter. Katrin had seen Jaime just once but had talked herself into an obsessive romantic love that set courtiers wondering, in whispers, about her sanity.

Helspeth was pleased by it all. In the sense that anything deflecting attention from herself was pleasing.

She was able to participate in life at court. Friends were not afraid to be seen with her, particularly Lady Hilda Daedal of Averange. Lady Hilda joked that Helspeth was more likely to be stained by her adventures than by any of the Princess Apparent's own.

Court gossip suggested that Lady Hilda was involved with three different gentlemen of the court. Each believed that rumors about her and the others were vicious lies retailed by Lady Hilda's enemies. "Men are fools," Hilda insisted. "They're stupider than puppies."

"Then why get involved with them?"

"I like variety. And I have fun manipulating them. If you weren't a princess you'd have a chance to understand. Might still, after you get yourself a husband and give him a couple of sons."

"I'm not going to marry. I've decided."

"So you say. And you might make it work. For a while. As long as Katrin is frazzled." Lady Hilda smirked. "I had a letter from my cousin." She did not say which cousin. But her smirk expanded when Helspeth responded with an excited start.

The Empress was not the only Ege daughter with an obsession.

Lady Hilda's cousin Culp was a priest. He was secretary to Principaté Barendt, living in the Chiaro Palace in Brothe. Cousin Culp was one of Hilda's game pieces. Helspeth feared there was a totally wicked side to their relationship. Maybe.

"Now you're trying to play with me."

"Only a little. Just making sure I figured it out right."

Helspeth frowned but said nothing.

"You aren't as obvious as Katrin."

"Katrin will get what she wants."

"If Jaime survives."

"So?"

"Your fixation is back in Brothe. And the Collegium is scared. Pacificus Sublime tried to do the Captain-General dirty by giving him an impossible job. He did it in record time, then came over . . . What's that goofy look, girl?"

"What? Excuse me?"

"You look like you think he'll be in your bed when you get back to your apartment."

"He might be. In my mind."

Helspeth felt the heat hit her cheeks. How could she have said that, out loud, in front of anyone? She was Princess Apparent of the Grail Empire. She was not supposed to have fantasies.

Lady Hilda broke out laughing. "One of you girls is human, then."

"What?"

"Your father had appetites. They say."

"He was a man. Men are that way."

Lady Hilda nodded but did not pursue the subject. She shifted to the mundane. The usual stuff of women at court.

HELSPETH FOLLOWED ALL THE FORMS WHEN SHE RESPONDED TO HER SISter's invitation to visit her in her quarters.

"Get up. Get up, Ellie. There isn't anybody here to see. We don't have to play the game."

Helspeth did as she had been told, clinging to Ferris Renfrow's instruction about being pliant. She could not restrain a gasp when her sister moved into a stronger light, though. "Have you been eating right?"

Katrin had aged terribly. Katrin gave her an ugly look. "Being Empress isn't what I thought it would be. Father made it look easy. People did what he told them."

Helspeth said nothing. She did not know what to say.

"I wish I could call down the lightning. I'd rid myself of these vultures."

"I agree with you on that." Though maybe not on who ought to be stricken.

"And Jaime . . . Helspeth, you can't imagine how awful it is, worrying all day and most of the night, terrified about what might happen."

And Helspeth could not. She worried, but not with the self-consuming intensity Katrin showed. The worst disaster imaginable in Direcia was unlikely to affect her personally. Other than in the misery her sister might choose to pass along.

"I can't eat. I can't sleep. I can't focus on being Empress."

"Will it get any better after you know how it turns out?"

The question caused Katrin's hysteria to stumble. "What?"

Helspeth decided she had asked the question wrong. "Uh . . . I just wondered if you haven't gotten yourself so worked up that no matter what happens . . ."

Katrin's expression hardened. She heard criticism. She did not take criticism well.

Anger did distract her from her growing lack of control.

Helspeth reminded herself: stick to Ferris Renfrow's formula. Give Katrin no provocation.

It was hard. Her sister had grown so mercurial it was impossible to guess what might set her off. In the greater court that did not matter. If Katrin shrieked absurd orders the court pretended to carry them out. She would calm down eventually. If she had done something egregious she would become deeply contrite. Then the object of her fury could be trotted out and forgiven.

Helspeth wanted to believe Katrin was a victim of cruel mood swings, from near deadly paranoia to unpleasantly deep depression.

A cycle of crude humor steeped Alten Weinberg. What could young Jaime do to relieve Katrin's moodiness?

Katrin went through one of her changes. "We've had feelers from Salpeno about an alliance for you with Regard."

"No!"

"Ellie . . ."

"The man is a bastard. His mother is a whore!" Helspeth flared despite the damper on her emotions, though not half as loudly as she was inclined. She did not mention Sublime V's role in supplying Anne of Menand's feeble claim to legitimacy. Sublime was Katrin's hero.

Katrin soothed her irritation at Helspeth by being catty about Lady Hilda. Then, sipping brandy brought up from Helspeth's Plemenza, through the pass that Helspeth had suffered so for opening, the sisters relaxed, came closer, and began to relive the gentler, warmer days of their childhood. They had a good cry over Mushin.

ALTEN WEINBERG ENTERED A TIMELESS SUMMER OF WAITING. NOTHING happened because everyone, of every political allegiance, was focused on the Almanohide campaign in Direcia. Every Brothen Episcopal family backing the Empress had someone gone to crusade with King Peter.

Most families in Arnhand and many in Santerin enjoyed the same purgatory. To a lesser extent, so did those of Firaldia, Ormienden, Grolsach, the lesser Brothen kingdoms and principalities, and even the Connec.

Helspeth guessed that similar tensions might grip the Praman world, at least in the Kaifate of al-Halambra.

The outcome in Direcia was more certain to shape the future than were either of Sublime's crusades.

Katrin told Helspeth, in a whisper no spy might overhear, "If God grants victory to Peter and Jaime, I swear by the Grail crown that I'll undertake my own crusade to free the Holy Lands."

Helspeth shuddered. The Night would be listening. The Night would amuse itself by pushing the Empress to ruin Episcopal Chaldarean humanity by launching another hopeless war in the east.

"Father had that dream," Katrin said. "Once he united Firaldia and brought it all into the Empire."

"What? Really? I never heard him say that."

"Really. Father Volker told me." And Father Volker was Johannes's confessor before assuming the same role with his successors.

Helspeth sighed, defeated. Katrin would not hear a word against Volker or his master, Bishop Hrobjart. Nor could she pray for guidance in mellowing Katrin's bloodthirsty ideology. God might be the Almighty but He was Born of the Night.

THE SISTERS ENJOYED WEEKS OF INTIMACY UNMATCHED SINCE THEIR FAther's passing. Brandy helped. A lot. The obsession of the court with Direcia quieted the usual politics. Helspeth did not miss the whining, backbiting, and name-calling. She did enjoy the time with her sister, just being sisters. Though she found the adult Katrin's powerful, obsessive, driving emotions frightening and her ignorance appalling.

GRAND DUKE HILANDLE WAS IN A FINE MOOD, GRACIOUSLY GIFTING EVERY-one he appreciated, for whatever reason. Helspeth faked a smile and wondered, for the hundredth time, why Hilandle was not in Direcia, commanding those Imperials who had chosen to reinforce King Peter. Lord Admiral Vondo fon Tyre was not suited to the task.

Hilandle began telling a hitherto unbored embassy from the Eastern Empire about the monster in the Jagos. Wonder of wonders, he credited the Princess Apparent with having engineered the beast's defeat. Then he produced the grasper he had lopped off the monster in his own encounter. The emissaries of the Eastern Emperor pretended to be impressed.

Those men were not interested in the Grand Duke's adventures. Rumors had leaked out. They had come to assess the likelihood that the Empress really would back another crusade in the east. Earlier crusades had not benefited the Eastern Empire. Especially those that originated in the Grail Empire. Those earlier crusaders had traveled overland, of necessity passing through the Eastern Empire. They had been more terrible than any locust plague.

These days the eastern emperors, however mad they might be in their beliefs, policies, and social notions, made sure the locusts of the west would not scourge their empire again.

"Time to find out what those not beholden to us think," Katrin said. Shakily. Because of too much brandy, not the uncertainty that ruled her secretly. She wanted to sit down with the strangely dressed easterners, whose beliefs seemed almost as bizarre as those of the Connecten dualists. She wanted what she could not have here, even with her confessor. She wanted to talk on into the night, as young people do, playing with ideas as though they were counters in some timeless game.

The chieftain of the eastern embassy seemed older than the world itself. He wore a huge, brushy black and gray beard. Katrin paid him little mind. She was almost flirtatious with his younger associates. Helspeth followed Katrin's lead, as much as her nature allowed.

There was no point, she thought. Katrin was amusing herself at the easterners' expense. They pretended to be good Chaldareans but were only slightly less damned than the Praman Unbeliever. They refused to recognize the divine supremacy of the Principaté of Principatés, the Patriarch of Brothe.

Fifteen minutes into the audience Helspeth knew the easterners were playing the Empress more than she thought she was playing them. The encounter consisted entirely of posturing and lying. She tried to suggest that the visitors be left to the droning mercies of the Grand Duke. She failed. They played well to Katrin's need for approval.

For the first time since her coronation Katrin was having a good time, Direcia forgotten.

The Direcian situation had not forgotten her.

An obsequious courtier came at Katrin like a bowing, puling crossbow bolt, clearly the harbinger of great news. While having no idea what that news might be.

As her sister fell into a chair, crying, Helspeth spied Ferris Renfrow weaving through the parasites of the court at Alten Weinberg. He looked like he had just stepped off the battlefield. He was filthy. Heavily bearded. His clothing in tatters. Under a mail hauberk in worse shape than a shirt ripped and torn by squabbling dogs. He had been leaking blood recently. He was pallid. He approached in a controlled stumble.

Where had he been? Helspeth had not seen him since last winter. Nor had anyone. Mainly to their pleasure. Many creatures of the court considered Ferris Renfrow a tutelary, not just a man whose labors on behalf of the Grail Empire had been appreciated by no one other than Johannes Blackboots.

At Helspeth's urging, Katrin brushed aside her tears. She recognized the spymaster and beckoned him. "Hurry!" she insisted. "Tell me! What news? How awful is it? Must we go into mourning? Are we in danger from the Unbeliever? Why aren't the bells ringing?"

The bells in every Chaldarean church were supposed to ring if the news from Direcia was good.

Ferris Renfrow seemed to gather strength. He dispensed with the usual honors. He treated his Empress, her sister, her courtiers, and the nearest easterners as though they were companions on campaign. "Not at all, Highness. The news is good. God stood with the Chaldareans in Direcia. He gave us a victory for the ages. The Unbeliever may never be a threat there again. Unless he gets help from the eastern kaifates. His champions are all dead. Every Praman of substance who rode with Sabuta. Gone."

Katrin seethed with impatience. She did not care about the battle's outcome. She wanted to know, "What about my Jaime?"

"He survived, Highness. He was one of the heroes. A timely charge by the Castaurigans sealed the thing."

"I sense reservations, Ferris. Don't toy with me. Tell me. I am the daughter of Johannes Blackboots." And for a moment everyone within earshot believed, except Helspeth. Helspeth felt the fear devouring the inside of this girl who pretended to be the despot of the Grail Empire.

"You are. My apologies. Jaime suffered numerous wounds, two of which were not inconsequential. He'll be a while recovering but there's no reason he shouldn't. And, despite his injuries, he hopes the nuptials will happen on schedule this time."

Helspeth kept her expression blank. She was unable to believe that handsome Jaime of Castauriga could be infatuated with her horse-face, insecure sister. Other than as a means by which he could elevate his own status, especially inside the Grail Empire. Though the marriage contract kept Jaime from becoming more than Katrin's consort, he would father the next Emperor.

Ferris Renfrow glanced at Helspeth. She smiled weakly.

"When can I expect my beloved?" Katrin asked.

"Not soon, Highness. But as soon as he's physically able. He's as eager as you are. He'd be headed this way now, but for his wounds." Renfrow glanced at Helspeth again, caught her frowning. She thought he was just telling Katrin what she wanted to hear. He showed her a tiny smile she took to mean that he confessed the action but not the crime. What he said was true, although it did fit in with Katrin's wishful thinking.

The Empress swallowed a draft of brandy that dismayed everyone and made it plain she had lost interest in the easterners. She did not care if they were affronted. In a soft voice she spoke to the chief of the serving staff. That man began shooing pages and servers out of the hall.

Katrin could have been more directly offensive only by shouting, "Get the fuck out of here, you assholes!" By the standards of the easterners. Who did understand that she was not creating an incident willfully. She was female, after all. At her best, most brilliant moments she was certain to be distracted and emotionally confused.

The easterners withdrew. Other guests departed. Members of the Council tried to assert themselves. Just a scowl from Ferris Renfrow sent them scurrying.

Helspeth watched in wonder while the grand hall shed ninety percent of its occupants.

When Renfrow came so close that no one would overhear, Helspeth asked, "Who are you, Ferris Renfrow?" Getting no answer, she added, "I bet that battle isn't more than a day old. How can you possibly know?"

"Why do you care, Princess? Isn't it enough to know?"

Helspeth did not respond. But she had ideas that would not please the master spy. She shrugged, pretending it was only adolescent curiosity.

Renfrow went on, indifferent to the sharp-eyed suspicion of the younger Princess. He told the story of the battle. "In the central highlands of Direcia there's a blistering plain known by several names. Plano Alto is the most common. It's been a no-man's-land between Chaldarean Direcia and al-Halambra since King Peter overcame the Praman principalities farther north. It's set off by a range called the Brown Mountains. The most direct approach to al-Halambra is over those mountains, across the Plano Alto, then down to the river valley of the Plata Desnuda. Which means something like naked silver and makes no sense. But that's not germane.

"Four kings joined Peter of Navaya in responding to the threat of the Almanohides. With them rode the chivalry of many other kingdoms, great and small. Meaning our ever-prickly contemporaries *can* recognize a real threat. As opposed to one contrived." Just to make his point clear. Without naming any recent Patriarch. "Eighty thousand gathered. The Pramans were overawed. Counsels of caution prevailed. They decided to defend the passes through the Brown Mountains instead of invading Navaya until Peter's allies went home."

Ferris Renfrow glanced round, found his audience content to listen. "The Almanohides thought they had the advantage. But a Chaldarean shepherd knew a way through the mountains that the Pramans hadn't found. We got through, behind, defeating numerous Praman bands before Sabuta abd al-Qadr al-Margrebi gathered his forces near a village known, in Direcian, as the Baths of the Spirits. There are healing hot springs there, of which King Jaime is taking full advantage. Each spring is an extremely feeble well of power. Kaif Sabuta's personal guard attached themselves by chains and shackles to posts driven deep into the ground all round their master's tent. So they couldn't run away if things turned out the way our side hoped.

"That was all for show. They didn't think their god would turn his face away. I expect they're asking him about that now.

"The Chaldarean victory was overwhelming. King Peter was the great hero. With King Jaime playing a smaller but still very big role."

Helspeth said, "So, once again Peter of Navaya is made stronger."

Renfrow said, "Some think he must be especially beloved of God. Each time he responds to the will of the Patriarch, his fortunes soar."

Helspeth kept her opinions behind her teeth. Not needing Renfrow's warning glance.

Katrin would not tolerate criticism of the Patriarchy. Although Boniface VII was doing bizarre things, like making overtures to Viscesment, canceling the charter of the Society for the Suppression of Sacrilege and Heresy, trying to open the Collegium to a broader range of prelates, and, especially, striving to revitalize the Church in its role as Protector of the Small. Meaning taking up its ancient obligation to shield the poor and the weak from the Tyranny of the Night. Boniface was making himself unpopular by absolutely insisting that Mother Church do all those good things that, supposedly, Mother Church had been created to do.

Every new Patriarch offered surprises. This one was the terror of all clerics of standing: an honest, God-fearing pontiff.

Because Katrin was not interested, Helspeth asked questions. "What's he done to make secular people unhappy?"

"He's about to send the Patriarchal army back to the Connec. But this time to hunt down the Instrumentalities running loose there."

"Instead of heretics?"

"It could be open season on dualists, too. But only if the troops want to bother. They call the Captain-General the Godslayer, these days. And that's what he'll be doing. Destroying things freed by the Artecipean pagans. Instead of just binding them."

Helspeth understood, tactically. Having witnessed the destruction of an Instrumentality.

The Captain-General's falconeers had, supposedly, refined and honed their methods dramatically since the encounter in the Jagos. Still . . . "How can the Church afford that? I saw the ammunition they use. It's expensive."

"The Deves of Brothe, who are allied with the Captain-General for reasons only they understand, have developed munitions that include only a twentieth of the silver needed when you attacked the monster in the Jagos."

"But . . ." She did note the use of "attacked" in preference to anything more absolute and final.

"Yes. You're right. It will be expensive to wage war on the Night, even so. Boniface will finance this campaign by the means used to fund the original crusades in the east. Every church, every monastery, every nunnery, every living, every instrument of the Church that produces revenue, will have to forward another tenth to Brothe to finance the scouring of the Connec. If that works, the compulsory donation could become a permanent weapon in the struggle against the Night."

"That's sure to cause him trouble."

"The Special Office will be thrilled."

"Are we going to trade in the Society for the Witchfinders?"

"Possibly." Renfrow shrugged. "Boniface's reign will be characterized by an inflexible adherence to canon law. He'll root out corruption wherever it's found. He's issued a bull saying the Church must put its house in order. That it must be beyond reproach when it makes demands of the secular realm. He might well loose the Captain-General on any bishop who remains obstinate."

"A great wind of reform, eh?"

"As Aaron declaimed on the steps of the Home Temple. It could be. Unfortunately, Boniface is older than the moon. He was a compromise, chosen to take up space while the factions agree on a younger man. A more flexible, more amenable man."

"Boniface won't live long enough to reform the Church?"

"That would require an immortal. Your Highness? Katrin? You haven't said a word."

"Jaime is all right?"

"He'll recover. Expect him here before winter closes the passes. His journey may be slow and painful but he's eager. You shan't have to endure virginity many months more. And now I must take my leave, sweet ladies. I'm an old man. I've come a long, hard way to bring the news. I need rest."

Katrin made a faint gesture, giving Renfrow permission to leave.

Helspeth surveyed those of the court who remained. They had closed in in order to listen. A few, old men of the Council Advisory, were not pleased. Not that they had hoped for a Chaldarean defeat. But they had hoped that King Jaime would embarrass himself somehow. This Imperial marriage, however much they had been part of making the arrangements, would only reduce their influence over Katrin.

Plotting. Always plotting. Helspeth fumed. And wondered how her father had controlled them.

Their natures must have compelled them to play the same games when Johannes was Emperor. Therefore, perhaps, one nickname: Ferocious Little Hans.

They did respect power. When it was employed.

Katrin employed her power inconsistently. She had trouble keeping her mind made up, except in the matters of Jaime of Castauriga and her allegiance to the Brothen Patriarchy.

Helspeth wondered what Katrin would do if Boniface tried to take over Imperial holdings in Firaldia. Lothar had come near war over Clearenza. Would have gone to war if he had lived. Katrin had accepted the Clearenza situation, urging that city's Duke to be more obedient to Mother Church.

Sublime's cronies did make sure the Duke's loans got repaid.

THE CHANGE IN KATRIN WAS DRAMATIC. IT INFECTED THE COURT, THEN Alten Weinberg as a whole, though hundreds of families still waited anxiously for word of those they had sent to Direcia.

Helspeth hoped to manage a private conversation with Ferris Renfrow. That did not happen. The spymaster slept twelve hours, ate a huge meal in the palace kitchen, then vanished. The gate guards did not see him go. Nor had any seen him arrive, either.

Helspeth worried about that often over the next six days, though without real passion. Ferris Renfrow had been an unpredictable enigma all her life. And all her father's life before her, insofar as she knew.

Church bells began ringing the sixth afternoon after Renfrow disappeared. The racket puzzled Helspeth. It was not a holy day, a feast day, a church day, or time for a call to prayer. Then it struck her.

News of the victory had come. Officially so, by courier. Each parish was proclaiming the celebration, as had been the order since war in Direcia became unavoidable.

Helspeth calculated distances and how hard the couriers must have ridden. They would have done relays, changing horses frequently, pausing just long enough to tell local bishops to spread the glad news in their dioceses.

So how did Ferris Renfrow manage to arrive six days early, rank, ragged, and bleeding? As though he had stepped through a doorway directly from the battlefield into a courtyard in the Imperial palace?

Something surpassing strange was afoot. And much as she wanted to know what that was, Helspeth did not discuss it with anyone. She might have stumbled over something no one else had yet noticed. No one ever accused Ferris Renfrow of having anything but an eerie mundane knack for slipping around unnoticed.

She had asked Renfrow who he was. The better question might have been, what was he?

22. The End of Connec: The Master's Release

The interminable months in the misery of the Altai ground souls into spiritual dust. Winter isolated Corpseour for three entire months. It was a winter beyond the prior imaginings of anyone trapped there. The sole focus of the colony became keeping warm. Those who had stocked the fortress had done well with food and water and weapons, but they had failed to foresee the fuel demands of an unnatural winter.

Rationing was necessary. Fuel had to be reserved for cooking.

The refugees did everything to soften winter's bite. But up there, in a narrow, draughty edifice built beam-on to the prevailing wind, it was impossible to hide from the cold. Nor was it possible to leave. Worsening weather closed the path to Corpseour. Those who tried it inevitably lost their footing. Several fell to their deaths.

The dark running joke was that they could thank the Light that the Instrumentalities of the Night haunting the Connec would not trouble Corpseour. Those were smart enough not to climb into that icy hell.

"Lessons learned," Brother Candle muttered. "Next spring they'll bring up mortar for chinking, and firewood, too." He was talking to no one in particular but was cuddled up with Socia, the Archimbaults, and half a dozen others, buried under a communal spread of blankets, trying to keep warm. It was not bad for him. He was in the middle, holding Kedle's baby, they being the weakest of the group. The baby was not doing well. Brother Candle feared it would not survive. Kedle was not producing enough milk. If the baby did make it, it would always be a weak child.

Kedle knew. Kedle cried a lot, despite knowing that she would always be sheltered by the Archimbault tribe and Seeker community.

There had been no news about Soames.

THE WORST WEATHER FINALLY BROKE. A WARM SOUTHERN WIND CAME. ICE began to melt. Brother Candle risked going to the battlements, being careful of his footing. Meltwater only made that more treacherous in shady places.

One glance told him it was warmer down by the lake. Warmer and less windy. People were harvesting ice. They would store it in caves, carrying a little winter into the summer. Birds drifted and soared at several levels between Corpseour and Albodiges. One species seemed unusual. The Perfect supposed it had come from the north, fleeing the permanent ice.

Cold came and went several times before spring achieved ascendance. And news came through.

It was a new world. There was a new Patriarch in Brothe. The Captain-General and his army had gone. A new war was taking shape in Direcia. This one posed a mortal threat far beyond those Chaldarean kingdoms in the direct path of the Almanohides.

The Maysalean Heresy had not been forgotten—the Society was making its notes and accusations—but in the larger picture the dualists had become insignificant. Had become annoying blowflies because wolves were running the borders.

Socia was put out. "We went through all that up there for nothing!" And Kedle backed her up, almost viciously.

"Indeed?" Brother Candle responded. "And which of you girls was prescient enough to foresee all those changes?"

"Bah!" Socia snorted. Knowing the argument could not be won.

"We make the best decisions we can using the information we have. In time to come you'll realize that one never has enough information to make the perfect decision. You do the best you can, and hope. Or, like Duke Tormond, you try to wait till you *can* make the perfect choice."

"Grr!" Socia said. "And then it's too late. I get it. But I sure as hell don't have to like it. What're we gonna do now?"

"Go back to Khaurene. Help these folk reclaim their places there."

The Society must have tried to seize the properties of Seekers who had not stayed to protect them.

But, Brother Candle soon learned, the Society's influence in Khaurene had guttered and gone. Known members had paid dearly for the successes of the Patriarchal forces in the fighting outside Khaurene. Brothen Episcopal churches had been looted and their priests driven out. Members of those parishes had banded together to protect themselves. They called themselves the Scarlet Cross. They wore black robes with red crosses sewn on when they roamed the streets.

Chaldareans who supported the resurgent Bellicose in Viscesment wore pale robes with black, blue, or even purple crosses sewn on. Some younger, more spirited Seekers had adopted white robes with a yellow cross for their vigilance bands.

A seamstress told Brother Candle that the militias chose the cross because that was the most efficient way of making a symbol using costly colored cloth. Other shapes left waste material.

KHAURENE HAD CHANGED DRAMATICALLY. IT HAD BECOME ABIDINGLY FACtional. Street brawls happened almost every day. Duke Tormond made ineffectual efforts to stifle them with insufficient resources.

Socia sneered, "I thought all the fools got wiped out in that battle last fall."

Brother Candle said, "Human nature being human nature, the fools were the more likely survivors. And, pray, don't say that in front of Kedle."

Still no news of the Archimbault daughter's spouse. His battalion had been overrun by the Captain-General's handful of heavy cavalry. Most survivors did not want to talk. Which suggested that they might have had their backs to the enemy by then. No one who would talk knew what had become of Soames.

Socia said, "He'll turn up if he survived. He looked forward to becoming a parasite. If you ask me."

Brother Candle's estimate of the man had been somewhat higher. But not much. He wondered what Raulet had hoped to gain from the match. "Not kind, girl."

"But true. All right. All right. I'll be a good Seeker and look on the bright side. We won't have to stay with that foul baker again." Spoken with Madam Scarre standing scarcely two yards away.

Brother Candle sighed. The child was hopeless. But, after all this time, she was almost a daughter. Or even a chaste young wife. He had difficulty imagining life without her. But that day was coming. He had to take her back to Antieux.

*   *   *

KHAURENE WAS A SIZABLE CITY BUT WORD GOT AROUND. THE SUMMONS TO Metrelieux reached the Master his third afternoon back in the city.

Socia refused to go up the hill with him. She had no faith in the good behavior of the local gentry, probably because her own nature was wholly predatory.

Unfamiliar men guarded the gate of the ancient fortress. Younger than their predecessors, they might actually have offered a moment of resistance. An unfamiliar chamberlain greeted Brother Candle. Inside, the Perfect saw unfamiliar faces everywhere, mostly strangers dressed in Direcian styles. He wondered why they were here when so critical a campaign was taking shape in their homeland.

Securing somewhere to run to if the worst happened?

The chamberlain led him to a hall he had visited several times before. This was well stocked with familiar faces. "All the usual miscreants, I see," he said as he arrived.

"Welcome, Charde," Duke Tormond said, coming to meet him. With his usual overestimation of the warmth of their relationship. Tormond had aged horribly. He would not last much longer. Which might explain the Navayans another way. Was Isabeth somewhere handy, ready to step in?

Then the Direcians would be here to enforce her claim to succeed Tormond, despite the law?

The Duke continued. "Not all the usual gang. Sir Eardale perished in his ill-starred battle. He just had to fight. And Tember Sirht isn't with us anymore. He took his people into exile in Terliaga."

Duke Tormond seemed resigned to the Terliagan Littoral's defection. The man seemed resigned, in fact, to anything.

The effort to poison him had been a waste of ambition. When you came right down to it.

"You wanted to see me?" Brother Candle asked after he shed the Duke's embrace.

Bishop Clayto told him, "We need your wisdom. Great things will soon happen in Direcia. The backwash may drown us."

"I've just spent four months on top of a mountain. Freezing. Plus time going and coming. I have no idea what's happening."

"There's a new Patriarch in Brothe. Another new one. Boniface VII. We don't know what he'll be like, yet. The Captain-General destroyed the pagan revivalists in Artecipea that the last Patriarch forced him to attack, hoping he'd get bogged down. Because he'd become strong enough to be feared by his masters. Meantime, the flower of Chaldarean chivalry is flooding into Direcea. We expect to hear of a battle any day now. And we fear that, no matter the outcome, what follows won't be good for the Connec."

"How so?"

"If God averts His countenance we'll soon see Almanohides horsemen outside the walls. If King Peter is victorious, it'll be Arnhanders out there doing mischief as they trudge on home. Anne of Menand certainly had that in mind when she sent Regard down with half the feudal levy of Arnhand."

"Regard?" Brother Candle asked. "She dared let the boy out of sight?"

"She had no choice. Strong as she is, fierce as she is, Anne's position is still fluid. And will never get any more solid if Regard doesn't win the respect of the fighting nobility."

"I see," Brother Candle said. "To tighten her grip Anne has to let her baby go off to war. Suppose the worst happens? Who succeeds? The younger brother?"

"Anselin? Probably. Though Anne hasn't thought that far ahead."

Duke Tormond chipped in, "Anselin is on crusade in the Holy Lands. Or that was his plan when I visited Salpeno. He wasn't happy. He didn't want to go. It was the only way he could get away from his mother."

"Then Regard's fall throws Arnhand into chaos. The nobility would never let Anne take charge directly. Might not even accept her as regent while Anselin was recalled."

Bishop Clayto said, "So you're suggesting that we could experience several years' respite if Regard doesn't make it back from Direcia."

The Master protested, "That's not what I meant at all!"

The Duke said, "You see, gentlemen? I told you it would be worthwhile to drag Charde up out of the stews."

Brother Candle protested again. And was ignored. The Council, including the Brothen Episcopal Bishop, began amusing themselves by conspiring to cause the premature ascent to paradise of King Regard of Arnhand. It was not a conspiracy with any heart. It was a wishful thinking game played by a covey of weak men who had been drinking too much wine too early in the day. Men, Brother Candle concluded, who would shepherd an ancient culture into oblivion not because they could not withstand predators from without but because they could not get up on their hind legs and take charge within.

Not once was his advice actively invited. He went away again after a few hours. No one seemed to notice or care.

BROTHER CANDLE AND SOCIA RAULT HAD JUST SETTLED IN TO REST WITH the resurgent Seeker community in Castreresone. The city's bells began ringing joyously, celebrating the Chaldarean victory at Los Naves de los Fantas. Word spread fast. No one believed the news was not exaggerated. Al-Prama's worst defeat in four hundred years? Impossible.

"And now the torment of the Connec resumes," Brother Candle observed.

"When did it let up?" Socia demanded.

Reaching Castreresone had taken nine days. Not so bad as the trek westward, yet fraught with danger from bandits and men serving surviving local lords who were little better than bandits. Not to mention things of the Night.

The pagans of Artecipea had released more dark spirits than they anticipated. When the ghost of a Shade or Rook or Hilt began to crawl the earth again, and reached a breakthrough level of restoration, it began to call up and release its own satellite Instrumentalities. Scores of which now roamed the wilderness, frail and blind but perfectly capable of preying on the incautious and unwitting.

Brother Candle stayed a while at Castreresone to relax and recollect his strength. He was there longer than he hoped. He wanted to send a message to Antieux. Socia would not hear of it. He hoped she would not be as surprised as Count Raymone might.

He looking forward to turning his charge over. That would free him, finally, to tend to the cleansing and healing of his soul.

The pause at Castreresone seemed endless. Just when Brother Candle felt ready to go on, he fell sick. Then the situation outside became so nasty the consuls locked everyone in till patrols cleared the danger. That danger did not keep news out: Neither Regard nor his chief followers were interested in more war after what they had survived in Direcia. They just wanted to go home.

Eventually, the old man and girl did return to the road, he observing, "I expect Regard will get a real scolding when he gets back to Salpeno."

"Or his mother will. He's a veteran, now. He's been tempered in the flame. Maybe he's developed a backbone."

Socia was dressed to look like an older boy. As always when they were on the road. And a good choice it was. Maysalean pilgrims, a Master and his student, were troubled by none but the frenetically insane. Masters disdained money. Their only currency was wisdom. Any student companion would be poorer still.

Later, they learned that a few Arnhanders did, indeed, indulge in looting and terror tactics, ignoring the distinction between heretics, Unbelievers, and Chaldareans of various allegiances. They just took whatever had not been taken already by previous invaders or predatory neighbors. They captured few towns or castles, nor did any great slaughter, but they did guarantee that they would find no allies if they returned.

Antieux was in sight when the old man and girl met a frightened traveler who shared what he believed was terrible news. The new Patriarch, Boniface VII, intended to send the Captain-General back to the Connec. He would have fewer men but all of them would be hardened veterans.

Antieux had begun preparing for yet another siege already.

Socia was grim. "How will we manage? There was almost no harvest last year. And the enemy isn't likely to let us get many crops in before he shows up this year."

Brother Candle had listened to the traveler more closely than she. "This is a new Patriarch. Not that lunatic Sublime. My guess is, he really does want to clean up the Instrumentalities that got loose here."

"We're talking about a man who said he would put an end to the Society's wickedness. Have you heard of any changes for the better, there?"

He had. But Socia was not about to hear it. He saved his breath. There were miles to be walked and his old joints ached. He thought about retiring altogether, not just dallying in a cloister while he rebuilt his spiritual center. Some Perfect did withdraw permanently, generally into one of several fastnesses down in the mountainous frontier counties between the Connec and Direcia. Even devout Episcopals there scorned the rule of Brothe and loved their neighbors more.

From crusty and bellicose, Socia turned concerned. "Are you all right?"

"I'm fine, child. It's just age slowing me down."

She eyed him suspiciously. She had been his companion long enough to follow the weakening of his flesh.

"I'm just tired." But he knew a hint of fear. His fiercest will could not push him forward at as fast a pace as he could make just last summer. He thought his decline had begun during that terrible passage from Castreresone to Khaurene. The miserable sojourn in Corpseour had not helped.

He despised his own weakness. Not his physical failing. That came to every man fortunate enough to grow old. No. He detested the fear that slipped foul tendrils through the armor of his faith. Death should not be dreaded. Death was no revenant creeping through the night, spreading corruption. Death was the doorway to the Light.

"I just need to get my feet back on the Path."

Socia understood that side of him, however weak her own faith.

Someone riding, who had passed them heading east, must have recognized Brother Candle. Socia's surprise did not materialize as planned. As they began the last mile downhill, Antieux's gate spilled a covey of horsemen. The Perfect recognized Bernardin Amberchelle almost immediately, then several Rault brothers and Count Raymone. "Looks like they mean to run us off before we can pollute their city."

"Smart-ass." Tearful, Socia began to run.

There was no run left in Brother Candle's old corpse. He trudged on, considering the countryside around him. A determined effort at restoration was under way. It appeared amazingly successful. The siege must not have been as harsh as rumor insisted. Or . . .

Or Count Raymone had done something extraordinary. And what that was became obvious after a study of the people in the fields and on the hillsides.

Raymone was using forced labor to restore his county. He must have rounded up all the Grolsachers he could find.

The Perfect would learn, later, that not just refugees had been forced into the labor gangs. Prisoners of war, criminals, captured bandits, and members of the Society were slaving out there, being used up with grim indifference to their humanity. And Count Raymone's logic was hard to refute. Those were the people responsible for the damage to the Connec. Let them die undoing the evil they had wrought.

The reunion was well under way when Brother Candle caught up to Socia, who was pummeling her brothers severely in her excitement. Of them, only Booth seemed the worse for wear. He had suffered a fierce wound to the left side of his head. Part of his ear was gone. The scar itself remained puffy and purplish. It was one of those that might take a decade to subside into normal scar tissue. The Perfect noted that Booth's left eye did not track, either. But the youngest Rault was wearing one huge grin.

Count Raymone came to Brother Candle. "I don't know how to thank you, Master. I didn't mean for Socia to become your whole life. You kept faith through hardships I can't begin to imagine. Till yesterday I feared you were lost. Bernardin has been keeping my spirits up since he came back from captivity. He was more confident of you than I was. I'm sorry."

The warrior enveloped the old man in his powerful arms. "I owe you, Master. I don't have much anymore, but anything I have is yours. For the asking."

"Peace, then."

"Master?"

"Make peace with the new Patriarch."

"I am at peace with him. And shall ever be. So long as he stays in Brothe. If he comes to Antieux to tell us what to do, then it's him who breaks that peace."

Brother Candle abandoned the argument. For the moment. There would be a better time. A time when reason might practice its subtle sedition against prejudice.

Count Raymone said, "Socia tells me that you're eager to get back to the intellectual harbor of Perfect companions. But I hope you'll stay for the wedding."

"I can do that. Unless war comes. I'm done with war."

Count Raymone's conviction that that was silly shone through. Then he grinned. "Done. If it looks like we can't get along with somebody, I'll slap your skinny ass on a donkey, point it west, and give it a whack on the rump."

Brother Candle considered the possibility that, even now, his outlook was too naive. If he lived much longer he would see more war. The Arnhanders would be back. They sensed the weakness and rot in the Connec. The province's hope was not Tormond, never Duke Tormond, nor even Count Raymone Garete. Count Raymone did not have the resources. Hope lay beyond the Verses Mountains, in Direcia. In Peter of Navaya.

"All right. Who could resist that offer?"

THE WEDDING CAME OFF PERFECTLY, WITHIN THE MONTH. TWO NEWLY-weds could not have been more thrilled with one another. And Socia won the hearts of the obdurate people of Antieux with her fierce talk.

Following the wedding Count Raymone sent Bernardin Amberchelle and a hundred men to take the Rault brothers home. Caron ande Lette was in the hands of Grolsacher squatters. The expedition did not go well. The squatters were more numerous than expected. And the Night haunted the land. It was no longer a place for a man who had not surrendered to the will of the Night.

When the tattered survivors returned to Antieux Count Raymone decided, "I'll send word to the Captain-General. He can muck out that cesspool for us."

Brother Candle stayed in Antieux way longer than he planned. Worldly things had a definite hold. He was reluctant to leave companionship he had enjoyed so long. As though Socia had become the family he had put aside to walk the path to Perfection.

But he could not stall forever. The Seekers of the west needed leadership and encouragement. And he needed his refreshment of the soul.

"Raymone," he said reluctantly, accepting the lead of a pack donkey the Count had nicknamed Socia for its stubbornness, "I've decided how you can repay me. Other than with this tragic beast, who will no doubt be taken by bandits before I'm out of sight of the wall."

"Not while you wear the pilgrim's robe, Master. They're superstitious, living out there with the Night so close. They won't trouble you."

"Yes. Only the Church will dare. Eh?"

"As you say. What boon would you have of me?"

"Peace being impractical, protection for those who follow the Path."

Count Raymone lowered his face as though to a king. "So shall it be, Master. So long as I have breath."

Socia, standing by quietly, reluctant to speak because she feared she would burst into tears, repeated the formula. "So shall it be, Master. So long as *I* have breath. And an arm to raise a spear." Which remark sparked an immediate squabble between powerful personalities.

Smiling in spite of his sorrow at parting, Brother Candle tugged the donkey's lead and took a step down the road to his future. First destination, Khaurene. After that, somewhere to reclaim Perfection. In essence, out of history, having shaped the minds of several people who would sculpt it with sharp steel.

23. Dreanger: At al-Qarn, in the Palace of the Kings

The old house slave, Gamel, strained under the weight of the burden he carried across the polished serpentine floor of the vast hall where Gordimer the Lion was holding the autumn assizes. Er-Rashal al-Dhulquarnen was present, evidently having an interest in some case due to come before the Grand Marshal. Likewise, Kaif Karim Kaseem al-Bakr, who dozed on a chair nearby. He was there for a case with religious implications.

The slave had little time left in this hard vale. Decades ago he had been a fierce young Sha-lug. Time, luck, and an amazing knack for healing had conspired to rob him of a battlefield death. Sha-lug who grew old despite the endless wars had to earn their keep managing the work of the Palace.

Gamel was well known to Gordimer. Gamel had taught him the lance when he was a pup. The Marshal concluded the case at hand by ordering the defendant strangled for defiling the daughter of his sister. Sentence was carried out on the spot. Gordimer then ordered the daughter stoned. Both corpses to be thrown to the crocodiles.

Then he sent two lifeguards to help the old man.

"Forget all that, Gamel. Your life has earned you the right to stand in the presence of the Marshal." Though not, perhaps, in that of the Kaif. If the Kaif were anything but an extension of the will of the Sha-lug, and awake. "What is this?"

It had to be critical if the old slave came here, now, during the height of the assizes.

"This box was given to me to bring to you. I was told it had to be delivered immediately."

"And what is it?"

"I don't know. But it's been dripping cold water."

"Who gave it to you?"

"General Nassim. Nassim Alizarin."

"The Mountain? He's here? In al-Qarn? Er-Rashal. I thought Nassim was dead."

Shaken, the court sorcerer replied, "I was sure he was no longer among the living."

"Let's see what it is. You two. Bring that box here. Open it."

Er-Rashal faded into himself while the lifeguards carried out instructions. Suddenly, he snapped, "Don't open that!" An instant too late.

"What do we have?" Gordimer demanded. He glowered at the scores of supplicants and defendants, all of whom leaned toward the scene.

"A head. In melted ice." The lifeguard lifted a severed head from the box by its hair. His companion retrieved a wooden tube about six inches long and an inch in diameter, covered with wax. He handed that to the Marshal.

Gordimer twisted an end off the cold tube, fished out a piece of paper. He asked er-Rashal, "What's the matter?" The sorcerer stared at the head. "You've turned gray." The Lion unrolled the paper. And read aloud, " 'To my lord the Grand Marshal of the Sha-lug, Gordimer, called the Lion, and to the sorcerer er-Rashal al-Dhulquarnen. Greetings. A gift. All that remains of the pagan sorcerer Rudenes Schneidel, by whose order my son Hagid was murdered. He was the first to pay. His partners in wickedness will follow.

" 'Nassim Alizarin, once a friend.

" 'In recollection of friendship, O Lion. A courtesy. Be warned. The storm from the north is rising. I have seen it with mine own eyes, and it is of your own construction. Nor even the Almighty Himself shall stand before it.' "

Gordimer the Lion closed his eyes. This was the voice of prophecy. Half a minute later, he said, "Clear the hall. The assizes will resume tomorrow morning." He roamed his own mind till the hall fell quiet.

He opened his eyes. Er-Rashal was no longer present. The Kaif still slept. Gamel had retired. He addressed the lifeguard still holding the head by its hair. "Glaid. What do you make of this?"

"That General Nassim disappeared because he heard his son was murdered. But Hagid was supposedly among those Sha-lug lost in Calzir."

"Where he was not supposed to have been."

The lifeguard nodded. "There are evil rumors about what happened over there. About Sha-lug who were abandoned, denied the chance to board ships carrying survivors of the disaster away from Calzir."

"Is that so? I haven't heard anything like that. Sidiki. You look like you're about to explode. If only you dared. Dare."

"There is much that you do not hear, sitting here in the Palace, O Lion." Sidiki carefully avoided the least implication of criticism, though the lifeguard complement were scandalized by the behavior of the Marshal in recent years and even those nearest him thought he had ordered those Sha-lug abandoned to the mercy of the Infidel because of their connection with Else Tage, the once-popular band leader whom Gordimer feared for no reason anyone could fathom.

In the end, the lifeguards, and those Sha-lug who spent much time around the Palace of the Kings, chose to blame all misfortune on the sorcerer er-Rashal el-Dhulquarnen.

"Enlighten me."

24. Brothe: At the End of the Day

After a week of loafing Piper Hecht started half days at the Castella. Nothing official had come out of Krois. But rumors ran hot and fierce. There would be another invasion of the Connec. For sure. To war against the Night. So staff work did go forward.

Ships were at sea, collecting the troops from Artecipea. Titus Consent made sure those men knew that it was Piper Hecht's fault they were coming home. The Captain-General and Boniface VII had an understanding. The Patriarchy's soldiers would be treated well, henceforth. With a big *or else!* implied.

Pinkus Ghort visited Anna's house briefly. After losing to her at chess, he told Hecht, "Take care how forward you are about your soldiers, Pipe. You got people in the Collegium putting you on their shit lists just because you're in a strong place."

Hecht had seen the signs. Wherever three or more people got together somebody developed a need to drag somebody else down.

He was about to snap defiantly, arrogantly, but caught himself.

"What?" Ghort asked. "You don't believe me?"

"No. I do. I'm having trouble believing me."

Ghort gave Hecht that look he reserved for times when he had no clue what Hecht was talking about.

Hecht asked, "One of them wouldn't be your boss, would it?"

"One of them would. He's developed a hard-on for you."

"He always had one. I wouldn't be his running dog."

"He figures you owe him."

"Really? Because he got us out of Plemenza?"

"Yeah. And some other stuff."

"Despite the fact that he wouldn't be alive if I hadn't wakened him in the Ownvidian Knot."

"I won't make excuses for the man, Pipe. I'm just saying. I tell you this, he's gonna push for enforcement of the quartering restrictions."

Which Hecht had anticipated. Bronte Doneto being consul or not, the city senators would have gotten to that. Maybe just not as soon. No one not part of the Church hierarchy wanted the Patriarch's soldiers stationed in the city.

"I think we're in compliance already." By sleight of hand. By means of a deal with the Brotherhood of War whereby the Brotherhood claimed those of Hecht's men quartered in the Castella.

"Not with the spirit of the law. You could have five thousand armed veterans here inside four days. And a hell of a lot more handy once the rest get over from Artecipea."

"And that's a bad thing with the troubles you're having here?"

"Hey, Pipe, I'm not trying to pick a fight. I'm just saying. And I'm wondering. What's your pal Principaté Delari been up to? We haven't seen hide nor hair in a rat's age."

"I don't know. Why?" Hecht smiled at Vali and Bit's daughter, Lila. The kids kept finding excuses to wander through. They were both curious and hoped that Ghort had brought treats. He did that sometimes.

Lila had recovered physically from the attack that had injured her and killed her mother but she was not yet over it inside. Though older and bigger, she had become Vali's timid shadow. She seemed to have put her harsh early years aside. Anna described her as well mannered and industrious around the house, but remote. She was more bookish than Pella. And could bring Vali out of her shell.

Hecht had overheard the girls talking himself. Chattering, even, almost like kids who had enjoyed a normal childhood.

"Doneto is really interested," Ghort said. "They aren't good buddies. Were almost enemies back around the time the hippodrome fell down. But they patched it up somehow. They tolerate each other, now."

"The way Delari tells it, it was all a misunderstanding. Too many people talking when they should have been listening ended up with them squabbling when they were both trying to get the same job done. Which was to destroy the monster that was murdering people."

Ghort frowned.

Anna said, "I don't think they got it, Piper."

"What? Of course they did. Principaté Delari . . ." He stopped. He could not explain.

"Then the monster's little brother came round to take over the family business."

Ghort was as taken aback as Hecht. "Anna?"

"The murders started up again. Like before."

Hecht watched color drain from Ghort's features. "Pipe. You said Delari dealt with it."

"That's what he told me."

"Did he produce a body?"

"Not for my benefit. And I wasn't interested in seeing one. I was dodging assassins and getting ready for a war."

"You need to find him and see what he thinks."

"Your boss is a consul. And a pretty potent sorcerer."

"You're right. It would be his job. But you still might want to consult Delari."

"I will. We're supposed to have supper at his town house tomorrow night. I assume he'll be there."

"All right. When are you heading back to the Connec?"

"I haven't been told. It's all still rumors. Boniface . . . I have an abiding suspicion that the bureaucracy around the Patriarch is so dense and so tangled that even though the Patriarch is God's dictator on earth he has to hack his way through a jungle before he can work His will."

"You ask me, it's just a bunch of assholes being obstructionist. He ought to have you clean them out. There's people at Krois belonging to families that have been underfoot there for fifteen generations. All of them take bribes from anybody with a piece of silver."

A conversation about corruption in high places got the attention of all the kids, and Anna, too. Before Hecht could caution Ghort about little pitchers, someone knocked on the front door.

Anna told Pella, "See who that is."

It was Titus Consent, Noë, and their brood.

Hecht said, "Titus, I completely forgot. Let me see the baby." He had not yet met Avran.

Noë passed the infant over, but hovered. In case he decided to take a bite.

"No doubt who was this one's daddy. Look at those eyes. Already calculating." Hecht passed the baby back. His mother proceeded round the room, giving everyone the same opportunity. Except for Pinkus Ghort. Noë Consent was seriously nervous about Pinkus Ghort. Ghort was too outgoing. She was a mouse, the most timid woman Hecht had ever met. Only a powerful pride drove her here.

Hecht said, "Pinkus, I completely forgot about Titus. We have business at the foundry."

Ghort faked a scowl and said, "I can tell when I'm not wanted."

Anna offered, "You can stay and play chess."

"Sure. I love getting my head kicked in."

"Shame on you, Pinkus Ghort. You win sometimes." Anna indicated the children. "And none of these miscreants can survive ten moves." Because they were children and could see no point to the game. Though when she focused Vali could be a deadly opponent.

"I've got work of my own that I let slide so I could come down here to talk my best buddy into keeping on being careful."

Titus said, "Noë could play you, Anna. She holds her own against me."

Consent's wife turned bright red. She murmured some sort of demurement and refused to meet the eyes of anyone but her baby.

Still insisting that Hecht remain cautious, Ghort let himself out. "Best buddy?" Consent asked.

"Not quite hyperbole. We've been friends a long time," Hecht said. "Unfortunately, we find ourselves with different employers. I hope we never butt heads."

"We should get moving." Consent started to say something to his wife. Hyperactive toddler Sharone had vanished with Vali and Lila in hot pursuit. The baby was working his magic on Anna. Pella stared over Anna's left shoulder, fascinated.

Hecht said, "Pella, come on with us."

Anna shot him a startled, questioning look.

"He's old enough."

HAVING THE LIFEGUARDS ALONG FRUSTRATED HECHT. BUT THEY WOULD not go away. Titus said, "Resign yourself. You're the most important man in Brothe. After Boniface VII. Bodyguards are the price you pay."

Hecht vented his irritation with rambling nonsense about how Duarnenians never had to suffer this kind of crap. Pella walked alongside, nodding as though he agreed with every word.

Their destination was the workshop and foundry of the people who now manufactured all the firepowder and firepowder weapons for the Patriarchal army, a consortium of leading Devedian families.

Ironic, Hecht thought. If that was the proper word. Unbelievers manufactured the weapons and munitions by which the Chaldarean Patriarchy would enforce its will upon the Faithful.

"The Faithful?" Titus asked. "Mainly things of the Night will be affected by what these people make. You want to whip up on an Imperial town or one of the petty duchies, you'll need to do it the old way."

Hecht did not argue. But Titus was only mostly right. Drago Prosek and Kait Rhuk had a hundred ideas about how firepowder weaponry could change the ways wars were fought. Few involved the Instrumentalities of the Night.

Prosek and Rhuk, with a couple more falcon specialists, were there already when Hecht, Pella, and Consent reached the Krulik and Sneigon Special Manufactory. Consent told Hecht, "We've consolidated firepowder and falcon production here. These people are wonderfully cooperative in helping work out new ways to kill people. And things."

"Especially things," Shimeon Krulik told Hecht soon afterward. "You understand, we Devedians aren't overwhelmed by a compulsion to make life easier for Brothen Episcopal Chaldareans."

"Of course. But we have common interests."

"Indeed. Crippling the Instrumentalities of the Night."

Hecht nodded. Not sure of that at all.

Shimeon Krulik handed Hecht, Pella, and Titus off to a Moslei Sneigon. Sneigon was in charge of production and testing. He was a bent little man who would have been right at home in an ethnic joke. But he was brilliant when it came to knowing what was going on inside his business.

"We've cut costs and improved effectiveness by nearly a hundred times this year, Captain-General. Look. We drip molten iron through these star forms. It comes out cooled just enough so each dribble is a rough arrow shape two inches long. That falls into water. The sudden steam expands and distorts the dart's surfaces."

Sneigon produced a severely irregular iron dart just under two inches long. "We pack these in fine sand treated with a vegetable gum inside these wooden forms that are the same diameter as your falcons. The shock and heat of the exploding firepowder breaks up the charge."

Sneigon showed them workers dipping the tips of the little arrows in molten silver. "We produce the darts fast. The bottleneck is silver application. Quantity doesn't seem to matter with the silver. As long as it's there. One tiny bit on the tip is enough."

"We can save a lot on silver, then?"

"Fortunes. Given time, I think we'll work out how to use a hundredth of the silver we're using now. You'll be spending way more for the iron, the firepowder, and, especially, the falcons themselves."

Hecht was amused by how well Pella managed to fake an understanding of the discussion.

Hecht was fascinated by everything at Krulik and Sneigon. These people were determined to produce new and ever more amazing weapons for deployment in the struggle against the Tyranny of the Night. The darts amazed him. Their battering by steam dramatically expanded their surface area, which meant that more iron would be brought into contact with whatever Instrumentality the missile hit.

Hecht said, "I understand what you're doing. But these darts won't go far, or fast. And the reason firepowder weapons work is, the shot moves too fast for the Instrumentalities to get out of the way."

"Smart man," Sneigon said. "And right. These charges are for when you're up close, smelling their bad breath and seeing the whites of their eyes. Which we figure would be most encounters. We're looking at a variety of other projectiles for longer ranges."

"Very good," Hecht said. "How are we coming with the firepowder?"

"Substantial improvements there, too," Sneigon told him. "We've developed three distinct formulations suitable for several different tasks." He grinned a big white grin behind his black forest of a beard. "You leave these boys free of worries about where their next meal is coming from, then hand them a big intellectual challenge, they end up going after it fifteen hours a day. Besides, it's fun, making all the stinks and bangs."

Hecht looked sideways at Titus Consent. Consent shrugged. "Curse of the breed."

"You stereotyping your own people?"

"Not mine anymore. Except by blood."

"Sorry."

"Mr. Sneigon," Titus said. "You were there when my uncle committed suicide?"

"I was, young Titus." Sneigon turned grim. "That was a dark day. It made no sense. He started babbling about the ravens of wickedness coming home to roost . . . Really! Those were almost his exact words."

"Bizarre. But I believe you. Now here's the thing. Seven elders have committed suicide since the end of the Calziran Crusade. None of them were the sort we'd consider likely candidates. Four were men who fled Sonsa after the riots there. Some time ago, when I was especially rattled by the suicides, the Captain-General asked me if they were all rich. And if they were, how did they get that way? A silly question, I thought then. But now I'm thinking he was more profound than he knew. I don't have the resources in the community that I did before I converted, but I was still able to work out that the men from Sonsa and at least two from Brothe knew each other when they were young. It looks like they were involved in something that made their fortunes. And that might be something they don't want anyone to find out about."

Moslei Sneigon and Titus Consent looked one another in the eye.

Seconds clicked away. Sneigon broke eye contact to glance at Hecht. "There was a rumor, a long time ago. That they made their fortunes slave-raiding. One quick summer, making fast raids where nobody expected slavers, disguised as Praman pirates." He glanced at Hecht again. Hecht had close contacts inside the Brotherhood. The Brotherhood hated pirates almost more than they hated Pramans.

Hecht said, "That's interesting. I heard something similar from Principaté Delari. His illegitimate son, Grade Drocker, had a secret family tucked away in a harbor town over in the Eastern Empire. They got carried off in that kind of slave raid. Drocker spent the rest of his life hunting the slavers, using all the power of the Brotherhood. He died distraught because he never got all the men responsible for his despair."

Sneigon and Consent both were taken aback.

Hecht said, "So Delari says. He didn't understand. I don't, either. But Drocker definitely was a driven man. Obsessed with revenge. So I'm told. I never really saw it myself."

Consent said, "All these men died after Drocker did."

Sneigon suggested, "Delari might have . . ."

Hecht interrupted. "Might not have. Unless he could manage it from over there in the Connec."

Consent trampled Hecht. "That's right, Moslei. You can't blame Delari."

"You think those men would even know what a conscience was? And I'd dispute you, Titus. Three of the suicides probably weren't involved in the old-time slave-raiding thing. But they might have known. They were all friends."

Hecht asked, "Why are we worrying about it? Why aren't we worrying about going forward? None of this means anything to us, now."

Was Cloven Februaren carrying out Grade Drocker's revenge? He *was* sure Muniero Delari was not.

"And, whatever else," Consent said, "we can't get around the fact that those men did take their own lives. In front of witnesses, every one."

Moslei Sneigon made a noise Hecht put halfway between a cat's purr and a dog's growl. Disappointment without disagreement.

Sneigon demonstrated several more experimental notions. Hecht smiled and nodded and pretended enthusiasm. His smiles never reached his eyes. He knew that Krulik and Sneigon would reserve the best weaponry for defense of the Devedian quarter. Which, Titus Consent later assured him, was suspicion entirely misplaced. He needed to get beyond his traditional prejudice. Krulik and Sneigon were getting filthy rich producing godkiller weaponry. According to Consent, chances were good that it had not occurred to them to hold anything back. They were interested only in the profits of the moment.

Hecht did not divorce his traditional prejudice.

"IF IT WASN'T FOR YOU I DON'T THINK I'D SPEND TIME IN THIS CESSPIT CITY," Hecht murmured. He lay on his back in the dark, Anna's head and left hand on his chest. A hot tear hit his skin. "I'm just a soldier. But everybody thinks they've got to get something from me."

"You aren't just a soldier, Piper. You've never been *just* a soldier. I wouldn't have come here from Sonsa if you were just another thug for hire."

Anna was being very serious. Neither of her hands were urging him to demonstrate his manhood again. He was nervous. What should he say?

He was distracted, anyway. On his return from the Devedian quarter he had learned that he would have an audience with the Patriarch in the morning. The Arnhander ambassador to Krois wanted an interview. Likewise, the ambassador from the Grail Empire. And his people at the Castella needed him to come make some decisions. And Bronte Doneto wanted a few minutes of his time.

Down deep inside him lurked an inclination to grab control of everything so he no longer owed anyone any part of his soul or time. Only, he knew that making himself lord of everything would just pile on more responsibility and suffering. He could never just avert his face and be done.

"I suppose. I'm thinking tomorrow may be the worst day of my life."

"How can that possibly be?"

"I have to see the Patriarch. I have to talk to the ambassador from Arnhand. I have to see Bronte Doneto. Redfearn Bechter was generous enough to make all the arrangements. I threatened to cut his ears off. He told me he'd saved me having to see some fanatical moron from the Society." He explained, "The Brotherhood doesn't get along with the Society."

"Piper, I don't care about any of that stuff. I just care about you. And the children. They aren't my own flesh, but they've grown on me to the point where . . . Hell. Never mind. We're as makeshift as it gets, but we're a family. But I would appreciate it if you didn't send me any more strays."

"I thought Lila wasn't a problem."

"She isn't. She's very helpful, especially with Vali. But she's another body to clothe and another mouth to feed. And your pals with the purse haven't been good about looking out for my expenses."

"I'll take care of that tomorrow, too. You ought to be up to your hips in money. I've been doing damned good."

After all the people he had to face during the day, he would have to deal with family in the evening. With Muniero Delari and Cloven Februaren. And Heris, probably.

Despite his worries, he fell asleep. And enjoyed uncomplicated, pleasant dreams.

HUGO MONGOZ WAS SHARPER AND MORE FOCUSED THAN EVER IN HECHT'S experience. And was amused by his surprise. "It does come and go, Captain-General. I am half as old as time. But it does become easier to focus when you know that millions are counting on you to stand in for them before the Throne of God."

Hecht said little of substance.

"You're uncomfortable here."

"I've visited Krois only once before. Briefly. Sublime was almost completely irrational."

Mongoz, as Boniface VII, had shooed his hangers-on out, then had ordered his Captain-General to abandon ceremony.

"Almost? You're too generous. But let's get to it. My keepers won't leave me unchaperoned long. I'm sure you've heard rumors. A few I've set free myself. A lot more were their own mothers. Let me assure you directly, I do mean to cleanse the Connec of the million shadows that have escaped there these last few years. I'm not determined to enforce a rigorous Episcopal orthodoxy. The Church doesn't need to find itself any more enemies. I'm also interested in conciliation, not just there but with Viscesment and our eastern cousins."

Hecht's surprise was so obvious the old man chuckled. Mongoz said, "I am a different man indeed. And totally surprised to be here. In younger days I considered myself too rational to be welcomed into the Collegium, too. So I mean to use my few hours as Patriarch to try to enforce reforms that will help my Church avoid extinction."

"That seems a little harsh."

The old man launched a protracted homily: He was engulfed by circle upon circle of functionaries possessed of the imaginations of pretty marble slabs. Their views sprang entirely from wishful thinking and "This is the way things have always been!" Never mind that the world was going through dramatic changes all round. Never mind that the faithful had lost their tolerance for bad behavior by their spiritual shepherds.

Mongoz touched on several points that had worried Hecht since first he became an agent of the Church. In a way that would make Boniface toxically unpopular with most of the clergy.

Amused, the new Patriarch said, "I have nothing to fear, Captain-General. I have nothing to lose. It won't be long before God calls me home. While I wait I'll cleanse His Church of the evil within and I'll make war on the renascent evil outside. And I'll beg our great, good God not to take me till I've finished."

Hecht shut out what he considered a righteous rant of little substance in the world where he had to work.

He pressed for specifics about what he was expected to accomplish. With what men and resources.

He heard little that had not been part of some rumor already reported by Titus Consent.

HECHT TOLD HIS STAFF, "THIS ONE IS JUST AS LOONY AS SUBLIME WAS. BUT his ambitions are less mean. He's honestly determined to make the world a better place. For everyone, not just for himself and his cronies. Hell, for as old as he is, he's ridiculously naive. He thinks all the evil accumulated over the last few years will clear off if we're just men of goodwill. Ready to invade the Connec again. And, just like the rumors say, we're supposed to use our new tools to render that land free of its revenant Instrumentalities."

The expressions he saw ranged from baffled to unbelieving. His officers were unable to comprehend. "Never mind. It signifies nothing. Just get ready to enter an environment where the Night is used to having its own way."

Hecht's companions gawked.

They did not understand.

Nor did he, really.

He said, "We're getting paid. Prosek. Take delivery on as much weaponry as possible. Get your new crews trained up."

"Yes, sir." Prosek grinned from ear to ear. He loved the bangs and stinks.

COMING OFF ONE OF THE BRIDGES FROM THE CASTELLA, LOST IN THOUGHT, Hecht found himself suddenly seized and dragged backward. Lifeguards rushed past, responding to some threat he did not see. Then Madouc announced, "False alarm, men."

The bodyguards had pounced on two civilians, now shaking in terror. "Stay here, sir." Madouc went to ask why the two had gotten into the Captain-General's path.

Madouc returned. "They've been hanging around, waiting to take you to the Arnhander ambassador."

"Is it that time already?"

"It is."

"Damn. I was hoping to sneak into the Chiaro Palace and get some coffee from Delari's cook."

"I've never had that pleasure," Madouc informed him. "I have smelled it. Delicious."

"It smells better than it tastes. Tell them to lead on. And I hope it isn't far. Bechter has me loaded down all day."

"Sergeant Bechter took time into account when he filled your schedule."

Of course. Bechter would have consulted Madouc.

He needed to talk to Bechter about the lifeguard situation. Madouc was a good man. But he and Hecht had begun to resent one another simply because of the demands their relationship placed upon them. That was not good.

HECHT'S FACE WENT STONY THE MOMENT HE SAW THE PURPORTED AMBASsador. He had not met the man before but recognized him by his hunchback. Rinpoché. One of those thoroughly corrupt priests that Sublime had so favored.

The man had a knack for surviving the disasters he authored, apparently. Morcant Farfog had had, too. For a time. Never really interested in Arnhand's efforts in the Connec, Hecht had paid little attention so long as that kingdom's agents stayed out of his way.

Rinpoché smiled. "Thank you for seeing me, Captain-General."

The smile went unreturned. Hecht said, "You aren't the Arnhander legate. I was told I'd be seeing King Regard's man."

The hunchback smirked. "I may be closer to the heartbeat of Salpeno than the Count d'Perdlieu."

"I doubt it. I recognize you. I know your reputation. Neither the Church nor I have any business with you."

Rinpoché's expression hardened. "Remember who you're talking to. Remember whom I represent."

"I am. I'm not impressed. You should recall whom you're talking to and whom I represent. Sublime isn't Patriarch, now. His follies are being addressed. Incompetence and corruption are no longer tolerated. Any odor whatsoever out of Arnhand could cause this Patriarch to review his predecessor's decisions concerning the legitimacy of marriages."

A man in brown turned into being behind the gnome. He grinned and waved and twisted away into invisibility again.

The hunchback visibly controlled himself. He was unaccustomed to being thwarted. Anne of Menand must see something in him that remained invisible to the rest of humanity. Else why invest him with so much power that he could not imagine disobedience?

"Perhaps. But this Patriarch will not be with us long."

True. And Hecht had a few ideas he wanted to kick around with Principaté Delari and Cloven Februaren. He liked having Hugo Mongoz in charge.

"As may be." No leading candidate to succeed Boniface VII said anything good about Anne of Menand. Some Principatés from neighboring states argued for a successor who would withdraw the Church's blessing from Regard and his mother. Hecht did not expect that to happen. Arnhand, lashed by Anne, provided the majority of the Church's income. And most of the warriors who went to defend the Crusader states in the Holy Lands.

"The situation in Salpeno won't be your problem, Captain-General. I want to talk about things you will have to deal with."

Hecht felt obligated to give the man his say. "I'm listening." He might learn something.

"Boniface means to send you back into the End of Connec."

"I hear rumors to that effect. I have no orders yet."

"This Patriarch withdrew the charter of the Society. He's ordered its dissolution."

"Yes." Reserving his approval of that.

"He might expect you to enforce that."

Hecht nodded. It would be enforced. He meant to see Society members who defied Boniface VII returned to Brothe for ecclesiastical trial.

"We urge you to look the other way. Those brothers are doing the work of the Lord."

"In defiance of the Infallible Voice?"

Flash of irritation.

The hunchback had swum so deep in corruption, for so long, that he had no grasp of the notion that others might not be equally corrupt. Or, at least, useful in their peculiar honesty.

Rinpoché said, "The Connec will be cleansed of heresy. My lady will see to that. I'm offering you the opportunity to be part of the solution to the heresy problem."

"If that's the will of the Patriarch and the Collegium, then that's what will be."

More irritation. "The King is young. He has many years ahead. Before the end of his days the Connec will be subject to Arnhand's crown."

"We have nothing to discuss. You're living in a fantasy, disconnected from all political and religious reality. I suspect that it's impolitic of me even to have spoken with you."

"You'll regret your attitude."

"I doubt it. So long as Anne trusts men like yourself to further her ambitions she'll go on enjoying successes like Caron ande Lette, Calour, and the Black Mountain Massacre. Good day."

"There'll be a new Connecten Crusade, Captain-General. With or without you."

"Without, most likely. But the Patriarch will make that decision."

MADOUC FELL INTO STEP BESIDE HECHT. "THAT WENT FASTER THAN I EX-pected."

"It wasn't the Arnhander ambassador. It was an agent of Anne of Menand. He wants me to ignore her mischief in the Connec. Wants me to let the Society run wild there, again."

"You told him where to insert his idiot ideas?"

"I was more circumspect. But not by much." He wondered if Cloven Februaren would do anything to add misery to the hunchback's life.

"An ambitious woman, Anne. Up to her ears in enemies, inside Arn-hand and out. She just ignores them. That has to catch up someday."

"How long before we need to show at the Penital?"

"Two hours. Because this visit was so short."

"The Castella is on the way. I can get some paperwork done."

"Why not just relax?"

"I can relax forever after I'm dead. Besides, I want to get today wrapped early. I'm supposed to join Principaté Delari at his town house tonight. It would be nice to show up on time."

THE PENITAL, THE BROTHEN PALACE OF THE GRAIL EMPERORS, WAS AN-other immense stone pile, eclipsed in size only by Krois, the Chiaro Palace, the Castella dollas Pontellas, and several half-ruined city-managed edifices dating from classical times. The Penital was only as old as the Grail Empire itself. It had been erected on ground once featuring a prison and, farther back, a gladiatorial school where men condemned to die in the arena trained to suffer their fates in style. The name was a play on an Old Brothen word. That had to do with the dim view of service in Brothe nursed by those sentenced to represent the Emperor in the Mother City.

A majordomo met Hecht in the vast foyer, after he had been passed on by several committees of Braunsknechts. At each layer he lost some of his lifeguard. Only Madouc was with him when the majordomo led him away for his interview with the ambassador.

Then Madouc had to stop. And just hope the northerners would not start a war by doing something stupid.

Piper Hecht stepped through a doorway. And spied Ferris Renfrow at the far end of a long, narrow, richly appointed room. "Everyone is ar-ranging meetings under false pretenses today."

Renfrow looked surprised. "Really?"

Hecht described his meeting with Rinpoché. The Empire might be interested in what Anne was thinking.

"I see what you mean," Renfrow said. "I'm not out to get you to serve the Empire's interests. Not directly. We're all happy as clams the way things are."

Did sarcasm lie beneath those words?

"I just wanted to deliver your invitation to the wedding of the Empress and King Jaime of Castauriga."

"Again?"

"Again. It will come off this time. Barring another Direcian crisis."

"Why?"

"Why a wedding? Or why an invitation?"

"The latter."

"I don't know. It was the Empress's idea. I was surprised. Another source seemed more likely."

Hecht showed nothing. He had no idea what this man knew. Or did not. Irregular letters slipped back and forth between Alten Weinberg and wherever life dragged him.

Renfrow's cast-iron expression suggested that he knew more than he should. Possibly even some content. Though a letter that went astray would do little to compromise its sender.

Helspeth stopped taking risks with the letter delivered by the Braunsknecht who had come to beg the loan of Drago Prosek. Exile had taught her caution.

Hecht said, "You'll have to present an invitation formally, through the Holy See. To get leave of the Patriarch. I expect to be campaigning against revenant evils in the Connec by then."

"Maybe you'll see King Jaime when he passes through."

"It could happen."

"Did you ever learn the truth about the child you brought home from Sonsa? The niece or daughter or whatever it was you were faking at that inn?"

"She was a clever liar. She convinced the women of the sporting house that she'd been kidnapped by Special Office types. In fact, her mother sold her to the house. Why are you here? An invitation doesn't need the infamous Ferris Renfrow."

"Infamous?"

Flickering, an old man in brown appeared behind the Imperial spymaster. Renfrow was looking directly at Hecht when it happened. He spun around. And around again. "What was that?"

"What?"

"Behind me. Something happened. You were looking at it. Tell me."

Hecht put on his best baffled face. "What are you talking about?" And, "If this is all you want, I have real work that needs doing. This Patriarch has strong ideas about his armed forces."

Ferris Renfrow had lost interest in Piper Hecht and whatever else had led him to arrange a meeting with the Church's leading warrior. He was off on a small, local quest, determined to unravel this sudden mystery. He mumbled, "What's become of Osa Stile? Why haven't I heard from him?"

Hecht did not respond. The question had not been addressed to him.

The Ninth Unknown showed himself just long enough to flash a grin and an old-fashioned thumbs-up. Renfrow spun around again.

MADOUC SAID, "AGAIN YOU'RE OUT OF AN INTERVIEW WITH AN IMPORTANT legate earlier than I expected."

"This one was crazy."

"Based on all I've seen lately, sir, most of the world fits nicely into that category. Meaning us three or four normal guys maybe better get to work making sure wickedness doesn't have its way completely."

"And you aren't so sure about me being one of the three or four. Right?"

Madouc grinned. Hecht suspected the man was not joking.

HECHT SAW TITUS CONSENT BRIEFLY BEFORE HE MOVED ON TO HIS INTERview with Principaté Doneto, who, after an exchange of messages, had agreed to move their meeting up. But he would have to see Doneto at his city home.

"There have been two more deaths," Titus whispered.

"Suicides?"

"The one in the quarter was. The other, probably not. Though it wasn't murder."

"Tell me."

"Syphon Credulius. In the quarter."

"I don't know the name. Who was he?"

"A recent immigrant. Came while we were on Artecipea. Supposedly from the Holy Lands. But he didn't have the accent. He spent a lot of time nagging people for details about what happened in Sonsa. During the riots."

"Sounds like a spy."

"And a stupid one. Him killing himself made me think about what he was looking for. Which led me to a connection between most of the dead men that doesn't rely on them having been part of a slaving ring."

Hecht's heartbeat increased slightly. Titus seemed to have found his way to the conclusion Hecht himself had reached not long ago. "And?"

"I believe they shared a common thread of knowledge. I wonder how deadly having any grasp of that knowledge might be. And I wonder who it worries so much that he has to execute anyone who might be in on the secret."

Titus did seem to have worked it out. People who knew that Piper Hecht was not a fugitive from Duarnenia had been killing themselves. Only . . . "I don't know who's doing what to whom, or why, Titus. I once thought I saw the same connection you're seeing now. But a third of the dead men just won't fit. And, I gather, there have been similar deaths overseas. A whole rash in one port once famous for its slave market. Do you want permission to dig? Go to it. Maybe Bechter can enlist a Witchfinder to help. Whatever is going on, there's got to be sorcery involved."

Titus looked puzzled. But only for a moment. "I'm more worried about Noë and my children. They'd be lost if anything happened to me. None of our relatives would take them in. Because of our conversion."

"I can't see any reason for you to worry. But, I do admit, I don't know what's going on. I'll look out for you the best I can."

Titus was not reassured.

"There was another death?"

"Polo. That was your man, then Ghort's, and got crippled in that ambush."

That startled Hecht. He let it show. "Polo? That's sad. He was a good soul, if slow and inclined to pocket small coins and trivial bits that didn't belong to him. What's the story?"

"He fell down a flight of stairs. At home. No obvious signs of foul play. He'd been drinking. He'd been doing that a lot. But the Bruglioni are suspicious."

Hecht was suspicious. Polo was another someone who knew things about Piper Hecht. Possibly things he did not know he knew.

"Was this recent?"

"Day before yesterday. Paludan had him interred in the Bruglioni crypt. In the servants' area."

Hecht shuddered. "I started to go down there once. Got as far as the wine cellars and whatnot. Polo talked me out of going deeper. He said there was nothing to see but bundles of bones."

"That would be typical."

"And now I have to see Doneto. I'm not looking forward to it."

PINKUS GHORT GUIDED HECHT INTO THE LITTLE ROOM WHERE BRONTE Doneto waited. It was overfurnished and overheated. Hecht had visited it once before, following the Plemenzan captivity. This was Doneto's ultimate refuge. Here the man felt safe to be whatever he wanted. Undoubtedly, the walls included stone from the Holy Lands.

Ghort did not leave. Neither did he appear thrilled by having to stay. Hecht did not question his presence.

Doneto said, "Make yourself comfortable. Coffee will be up momentarily. Your only vice, as I understand it."

"That and, according to some, being steadfast."

"A trait highly respected in Duarnenia, I hear. A title of high respect, Steadfast Guardian."

"Steadfast Guardian is what they call the Chief Castellan of the Grail Order. But, you're right, it can be given as a honor, too. Generally to somebody who has slaughtered an impressively large number of savages."

"Such is the way of the . . . What?" Doneto sat straight up, reminding Hecht of nothing so much as a hound startled out of sleep. "Pinkus. Did you . . . ?"

Ghort asked, "Principaté?"

"Something just happened. A force stirred. But I don't feel it now."

Hecht suspected someone in brown might have tried to enter the room. Something in the doorway had made his amulet react when he arrived.

Hecht put on his best perplexed expression and waited.

Doneto relaxed. He said, "Colonel Ghort tells me you feel we have a neutral balance of obligation between us."

"Essentially. I wakened you in the Ownvidian Knot. You got me out of captivity in Plemenza. Most would consider a life of slightly more value, but I'm content."

Doneto nodded. To himself. "And how do you feel about Principaté Delari?"

"I owe him a great deal, professionally."

"Indeed. And many wonder why."

"It's worked out well for everyone. So far."

"I think Rudenes Schneidel would demur."

Hecht chuckled. "And well he ought."

"Were you aware that Muniero Delari and I were once great enemies?"

"He mentioned having had a problem with you, yes. He said it was all a misunderstanding. That you'd discovered that you were both working toward the same objective."

"Not quite true, but a good foundation for a truce. Where has he been lately? He's been invisible since the election."

"I don't know. I haven't seen him. I'm supposed to take the family to his town house this evening."

The coffee arrived. The old woman who brought it was shaking.

"Hannah?" Doneto asked. "What is it?"

"A ghost, Your Grace. Or something of the Night. Right out there. Cold, Your Grace. Cold as the grave."

Doneto scowled at Hecht. "What did you bring into my house?"

"Nothing. You know I'm stone deaf to anything sorcerous."

"Except when it's about to murder you in the mountains. So. The question would seem to be, what follows after you? The answer would interest a lot of people."

"Sir?"

"You live a charmed life, Piper Hecht. Neither Death nor the Night seem able to find you, however hard they try."

"Praise the Lord."

"Enjoy your coffee. Hannah, show me where this happened." Doneto left the room.

Hecht asked Ghort, "Want some?"

"Only two cups there, Pipe."

"Only two of us here."

"I can't get away with the games you play, Pipe."

"Speaking of, what's he up to? What does he want?"

"Honestly?"

"Of course."

"I think he's trying to get a feel for how much trouble you'll be down the road."

"He's known me almost as long as you have."

"And I'm wondering, too. Things happen around you, Pipe. You maybe don't have a friggin' thing to do with getting them started. Like them soultaken that turned up at al-Khazen. You didn't conjure them, but according to anybody who looked into it, they was there on account of you. Them and Starkden and Masant al-Seyhan. Then you got Rudenes Schneidel making a career out of trying to kill you. And a giant-ass worm crawling up out of the ground, fixing to eat your ass. And that's just the shit I know about. What all else have guys like Doneto spotted?"

"So I'm like, what? The Chosen One of Legend? Something like that? And God, or the gods, haven't bothered to let me in on the secret?"

"Hey. That could be." Ghort stepped over to where he could look out the doorway. Then he stepped back and helped himself to a long swig off a bottle of liqueur he took from a sideboard near where he had been standing. A dozen bottles in various shapes stood there. Glass bottles. Those alone bespoke wealth and power. "I'm not the expert." He did the peek-out-and-duck-back again, drank from a different bottle. "Ugh! That's foul."

"What do you think is going on?"

"I told you. Sizing you up. Him looking farther down the road than most of the Collegium. Those others just want to get you gone to the Connec. You can do some good there and be out of the way at the same time. Doneto is maybe worried that you might turn into the kind of threat that Sublime Pacificus feared."

Hecht wondered how rehearsed this might be. "Why would people consider me a threat because I do my job?" It had to be his fault, somehow. It kept coming up.

Doneto returned just after Ghort helped himself to a third draught of liqueur. He stopped halfway across the room, sniffed, frowned, seated himself. His glance darted to the bottles. "How is the coffee?"

"Excellent."

"Pinkus, you should have taken the other cup. It's getting cold."

"I'd never presume, Your Grace."

Doneto almost smiled.

"Hecht, I'd hoped to spend a few hours getting a better feel for your views. But I have to deal with something that's gotten into the house. That's a real problem right now. I'll have to take the rest as it comes."

Hecht hoped he looked suitably bewildered. And just irked enough, with a dark glance at Ghort, to make Doneto think he believed the interruption had been staged.

He hoped Cloven Februaren had gotten a running start.

"IT MUST BE YOU," MADOUC SAID AS THEY DESCENDED TO THE STREET OUTside Doneto's town house. "You go in anticipating a long session and they bounce you right back out."

"This time the guy had a paranoid seizure. He suddenly decided that something awful had invaded his house. He had to get it out. Nothing else mattered."

"And he wasn't looking at you when he said it?"

"You're in a feisty mood. He was not looking my way."

"Got to do what I can to keep my spirits up, sir. This will be my longest day since we got back from Artecipea."

"Take the rest off. I don't need a shadow."

"How can you be bright about so much, yet persistently dumb about your own safety?"

Hecht started to argue.

"Sir! There are people and things who want to kill you. Wishful thinking won't change that."

Hecht grumbled something to the effect that somewhere Anna Mozilla was cackling and rubbing her hands together. Anna had started hinting that he should consider retirement. He owed no one. And the Connecten campaign had brought wealth his way. Not a vast fortune such as Sublime had hoped to gain but enough to live comfortably.

He could not do that. He was not made that way. Chances were, he would follow Grade Drocker's example and die in service. Possibly equally miserably.

Hecht grumbled some more. Without point. It was unreasonable to expect the anonymity he had enjoyed when he, Ghort, Bo Biogna, and Just Plain Joe joined the first expedition into the Connec.

"Madouc, I understand. Intellectually. But I'll never like dragging a mob around."

"We could solve that by letting you get got once. Not fatally. Just enough to get the message pounded into your soul."

"Yes. That might do it." Really? After the attempts he had survived already?

There was only one way he could get what he wanted back. Rid the world of er-Rashal al-Dhulquarnen. Or pray that Nassim Alizarin would do so.

"Well, Madouc, I'll try to uncomplicate your life. I'll stay inside safe places as much as I can."

Madouc did not appear mollified. Presumably because he recalled the firepowder attack on Anna's house.

"At least learn to delegate." Madouc did not trust his own men to do their jobs without him watching over their shoulders.

"A shortcoming of my own."

"WELL, THAT'S INTERESTING," HECHT SAID AS HE HELPED ANNA BOARD Principaté Delari's coach.

"What's that?" She was ravishing. She had commissioned a new gown. Hecht wished he could parade her through the Chiaro Palace, just to make those cranky old men drool.

"Madouc. He found a way to compromise with his conscience and let his men do their jobs."

"Does he have a family?"

"The Brotherhood. Come on, kids. Vali, you look stunning." Vali had a new gown, too. She would be a beauty in a few more years.

"And you, Lila." Lila wore a gown of Anna's that had been refit for her. Her idea. She loved the particular piece. It was the richest thing she had ever worn.

"Pella, you look like a young lord."

"An' I itch like one, too."

Pella did not want to go to Principaté Delari's town house. He felt too self-conscious.

"It's the price you pay for the life you live. You want to be comfortable, you have to dress up and be uncomfortable. Look at me."

Hecht was an adult reflection of Pella. Though Pella was heavy on green and Hecht wore dark blue. Both preferring one main color to the flash lately shown by Pinkus Ghort. "I always feel silly in hose."

Though he protested dressing in style, Hecht had grown accustomed to doing so. The west had seduced him thoroughly.

He climbed aboard the coach and settled beside Anna, opposite the children. Lila was terrified. Vali took her hand and tried to look bored. Hecht observed, "We'll need to get Pella a razor pretty soon."

Anna grumbled, "Did you have to bring that damned sword?"

The hilt of his weapon pressed the outside of her thigh. "I did. Yes. I'll move it."

He had a bad feeling, suddenly. Like mentioning the blade might conjure a need for its use. Just when Madouc decided to take time off.

It was a tense ride. And for naught. They reached Muniero Delari's town house without misadventure. There was still some light when Hecht began handing the other passengers down.

Noting his stare, Pella said, "That's where part of the house fell down. They got it almost all fixed."

"You've been over here?"

"I go exploring. When there ain't nothing else to do."

"Interesting." Hecht was inclined to go look. He did not, despite being early. Nothing of the original disaster remained to be studied. And the lifeguards were getting that strained look.

Heris came out, followed by Turking and Felske. In case anything needed carrying, Hecht supposed. "We're early."

"Grandfather will be pleased. There'll be more time to talk." She embraced Anna. Anna had no trouble with that. Her negativity had faded. "Anna, you look like a queen. And the children like young lords and ladies. You didn't need to go to so much trouble." She eyed Lila, plainly curious.

"Nor did you, then."

Heris had made an effort. "Grandfather's idea. He wants me to become more social. I'm starting small."

Anna said, "This is Lila. She lives with us, now."

"I see." Heris would know about Lila. Given her own history, she was unlikely to be judgmental.

They entered the house. Heris said, "Make yourselves comfortable. Grandfather will show up whenever he can tear himself away from his sorcery." She squealed. "Damnit! Stop doing that!"

She had turned to follow Turking and Felske. And had bumped into an old man dressed in brown.

Cloven Februaren flashed a big grin. "It's juvenile but it never stops being fun. So, Piper. Introduce me."

Hecht was not quite sure how to do that. When he did nothing, Februaren stepped up to Anna. "The boy must be tongue-tied. I, lovely lady, am Muno's grandfather, Cloven Februaren."

Pella blurted, "You can't be! Nobody is that old."

Hecht said, "Pella. Manners."

Februaren said, "He's right, Piper. Almost. Hardly anybody human is as old as I am." To Anna, he said, "You don't know about me."

Anna shook her head. "It seems like I should, though."

"Admirably closemouthed, our Piper. I'm his guardian angel. I follow him around and protect him from assassins when he's too stubborn to listen to his bodyguards."

Pella blurted, "You were the Ninth Unknown!"

"Still am. You'd be the literary character, eh? Pellapront Versulius. Have you read *The Lay of Ihrian?*"

"There's only one copy in Brothe, Your Grace. Principaté Doneto owns it. Colonel Ghort tried to get him to let me read it. He wouldn't let me, not even if I did it in his house."

"Wish I'd known that this afternoon. Piper and I were there. I could've borrowed it."

Hecht said, "I'd bet it was in that room you couldn't get into."

"I could have. But it would've made a mess. And would've gotten Doneto more upset than he is. Which is upset enough to launch an effort to trace back the true history of the Duarnenian sellsword, Piper Hecht."

Anna betrayed herself with a sudden intake of breath.

"Not to worry. Duarnenia and the Grand Marshes are under the ice. Your friend Bo Begonia won't wrestle the Windwalker to find some dirt."

"Biogna," Hecht corrected. "So. He's back with the City Regiment."

"I imagine he became a Patriarchal because Bronte Doneto insisted. And to be around his friend Joe. Again, not to worry. Hardly anybody remembers you passing through, headed south. But he'll find your name in the pay books some of the places you worked." The old man grinned.

"I need to talk to you about a couple of things. Privately."

"They'll have to wait. Here's Muno. And he looks hungry."

Hecht thought Delari looked distracted. He did not have much to say, then or during the prolonged dinner that followed. The company took their cue from him. Even Pella remained subdued.

At one point Delari looked up and seemed surprised to see them all. Apropos of nothing that had been said at any time since Hecht's arrival, he announced, "I don't think it's a war that we can win." He withdrew into himself again.

Cloven Februaren shrugged, signaled Felske to pour more wine. He was putting it away. To Anna he confided, "I can take the night off. Piper is safe here."

Anna glanced toward Hecht. A joke?

Hecht shrugged. He had no idea how the old man's sense of humor worked. Except that he enjoyed practical jokes.

Hecht said, "Your Grace, I have a question about the killer we hunted down back before the Connecten Crusade started. The one underground."

"Hunh?" Delari was in touch enough to understand that he was being addressed.

"The same kind of murders are happening again. In the same neighborhood."

Delari forced himself to focus. "It's back?"

"Something is."

"What did Doneto say about it? You saw him today."

"The subject didn't come up. There was an intruder in the house. He cut the interview short."

"Intruder." Delari eyed his grandfather. "I see." He smiled wearily. "Good. If he's chasing his own tail he can't get up to any other mischief."

"Mischief? Like what?"

"We'll talk later. Heris, be a good girl, make the coffee, then join us in the quiet room."

Dutifully, Heris left, taking Felske. Turking began to clear away. Anna and the youngsters were at a loss. What now?

Delari started to leave, recalled his guests. He came back. "Anna. Pardon me. I've been thoughtless. I'll have something done about that monster. I wish I could tell you how to entertain yourselves while we spit and roast Piper. I've been in another world since I got back from the Connec. Turking. You've got the rooms ready?"

"Yes, Your Grace."

"Then we're not doing everything wrong. Piper, Grandfather, we should get there before Heris and the coffee. Turking, see if our guests would like some, too."

"Yes, Your Grace."

Climbing upstairs, slowly because neither Delari nor Februaren were especially spry, the Principaté observed, "She's quiet about it but she's angry. Anna."

Hecht said, "She thought this would be a major social event. She had a new gown made. She worked hard to make the kids look good."

"My fault. My fault. I should've seen that. I'll do what I can to soothe her."

Heris did almost beat them to the quiet room. Delari closed and locked the door while she poured. They settled at the sides of a small, square table, new since Hecht's last visit.

Hecht sipped rich coffee and waited. Heris and the Ninth Unknown did the same. Delari started to speak several times, backed off to get his words right.

Februaren finally said, "He can't get to what's on his mind, I'll go with what's on mine. Piper, I need you to get rid of the ring. Take it back to the Bruglioni. Make up a story."

"What ring?"

"Sainted Eis. Here we go again." Once he had reminded Hecht of what he was talking about, he said, "Give it back. It's becoming a liability. They know you have it. The servant, Polo, remembered. You don't want to provoke them more than you have already."

Hecht started to protest that he had done nothing . . . "They don't know about that, do they?"

"Gervase Saluda has suspicions. He's mentioned them to Paludan. Neither believes it. Yet. They can't get it to make sense. They don't know the history that brought Divino Bruglioni low. Returning the ring ought to disarm them."

"And the Night?"

"We'll find another way to blind or distract them."

"The Night. That war can't be won."

"Muno?"

"Grandfather?"

"You can only kill the older gods. The discrete Instrumentalities. Not the diffuse modern ones."

Delari had his audience. Only Heris moved at all, slowly lifting her coffee cup to her lips. He asked, "Piper. How would you kill God? Our God, not something like Rook or Weaver."

Hecht intuited the problem. "I'd have to get Him to manifest so I could shoot Him."

"But that can't happen. Not with our God, the God of the Pramans, or the God of the Deves or Dainshaus. Pretty much the same God wearing different masks for the benefit of the faithful. The problem is, unlike Ordnan or Seska or whichever, this Instrumentality is *expected* to be everywhere at once. He does that by putting a little bit of Himself into each place that is consecrated to Him. Which is God doing to Himself what the sorcerers of the Old Empire did to the most powerful Instrumentalities of their time."

"Which might be why there's no credible example of God stepping on stage since back when the Dainshaukin murdered goats in His honor." Cloven Februaren stabbed the air and grinned. He had marvelous teeth.

Delari said, "To destroy God you'd have to visit every church and shrine in the world, find the bit of God consecrating them, and treat it. A thousand Witchfinders working for a thousand years might only get to the point where the surviving fragments could pull themselves together from places you didn't know about and places you couldn't reach because they're under the ice."

"No one wants to destroy God," Heris said. "Just the Instrumentalities. The things that make human life awful."

Februaren said, "Humans make human life awful, girl. Instrumentalities are a handy excuse."

"Speaking of making life awful," Hecht said. "Have you been making people kill themselves?"

"I? Why? Who killed himself?"

Hecht explained.

"Interesting. Maybe you have more than one guardian angel."

Hecht did not believe that. Nor that the old man was innocent.

"It matters not, if they belonged to the ring that sold you into slavery."

"It matters . . ." Hecht noted real emotion in Heris. For the first time. The hatred rolled off her like clouds of black steam. "Not those men. The others."

Februaren looked like he might really be surprised. "Others?"

"Men have died, by their own hands, who had nothing to do with slaving."

"You're certain?"

"Yes."

"Possibly their lives had lost meaning. Better yet, name me three you know were innocent."

Hecht could not do that.

"Better still, give me another motive."

While Hecht and the Ninth Unknown glared at one another, Principaté Delari visited a small sideboard, took a scrap of greenish paper from a thin drawer. It had been folded once, crosswise. He dropped it in front of Hecht. "That's your father's list. Exculpate whomever you can."

It was a long list inscribed in tiny characters in the crabbed hand of a man near the end of a painful terminal disease. Tick marks had been placed beside a score of names. Hecht recognized only a few. He knew several of the unchecked names. "There'll be another list with check marks."

The man in brown pulled one out of his sleeve, pushed it over. It was on slightly tan paper. Heris snatched the green list. "Oh! These two. We worked in their houses in Shartelle. Mintone was particularly cruel to Mother."

The old man in brown said, "Josuf Mintone died last year. His house burned down. He was inside. It took him a long time to die. He understood why."

Hecht could see there was more. Februaren did not tell it.

Hecht consulted the old man's list. It matched the unchecked names from Grade Drocker's, with two additions. Just one name remained unchecked.

Heris took that list. Februaren indicated the unchecked name. "He may have gotten away by dying on us. Or he may have been smart enough to see what was coming. He was last seen on a barge on the Shirne headed toward al-Qarn, whining because he had malaria."

"There are names missing," Heris said. She was alive now, like some vengeful harpy Instrumentality.

Hecht said, "I thought shared knowledge might be a thread linking some of the dead."

Februaren observed, "And it would be right to leave them rambling around sharing that thread with anyone who wants to listen."

"I didn't say that."

"You're thinking it. If only obliquely. Being dishonest with yourself."

"You can't kill everyone who knows about me."

Muniero Delari said, "You can't kill Armand."

"And why not, Muno? He's a spy. A slimy spy."

"I know that. I always knew that. When he was in my household I controlled what he reported to Alten Weinberg."

"Anna and Titus Consent are immune," Hecht said. Ferris Renfrow he was not so sure about.

Heris muttered to herself as she continued to glare at Cloven Februaren's list. "I said there are names missing, double-great-grandpa."

"I'm listening, sweetheart."

Heris named three men and a woman against whom she enjoyed abiding grudges. After questioning her, Februaren concluded, "Only the woman Hasheyda fits. The rest were just slaveholders. They treated you the same as their other slaves. The woman, though, has come up before. She may have helped finance the slaving expedition. Her front man paid his due before she became suspect. She'll be interviewed."

Heris muttered, "I'd like to interview her. For about a year, in a torture chamber."

"You wouldn't come out any happier."

Hecht changed the subject. "Principaté. Where have you been since you got back? Everyone keeps asking."

"They don't need to know."

"I wouldn't tell them. But the asking leaves me curious."

"I've been down under. With the Construct. And in the catacombs."

"Staying out of the way?"

"I came up to vote. Twice. And to campaign against myself in the second election. The world is getting harsher every day. I have no time to waste socializing with idiots who can't see what's coming right at them."

Februaren suggested, "If you spent time with them you might open their eyes."

Delari snorted. "The only one out there interested in anything but his own power and pleasure is Bronte Doneto. And he's interested for the wrong reasons."

Hecht said, "I was impressed by Hugo Mongoz. Though our interview wasn't as thorough as it might have been."

"I'll give you Boniface. But the man won't be around long. And most of what he gets done is because people are humoring an old man."

"Fix him up with enough time to do some good."

"Eh?"

Hecht pointed at Februaren. "He's figured out how to hang around forever. Fix it so the Patriarch stays with us for a while, too."

"Nice idea. In theory," Februaren said. "Probably impractical. But I'll think about it. The ring, Piper. Tomorrow. Get shut of it. It's important. The Instrumentalities are about to figure it out."

Hecht nodded. He asked Delari, "Do you know the whole story about Osa Stile?"

The Principaté frowned. "Osa Stile?"

"Armand? Osa Stile is his real name."

"How would you . . . ? He's an agent of Ferris Renfrow, the Imperial spy. He arranged embarrassments for the Church in the Connec before I inherited him."

"Osa was a gift to Ferris Renfrow from Dreanger. He was made by er-Rashal al-Dhulquarnen. He's almost my age. His first loyalty is to the Rascal, not Renfrow. Nor his lovers. I believe er-Rashal subtly suggested Osa's use in the Connec. Where al-Dhulquarnen and his allies would experiment with resurrecting banished gods. They didn't count on Bishop Serifs being so awful that a Braunsknecht would fling him off a cliff."

Delari asked, "You know this for a fact?"

"About Osa Stile? Yes. I'm speculating about er-Rashal's conniving."

"And where does your loyalty lie now, Piper?" Februaren asked. "Since you were sent west to die, and have been attacked repeatedly because you won't stop breathing."

"I don't know. Honestly. Intellectually, I know I've been betrayed by Gordimer and al-Dhulquarnen. They've made enemies of themselves. But I haven't been betrayed by the Sha-lug. My own company, that I commanded before I came over here, were at al-Khazen. And, later, at Arn Bedu. They were betrayed, too. Because of their association with me. They didn't turn on me. Neither, I suspect, would most Sha-lug." Though he had been away so long that few would remember him.

Februaren nodded. "The one called the Mountain. Hiding amongst the Pramans at Arn Bedu. He's in Lucidia, now. Supported by the Kaif of Qasr al-Zed. He's gathering Sha-lug willing to turn on Gordimer and er-Rashal. But he's gotten less sympathy than he expected. He's survived several assassination attempts. He'll need luck to keep on."

"Tomorrow," Delari said. Evidently lost inside his own head.

Everyone stared. He did not go on.

"Muno? You were going to say something." Februaren put an edge in his voice, adult to inattentive youngster.

"Uh? Oh. Yes. Tomorrow. Heris. You start Piper's education with the Construct."

"Piper has to visit the Bruglioni."

"Afterward, then. But tomorrow. We need to get on with it. It can't be that long before he has to go off to the Connec again."

"I don't have time!" Hecht protested.

"Make time, Piper," Februaren said. "Trust your staff. This is important. Muno and I aren't immortal."

"I have no talent for sorcery."

"Talent not required. No more so than to throw a rock. We'll both be there to instruct you. Right, Muno?"

The Principaté nodded. But he was drifting again.

"WHAT DID YOU TALK ABOUT?" ANNA WANTED TO KNOW WHEN HECHT slipped into their borrowed bed.

"Yesterday, today, and tomorrow. Depressing stuff."

"And secret?"

"Naturally."

"Politics?"

"That, too. But you'll get help with the killer in your neighborhood."

"And you have to . . . ?"

"I have to study something with Delari before I go back to the Connec."

Disappointed, she murmured, "How soon will that be?"

"Depends on Boniface. He doesn't seem to be in a hurry. Certainly not till all the troops from Artecipea are over and rested and refitted."

Anna pressed against him, head to toe. "I don't want you to go."

"I know. But I can't not."

"I know. You can't stop being you."

That was not really it. Or, maybe it was.

"YOU'RE THE LAST PERSON I EXPECTED TO SEE," PALUDAN BRUGLIONI SAID, looking startled. "You've gotten us out of your life." The man was nervous. He had trouble meeting Hecht's eyes. He had lost hair and gained weight.

"Not at all. I owe you. You gave me work when I was new here. I gave you my best while I was here."

Grudgingly, Paludan admitted, "You did turn us around. You did win back the respect we'd lost." Lost because of Paludan Bruglioni's indifference toward management of the family he had come to head at too early an age.

"But you were unhappy with me anyway. So I hear."

"You say you have something . . . ?" Paludan lost focus. He stared at a shadowed corner, the color draining from his face.

"I may have found the ring I was so sure I didn't have." He had a note on paper fixed to his left wrist. Writing never forgot. "If this is it." He handed the gold band to Bruglioni. "I found it with some coins and jewelry I brought back from Artecipea. I don't know if I picked it up there or if I had it all along. All along makes more sense."

Paludan glared as hard as a frightened man dared.

"I showed it to Principaté Delari. He said there's a spell on it that makes you forget it. I wrote it all down." He showed his wrist.

Bruglioni studied the ring. "It looks like the one Divino had. And he always claimed that only people who had seen it but didn't actually have it could remember it."

"So what's the point of it if you don't know you have it? What kind of lunatic sorcerer makes a magic ring like that?"

"I couldn't guess the reasoning. Maybe the ring did what it was supposed to do way back when and is still around because nobody remembers it long enough to melt it down."

"That fits. The Principaté thinks it goes back to antiquity, even before the Agean Empire. But he couldn't guess why it was made."

Bruglioni had been turning the ring over and over. Now he slipped it onto a finger. "Uncle Divino didn't know. Didn't remember he had it till it was gone."

"I'm really pressed for time. I just wanted to do right after I found out I'd been wrong and really did have the ring. And I wanted to see for myself that everything was going good here."

"Still better than before you came here. Gervase prods me when I backslide. He shows me the youngsters coming up. That reminds me what might be—if I don't pay attention. I'm sorry I shoehorned him into Divino's seat. He isn't around enough, now." He shrugged. "Gervase is the best we have."

Hecht offered to shake hands. Bruglioni passed. It was not a current custom. He told Hecht, "Good luck in the Connec. Clean them out this time."

"I mean to try."

Paludan let out a startled squawk soon after Hecht left him.

That old man was going to get himself into something he could not handle, someday.

PRINCIPATÉ DELARI WAS IN A DARK MOOD. "YOU'RE LATE."

Hecht said, "Your grandfather played one practical joke too many. We almost didn't make it out of the Bruglioni place."

Februaren managed to look sheepish. For a moment.

Hecht joined Heris. She was looking down at the giant map of the world. "There've been changes." Heris was grubbier than usual.

"The ice line?"

"That." That was obvious. "But some more subtle things, too."

"There's the sea levels rising in the Negrine and those two lesser seas farther east. More snowfall to the north means more meltwater during the spring and summer."

"You're well informed."

"Grandfather has been sneaking me in here all year. To learn the Construct. Hoping I'll be able to work it someday. Now he wants to crash train you, too."

"What? We don't have an ounce of talent for sorcery between us."

"He claims it doesn't matter. The sorcery is in the engine. You just have to know how to tell it what to do. Februaren is a true master. He doesn't even have to talk to it. Maybe he'll teach us. Grandfather isn't good at getting ideas across."

"If Februaren can stop pinching bottoms and tugging ears. How did you get here? Bribe the guards?" The only women allowed in the Chiaro Palace were nuns of the Bettine Order. And those nuns down there, updating the map.

"I come in underground."

That explained the dust and grime. "Wow. You have more guts than I do. I've only been down a few times. I won't go again unless I have to."

"Grandfather told me. But it's tame, now. He's made sure. The old man helped."

Hecht sighed. "I don't know how he gets around and gets all those things done."

"The Construct." Heris gestured at the map. "He's a virtuoso."

"That's how he skips all the walking in between?"

"Yes. He's the only one who can do it today. The wells of power are too weak and too many revenants are competing for what power there is. Your work in the Connec should help. Grandfather really wants the good old days back. He couldn't even get himself out of that hole where you found him that time. When he still thought *he* was Lord of the Silent Kingdom."

While they talked Cloven Februaren sparked around the vast chamber, looking over the shoulders of people working on the Construct. He restrained his urge to startle.

Principaté Delari did the same, using ladders and catwalks.

Heris said, "If the wells come back strong, you and me, we should be able to do what the old man does. If we study hard enough and want it bad enough."

Heris wanted it badly enough. But her motives might not be pure.

"What?" Heris asked. "I didn't hear the joke."

"Thinking of motivation and purity. In this city. In this palace."

"That would be a joke, wouldn't it?"

SIX WEEKS MORE PASSED BEFORE BONIFACE GAVE THE ORDER THAT SENT PA-triarchal forces into the field. Piper Hecht spent five hours each day beneath the Chiaro Palace. He did not believe he was doing any learning. Delari and Februaren disagreed. "You're becoming attuned," Februaren insisted. "Eventually, we'll be able to communicate from afar. I can watch you from afar already. I won't have to tag along quite so much. So. Go on out to the wild country, where the people talk funny, and kill some gods. I need the power they're sucking up."

FOUR DAYS BEFORE LEAVING FOR THE WILD COUNTRY HECHT RECEIVED A RE-quest that he visit the Penital, a direct appeal from the Imperial legate himself. With assurances that no misdirection was involved.

Rumors that the Imperial nuptials had grown shaky abounded. Hecht supposed the legate wanted to set the record straight.

He supposed right.

The legate told him, "The wedding has been postponed again. Because of complications with King Jaime's recovery from his wounds. He was less ready to travel than he believed. He collapsed as his party neared Khaurene."

"Is he trying to elude the commitment?"

"Not at all. He's *too* eager. Her Majesty will contact you as soon as we set a new date." The legate smiled at some private joke.

"My appreciation, My Lord." Hecht left the Penital bemused yet again by the Empress's evident interest. Why?

The legate had shrugged and shaken his head when asked the question direct.

THE PATRIARCHAL ARMY APPROACHED THE DECHEAR RIVER WITH TWENTY-four hundred men, all Boniface VII would approve for the campaign. The Patriarch believed a larger force might spark a Connecten resistance while fewer soldiers would not be enough to handle the anticipated supernatural chaos. The Captain-General had no Principatés underfoot. Members of the Collegium were sticking close to Brothe. The next Patriarchal election would be a critical one. It would be fought to the bitter end. There would be no antique compromise to fill the slot while younger men maneuvered.

Hecht hoped there would be no election for years. He liked Hugo Mongoz as Patriarch. He hoped Principaté Delari and Cloven Februaren would use the power of the Construct to assure his longevity.

"Rider coming in," Clej Sedlakova announced. "I'd guess down from Viscesment."

Hecht spotted the man. He wore Braunsknecht dress. "Good guess." Despite Empress Katrin's rapprochement with the Brothen Church, a small band of Braunsknechts still guarded Bellicose.

The man drew closer. He picked up shadows from among the outriders. Hecht observed, "We've seen this one before." He urged his mount farther from the road, where the troops were heading down to the Dechear in no particular hurry. Sedlakova, Smolens, Consent, and several others stayed with Hecht.

"Algres Drear," Consent said. "That's what he called himself when he came to borrow Drago Prosek."

Drear approached carefully, though his caution was of no value. "Captain-General. I bring dispatches."

"Captain Drear. I thought you attended to Princess Helspeth's safety."

"Once upon a time. In another life. Before I let her get away with going into the field against the Remayne Pass monster. Where the chit embarrassed the heroes of the Empire by actually slaying the dragon. I got rusticated. I'm being rehabilitated, now. Allowed to work my way back. As commander of the six-man company protecting someone the

Empress would rather not protect. But we have to observe Imperial tradition."

"I see. Dispatches?"

Drear produced a fat, wheat-colored leather courier's case. "Long-winded, I'm sure. But the gist will be, Bellicose and Boniface have a deal. Bellicose will end the Viscesment Patriarchy. He'll succeed Boniface in Brothe. Once he's gone, there'll be just one Patriarchy."

Hecht's staff refused to believe it. Those with deep ties to the Brotherhood indulged in some derision. Hecht read the dispatches. "The Captain is right, gentlemen. It's all right here, in Church legalese."

Colonel Smolens said, "The whole goddamned Collegium will be shitting square turds over this."

"Probably," Hecht said. "But first, Captain, how old would Bellicose be?"

"In his fifties. And full of ambition. But he's a cripple. Polio when he was little. It's a miracle he's lived this long."

"I see. So. The Collegium might go along. If cool heads prevail and enough men want to end the multiple Patriarch problem."

Not many men accounted the Collegium collectively capable of making mature decisions. Hecht counted himself among the skeptics. Those old men all behaved like spoiled eight-year-olds.

Drear said, "A further consequence of the agreement is that Bellicose is now your ally. The bridges over the Dechear are now available. Bellicose hopes you'll make Viscesment your base for operations in that part of the Connec. That would stimulate the local economy."

Interesting. "Colonel Smolens. An opportunity to return to the scene of your crimes. Take our main force north and cross at Viscesment. That will put us right opposite the country we need to clear."

Madouc was scowling already. He knew he would not like what he was about to hear.

"I'll stay with the battalion already crossing here. We'll follow the west bank north. Madouc, I don't want to hear it. Where's my kid? Why the hell does he keep disappearing?"

"He's with Presten and Bags," Madouc replied. "He wanted to see where the worm came out of the ground."

Hecht glanced southward. There was no sign now of what had happened last year. "You lose him, you won't have to explain to me. I'll just feed you to Anna. What now?"

A rider was headed back alongside the road, as hard as he dared without trampling anyone. The soldiers had begun stopping and falling out as word spread that a change of plan was in the works.

The rider was one of Drago Prosek's falconeers. They had been first to cross the river.

"Captain-General. Sir. Some Connecten nobles want to talk. One is that Count Raymone Garete."

"Never stops raining," Hecht said. "Captain Drear, stick with me till I can deal with you more fully. Sergeant Bechter, make Captain Drear's visit pleasant. Madouc, I wasn't kidding about the boy. I had a letter from Anna yesterday. She isn't happy." She also reported that Principaté Delari and Principaté Doneto had enjoyed less than complete success at destroying the killing beast underneath Brothe. They had gone below with silver and iron and borrowed falcons. The thing had flown after one debilitating encounter. Since then it had evaded them. And had not betrayed itself by coming to the surface to practice its horrors. Now there were rumors of terrible things happening to those who lived underground. Pallid adults had dragged themselves into the hateful sunlight for the first time in their lives. The Principatés feared the killing thing was a more potent Instrumentality than originally suspected. Research was under way. Other members of the Collegium were being enlisted in the hunt.

Principaté Delari still guaranteed its extermination.

The Principatés now feared the thing was the queen of a terrible brood. They had caught and destroyed a dozen smaller, murderous evil things like it—all summoned into being by the hateful imaginings of the refugee populace.

So. Instrumentalities could be created by the pressure of the irrational fears of too many people crowded into too narrow a space.

Hecht supposed that should have been no surprise.

Madouc said, "It's not the boy we need to worry about. He's tractable enough when it comes to the wishes of his lifeguards."

"Yes. Yes. I know that psalm by heart. Let's go, gentlemen. I want to meet this paragon of Connecten nationalism, Raymone Garete."

COUNT RAYMONE DID NOT SEEM REMARKABLE. A REASONABLE MAN, APparently. He just wanted to be sure he understood what the Patriarchal forces meant to accomplish.

"In that case, Captain-General, I can lend you some of my own people. In particular, those who fled the counties where the Night holds sway now. I hope you go after the invaders with as much zeal as you came after us last year."

"You're welcome to join me. I can't support you financially, though. I can barely support myself, that way."

"That isn't a problem."

Hecht eyed the woman beside Count Raymone. The former prisoner, working hard to keep her mouth shut. Raymone's wife, now. Presumably, some of the Count's companions would be her brothers.

"I expect another hard winter," Hecht said. "We'll operate out of Viscesment." That startled Count Raymone. "Boniface and Bellicose have made peace."

The wide man, the cousin, Bernardin Amberchelle, barked malicious laughter. "Open season on the Society, brothers! Open season."

"Indeed," Hecht said. "The new Patriarch has a fixed loathing for the Society. But I don't think we'll find many of those where we'll be campaigning. They lack the nerve to operate under the nose of the Night."

"I like this guy," Amberchelle said. "Even if it wasn't all that comfortable being his prisoner."

"Enough!" the woman said.

Hecht said, "I trust you found your captivity less taxing, Countess."

The woman loosed a jackass bray of laughter. "Stupidest thing I ever did was run away. I was warm and I got fed regular. After I escaped I froze for weeks and almost starved to death. But, by damn! I was a free Connecten."

"I've been there. Count Raymone, I want to make it plain that I haven't been sent here to recover your lost territories for you. I'm here to get rid of rogue things of the Night. I will, however, keep those things away from you while you deal with squatters. I'm told a previous attempt bogged down because there are so many Night things up there."

"There was that. And the fact that I only sent a few men. I'll have no trouble working with you that way. I look forward to everything but winter. Which looks like it's going to come even earlier this year."

It did. And it was fierce.

CAMPAIGNING OUT OF VISCESMENT MADE FOR SOME COMFORT. THE Captain-General and Count Raymone moved from strongpoint to strongpoint, eliminating their respective targets, seldom spending much time in the cold. Neither the squatters nor the Night offered any challenge. Both fought in furious despair, to little effect. Arnhander knights in captured castles were more difficult at first, but faced with a choice between instant surrender or certain extermination, they abandoned resistance and began migrating northward before Nemesis overtook them.

Drago Prosek and his henchmen had a wonderful time with the stinks and bangs. "But this isn't much harder than butchering chickens," Prosek averred. "Big or little, these Night things suffer from an abiding plague of stupid."

Months based in the onetime seat of the Anti-Patriarchs allowed the Captain-General to become familiar with the local offshoot of the Chaldarean faith. And to meet and grow partial to the man Rocklin Glas, a man much like Hugo Mongoz. Hecht made a point of reminding Cloven

Februaren, who turned up randomly, that Bellicose was a good man. He wrote Boniface and the Collegium to report the same thing. Never failing to remind the latter that Bellicose could not possibly survive Boniface by long.

Come spring Titus brought word: "King Jaime is on the move. His advance riders just arrived. He'll use the Viscesment bridges. If you want to attend the wedding you can join up with him here."

Hecht had Boniface's permission to attend. Indeed, he would stand in for the Patriarch, Boniface being too frail to cross the Jagos.

Colonel Smolens overheard. "Go ahead. Sir, you'll never enjoy a grander honor. Sedlakova, Brokke, Consent, and I can keep the outfit from falling apart."

KING JAIME OF CASTAURIGA WAS JUST TALL ENOUGH NOT TO BE ACCOUNTED a dwarf—in Piper Hecht's opinion. He disliked the Direcian at first sight. The man had a dramatically inflated notion of his own worth. So much so that Cloven Februaren proved incapable of restraining his inclination to deflate swelled heads.

After just two days of sharing the road with the future Imperial consort, Madouc observed, "They say the Empress is mad about Jaime. She'd have to be."

Pella cackled like an old woman. Hecht said, "We'll reach Alten Weinberg a week before the wedding. That should give Katrin time to see through the dusky little bastard."

He knew that was wishful thinking, though. Katrin had her mind made up and her heart set. Her Council Advisory were not, supposedly, even a little thrilled. Especially not those members who had seen Jaime at Los Naves de los Fantas.

Piper Hecht did not worry about Katrin. He could not drag his thoughts away from Helspeth. In just days he would see her again. How much had his imagination run away from reality?

He felt like a callow youngster. And wondered what the Princess might be thinking. Might be anticipating.

And never stopped worrying about the soldiers he had left behind, tasked to tame the Connecten Night.

How could they possibly manage without him?

CPSIA information can be obtained
at www.ICGtesting.com
Printed in the USA
LVHW01s0143231018
594411LV00011B/351/P

9 780765 326058